SOME SAW AN *Angel* IN LAS VEGAS

—————— •ı• ——————

S. A. Craig

To my husband

No one on this earth is as blessed as I am to have you.

ACKNOWLEDGEMENTS

I wish to acknowledge all my family members and the wonderful friends who helped me along my journey in writing this book and gave me great encouragement...

First off, this book could never have been written without the help of my very intelligent husband who listened every night to my ongoing chapters and provided valuable and fruitful comments.

I cannot thank the following people enough who were there to give me support and insightful feedback: Richard and Sue, my awesome brother-and-sister-in-law; Brig, my very amazing sister; Timmy, my dear nephew; Tim and Diane, my special brother and his wife; and Jeff, my other fun brother-in-law. Also, many thanks to Ronda, my best friend and Jean, another great friend. I also want to thank my fantastic editor Kara for all of her help and hard work.

But most of all, I want to give all of my thanks and praise to my LORD and SAVIOR JESUS CHRIST.

S. A. Craig

The Players
of
Some Saw an Angel In Las Vegas

	John Sanger	A wannabe poker player
	Jill	A dancer hell-bent on making it big in Las Vegas
	Roy Garner	Houstonian country-line dancer
	Leroy Hart	Taxi driver known for his wild antics
	Rip Rumple	Billionaire businessman
	Nadine	Single mother who works at a cosmetic counter
	Lucy Faulkner	Seattle nurse looking for a change in the weather
	Hank Mariotta	Father and eclectic entrepreneur
	Bruce "Rebel" Rebenack	Handsome, professional quarterback
	Christianna Mariotta	Beautiful daughter of wealthy magnate Hank Mariotta
	Mindy	Talented curly-haired country-line dancer
	Ty Amaya	Commercial advertising photographer
	Sean Stevenson	New York City advertising agent

	Becky Dean Silas	Fantastic singer who heads out to Las Vegas for a piece of the pie
	Father Lawrence	Catholic priest with a true heart of gold
	Mary	Galveston, Texas girl with big poker dreams
	Lee Murphy	Lead guitarist of a band in Madison, Wisconsin

THE GAS & GO

John drove into the Gas & Go lot at street-speed. His girlfriend Jill screamed as he jammed on the brakes beside a gas pump. The Jeep Sahara was still rocking as he got out and slammed the door behind him. Jill watched through the side view mirror as John angrily shoved the pump nozzle into the car. They were fighting. Again.

When he got back inside the car, Jill asked accusingly, "How much this time?"

"What does it matter?" John answered.

"There go my new pair of jeans. Why did you get this gas guzzler in the first place?"

"At least I have a clear title to it."

"Little boy Johnny and his stupid toy truck!" she mocked.

John muttered under his breath, "Like you really need any more clothes. You're already crowding me out of my closet."

They ignored each other the rest of the way back to their apartment. John found an empty parking space and pulled in. He turned off the jeep and leaned forward, putting his hands on the dashboard. Turning to his girlfriend, he asked, "Look, can we just call a ceasefire? I'll grill up some dogs."

Jill relented. "I'll mix us some margaritas."

During dinner they watched Fox News and got into a fight over Geraldo Rivera. "He's so smarmy. He makes my skin crawl!" Jill shuddered.

"I don't care either way. But I wish I had his mustache. Maybe I'll grow one like it."

"Over my dead body!" Jill threatened.

"That can be arranged," John said matter-of-factly.

Jill looked startled. "It sounded like you meant that."

John just smiled and changed the channel.

Later that night Jill lay in bed, kept awake by John's heavy snoring. But maybe it was the moon. It was full and hanging big and round in the sky. She shook him to get him to stop, but that only made the snoring worse and she half-expected the neighbors to start banging on the thin wall that separated their apartments.

As the margaritas began to wear off, Jill's head started hurting. Running to the bathroom, she shook out two Advil from a plastic bottle and swallowed them. Mercifully, the pills helped her fall asleep.

She dreamed she drove John's jeep to the Gas & Go. The engine was idling. She plunged the gas pedal to the floor with her six-inch spike heels and slammed the shifter into drive. The jeep lunged forward, veered left, and knocked one of the fuel pumps off its mount. Gasoline geysered into the air. A spark ignited it and the Gas & Go exploded in a furious inferno. It rained molten ashes.

Her heels had become weapons of mass destruction.

WALGREENS

Frank was an old man. His clothes were frayed and dirty and his face was heavily wrinkled. He smelled. To some, he looked like he was steps away from entering eternity. Most people, however, just looked past him.

Frank had had a two-pack-a-day habit since he was a young boy and was one of those hardcore smokers who ate with one hand and took deep drags between bites with the other. He liked his tobacco straight and never let gimmicks dilute his pleasure. He smoked unfiltered Camels and never compromised; it was Camel or nothing.

He wasn't fond of talking, so when he did say something, it mattered. He figured that since he was retired, he no longer needed to speak unless it suited him. Most days, the few sentences he offered up to anyone who cared to listen revolved around the refrain that he liked his cigarettes smooth but strong. But because most people avoided Frank, some days he had difficulty satisfying even that meager verbal allotment.

That all changed at a Walgreens one day as Frank purchased what he swore would be the last two packs he would ever smoke. The clerk, who was quite familiar with his habit, retrieved his usual packs of Camels and asked, "Will that be all, Frank?"

Frank gazed into her sparkling blue eyes and said with a raspy voice, "No. I have something I just got to run by you!"

Her name was Nadine. "What's that?"

"I want to marry you, Nadine!"

She stared at him, frozen mid-scan.

"That's right. And to prove it, I'm going to kick the smokes just for you. But if you don't want to marry me, then I won't get to see you anymore because I'd have no reason to come around since I aim to give cigarettes the cold turkey today."

Nadine thawed some, finished scanning the pack, and asked sarcastically, "And that's why I'm ringing you up two packs of butts? Frank, you ain't got a brain in that ole head of yours. I don't care one way or the other if you quit those nasty things. And I can't say if I want to marry you or not. I'm about to get a promotion to the makeup department so I wouldn't be getting you those cigarettes anyway." Nadine had a way of being blunt.

"Well," Frank pressed her, undeterred. "What's it going to be?"

Nadine took a long look at Frank's old, creased face and reckoned it was the cigarettes that probably gave his pallor that gray look. She thought to herself that Frank probably didn't have long to live; maybe he had some money stashed away – even if it was a paltry amount. Still, from what Nadine could see, Frank looked like he was just a step away from setting up house under a freeway bridge. But she got to thinking that two incomes were better than just her one from Walgreens. It was a struggle bringing up two young children on her wages. And if he brought even a little to the table, it would be better than her present situation.

Nadine played with her dangling earrings and gave them a twist. Her young daughter and son came to mind and how she was sick of mac and cheese and Hamburger Helper. Moreover, the dating scene in town was pretty bleak. She hadn't met one man who could stay sober for longer than a week.

At least she wouldn't have to hear Frank go on and on, boring her with inane chatter. The man hardly spoke. Besides, if it became unbearable, she could always reach for her old-reliable rum and Coke; only instead, Nadine poured Pepsi into her rum to get a better fizz. That was her secret recipe and one she never divulged.

Nadine looked up at Frank and said, "Okay. Yeah, sure, Frank. When do you want to do this?"

Frank took her hand and smiled up to the ceiling. "Oh Nadine, there is so much I want to tell you!"

TRUDY'S ROADHOUSE

Roy walked along the long road toward Trudy's Roadhouse, his boots growing dustier with every step. Boy, he was thirsty. A cold brew would taste good right about now. He liked Shiner Bock – and Shiner Bock sure liked Roy.

It was nothing for him to down a six-pack a night, even if it did bloat him and keep him running to the bathroom between dances. Mindy, his dance partner with long, blond disheveled curls, would impatiently roll her eyes. "Boy, you just got to have that bladder checked. You might as well strap a porta-potty on your back."

It was Houston-hot and muggy and Roy just wanted to be dancing. Walking in this heat made him feel like a rube, especially when some shiny new Mercedes with tinted windows sped past, sending a blast of hot exhaust swirling around his face. The humidity curled his hair and he felt uncomfortably damp all over.

Damn that car anyway. He could only guess why his twenty-year-old Lexus wouldn't start this time. He should have junked it long ago. The paint was peeling off this once beautiful car in nasty chunks. It looked like it had a bad case of rosacea. The chassis was out-of-line and when it started, the car pulled hard to the right. The brake lights hadn't worked in two years and Roy counted on luck to keep a cop from coming up behind him at a traffic light. It wasn't as if he was broke, but he wasn't exactly flush with cash either. So, as long he could keep the beast alive, he would. But now, Roy was beginning to second-guess that decision.

On foot, with the hot Texas sun thwarting his every step, Roy was heading for the best cowboy bar in all of Houston. He was eager to hit the dance floor and boot-scoot with Mindy.

He didn't like Mindy; he didn't like her hair or style or the way she talked, but when she danced, *boy-howdy*, something happened. Roy became mesmerized. Mindy was the best country dancer in H-town. He was pretty good too. But when they danced together, it was almost like they lifted each other to a higher plane. They always received lots of attention and accolades whenever they hit the dance floor together.

With less than a mile to go until he reached Trudy's, Roy settled into the dusty footpath parallel to the street and picked up his pace. His boots were a mess and his shirt was open and sweat-stained. He knew

Mindy would be there to greet him with a nasty quip or two. Something needed to change in his life and Roy knew it.

As if to answer his prayer, a taxi slowed alongside him and screeched to a stop. "Hey, you want to ride in my cab? 'Cause you sure look like you could use some A/C. Where are you going? And oh, by the way, I hope you have some money or at least a credit card on you."

Roy walked over with some hesitation and studied the driver suspiciously. "I want to go to Las Vegas and go to the Western Nugget and gamble. Can you take me there?"

The cabbie looked confused and exclaimed, "Are you crazy? I'm not sure what to think about this scene. You saying you want me to drive you all the way to Vegas? You got the cash to pay for it? Brother, I'm sorry I even stopped for you."

"I'm sure. And yes, I do have the money for your information." Then, Roy asked the cabbie, "Do you know if they have line dancing there?"

"Are you kidding me? That's where some of the best line-dancing clubs and biggest dance contests in the country are. I was born there and I consider myself a closet cowboy disguised as a taxi driver. Do you want to find a place with some serious line dancing? Well, bud, I am your go-to man. Yee-haw!"

Roy was skeptical; he didn't have time to waste on a bullshitter. "What's a Houston cabbie from Vegas know about dancing anyway? You think you know so much, then how about you telling me a little bit about the Bronco Step or the Applejax?"

The cabbie nodded so hard Roy thought his head would fly off his skinny neck. "Come on, man. Them's baby steps. Do you know the Boogie Roll?"

Maybe it was the heat, but thoughts started whirling in Roy's head as he imagined himself dancing at a country-western club in Vegas. There wasn't much of anything to keep him in Houston, certainly not Mindy. She could have Trudy's Roadhouse. Sometimes they'd pull day-old beer. If there was one thing that pissed him off more than Mindy, it was flat, day-old Shiner Bock. Suddenly Roy decided, "Hell, why not!"

He charged the cab like a stampeding Texas longhorn and climbed into the back. He wrestled out a credit card from his damp wallet and looked squarely at the astonished cabbie. Handing him the card and pointing west, he exclaimed, "Wagons, ho!"

THE GUITAR SHOP

Her name was Rebecca Dean Silas, but she would only answer to Becky Dean. She didn't like Becky and hated any variation of her full name and demanded that people pronounce it as one name, Becky Dean.

Becky Dean was on her way to The Guitar Shop to buy some picks. Thinking the name was generic and boring, it nevertheless held the honor of being the best guitar shop in all of Madison, Wisconsin. She rarely used picks on stage, but she was working on a new sound and had broken the few picks she did have. She wanted to expand her band's repertoire and introduce a new musical style.

Her group consisted of herself and three others. She was the lead vocalist, but played keyboards and sometimes lead guitar when the song required it. Lee was their lead guitarist. Javier played bass guitar, and Basil was on drums. Together they formed The Madison Four.

She had been in this rock-and-roll, blues, country-western, southern-rock band for the last five years. It was a mouthful, but that was how Becky Dean described her group. And she berated the other members if they didn't see it the same way. Lord, she could be a stickler; Lee described her affectionately as one considerable pain in the backside who typically got her way.

It was her idea to introduce a bit of Flamenco flare into their playlist with the notion that they should try to mimic Ottmar Liebert's sound. Lee had tried to explain that Liebert was one-of-a-kind and it would be hard to emulate him since no one in the band could play classical guitar. "Besides," Basil and Javier had argued, "copying someone else's style was never a good thing." But Becky Dean wouldn't hear of it.

At first, playing in The Madison Four had been fun and exciting, but the novelty had worn off long ago, and Becky Dean was restless. The odd part was that the other band members were still okay with it all. She was always the one cajoling and motivating, pushing and urging. And she was tired of it. Still, she considered herself a professional and managed to feign interest in the band so that when they performed, no one would ever guess she found her bandmates extraordinarily dull and their music uninspiring. It had all become a tedious bore.

If it wasn't for her, those dolts would be happily vegging out in Lee's apartment, drinking beer, and watching reruns on MeTV. She booked all their gigs; it was her persona, her personality, and her songs that brought in their paychecks. They did nothing.

Thinking of all she did for the band made her angry and she even began seeing them as the reason for her constant hunger. Although considered skinny by some, Becky Dean still had a fit and alluring figure. That was because she barely ate. After paying the rent and utilities, she never had enough money for groceries. Although her income, or lack of it, qualified for public assistance, food stamps and food banks were out of the question, and she'd be damned if she would ever be caught using either. No sir, Becky Dean was proud! Her idea had been to give herself five years to make it and those five years were up. She was sick of barely getting by and she resented the fact that five years later, they were still playing the same dives and low-life bars as when they had started. If they weren't going to agree to her new plan, then that would mean splittsville. Becky Dean had had enough.

So what if she wanted to incorporate a little Spanish sound into the mix? What was the big deal anyway? Who were they to stop her? She didn't need their approval and wasn't about to ask their permission. Tonight, she would grab the mic, whip up the audience, and start picking away like she was the flamboyant vamp, Delinda Delgado.

Delinda, now in her eighties and looking pickled after years of facelifts, had been one of the world's most renowned Flamenco guitar players and been involved in a scandalous love affair with a famous Hollywood movie star four times her age. They had married in Mexico when Delinda was just 15 years old in what the gossip columnists called "The Shotgun Wedding of the Decade." Even then, she had looked as fake as a plastic pearl, but that irony wasn't lost on Becky Dean because Delinda Delgado could play, *really* play.

Becky Dean wasn't just smitten with this Latin tart; she was borderline obsessed. A smile crept across her face as she thought about it more. Given a little time, *she* could become the next Delinda Delgado and no one would even know who she was copying. After all, Delinda was from another generation. Actually, two generations removed, if anyone was counting.

So much for the repeated lectures from the rest of the band always harping that the pathway to success was to innovate and be original. "Be authentic!" Lee would insist emphatically. It angered her how they chose to dwell on that point instead of exploring new musical styles.

Ready or not, tonight she would debut the new Becky Dean and unleash Becky "Delinda" Dean on the world.

Sporting high-top Converses and calloused fingers, she strode into The Guitar Shop. After rummaging through the guitar picks, she noticed the store was now selling used albums. She was a fiend for used records and considered herself an aficionado of old music. Too bad she was on a tight schedule today because there were crates and crates of old vinyl to pick through. And with what little money was in her purse, she would rather spend it on music than use it for her next meal. Most of the time, she didn't know how she was going to fill her belly but never seemed to be short when it came to paying for her next used record.

Becky Dean chuckled as she thought of the many trips she had taken to Book Me, which, up until now, had been the only store in town that sold old vinyl records; she was a Book Me regular. She was always searching the bins for obscure artists or forgotten gems and often left the store carrying an armful of musty old albums, even if it meant scrimping on groceries.

Now The Guitar Shop was giving Book Me some competition, and she quickly thumbed through the crates of records at the back of the store. Becky Dean already knew what her first errand for tomorrow would be. She bought a few dozen assorted picks and the clerk told her to have a good day as she left. Becky Dean smiled as she looked forward to tomorrow when she would be on the prowl for some new, old albums.

But tonight, she was going to unveil the new Becky Dean and she hurried off to a club named The Blue Goose where they were going to be playing. The Goose, as it was known by the locals, had a reasonably large stage and that was where she plopped herself. Caught in a daydream, she envisioned how that night would unfold. But first, she had to bring on the razzle-dazzle by dressing teasingly.

Becky Dean googled Delinda Delgado on her smartphone and a second later there she was, Delinda Delgado in all of her colorful, full-bloom splendor. Her bleach-blond hair piled high into a puffy beehive, Delinda Delgado had ruby-red lips and wore so much eye makeup it was a wonder she could keep her eyes open wide enough to see the strings on her guitar. Like most Flamenco guitarists, she had long fingernails and Becky Dean wondered how Delinda kept from poking her eyes out with those claws.

Oh well, Becky Dean thought to herself. *I've just got to do it and get a blond wig.* She knew she could scrounge up some tight-fitting clothes; tonight, she would barely button her shirt, exposing more of herself on stage than ever before. She could sex it up with the best of them and tonight her valuables were coming out.

Her daydream was interrupted by Lee and the others as they came barreling onto the stage with bags full of used records. From the logo on the bags, it looked like they too had recently paid a visit to The Guitar Store. Becky Dean's eyes twinkled as she watched them, thinking in amazement that maybe they had finally decided to expand their musical tastes.

"Man, did we make a killing!" Lee was breathless. He seemed to be in an unusually good mood despite his default even-temperedness. *Maybe that was the problem*, Becky Dean thought. *Lee and the others needed more emotion, more passion, instead of always relying on her energy.*

Curious, Becky Dean asked, "What's up, Lee?" and cocked her head toward the bags they were holding.

"Well, we went to The Guitar Store and, Becky Dean, you would love it! They've started to carry old vinyl. They said they are going to compete against Book Me and they aim to win. We bought a boatload of old albums. They even had Flamenco. I couldn't believe they would have anything like that. You got to admit that it's a pretty obscure genre. They knew about Ottmar Liebert, but said they could turn us on to someone even better!" Lee and company stood before her eagerly.

Becky Dean felt a sense of accomplishment. They had listened to her after all. It was about time; she knew a lot more than they did. She flashed them her trademark look: a deadly mixture of haughty condescension and superior arrogance. "So, who, pray-tell, did they recommend? Carmen Miranda, that chick with all the bananas on her head, or maybe Ricky Ricardo, that crazy cat bongo player from Cuba?" Lee's eyes went cold as Basil and Javier stared into space.

Lee went on, "No, you've probably never heard of her; we sure never had and what a bangin' poptart she was! But how could anyone play a guitar with nails like hers? They're as long as machetes. She'd cut through half of her strings before she got through the first bar."

"But she's got a rack on her and that's all that matters!" Basil interjected. Javier nodded in agreement, wearing an impish grin.

These three always reminded Becky Dean of *The Three Stooges*.

"She was some fifties darling! You never know what was in back then, but the guy at The Guitar Store said she married some filthy-rich, B-movie dude. He said we should listen to her and that we'd be surprised."

Becky Dean's plan ended in a big fat fizzle. She swallowed hard on the lump building in her throat and managed to ask, though barely audible. "Okay, who is it? I am all ears."

"Her name is Delinda Delgado and have a look at her!" Lee pulled the album from his bag to reveal Becky Dean's idol in all of her bouffant glory replete with blood-red dagger-like nails. Completely deflated, Becky Dean nodded.

At that moment, her stomach chose to grumble; she was hungry. She would rather have the two-dollar spaghetti special at the church down by the train tracks instead of splurging on a teased-up blond wig anyway. Besides, where would she find a wig like that?

"Well, I'm glad you all listened to me. Maybe now we can get started on something new."

59 DINER

John woke early the next morning and quietly slipped out of the apartment while Jill slept. He drove his Sahara Edition Jeep to a nearby McDonalds and stopped at the order screen. It was early and the restaurant was not yet open. He felt almost embarrassed sitting by the dark menu board, waiting for the lights to come on. All he wanted was a Sausage Egg McMuffin – that was it. Just a Sausage Egg McMuffin.

"What am I?" he wondered aloud into the silence of his car. "Some kind of stupid rooster to be getting up this early?" Maybe it was his snoring that according to Jill, gave him quite a workout. Or perhaps it was their constant bickering and fighting that affected his metabolism. Whatever it was, all John could think about was his stomach. And for him, hunger was a powerful motivator.

It seemed like it took forever before the menu board flickered to life and a tinny, staticky voice acknowledged his presence. John ordered the number three and pulled up to the takeout window where he connected the voice to a face and immediately wished he had not.

When the cashier leaned out of the window to robotically announce that they were out of eggs, John saw the man's entire face had been drilled with holes and plugged with barbell studs that glittered under the restaurant's overhead lights. The piercings were everywhere, around his eyes, nose, cheeks, and lips. The holes in his earlobes were wide enough to stick a thumb through.

"You're telling me that McDonald's is out of eggs?" John asked impatiently.

"That's what I said."

Realizing he would have to get his breakfast somewhere else – how could a restaurant *not* have eggs and be *open* for breakfast? – John smashed the gas pedal into the floor board and raced out of the parking lot. The hard right he made entering the street toward the 59 Diner put the jeep on two wheels.

He eased off the gas and the car landed solidly back on terra firma. Surprised but proud of the maneuver, John pictured himself as a stunt driver in the *Fast and Furious* movies. Afterall, he had pulled off a two-wheel balancing act in a jeep.

Maybe it was Jill that was getting to him. She had become difficult to live with. They had nothing in common anymore. The only thing that interested her was a twenty percent-off sale at Ross. Jill was pretty, but the attraction that had once drawn John to her was gone. He had lost interest not only in Jill but in just about everything else the city had to offer.

John had a job at City Lights Mercedes selling Benzes to well-heeled Houstonians. The irony of selling expensive foreign luxury cars while he drove around in a quintessential American off-road monster was not lost on him. Nor was it on Jill. She nagged him every day how he should strike a deal with the owner, Heinz Krueger, to at least get a loaner Benz to bring home at night; at least then they would look like they were somebody.

Jill had always been hostile about his wheels and acted embarrassed whenever he came to pick her up at work. It wasn't as if the jeep was cheap. He'd paid almost forty grand for it, and with the custom burgundy paint job, it was actually quite the showpiece. It just wasn't Jill's style and as she put it, he "was just a little boy playing soldier in his stupid jeep."

So, she thought he was playing soldier? Fine – he'd enlist and come home a *real* GI. That would show her.

Then again, maybe not.

John tried to get Jill off his mind. He couldn't decide whether he needed to put a fork in their relationship or into a plate full of food. He decided that his hunger might be keeping him from seeing things clearly and that a few scrambled eggs, waffles, and some greasy sausage and bacon would help him navigate his emotional confusion.

The parking lot was already full when he pulled into the 59 Diner and he saw a waiting line forming outside the door. He flirted with the notion of crashing into the line and scattering the crowd but decided not to risk damaging his beloved car. He pulled into a no-parking zone and stopped, suddenly feeling hopeless.

It was then John determined, *I need to get my sorry ass down to the recruiters and get on over to Afghanistan. They need me and I want to fight for the good ole U.S. of A. They take good care of you and at least there, I'll get a decent breakfast. I'm sure they never run out of eggs! And who knows, I might even find a good game of poker there.*

Unwilling to suffer the line, John tore out of the parking lot and drove down the road a mile or so to a small cafe with a sign blinking the word "BREAKFAST." There was no line that John could see, so he pulled in the lot. He would get some food and then head for the nearest recruiting office to join the US Army. He was going to take control of his life again.

ELIZABETH'S HOUSE

Mary intently watched her mother's eyes which were barely flickering today. When they were open, her pupils had a grayish pall to them and were set on something in the distance. Her mother hadn't said a word all day; Mary knew the time drew near. Although hospice had kindly instructed her to prepare for the inevitable, Mary felt she could never be ready for it even though the last five months had been heartbreaking and exhausting. She hired a hospice team to care for her mother at her house because she wanted her to be comfortable and in a familiar environment, but facing death remained part of the process.

As she took her mother's hand, she observed that the woman felt cold, something hospice said would happen. Her mother Elizabeth had suffered a heart attack while swimming in the Gulf on Galveston Island. At 39 years of age, a heart attack was unthinkable, but Mary's mother had always been susceptible to heart disease since childhood and suffered from a heart murmur as well as a hole in her aorta. In the past few years, she had endured 12 operations.

Mary, who had just turned 18 the month before her mother's heart attack, was Elizabeth's only caregiver. Actually, Mary had always taken care of her mother because of the woman's poor health. She never knew a time in her life where she had not looked after her mother. In a cruel twist of fate, their roles had reversed, making Mary the caregiver and her mother the feeble and mostly disabled dependent, a pity to witness.

There was a tight bond between them. Mary's mother wanted her daughter to find her future. Her mother always urged Mary to pursue what was really in her heart. She had known of Mary's want. Mary still yearned for something big but was unsure what form that would take. Whether a great love, fame, or some profession, Mary did not know.

The one thing Mary was certain of was her fondness of poker. All her life she had fantasized about being in Las Vegas and playing real poker. The daydream consumed her. All the while caring for her mother, Mary took to playing games of internet poker and in a short time had accumulated a bank of over a million dollars. Of course, it was all fake money and her anonymous opponents were likely only slightly more inept than her. Nevertheless, her rapid success added fuel to her dreams of becoming a professional card player.

Mary was just a child when her Uncle Tad had taught her to play Texas Hold'em. Instead of playing FISH or Old Maid, he would stack colorful chips in front of each of them and tell Mary to ante by tossing a few pieces into the center of the table. Mary loved the clinking sound the chips made and at five years old remembered being told to either check, bet, or fold on the river.

Oh, how Uncle Tad liked to bluff. He often let Mary wear his sunglasses when they played together, explaining, "They help hide the lie you are holding in your hands." Mary didn't understand what that meant at the time, but felt grown-up wearing her uncle's sunglasses. Years later, she realized the sunglasses helped hide her pupils and prevented opponents from seeing her eyes widen and her pupils dilate, an uncontrollable tell when she was on a bluff.

It was her Uncle Tad who had put the idea in her head to move to Las Vegas where she could watch and take notes from some of the greatest players in poker. Now, moving to the desert city was all that occupied her thoughts. Her mind was made up.

The end came precisely as the hospice team had told her it would. Her beautiful mother died in her home with Mary holding her hand and telling her how much she loved her. Elizabeth squeezed her daughter's hand weakly while laboring for breath. With a fading pulse, Mary's mother whispered, barely audible, "I love you, Mary. Go and do what you need to do; I will be there watching over you."

Elizabeth, Mary's mother, closed her eyes for the last time. Mary knew she would be guiding her.

THE WOODLAND
APARTMENTS

Where the hell had John scrambled off to this morning?

Jill pretended to be asleep, but she was quite aware that John had showered, dressed, and left well before 6 a.m. She thought maybe he was sporting a hangover because while she drank margaritas, he drained the last of the beer from the fridge. It had been one beer after another as if he was on an IV. She also noticed that he barely ate even though he loved working the grill. It was like he enjoyed the cooking part of dinner, but when it came to the eating part, John just shoved the food around his plate with his fork. Where could he be? And what did he think he was doing treating her like this? He just up and leaves? No kiss goodbye, no farewell, nothing!

Sure, they'd fought yesterday, but they had followed that argument with a serious make-up session. Shortly thereafter, however, they had ripped into each other again when John asked her to get him another beer. She had told him she wasn't his "step and fetch" and to get it himself. He became angry and said he was bored and sick of her. How dare he be bored with her? What the hell did he have to offer her, a freaking jeep? He was crazy over that useless piece of crap.

She'd had her share of men and John was kind of in the middle. Sometimes Jill loved him and other times she felt that she could toss him away like an empty gum wrapper. If he wanted to skip off on her and play the scene from Five Easy Pieces where Jack Nicholson leaves his girlfriend stranded at a gas station, well, she could live with that.

There were still a few months left on their lease, but Jill didn't want to wait that long to leave this damn town and be free of everything. The manager at The Woodland Apartments where they lived was always pretty flexible when it came to her. In fact, Jill was sure she could get him to let her out of the lease early and still get her deposit back.

Jill began to form a plan. She had always dreamed about living in Las Vegas and now seemed like the perfect time. Maybe she could land a job as a showgirl. Entertaining the idea for a moment, she posed in the mirror to admire herself. She certainly had the package to be one of those showgirls who strut around wearing nothing but feathers. Why not? She was determined to go to Vegas. Even if John did decide to come back, the simple truth was that he no longer mattered to her.

KOA CAMPGROUND

Remembering his past, Father Lawrence often felt saddened. It remained in his mind like unpicked fruit slowly decomposing on the vine. It was his childhood. His father was an abusive man and became more so while drinking. It was those times Larry remembered, hiding in the attic behind musty boxes, trembling with fear and hoping his drunken father would pass out before discovering his hiding place. As Larry grew older, he developed other strategies to avoid his father. One was to participate in any after-school activity he could find; another was to do odd jobs for anyone who would hire him.

Larry's first job at eleven was cleaning out old Barney Cane's barn just down the road from where he lived. Barney's barn didn't really need cleaning, but the man knew about Larry's father and, looking back on it now, Father Lawrence realized Barney Cane had offered him sanctuary. That was the only way he could avoid the violence of a drunken father.

Finally, after spending too many nights hiding in the attic while his mother endured her husband's savage fists, Larry decided that running away was his only option. And to this day, years later, Father Lawrence knew it was God's hand that had delivered him.

One morning, Larry hid by the corner of his house and watched the school bus pass his stop. He crossed to the other side of the highway and stuck his thumb out to hitch a ride. After a few cars passed him by, an old lady wearing a broad-brimmed hat pulled over in a beat-up Honda and swung open the door. The first thing the old lady said to him was, "Well, what are you waiting for? Get in, scrawny." For a moment, Larry hesitated, marveling at the power of his magic thumb, but then climbed into the car. He pulled the door closed and he was gone.

The lady was heading west toward… somewhere. An open map of "The Western United States" was draped across the console between them. She kept looking over at him before finally asking, "Say, aren't you a little young to be hitchhiking? Shouldn't you be in school?"

Larry answered curtly but mannerly, "Yes ma'am." And that was it.

With big round eyes and a hat brim that flapped in the breeze from the open window, she didn't hesitate for a second, "My name is Mabel and I'm going all the way to San Francisco, California. Where on

God's green Earth are you going, young 'un? Are you going over to the next town?"

Larry gave the lady a quick nod. "No ma'am, I am going to Las Vegas. Can you drop me off on the way? That is, if you'll be going in that direction."

"What-in-the-name-of-Pete are you gonna do in Las Vegas? You are probably in trouble and someone is probably looking for you right now. You know, scrawny, the only reason I picked you up is that I got a feeling in my gut that you were running, running from trouble. That right? How old are you anyway?" This lady Mabel wanted answers.

Larry hugged the door handle. He thought he might jump out of the car right then and there and try again. She wasn't the only get-away car on the road. Larry was quick to answer her, "Ma'am, I am running away cause my daddy is no damn-good and I am not taking any more from him. And yes, I am a young'un."

Mabel responded with a question bordering on interrogation. "Well, are you of age and do you have a mama?"

"No, ma'am." Larry was careful to answer her respectfully, hoping that might keep her from prying too deep. "I am sixteen years old and I ain't got no Mama anymore because she killed herself after taking all those beatings from my daddy." That was a bold lie, but he had no doubt that one day it would be true. Larry told himself he would return to rescue his mother as soon as he made a few bucks. He loved his mother and felt guilty about leaving her behind, but why in the hell did she marry that old drunk? He had no choice but to run.

"Well, scrawny kid, after hearing all that, I've half a mind to take you with me."

Scrawny kid – scrawny kid – scrawny kid.

The tag buzzed through his mind like an annoying fly. It was an insult that needed a response, but Larry remained quiet.

"Scrawny kid, if this is what you want, then you got it. I am all for enabling the unfortunate child who needs some help. God told me to pick you up; I'll be your angel." Mabel settled down a bit as she began to accept her role as his guardian angel. She seemed to have a direct line to God, but Larry didn't know what to believe.

Raised in a strict Pentecostal church, he and his mama had gone to church every Sunday no matter what the weather brought. She never missed service, but the old man, of course, stayed home. He was either on an early-morning binge or was nursing a Saturday-night hangover. So, Larry didn't know what to think when it came to having an angel looking over him, let alone one who arrived in the flesh driving an old, beat-up

Honda Civic ready to drive him to Las Vegas. All he cared about was escaping Jackson, Mississippi and starting a new life.

Throughout that first day, the old lady spent more time stopping at restaurants, insisting that he eat something, than driving. Larry believed she was doggedly determined to fatten him up. But for what?

Mabel also talked. A lot. She told him how a virus had been going around where she lived in some small town in Northern Mississippi, almost into Tennessee. Her husband of 40 years had caught it and died. After she'd buried him, God told her to pack her things and leave Mississippi. She had lived like a vagabond ever since, staying in cheap hotels and sometimes even in campgrounds where she would sleep in her car.

Always professing her deep faith in God, Mabel said He was getting her through the hard times. She declared God had told her to settle down in San Francisco and, finding it agreeable, she had set off. Mabel said there were a bunch of sinners in San Francisco and it was up to her to bring them to Jesus. She was strapped for money and always frightfully tired. Larry figured it was because of all her talking. "Boy!" she continuously touted, "I am gonna take care of you and, who knows, I might even adopt you." Mabel could talk herself silly.

At the end of a particularly loquacious day, Mabel suddenly exited the highway, proclaiming she was too tired to keep going. Larry, who had been dozing, peered up at the sliver of a moon hanging in the twilight sky. He was tired too.

As Mabel eased off the accelerator and turned onto a gravel road, she said, "I ain't got but about 20 bucks for tonight and I can't believe what I see up the road. Praise God and my lucky stars. It's a KOA! I hope you don't mind sleeping in the car, scrawny, because we're in luck!"

The car crept up the road until a neon yellow sign with a teepee and three giant letters – K O A – came into view, lighting up the night sky. That night, as Larry drifted off to sleep in the back seat, he thought that maybe Mable could indeed be an angel sent from heaven.

ST JOSEPH'S HOSPITAL

Lucy had been a nurse in the oncology unit at St. Joseph's for the past 8 years. Her schedule was unrelenting. She worked 12-hour shifts five days a week, but there was no discernible logic to what the hospital defined as a week. And the days she worked were never the same. Lucy was sick of it all – pun intended. The smell of antiseptic began in the parking garage and permeated every ward in the hospital, but it could not mask the underlying odor of death. She couldn't quite understand where her restlessness came from; she just knew she needed to step away from nursing for a while.

Most of her oncology patients had dismal prognoses. Regardless of the treatments they received, in the end, the majority of them died. Sure, they lingered for a brief period and utilized various life support to ease their suffering, but no matter how much she cared for them, they only seemed to die. It was, in a word, depressing.

Only two good things came from her enervating job. Firstly, she made a reasonably decent living which allowed her to support herself and her wayfarer boyfriends. Lucy also liked the fact that she lived about a half-mile from the hospital, making it easy for her to ride her bike to St. Joseph's.

She lived in Seattle where the weather was monotonously gray. Winter was the worst. A chilly rain could quickly turn to sleet and occasionally snow; twilight began at three in the afternoon. Lucy missed having a warm summer because Seattle never had them. She was so sick of the incessant rain. Her persistent pessimism made her wonder if she had contracted a seasonal disease where the rainier it got, the more morose she became. Lucy needed to leave Seattle and do it quickly for the sake of her mental health.

At her apartment, she had a large, coffee-table book describing all of the United States. She loved perusing the book late at night and even made up a game to go along with her leisurely reading. Closing her eyes, she would open the book and let her finger randomly drop on a page. Wherever her finger landed, that would be her new home. Lucy enjoyed playing the game, and it almost always turned up somewhere new and interesting for her to think about.

After the day she had had, Lucy vowed that tonight after work, she would play 'State Roulette' again, but this time, she would leave Seattle and actually move to wherever her finger landed. The book was useful for this type of quest since the states were not listed alphabetically. Lucy deliberately never became too familiar with the order so she could be surprised every time she played. Anything else would be cheating. She finished her shift in a feverish excitement and peddled home like a maniac, pumping through stop signs, hoping her finger would assign her a warmer location.

Lucy felt thirsty but decided that reaching for a diet coke could wait. In high anticipation, she rushed over to her book, almost tripping on her braided rug. She didn't bother to change out of her hospital scrubs, which was her usual order of business when she got home. Instead, she knelt at the coffee table and slid the book in front of her, closed her eyes, and said a little prayer, asking God to pick her a good one. Flipping the book, she jabbed her finger onto a page almost as if her finger had magical power. To her great dismay, she landed on Alaska.

"Oh, no! No way!" Lucy exclaimed. "This can't be happening. Alaska! Are you kidding me? It would cost me everything I've saved even to live there. I have to break my rule, and I am going to put my flipping finger in that damn book one more time. I don't care. It is between God and me." With bated breath, Lucy grabbed the book roughly for one more fling. Her repeated performance landed her in the southwest state of Nevada. "That's better. But the only two towns worth a darn in Nevada are Las Vegas and Reno."

Of the two, it would have to be Las Vegas. A smile of anticipation overcame Lucy. With a new zest for life, she pictured herself being a dealer in some fancy casino. She could rule over a blackjack or craps table, or maybe even baccarat where the stakes were high and the tips were enormous.

Talk about a career change! Lucy knew one thing. No one ever died from going to Las Vegas, and if they did, they expired from too much excitement. Tomorrow, she would give her two-weeks' notice.

RILEY'S LIQUOR STORE

In his mid-twenties, Ty was alone in the world. Both of his parents had been drug addicts; cocaine had consumed them. While Ty was still an infant, his grandmother sued his parents for guardianship and subsequently raised Ty as best she could. He lived with her in Brooklyn, poor but cared for until, when he was a college senior, she died. Except for the one wedding photograph of his parents that his grandmother kept on the fireplace mantel, Ty never saw his parents. Although the New York streets toughened him, somehow he managed to avoid becoming caught in the downward drug spiral that snared so many of his friends.

A talented artist with an innate ability, he was offered a scholarship to the prestigious School of Visual Arts in Manhattan. After graduating, Ty accepted a job in the art department of a prominent marketing and advertising firm. His artwork and photography were recognized by his peers and encouraged by his superiors. Everyone knew that success for Ty was all but assured.

Like Ty, Sean was another prodigy the firm was grooming for the future. Talent-wise, he and Ty had much in common. Arriving within weeks of one another, they became wary allies in a system they knew would eventually pit them against each other. Sean made that point perfectly clear to Ty one afternoon during a lunchtime run together in Central Park. "You know, Ty, the firm can't have two up-and-comers. One of us is going to lose and I'm telling you now, it *ain't* going to be me, man!"

Privately, Ty considered Sean a parasite who was not above stealing ideas and presenting them as his own. He certainly was no friend. Sean was in perpetual competition. Even out of the office, the man never let up. He could turn a quick twenty-minute cardio run through Central Park into an all-out Olympic event.

Ty knew he could beat Sean in just about anything, but tired of the competition. Even when they entered the ring for a friendly boxing bout, Sean inevitably turned it into a prizefight. Ty felt the jar of Sean's competitiveness through his sparring helmet. These were not just friendly jabs. They had a purpose.

In their company touch-football games, Sean put a hit on him like he was a lineman for the NY Giants. But even in pro-football, it was illegal to perform a body slam like that on your opponent for concern about concussions.

In Sean's world, there was no room for friendly competition. He was either the victor or the vanquished. It seemed losing to Ty at anything meant abject failure to Sean. Even when drinking, Sean had to drink Ty under the table or score all the women when they were out. Ty began to see Sean's compulsion to compete as abnormal; even bordering on the psychotic. Someone like that was capable of doing just about anything to win and Ty realized he needed to lose Sean from his life.

Ty's girlfriend Emily echoed Ty's sentiments, saying, "Sean isn't a good friend. He's got issues. He's a jerk and a major creep. He's always trying to keep you from succeeding. He's always trying to one-up you. Oh my God, he's no good and he's only going to bring you down if you keep hanging around him." Ty ignored her characteristic rantings even though he knew she was right.

And considering Emily, it wouldn't be such a devastating loss if he dumped her too. She had an over-inflated opinion of herself but aspired to nothing. Emily worked at the shoe boutique of an upscale department store and seemed to care about only shoes. The woman had so many shoes that she stopped counting after her four-hundredth pair. Shoe boxes crowded the walls of every room in her small apartment; they were even in her bathroom. Nothing else motivated her, not even sex. The woman was vain, self-absorbed, and disgustingly materialistic; Ty wouldn't miss her.

New York City might be the Big Apple, but to Ty, it was turning out to be the Big Nothing. He had no ties or family there. The promise of a successful Madison Avenue career was no longer enough for him. He seldom traveled outside of New York City – that thought alone made him feel confined. Ty was impatient for change. What was he waiting for? Knowing things wouldn't change unless he did something about it himself, he began to update his résumé and portfolio.

Without thinking, Ty left his Greenwich Village flat and headed for Riley's Liquor Store. He needed to quench his thirst and a bottle of Tanqueray was the tonic for all that ailed him. As he crossed mid-street, three different taxi drivers blew their horns at him and a furious woman with an Italian accent hollered and threw him the finger. Ty paid no notice. He could already taste the gin going down and thought to himself, *Yep, a little Tanqueray will help focus my brain.* For Ty, gin was the gods' pure nectar that helped him make crucial decisions. Besides, it always helped him seduce women.

WALGREENS AGAIN

Nadine and Frank married shortly after his proposal. The courtship was quite brief and they were wed in a five-minute civil ceremony a week later.

Not wanting to uproot Nadine's kids, Frank moved into a small spare room Nadine had been using as a dump room. He kept his word and gave up cigarettes, but not without aid as Nadine now found herself picking up Frank's discarded nicotine patches strewn around her crowded house. Their marriage so far had been nothing but Frank's ill-tempered demeanor due to his kicking cigarettes.

Nadine's two children Dorothy and Robert pretended he wasn't there and avoided him whenever he was around. Similarly, Frank barely spoke to them but when he did, he was churlish and impatient. He showed no interest in them, refusing to even interact with them. And as far as Frank having "So much to tell her," well, that never happened. He lived in her house like Nadine imagined he had lived before they were married – quietly and scarcely speaking. It was like a gossamer specter, whose presence made itself known in only fleeting glimpses, had come to live in her house.

Frank's routine was predictable. Long before she woke, Frank brewed a pot of the most grind-full, muddy coffee she had ever tasted. It was so caustic that after her first initial sips, she swore never to subject herself to it again. Like his cigarettes, the man didn't use filters. And by the time he headed out for his morning walks which usually lasted hours, the only thing left in the coffee maker was a pot full of grounds.

Nadine often wondered if her new husband was really taking walks. Perhaps he was up to something else. Either way, she was mad. She couldn't even count on the old man to be there to babysit her children. Instead, she had to continue to rely on her best friend Phyllis to sit for her. Phyllis was as flaky as the trail of dandruff that wafted behind her. Sometimes she'd forget to feed the children their lunch and other times she would feed them an ice cream cone or candy bar in place of a healthy meal. Another contentious issue with Nadine was that Phyllis incessantly swore in front of her kids, using every foul and profane word imaginable. No matter how often Nadine told Phyllis to watch her language around her children, her friend continued to pull from her treasure chest of profanity

Early November on a bitterly cold day, Nadine found herself escorting her children to the Bible Daycare shuttle parked along their street. Shivering against the horrible wind, she waved at the bus as it pulled away. It was unusually cold, even for Wheaton, Illinois, a Chicago suburb. Located right off Lake Michigan, winter temperatures could fall well below zero; when combined with the wind chill, the cold could turn deadly.

Folded against the wind, Nadine hurried back into the house, pausing to peek at the thermometer nailed by the garage. It was a beat-up old thing with chipped corners and faded colors. There used to be a picture of a hummingbird on it but now only a barely visible shadow remained. She imagined that the bird materialized over night and was now flying south to escape the frigid cold. Eight degrees below zero – that was one smart bird! Wearing only pajamas and a light, ripped up old bathrobe, Nadine was highly aware of the icy air. She rubbed her arms vigorously trying to warm up. "I can't believe this! In November! Is this the North Pole or what?"

A disturbing thought came to Nadine. Her stomach seized with stabbing pains that came in waves. She was used to dealing with the pain of her stress-related ulcer, but this flare-up erupted faster than most. Where was Frank in this cold? As usual, her husband had left at first light. She had only heard the front door close. What time was that? Maybe around six-thirty? Where was he?

Now it was now two in the afternoon and still no Frank. It was not like him to miss lunch. Frank did not have much of an appetite, but skipping lunch was not a part of his routine. Nadine began to panic. She had to find him.

She called Ronald, her manager at Walgreens, who told her to come down to the store. His shift was just about over and they could take his car to search for Frank. Nadine gratefully agreed as she didn't have a car and always walked to work. She lived just a few blocks from the store and dreaded the idea of even walking to Walgreens in this bitter weather, but at least it wouldn't take long. She quickly dressed in a pair of jeans and a warm, cashmere sweater. There would be no hibernating from the cold today. Finding Frank was all that mattered now.

As she pulled on her fleeced-lined boots, Nadine thought she heard the doorbell ring. She cocked her ear in the direction of the front door and assumed that it was Frank. She thought what a fool he was to walk out without his key. But when she opened the door, instead of Frank, two blue-uniformed men stood in front of her. A sense of dread overwhelmed her. Her heart was pounding because she knew. With shaking hands, Nadine let them in.

25

"Ma'am, are you Mrs. Nadine Wall-Spencer?"

Nadine had hyphenated her name when she married Frank because she loved the sound of it. The name had personality. She thought she sounded like somebody, maybe even a celebrity. But now, as spoken by the officer, the name had a foreboding sense to it.

"Yes, that's me." Her voice shook so severely the bigger cop had to lean in.

"Ma'am, we have bad news to report to you. Your husband has been found dead. He was found lying by a tree near Oswego Pond with a pistol by his side. It appears he died from a self-inflicted gunshot wound. We also found something on his person that might be of interest to you." He placed a letter in Nadine's trembling hands.

The smaller bespectacled cop with jet black hair told her, "We are so sorry for your loss."

BLINKER BAR

Keith and James walked along the banks of a muddy park lake in Macon, Georgia. In a great mood, Keith would occasionally pull out his harmonica and start playing. He could blow the blues and once he got started, would throw his whole body into it. James would start swaying back and forth to the rhythm while singing the blues to Keith's playing. Together, they were pretty good. There was no reason that with a little practice, they could not turn their act into a steady job somewhere.

For the most part, the park was empty as they walked along the path improvising melodies. The few people they did pass clapped their hands to the beat or gave them an approving thumbs up. Now and then they would stop to perform for a small but appreciative audience.

After a short while, Keith set off to pester James yet again. "Man, let's get serious and form a band. We could be called K & J!" James rolled his eyes. "Okay, okay, man! *J* & K!" Keith went on about his connections and how they could line up a few paying gigs at a local bar for them on Friday and Saturday nights. The dive bar to which Keith referred – known as The Blinker – had been the scene of four murders in the past year.

James shook his head adamantly. "There's no way I am going to get up on stage at The Blinker and put my life on the line for a bunch of drunken assholes. They should have shut that place down years ago."

Keith groaned. "Just go fuck yourself. Who needs you anyway? I can find another partner easy. I wouldn't mind having a good-looking woman to front the band."

James had known Keith his whole life and recently started thinking that hanging around Keith put him on the losing side of nowhere. All they ever did was score drugs and get into trouble. Now that he was twenty-two, James had grown bored with Keith and his antics. He knew he could sing and wouldn't mind forming a group, but he'd be damned if it was going to be in some podunk town like Macon, Georgia. And it sure as hell wasn't going to be with Keith.

James was still pissed about the last time they had been to The Blinker. They had gotten into an altercation that landed them both in the county jail on assault and battery charges – not for the first time. Fortunately, Keith's gorgeous stepmother Sally, once again came to their rescue and bailed them out.

It always started at The Blinker Bar and ended with jail.

Sally was closer in age to Keith than she was to Keith's father Floyd who had divorced Keith's real mother in favor of some "eye candy." As his mother had approached 50, Floyd began crowing around other hen houses and out came Sally. Young, pretty, and materialistic, Sally became infatuated with Floyd's charm and sophistication, not to mention his success and the fat bank account which accompanied it. But from the beginning of their marriage, Floyd put his new wife on a strict allowance and Sally was not shy about constantly voicing her resentment of it.

Why Sally continued to come to Keith's rescue puzzled Keith. He knew she wasn't happy with his father. So why bother rescuing the man's son from jail? Particularly when they both knew that Floyd would rather let Keith decompose like a rotting potato in that cell before he wasted his hard-earned money on that disappointment called "Son."

As Sally rescued Keith and James from their latest incarceration, she said while ushering them out of the police station toward her car, "I get scared just driving by it, let alone going inside for a drink. The cops are always there. I don't understand why they don't just shut it down. Why do you keep going there?"

Keith answered simply, "For the good times." Sally looked at him coyly. James just smirked.

"Well, Keith darling, if it's good times your looking for, you know I've always had a soft spot for you. There isn't *anything* I wouldn't do for you. I'm so sick of your old daddy and how tight he is with his money. He's got nothing on you. I'll be your Blinker Bar Babe and rescue you any time you get your hot little butt in a fix."

Sally looked over at James and told him alluringly, "And James, I wouldn't never leave you out of our little party. Feel free to join us anytime." She tossed her head back and began laughing hysterically and added, "I wonder what Floyd would think about all this family love I'm showing. I'm even sending love to James, our extended family."

The Blinker Bar boasted "The Skeeter," Macon's biggest and meanest badass bouncer. He stood six feet, seven inches and weighed well over three hundred-fifty pounds. Made mostly of muscle, he had a jagged scar on the right side of his face which, rumor had it, was the result of a prison knife fight. He could throw his fists like lightning; when he landed a blow, his victim crumbled to the ground, not likely to stand up and ask for another. The Skeeter was the only bouncer The Blinker employed.

Everyone talked about The Skeeter turning professional heavyweight because as far as anyone knew, once he landed his right on an unruly patron, they were out for the night. The Skeeter was fearless.

He could fight anyone anytime; he never lost. The owners paid him well, making him an odd kind of celebrity among the rough roadhouses of Georgia. But nobody messed with The Skeeter.

Fortunately for James and Keith, The Skeeter liked Keith. So, whenever Keith got into a mess at The Blinker, The Skeeter would come to his rescue. First, he would destroy Keith's adversary and then drag Keith by the shirt collar to the door and send him flying, making sure that Keith ate some dirt when he landed. It was always a hard fall meant to teach Keith a lesson. Unfortunately for James, once the bouncer had disposed of Keith, he delivered the same painful lesson to James.

The Skeeter's schooling never seemed to sink in with Keith and each class became more difficult than the last. The next weekend, Keith and James would return to The Blinker only to feel The Skeeter's muscled grip around them mid-evening. They would both be launched out the nearest exit.

Now, as they walked down the park trail, Keith droned on about forming a band. James ignored him and let Keith's voice drift into a distant mumble. "Yeah, whatever you say, Keith." James pulled his phone from his pocket with the hope that it would have a good signal. He had seen a television commercial about it last night and now he all he wanted was to book a one-way ticket to Las Vegas. He was done with Keith.

PINS & THINGS BOWLING

ALLEY

Hank Mariotta stood on a small hill to survey his land which included the town named after him – and that he owned. In a time when many small Texas towns were dying, Mariottaville of Central-West Texas was the exception. It was thriving, expanding, and building. Hank was pleased; his life was blessed. Not only did he own Mariottaville, but he was also the proud proprietor of the franchise football team the San Antonio Antelopes. Of all his achievements, however, he was most proud of being responsible for designing and manufacturing the iconic American motorcycle, the Mariotta Maverick.

A gear-head all his life, Hank had amassed his fortune by pursuing his passion for motorcycles. When he was seven years old, he built his first bicycle from parts he had scrounged up around town. At fourteen, Hank started working at the Pins & Things Bowling Alley in San Angelo, Texas. His job was to reset bowling pins by hand. Finding that he didn't need an education to make money, he dropped out of school during his freshman year. By the time he was seventeen, he owned a small garage that he had bought after saving his earnings from the bowling alley and later from what he made repairing his neighbors' cars in his driveway.

Despite his age, Hank already had a reputation going for him. The townsfolk thought he was some sort of mechanical genius with an exciting future ahead of him.

But to Hank, it was instinctive. He was a high-school dropout, born into poverty, and destined for rarefied success.

In addition to an innate mechanical aptitude, Hank was also a gifted designer. He was never without his small three-ring notebook filled with sketches of various motorcycle designs. He obsessed over his design work and endeavored to create the most ubiquitous of all-American cycles. He wanted to be the Henry Ford of the motorcycle world! Relentlessly driven, discipline was the engine of Hank's achievements.

And by his side from the very beginning was his girlfriend Matilda. While Hank was gifted with working with his hands, Matilda had a keen sense for business. She encouraged him to patent his motorcycle designs and to ultimately convert his auto repair shop to focus exclusively on the building of his motorcycles.

At first, the business had been slow. But motorcycle enthusiasts began to notice a new machine trending on the streets. Whenever they asked about a bike that impressed them, the name of the builder was always the same – Mariotta's Cycle Shop out of San Angelo, Texas.

After four years of exhausting, non-stop work, Hank's effort paid off with the introduction of the Mariotta Maverick. The Maverick's radical new design not only transformed the motorcycle industry, but its performance and ride were such that it became an instant success. Soon more orders than his small shop could handle flooded in from dealers and individuals around the county. It was a nice problem to have.

With his business growing, Hank needed to find a manufacturing plant. He knew about a mothballed machining factory in San Antonio. It was built to manufacture auto parts for Detroit that had been hailed by the press as the beginning of the return of American manufacturing. Suffering from mismanagement and corruption, it soon became clear that the factory would never realize the hope and hype promised at the opening day ceremonies.

The plant manager had gotten himself embroiled in scandal. He had been caught colluding with the quality assurance manager to fail perfectly good parts coming off the line. They would then secretly ship them off to Louisiana for resale by an unsavory third accomplice. Predictably, management pointed the finger at the employees. It was a union shop, and maybe the workers were taking too many breaks and too long lunches. Perhaps they were not doing their jobs or meeting their quotas. And for a time, that explanation worked, but it could not explain the glaring fact that the parts rejected by the QA manager were missing. No one was able to solve the mysteriously missing defective inventory.

The Louisiana partner was also involved in other nefarious activities in New Orleans and one night had been found floating face-down in Lake Pontchartrain. It seemed the Dixie Syndicate caught him skimming the till from three of their strip clubs.

The murder investigation led New Orleans detectives to a warehouse in an industrial park located in River Ridge, Louisiana where they discovered racks full of auto parts. Shipping documents indicated they came from Texas. That fact meant that this was now an interstate crime and the New Orleans police were happy to turn that part of the investigation over to the FBI.

FBI agents quickly traced the parts back to their San Antonio source, and the factory owners found themselves embroiled in a scandal that became the lead story on all the network news shows. Almost immediately, customers began canceling longstanding parts orders. This forced layoffs. More canceled orders, more layoffs. By the time those involved had been prosecuted and introduced to their prison cells, the business was beyond recovery. The owners had no choice but to declare bankruptcy and close their doors forever.

The factory had lain vacant for over a year when Hank finally walked through the plant's door. It was perfect for his plans. Fully aware that the banks were eager to unload the property, he made an absurdly low offer for the factory and everything in it. It turned out just the way Hank knew it would; the bankers immediately agreed to Hank's terms and the Mariotta Motor Company was born.

Amid all of this drama, Hank and Matilda married and began a family. Over the years, Matilda gave birth to twelve sons and one precious daughter. Eleven of his sons were named after Jesus's apostles. The twelfth they named Luke. His only beloved daughter, whom he doted on, was named Christianna. Their fourteenth died at birth and Matilda died shortly afterward from childbirth complications. Her untimely death devastated Hank; some say he never returned to what he had been. Hank's world had revolved around Matilda. Now that she no longer walked by his side there was a tremendous void in his life, one he was certain could never be filled.

As was characteristically Hank, he turned his energy and focus back to business and acquisitions with greater determination than ever before.

Years later as Hank stood on the bluff overlooking the town that bore his name, his only regret was that his beloved Matilda was not there to share that moment with him.

THE SAN ANTONIO
ANTELOPES

What turned out to be Hank Mariotta's boldest and most successful acquisition came with his purchase of the San Antonio Antelopes NFL franchise. It was a shrewd move that required unmitigated nerve. Hank Mariotta knew nothing about owning a professional football team but treated the business venture as just another challenge to overcome.

The San Antonio Antelopes were one of the original eight teams in the American Football League when the upstart league debuted in 1960. The team's founder Louis Paul Dean was a prominent San Antonian whose family roots could be traced back to the Alamo. The Antelopes remained under the Dean Family throughout the decades; there was always one member of the Dean Family at the helm, making the Antelopes the longest-held franchise under a single family in NFL history. Unfortunately, under the Deans' control, the Antelopes were, at best, mediocre. The team rarely played above five hundred. There was general agreement that the Antelopes could never reach their potential due to lack of investment in the franchise by the Deans.

The Dean family always seemed mired in financial difficulty and reports of their imminent bankruptcy abounded. To make matters worse, Cyril Dean, the last family head of the team, had a reputation that only exasperated the public's perception of the family. An A-list partier, Cyril was known for throwing lavish soirees rivaling F. Scott Fitzgerald's character Jay Gatsby. It was also a well-established tabloid-fact that he, as well as many of the other members of the Dean family, were involved with drugs. Cyril's twin brother Cyrus was alleged to have been so strung-out on cocaine that he had to have his nose cauterized. And when his private life exploded into a public scandal that threatened to smear the NFL's reputation, Cyril Dean was strongly advised to sell the Antelopes.

Under the Deans' ownership, the Antelopes made it to the playoffs only twice. Each time they were eliminated in humiliating first-round defeats. For the fans, a 'Lopes' loss came to be the expected outcome on any given Sunday. Fingers pointed the blame unanimously at mismanagement under Cyril Dean's ownership who, instead of investing in the team and recruiting top talent, squandered money on inconsequential affairs. There were even allegations of sports gambling that, if proven, would force the Deans to relinquish ownership. The league quietly made it known to Cyril that unless he sold the team, they would launch an investigation into these grave charges.

After years of mismanagement and underfunding, the San Antonio Antelopes were not worth much. Gate receipts for their games were some of the lowest in the league and licensed sales were almost non-existent. Nobody wanted to wear an Antelopes jersey much less pay for one. They were a joke and the line of bidders looking to buy the team was about as long as the line in front of the ticket box on game day, which is to say that there were no takers – except Hank Mariotta.

Seeing a rare business opportunity, Hank leapt in to buy the beleaguered team. And after several months of intense negotiations, Cyril Dean signed the contract ending more than forty-five years of Dean ownership. Hank Mariotta became the sole owner of the San Antonio Antelopes.

Hank wasted no time rebuilding the franchise. Seconds after the contract was signed, Hank summarily fired the Antelopes' general manager and shortly after that, the whole front office. By the end of that first day, the only people left from the Dean-era Antelopes were the players under unbreakable contracts. Hank brought in a new general manager named Lou Danner who staffed the front office with talented and experienced veterans. Next, he hired Curt Colby as the Antelopes' head coach who immediately tackled the challenge of instilling confidence in a team that accepted losing as a foregone fact. After Hank's general manager convinced Hank to sign Allan DeGreer, the great free-agent quarterback, the Antelopes underwent an impressively swift regeneration. That first year under new management, when the NFL still played a sixteen-game season, the Antelopes went twelve and four and made it to the playoffs.

From then on, the Antelopes walked with pride over what they had accomplished. Under Hank's ownership, the San Antonio Antelopes became a formidable team. Gate receipts routinely broke records and it became a familiar game-day sight to see citizens of San Antonio sporting the jerseys of their favorite Antelopes players.

As the Antelopes' success grew year after year, Hank never hesitated to reinvest his sizable profits back into the team. His goal was to build a football powerhouse as enduring as baseball's New York Yankees. Hank Mariotta was all about creating a legend and a dynasty.

Anything he decided to embark on, Hank inevitably achieved. Each season, his Antelopes were ranked in football's top tier. For a time, Hank was satisfied with the success he had brought to the Antelopes. But after the wins started becoming routine, Hank became restless and began searching for new challenges. For Hank, it was all about the quest.

MARIOTTAVILLE, TX

Hank Mariotta became a business legend. Mariotta Motors produced the most iconic motorcycle in the country. And in a few short years, the San Antonio Antelopes staged an epic turn-around that took them from being the subject of merciless ridicule to Sports Center talk as possible Super Bowl contenders. All this made Hank the frequent subject of many TV sports shows and business magazines. Original as the media was, they began collectively referring to Hank as "The Midas Man," a moniker Hank deplored.

Despite his success, "The Midas Man" Hank felt unsettled. The Antelopes and Mariotta Motors no longer demanded his constant attention. He'd staffed his businesses with managers whom he knew would not fail. To appease his restlessness, Hank began searching for something new to occupy his drifting attention. Subsequently, he hatched a venture so audacious, so ambitious that, despite his past successes, even some of his closest business associates thought impossible to accomplish. He would build a town.

People often joked about it, and it became town lore as to how Hank Mariotta put his plan forward. According to the story, it all began in a run-down San Angelo restaurant. Between bites of a roast beef sandwich, Hank sketched out on his napkin the beginnings of a new town to be named Mariottaville. It was to be built a few miles southwest of San Angelo between the westernmost fingers of Twin Buttes Reservoir. The myth continued to grow until the Hank-Mariotta-gossip train had him buying up half of West Texas to build it. This, of course, was absurd. Only a Texan or those who have taken a Greyhound bus across Texas can appreciate how big Texas is. West Texas alone encompassed over ninety thousand square miles in which ten New Jerseys could comfortably fit.

Mariottaville would be built on land Hank was very familiar with, and he knew what it would take to develop it. Hank already owned sixty-five hundred acres, about ten square miles but to realize his vision, he bought ninety more square miles of mesquite-filled prairie. On the eastern boundary was seventeen miles of undeveloped waterfront. The town would zigzag around this crown jewel of a lake that boasted some of the best catfish, crappie, and white bass fishing anywhere in Texas.

Once again, it was the challenge of turning the dream into the reality that animated Hank, and soon the planning of Mariottaville consumed him.

In his imagination, Hank envisioned a Disneyland of sorts, only Texas-style. It would take years to complete, but eventually, it was Hank's hope that Mariottaville would become an artistic and cultural oasis. It would offer mini-ranches from ten to one hundred acres to the affluent. It would have an exotic animal habitat, numerous parks, boat ramps, historical museums, and countless other amenities. There would even be a pavilion for hosting concerts and cultural events.

Hank enlisted the help of his family and relatives who were put to work in some capacity. Some assisted him in procuring the tracts of land Mariottaville needed while others helped design a master plan for the community. Even more of the extended Mariotta family were engaged to help develop the infrastructure necessary for a town like Mariottaville. There was the water supply, power sources, sewage processing, and all manner of complicated engineering problems to resolve. It was precisely the kind of work that Hank Mariotta loved, and it absorbed him.

To show his appreciation to those family members and friends who helped him, Hank gave them the right of first refusal for prime property around the lake. Half of the first families to call Mariottaville home came from Hank's immediate and extended family.

It took seven years, but by the time the town was incorporated, Mariottaville was on its way to becoming everything Hank had originally envisioned. It boasted a public library with a West Texas historical reference department that rivaled even some of the best universities in the state, and had its own fire and police station. An elementary school and a high school were the first to go up due to the rapid influx of young families from nearby San Angelo. Of course, numerous small stores and restaurants opened to capitalize on the upstart community. Antique stores, art galleries, eateries, specialized boutiques, and more lined the streets of the town center. Visitors to the village remarked to their friends and neighbors that Mariottaville oozed charm. Still, for Hank, Mariottaville lacked the one thing that was most important to him, a Catholic church. His Catholic faith was his constant counsel and at the core of every decision he made.

THE CONCHO RIVER

Hank was proud of his Italian heritage. His great-great grandparents Giacomo and Lucia Marietta were barely eking out a living as sharecroppers in their small village in southern Italy when what is known as the Risorgimento began in 1860. A period of unification between the northern and southern regions of the country, Risorgimento marked the beginning of what is now considered Italy.

Because most of the wealth was concentrated in the north, the northern cities dominated the newly formed Italian government. These politicians enacted higher taxes, excessive tariffs, and trade regulations that unfairly impacted the people of southern Italy and had devastating effects on them. Life had been hard before, but with the Risorgimento it was an outright struggle. No longer seeing a future for his family, Giacomo Marietta convinced his extended family members to pool their meager resources to fund passage to America for his and his brother's Ernesto families. There they would make good and send for the rest of the family as soon as they could.

The Marietta brothers reached the shores of the United States in the spring of 1867, entering through the city of Galveston, Texas. It was there that port officials misspelled the brother's surname by replacing the 'e' with an 'o' in the official immigration records. Thus began the long history of the Mariotta family in the United States of America.

In Galveston, the Mariottas joined a group of immigrants heading north where it was said that the land was open and free to claim. After nearly two months of difficult travel punctuated by the birth of Luis Mariotta, the group finally made it to where the north and south branches of the Concho joined to form the Concho River – the confluence of America's Manifest Destiny and the hard edge of the western frontier. It was there the Mariottas chose to stake their families' futures.

And fate smiled down on them. With constant work but not without the vigilance of the soldiers at Fort Concho to protect them from frequent Comanche raids, the Mariottas transformed wild, formless acres into the most successful sheep ranch in the territory. As promised, the brothers began sending for the Mariettas remaining in Italy.

In the intervening generations, Mariotta family history became inextricably woven into the fabric of the history of San Angelo and the name Mariotta was as common as the mesquite brush that filled the Texas prairie.

Though the Mariotta family adapted to the customs and ways of their new land, they still held onto many of the traditions of the old country. One of these traditions was a constant commitment to the Holy Catholic church. In a land where faith was either non-existent or the nearest priest was more than one hundred miles away, the family held mass as best they could. Without an ordained priest to administer the sacraments of the Holy Eucharist and Reconciliation (confession), they could not fully practice their faith. A top priority for the Mariotta patriarchy was to establish a parish and bring a priest permanently to San Angelo.

Unwilling to wait for the Catholic Church to send a priest to San Angelo, the family financed the reverse immigration of the first American-born Mariotta, Luis Mariotta, back to Italy to become ordained into the priesthood. It was a dangerous trek and there was no guarantee Luis Mariotta would ever return. But eventually he did. Returning as Father Luis Mariotta, the priest brought with him the ability to confer the holy sacraments to his family.

In 1961, more than eighty years later after Father Luis celebrated his first mass, the diocese of San Angelo was established. No one could argue that the Mariotta families had not been the dominant force in its creation.

HENDERSON, NEVADA

In keeping with family tradition, Hank wanted to establish the first Catholic church in his newly incorporated town of Mariottaville. It seemed preordained and it was no coincidence that as soon as Hank began laying the foundation for the new church, a beleaguered stranger passed through town.

On that hot summer afternoon as Hank was driving home to his ranch, he noticed a man walking along the road in front of him. The man's back was sweat-soaked and his feet dragged from exhaustion. Hank pulled alongside him and asked, "Is there anything I can do to help you?"

The man appeared to be in his forties. His salt-and-pepper hair was matted to his forehead with sweat and his lips cracked. Gratefully, he said, "Yes, my car ran out of gas back a'ways. Do you know where I can get some gas?"

Hank told him there was a Shell station a few miles down the road. The only other gas station was a Chevron about twenty miles away and Hank wasn't about to send this guy off on a two-day hike in this heat. "If you want, I can run you over to the Shell station. I'm heading that way and it would be no problem. You shouldn't be walking out in this heat."

The stranger, who was dripping sweat off his upper lip, said, "Well, thank you so much. I will take you up on your offer." Heat-ridden, the man almost fell into the car.

Hank asked bluntly, "What brings you here? Too bad you ran out of gas during the hottest part of the day. You don't want to be walking anywhere in West Texas during the summer without water. This place is like a blast furnace. You'll dehydrate so fast you'll be a shriveled prune in no time." Hank exaggerated the danger in his attempt to lecture this stranger about the perils of the Texas heat.

"I was down in San Antonio on business."

"Yeah? What kind of business?"

"I was visiting the San Antonio diocese."

"Really, what was your business with them?" Hank couldn't hide his sudden curiosity.

"I am a Roman Catholic priest; my diocese is in Henderson, Nevada. I came for a seminar and someone suggested that I check out

Mariottaville on my way back home. They said it was new and I would enjoy taking in the scenic lake and small shops. My name is Father Lawrence." He put out his hand for a firm handshake. "And what is your name?"

Hank returned the priest's handshake with an even firmer grip. Then with a twinkle in his eye and a somewhat puffed up chest, replied, "Welcome to Mariottaville. I'm Hank Mariotta." Hank was astounded that what he had prayed for so long might be happening. "Excuse me, did you just say you are a Roman Catholic priest?"

Amused, Father Lawrence replied, "Last time I checked, I was. Actually, I am a retired priest. Why? Is there a problem?" He searched Hank's face, waiting for an explanation.

"Well, you won't believe this, but Mariottaville is coming around nicely and we are building a church. But I've been told that there are no priests available to shepherd it. I'm a cradle Catholic and The Faith is an essential part of my life. Retired, you say? Is there any way you can talk with your diocese to be our priest?" Hank poured his heart out to Father Lawrence.

"Well, if your bishop could help petition my case, there is always a chance I'd get the necessary permissions," Father Lawrence admitted. "What a twist! I came here to Mariottaville as a tourist and now I could be coming out of retirement. All because I ran out of gas."

Hank threw back his head with a good laugh. "It appears that there may be a divine reason for our meeting. It proves that not only does God have a good sense of humor, but He's got a plan. I am actually in the middle of pouring the church foundation. We plan to complete it in about seven months. Father. It would be my pleasure to show you around. Perhaps we could even grab some lunch." With a grin, he added, "Then we could talk about how to go about getting you assigned as the priest for Mariotaville's new parish."

Later that evening, Hank and Father Lawrence walked the church site. "I do have a question for you," Hank said quizzically. "Please don't take this the wrong way. But you only look to be in your forties." He paused for a moment and then blurted out, "So how is it that you are retired?"

Father Lawrence looked down as if Hank had slighted him in some way. "I'm not exactly retired. It's just that I have a disability and the diocese uses me as a pinch hitter, so to speak. I have a bad back and sometimes I cannot walk or even get up. My bishop deemed me to be in too poor of health to have a parish of my own. That might be true, but the problem would be fixed if they would buy me a wheelchair that would allow me to get around on my own." The Father replied with a melancholy sigh. "But then they said I would need a handicap van to accommodate my needs and they don't have the funds for both. They have a point, I guess."

Hank didn't know what to think. The father appeared perfectly fine, at least for now. "But you seem okay. I mean, you ran out of gas and were walking around in the hot sun. Are you in any pain right now?"

"Today, my back was cooperating but my car was not. I have good weeks that sometimes go into months, and then my back acts up again and I am laid out for long periods. I have a disease called 'ankylosing spondylitis.' It's a form of arthritis that causes inflammation of the joints in the spine. I know, it's a weird-sounding name."

Hank chuckled and then posed a serious question to Father Lawrence. "Suppose I bought you the fanciest wheelchair and added the latest and greatest van to give you complete mobility. Wouldn't that sweeten the deal to let your bishop release you?"

Father Lawrence pondered the question and after what seemed to Hank like an eternity, exclaimed eagerly, "Yes, I think that might. I think he would!"

Six months later, Hank Mariotta received word from Father Lawrence that the diocese in Las Vegas was talking with the diocese of San Angelo. Together they agreed to transfer him to the San Angelo diocese with the express purpose of pastoring the first Catholic parish of Mariottaville.

The bishop of San Angelo presided over the dedication of St. Lawrence Catholic Church and installed Father Lawrence as its pastor. Eager to nurture the infant church and its new priest, both dioceses supplied interim deacons to assist with the operations of the new parish. The beautiful, solemn christening of the church brought in parishioners from Dallas to San Antonio. Hank was overjoyed.

At the celebration after the mass, Hank joked with Father Lawrence, "Well Father, I bet you never thought you'd pastor a church named after you."

Lawrence smiled and said, "Well, I'm certainly no saint. Saint Lawrence left some mighty big shoes to fill, but it does give me something to aspire to."

In the year 257, despite his young age of twenty-three, Pope Sixtus II ordained Saint Lawrence as a deacon and charged him with the responsibility of managing the church treasury and distributing charity to the poor. A year later, Sixtus was martyred. Saint Lawrence was arrested and ordered to turn the church's wealth over to Rome. Legend has it that he said he would need three days to gather it all. During those three days, Saint Lawrence gave away all the church's money to the poor. He even sold sacred church relics to increase what he was able to give to the poor. When the three days were up, he invited Roman authorities to come to the church. All around them were lepers, orphans, widows, the blind, maimed, and lame. Lawrence, spreading his hands toward his congregation, told the Romans that these people were the Church's real treasure. Greatly angered, the authorities ordered his immediate execution over a bed of hot coals. Legend says that after some time over the coals, Saint Lawrence joked with his executioners, saying, "I'm done on this side. Turn me over." Saint Lawrence became one of seven martyred deacons during a period of brutal Christian persecution under the Roman Emperor Valerian.

The name of Mariottaville's church had been decided on long before Hank and Father Lawrence had crossed paths, but the strange coincidence of their meeting did not escape them; they saw it as confirmation that this was God's will. The two joked that Father Lawrence's car running out of gas turned out to be God's biggest blessing.

Hank could rest easy knowing that the town of Mariottaville was finally complete and that the first Catholic church of his town would flourish.

HOLY GHOST MONASTERY

Father Lawrence found himself given to frequent reflection and introspection. He couldn't help but think that his life began the day he decided to run away from home and Mabel stopped to pick him up. Through the years, Mabel stressed to him that God had told her to pick up that young hitchhiker and be his angel. Father Lawrence always felt her presence throughout his life.

One of Father Lawrence's fondest memories was when Mabel let him take the wheel of her old car and drive around that KOA campground. He had told her that he was sixteen years old, but the truth was that he was barely fourteen years of age. He was small, even for fourteen, and could barely see over the steering wheel. The first thing he did behind the wheel was blast the radio. Father Lawrence remembered Mabel throwing her head back and laughing hard as he steered the beat-up car around the campground's gravel road.

"Scrawny, you're a mess, but I gotta say, you got a handle on things. You're driving just fine. You got a take-charge attitude turning on that radio, making that your first order of business. Someone must have taught you how to drive. I bet I'm right. Did your daddy teach you how to drive?"

Larry thought better of telling Mabel how he and his friend Les had often sneaked Les' daddy's 1964 Oldsmobile out at night and joyrode around the back roads of Mississippi. One time they got caught by Les' daddy, Popeye. His real name was Lester Senior, but everyone called him Popeye because of the corn-cob pipe and sailor's cap he wore as natural as his mustache and full head of hair.

That one night so long ago, Popeye had been waiting for them when Les pulled the car into the garage. Les' daddy flung open the door and dragged Les out by his shirt collar, forcing Les to hold out his hand. He took his smoking pipe and slammed it into the palm of Les hand, emptying the burning tobacco into it. Les screamed in pain. "Maybe that'll make you think twice about wrapping your hands around the steering wheel of my car ever again," the man warned.

When he was through with Les, Popeye made a grab for Larry, but Larry turned and ran out the door faster than he ever thought possible. He heard Popeye yelling behind him, "Your old man is gonna hear about this one, you good-for-nothing brat." But Popeye's threats never stopped them, and they were careful not to get caught by the cops and especially

Popeye again. It was what they did on the weekends for fun and years later Father Lawrence could still see Les sitting behind the steering wheel of Popeye's Oldsmobile, saying, "Let's go get some kicks."

But Larry never revealed his clandestine cruises to Mabel. Instead, any time she asked about his driving skills, he said, "No ma'am, I guess I was just born with a steering wheel in my hand. I know I'm gonna be in the Daytona 500 someday and I'll probably win too."

"Scrawny, you sure are a stitch saying you're going to win the Daytona 500." Mabel held on to her side and said it hurt from all her laughing. Larry had never seen anyone laugh quite like Mabel. She laughed so hard that she started to cry and her tears ran down her fat rosy cheeks.

Often, he would close his eyes and remember their trip to Las Vegas. But once there, Mabel told him that there was no way she was going to drop him off in that godless place. "My God," "It's called *Sin City*, scrawny."

Someone once told her about a Catholic monastery in the desert east of Las Vegas and Mabel announced God was telling her that was where they would go even though she admitted that she had no idea where it was or if it really existed. When they stopped at a dilapidated gas station in a remote town outside of Las Vegas for directions, it turned out that they were just about there. A few miles later, Mabel turned onto the side road that led to the monastery. After cresting a small hill, it seemed like they had entered a new world. Below them spread a sweeping valley bounded by barren mountains that splattered the horizon. In the center of the valley was the monastery, a low, sprawling adobe complex surrounded by a grove of olive trees. From the top of the hill, it looked like a desert oasis in the dry brown of a Nevada desert.

The monastery sat on a few hundred acres of which about one hundred acres had been cultivated and consisted mostly of olive trees. The produce from the olive grove was how the Benedictine monks financially sustained themselves. The olive trees they planted were used to produce olive oil, but not the bread-dipping kind. Their trees did not produce saleable fruit in the form of edible olives as the soil chemistry made the olives far too bitter. Instead, the monks used the fruit to create facial creams and beauty products. They had purchased specialized equipment and presses to cure and process the olive crop into healthy lotions. They produced an entire line of topical creams to heal dry skin, wrinkles, and scar concealer, as well as a host of other beauty treatments.

Over the years, the friars had developed a sizable mail-order business for the sale of their creams. But with the advent of the internet, orders for their products exploded and they found they could barely keep up with the demand. Their flagship product, a small jar of greenish cream they described as the "Desert Fountain of Youth," pictured a kind, old monk wearing a brown robe. Above him read:

Do you want Monk-tastic skin?
We guarantee you will experience
Amazing, Age-eliminating results when you use

St. Benedict's Desert Skin Cream

Each jar has been blessed by our beloved Abbot Karl Schmidt
Presiding over our monastery for 20 years!

Abbot Schmidt of the Holy Ghost Monastery agreed to shelter Larry and Mabel for three months, and no longer. But the monks quickly took a liking to Mabel and began calling her "Aunt Mabel." Three months turned into three years. The monks loved Mabel. She was an excellent cook and her gardening skills allowed them to grow a bountiful garden of different vegetables year-round. Mabel even sewed and darned the monks' socks, joking that they were *holy socks*. And then she would laugh at her own silly pun. Her laughter was contagious and soon the whole abbey caught her affliction.

Mabel never did adopt Larry. But that was only a legal technicality to him. He considered Mabel as much a mother to him as his real mother. He often overheard her speaking with the monks about "her son Larry" or "her boy." And Larry was sure that in her own mind, Mabel looked upon him as her adopted son.

Larry found he enjoyed life with the monks and they taught him many useful skills. At first, he had helped Mabel in the kitchen and garden, but later worked in any capacity the monastery demanded. From carpentry to plumbing, olive harvesting to facial cream chemistry, manufacturing to mail room duties, Larry engaged in every aspect of monastic life.

He particularly enjoyed the frequent long hikes he took with the monks traipsing through the desert. There he learned to identify the surprisingly large variety of desert plants and wildflowers. He learned to observe tiny movements and out-of-place textures in a sea of monotonous shades of brown and realized that the desert was teeming with animal life; lizards, jackrabbits, Gila monsters and mule deer, along with the coyotes, and rattlesnakes all found ways to make the desert their home. The ubiquitous rock outcrops too were more than just rocks. They told their own stories about an ancient Earth that existed millions of years ago. He grew to love the hot, dry sun on his back during the day.

And during moonless, star-lit nights, with the coyotes howling off in the distance, he could almost convince himself that this was heaven.

During those years, Larry also tended to his studies and excelled; Mabel and the monks made sure of that. Their care and concern for his welfare brought new order and stability into Larry's life that kindled his growing faith in God. Undoubtedly, God was answering the prayers and devotions of the doting monks and his adoptive mother Mabel.

At the age of sixteen, Larry legally emancipated himself from his parents in the state of Nevada. During the process, the state found out his mother had passed and his father had gone missing. The only requirement was to prove to the state that he could take care of himself financially. Mabel and the Holy Ghost monks vouched for his veracity on that count which led to the State of Nevada granting his petition. Free to pursue life any way he saw fit, Larry asked if he could continue to stay at the monastery with Mabel and the monks. Of course, they said yes.

When Larry turned seventeen, he announced his decision to become a priest. One dilemma faced him, however; he was afraid to tell the Abbott that he did not want to become monastic, but instead wished to serve as a parish or community priest. The Abbott explained that although they had hoped Larry would join their order, his calling came from God and the monks would support him wherever that calling led him. Larry applied to and was accepted at a nearby college where he could divide his time between work at the monastery and complete his undergraduate studies before heading off to seminary.

One morning at communal breakfast, Mabel announced matter-of-factly that God had told her it was time for her to continue her journey to California. That same afternoon, Mabel left the monastery without saying goodbye to anyone.

Mabel's departure left a void at the monastery that Larry found difficult to adjust to and he added a part-time job as a convenience store clerk to his already busy schedule. Larry was accustomed to hard work. In Mississippi, he had worked to escape his father's cruelty. But now, the extra work was to avoid the monastery's lonely silence that replaced Mabel's cheerful presence.

After Mabel left the monastery, Mabel and Larry corresponded in frequent letters. On rare occasions, whenever Mabel could find a telephone and the change, she gave Larry a call to update him on her nomadic life on the road. While she had made it to California, she wrote that she was stranded in Los Angeles and had not yet made it to San Francisco. Time went by and although Larry became caught up in the business of living his life, he always found the time to correspond with Mabel.

When Mabel failed to reply to his latest letter, Larry became concerned. It had been months since she last wrote. Unable to locate her, all he could do was wonder and worry. One early winter day while working at the Quik-Stop, Larry picked up the latest issue of *USA Today* and skimmed it. It was the usual stuff of politics, scandal, and crime. On page four, however, he found the mini-headline "Women Dies in Car from Carbon Monoxide Poisoning Trying to Stay Warm." Larry dreaded what came next. Mabel was found in her car, dead, on a forest service road about seven miles from a campground near Mount Shasta, California.

The newspaper revealed scant detail about what had happened to Mabel but after contacting the California Highway Patrol, Larry learned the tragic truth.

Witnesses reported that an elderly woman in her late-seventies driving an old Honda had pulled in front of the Camp Shasta campground office. The camp may have needed some basic maintenance and repair, but it boasted of the most spectacularly scenic view of Mount Shasta available from any vantage point. During a full moon, the effect of the soft and silver light on the mountain was positively sublime.

Shortly after the elderly woman had entered the rustic, cedar-planked office, a caravan of shiny new Cadillac Escalades pulled into the campground lot, each of which was towing an equally polished and new Air Stream trailer. The drivers had gotten out of their cars and walked into the office to register.

They waited impatiently behind the old woman who was explaining to the folks behind the counter that she had no money, but hoped to indulge the owner's kindness and let her use one of their hookups to plug in her electric blanket to guard against the night's expected cold. The weather forecast had called for the first hard freeze of the season and temperatures at their elevation were forecasted to dip into the teens. Except for a fifth wheel and a mini motorhome whose generator sounded like it was about to lose a bearing, Camp Shasta was all but empty.

The owners of the camp, a husband and wife team, were suspicious of the old woman and made up a story that park rules did not allow sleeping in your car; there were rest stops for that.

"You must have some kind of trailer," the husband told her.

Mabel had pleaded with them to let her stay. "I promise I won't be any trouble." One of the Air Stream drivers had muttered impatiently for the old lady to get on with it. The other had complained loudly about being exhausted.

The woman repeatedly tried, begging the owners to let her stay in the campground. Again, they had told her, "No." They had state campground guidelines that they were to follow. Then they turned their attention to the Air Stream duo and barely noticed as Mabel left the office.

Larry envisioned what a resourceful Mabel must have done next. She had probably thought that she would find a spot on a back road to pull over, catch some sleep, and stay warm by keeping her car running. Larry grieved as he thought of her on the side of some deserted dirt road, alone. The autopsy determined that she had succumbed to carbon monoxide poisoning, falling asleep peacefully without realizing she was suffocating. At least she had not suffered from hypothermia.

Enraged, Larry thought, *What kind of people were these that had no compassion for this poor woman down on her luck?* He thought of Jesus' parable of the Good Samaritan in which robbers attacked a traveler and took everything he had, even his clothes, and left him for dead on the side of the highway. Two holy men came along and, seeing the man, moved to the other side of the road as they passed. A third man not of God passed by and, seeing the beaten man, took pity and immediately cared for him. If any good was to come out of Mabel's tragic death, it was Larry's renewed determination to enter the priesthood and to serve other people as God commanded. Mabel had been his Good Samaritan and this was Larry's way to honor her memory.

From then on, Larry's life followed the orderly succession of steps necessary to become a priest. He completed his undergraduate degree at the Franciscan University of Steubenville and graduated with a double major in theology and philosophy and a minor in Latin. Then, it was off to seminary for further studies in Greek, Latin, canon law, the history of the Roman Catholic Church, and, of course, the Bible. He excelled and, after four years, graduated with a Masters of Divinity degree. After serving a year as a deacon at a local parish, Father Lawrence made his final vows for the priesthood. He was ordained at age twenty-five after eight intense years of discernment and training.

After his ordination, everything fell rapidly into place for Father Lawrence. In his first job, he was sent to a small parish in Henderson, Nevada named St. Michaels. There, he stayed for fifteen years overseeing its growth from a few hundred families into one of the largest parishes in Clark County. It seemed that he would be at St. Michaels forever until he was suddenly and inexplicably stricken with a severe arthritic malady called *ankylosing spondylitis*. His pain became so severe that he could no longer reliably complete the celebration of the mass. The bishop reluctantly put Father Lawrence into semi-retirement, asking him to assist with services around the diocese as needed. Despite his disappointment, Father Lawrence dutifully complied with the bishop's assignments.

And then one day, he was sent to San Antonio, Texas to attend an annual conference of Catholic laymen and clergy to discuss ways to make the Catholic Church more appealing to young people. He would never forget that day when, in casual conversation during a session break, someone suggested that he return to Las Vegas by way of a little Texas town called Mariottaville. Father Lawrence had intended to make a brief stop there before continuing home, but God was at work and had other plans for him. Mariottaville would become his new ministry.

Father Lawrence saw God's hand directing his every turn in life and was humbled. Looking upwards, he clasped his hands together and prayed an intercessory prayer to Saint Lawrence for continued guidance. With Mabel and his patron saint St. Lawrence at his side, he felt invincible.

1414 BIG SKY RANCH ROAD

Christiana Mariotta had everything she could ever want – Hank made sure of that. Born the youngest of thirteen, she was Hank's only daughter. From the moment she was born, Hank worshipped and adored her. After his beloved wife Matilda died, Hank deflected his grief by pouring his love and adoration onto the only woman left in his life, his Chrissy.

But in addition to a doting devotion, Hank conducted Chrissy's life with the same meticulous control that he did in all of his business ventures. Whether it was who she could be friends with or how she occupied her after-school time, he decided it for her. Chrissy grew up insulated and isolated, oblivious to the fence her father had built to keep her safely corralled.

One Saturday morning, Hank brought his marketing team over to his ranch to discuss Mariotta Motors' latest advertising campaign designed to continue to drive the Maverick's impressive sales into the future. Hank's team argued that they needed to appeal to a younger audience. The Maverick already dominated the hardcore cyclist market, but to continue to grow sales, they had to appeal to a new demographic. Hank looked at the flattening lines on the graphs and charts his team had thrown up on the makeshift easel and immediately understood the issue without the need for further explanation or interpretation. "Thank you, gentlemen; I've got it. What do you propose?"

Before the team had a chance to respond, Chrissy burst into the room dressed in riding gear and visibly distressed. "Daddy, Chico bolted and I can't get him to come back. You've got to help me round him up."

Hank looked at her and smiled. "Okay Chrissy, as soon as I finish here, we will go corral Chico. For now, have a seat while we finish our meeting." Chrissy sat next to her father on the soft leather couch.

Turning his attention to his staff, Hank said, "I'm sorry for the interruption, gentlemen. Cooper, you were just about to tell me your proposal for appealing to the younger set." Cooper did not respond. Instead he appeared distracted and was staring at Chrissy with an odd expression on his face. Chrissy didn't seem to notice, but Hank certainly did.

"Cooper!" Hank barked impatiently.

Cooper rattled his head and shook himself back into focus. "Uh. I'm sorry, Mister Mariotta. Yes, we feel that to build up interest in the younger market, we need to soften up the Maverick's image. Make it more like a girl magnet. A guy that age thinks about only one thing, and if we make it the *cool* ride that girls respond to, we feel that this is the kind of appeal that will open the door to a whole new market for us."

Hank was silent. He stared at Cooper for a moment and then turned his attention to the men standing next to Cooper. "So, you want to sex it up? What are we going to do, have bikini-clad Playboy bunnies stretched out along the bike?" Hank paused, clearly unimpressed. "No! That is *not* Mariotta Motors."

Cooper responded quickly. "No sir, that's not our idea at all. We want to showcase the Maverick as innocent fun for the younger crowd. All straight up and proper, but implying the freedom and independence that they can only get by riding a Mariotta Maverick. We do envision using a female model, but not the type you see in the usual biker magazines. Our girl will be the quintessential 'Girl Next Door,' attractive, fun-loving, but innocent. Something like the Ivory Girl image, if you recall those commercials from years ago."

Hank did remember those old commercials and was beginning to see the possibilities of the campaign. "I like it. But where do you find a girl like that? Nowadays they all have tattoos and nose piercings and pink and green hair." Everyone laughed at this.

"Well sir, I think we've found her." Cooper motioned to Chrissy. "And she's right here in this room."

The room went cold. Hank sat rigidly on the couch, dumbfounded. Cooper's colleagues glared at him in horror as they saw their careers disintegrate like a Star Trek teleporter. Cooper fidgeted nervously evidently unsure about what he'd said.

After a long and unnerving pause, Hank jumped off the couch and approached Cooper. "Let me get this straight. Are you telling me that you want to make my only daughter the spokeswoman and figurehead for The Mariotta Maverick? You want *my* Chrissy to star in a bunch of commercials and use my pride and joy, *my baby girl*, to help me sell motorcycles? For God's sake, man, she's only fifteen years old!"

Copper appeared paralyzed but managed to sputter a reply, "Well sir, I mean no disrespect, but the moment your daughter came into this room I thought she had the exact qualities we are looking for: youth, innocence, and authenticity."

Chrissy jumped up and tugged at her father's arm excitedly. "Daddy, please? It would be the greatest thing that ever happened in my entire life. Please, Daddy? I won't let you down. Please let me do this."

"Absolutely not!" Hank replied emphatically. Then addressing Cooper, he said, "This meeting is over. We'll take it up again on Monday.

Good day, gentlemen." Hank left the room abruptly, dragging Chrissy alongside him.

From that moment on, there was no peace for Hank in the Mariotta household. Chrissy pestered him mercilessly, pleading to allow her to do his commercials. And in the end, Hank had no choice but to relent and reluctantly agree to use Chrissy in his new advertising campaign. So, at the tender age of fifteen, Hank's beloved daughter set off for California to become the face of the Mariotta Maverick.

Of course, Hank was not about to rely on the integrity of the Tinseltown crowd to shield his only daughter from the temptations that Hollywood had to offer. He insisted on maintaining complete control of every aspect of the campaign shoots and frequently demanded script rewrites and wardrobe changes, much to the frustration of the commercial's director. Most of the time, Chrissy was cloaked from head to toe, but none of that mattered. The camera loved Chrissy; no matter what she wore, her natural beauty and disarming innocence always shone through. Cooper had been right – Chrissy was the perfect choice.

After the release of Mariotta Motors' initial set of commercials featuring Chrissy, Maverick sales turned north again. Hank's daughter had an undeniable appeal that went beyond her looks. With her alluring sapphire eyes and stunningly high cheekbones, Chrissy was the girl every Maverick rider dreamed of sitting on the back of his motorcycle with, her arms wrapped tightly around him as they cruised off into the sunset together.

The commercial scripts were sparse on dialogue, assigning Chrissy only one or two simple lines which read: "What a treasure the Maverick is. Don't you think? Wouldn't you like to ride one?" It was playfully suggestive but still prim and proper. Whenever his schedule allowed, Hank accompanied Chrissy to Los Angeles and never let her out of his sight during the commercial shoots. When he could not be there, he sent one of her brothers to protect her. She was not allowed to make personal appearances at any promotional or media events and Hank forbade her from speaking with the press She might have been the face of Mariotta Motors, but she was still *his* daughter.

For Chrissy, it was good and bad. The bad being she could never experience any of life's lessons and knew little of the world except for what her father allowed her to see. The good being that at least her father let her do the commercials.

The problem with Chrissy was that if anyone outside of her large extended family did talk with her, she was unable to engage them in even the most casual of conversations. Chrissy was painfully shy almost to the point of exhibiting hints of autism. Even at fifteen, she seemed to have the maturity of a little girl. Among family too, she wasn't exactly talkative. It wasn't that Chrissy had a low IQ. She had tested on the high side of average. No, Chrissy was just about as normal a young woman one could expect from being raised by a loving but over-protective widowed father and his twelve sons. Chrissy wasn't one to talk about herself, no matter the problem. She was very affectionate with Hank and her brothers, but she never confided in them. She had a reserve about her as well as a natural desire for privacy that kept her from becoming close friends with anyone. This, compounded by her dominating father, only served to exacerbate and amplify what many perceived as an arrogant aloofness.

Chrissy turned eighteen the same year her father acquired the San Antonio Antelopes. And though now legally an adult, Hank continued to shield Chrissy from anything connected to the outside world, especially anything related to the National Football League.

Her name and face had become synonymous with all things "Mariotta Maverick," and it was inevitable that many players on the Antelopes would be interested in Hank's beautiful daughter. He was determined to keep her a mysterious ingénue, and nobody could recall having ever seen her attend even one of the Antelope's games.

The decision to use Christianna Mariotta as the spokeswoman for the new Maverick advertising campaign was wildly successful. First suggested by Cooper Jansen several years earlier, now the company's lead marketing strategist, sales of the Maverick continued to grow as a whole new market opened up to Mariotta Motors. It was all thanks to Christianna, who became the face of Mariotta Motors.

Every few months she'd fly out to Hollywood to film the latest Maverick commercial. Despite Chrissy being familiar and in many ways a veteran of the entire commercial making routine, Hank always sent her with a full contingent of keepers to watch over her. Her entourage included at least two of her brothers and occasionally someone from her extended family. For her part, Chrissy was professional, knew her lines, and rarely made mistakes.

Her brothers kept her from making friends with anyone other than the director and fellow actors. Once a shoot wrapped up, Chrissy was immediately hustled into a limo and onto Hank's private jet waiting on the tarmac, all fueled up and ready to fly her back home. The funny thing was that Chrissy did not object to the smothering oversight, and she was always most content to hang out with her favorite brothers Luke and Bartholomew.

While Chrissy enjoyed her excursions to Los Angeles, she remained peculiarly ambivalent about the success of the commercials she made or the mystique they generated surrounding herself. Making a career out of acting never crossed her mind and at home in Mariottaville, she remained the unaffected Chrissy Mariotta who openly talked of entering a convent to serve the Lord.

For as long as she could remember, Chrissy had dreamed of becoming a nun. And every time she spoke of it, her father was very supportive and encouraged her to pursue her calling. "Your mother would be pleased," he would tell her. The idea had become so much a part of her for so long that she had convinced herself that it was what she was going to do with her life.

About that same time, Hank arranged for Chrissy to visit a convent near San Antonio named "Our Lady of the Mission."

After interviewing with the head Abbess, Mother Ruth, and touring the facility, Chrissy was asked to wait outside an office while the Abbess and her father spoke.

"Mister Mariotta. I'll be frank and to the point. Your daughter isn't a good candidate for a religious vocation," Mother Ruth explained matter-of-factly to Hank. "She lacks the discipline and clarity of purpose to become a nun. The calling she thinks she feels coming from our Lord is, in my view, actually one that has been pounded into her since she was a child."

Hank felt sucker-punched by Mother Ruth. She was accusing him of forcing the idea of Crissy becoming a nun on his only daughter.

Hank sat silently as Mother Ruth continued. "Furthermore, Christianna is immature and over-indulged with material things." Hank had to admit to himself that maybe Mother Ruth was right about this as well. He had never denied his daughter anything. Nor had he ever given her any responsibilities or chores to perform. Her only life experiences were a few shallow modeling jobs and television commercials; hardly the challenging work that would instill a determined work ethic in somebody. Christiana was spoiled, and Mother Ruth worried that she would not be able to adapt to life in a convent. In other words, Christiana had a case of arrested development.

She thanked Hank again for his generous contribution to the order and recommended that she wait a few more years to see what the future might bring. "The Lord has his ways you know," she concluded.

SAN ANGELO, TEXAS

Bruce Rebenack, the sophomore quarterback for the San Antonio Antelopes was coming into his own. Already he had generated media interest and rapidly became a legend with his fans. Along with his classic movie star looks, his enthusiasm, discipline, and vigor helped to complete his character. He had a natural talent and could launch a football into the air at rocket speed. Nicknamed "Rebel," he approached the game of football as he did everything else in life – passionately independent. Teams never knew how to play him as he was as predictable as a tornado. It was this that confounded his opponents and usually left them on the losing side of any given play. The moniker "Rebel" suited him well; living up to it came as naturally to him as breathing.

Hank thought well of his young quarterback. Although unconventional, Rebel had a clean past. At a time when most ballplayers of his stature carried some sort of baggage in the form of cocky attitudes or indiscretions of mild delinquency or of a criminal nature, Bruce Rebenack was the exception. Rebel had none of it, and as it turned out, Rebel was a devout Christian. But while this gave Hank and his star quarterback something in common, Hank nevertheless wanted Bruce "Rebel" Rebenack nowhere near his family, especially his precious Chrissy.

Recently, Hank had noticed a disconnect between Bruce and his rookie tight end, Darius Michael. He knew Rebenack had great chemistry with his wide receiver JC Stewart who was Rebel's favorite receiver; they usually connected to put points on the board. But there were problems when it came to the new tight end.

He had discussed the matter with both his general manager, Lou Danner and, of course, Coach Curt Coby. Both had seemed to be indifferent to the problem, claiming the tight end was merely green and still learning the Antelopes' system. After all, he was new to the team as well as the NFL. Danner and Coby did not seem to see a problem they could not resolve as the football season progressed. Still, Hank felt this needed to be addressed and so went around his coach and staff. And though it was extremely rare for an owner to get involved with the mechanics of the game, he took the unusual step of inviting the young quarterback to his ranch for a private conference. The Antelopes' continued success was on the line.

      Bruce felt a certain amount of anxiety over being invited to the owner's house. Like everyone else on the team, he had heard about Big Sky Ranch but had never been there. He was apprehensive as he made the long drive up to San Angelo.

      Why was he being summoned to an audience with the great Hank Mariotta? Had he not delivered? Where was Hank's wingman GM Lou Danner? Would he be there? And if not, why? And what about Coach Coby? Bruce was perplexed and didn't know what to think.

      He followed the directions he had been given and turned onto Big Sky Ranch Road. As he continued along the empty road, he spotted a large wrought-iron gate, over which spanned a massive metal arch that read BIG SKY RANCH.

      He pulled to a stop outside the gate and leaned on the steering wheel to appreciate the intricate metalwork when a sudden movement caught Rebel's attention. *God!* he thought to himself, eyeing the girl leaning against the gate. *She is exquisite.* Instantly, he knew who she was. She was the mysterious Christianna of Mariotta Maverick fame, the lovely daughter Hank kept to himself and his family.

      Of course, Christianna was the topic of a lot of locker room chatter, but no one had ever seen her in the flesh. It was an unspoken rule not to even mention her name around Lou Danner or Coach Coby – and especially not Hank Mariotta. And yet, there she was, walking toward his car like a vision. She had a curvaceous body and cascades of blond hair blanketed her shoulders. With the flash of a smile, she stopped at his car. Rebel mumbled to himself, "Can this really be?" She had to be the most coveted and elusive woman on the planet, and yet, there she was standing in front of him. He could not believe his eyes or his good fortune.

      "Do you need to get in? Who are you here for?" she asked. Rebel thought she had a childlike voice. "I am Bruce Rebenack and I have a meeting with Hank Mariotta." He could not stop staring and seemed to enter into another dimension where time no longer mattered. He was certain that if he looked away for even a moment, she'd disappear into the night like a mythic wood nymph.

"Oh, okay, he is my father. I'll let you in. Let me buzz the house to let him know you are here." Rebel took note of her Texas drawl; it had a melodic rhythm. He was mesmerized. He reached out to take her hand.

"Nice to meet you. What is your name?" He felt like such a fake. Of course, he knew her name from all of her TV commercials, but he wanted to hear it from her own lips. He worried that she would see through his transparency. You would literally have to be dead not to recognize Christianna Mariotta. Hers was the face everyone talked about. Her picture was on the cover of more than one fashion and beauty magazine. *People* magazine had featured her in a cover story even though they admitted that Christianna Mariotta had not participated in any way. And without a Twitter or Facebook account to reference, everything in the article about her relied on unnamed sources. And Rebel remembered how the article described her as one of the most beautiful yet intriguingly enigmatic women since Greta Garbo. He now understood why.

Christianna took his hand ever so lightly and said, "I am Christianna Mariotta. It's nice to meet you too."

Wow! was all he could think.

After parking, Bruce floated across the wide limestone porch that encircled the house through the open front doors where Hank waited. The home or, more precisely, ranch, was spectacular. Bruce had heard talk of Mariotta's big house, but even Bruce's wildest dreams could not have conjured this.

Upon entering the mammoth foyer, Bruce marveled at the soaring limestone walls and the marble floors streaked with intricate veins of pink and grey. The house was stately, unique, yet comfortable. Everything about it suggested class without pretension, much like the owner himself.

As Hank led him to the library, Bruce peered into rooms and down hallways. The house took Bruce in and made him want to explore it. All of the building material in the home was indigenous to West Texas. The soaring limestone walls supported massive rafters of sweet-smelling pinyon pine that reached even further for the sky. Hank guided him past a winding staircase built from mixed red and live oak and through two massive, hand-hewn cedar doors into the library, an enormous multi-level room with staircases that stepped down to the main sitting level. On the far side of the room was a sculptured wall of cut limestone interspersed with slabs of pink Llano granite that created a grand fireplace which consumed one whole side of the room. Pictures of the Mariotta Clan adorned the walls and shelves.

There were also western and cowboy-themed paintings and photographs scattered throughout the room. One wall devoted entirely to books stretched upward like a vertical library, boasting four levels with winding brass staircases connected by oak-paneled scaffolding between them. Despite the extravagance of the architecture however, the focal point of the room was a life-size, oil painting of Matilda Mariotta, Hank's deceased wife. She had been a beautiful woman and Bruce could feel her arresting blue-green eyes staring at him. This was Hank Mariotta's private world. Bruce felt privileged to have been allowed into it and doubted he would ever experience anything so extraordinary in his life again.

Rebel's meeting with Hank, however, did not come close to matching the grandeur of the house. It turned out that Hank wanted to make sure Bruce understood how important it was for their new running back Drew Perry to learn the Antelopes' play calls. Hank wanted to see more running plays and he wanted Drew Perry to lead the attack. Perry showed promise but needed to learn the signals as well as the Antelopes' play-calling system. "Bruce, that's why I called you here today. As the team captain, it is incumbent on you to mentor your players and recognize and address issues as they arise. This disconnect has to be corrected immediately. Son, I need you to step up."

Rebel had heard all of this before from Coach Colby and was already working with Drew on learning the Antelopes' playbook. "Yes, sir, Mr. Mariotta. I understand."

"Thank you, son. I hope you do," Hank said, ending their meeting.

As Bruce stood to leave, he felt relieved. Now that he knew he wasn't in trouble, he wanted to take in the house in its entirety and store its details in his memory. But that plan came to a quick end when the doors to the library flew open and in walked, or rather, in bounced, Christianna Mariotta. Instinctively Hank jumped between them almost like a defensive lineman ready to protect his QB from a hard-rushing tackle.

"Um, ah. This is my daughter Christianna. Christianna, this is Bruce Rebenack who plays quarterback for the Antelopes as you well know."

Bruce's eyes met hers again and they both said in unison, "Yes, we already met."

"And just how did you two meet each other?" Bruce didn't miss the accusatory tone in his Hank's voice or the irritated look on his face. His polite composure from before had all but disappeared.

"Daddy," grinned Christianna. "We met outside by the gate. I was taking a walk and I let him in."

"Well then, Chrissy, why don't you walk Mr. Rebenack out to his car?" asked Hank, turning to shake hands with Bruce once more. Bruce wiped the shadow of surprise from his face. "Okay, son, get on with it, and I don't want to see any more missed signals."

"Yes sir, Mr. Mariotta. Thank you for having me here." Bruce turned and walked out with Christianna. Following her, he reveled in his fantastic luck.

As they left the porch, Christianna added a playful sway to her walk out to his red Corvette. Then without warning, she turned and asked him in a very casual tone, "Well, how did you like my daddy?"

"Your father is awesome, and so is this place." Rebel looked up again at the house pretending to take it in one last time. He hoped Christianna knew that he was really referring to meeting her. "Do you know how many acres it covers?"

Christianna blushed a little, seemingly embarrassed at her father's opulence and wealth. Her modesty made her all the more appealing to him. "The ranch alone is sixty-five hundred acres, and as you know, Daddy owns the whole town."

Without hearing what she said – and without thinking – he blurted out, "Hey Christianna, what are you doing this Friday night? Would you like to go out to dinner? How about it?"

Christianna turned bright pink and in a small, barely audible voice said, "I'll think about it. I don't know yet. Maybe."

Bewildered, Bruce puzzled over her response. Was she playing hard to get or had her friendliness been a trick? It occurred to him that maybe she was just a shy young girl. No, that couldn't be it. Why would somebody like her be shy?

Bruce could not get into his car fast enough, stammering out an obligatory and polite goodbye, "Well, okay, it was nice meeting you anyway. Maybe I'll see you around sometime." He raced down the driveway, leaving a bewildered Christianna behind. He would have to concoct a plan to see her again. She was well worth it. But her rejection put him in a lousy mood.

He accelerated down the drive, nursing his wounded pride and almost smashed through the now closed Big Sky gates. He jammed on the brakes and skidded to a stop just inches from blasting through them. He backed up and reached out to push the intercom button to ask for the gate to be opened. But before he could, the massive gates swung open and Rebel raced hard down the road, not caring to look back.

Christianna waved goodbye as Bruce sped off. Feeling awkward and ashamed, she ran back inside the house. Once inside, she pushed the gate button so it would be open when he got there. She didn't want to take the chance of speaking with him again even if it was through an intercom. Christianna's stomach churned.

She had seen the confusion on Bruce's face when she had turned him down. But how could she get this past her father and brothers? She knew they would sabotage their date if they ever found out, but all she wanted to tell Bruce was, "Yes. Yes. *Yes!*" She could never tell Bruce the truth about why she couldn't go out with him and suddenly felt embarrassed.

She needed to talk to somebody, but in whom could she confide? The only person she had ever opened up to was her priest Father Lawrence. But that had always been about vain, little girl problems. How could he possibly help her with something like this? He was a priest, after all.

They would meet again, she was certain. Next time, she'd be ready. Christianna began working on her plan.

DAVY CROCKETT STADIUM

For as long as her father owned the San Antonio Antelopes, Christianna never wanted to attend a game. Football didn't interest her. On occasion, her father invited her to come to a home game as long as she stayed by her brothers. But she always declined. It was just something her father, and most of her brothers and uncle did for a living. It seemed everyone in the Mariotta family held positions in the Antelopes organization except for her. She remained an outsider. She planned on changing that. Now Christianna devised a plan she knew even her overbearing father couldn't help but approve. One evening at dinner, she sprang her idea.

Knowing the Antelopes had a home game in two weeks against the Carolina Panthers, Christianna asked her father if she could watch the game from the sidelines with her brothers. Luke, one of her favorite brothers and a team doctor, told her he would be glad to take her to the game. He also assured Hank that he would keep a watchful eye on Chrissy.

Phillip challenged his brother. "How can you play chaperone to Chrissy *and* be on the sidelines doctoring the team at the same time? That won't work. How 'bout Bart and I babysit Chrissy and leave you to your work?"

Luke agreed, which suited Christianna just fine as she and Bartholomew – or "Big-Hearted Bart" – always had fun together. He was her favorite brother, second only to Luke. She loved her brother Philip as well, but he had a temper that could ignite at the slightest provocation and that frightened Christianna.

Hank Mariotta seemed to be rendered speechless and she could see the mild surprise in his face. "Why all of a sudden have you seen the light?" he asked jokingly.

Christianna bounced over to her father and threw her arms around him, "Oh Daddy, it's about time I learn what you do for a living!"

"All right, but one rule I have is that you don't talk or interfere with any of the players before, during, and after the game. I don't want you to be involved with any of them. They need to be concentrating too. And make sure to stay with Philip and Bart at all times. Do you understand?"

Christianna smiled coyly, she had to think fast. "But Daddy, how about that quarterback I met last week? It was your idea to have him come to the house and you *did* introduce us. Do you mean to tell me I can't even say 'Hello' if I see him? What harm could that do? Besides," Christiana emphasized the 'besides', "you don't need to worry. He's not really my type. Why would I go for a football player? They just aren't at the top of my list." Before last week that had been true and so she did not count that small omission as lying to her father. But now, she felt different and couldn't wait to see Bruce Rebenack again.

That appeared to appease her father but he stressed his concern to Chrissy, "Okay, you can wave to him. I don't want anything to distract Mister Rebenack. He needs to focus on one thing only, and that is winning the game." Christianna gave her father a hug and pecked his cheek with a kiss. "Thank you, Daddy. You're the best!" She always knew how to butter him up.

Two weeks later, the Carolina Panthers arrived in San Antonio for the Sunday game. The day before, Christianna joined her brothers in the four-hour drive from the ranch to San Antonio. They stayed in the family condo near Davy Crockett Stadium and that evening, Bart, Philip, and Christianna strolled along the River Walk and had dinner on the patio of a Mexican café.

With kick-off scheduled for noon, Christianna arrived at Davy Crockett Stadium around nine-thirty a.m. with Bart and Philip. Luke and her other brothers were already there, too busy with their work to notice her. All around her was the buzz of activity. Television crews set up their cameras and reporters performed sound checks with their producers in the booths. Groundskeepers laid the final lines on the field as a steady trickle of fans filled the stadium.

Around eleven forty-five, everything was finalized. A loud voice reverberated through the stadium, "Ladies and Gentlemen. Please welcome your San Antonio Antelopes!" A cloud of smoke and flashing strobes introduced the Antelopes. As they came running through the tunnel into the stadium with Bruce "Rebel" Rebenack leading the pack, the crowd erupted with thunderous applause. Fireworks exploded around the stadium.

Among the swarm of activity around her, Christianna saw Bruce who was pumped up on adrenaline and obviously feeding off the cheers of the crowd. She watched her father and the Antelopes' coaches clasping their heavy-looking clipboards. They all wore headsets and were talking to faceless assistants in upstairs booths, engrossed in finalizing their game plans.

When Chrissy was younger, her father used to try to explain the game of football to her in terms of X's and O's. It never made much sense to Christianna. Football to her was just a weird form of tic-tac-toe.

And although she found the whole game experience unexpectedly exciting, the game of football itself still didn't interest her.

After high-fiving his fellow players, Bruce moved off to the side to practice throws with the backup quarterback. He had a look of fierce intensity and Chrissy was certain that nothing could break his concentration. Still, she didn't want to take the chance of distracting Rebel so she slid behind Bart and Phillip but continued to watch Rebel from behind her brothers.

Christianna saw Thomas, another of her brothers, out of the corner of her eye. He ran by her making odd signals with his arms and hands. She could hear him yelling in a fiery voice for the team to listen up. Thomas was the Antelopes' assistant defensive line coach and had a reputation for being quite the taskmaster. His ambition was to be appointed head coach. But for now, Curt Colby had a firm hold on that job, especially with GM Lou Danner backing him. There was a tension between the three of them, and Thomas knew the only reason he remained there was because his father owned the team.

But Thomas was not above leveraging his family relations to further his ambition. It seemed that whenever his father was within hearing distance, Thomas would loudly criticize Colby's play calls, or his coaching style, or something else intended to undermine his fathers' confidence in Coach Colby. But Hank ignored his son's machinations. Thomas just wasn't ready to be a head coach, and Hank wasn't about to upset the delicate team balance Colby created because of blatant nepotism.

Besides, Coach Colby did well with the Antelopes. Two years before, he had taken them into the postseason playoffs for the first time in their history. And though they were eliminated in the first round, San Antonian's enthusiasm was overwhelming and Hank publicly announced his support for his head coach, giving Colby much of the credit for the increased revenue just that one postseason game had generated. Curt Colby's claim as the Antelopes head coach was secure but Thomas continually strived to work himself into the position he considered rightfully his.

Bruce "Rebel" Rebenack was playing a good game. At half time he had already thrown two touchdown passes, and the Antelopes were beating the Panthers by fifteen points. Rebel's play calls had confused the Panther's defensive line and his signal for a last moment play change was picked up by both Darius Michaels and Drew Perry. Rebel could spot even the most well-disguised blitz, and Coach Colby trusted Rebel to change play calls whenever he saw a defensive formation his line was not prepared to repel.

Rebel was also agile. He had a quick release and was mobile out of the pocket. His arm was strong and his throws were accurate. On short-yardage passes, the ball shot from Rebel's hand like a bullet, and it was nothing for him to lob a long bomb downfield to connect with his reliable wide receiver JC Stewart on the five-yard line. It was an alliance that rarely failed, and Rebel could always rely on "Velcro Fingers" JC.

The half-time show featured the United States Marine Drum and Bugle Corps which consisted of 80 active-duty servicemen dressed in their finest ceremonial garb. A sea of white and red, the band produced a powerful sound and played several favorite and crowd-pleasing songs. Upon concluding with a medley of military classics by John Philip Sousa, fans rose to their feet and excitedly cheered. The noise deafened Christianna as she gaped first at the band and then at the thousands of fans around her.

Sitting about fifteen rows behind the Antelopes' bench was a large woman dressed in an Uncle Sam suit wearing a tall red, white, and blue stovepipe hat with two American flags jammed into the sides. The splendor of the Marine Drum and Bugle Corps must have filled her with such a patriotic fervor that she jumped out of her seat and came bouncing down the aisle toward the field. The woman built up so much momentum as she descended the stairs that the railing was no match for her two hundred pounds hitting it at full throttle. She flipped over the fence and fell onto the field with a thud in front of Christianna and her brothers. As the wind carried her hat and flags into the air, the woman lay on the ground motionless, curled in the fetal position, and apparently in pain. She emitted a shrill piercing moan.

Christianna, Bart, and Philip rushed to help the woman up. But the lady took offense and waved them away as she rose to her feet, snarling, "I don't need your stinking help. I may be fat and out-of-shape, but don't count me out. I'm just fine, thank you very much!" The woman ripped the Uncle Sam hat from Christianna's hands and flashed her a venomous glare. The Mariotta siblings watched bemusedly as the woman suddenly dashed onto the field. Running up to the marching band, the woman launched herself in the air, tackling one of the horn players to the ground with a ferocious bear hug.

It all happened so fast. A gleaming, brass trumpet shot into the air as its owner, once so resplendent in his Marine dress blues, tumbled to the ground with a two hundred fifty-pound woman dressed as Uncle Sam sprawled atop him. The two marching Marines next to him bore the collateral impact of the robust lady's leap into their formation, sending them staggering into other musicians. In the entanglement, another horn became a casualty as it was trampled deep into the natural grass field on the fifty-yard line. What was once a shiny and glorious piece of brass that produced a triumphant sound was now a twisted pile of muted scrap metal.

Within seconds, a battalion of security guards and police poured onto the field to subdue the lady. Struggling to remove her, the woman met them with kicks and blows. Through the chaotic noise, Christianna heard a cop crack that she had a powerful uppercut after being the recipient of one her punches. Finally, the security detail handcuffed the woman and marched her out off of the field to a chorus of cheers and taunts from the crowd.

Christianna had a front row seat to the spectacle and had been watching from the sidelines with astonishment when suddenly a burly cop stood menacingly in front of Christiana, obstructing her view. She recognized him as one of the policemen who wrestled with the demented lady. He was in an ornery mood and with his face freshly scratched, looked like he had taken worse than he had given. To Christianna's alarm, her brothers were nowhere in sight.

The policeman peppered her with questions. "Do you know that woman? What did you say to her when she first fell? Did you incite her. Have you been drinking?"

Christianna stammered, flushing under the interrogation. "How do you, uh, know I even tried to help her?" Christianna managed to reply.

The policeman answered her sarcastically. "Uh ma'am, you were on the Jumbotron. Who *didn't* see you?" Christianna looked up at the big screen and staggered under the crushing humiliation she felt. Wishing she was invisible, she wondered why she ever wanted to come to this game. Where were Bart and Philip? She laughed mockingly after remembering how they had promised her father they would look after her. Christianna was working herself into quite a foul mood.

Things only got worse for Christianna when Bruce Rebenack and the rest of the team returned to the sideline to begin the second half. Everyone in the stadium stood to welcome their team back. The clapping and cheers had reached such a crescendo that the cop was forced to postpone his questioning. But Christianna tried to explain that she had no information to give the officer about this unstable lady. She and her brothers were only playing the part of the Good Samaritan.

The officer, however, showed no intention of leaving when all Christianna wanted to figure out was how she could *accidentally* run into Bruce after the game. Humiliated over the debacle of their last meeting, Christianna wanted a chance to redeem herself. But could she make this happen? And if she did manage to see Bruce, would her social ineptness turn her into a blathering adolescent again?

She looked over at the bench and saw Bruce. Their eyes locked. He saw her too. She looked up and once again she was the star of the Jumbotron. The caption on the bottom of the screen identified her: "The daughter of Hank Mariotta, owner of the San Antonio Antelopes." Some in the crowd let out wolf howls, and Christianna's heart started hammering in her ears. Could one die from sheer humiliation?

Meanwhile, the brusque, pesky cop must have realized who she was because he disappeared. Christianna thought he left when he saw her face plastered on the Jumbotron. She was relieved that he was gone and guessed that he had finally figured out she had nothing to do with that half-brained Uncle Sam or patriotic Aunt Samantha. Now, hopefully the second half of the game would continue without her becoming part of the entertainment.

Luke and Bart had conveniently disappeared during her ordeal with security and now returned. Bart held a tub of popcorn while Phillip carried a tray of hot dogs, fries, and drinks. Even though the gesture was kind, Christianna was irritated that they had taken off without telling her, leaving her alone to defend herself against the cop's intimidating questioning. When she pressed them on why they had run off on her like that, she received different answers. Bart said he was so hungry that he couldn't see right. Phillip told her that he was answering nature's call.

During the second half, Christianna occasionally glanced over at her father. Unlike other NFL owners who watched their teams play from the privacy of luxurious suites with catered delicacies and top-shelf liquors, Hank Mariotta preferred to be on the field. He could always be found on the sidelines taking copious notes on a clipboard that became his third appendage on game day. Her father was animated and prone to outbursts of either anger or excitement. When an official flagged one of the Antelopes' defensive players for being offside and given a five-yard penalty, Hank threw his clipboard in a fit of rage. A bit later, her father exploded on one of his players after the athlete fumbled a punt that was recovered by the Panthers. Capitalizing on the mistake, the Carolina Panthers ran it in for a touchdown. Christianna watched her father swear wildly at the unfortunate player. Hank's public behavior was something she had never witnessed in private. Christianna was seeing another side of her father that she neither recognized or knew existed. She had to admit that it frightened her.

The game ended with the Antelopes demolishing the Panthers. The Antelopes scored thirty-five and the Panthers only six. The Panthers kicker, whose big claim to fame was kicking barefoot, shanked the twenty-yard extra point as the pigskin veered far right of the uprights. The mortified kicker blamed it on the wind and a cut on his foot. He hobbled back to the sidelines while the crowd jeered with chants of, "Where are your shoes? Where are your shoes?" He was no match for the Antelopes' placekicker, Edmund Gerry, who was the best in their entire division. The whole Antelope offense was outstanding. Even Drew Perry, the Antelopes' new running back had proved his worth. He had a one hundred twenty-yard rushing day with twenty-five ball carries, all of which helped to alleviate Hank's worries about his newest acquisition.

Watching the Antelopes file into the locker room from the stadium, Christianna was determined to see Bruce even if she had to set up camp by the locker room and spend the night at the stadium. Her only problem was how to dodge her father and brothers. Fortunately for her, they had already gone into the locker room eager to join the victory celebration. Of course, the media would be waiting for Bruce Rebenack. She was surprised they hadn't snagged him midfield for a few words about the game already. But that didn't happen. Instead, the media stationed their cameras and reporters outside the locker room to ambush the game's star quarterback.

Suddenly, there he was. Christianna craned her neck to see Bruce. How was she to intercept him? She hadn't moved since the game ended and she was sure he had hastily run into the locker room with the rest of the players. But to her surprise, the press had set up their ambush right next to her. He swept past the reporters, but became tangled in the scrum of sports commentators calling out to him, begging for some of his time.

"Hey Bruce, come on over here. We're live. You played a great game. Come on over here and join us. We promise to take only a few minutes of your time." Christianna thought the sportscaster looked familiar; she had seen the woman many times on ESPQ. She was tall and skinny with a horse face framed in bleach-blond hair. And if Christianna remembered correctly, the commentator had scored big, recently signing a lucrative multi-year contract with the network. The camera crew representing ESPQ had arranged seven chairs on a makeshift dais on the field for the various post-game interviews they were planning. Christianna overheard someone from the camera crew saying they would be cutting for a commercial in seven minutes.

Ignoring their calls, Bruce blazed through the gaggle of reporters, hurrying to Christianna. "I can't believe you're here. We have to go out for dinner, and I won't take no for an answer." Bruce stared into Christianna's eyes as if it were just the two of them standing there alone. He ignored the camera crews and sports reporters watching them intently. Turning their cameras on Christianna and Bruce like a firing squad, this was the most sensational story of the day, and they were not about to miss it.

Bruce seemed to be toying with these so-called sports journalists. In fact, he seemed to enjoy it more than playing for the Antelopes – and he was dragging her into it.

"Well, give me your answer. Are we on for Tuesday night?"

Christianna noticed the cameras now planted right in front of them and understood that the reporters wouldn't be satisfied until she gave Bruce an answer. Christianna had no choice but to engage in this game with them because she knew that she and Rebel were now part of the entertainment for everyone watching ESPQ. She was now centerstage.

Christianna was terrified, but couldn't panic. She had to stay calm. She began to pretend the same way she did when she was doing commercials for the Mariotta Maverick. She took a deep breath and whispered to herself, "Action!" Now she was in acting mode, and she fluttered her eyes at Bruce and said in the calmest voice she could, "That works for me, Rebel. Who wouldn't want to go out for dinner with the most amazing quarterback of the NFL? Of course, I may be a little bit partial!"

Bruce grinned and flung his arms around her, kissing her. Christianna felt light-headed. It was a tender kiss that was also broadcast for all America to see. *My God*, she thought, *two times on the Jumbotron and now on coast-to-coast live television!* It had been a crazy mixed-up day, and it seemed everything was out of her control.

The skinny, long-legged blonde teased Bruce, shoving a microphone in his face. "Is there anything you would like to comment on, Rebel? It seems you are scoring in more ways than one. Do you get extra points because she is the boss' daughter?"

Intuitively, Christianna felt that this lady had had something in the past with Rebel and she was looking to exact some kind of revenge. The question was soaked in animus, and when combined with the sneer on her long, thin, drawn-out face, she was sickening. Fortunately, Bruce knew how to handle himself in front of the media.

"Well, who wouldn't want to eat dinner with an amazingly beautiful woman like Christianna? Just saying!" Bruce answered with a glint in his eye as the camera turned for a close-up of Christianna. "The Boss would encourage me to eat dinner. He knows I need proper nutrition to lead the team. So, I guess he would give me extra points." Bruce's answer oozed with sarcasm and served to put an end to the woman's snarky questions. She had no choice but to proceed with legitimate questions about the team's victory over the Carolina Panthers. Bruce answered them quickly and ended the interview when they broke for commercials. Once the show was over, he went to Christianna and apologized for what just happened.

"Sorry about that. The press tries to get into our personal business all the time. They want a story and don't care who they steamroll to get it. Don't worry about them. Let's just make sure we go to dinner this Tuesday, okay? I know a great little Italian restaurant with the best lasagna and spaghetti. I can pick you up at five-thirty. Is that okay?" Peering over his shoulder, he added, "I've got to get to the locker room or Coach Colby will send his posse after me. We are on, aren't we?" Bruce was rushing her, but she didn't care. She was careful not to make the same mistake as last time.

"That will be fine. I love lasagna." Christianna didn't care what they ate. Lasagna or hamburgers at McDonalds, she was just pleased to be given a second chance! She was so happy she felt she might burst.

Then an ominous thought cast a shadow on her excitement. Christianna felt her heart start to race again. Rebel asking her out on a date, the kiss – it was all on television. What would her father say? She could never keep this from him. Either he would see it later or word would somehow get back to him. Christianna had some damage control to attend to.

US ARMY RECRUITING

OFFICE, HOUSTON, TEXAS

John was ready. Ready to report. After eating his long-awaited breakfast at the café the day before, John could not get the idea out of his mind. All of his life he had thought about joining the Army or Marines – whichever made him the best offer. He loved the idea of being in the military and being a soldier; he knew he'd make a good one. Not only did he have physical prowess on his side and could fight, but he was handy with a gun. He wanted to see some action. Anytime he saw a soldier dressed in army fatigues, he felt a rush of admiration followed by a flush of envy. He wanted to be *that* soldier. He wanted to serve his nation.

Smiling to himself, John was prepared to meet with a recruiter and would probably sign the enlistment papers. Driving in his jeep – the one Jill hated – John was ready to trade up to an Army Humvee and pictured himself hopping out of a chopper shouldering an M-16 on a covert special ops mission. He spoke briefly over the phone to a recruiter the day before and, although had found the recruiter pushy, had set up an appointment for the next day. John sped his jeep into the parking lot of the Army recruiting office. He leapt out of his ride and bound into the office in eager anticipation. The recruiter engulfed John's outstretched hand with his own and welcomed him with a powerful handshake. "I am Staff Sergeant Andy Mara. Nice to meet you, John. How are you doing today?"

John replied, "I couldn't be better, sir. It's nice to meet you too."

They sat at Sergeant Mara's desk across from each other and Mara began reading a litany of the usual questions:

"Have you inquired about joining the Marines, Navy, or Air Force?"

"Have you ever, or are you now, using drugs?"

"Did you graduate high school?"

"Do you have any venereal diseases?"

"Do you have any felony convictions?"

John answered the staff sergeant's emphatically, "No. No. Yes. No, and no."

John had prepared his own list of questions, but when he attempted to ask them, the sergeant would not allow any interruption. "Young man, I am speaking. Your job now is to listen and respond with a simple yes or no." Sergeant Mara then proceeded to bombard John with more prying questions.

"Father living? Mother? How did they die? Do you have any brothers? Any sisters? Do they have any chronic diseases? Do *you* have any chronic diseases?"

John was tiring of the interrogation, but when Mara asked, "Are you homosexual?" John had enough. "No!" but wondered to himself, "Whatever became of Don't Ask, Don't Tell?"

John interrupted the sergeant. "Sir, I'm just not sure I'm ready to join the Army. I also am interested in looking at the Marine Corps."

Staff Sergeant Andy Mara regarded John with an icy stare. "Young man, any service branch you talk to will ask you the same questions. So, let's cut to the chase; how quickly do you want to join the Army since the Army is your obvious first choice?"

"Sir. I'm not sure it is."

Sergeant Andy Mara ignored John. "Well, let me reiterate that you seem well-suited for the Army. Let's get you started taking the vocational aptitude test. We call it the ASVAB test, short for Armed Service Vocational Aptitude Battery. It's the procedure. You sign this paperwork before you take the test. The results determine what kind of job the Army will give you. Of course, other criteria, such as physical fitness, eyesight, and level of education, et cetera are also taken into consideration."

John frowned. He was beginning to feel pressured. He had met many people from the military who had told him that most recruiters were very professional. They did not receive any bonus when they signed someone up, but worked hard to convince you that their branch of service was the best. The enlistment process was involved and usually took time. But with the speed Sergeant Mara was moving, he'd have John packed onto a bus and off to basic training by nightfall.

Suddenly John sprang to his feet but was not quite sure why. "Thank you, sir, but I am going to go over and talk with a Marine recruiter. I am actually more interested in the Marines and I have questions I would like to ask before I even take a vocational aptitude test and that would be...." John realized he was rambling and knew he had to get out of there. He extended his right hand to Staff Sergeant Andy Mara for a final handshake.

Sergeant Mara unleashed on John. "Young man, you have wasted my time. You are disrespectful and discourteous, and from what I have witnessed, you would never last one minute in any branch of the military."

Trying to remain composed, John responded, "Sir, I am sorry you feel that way, but I appreciate your time." He let his hand linger in the air for a moment longer until he realized that there would be no farewell handshake with Sergeant Mara.

John turned to leave, and could see his jeep through the office window. He felt like doing the hundred-yard dash to get to it. On his way out, the recruiter remarked pedantically, "By the way, my name is not '*Sir!*' It is Staff Sergeant Mara to you."

John looked back to see Mara snarling and spitting out his words. Hell, this guy was a real jerk. If Sergeant Mara was any indication of what the Army would be like, then they could have it. John felt his first taste of Army discipline and didn't like it. *What's next?* he thought. *Do I get thrown in the brig if I look at somebody the wrong way? Afghanistan can wait.*

WAYNE'S CAR WORLD

After the fiasco with Sergeant Mara, John decided he did not want to become a flunky for the US Army. He figured that Sergeant Mara was just the first of many constipated officers he would encounter and he wanted no part of them. He now began to have his doubts about the Marines. They were sure to have Sergeant Mara's of their own. Maybe worse. John wondered if there was something else he was supposed to do with his life.

He did have a backup plan though and that was gambling. He could always default to poker. Man, he could play a round of Texas Hold'em – so he thought. His friends called him the "Pot Stealer." If he knew there was a poker game going on, he'd find it and be there. He didn't care where. Even if it was in some grimy, back-alley game room, John would show up and, most of the time, leave the game with more money than when he had begun.

His poker obsession was just one more thing that annoyed Jill and she constantly nagged him about it. It was funny. When he lost, Jill wouldn't talk to him for days afterward. But she sure knew how to collect when he came home a winner. Her hand was always out, and the next John knew, Jill was heading for the mall.

Recently John had begun to rely on his poker winnings to help supplement his income. Unlike his poker game, John had lost his ability to close a sale. He hadn't sold a Mercedes in weeks and the owner Heinz Krueger was growing impatient. John knew that without landing a new contract or two, he'd soon feel the sole of Heinz's boot kicking him off the lot. Deciding he'd get ahead of Heinz, he aimed to be the one to do the firing. John always felt sleazy selling overpriced luxury to some gullible John Q. Public or like a sycophant kissing up to pretentious snobs who chased status by leasing their Mercedes two years at a time. John's hawking days were over.

Once at the dealership, he turned in his two-weeks' notice. With a sneer, Heinz bellowed, "Consider *now* the end of your two weeks. You can go, boy. Pack up your stuff. You haven't put squat in the register in ages." The grim-faced Krueger pointed to the door and added, "And put some speed on it."

John laughed at Heinz as he left the office, "You want speed? I'll give you some speed!"

He hopped into his jeep and drove a fast lap around the lot, burning tire tread into the pavement. Kreuger mouthed something through the salesroom window as John made his exit, yelling, "So long, sucker! Is this fast enough for you, asshole!" He smoked his tires out of the lot, leaving black streaks on the pavement and flipped off Heinz Krueger. That felt good.

When he got home, he pulled out a suitcase and tossed in a few items and then cleared out of the apartment he shared with Jill. He didn't have much and she could do whatever she wanted with the rest of his things. He didn't care in the least. John was getting out of Houston, Texas. He made a quick online reservation with Southwest Airlines and printed a one-way ticket to Las Vegas.

The next matter in front of him was to sell his much-loved Jeep Wrangler Sahara for the best deal he could get. Knowing the ins and outs of selling cars, John went to Wayne's Car World. Wayne's World was a used-car dealership that had been in operation for some thirty-odd years and it had a reputation for paying good cash as long as the seller presented a clear title.

Within a few hours, John sold his beloved Jeep Wrangler Sahara and was now sitting in the back seat of a taxi heading for Hobby Airport to wait for the red-eye flight to Vegas. He signed over the title to his jeep and had in his pocket a fat check from Wayne's Car World. He had struck a pretty good deal with Wayne. His last tie to Houston was severed.

It was an impulsive decision, but John knew he had finally made the right one. He hoped to see his dreams come to fruition in Las Vegas. There was a big Texas Hold'em poker tournament going on at the Laredo Casino in a few weeks and John intended to buy a seat. He was already counting his winnings.

MCCARRAN INTERNATIONAL AIRPORT

John's plane landed with a thud and his first concern was his stomach. It had been growling since take-off. He didn't care if he ate in one of those rip-off airport restaurants, he was hungry. He'd eat first and think poker later. He walked briskly into the first restaurant he saw. Though crowded, he found a table in the corner. A waitress came over, slapping a menu and an empty coffee cup down on the table.

"Can I pour yous' some coffee, honey?" she asked with a booming Brooklyn accent, proceeding to pour a cup before waiting to hear John's answer. He ordered up the "McCarran Triple Jackpot" consisting of 3 eggs over easy, three sausages, three pancakes, three slices of bacon, juice, and, of course, home fries. John sipped his coffee and did a little people watching.

To his right, sitting alone, was a young girl who looked very lost. She was kind of pretty from what John could see of her. As he peered around the restaurant, he saw a cross-section of human beings who had come to Vegas for reasons of their own. Where did they come from? What was their story? His thoughts drifted back to the girl. Why was she alone? He imagined the worst, hoping he was wrong. Furtively, he glanced at her again in an attempt to see more of her face. So angelic and sweet, she appeared as though she had parachuted in from heaven. He wanted to know more about this girl and began to imagine all sorts of scenarios surrounding her.

His daydreams were interrupted when the waitress slammed plates filled with the Triple Jackpot in front of him. The girl could wait. He ripped into his breakfast like it was the first decent meal he'd eaten in days and soon mopped up the last of egg with his final bite of pancake. The nourishment recharged him and focused his mind on why he was there – to play poker.

Wasting little time, he slung his carry-on pack over his shoulder to leave. John had other eggs to fry, but not for eating! He had to get over to the Laredo and see about getting a seat at the Big Texas Hold'em tournament.

As he crossed the room, the young girl hurried in front of him toward the register. She seemed oblivious to John as she ransacked her purse, searching for money to pay the bill. He heard her tell the impatient cashier whose horn-rimmed glasses were balanced precariously on the tip of her nose, "I'm so sorry, I didn't realize I was so short of cash. I could have sworn I had a ten-dollar bill, ma'am. I am so sorry. Can you take my eight dollars for now? I promise I will pay you later. I swear I'll come back with the two dollars. *Honest!*" The girl seemed embarrassed, genuinely sorry, and even a little bit panicked.

The cashier flashed her a not-this-again-look and pushed her glasses back up her nose, giving her a hostile stare. "Forget it, missy, I'll cover it. Oh yeah, I just *love* working so I can cover every loser's meal. I can't wait for you to bring me two bucks. What do I tell the manager when he comes for the hourly till check?" The girl looked like she was about to burst into tears.

John pounced on the situation. "Hey ma'am, I couldn't help overhearing. I can cover it." Time stopped for John as both the annoyed cashier and the angelic girl stared at him.

The girl cried out, "Oh, thank you so much. I really appreciate it!"

"No problem. It's no big deal. My name is John. What's yours?"

Most demurely, almost to the point of being coy, she told him her name was Mary. John settled Mary's and his bills. Outside the restaurant, they continued their conversation. Mary explained that she had just gotten off the plane with the sole intent of entering the Texas Hold'em tournament at the Laredo.

"No way. Get out of here!" John could not believe it. "That's why I'm here too! I'm on my way there now. Do you want to share a cab?"

They flew through baggage claim, grabbed their bags, and dragged them outside to the taxi stand to wait for the next cab. A white taxi painted with red and blue stripes pulled up to the curb. John and Mary excitedly jumped in and struggled to yank in their bags behind them.

The driver barely grumbled a hello to them. "Where to?" Not answering soon enough for the impatient cabbie, he said again, "Where to? Hurry up." He seemed to be angry at them almost to the point of loathing them. John told him that they wanted to go to the Laredo and the cabbie groused mockingly under his breath, "Another internet poker-player wannabe." And with that, they took off.

As the cabbie navigated through the morning traffic, Mary pulled a pair of Ray Bans out of her purse and put them on with a great deal of theatrics. She told John that they were her secret weapon. "My Uncle Tad always told me that when it comes to poker, dark glasses are about as indispensable a piece of equipment as a goalie's mask is to a hockey player." With an air of playful mischief, she asked John if he wanted to know about her fool-proof plan to win the Texas Hold'em tournament. Then she asked him what his name was again. "I hope you won't take offense, but I don't remember your name." John didn't mind because she had the sweetest way of saying things. "So," she went on, "Your eyes give everything away.

Mary explained to John about pupils. "They dilate when you are lying or bluffing. And that is your tell. At least it's mine. That's why you see all the great players wearing sunglasses - so the other players at the table can't see their pupils dilate and know a bluff." As she prattled on about her Uncle Tad, it became evident to John that she had no intention of removing her sunglasses.

John noticed something fall onto the taxi's red leather seats. It was a fifty-dollar bill with the eighteenth U.S. President Ulysses S. Grant's face staring at John. It had fallen out of Mary's purse and got John to thinking that maybe Mary didn't need those shades after all. She had delivered a convincing performance at the restaurant. He began to suspect that she was playing him for a sucker.

Believing he was sharing a cab with a con artist, John almost wished he was riding shotgun with the sullen cab driver instead. What was her game? He was certain of one thing – there was no way he was going to pay the cab fare and be a fool again. He picked up Mr. Grant and handed it to her with an incredulous look.

"Oh, there it is," she said calmly. "I was going to use it to pay for the taxi." She didn't flinch. It was like she did this every day. John knew one thing was for real. He couldn't tell if her eyes were dilated because she was still wearing those stupid glasses. Did she intend to use the fifty dollars to pay for the cab? Maybe the sunglasses weren't so crazy after all and perhaps Uncle Tad had a point.

The cab pulled up to the entrance to the Laredo with a jerk and the driver told them it would be forty dollars for both of them and there baggage. Mary looked at John and smiled. She fumbled through her purse for a moment and said she seemed to have misplaced the fifty-dollar bill. By this time, John had grown weary of her stunts, and waited while she rummaged through her purse again. The cabbie repeated the fare and said that he'd turn the meter back on if he didn't soon see some money.

Mary turned around in the seat, her eyes searching the red leather again. "Maybe I dropped it again on the seat. Oops, I can't seem to find it. I hope I didn't lose it. This is crazy. You must think I've lost my mind, John."

John was sure she was acting, but again, couldn't be sure. She still wore those damn glasses. Then he got his first taste of "Lady Luck" in Las Vegas. As Mary went through her mock search, he saw the fifty-dollar bill fall out of her purse onto the floor of the cab. To John, it seemed the money had floated down in slow motion. He smiled wryly; this time he had her.

"Look here, Mary. Why, it's your fifty-dollar bill! Well, what do you know?" John teased with triumphant. He nimbly swooped up the cash before Mary had a chance to lose it again and gave it to the cab driver. "Here you go. Keep the change."

The annoyed cab driver took the money and looked at them as if to say, "What, that's all?"

He muttered something unintelligible and drove off, no doubt ready to brighten someone else's day.

Mary looked up at John with a sweet smile. "I am so glad you found it. I swear I couldn't find it anywhere in my purse."

And yes, she was still wearing the sunglasses.

THE LAREDO

John was disappointed with the Laredo Casino. Instead of the opulent palace he expected, the Laredo was unimpressive. Off the main strip, it was small and dingy, and clearly, its best days were well past. The Laredo begged for a wrecking ball to take it out of its misery.

But that didn't matter. He and Mary entered the casino lobby, checked their bags with the bell captain, and headed straight for the Doc Holliday Poker Parlor. It was where the poker tournaments were played and where next month's "Texas Hold'em Celebrity Showdown" was to be held. But when John and Mary stepped through the swinging saloon doors, it was anything but a quaint parlor where one could enjoy a quiet, private game of cards with a few friends. The gaming hall was massive and dark except for the bright lamps focused over each playing table. There must have been over three hundred tables of all shapes and sizes around the room. Numerous LED signs floated magically above the tables to indicate the game played at the table.

Mary grabbed John's arm and pulled herself firmly next to him. There were signs for every version of poker imaginable – Omaha, Cincinnati, Pineapple, Stud 5, Stud 6, Stud 7, Draw 2, Draw 3, Straight, and even One-Eyed Jacks, which also happened to be the name of the room. Under every sign stood a dealer surrounded by several seated players who were intent on being the best in their chosen brand of poker.

Mary looked up at John and said, "Have you ever even heard of all these games? My Uncle Tad only told me about Texas Hold'em. Maybe we should roam around and take it all in before we get into a game."

But John didn't want to wait. Besides, he still didn't know what to think of this girl hanging on his arm. Was she the grifter he thought she might be or Uncle Tad's little innocent? At least she had finally removed her sunglasses. But it was so dark in the room that it hardly mattered; he couldn't see her pupils to spot her tell no matter how hard he looked. For now, John knew he needed to forget about her. In fact, he wished she was wasn't there. Ignoring her, he scanned the great hall for the Hold 'em tables, hoping that she would go away. But Mary continued to cling to John, seemingly ignorant of his obvious impatience with her.

John finally spotted what he was searching for – the Texas Hold'em tables. Unsurprisingly, they were in the busiest part of the room.

He pointed in the direction of the Hold 'em tables and told Mary, "There they are, over there. Let's go."

The number one thing he wanted to do was to get a seat at a game. He counted about a dozen active tables, but they were all full. At this point, Mary was the last thing he wanted to think about, but she had attached herself to his arm, like an unintended and unwanted growth named Mary. He called it the "Mary Factor." John dragged his new appendage to a long bar in the center of the room. Until a table opened up for him, this was the perfect observation post where he could study the table action first-hand. A panel of televisions showcasing various poker games filled the wall behind the bar. He would keep track using those.

One of the screens replayed last year's big Texas Hold'em Celebrity Showdown. John watched as poker legends Solomon Bronstein and Phillipe Marche played a one-on-one shootout for a sizeable pot. Bronstein's manic eyes seemed to confound Marche as Bronstein pressed the river bet. That seemed to make no sense to Marche as he held a jack and a queen; the only face in the community cards was a queen. The odds were with Marche but Bronstein immediately threw down an unlikely straight and hauled in a pot that took him to the final table and into the big money.

Marche exploded with angry frustration, complaining to Bronstein that he should have folded before the flop with those hole cards. Marche stormed away from the table, leaving Bronstein wearing what could only be described as a shit-eating grin. The next tournament was a month away. Though the buy-in was $10,000, nearly half of his savings, this was why John had come to Las Vegas.

The other video screens focused on the plays happening in real-time at the tables surrounding the bar. It gave John a chance to watch the players and learn how they played their hands. Of course, when a player folded, he didn't know what they were holding. But those who did play out the hand, gave him a sense of how they bet, and he was able to develop a feel for how he would play when a table finally opened up.

The larger screen set in the center of the displays suddenly caught John's attention as the camera focused on an older gentleman sporting a crisp tan Stetson. John recognized him immediately. It was Brandon Foyle, a Poker Hall of Fame inductee and legend. He was known for his crusty personality and disarming table banter and witty barbs, and a career spanning fifty years; he knew how to win.

Keen on watching him in person, John searched the tables around the bar. His eyes settled on the man with the iconic Stetson just as Foyle pushed his entire stack into the pot. John spun around to watch them finish the hand on the screen. The other players quickly folded. John smiled as Foyle raked in his winnings.

John felt Mary poke him in the ribs and she turned his attention to a table near them. One of the players threw his cards on the table and scooped up his minuscule pile of chips. John saw his chance. He quickly unhinged Mary from his arm and moved in behind the man. The player turned to John and pointed to his seat, "You want it? Go ahead and take it. Maybe you can do better than I did. Good luck." The man vanished into the casino darkness, and John anxiously took the loser's seat for his first game of poker in Las Vegas.

The game was five-ten no-limit, which meant that the small blind's ante was five dollars and the big blind's ante, the player seated to the left of the small blind, was ten dollars. But there was no limit to the size of the bet one could make once the hand began. No-Limit suited John just fine since it meant the pots could grow quite large, which made it all the more exciting. The flip-side of No-Limit was that one losing hand could wipe a player out.

John decided to play it safe. After all, he just wanted to get a *feel* for Vegas poker. He handed the dealer ten Benjamins who slid John over a stack of chips. Including John and the dealer, ten people sat at the table. He greeted them all with a "Hello, everyone." Most at the table acknowledged him with a friendly wave, though there were a few who ignored him completely.

He sat between the small blind which was on his left and to his right, a girl who introduced herself as "Candy Land." And her candy land was indeed on display for all to see. With a skin-tight, low-cut V-shirt, Candy's ample breasts spilled out to adorn the table. She smiled at John as he pulled in his chair to sit next to her. Candy's presence was a distraction to the other guys at the table and John forced himself to keep his eyes on his cards and his mind on the game.

He was lucky to be starting next to the small blind. He would have the luxury of playing several free hands before the big blind came around to him, and he would have to ante. It gave him the chance to see how the other players played before having to commit anything to the pot. Meanwhile, he didn't notice when Mary wandered away from the bar.

The dealer shuffled the deck and dealt the players their hole cards. John watched each player stealthily slide their cards to the edge of the table and draw them close to their chests to take a quick peek at their hand. When the dealer laid his second card down in front of him, John shielded his cards with one hand while pulling up the corners of them with the other. "Lord have mercy!" a voice inside him screamed. John was staring at two beautiful aces. Then it hit him; he wished he had a pair of sunglasses.

The pre-flop betting started with the players to the left of the big blind. The first man folded while the next called the ante and tossed a $10 chip into the center of the table. The following two players also called the ante. The man sitting on the other side of Candy then called and raised the pot $50. Candy called and tossed in $60 worth of chips.

Then it was John's turn. He knew he had the best hand at the table, at least at that moment. After the flop, everything could change and his top hand could quickly turn to lead. He was tempted to go all in. But he suddenly decided to call and followed Candy's lead, tossing $60 into the pot as well. The bet was too much for the small blind and he folded. The big blind, however, pushed in a $50 chip to call. The bet went back to the three who called the initial ante. They now had to either call the raise or fold. The first called, but the other two tossed their cards onto the table. At the end of the first round of betting, the pot stood at $325 – and this was even before the flop.

The dealer burned the top card from the deck and turned the next three cards face-up on the table. It's called the flop and these three cards are communal and used by all the players to make the best hand they can when combined with their two hole cards. The dealer flopped a seven of clubs, three of hearts, and to John's disbelief, the ace of spades. John had three aces, a very strong hand.

The betting began again with the same man who had started the previous round. He was taking a while to decide what to do when Candy Land blurted out, "Come on, Oscar honey, I am running late for a date." She giggled and then began babbling about her date that night. Oscar raised $25 and the next man quickly folded. The bet moved to Candy who was still chattering away when she nonchalantly saw Oscar's raise and raised the pot by another $50. It was now $75 to John.

Candy continued with her drivel like she was at a girls' night-out party. "He's okay, I guess. Should I go, or should I not go?" She paused and then said loud enough for everyone at the table to hear, "He wants to be my sugar daddy, but I wonder if he's any good in bed?"

John did his best to ignore her, but could tell that this was part of Candy's tactic. She was quite the strategist. Between her ample breasts and incessant mouth, Candy Land was well-armed. John saw the $75 and pressed the bet another $25. The big blind called the $100 and Oscar also called, tossing in the $75 he owed the pot. It was the end of that round of betting; the pot now stood at $725 dollars.

On the turn, the dealer flipped a seven of diamonds and John knew he had won the pot. Now, he just needed to play it slowly so he wouldn't scare his opponents into folding. Again, Oscar began the betting and led by raising $100. Candy, who hadn't yet stopped jabbering, pushed another $350 into the pot without taking a momentary pause in her mindless conversation with no one.

The bet was now $350 to John. He was in the biggest game of his life. All he had wanted was to get a sample taste of Vegas poker action, but now he was getting the full five-course dinner. John pushed $350 into the pot and said, "Call." Candy Land didn't notice as she continued talking to the air.

The big blind scrutinized Candy and shook his head. Then he stared at John for a full ten seconds, looked at the cards on the table, and then at his hole cards supposedly to make sure they hadn't changed since the last time he saw them. He carefully counted a stack of chips and pushed them into the pot. But for all of his theatrics, the big blind just called.

Oscar was already committed to the pot through his opening raise and tossed in the $250 he needed to call. The pot had now grown to over $2,000 and Candy Land still chattered away.

The dealer turned over the river card – a four of clubs. It was a good card for John as it could be the straight John thought Oscar and the big blind were trying to play. At best, he put the mouthy Candy on a sinking boat, a full-house but more likely, two pair.

The bet was to Oscar who tapped the table with his palm to indicate he checked. Candy, apparently uninterested, checked. John had to move and so pushed his remaining stack into the pot. The big blind immediately called John, so did Oscar. And John was not surprised when Candy, suddenly interested, finally stopped talking and also called. The pot now stood at almost $4,000.

John turned over his pair of aces and smiled as he watched each of his opponents toss their hole cards onto the table admitting defeat. John won and couldn't believe the pile of chips he pulled in after his first game of Texas Hold'em in a Las Vegas casino. With one fifteen-minute hand, he had nearly tripled his investment; not bad for a rookie. Maybe this Vegas-thing was going to work out after all.

John stood up and said, "I hate to win and run, but I just got into Vegas two hours ago and I have to find a place to stay." He tossed the dealer a $100 chip as a tip and gathered up his winnings. As he headed toward the cashier's cage to cash in his chips, he heard sweet little Candy Land mutter behind him, "Motherfucker!" John thought to himself that Candy's candy had just turned bitter to the taste.

Now about that Mary.

JULIAN VILLA APARTMENTS

Selling the jeep had given John the cash he needed to keep going in Las Vegas, at least for a while. And after winning that hand at the Laredo, John momentarily inflated his poker prowess and imagined himself a professional card shark. But it bothered him at how casually he'd thrown down a thousand dollars into a single hand of poker he could just as easily have lost. But that's why it's called gambling. He knew luck was fickle and that if he was going to make a paying career out of poker, he needed to learn how to *really* play.

John had entirely forgotten about Mary and was on his way to collect his bags when he glimpsed Mary chatting it up with a small group of people in the lobby. She flashed a smile at him and hurried over to announce that the few hands she had played hadn't gone at all well. She lamented how she had already lost seventy five-dollars after just one game.

"I never even got to the river. I guess my Uncle Tad didn't teach me very well. Even the sunglasses didn't work. What I need is a pair of magic glasses that let me see what the other players cards are. Anyway, I need to get going and find a place to live. Do you want to go with me?"

John studied her face and, for a fleeting moment, saw the innocence that had first drawn him to her. He squelched the nagging voice in the back of his mind warning him that she was just another Candy Land. Maybe it was her voice or the way she seemed so casual about things. He was beguiled and what she said next bewitched him.

Batting her big blue eyes, she asked coquettishly, "Hey Big Shot, do you think you could teach me a thing or two about poker?"

Not thinking, John broke down with a quick reply, "Heck yeah. It'd be my pleasure." He was strangely infatuated with her and couldn't quite figure out what was happening. "But first, we've got to find a place."

Mary was quick with her rebuttal, "What's with this '*We* got to find a place?'"

John answered as if it was an already settled deal. "Hey, look at it this way. We can split the rent and I can teach you poker."

Mary seemed to accept the inevitable and together they went to find an apartment close to the action of the strip.

The people Mary had been talking with told her about the Julian Villa Apartments just four blocks east of the strip on Koval Road along the bus line. It was a sketchy area, but a lot of beginning players lived there; there was always a game going on somewhere in the complex. The manager at the Julian showed them his only vacancy. And although it was not exactly what either of them had in mind, the rent was reasonable. John and Mary signed a twelve-month lease for the two-bedroom apartment.

Standing outside the entrance of their new apartment, John glanced at Mary. "Look. You know we both like each other. How about you share my room and we turn the other into a game room?"

Acting surprised, Mary smiled and, "A game room is a good idea. I suppose if it doesn't work out you can always sleep on the couch."

"Fair enough. I've been in the doghouse before. You know, right now I just want to take you into my arms and give you a kiss," John said as he fumbled the key into the lock and opened the door. Mary smiled coyly, stepping into their new home.

Deciding to try out a trial run at cohabitating, they made a steadfast agreement and put it in writing that if they didn't work out together as a couple, Mary was allowed to move into the other bedroom to live independently as a roommate. With both of them splitting the rent, it was a win-win situation no matter what happened to their relationship.

For the time being, the other bedroom was set up for learning and practicing poker and was poker central for them. It was an eight hundred-square foot apartment, and Mary took to the ambitious job decorating it as best she could. It was a furnished apartment, and she tried to make it as homey as she could for John.

Mary's mind whirled when she thought about what she was doing – moving in with some guy she had just met at an airport restaurant. But she was cavalier about it all. Even if she couldn't remember his name half the time, she'd go anywhere with him. Heck, she had followed him to the Laredo, so why not move into a new apartment with him? Afterall, he was a poker player, wasn't he? There was something about him she liked and she liked those odds.

Mary had never dreamed her life could move this fast.

WOODLANDS ' MAIN OFFICE

Jill finally realized John had dumped her.

Since their fight a couple of days before, John had been distant. He had barely been home and, when he was, he had avoided her. After finishing her shift as a hostess at a nearby restaurant, Jill returned home to an apartment that seemed strangely different; something was missing. At first, she couldn't quite figure out what it was. But then she noticed all of John's sports caps were missing from the oak hat rack that stood by the nook where the washer and dryer were located.

When she checked the closets, she found most of John's clothes were also gone. He didn't own much, but what he did have, had now mostly vanished. There were a few embarrassingly out-of-style shirts still hanging in the closet along with a pair of worn-out boots tossed haphazardly on the floor. He had also left behind an old tennis racket and a small bookcase. It was junk made out of particle board and falling apart. He had left five books on the bottom shelf.

Jill remembered John bragging about how all their money problems would be solved if he could only get to Las Vegas. He could become the next Solomon Bronstein. Yeah, sure. And all his talk about enlisting in the Marines was just that, talk. No, John was definitely in Vegas. And she knew at that precise moment that she would head for Vegas too. Not to get him back. She didn't give a *damn* about him *now*. She wouldn't stand for the way he left her and would settle for nothing less than telling him off one final time. Oh yeah, she would find him; she was sure of that. He pissed her off, and she wasn't going to let him get away with leaving her this way. Nobody dumped Jill, especially John.

First though, she had to connive the manager into allowing her to break the lease on her place at the Woodlands Apartments. He was always sneaking around the complex, letting himself into the apartments while the tenants were gone. And the way he always leered at her convinced Jill that he had installed hidden cameras all over her apartment and spent his evenings watching her and John. John just laughed when she told him about her suspicions, but every time Jill thought about that smarmy, crotch-scratching deviant she felt like a thousand Texas-size wood roaches were crawling all over her bare skin.

But she would do whatever was necessary to move out of there as fast as she could. Fortunately, she didn't have many possessions to deal with; in fact, her biggest concern was her wardrobe. She had too many clothes to carry on the plane so she would store them at her sister's house for the time being. And if all went according to plan, she would soon be running down an airline gate with her five-inch Jimmy Choo high heels to board the next plane to Las Vegas.

Jill worked her plan with a streetwalker's purpose and followed the narrow cement pathway that led to the manager's office. A dusty summer wreath was nailed to a red door and below it was a sign that read "Woodlands Apartments Main Office." The loud *click-click-click* of Jill's high heels on the pavement announced her coming. The landlord greeted her with a lascivious grin as he moved his hands from the top of the desk to something beneath it. Repulsed by the thought of what he was doing, she tried to hide her disgust. *God, this guy is gross!* she thought.

She could see the oval-shaped swimming pool through the back window. A bed of giant liriopes surrounded it, creating a sort of low fence. The manager told her she looked great and asked what he could do to help her as he fiddled for something under the desk.

She had changed into her shortest skirt and tightest shirt to purposefully distract and disarm. And as Jill explained her situation to the manager, she leaned forward so her cleavage loomed dangerously close to the manager's face. That was all it took. The manager released her from the lease two months early and even agreed to return her deposit. On her way out, Jill thanked the randy landlord with a peck on his cheek which prompted him to squeal with delight.

As she left the office, she wiped her mouth and said aloud, "I could throw up." Then a sly smile swept over her face and she said triumphantly, "Vegas. Here I come, baby!"

LONGVIEW HOTEL

Jill was on a plane that was about to touch down at McCarran International Airport in Las Vegas. Thinking about how she would exact her revenge on John when she saw him, a smile came to her face. But first, she had dreams of her own to realize. Her immediate priority was to find a hotel where she could pamper herself and change into something modestly alluring. Afterward, she would be off to the Malai Casino for a job interview.

The Malai was known for having some of the most talented showgirls on Earth and Jill wanted to become one of them. She knew it wouldn't be as easy to get an audition as it had been to con the landlord into letting her out of her lease but it was worth trying. Jill thought carefully about what to wear. She had just one shot at this and knew she needed to dress interview-appropriate yet still suggesting the right amount of tease.

She decided to stay at the Longview Hotel, which was an enormous leap down from her former apartment. But it boasted easy access to the main strip and she didn't mind the meager accommodations. At least she wasn't renting a room by the hour. Right now, she had to be frugal; there wasn't much in her account. But it wouldn't always be that way. She was going to make her name in Las Vegas.

The following morning, she woke to start her beauty routine at the Regal Casino as it was close to the Malai. She got her hair done and then completed the look with a mani-pedi. Jill had already called the manager at the Malai Casino who had arranged for an interview with Derek Martin, the entertainment manager in charge of the showgirls. She was told that, although all candidates had to audition, the entertainment manager liked to interview girls personally to learn of their experience and get a better understanding of their personalities. As her conversation with the hotel manager came to a close, the man stressed to Jill not to be late.

"Derek vill not even vait von minute for you, so girl, come in early," he said with a very thick German accent. "That vould not be gut."

Jill took heed and showed up at the Malai with fifteen minutes to spare.

Derek Martin walked into the room with an air of conceited superiority. He could have been the original inspiration for the trope "tall, dark and handsome." As Derek kept glancing at his watch, Jill knew she had done the right thing by showing up early for her interview.

Upon asking her to walk for him, Derek graded her with his eyes, tracing her every movement and curve with veteran discrimination. Abruptly he motioned for her to sit down. "Why do you want to be a showgirl? Tell me about your experience and how it relates to this industry."

Jill wasn't prepared for Derek's questions, but should have expected them. The truth was that, though she had some basic dance training in her past, Jill had zero professional experience. She thought that all she would have to do was show how well she could dance. Fumbling for an answer, she said, "I can dance and I can always learn what I need to. I'm a quick study."

"Where are you from?" Derek inquired.

"Houston, Texas. I think I can dance and I am in great shape."

Derek snorted back, "You think you can dance? Why are you frittering away my time?"

Jill stood up from the soft, cushioned wicker chair she was velcroed to. "Well, what do you think?" She twirled salaciously so he could take in the full picture. Jill knew it was a bold move, but she also knew she had a product to sell – and right now Derek Martin didn't seem to be in a buying mood.

"Well, can you dance? And are you an evening person?"

"I can be whatever I need to be," she said, trying to sound convincing. Derek looked her over again and Jill knew she knew had closed the deal.

"Okay then, I am going to hook you up with Patty, our lead choreographer." Derek grabbed the phone and growled, "Rene, get Patty down to the second floor. I have someone I want her to see."

Five minutes later, a tall lady balancing a Starbucks in one hand and her phone in the other came into the room. "Stand up!" the woman ordered. "How tall are you? This job has a height requirement. You have to meet the standard. Don't get me wrong; I totally don't think being tall is that great. Most men like their women small and petite and that's always been my problem. I have issues and that is, like, my hang-up. Like, I feel like a giraffe totally reporting for zoo duty. I hate being tall, especially, like, six-feet-tall. And, like, my feet are totally as big as boats." This Patty was a Valley Girl. Jill stood, hiding a slight grin, and thought Patty did indeed resemble a giraffe. She had an extremely long neck and yards of arms and legs.

Jill answered, "I am five foot eight and weigh a one hundred fifteen."

Patty sized her up and down and then finally took a sip of her coffee. "Follow me. I will show you the drill."

She had passed the first stage of the interview; Jill knew what was next. Patty wanted to see if she could dance. They took an elevator up to the tenth floor where Jill was awestruck by the spacious room that opened up in front of her. With its hardwood flooring, the hall was perfect for dancing. On the shiny floor, several young ladies stood in a straight line, all wearing different colored workout outfits. Yet despite their apparel differences, every girl was the identical height and wore her hair up high in a ponytail. Their sameness reminded Jill of clones. There was no parity in their ages, however, so Jill guessed they were between eighteen and into their early thirties.

The choreographer, an older woman wearing fishnet legwarmers, directed the line. She commanded them in an aggressive tone, "Step right! Rond de jambe! Face forward! Transition to a grand battement! And finish with a high jet`e!" Each command became louder and harsher. She finished the routine by signaling for them to form back into a line and drop back three steps.

The woman was a merciless taskmaster. Clapping her hands, she barked, "Move it faster to the line. Keep your head up high. Maintain eye contact. Don't look down. Remember your posture. Your outfits weigh a ton and you need to maintain good balance!" After that, she cued them to flare out their jazz hands as they practiced their high kicks with such synchrony that they rivaled the Radio City Rockettes. Again, she shouted to the girls, "Remember, you are balancing a heavy headdress full of plumes. You need to straighten up; keep your back straight." The girls complied, unaware of Jill's presence. She was invisible to them.

"Point your toes, Natalie!" the choreographer bellowed at a younger dancer who seemed shy and lacked confidence. Natalie was trying hard but not hard enough for this demanding disciplinarian. "This is the second time I've told you." She pointed a vehement finger at Natalie as she crossed the room to address the girl. "The second time! This is the last. Do you hear me?" But when she brought it up to reprimand her, her fingernail caught on her legwarmers and pulled a small rip in them. The split turned into a large hole when she danced the last steps with the girls trying to demonstrate the steps. She was angry when she looked down and noticed the gaping hole in her legwarmers. "I *just* bought these fishnets!" she shouted at Natalie. "This is your fault." Natalie looked mortified and stood paralyzed with her mouth open. Then the unexpected happened.

Jill, who had been watching, came to Natalie's defense. "They're fishnets, aren't they?" Don't they already have holes in them? What's the big deal?" All eyes suddenly turned to the new girl standing by the elevator and a few dancers stifled their laughs. Before the situation could get out of hand, Patty surfaced onto the scene before the stern instructor could take umbrage with Jill. Miss Fishnet stepped back but not without first shooting Jill dagger eyes.

Patty said, "Ladies, this is Jill. She is going to join you in the next dance segment. Give her some room in the middle; I'd like to see what she can do." Patty motioned to Jill who moved quickly to the center, joining the other girls in their rigid line. Butterflies flared to life and flapped frantically in Jill's stomach. Patty walked over to where Miss Fishnet had been standing and began guiding them through various dance moves. Snapping her fingers in tempo, Patty didn't let up.

Although nervous, Jill told herself, *Get it together, girl. The game's on.* At first, she kept up and did okay, remembering her dance basics with little trouble. But then Patty accelerated the steps and the tempo. It was then that Jill fell off the beat and, for that matter, her feet. Looking up at Patty, Jill saw her dreams vaporize.

To Jill's surprise, however, Patty seemed unfazed and merely said, "Girls, let's try that again. Jill, you give it another try. You can do it." Snapping her fingers once again, she let out a, "One, two, three, and four…"

Patty was right. Jill was once again nimble on her feet and this time she was able to keep up with the beat. No longer did her feet betray her and Jill worked through the routine mistake-free. Patty had them dance a chorus line for a few more measures and then called for a break.

Jill walked toward Patty who had half a smile on her face. "We'll see you the same time tomorrow, Jill."

Jill asked brazenly, "Does this mean I have the job?"

In a suddenly terse voice that matched her now steely face, Patty snarled back that there was a lot more involved. She waved Jill away, dismissing her abruptly.

Confused, Jill's confidence shattered. She was utterly humiliated but was determined not to let it show. She threw her shoulders back and sauntered into the waiting elevator. Part of her wanted to flip Patty off, but she knew she would have to persevere. Her future depended on it.

As the elevator door closed, she murmured, "Just wait and see tomorrow. I'll come back with a vengeance. This girl isn't done just yet!"

BEBE'S BAGELS

The next day Jill unexpectedly ran into the dictator-like instructor at Bebe's Bagels. It was weird luck, just bad juju. Of all the people to cross paths with, it had to be Miss Fishnet. Still, the woman seemed to know what she was doing and had imparted some sensible tips. Jill remembered how she had emphasized the importance of keeping their backs straight, especially when wearing their beautiful but heavy outfits. As a result of this, Jill was conscientious about maintaining a straight posture. She even practiced in her room at the Longview, walking back and forth across the worn carpet, balancing the only book she could find, a Gideon Bible, on her head.

Unable to resist, Jill hurried across the small shop to the instructor who was in the process of devouring her bagel. "Hi! Do you remember me? I'm Jill."

Jill's intrusion was met with a blank stare. Miss Fishnet struggled to swallow her bagel and then brushed away crumbs from the side of her mouth. Suddenly recognizing Jill, her stare turned to a scowl.

Jill ignored the chilly reception. She had some important questions to ask. Putting on the sincerest fake smile she could muster, she asked, "Hey, how are you doing? Thank you so much for all your great tips yesterday. It really helped me." Jill heaped on the Sweet and Low.

She could see from her face that she was starting to defrost. She replied to Jill with a tepid, "Thank you."

Jill proceeded, "Um, why did that girl Patty yesterday tell me to come back again today at three for practice, but would not tell me if I had made the first cut?"

The woman stared coldly; her unyielding eyes fixated on Jill. She had reverted to her old mean self. "Don't you get it? The real auditions start on Saturday and finish on Monday. These are just practices that don't count for anything. They're just a chance for you to practice and get ready for the auditions that *do* count. It's like summer camp for football players. You come and practice and workout. Then, some make it and some get cut. It's a chance for them to get their sea legs." She told Jill that practice continued through the week; Saturday at noon was when the real auditions began. The combined score for both of those days would determine who made showgirl for the "Malai Casino Show Girl Extravaganza."

It was the excellent news Jill needed to hear. She had three more days to practice; hopefully, that would be enough. She thanked the instructor profusely and told her she would see her later today. The instructor didn't bother with personal pleasantries, like saying "Goodbye." Jill hoped she wouldn't be on the judging committee, muttering to herself, "To think this is over a pair of fishnet legwarmers! Who the hell still wears them besides Madonna?"

As Jill sat to enjoy her bagel, she glimpsed someone familiar pass outside the window. She lost her appetite. It was John and he was holding hands with a very young girl. Tossing the rest of her bagel into the garbage can, Jill ran out and confronted him right there on the sidewalk. It was the chance encounter she had hoped for but never really expected. She wanted to rip John into little pieces.

"Well, if it isn't John and, let's see, he's with his long-lost daughter." Then she launched into an obscenity-laden tirade. "You are such a *fucking* asshole! You thought you could just up and leave me, but your little plan misfired, didn't it? You little shit! Where did you find your daughter? She's cute. Where are you going? Off to Toys 'R' Us to buy her a new rocking horse? Or maybe a pacifier?"

John stood speechless, mouth agape. The shock on his face was delicious. It didn't matter that she was making a scene and that passersby were gawking at them. She *had* him!

After a moment, the young girl accompanying John turned to him and, unfazed by Jill's sudden appearance, asked, "Who is she, John? Does she work as a stripper or is she one of those ladies-of-the-night workers? You never told me about her." The girl's voice was as sugary as cotton candy and her inflection was even-keeled and slick as ice. It made her insult that much more devastating. Jill went ballistic.

"How *dare* you, you little slut. You're the one who looks like she walks the street. I'll have John thrown in jail for robbing the cradle and walking around with you, you jail-bait runaway. You are a teenage runaway, right honey?"

John grabbed the girl's arm and tried to push past Jill, but Jill wasn't finished. No. Now, she had one more reason to unload on John. She was going to embarrass him in front of all of Las Vegas.

"Hey runaway, you got yourself hitched up to a nobody. All he does is run around and want to play soldier. But I guess he couldn't make it as a Marine, so here he is trying to be a big poker star like the kind he watches on TV. As if he could ever win anything. Only now, he's got this little problem with an underage street troll. You sure are doing some fucking dumpster diving with this little tramp. Did you find her underneath a bridge with a rattle in her mouth?" For extra points, she trashed the both of them for the next minute, using every expletive she had learned from late-night reality shows.

Jill finally stopped, flipped them the finger, and stormed down the sidewalk. She had gotten some of it out of her system. But she wasn't finished. This was round one. She knew, John knew, the underage street troll knew, and half of Vegas knew that Jill would be back for more.

She had bloodied him and won the battle, but the war still raged and Jill would make him pay for running out on her. He was in for more. And the funny thing was that Jill didn't care that much about John.

John was in shock and tried to process the reality that Jill was in Las Vegas. What was she doing there? And more to the point, how had she found him? Finally, his brain began working again and he began to wonder what he had ever seen in Jill. John was embarrassed; he didn't like everyone staring at him and his new girlfriend Mary.

Mary turned to John and asked, "Who *was* that? She sure has quite a mouth on her. Is there something you need to tell me, John?"

THE DOLLAR STORE

Jill went to the practices, attacked the challenge with an unrelenting determination, and improved with every step she took. Her intuition told her she was going to ace the auditions so she began to relax. Picturing herself wearing a showgirl outfit with fancy feathers and sequins, she could feel her dreams coming true.

On Friday, the last day of practice before the three days of final auditions, Jill ran into Derek Martin as she walked through the Malai lobby.

"So, Jill, are you ready for the auditions this weekend?"

"Oh. Hi Derek. I'm a little nervous, but I'm feeling good about it," Jill responded, trying to hurry past him. She did not want any kind of relationship with him — not even a casual friendship. Something about him unnerved her. And though he had the power to squash her career before it started, from her viewpoint, she was doing okay on her own and knew it would be an unmitigated disaster if she got involved with him in any way.

"Do you want any coaching or help? Today is your last opportunity. I can open up a private workout room in the gym where we can go over some of the dance steps and moves I know you will be asked to perform. Are you up for it?" The look on his face irked her. Derek had something in mind. "You know Jill, I do have a lot of pull on who makes it and who doesn't. I'm easy-going if you cooperate." His eyes darted down the length of her. "So, what's it going to be?"

Stunned and momentarily numbed, she gazed at him. She could not believe his arrogance and, for that matter the blatant sexual harassment. Still, she couldn't risk antagonizing him. After collecting herself, she responded evasively, "Well Derek, that is so nice of you." She sidled up to him, rubbing against his hip and touching his arm seductively. She brought her face close to his and lustfully put her finger to her mouth. "Can I take you up later on that? How about a rain check? I've got to be somewhere in about twenty minutes, so I can't do it today."

Obviously disappointed, Derek replied peevishly, "Then why are you walking through the lobby of the Malai. Why are you here?"

Jill made up something quick. "I lost my sunglasses during practice last night and wanted to see if they were down here in the lobby."

Not backing down, Derek countered, "Jeez, there wasn't even any sun yesterday, and you were wearing sunglasses?"

Growing impatient and agitated, Jill retorted, "What is this, an investigation? I take them with me everywhere, no matter what. Is that okay with you?" Then, realizing she may have sounded bitchy, she changed her tone and suggestively brushed against Derek, hinting he try another time. "But now I really do need to be going."

As she walked away, Derek told Jill he would look for them when he went upstairs to see Patty. "By the way, what kind of sunglasses are they?"

Over her shoulder, she said, "Cheap! I got them at the dollar store." She smiled at Derek. "That's why I need this job."

MALAI CASINO

It was time for the auditions. Jill had put in the effort, but something else had helped her focus during those long hours of rehearsal. She had read about famous athletes who incorporated visualization skills into their training regimens. It was important to imagine yourself winning, to make a mental picture of that in your mind, to convince yourself that winning was not only attainable, but inevitable. This was like a narcotic to Jill. In her imagination, she saw herself flawlessly executing various dance steps in perfectly timed rhythm.

A half hour before noon, Jill stepped into the elevator that would take her to the tenth floor of the Malai Casino. She was resolutely fearless, confident that she could overcome anything thrown at her. She was ready.

As the elevator opened up on the tenth floor, Jill sensed the nervous excitement in the room. The folding walls of three adjoining rooms had been opened to make room for the two hundred fifty auditioning ladies. Except for a few card tables and chairs for the judges, the room was stark and bare. The audition began promptly at noon at which time the women were told to sit on the floor until they were called. In fairness, those auditioning had been advised to bring a towel or a small mat to sit on while they waited.

A woman with tall hair styled in a puffy, fifties-era beehive ran back and forth between the four rooms, instructing the ladies that she would be the one calling them when it was their time to come to the main hall for their auditions. The low hum of hushed talk and anxious chatter pervaded every inch of the room.

Out of nowhere, a husky man with several tattoos on his bald head wearing a sleeveless T-shirt with a picture of Count Dracula on the front and one of Frankenstein on the back appeared before them. He held out a stovepipe hat upside-down. For a moment Jill thought he was there to provide some comic relief and that his ludicrous appearance might be the casino's attempt to calm the girls down. But there was a purpose, and the crazy beehive lady explained that all the women were required to reach in and pick a number out of the hat. After that, she called for those holding the numbers one to twenty-five to step forward. They were the first audition group. She lined them up against the wall on the left side in the correct order. As order fell across the room, the girls were divided into ten groups of twenty-five ladies.

As luck would have it, Jill had picked number one hundred twenty-five, right in the middle of the pack, which she thought could work to her advantage. She figured that all the pressure would be on those at the beginning and by the end of the day the judges had probably already made their decisions and were ready to call it a day, especially with a group this size. The coordinator with the bloated beehive ordered them to move fast because of the large number of ladies auditioning. "No lollygagging, no shilly-shallying, ladies. Get in line!"

She yelled so loudly and so enthusiastically that her beehive started to unravel. Jill noticed that two of the barrettes she relied on to keep her peculiar coiffure in place had fallen to the floor. The tattoo-headed man walked over to pick them up, but when he bent down there was a loud rip. The man had split his pants and started laughing with a broad toothless grin. Jill stifled her laughter, but could not get the picture out of her mind. Looking around, she noticed other ladies trying to hide their amusement as well. Jill, thinking she was at a circus show, relaxed. This sideshow was the funniest thing she had witnessed in a long time.

Two very muscular women joined Beehive Lady as she told the first group of twenty-five to follow their directions as she called them out by number. They were to take a step forward, introduce themselves, and explain why they wanted to be a dancer with the Malai Showgirl Extravaganza. One girl, who was obviously high on something, introduced herself and slowly explained that she wasn't sure why she wanted to be a showgirl. "I guess it's the next step up from turning tricks." The girl began laughing and told the two muscular judges seated at the front of the room that she had the "right stuff" and pulled off her shirt to prove it.

The judges' faces reddened and it was apparent that they were not happy with the girl's stunt. One of the muscular ladies whose nose was adorned with a crystal stud warned her to take this audition seriously and not to waste their time. "We are not some reality talent show where you think you can get your fifteen minutes of fame."

The audition process consisted of twenty separate stages held over three days with each successive stage proving to be more complicated and longer in duration. Group after group came in and performed their steps; the muscular women pointed at whom would proceed to the next round. It was a simple process of elimination. But with so many competing, there was a lot of downtime between actual tryouts. After a while, Jill became bored with just sitting on a mat and began to talk with the girl next to her.

The judges immediately discouraged any conversations between the participants. "You must be quiet and respect the ladies coming up to perform. You will not be told again," The beehive hair lady chided. Jill was beginning to feel that she was in some sort of prison. Her butt hurt and the flimsy towel she sat on provided no comfort against the hard wood floor. It was the property of the Long View Hotel as was clear for anyone to see with the hotel name emblazoned down the length of the towel.

After four hours, Jill was still in contention and was performing even better than she had ever thought she would. However, she was getting fidgety and even worse, hungry. Her hunger was all-consuming and Jill began counting off the minutes until Saturday's audition concluded. As far as she was concerned, she knew she'd be back for round two the next morning.

Jill's last dance routine was predictably the most complex. Asked to incorporate two minutes of fluid ballet steps with a pas de bourrée move in fifth position or relevé, she and the other participants were expected to execute these tiny steps in rapid progression while following the instructor throughout the three exhaustive minutes. After the taxing repetitive pas de bourrée steps, she then found herself leaping in the air as she emulated the instructor. In two minutes, she performed a series of jetés with the grand jeté, a long jump with a full leg split in midair, being the most challenging. Her last move was an entrechat leap, where a dancer jumps into the air and quickly cross their legs in front and behind.

Feeling weak with hunger, Jill had to reach deep inside herself to find the energy to perform the strenuous and complicated moves proficiently. The affirmation "Just one step at a time, one step at a time" ran through her head on loop. After all, it was what she really wanted in life. Why else had she even come out to Las Vegas? She wanted to become a Las Vegas showgirl and she was going to make it happen no matter what. In those final moments, Jill executed the steps faultlessly and smiled with confidence in the judges' direction when she completed her sequence. Standing breathless before the judges, she was ready for tomorrow, certain she was going to be asked to continue to the next phase of the tryouts.

After the final group completed the tenth stage of the auditions, only a hundred ladies remained to compete for the coveted showgirl positions; Jill was one of them. And as she gathered up her gear, Jill wiped her brow with relief.

APHRODITE'S PLAYLAND

After the final group completed the last sequence, the ladies were dismissed and told to return the next day at the same time. Jill raced out of the Malai Casino toward the nearest eatery she could find. She hadn't eaten since early morning and the hunger pangs she felt required immediate attention. She walked along the sidewalk connecting the Malai and another casino called the Palm Tree.

Wedged between the two gaming palaces was a string of boutique shops offering passersby a variety of retail opportunities. There was an adult novelty store named Aphrodite's Playland with a guy in a condom suit standing in front handing out free samples.

Next to Aphrodite's was a small sandwich shop. A banner in the window boasted "Voted Best Pizza by The Slice on the Strip." The menu board promised a smorgasbord of international fare ranging from Italian meatball sandwiches, French dip (or what some called 'beef dip'), and Philly Cheese Steak Sandwiches. It was all sweet music to Jill's stomach which grumbled with anticipation. Jill walked into the sandwich store and ordered the roast beef sandwich platter that included a bag of chips and a cookie. She carefully picked through the cellophane-wrapped cookies next to the register to select the one with the most chocolate chips in it.

She found an empty stool and unwrapped her sandwich, anxious to begin her feast. But no sooner had she taken her first bite than she saw Derek Martin stroll into the deli. In no mood to mix it up with him again, she hastily wrapped her meal and stuffed it into her bag. Jill popped off the stool and, in her panic to flee, slammed right into him. "Oh! Hey Derek," she laughed nervously. "Oh, I'm so sorry! I just got a call and I don't have time to talk to you now. I've got to get going. It's an emergency. One of my friends was just rushed to the hospital." Jill stepped to move past him when she felt his cold hand on her wrist.

"What else is new, Jill? Why are you always in a rush and trying to leave whenever I come around?" Jill noticed his eyes were red and he reeked of alcohol. There was an intimidating don't-mess-with-me look on his face.

"I told you already, Derek. My friend is in real bad shape and I need to get going."

She shook free of his grasp and fled out the back door of the deli. Suddenly Jill found herself alone in an empty alleyway. She walked briskly toward the main sidewalk hoping to lose herself in the crowds of the Palm Tree. This way she could evade Derek, at least until the tryouts were over. But once the tryouts had concluded, she would report him to the Malai management and accuse Derek Martin of stalking her.

Or maybe she wouldn't. Would they even believe her? And if they didn't, she risked losing her opportunity to become a showgirl with the Malai. Pushing this to the back of her mind, she broke into a sprint.

Unfortunately, Jill was a few steps too slow. She felt Derek's hand grab her right shoulder and spin her around violently. "What's the matter with you anyway? All I wanted to know was how you did today?" he shouted angrily at her. Facing a furious Derek, the features she had once thought made him handsome were now sullen and menacing.

"Derek, I told you I got to get moving, and you are now in my way. Let me through." She couldn't hide the panic in her voice.

But Derek moved in closer and, taking hold of her arms, roughly pinned them against the wall. "What's up with you? I'll ask you again. How did it go for you today?"

It was dusk and the main sidewalk looked like it was miles away. All Jill could think was that nobody seemed to be around to help her. Usually, even the side streets were jammed with people. But tonight, they were empty. Jill and Derek were alone.

Derek shoved her against the wall and began unbuckling his pants.

Jill struggled in his grip, "Let me go! Stop it!"

Derek smacked her hard across the face with the back of his hand. "Relax! You know you want this. I knew it when you did that little tease for me in my office. So cut the act, or I'll fix it so you don't stand a chance making the show."

The shock of being hit paralyzed Jill momentarily until the stinging in her face forced her to confront the reality of what was happening. She jerked her right knee up hard between his legs and delivered a heavy blow to his groin. Derek loosened his grip and began to crumble, wheezing, "Kiss off the chorus line, bitch!"

Calling her "bitch" only angered Jill and she yelled, "Had enough yet? You want me to break your other ball?" She launched her knee upward but Derek blocked her momentum and again smashed her body hard against the wall. He had her planted to the ruddy brick wall so that she couldn't move.

"Say you're sorry to ole Derek or you're going to wish you never met me, honey."

Jill let out a curdling scream that reverberated off the walls around them. Trembling, she struggled in his grip

To her astonishment, a blur of a man appeared behind Derek. He wrenched Derek off her, twisted him around, and smashed his fist into the entertainment manager's face. Derek buckled but remained on his feet. Holding his face with his left hand, he appeared dazed. But he was up again like a jack-in-the-box, leveling a series of body punches to the man's gut.

As Jill stumbled away from the fray, her defender retaliated with a flurry of blows to the head, a left jab then a straight right, followed by a punishing left hook.

Derek weakened but tried to throw another punch. The man blocked it with ease to deliver a counterpunch with a disabling uppercut to the left jaw. Derek fell to the ground in a writhing heap.

No longer a blur, Jill stared at the man who had rescued her. His back was toward her but she knew who he was. She recognized his muscular body and athleticism. It was John.

PALM TREE CASINO

By now, a small crowd was gathered and two Las Vegas squad cars with lights flashing had pulled up to block the alley. The uniformed police sprang out of their cars and pushed their way through the crowd. Seeing Derek still lying on the pavement, John standing close by trying to catch his breath and Jill clearly shaken, it was obvious that there had been a fight. One of the officers asked if everyone was all right.

John had managed to come away without so much as a scratch. Derek, however, was a different story. His face was swollen like a mushy melon and decorated with black and blue bruises. His jaw appeared dislocated; he could barely speak. The few words he uttered gave signs of missing teeth. Derek pointed at John accusingly, telling the police with slurred words that John had jumped him and tried to rob him.

Immediately Jill ran over to the police and pointed at Derek. "No, he's lying. This guy tried to rape me when this other guy came to my rescue and pulled him off of me. That's when the fight started. Don't believe his story. He's a fucking liar and he would have raped me if it hadn't been for this guy." Now she pointed at John.

The other officer took a look at the pitiful, bloodied Derek lying on the ground and, apparently out of sympathy, promptly handcuffed John. He marched John out of the alley, pushed him into the back seat of his squad car, and drove off. Distressed, Jill chased after them. "Wait! Why are you taking him? I told you what happened!"

Jill glanced at the swelling crowd. Where were these people when she had needed them earlier? Now, they were just gawking vultures. One of the cops scribbling in his notebook asked Derek if he needed to go to the hospital. Derek rubbed his jaw and uttered something incoherent. The cop interpreted Derek's response as confirmation and proceeded to radio in for a "bus," which was police shorthand for "send an ambulance."

The policeman then directed his attention to Jill. Starting with asking her name, address, and some other pertinent information, he instructed her to go through exactly what had happened step-by-step. He was fastidious in his questioning and seemed to scribble every detail in his notepad. When she was finished, the officer asked if there were any witnesses to corroborate her version of the story. Jill knew she had a problem. To her knowledge, there had been no witnesses, and she could see skepticism etched into the officer's face.

The policeman retorted, "Ma'am, this is Las Vegas. We're on Las Vegas Boulevard, one of the busiest streets in the world and you're going to tell me that no one saw anything? I find that almost impossible to believe especially on a Saturday night.

"I'm telling you, he followed me out the back door of the sandwich shop. I tried to get over to the Palm Tree as soon as possible and was hurrying out of this alley when he grabbed me from behind."

This got the attention of the cop and he stopped writing in his notebook. A new idea began a different line of questioning. "Do you think anyone from the sub shop might have seen anything? He did come in there, right? Isn't that where you first saw him?"

Jill, feeling that the cop thought her story was full of holes, hung her head to think. It was dinner time and the sandwich shop had been busy when she walked in. It might be a customer or worker, but *somebody* was sure to have seen or remembered something. Jill nodded. "Yeah, I bet someone saw Derek come in and then follow me out."

Then for the first time, the policeman began to soften and show some concern for her well-being. "I am sorry, ma'am. I have been remiss in asking you how you are doing. Are you hurt in any way? You seem to be doing okay, and maybe that explains why I didn't ask you earlier."

Her mood toward him began to thaw. She had been offended by his accusatorial tone. "I am fine, just in shock. I am also upset that you hauled away the wrong guy."

The cop gave her a blank look. "Let's go back to the sandwich shop and see if there are any witnesses?"

It suddenly occurred to Jill that she had never gotten to eat her sandwich and that she was still quite hungry. All at once she felt bone-tired and drained from the events of the day. From the arduous tryouts and now Derek's brutal assault, it seemed to hit her at the same time. One thing was sure, Derek was sick and twisted, and she would see to it that he would do time.

But before that, she needed to get John out of jail. What was he doing there near the Malai? Of all the places for him to be walking by, why would he be on some out-of-the-way side street? An overwhelming feeling of guilt came over her as she thought back to Bebe's Bagels when she had called him all those awful names and caused a big scene about him and his new girlfriend. Why would he even want to come to her aid? Did he still care about her and did the same apply to her? Maybe she still wanted him.

SALDINI'S SANDWICH SHOP

It was hard for Jill to keep up with the long-legged policeman as he raced out of the alley toward the front door of Saldini's. Before they entered the restaurant, Jill broke their silence and asked if she could finish eating her sandwich. She was thinking about the roast beef sandwich that she had stuffed in her bag before all this had begun. She was weak with hunger and it was calling to her, "Eat me."

The officer wore a puzzled look. "You know, I've handled a number of assault cases and I've seen the victims all respond differently. But you are the first one that has asked if she could finish their sandwich. Just kind of odd to my way of thinking." But the moment they stepped into the shop, a man with frizzy hair accompanied by a lady in her sixties with a hair-sprayed helmet of gray came running toward them.

"I'm Marjorie Lavelle and this is Hamilton Ford. We saw it all officer. There was a good-looking man that came in here. I could tell he had upset this girl because she had just ordered a sandwich and suddenly, she gets up and runs, and, I mean, she runs scared to the side door. I bet she hadn't even taken one bite out of her sandwich and the next thing you know she's trying to get away from this guy like the plague." Marjorie Lavelle was animated to the point of being cartoonish, but Jill was grateful. The woman's story corroborated everything Jill had said.

Hamilton Ford stepped in with his version. "She ran out fast. Out the side and he followed her to the side street between here and the Palm Tree.

"Yeah, then he…." Marjorie broke in, eager to get back into the conversation, but Hamilton spoke over her. Exasperated, she demanded, "Come on, Hammy, let me talk."

"One at a time, folks. Sir, please continue," The policeman said, trying to assert some order.

"Shit! He slammed her up against the wall and smacked the piss out of her face. Then she kicked him and it looked like she had gotten him pretty good. Yeah, he was sliding down some and then he got crazy mad. He grabbed her again and shoved her back up against the wall."

"Why didn't you try to stop him?" The policeman scolded. "You do know that we have Good Samaritan laws here and you're expected to help someone in peril."

Marjorie jumped in, fiercely defending herself and her friend. "It all happened so fast. And before we knew it, some other guy had come up to take him down. He stepped in to help her. They started fighting and the good guy won. He was a real hero."

Hamilton followed. "Shit man, the guy was good. He took this guy to school to teach him a lesson. He put a pretty good hit on him. Dude had it coming. What happened to the Good Samaritan? He fought like a prizefighter. He was awesome."

The cop interrupted and asked them, "Well, exactly how long would you two say this whole thing took place? And…" His expression darkened into a stern and serious look. "Where were you two witnesses when we needed you? You were nowhere in sight. How come? Why did you leave the scene?"

Both of them looked flustered. Nevertheless, they answered quickly and with the same story.

Hamilton countered the insinuation in the cop's hardnosed query. "After we saw the girl was okay and the scumbag was on the ground hurting like a mother, we knew we had to get back to work. It's the dinner rush and we were getting slammed. We're the only ones running the shop. I knew people were waiting in line and we had to get back."

Marjorie looked at her co-worker in support. "I was worried we had been gone too long already. I just figured the girl was okay and we could go back to business as usual."

The tall policeman had been taking copious notes. His next question not only seemed to astound them both, but made Jill nervous. "Did you see him try to rape her or anything of that nature?"

Marjorie twisted her lip into a funny expression and said, "He moved in pretty close to her, but I didn't see anything like that. Only that he roughed her up and put her up against the wall. Like I said, it all happened so fast."

Hamilton Ford agreed, "I only know what I saw. He slapped her and jacked her up against the wall. And he was holding her arms so she couldn't escape."

The policeman looked at them soberly and said, "I will ask you again. Are you certain that this was a case of assault and not the attempted rape of this young woman?"

Hamilton ran his hand through his curly hair, but his fingers got stuck about halfway through. He looked the cop in the eyes and replied emphatically, "I never saw anything that looked like rape."

"Okay. Then ma'am, what do you have to say on this?"

"No sir, I never saw anything like that. Only physical abuse."

Then the policeman looked at Jill. "Ma'am, I don't know if what you say is true about the rape, but I can tell you that this case will go nowhere. It's a he said-she said matter. Without any physical evidence or eye-witnesses to actual rape, the DA won't even look at it. At best, you've got a good case for assault and possible attempted rape."

Jill's brain churned and protested, "What about John, the man you guys carted away? He obviously saw something. Why don't you ask him that? It seems to me that should be the first question put to him." She knew what that little prick Derek had tried to do and she wasn't going to collapse as if her dancing legs suddenly went lame.

"Yes ma'am, that is a fair request. I am going to head back to the station and you can ride with me to file charges – if that's what you want to do."

Jill said, "That's all fine. But I need to do one thing right now if you don't mind."

The cop rolled his eyes and seemed annoyed.

Jill smacked her lips and held her growling stomach. "Sir, I've got to get something to eat or I'm going to keel over. I just want to eat my roast beef sandwich."

The tall policeman seemed to soften. "I know the feeling. There have been many mornings where I've had to start my day driving past the donut shop without stopping even getting the chance to stop. I guess I'll join you. What's a good sandwich to get?"

CATCH A COWBOY

Looking back on it, Roy thought he must have been suffering from temporary insanity. He had stepped into a cab in Houston, Texas and told the driver to take him to Las Vegas. Did he have rocks in his head? Probably. But it *had* turned into quite the road trip. Together, Roy and the cabbie traveled almost fifteen hundred miles, the sojourn from Houston to Las Vegas taking two days and a night. The entire fare came very near to $5,000 once Roy included the cabbie's hotel cost, dinners, and incidentals. The cab driver gave Roy a discount since he downright enjoyed Roy's company, charging Roy's credit card just $4,800 while repeating, "Just call it charity, brother."

Since the cabbie was an independent, he didn't have to get permission from a dispatcher nor anyone of higher authority to drive clear across half of the United States. Roy's cab fare pushed his card balance to the limit. Funny how in an instant it had just become a worthless piece of plastic. Hell, he could easily have flown, and it would have only cost him a few hundred bucks and a few hours. But the cabbie claimed to be a Vegas insider and implied he could open a lot of hidden doors there for Roy. And yet, for most of the trip, Roy didn't know if the cabbie was full of crap or not. In the end, however, he was happy he had decided to make the trek.

About a hundred miles west of Houston, the cabbie skillfully swerved the car into a Buc-ee's, a Texas-sized chain of gas stops known for their clean bathrooms. He unexpectedly whirled around in his seat and stuck out his hand. "It's about time I introduce myself," he said. "I am Leroy Hart, and I just want to let you know that I'm packin'."

Roy straightened nervously in the back seat and replied, "Why the hell are you telling me that? Are you fixing to whack me or something?"

Leroy laughed heartily leading Roy to believe Leroy was crazed; it wasn't that funny. Roy grasped the door handle in the event he had to jump out of the shrieking lunatic's car, but second-guessed himself. Leroy could easily hunt him down and shoot his ass.

"Calm down, man; I use it for protection," Leroy chided. "I live in Houston and I have my CHL. Doesn't everyone carry? This is Texas, man. The only thing is if you do get stopped by a cop, you better let them know right off that you have a concealed weapon and be prepared to show him you're licensed to carry."

"Okay man, just don't point it in my direction," Roy replied with an anxious smile.

"No worries. Just don't give me a reason to." Leroy winked and got out of the car to fill it up.

It was nearing nine-thirty when they reached Lubbock, about six hundred miles from Houston. Over the noise of the radio, Leroy announced, "My ass needs a break!" Roy agreed.

They pulled into a Best Western and each got a room. Roy asked the desk clerk if there was anywhere in town where he could shake his tail. Leroy joked, "Forget the shaking. I want to *get* me some tail."

The clerk told them Catch a Cowboy was the best dance club in town and only a mile east of the hotel. "That's the place if you're looking for some serious line dancing."

Leroy quipped, "What about the chicks? I sure don't want no cowboy!" Roy shook his head; Leroy could use some duct tape for his mouth.

They grabbed a quick dinner across the street from the hotel at a restaurant called the Mesquite Steak House. Roy felt pretty full after devouring a sixteen-ounce T-bone steak smothered with sautéed mushrooms. For his part, Leroy made at least half a dozen excursions to the bread and salad bar to complement his blood-red ribeye. For dessert, they emptied their pitcher of beer and drove the short mile to Catch a Cowboy.

As soon as Leroy turned into the parking lot, Maxi the Taxi rolled through a pothole that launched Roy's head hard into the ceiling of the car. "Easy, man!" Roy said, rubbing his head.

"The hell with you. What about my alignment? By the time we get to Vegas, I'll need a new set of tires." They bounced along the crumbling parking lot until Leroy near about drove up to the front door. The paint lines had long worn away thus Leroy made a single parking space out of two.

They got out of the car and walked around to the front of the derelict building. Roy began to have his doubts about Catch a Cowboy. There was a ten-dollar cover charge to get in, and once they had paid, they immediately wished they had not. Roy seriously considered turning around and asking for his money back. Catch a Cowboy inspired an added dimension to the definition of the term "honkytonk." It was old, dark, and dank, just like the wait staff and clientele scattered around the room. Roy was beginning to think they had accidentally stumbled into a senior citizens' facility or Country Music Night at the VFW.

Leroy took a look at the aging waitresses and said, "Man, that's some ratty tail." Roy laughed and silently agreed. But the place had

Shiner Bock on tap, so it couldn't be all that bad. They walked over a bed of empty peanut shells which littered the floor, sat at the bar, and ordered beers. There were bowls of shelled peanuts on the bar so Leroy helped himself to a handful, tossing the spent husks on the floor.

After a while, Roy noticed the place was beginning to fill up. His cabbie kept an annoyingly focused eye on the entrance to note the girls filing through the doors. The dance floor set off from the bar was in desperate need of light; it was dark as a coal mine. Worried for the safety of the partying geriatrics, Roy hoped the bar staff had a hidden stash of carbide headlamps to hand out to them. How could anyone walk in here, let alone do some two-stepping? Roy felt like screaming, "Turn the dadgum lights on already!"

Peering through the dimness, he suddenly flinched as strobe lights flared to life and began flashing throughout the room. Squinting against their brightness, he could finally make out the band. The dancing began and a few couples ventured out on the dance floor. No one was line dancing yet though; those who swayed were just getting to know the music. Unlike Roy who was intent on surveying the room first, Leroy the cabbie stalked across the floor to a busty brunette wearing snakeskin cowboy boots seated at a table. As soon as the band started playing, Leroy approached her with an affected bow, asking for a dance. At first, she demurred, but Leroy was persistent and eventually coaxed her into his arms. Amused, Roy watched as the cabbie twirled and spun the chesty girl around the floor with vigor.

The band wasn't good, but it wasn't bad either. The lead singer had a long braid down his back and seemed to be high on caffeine. Jumping up and down, he announced, "Git ready. We're gonna kick off the dancing with a song by the one and only Toby Keith! You folks know the line dance for this. So, put your cowboy boots to good use and start stepping the 'Stroll Along Cha-Cha.' Come on, let's put Lubbock on the map. Get in line! Giddyup, let's get strollin'!" Roy watched as Leroy joined the line, hauling the well-upholstered brunette behind him.

Roy moved away from the bar and to a table where he watched as Leroy and his partner attempted to dance the Cha-Cha. It didn't take Roy long before he finally had to admit he'd been right about Leroy all along - Leroy sure couldn't dance, not even a little bit. But he *sure* thought he could. The cabbie made so many mistakes that for most of the song, the girl just stood still on the floor her hands on her hips, watching Leroy make a fool of himself – which, Roy also had to admit, the cabbie did quite well.

Roy's critique of his cabbie's lack of dancing skills was interrupted when an octogenarian waitress came by and asked him if he needed a beer. Roy had already worked his first beer down to backwash and was indeed ready for another. The woman scribbled his order on her pad and hobbled away. He watched as the woman old enough to be his grandmother, took an order at another table. He felt sorry for her and resolved to leave her a good tip. But hell, she was well past her expiration date and Catch a Cowboy should have recycled her years ago. He felt ashamed to think that way, but she seemed infirm. He thought she might be better off in an assisted living facility instead of lugging trays of beer around for thirsty drunks in search of a few tips.

Roy looked around the bar for someone to ask to dance. Across the room, he saw a woman in her mid-twenties adorned in a fringed blouse and tight-fitting Wranglers, sitting at a table with some other girls. And she was cute. He left a $20 tip on the table for the waitress and crossed the room.

The song ended with a guitar flourish and the singer shouted to the crowd, "All right, all right. Get in line and let's work it again. We're going to play a little 'Beer Money' by Mr. Kip Moore, and we're going to get it done with a little bit of Country Slide." Roy approached the girl's table, his eyes set on hers. That was a good sign, but he had to hurry. Already the other girls at the table had begun to partner up with a nearby group of guys.

Roy glanced at the stage to get some idea of when they'd be starting the next song, but his attention was drawn to his cabbie who was hassling a young waitress. With a tray full of drinks, she battled Leroy, shooing him away. When he grabbed her, she screamed, "Go away! Leave me alone, you asshole!" Undeterred, Leroy dogged the waitress across the dance floor. Whether he was drunk or not, Leroy was undoubtedly a man out of control.

Two beefy guys wearing ten-gallon hats intercepted Leroy mid-way across the floor and wrenched him up between them by the arms. They lifted him into the air and held him there like he was a sack of potatoes. The larger of the two demanded, "Apologize right now to Ms. Stephanie for causing her trouble."

Leroy flailed wildly, thrashing his legs comically in the air. "Ain't no way I am going to apologize. I didn't do nothing wrong. I was just trying to be friendly. Man, you people sure are testy around here. Put me down or you are going to wish you never met me before."

Stephanie the waitress seemed calmer now, and she told the big guy that it was okay and that they could put him down. "Hopefully, he's learned his lesson," she scoffed before hurrying away.

"Are you sure?" one of the men called after her, still holding Leroy in the air. She nodded. The bouncer let go and Leroy dropped to the floor with a thud.

Leroy pulled himself back to his feet and threatened, "Don't try that again or I'll introduce you to my friend, Mr. Glock-27. He's kind of small, but he gets the job done and I ain't fooling." The mention of a gun got the bouncers' attention and they surrounded Leroy in an apparent stalemate.

"What're you saying, boy? That you got a gun? Where is it then? Somebody call the cops. This guy's making threats." One of the bouncers came up behind Leroy and put him in a chokehold.

Roy, abandoning any hope of dancing with the cute girl in the tight Wranglers, rushed to Leroy's rescue. "Look, let me take his ass out of here, and I promise, you'll never see him again. We're just passing through on our way to Vegas. He doesn't mean it. But the guy just gets to drinking and turns a little nuts. Look, he's sorry." With the bouncers' eyes fully on him, he stammered, "He doesn't have a gun. He's just bluffing. He couldn't hit anything even if he did. The dude's blind as a bat. Let him go and we'll be on our way." He sure didn't want anything to do with this kind of trouble and knew he was talking a load of bullshit. But Roy had to do what he had to do to get out of the mess that confounded Leroy had gotten them into.

The bouncers searched Leroy's pockets only to come up empty-handed. They even pulled up his shirt. Nothing. Roy was puzzled, exactly where was Leroy's freaking gun? "Okay, you little freak. We're going to walk you to the door, and you can get your sorry ass out of here with your so-called friend." They each grabbed one of Leroy's arms and, ignoring his screaming protests, dragged him off the dance floor to the entrance where they heaved him out the front door.

This nut job cabbie had just ruined Roy's night. Roy was pissed. He had barely shut the car door behind him before ripping into Leroy.

"What in the hell were you doing? I feel like kicking the shit out of you. Were you trying to get us thrown in jail? I didn't want any dustups with the locals. I just wanted to dance. And just what was up with you bringing up that you had a gun? Why would you say that? You don't even have the gun on you, and you know it."

As Roy continued his tirade, Leroy shoved his hand inside his boot and pulled out the gun. Waving it around, he pointed it in Roy's face. "You need to shut up, man, 'cause here it is, fully loaded. One click and you're a goner. Say a prayer, brother."

Roy put his hands up in the air, familiarizing himself with The Lord's Prayer real fast. Feeling like he was in some old Clint Eastwood movie, he lowered his voice and said, "Man, I want out. I wasn't counting on any of this shit going down. Let's call this trip done."

Leroy stowed the gun back in his boot and threw his head back really cocky-like and had himself a good belly laugh. He was laughing so hard, he almost choked. With a cough, he said, "Hey man, I was just messing with you. You're all right in my book. I appreciate you having my back. Don't get yourself in a lather. Let's forget about this shit and just call it a little misunderstanding between me and my Glock."

He revved the cab and floored it back to the Best Western.

CANYON, TEXAS

Early the next morning, they left Lubbock. Leroy announced that he was going north to Amarillo to take Interstate 40 into Nevada instead of the more direct route over US-84. "Those old US highways take you through every little podunk hole between here and hell. Stoplights, speed traps around every corner with ticket-happy cops ready to slap a fine on you for doing a mile over the posted limit. And you don't even know what the damn limit is because they ain't even posted it," Leroy ranted. "No sir, that ain't for me. It may be a few miles longer, but we can do eighty-five, ninety all the way and be in Vegas by sundown."

Roy didn't have much of an opinion either way and just shrugged, still angry about the debacle at Catch a Cowboy. He settled into the back seat without saying a word. Leroy screeched out of the Best Western and headed north. Neither of them spoke until they were a few miles south of Amarillo and Leroy pulled up in front of a small café in Canyon, Texas. He told Roy, "Look, man, I'm getting an early lunch. You can stay here and pout if you want, but I'm hungry." Slamming the car door behind him, Leroy strolled into the restaurant. Roy followed a few minutes later and slid into the booth across from Leroy.

Being the obnoxious companion that he was, Leroy became enchanted with a saucy waitress named Louisa who came over to take their order. Louisa also showcased her interest, but not in Leroy. When Leroy mentioned that they were heading for Las Vegas, she instantly turned to Roy and pleaded, "Please take me with you. If I have to work another shift in this shithole, I know I'll die. You don't know how boring Canyon, Texas is. Why, I'd do nearly anything if I could hitch a ride to Las Vegas with you."

Her coquettish smile was suggestive and Leroy appeared more than willing to speak for both himself and Roy. "Why, sure baby. I'm down with it. You'll be a welcome change of scenery compared to my man Roy here."

Louisa smiled excitedly and said, "Just let me get my things and we can get going." Leroy watched her walk away with a sexy saunter and smiled as she untied her apron and dropped it on the floor as she pushed through the kitchen doors.

Leroy may have been accepting of Louisa's sudden ability to drop everything, but Roy was not. The last thing he wanted was another fiasco like Catch a Cowboy. Besides, Leroy was baggage enough. "Look, man, she doesn't even know us and here she is ready to toss it all and go to Vegas. That stuff only happens in the movies. For all we know, she's married and her psycho-killer husband might come after us." Leroy shook his head, his eyes set eagerly on the kitchen doors. "Leroy, do you hear what I'm saying to you? Let's just eat and get out of here!"

Leroy looked at Roy, annoyed. "Man, listen to what you're saying. 'That shit only happens in Hollywood.' What've you got against her? You're just jel because she's got the hots for me. Hell, you can get to Vegas on your own. I'll dump you here and take Louisa. She's a babe and is already spicing up this trip."

Exasperated, Roy replied, "So, you're going to throw away a couple of thousand in cab fare for someone you just met ten minutes ago?"

"Well, it's like this, brother. I met you yesterday and already I've had my fill of you. But Louisa? Man, we're just getting started." Then Leroy got all exaggerated and said, "Brother, this is the beginning of a *beautiful* thing. If you can handle it, then you can stay. If not? Hit the road. You're on your own."

Roy countered, "I got news for you, Einstein, she likes me, not you. She's going to be hanging all over me. That's the last thing I need right now."

Leroy laughed, "Snagging you would be like sinking the eight ball on the break."

Louisa burst through the kitchen doors, swaggered her way to their table, and announced she was ready. Leroy grinned wildly and said, "Hell, what are we waiting for? Let's go!" He jumped out of his seat, put his arm around Louisa, and rushed her toward the door.

Startled, she looked back at Roy still sitting at the table. Roy heard her tell the cabbie to pull his car up to the front; she'd be right behind him. Leroy dutifully obeyed, floating out the door with glee.

Louisa called over to Roy, "Aren't you coming with us, cowboy? I sure wish you would. I can make it worth your time." It occurred to Roy that this whole trip was one big stupid, impulsive waste of money that he didn't have. This was his chance, maybe his *last* chance, to get back to Houston and put things back the way they were only yesterday. But Louisa was waiting for him at the door and Leroy was out front honking the horn. What choice did he have? "Aww, what the hell!" Roy muttered, sliding out of the booth to follow Louisa out the café.

With Louisa sitting up front next to Leroy, Roy was all but forgotten in the back seat as Leroy tried to make his move on Louisa. "Baby, we're going to have us some fun in Vegas. You ever been there?

Just hang with me and I'll show you the time of your life." Roy looked out the window and watched the prairie roll by.

They reached Amarillo and merged onto Interstate 40 on the west side of the city. As they sped along at ninety miles an hour not far from the New Mexico border, a Texas State Trooper patrol car appeared behind them. There were two cops in the car. The driver maneuvered the patrol car into the lane next to them and kept pace with the cab while the other trooper motioned for Leroy to pull over. Growing increasingly frustrated, Roy just looked at his feet and shook his head. He should have gotten himself out of this mess when he had the chance.

The patrol car pulled ahead and dropped in front of them and braked, forcing Leroy to do the same. Leroy eased the taxi to the side and rumbled along the gravelly shoulder to a stop. The patrol car pulled to a halt in front of them. Leroy leaned forward and placed his hand's palms up on the dashboard and waited patiently. He had been through this before and knew the drill.

Two big cops got out of the patrol car and lumbered up to the passenger side of the taxi. They peered through the windows, casing the inside of the cab. One cop with bright, fire engine-red hair and pimples, braced his hand along his hip close to his gun and gestured for Leroy to roll down the window. Leroy moved his left hand slowly and deliberately to the window controls on the door. Roy and Louisa remained silent.

The other cop named Lieutenant Ramos "Jimi" Jimenez pointed to Louisa in the front. "I want the girl out of the car right now!" He jerked open the passenger door and pulled Louisa out. "Bend over, face down on the car. Hands behind your back." He pulled out a pair of handcuffs and clamped them onto Louisa.

While Lieutenant Jimenez apprehended Louisa, the red-headed cop demanded to see Leroy's driver's license. Leroy recited how he had his Concealed Handgun License and that he was carrying. He carefully handed the patrolman both licenses. The cop then asked him to produce proof of insurance. Leroy complied. The officer proceeded to question him about Louisa, a litany of accusatory questions that would have rivaled a trial under the Spanish Inquisition. Roy sat stoically in the back seat staring at Leroy's head, chiding himself for hooking up with this idiot.

Lieutenant Jimenez turned Louisa back around, read her Miranda Rights, and then grinned. "I bet you thought you could sucker these two men here. Honey, you thought you could run and hide. You thought you could give us the slip, didn't you?" He perp-walked her over to his patrol car and forced her into the back seat before jumping into the front to radio the dispatcher. Louisa turned to stare through the rear window at Leroy's taxi. She made faces at them like this was all one big joke.

The pimply cop seemed satisfied with Leroy's answers and turned his attention to Roy. He wanted to know how they knew Louisa. Before Roy could answer even one of the cop's questions however, he was asked another. Roy knew it was only a matter of time before they were both carted off and thrown into jail. On what charge? Roy didn't know, but he was sure he would be spending the night on a hard and stained cot in a jail cell in Vega, Texas.

Suddenly Lieutenant Jimenez jumped out of the patrol car and ran toward the taxi waving his arms in the air to signal to his partner. The heavy pounding of his shiny black boots on the gravelly pavement finally got the red-headed trooper's attention. Signaling timeout, he yelled for his partner to stand down and stop questioning Leroy and Roy. Leaning into the window so everyone could hear, the lieutenant wheezed, "We've got a confession. I Mirandized her and she admitted everything. She insists she just met these two while waitressing at the cafe and conned them into giving her a ride to Las Vegas. She said she had never met them before today. They are innocent."

The state trooper had some bad body odor and Roy was relieved when he moved away from the window. Damn, Lieutenant Jimenez needed a shower.

Leroy, not one to stay quiet for long, asked, "What did she do? Why'd you cuff her?"

The two cops looked at each other, deciding whether they should answer. "You really want to know?" Pimply asked.

Leroy nodded. "Of course, it looks like the bitch is toxic."

"Well, you hit the jackpot when you found her. She's wanted for five counts of felony grand theft of five restaurants where she stole their tills blind and is a suspected accomplice in a string of armed bank robberies from Sierra Blanca to El Paso right on the Mexican border. That's five-on-five, boy. We've been watching her for several months. You should count your lucky stars we got her or she would have played you stooges. So, get moving and enjoy Las Vegas. You're free to go."

Leroy didn't need to be told twice and beat it out of there just in case they changed their minds. After they were a few miles down the road, Leroy finally noticed Roy glaring at him from the back seat. Peering back at him, Leroy argued, "What? I don't care. I liked her. Maybe I'll come back and visit her in the clink."

HOLA AMIGOS

Their next stop was Albuquerque. Leroy was determined to make the two hundred seventy-five miles from Amarillo in a little more than three hours and maintained a steady speed of the limit plus nine all the way. And since Leroy was driving, there wasn't much for Roy to do but look out the window and enjoy the sights. At the Texas border, they were greeted by a large sign stretched across the highway that read: "Welcome to New Mexico – Land of Enchantment." Immediately the landscape changed from a flat, featureless prairie as far as the eye could see to undulating rolls in the earth. Each passing mile became more arid and desert-like. Mounds of prickly pear cactus sprouted between outcroppings of rock. On the western horizon, long escarpments and mountains slowly formed great purple ridges. It was a sparsely populated region, sporting only a few small towns between it and Albuquerque to break up the relentless rush into the desert southwest.

When Roy saw a mileage sign indicating Albuquerque was still an agonizing one hundred eighty miles away, he sighed. As they approached a small town called Tucumcari, Leroy began humming a vaguely familiar tune, eventually breaking into song.

> *An' I've been from Tucson to Tucumcari*
> *Tehachapi to Tonopah*
> *Driven every kind of rig that's ever been made*
> *Driven the back roads so I wouldn't get weighed*

Roy remembered the words from his childhood when his dad and his friends would party while he pretended to be asleep. He saw them sitting around the table holding their beers up in a toast to an anthem he didn't quite understand. Nostalgia calling to him, he helped Leroy finish the refrain, belting out in unison:

> *And if you give me… weed, whites, and wine*
> *And you show me a sign*
> *I'll be willin' to be movin'*

They sang it again as they whizzed past the exit for Tucumcari. "Little Feat sure were good. The music these days is crap!" Leroy declared.

"They were," Roy agreed.

"You know, Lowell George started Little Feat after Zappa fired him from the Mothers of Invention for writing that song because it talks about drugs?"

"You're kidding! Weed and wine? Today it'd be crack and fentanyl." Roy paused briefly and then asked, "Who's Zappa?"

"Just some old rocker from the sixties who named his kids Dweezil and Moon Unit. Lowell George OD'd long ago."

As the miles ticked by, Roy pondered on the remains of his life in Houston. Despite some run-ins at the hands of Leroy, he had no regrets and admitted that he liked this new adventure. In fact, he felt – somehow – that he would end up living in Las Vegas permanently. He figured he'd play for a few weeks in the Las Vegas sandbox and find out what it was all about. If he liked it, as he was sure he would, he would sell some of his stuff, pack up the rest, and ship it out. Roy owned his own small house; if he decided to stay in Vegas, he could always lease his Houston home for some extra income.

He hadn't worked for the past two years and had been living off the sale of the stocks he sold right before the housing market crashed. He was able to sustain himself by living somewhat frugally from his gains and picking up an occasional project. He was neither rich nor poor, but somewhere in the middle.

A finish carpenter by trade, Roy saw the building boom develop before most investors as evidenced by being thrown more work than he could handle. Often, he was called in to complete the final trim on a new house or hide some construction flaw that had gone undetected until the last minute. He had a reputation for being one of the best crown molding installers around. As a result, he was able to work on the high-end McMansion projects and name his price.

Investing in the industry he knew best, Roy had bought into homebuilder stocks at the very bottom of the market. But when he noticed that his phone stopped ringing with work, he dumped his stock and walked away with a return on investment of four hundred percent, a capital gain any hedge fund manager would be proud to report.

Watching the miles roll by his window, Roy became aware of how comfortable he felt. Leroy knew how to drive. The ride was smooth and he kept the car going at a constant speed without the herky-jerky braking and acceleration the average driver employed. Without pit stops, they rolled into Albuquerque right on schedule, both ready for a break.

Leroy pulled into a truck stop to gas up and to get a late lunch at a small Mexican restaurant named Hola Amigos attached to the gas station.

Hola Amigos offered every conceivable assortment of Tex-Mex food all served on an enormous platter. Roy's stomach growled noisily at the inattention it had received; they'd not eaten anything since meeting up with the felon Louisa and the Texas State Patrol. Roy ordered the "Five Taco Special" that included a big bowl of *frijoles negros* and Spanish rice and unapologetically consumed it with a couple of Tecates. Replenished, he patted his stomach and told Leroy, "Now I'm rearing to go. How far to Vegas? Do you think we can make it tonight? I'm ready to race."

Leroy stuffed the last of his chimichanga into his mouth and took a swig of beer. He looked at his watch and scratched his head. "Let's see. Around six hundred miles at eighty or eighty-five. Stops for gas. Food. That's about seven hours if we push it." He looked at his watch again. "It's 1 p.m. now. Hell, we could have dinner in Flagstaff and still be pulling into Vegas around sunset."

"Next stop Vegas! Let's move!" Roy announced, picturing himself strolling down the Strip before the day was over.

As they walked out of the restaurant, Roy noticed Leroy acting a little woozy. He said, "We still got a'ways to go; you want me to drive for a while?"

Leroy tossed Roy the keys and climbed into the back seat of the car, saying, "I'm going to catch some z's."

FLAGSTAFF, ARIZONA

Roy steered the cab down the entrance ramp and accelerated smoothly onto I-40. Once he brought the car to a steady cruising speed, he noticed Leroy's sudden and obnoxious snoring. Roy turned to tell him to shut up but decided against it, instead turning the radio on low to scan the channels. Finding a station playing an eclectic mix of old and new country songs, Roy made himself comfortable. They planned to stop in Flagstaff for some early dinner and then cross the high Arizona plains into Vegas just in time for some evening action. They were so close. It was as if they were about to cross the finish line; Roy could see the checkered flag waving him in.

Flagstaff was a beautiful town surrounded by the largest contiguous ponderosa pine forest in the continental United States. Looming over the city were the San Francisco Peaks, a volcanic mountain range soaring over twelve thousand feet north of the town. The scenery was spectacular and Roy marveled at the incredible difference between Houston and Flagstaff.

They were coming into Flagstaff when Leroy woke. "Brother, I need some nutrition again and I need it now. Stop at the first restaurant you see. I got needs. This one usually comes in second, but now it's jumped to first place. I got to feed my belly immediately or I'm going to waste away."

Roy eased the cab off the interstate and took the business loop through town. He thought there must be something weird going on in Leroy's stomach. It wasn't that long ago they had stopped at the Mexican restaurant where Leroy gulped down two bowls of chips, a double order of chimichangas with rice and beans, and three bottles of Dos Equis. As usual, the cabbie wasn't shy about demanding what he wanted.

Leroy leaned up behind Roy and pointed to a small, greasy spoon of a restaurant just ahead. "Pull in there."

Roy accelerated with the intent to pass it. "Come on, man. There'll be something else up ahead. You'll get the ptomaine if you eat there. Even the cockroaches would pass up this dump!"

"I don't care, man! Pull in," commanded Leroy.

Roy pulled into the dusty, littered parking lot where the small restaurant stood. It was hard to decipher the exact name of the restaurant. The top half of the sign was broken off. What was left of the paint on the bottom half had faded in such a way that it looked like they served "Goo_ Foo_."

Leroy quipped, "It looks like I'll be shoveling some Chinese food on top of that Mexican slop we had at lunch. They better sell Rolaids at the cash register."

Adjacent to the hole-in-the-wall was a motor court. From across the parking lot, they heard a door slam shut as a brawny man strode out of a room hefting a blood-stained, double mattress onto his shoulder. He had a long, jet-black plait that hung down to the visible split in his rear end. A folded red bandana was wrapped tightly around his forehead. Roy's stomach turned. The thought of eating dinner now repulsed him and he wished he had never pulled into this shit hole. For all Roy knew, he was in store for more trouble.

The man looked around and, spotting Roy and Leroy sitting in the cab, tossed the mattress into the dirt and stumbled toward them, his uneven gait revealing much about his earlier activities. To Roy's shock, the man came over to the driver's side and rapped hard on the window with his bloody, skin-scraped knuckles.

"Open up!" the demanded. "I need money, man." Roy pretended to ignore him, but Leroy did not hesitate to crack the back window.

"What ya need, man? I got a tenner. How's that work?"

The large and imposing man looked to be a Native American and murmured something in a language that both Roy and Leroy assumed to be Navajo. Pulling out a pint bottle of Burnett's vodka from his hip pocket, he swilled the last of the backwash and smashed the empty bottle on the asphalt parking lot, sending glass shrapnel in every direction. He winced and, slurring his words told them, "Dat shit tastes like battery acid."

Then he grabbed his braid and wiped his mouth with it. He was adorned with cuts and scabs and when he leaned in to speak, his breath filled the car with enough alcohol vapor to send them all into oblivion with a single strike of a match. "I need some money for tequila and I'm hungry too."

"So am I, brother," Leroy agreed through the window crack. He reached down into his boot and fingered his Glock. "Let's go in and wrestle up some grub, some vittles, man."

All Roy could think about was the blood-stained mattress lying in the middle of the parking lot. He wished he had just followed his instincts and driven to a Cracker Barrel.

"First, I want tequila," the man muttered, fiddling with one of the many scabs near his right eye. Spurts of blood splattered the car; some even came through the window to speckle Leroy. The cabbie leapt to the other side of the back seat, but the blood kept spraying through the window. "Brother, you are bleeding in my car. Please quit leaning in so close. My God, what is wrong with you? You need a doctor, man!"

Without thinking, Roy jumped out of the car and bolted toward the restaurant. He didn't care that it was the rankest place he'd ever seen; the stuff in Roy's stomach was beginning to come up into his mouth. However fast Roy thought he had been with his strides, he suddenly found himself face-to-face with this intimidating goliath. It was more like Roy running into the big man's naval.

Blood streaked from his cheeks and drool streamed from the man's mouth. He confronted Roy. "Do you know what I am?" His drool dripped on Roy. "I said, do you *know* what *I am*?" He towered menacingly over Roy, wavering slightly on his feet. As Roy stepped back, he noticed this spurting fountain of blood was now reaching for his right hip where a large buck knife was sheathed.

"Come on, whitey. Tell Big Chief what *I am*! All you know about me comes from John Wayne movies, right? Teepees, peace pipes, and eagle feathers. What a load of Hollywood bullshit."

This "Big Chief" was working himself into a rage and it appeared to Roy that he was about to pay the price for every poorly written clichéd Hollywood western ever made. What kind of trip was this man on? Blood still raining from his brow and dripping on his boots, his dark eyes nearly indiscernible from his pupils glowered menacingly at Roy. Roy couldn't help but look at all of his lacerations. God, he was cut up. Wanting nothing more than to escape, Roy gave the man the answer he thought he wanted to hear, "I believe you are Navajo. Look. I don't want any trouble. My friend and I were just fixin' to get after some dinner. We'll buy you some drinks if you want. What kind of tequila do you like, Jose Cuervo or Tres Agaves?" Roy recoiled at the thought of sitting down to a drink with this walking mess of blood.

As it turned out, Roy wouldn't have to worry about having a drink with "Big Chief" because "Big Chief" was now holding the knife to the tip of Roy's nose. "Ronnng answer, white boy! You wantem I talk like fake movie Indian? Okay, now I cut off your beak and make it necklace. Then I scalp you just like John Wayne movie. That's all you pale faces watch is John Wayne movies where Indians are bad. So, I show you shitty John Wayne movie. That'll teach you. Big Chief ain't no Navajo. I'm a proud Apache and attack like the army Apache helicopter. I come from the great warrior leader Geronimo. Why don't you bring *him* up? He's better than your George f'ing Washington.

"You know, whitey, you and I can't get along 'cause that's how this shit goes down. I gotta make it even with you 'cause of what you did to us. You threw us off our land and now you call me Navajo."

Roy told him he was sorry about thinking he was from a different tribe but that he meant no offense. "The Navajo people were the code talkers during World War II," he hastily explained. "Without them, the Marines would never have taken Iwo Jima. They helped to win the battle in the Pacific Islands. They were amazing."

Big Chief shoved Roy against the brick wall and spit out, "Shut your piehole whitey! What the hell do you know about it. Just another bullshit Hollywood movie.

Roy found it sad that this kind of animus still existed. Under different circumstances, he would have felt sympathy for the plight of the Native American. He had always had great respect for their extraordinary and unique culture. It was wrong to force them off their land, but Roy would be damned if he was going to be the fall-guy for their grievances. Roy knew he couldn't resolve past wrongs – he was just an unemployed carpenter on his way to a country line-dancing hall in Vegas after all. What did he know about mediating longstanding antagonisms between different people? He was no diplomat. But when Big Chief pulled his knife, there was one thing Roy did know for sure, he needed to escape the freaking slash-and-hack that appeared to be coming his way.

Despite his size, Big Chief was quick with his knife, leaving Roy no time to escape as its cold steel point swiped the tip of his nose. A thin line of blood ran down the blade. This time it was Roy who was bleeding and about to be carved up. Running on adrenaline, Roy launched his knee into the man's groin. Big Chief dropped his knife and buckled. Roy finished him off with an uppercut to the face that left him moaning in pain and writhing on the broken pavement holding his vulnerables with both hands.

Roy bolted back to the cab and dove headfirst into the car where Leroy was already behind the steering wheel. "Let's get the hell out of here before he comes to." Leroy punched the gas pedal, aiming for the bloodied mess struggling to rise to his feet. "No way, man, don't hit the fucker!" Roy yelled, trying to wrestle the steering wheel away from the cabbie. But Leroy kept on and Roy watched in horror as he imagined them running him over. At the last moment, before they bounced over him like a human speed bump, Leroy let out a yell and cut the steering wheel hard to the right. The cab fishtailed, barely missing the Apache sprawled out on the ground, burying him with a blanket of gravel. Leroy raced out of the parking lot, accelerated onto the highway, and sped out of Flagstaff, Arizona.

Neither of them spoke. While Leroy weaved around cars, Roy nursed his sliced nose. With some bitterness, he saw a Cracker Barrel whiz by a few minutes later. They were west of Flagstaff almost to Williams when Roy finally felt his insides relax. He had staunched the bleeding on his nose and reckoned that if the cops were going to pursue them, they would have done so by now. Finally breaking the silence, Roy asked, "What's the difference anyway between an Apache and us? Last I checked we're all American." Then waxing philosophic, he added, "It's kinda sad on both sides that we can't move on, but I guess I get it." He fingered his sore nose once more.

Leroy joked, "It all depends on how much tequila you've had, brother. Honestly, I don't know what to make of all this politically correct shit. It seems to be what's going on nowadays, everyone hating this group and that group. Don't ask me why. Just saying, there's good and bad in everyone. I will say this though – I sure do like playing in the reservation casinos. They got better odds than the ones in Vegas."

LA HACIENDA

Leroy drove them into Las Vegas. And as he had predicted, there was a glorious sunset to welcome them. The first thing Leroy did after they finally passed by the iconic "Welcome to Las Vegas" sign was to pull into a hotel called La Hacienda, a fleabag, but relatively cheap place to flop for the night. Of course, staying at the La Hacienda had been Leroy's idea. It was also Leroy's idea to take a quick rest before they hit the strip, telling Roy, "I'll swing by in a half hour, and we'll go out and tear it up, brother."

When Roy opened the door to his motel room, a mélange of noxious odors assaulted him. There was a faint but distinctive smell of formaldehyde that was overwhelmed by the toxic smell of mold. The combination of the two was lethal and had Roy fearing he was in danger of catching some disease. The room was a definite health hazard that required immediate remediation. Scanning the room, a hand over his nose, Roy noted that the formaldehyde seemed to emanate from the numerous cigarette burns that had melted through the laminate on the room's particle board furniture. The source of the moldy aroma was easier to locate as thriving colonies of fuzzy red and black mold spores papered the bathroom walls. As bad as it was, Roy nonetheless lay down on the bed and started making his plan to divest himself of the cabbie. Leroy had worn on him the whole trip like a annoying wart.

In the last two days, Roy had been through more life-threatening run-ins than he'd had in his entire life. He could still feel the hot pain of the knife sticking in his nose and had stewed about Big Chief the last stretch of the journey. Of course, it was *all* Leroy's fault. Trouble just seemed to follow him everywhere and Roy sure didn't need that crap dogging him in Vegas. He didn't even like the idea that they had similar first names. He figured he would settle up with Leroy in the morning and then watch with relief as the cabbie drove out of his life forever. Let him cause trouble for some other poor sucker. Roy drifted into a deep, narcotic sleep.

He woke up early the next morning. First on his agenda was to find Leroy, pay up, and ditch him. After that, Roy planned to head for the Western Nugget. When Roy went down to the hotel breakfast lounge, Leroy was already there slurping watery oatmeal. Having no choice but to join him, he sat down and said, "Leroy let's settle up. I need to move on." Roy tossed Leroy his credit card.

"No problem, brother." Leroy plugged his Square card reader into his phone and swiped Roy's Visa. "The meter clicks plus incidentals come to $4,972 and sixty-eight cents." Roy shuddered as Leroy punched the amount into the phone. "But brother, you've been my all-time best fare, so I'm going to give you a discount. And that's something this cabbie never does." He handed the phone over to Roy for approval.

Roy looked at the charges to find that Leroy's idea of a discount amounted to a whopping two dollars and sixty-eight cents. He looked at Leroy, "Wow, that's one hell of a break, Leroy. You sure you can afford it?"

Leroy smiled and said, "No need to thank me. Just call it charity."

With his account settled, Roy shook Leroy's hand and said, "Thanks, man. It's been quite a trip. Good luck, Leroy, and have a safe drive back."

"Hey bro, I ain't goin' nowhere. Thanks to you, I got an all-expense paid trip to Vegas plus five grand in my pocket. This boy's mama didn't raise no fool. No bro, I'm staying. But now that we're here, I'll take you wherever you want to go. I won't even start the meter."

Roy sighed inwardly. Why wouldn't the cabbie go away? He wished he could swat him away like a pesky fly. But it was clear Leroy had other plans. "I was planning on going over to The Nugget," Roy told him none too excitedly.

"Hell bro, I'll get you there in a minute, no charge. What the hell! You trying to get rid of me?"

Roy mumbled under his breath, "That's the general idea, yes." But he relented and followed Leroy out to the cab. Leroy sped them over to the Western Nugget.

The Nugget was located on the west end of the strip and didn't exactly have great curb appeal. Still, it had a reputation for offering the best slot payouts in Vegas. Rather than dumping money into lavish decorations and pointless opulence, the owners focused on a volume business for their profits. The Nugget catered to gamblers, not gawkers, and with the best odds on the strip, encouraged the real players to keep coming back. But the place was old and in sad need of an update. It especially needed a new air conditioning system because the hot air blowing through the vents smelled of stale cigarettes. It would probably be cheaper to tear the whole thing down and start over.

When it came to country entertainment however, The Nugget sure knew how to throw a good party. They brought in the biggest names in country music and boasted the biggest dance floor in all fifty states. They were serious about their country and their western line dancing.

Leroy headed for the nearest crap table and told Roy he'd catch up with him later. Snapping his fingers at the first waitress he could find, Leroy asked for a Bloody Mary, adding with a holler, "Let's get this party started! Las Vegas, Leroy's here!" It was 8 a.m.

Even this early in the morning, the casino was unexpectedly crowded. Roy suspected many were night-shift gamblers who had lost track of time. But a steady flow of people kept coming in from outside and soon Roy lost sight of Leroy. It was his chance to give Leroy the heave-ho.

Off to the left of the casino, a long dark hall caught Roy's attention. He decided he would follow the conspicuous passage to see where it led, hoping there would be an exit at its end. The hall seemed to melt into the dimness before coming to an abrupt halt at the feet of two giant, green doors.

Curiosity piqued, Roy peered at the doors for a long moment. He wasn't sure what lay behind them, but he hoped it was the famous Western Nugget dance floor. He tried to open one of the double doors, but it wouldn't budge. Roy, ever-tenacious and determined, jiggled the door handles while pressing his shoulder against the solid oak until there was a loud creaking noise; the doors swung open and a bright light escaped into the hall revealing the object of Roy's journey. As a great breadth of gleaming hardwood floor extended before him, he grinned like a fool. He felt as though he was having a spiritual revelation.

On the far side of the cavernous room, a rustic sign adorned the wall with silver-lined letters in a crisp, western font reading: WELCOME TO THE WILD BILL HICKOK DANCE HALL. Beneath it, an additional banner with gleaming red and gold letters read: COWBOYS AND COWGIRLS WELCOME HERE. A life-size picture of Annie Oakley, the famous sharpshooter who had starred in Buffalo Bill's Wild West show during the late 1800s, hung just to the left of the regalia. A similarly sized photograph of Buffalo Bill Cody decorated the opposite side.

As a dance hall, "huge" could not begin to fit the description of Wild Bill's. It seemed more like a coliseum. The stage where the artists played was wide enough to swallow a symphony orchestra. Pictures of past performers including Merle Haggard, Loretta Lynn, Dolly Parton, Hank Williams Jr., Tammy Wynette, Garth Brooks, and Kenny Chesney bedecked the walls. All were autographed with sentiments along the line of "After the Opry, once you play Wild Bill's, everything else is just small potatoes."

Roy couldn't wait to dance on those hallowed floors, and he wondered who would be playing there tonight; it was a Friday, after all.

Someone was surely scheduled. Leroy had said there was nowhere better for a cowboy to be on a Friday night in Las Vegas than The Nugget and Roy had to agree.

Unexpectedly, a burly guard materialized behind Roy to slap him back from the mystical plane to which he had transcended. "Hey you, where's your badge. If you don't have one, get out of here, now. We're trying to get it ready for Miss Reba McEntire and you got to go. Did you hear me? How did you get in here anyway? I ought to have you arrested for trespassing." The guard was bigger than Big Chief; his arms were thick as tree trunks. He stood about seven feet tall, talked like someone out of the movie *Deliverance*, and was missing most of his teeth.

Having long lost his sense of adventure thanks to Leroy, Roy backed out. "I'm sorry, sir. I thought this was an exit."

"Well, it ain't! Now get your ass outta here."

Roy wasted no time complying, running squeezing past the massive guard and down the long hall back to the casino. He knew he'd be back tonight to dance on that hallowed ground.

Making his way through the crowded casino, he tried to sneak past Leroy. Fat chance. Leroy, still at the craps table, spotted him with ease and motioned him over with more energy than he should have had so early in the morning. The cabbie grinned triumphantly as he pointed to the big stack of chips in front of him. "Roy, brother, Lady Luck is sure shining on me today!"

It was clear Leroy had been winning. He was the next shooter and asked the attractive brunette cozying up next to him to blow on the dice for luck. She leaned over and blew a lustful kiss on the dice before puckering her lips and pecking Leroy on the cheek. That's all it took. Leroy tossed the dice and hit a lucky seven.

Roy turned his eyes upward and around with disdain and told the dice-rolling cabbie he would catch him later. Roy couldn't bear the thought of spending one more night at La 'Fleabag' Hacienda. Finding a new place to live was now an urgent priority for him.

DESERT VALLEY HOSPITAL

It had only been a few weeks since Lucy had poked her finger in a book of maps to determine her future home. And while she didn't miss Seattle, the reality of life in Las Vegas was forcing her to accept that her dreams of a new career might not be attainable. Despite the sunny skies of Las Vegas, circumstances had already forced a change in Lucy's plans.

On the flight into Vegas from Seattle, she daydreamed about what it would be like to live in Sin City. She intended to become a dealer at a casino and prepared for it by treating herself to a manicure to shorten her fingernails and give them a more natural look. She'd read once in a woman's magazine that next to knowing how to deal cards, a presentable set of hands was paramount, and long nails only got in the way of dealing cards. With one of the two job requirements already attained, Lucy was ready to launch her new career working in the gaming industry.

She planned to stay with her aunt Rosalie, at least until she could find a place of her own. She had met Aunt Rosalie, her mother's sister, precisely once before as a child. But when Lucy called her aunt for advice about where to live in Vegas, Aunt Rosalie had insisted Lucy stay with her. "Why, Lucy-Honey, I won't hear talk of anything else. You're staying with me and that's all there is to say."
While it all might have sounded like Lucy had walked into the perfect setup, not everything turned out as she had dreamed it would. As usual, life's road presented Lucy with some unexpected twists and turns and one very troublesome speed bump in the form of her Aunt Rosalie.
She was not your typical sweet aunt from Schenectady. Everyday living at Aunt Rosalie's was trying, a real challenge for Lucy. The sweet and welcoming woman Lucy had spoken to in Seattle turned out to be a manic-depressive schizophrenic, prone to frightening mood swings and a roulette wheel of personalities that ranged from dark to darker. Lucy had heard Aunt Rosalie creep around the house in the middle of the night opening and closing doors, talking to herself. In the morning, the woman had sat at the kitchen table brooding and depressed. About what? Lucy could only guess because the only words Aunt Rosalie spoke were those she mumbled to herself. Lucy questioned why her aunt had not sought medical attention for her mental illness. After all, mental illness was nothing to be ashamed of. Two weeks after arriving in

Las Vegas, Lucy signed a lease on an apartment on the other side of the city – far, far away from Aunt Rosalie.

But there was another twist Lucy hadn't planned on. She soon learned that the life of a casino dealer was not full of the glamor she had imagined. Most casinos expected their dealers to work the weekends as well as all sorts of crazy hours – night or day, any day of the week. She would be have to be on-call, just like she had been while working as a nurse, but here in Sin City, she would have to start back at minimum wage. Every dealer she had spoken with told her the same story – the work was stressful and the casino management could fire you on a whim. In other words, they either liked you or didn't. Your first mistake was usually your last. Lucy was forced to reassess her plan.

Standing now at the proverbial fork in the road, Lucy took the one she knew best and applied for a nursing position at Las Vegas's largest hospital, Desert Valley Hospital & Medical Center, a multi-service acute care hospital. It boasted one of the most advanced oncology units in the West. After a brief interview with the doctors and a tour of the oncology ward by none other than the hospital's chief of staff, Lucy was asked to join their team. Round two on the oncology ward.

This time around however, because of Lucy's experience in oncology care, she was able to negotiate an impressive pay raise and a more predictable work schedule. Of course, the cherry topper was that she now lived in Las Vegas.

The pace of work on the oncology ward was always frenetic; there was very little time for nurses to rest, not even a second. Despite her increased salary, Lucy immediately returned to the grind of performing the same, depressing tasks on loop. Luckily, Desert Valley was able to provide her with some entertainment as – she quickly discovered – the local media paid special interest to the hospital. The oncology ward was often a frequent subject of local TV news stories, so it was not unusual to see reporters with their camera crews chasing after a rushing doctor or nurse for an interview or a lead on a story. The human-interest angle of the children's plight brought their broadcasts good ratings and seemed to help build Desert Valley's reputation. This was new for Lucy; it added excitement to her day, varying the pace of her work and schedule dramatically in some cases.

Another glaring difference Lucy found was the director of oncology's proclivity for asking for her personal input when it came to imagining new ways to promote an impressive new hospital wing. At first, Lucy had been suspicious and thought it all just a come-on. But she had soon learned that the director was gay and so had no choice but to conclude that he was sincerely interested in her ideas. Her job satisfaction rose exponentially as she slowly became acquainted with the business side of the hospital industry.

One morning early in her shift, Lucy was told to go to the meeting room on the first floor. It was in the main conference room where the nurses and staff came to receive their daily assignments. Like the others in the room, she was startled to see the hospital's chief administrator standing at the front of the room. Once everyone settled, he addressed the assembled employees.

"Thank you for coming this morning. Let me get right down to it. As you know, our new oncology unit is now humming along and the board of directors wants to launch a big advertising campaign to promote it as a source of pride for the community. The promotion will last for several months and involve all types of media poking and crawling around the hospital. You know a lot of those reporters might be a little pushy, but we want you to cooperate and accommodate them in every way possible. We are thrilled about the opportunity this gives Desert Valley Hospital to reach out to the greater Las Vegas community." After seeing a few approving nods from the audience, the director continued, explaining the extent of the media blitz heading their way.

It would begin with a publicity push that would plaster pictures of the doctors and nurses of the oncology unit on the sides of the metro buses servicing Las Vegas. The hospital had bought full-page ads in *The Las Vegas Sun* in exchange for a series of lengthy articles about the hospital and favorable editorial reviews in both their print and web editions. Along with the print blitz, they would be producing a series of television commercials featuring the testimonials of actual cancer patients who had been treated and cured at Desert Valley.

Lucy understood the effort. Millions had been spent on expanding the oncology ward so the board naturally wanted the citizens of Las Vegas to know they no longer needed to travel to Phoenix or Los Angeles to receive the most advanced cancer treatment available. Patients had full access right there in Las Vegas. The administrator ended the meeting with just one request, "Ladies and gentlemen, we are about to bring in the press to meet you. I trust you will conduct yourselves as exemplary ambassadors of Desert Valley Hospital." The doors swung open and a swarm of reporters with cameras and microphones spilled into the room.

One in the crowd was a man in his early thirties, a large, expensive camera dangling around his neck. He thrust the camera lens into Lucy's face and snapped several shots of Lucy to the point of being obnoxious. When Lucy protested, he quipped, "Why not? You'll get their interest. That's why I chose you."

Lucy prodded him, "What do you plan to do with these pictures?" She was embarrassed at being singled out by the photographer and by the stares of her coworkers.

"I'm an artist, not just a photographer and I am going to transform these pictures into art. I am going to make a canvas of these. Eventually, you'll see them hanging on the walls of the new hospital wing. But first, they'll be seen on every bus in Vegas." The man smiled widely allowing the small gap between his two front teeth to show.

He was gorgeous and Lucy had to get his name. Starting to preen for his attention, Lucy asked, "What do you mean you are going to make a canvas?" The photographer did not answer, but instead moved on to other people in the room, feverishly snapping pictures.

After a moment, he turned around to answer Lucy. "My goal is to turn these photographs into a mural that tells the story of Desert Valley."

With a loud voice, he directed the staff to gather together for a group shot. Everyone smiled and was more than eager to do their part in creating the "caring family" image they were expected to portray. They were excited at the thought of seeing themselves on the side of every bus in Las Vegas. After taking countless photos over a half hour, the photographer disappeared into the crowd of reporters and employees.

Before hurrying back to work, Lucy sneaked over to the vending area to get herself a Diet Coke. She jingled the change inside the pocket of her scrubs and then scrutinized it with a frown. She was short a quarter. "Dang!" she whispered, frustrated. It was an old machine and would not accept paper bills, an ironic twist. Here she worked at one of the most advanced cancer treatment centers in the world yet they still had vending machines from the 1970s. And what was worse, there wasn't even a bill changer anywhere in the hospital. As she rolled her eyes and digested the irony, she felt the presence of someone peering over her shoulders.

"Can I buy you a drink? I happen to have a lot of change." It was the photographer.

Lucy grinned. "Yes, I'd like that. Thank you." She was a little nervous; she could feel her hands were clammy. What power did this man have over her?

"Hi, I'm Ty Amaya. It's nice to meet you, by the way."

"Lucy Faulkner. Thanks for the Coke, I really needed it." She tried not to sound too interested, but she knew she was failing miserably. Her face flushed.

"Are you a nurse?"

"Yes, I'm a nurse in the oncology wing. Mainly I work the children's ward."

"That's a noble profession."

"Yeah, I guess so. I wouldn't know anything else. I've done this my whole life." She realized this trite dialogue was part of a script she had to follow. At one point in her life, she had entertained ideas of becoming an actress. So now, she just had to put on her acting hat and channel Meryl Streep.

This guy was spellbinding. He had jet black hair and stood well over six feet. He had perfect features and a chiseled nose and dancing brown eyes that were so dark they could almost be called black. It was his eyes. They either danced or twinkled whenever he talked. When he spoke, he had a way of making Lucy feel like she was the most important person in the world.

Lucy sipped at her Diet Coke, wondering if he could discern the slight tremor of excitement in her hands.

"Where do you work?" It was Lucy's turn to ask the questions.

"I work with an advertising company not too far from here. But then nothing seems very far away in Las Vegas. I'm from New York City and this place pales in size."

"New York City?" Lucy asked, bewildered. "Other than gambling, what does Las Vegas offer that the Big Apple doesn't? Are you a gambler?"

Ty chuckled. "No, since I've moved here, I've hardly gambled at all. It's not my thing. I'm like you, all I've ever done was work in the same industry. My area has always been advertising and marketing. I just moved here and I'm new on the job."

"Me too. I just came down from Seattle."

Ty smiled with a glint in his eyes. "Well, since we have so much in common, why don't we go out and discover more about Vegas together?"

"That would be great." Lucy worked to calm herself, keeping her voice even. "Where do you want to go?"

Ty flashed his eyes at her once again. "Well first off, will Friday work for you?"

She gazed at him, not quite sure what was happening to her. "Friday is fine. I don't have to work early on Saturday so that would be good."

"It would be fun to catch a show and then maybe go shoot some dice as a nightcap even." Using a mocking New Jersey accent, he asked, "Watta 'bout you's? You's wanna take in da Joisey Boys?" Lucy laughed as Ty dropped the accent and explained, "It's gotten great reviews but then again, what do I know?"

Lucy smiled demurely. It all sounded like too much fun. "I thought gambling wasn't your thing?"

Ty winked playfully and Lucy melted over his expressive ebony eyes. She texted him her address. They were all set for Friday night; first dinner, then the show.

Perhaps moving to Vegas had been just what she needed.

MARKS & FRANKLIN

ADVERTISING

Full of ideas for the Desert Valley campaign, Ty walked into the office of Marks & Franklin early the next morning eager to work. He was excited about his new assignment and anxious to download the pictures he had taken at the hospital. But he especially could not wait to see the photographs of Lucy Faulkner displayed on his high definition monitor.

The office was laid out in a typical open-concept format, supposedly to encourage closer collaboration between staff members, but everyone knew it was because cubicles were cheap and allowed managers to monitor their people through their windowed offices. Ty was used to it; back in New York, they referred to the office place as "Prairie Dog Village" because whenever someone walked into the room, every head would pop up in unison from behind their half-height cubicle walls to assess the intruder.

Since it was early, Ty figured he had a few hours to work alone before his coworkers began arriving. Indeed, when he walked into the office, no one was there except one person. It was a man, and he was sitting at Ty's desk with his back to Ty.

Something about the man was strangely familiar, and as Ty approached his desk, the form in the chair spun around and with a Cheshire grin, greeted Ty. "Well, hello, my old friend." It was his nemesis, Sean Stevenson.

"Sean! What the hell are you doing in here? What brings your ugly mug here? Vacation? And how did you get into the office?" Ty tried to disguise his anger, but already felt a dormant animus awakening inside him. Why *was* Sean here? What was his story? Ty was beginning to feel pangs of panic. After leaving New York City in pursuit of new opportunities, Sean Stevenson was the last person Ty wanted to see or hear from again.

Dressed in Brooks Brothers, Sean deflected. "Hey. How do you like my custom-tailored threads? It put me back five grand, but it was worth it. You're looking at one USDA-Prime babe magnet."

Ty was not amused. "No, Sean. Really! What brings you here to Marks & Franklin? There's no way you guys are doing business with us."

Sean threw back his head, laughing. "No, get real, Ty. You are looking at Marks & Franklin's *new* Director of Media."

"Media Director! Are you kidding?" It wasn't possible. Ty had more experience than Sean and held rank over him at their New York firm. How did Sean even know where to look for him? If Sean was telling the truth, it could only mean one thing – that Sean had come to deliberately interfere with Ty. Once again, Sean had trumped Ty.

It was like Sean could read Ty's thoughts and took great pleasure in confounding him. Goading Ty with his repeated obnoxious laugh, he said, "Come and check out my new state-of-the-art office. Talk about the Taj Mahal; wait 'til you see it."

Ty's face flushed red with fury and his thoughts turned dark. He fantasized about snuffing this guy out. He couldn't believe this was happening. "Uh, Sean, um, how did you even hear about this company, let alone get made the Director of Media? I never mentioned that I was leaving and I sure never let anyone know where I was going. So, how did you find out?" Instead of answering, Sean twisted in the chair and smiled self-satisfied. Ty demanded an answer, and repeated the question with sarcastic disdain. "Tell me, Director of Media at Marks & Franklin. How did you find out?"

Sean rose from Ty's chair and, getting into his face, said smugly, "I'll tell you what. It sure wasn't hard. You left a trail, man! The freakin' bread crumbs were everywhere. Like, leaving your acceptance letter in the fax machine for a minute when you went and answered the phone. Yeah, I saw it when I went to use the copy machine and I sure as hell read it. Hate to throw shade on you, but hey, I figured if you could do it, I could too. Only better. Face it dude, it was nothing to one-up you again. Bad move, man, leaving private docs on the company copy machine. Too bad I read it, huh? My bad!" Sean laughed viciously.

Ty was in a rage. He wanted to throw Sean up against the wall but thought otherwise. "Yeah, well you know – this company is going to find out real fast what you're all about and your sorry ass will be out the door before you know it."

There was movement from across the room and the two men looked up to see a short, mousey woman watching them warily. She had heard everything. You would have to be deaf or just stupid not to know that this was escalating into a heated row. Her presence silenced them and Ty stormed out of the office.

PARIS FRANCE CASINO

Ty showed up precisely at five forty-five p.m. to pick up Lucy. He wore a navy-blue sports coat and dark dress slacks. For his part, Ty wasn't quite prepared for the woman standing in the doorway inviting him in. She was more than beautiful, and he told her so. "You look amazing."

Lucy smiled demurely. "Well, thank you, kind sir. Won't you please come in?"

Ty entered, and the first thing he noticed was the sparsely furnished apartment. It was devoid of any furniture except a small kitchen table with two splintered oak chairs. In the living room was a Lazy Boy recliner with a ripped arm, and a floor lamp standing behind it.

Lucy motioned for Ty to take a seat in the recliner while she rushed into the kitchen to retrieve one of the broken oak chairs. She positioned the chair to face the Lazy Boy. Ty was somewhat hesitant to even sit in the damaged chair, fearing he would break it. But not wanting to appear snobbish, he sat ever so gingerly.

She asked if she could get him a drink and Ty said he could sure use one. From the kitchen, she called, "Well, how did your Friday end up?"

All Ty could think about was that dirtbag Sean. Seeing him had pretty much ruined life for him in Vegas. But he wasn't going to start their date by unloading his troubles on her. "It was good. Fridays are always good," he answered, forcing a smile as Lucy came back with a cold Heineken in one hand and a frosted mug in the other. She poured the beer into the glass and handed it to Ty.

"Let me go get mine and we can have a toast." Ty watched Lucy walk out of the room. He always liked it when women drank beer; it meant they were down to earth and unpretentious. When she came back, she raised her glass and said, "To Joisey!"

Ty laughed and clinked her glass. "To Joisey!"

From the moment he had seen her through his camera lens, Ty had been attracted to her. Lucy had curly hair like a Botticelli model and large, blue eyes as clear as a summer's day. She had alabaster skin and a shapely body that had been hidden by the loose hospital scrubs she wore when they fist met. He could feel the desire building between them. *Damn*, he wanted her. He wanted to get something going right then and there, and was sure that she did too. But he didn't want to spoil things between them by moving too fast. They had a dinner and a show to see first. Really though, the only show Ty wanted to see was the one he was in right now.

Ty made Lucy nervous, and she had some trepidation about their date. The problem was she was extremely attracted to Ty, and was afraid she might lose control of herself. One or two drinks and she could throw her inhibitions away along with the empty beer bottle.

She began taking large gulps of beer. Across from her, Ty was doing the same. But he was annihilating it. *My God, he drank it so fast. What in the world is wrong with him? Is he as nervous as I am?* Lucy thought to herself. She shook her head. It was funny that they were both acting the same way, downing their beers in an attempt to arrive at some level of inebriation that might help them navigate the tricky waters around the first hour of a first date.

With the beer beginning to have its effect on Lucy, she went to Ty and bent down in front of him. "Care for another?" Ty suddenly grabbed her and pulled her into his arms. He kissed her and she kissed him back.

His hands began to discover the curves of her body as they roamed over her tight-fitting dress. Lucy didn't resist and reciprocated by running her hands up and down his muscular physique. He wouldn't stop kissing her.

Lucy was surprised at his forwardness, but she had to admit she liked it. She had never met anyone like him and wished they were already through with the preliminaries of their date. But she didn't want Ty to think she was like that. She would have to tamp it down.

They would enjoy dinner and the show together. After that, well, that would take care of itself. Lucy grimaced as she thought that life was pretty much about pretending. She had to pretend that she didn't want to be with Ty right then and there. But there was time, and just now, they needed to slow it down.

She gently pushed away from Ty's embrace, stood and smiled. "Well, if we're going to dinner, I better touch myself up."

LA MAISON ON FREMONT

Ty hailed a cab outside Lucy's apartment. Being from New York City, he had taken taxis all of his life and doing the same thing in Las Vegas was second nature to him. But Manhattan wasn't Las Vegas and as Ty helped Lucy into the cab, he whispered to her, "Next time I will have a car and I'll be your chauffeur." He was pleased to see her blush.

After instructing the driver to take them to the La Maison on Fremont, Ty casually took Lucy's hand and held it all the way downtown. It was his way of letting Lucy know they were a couple, even if this was only their first date.

The food was excellent and plentiful. Starting with a delicious bowl of oyster soup, Ty and Lucy were on the way to a fantastic culinary experience – and one that Ty could afford. He ordered the New York strip cooked rare and it came out almost entirely raw. He thought it resembled steak tartare, but even so, it tasted good.

Lucy ordered a light salade aux lardons, a favorite French meal made with fatty bacon called lardons and finished with a poached egg atop a bed of greens. The atmosphere was elegant and Lucy told him, "I feel like French royalty even though my DNA doesn't have a trace of French blood in it. And I've never even stepped foot in France. Still, a girl can dream."

When the waiter brought her plate and set it in front of her, Ty couldn't help but remark, "That's a fancy name for a salad with a runny egg on top."

Lucy laughed. "I totally agree."

They shared a bottle of 2010 Chateau Maris Natural Selection which Ty thought went just right with his steak. Under the table, Lucy kicked off a high heel and ran her foot up and down his leg. Ty stirred and pressed his leg against hers. Smiling, he knew how this night would end. He only wished that the curtain had already closed on "The Jersey Boys." They hadn't even finished dinner.

"THE JERSEY BOYS"

Since Sean had just got into town, his temporary residence was the Staybridge Suites on Dean Martin Drive. He got a kick seeing his handsome reflection in the Laura Ashley modern chrome mirror in his room. Sean Stevenson was primped, primed, and ready. He had somewhere to go.

A proud Yankee from New York City, Sean always intended to see "The Jersey Boys." Sean's father had been raised across the Hudson in Newark, New Jersey and was a huge fan of Frankie Valli. It was the same city that had given the world The Four Seasons, a group made famous by the distinctive falsetto voice of their lead singer Frankie Valli. "The Jersey Boys" was a Broadway smash hit about The Four Seasons' rise to fame. And Sean's father regularly lamented the show's closing before he'd had a chance to see it. Now that it was playing in Vegas, his father ordered Sean to see it as soon as he got there.

As Sean left New York to begin his new position at Marks & Franklin, his father was there to see him off at Newark's Liberty Airport. They shook hands goodbye and Sean stepped into the long security line to board his plane. His father watched silently as his son slowly made his way up to the metal detectors. As Sean dropped his shoes in the plastic bin, he heard his father's roaring voice call out in a forceful ultimatum, "Sean! Either yuse go see Joisey Boys, or I'll fly out and kick yuse butt. Capiche?" Sean turned and waved, acknowledging his father's command.

Mr. Stevenson was a tough teamster. He had worked the docks for years and was never afraid to stand up for himself. He was ready to fight at the most innocuous dig against his character. Sean had learned early on never to cross him or bring disgrace to the Stevenson name. His father's fierce reprimand after losing a little league ball game he had pitched was a reminder to Sean to never question his father. He had given up several hits and his team had suffered a humiliating defeat. Choking back tears, Sean's father struck his son on the head with a hard fist. "Son, don't be a wimp; kick butt and take no prisoners. You always have to be one step ahead of whatever is in second place. Don't *ever* let me down like that again. Do you understand?"

It had been a hard lesson, but Sean had learned it well. From then on, he lived his life to win at everything he did. Perhaps this explained why he had followed Ty out to Las Vegas. Ty Amaya was just like him – he was never satisfied with being second and could never let Sean Stevenson best him in anything. And now, finally, Sean had won. From here on out, Ty would answer to him and that made Sean smile. Their roles had wholly reversed which gave Sean endless pleasure. He was determined to treat his former manager as hostile as he perceived Ty had treated him.

Still wearing a brash look on his face as he waved his hand out to catch a cab, Sean couldn't wait to fulfill his father's command – to see "The Jersey Boys." Now, as he rode in the cab to the theater, he phoned his father to tell him where he was heading. The call connected and after a few rings, Sean was greeted by the same curt recording that answered his father's phone for as long as he could remember, "I ain't here. Leave a message."

Ty laughed. After the tone, he left his message. "Pop, it's Sean. Just letting you know I'm on my way to see 'The Jersey Boys.' I'll report in tomorrow." Pressing the button to end the call, Sean stared at the phone's glowing screen in the darkness of the cab. He hoped his father would be pleased. Actually, he wished he was there to join him. But the next best thing he could do was to buy up every Jersey Boy souvenir available in the theater's gift shop and send them out to Mr. Stevenson.

The show started promptly at 8 p.m. The theater was lavish. Heavy, red brocade curtains which hung from ceiling to floor were tied back with contrasting ornate gold tassels to reveal black velvet walls. From the moment the curtain rose and the play began, Sean was captivated. The acting was superb, and in many ways, the storyline paralleled Sean's struggles as a young man. As expected, it featured all of The Four Seasons' big hits like "Can't Take My Eyes Off of You," "Big Boys Don't Cry," and, of course, "Sherry." In fact, the first half of the show moved along too quickly for Sean to fully appreciate its artistry. As the curtain fell on the first act, Sean hoped for a short intermission.

The theater lights came on and people dutifully left their seats to attend to whatever it was that called them out to the lobby. Sean followed the herd, filing into a busy line for a drink. He bought a glass of cabernet and then waited in another vending line for a small box of assorted petit fours. Sipping his wine and munching on the little cakes, he strolled through the lobby, following the photo mural along the wall of the Frankie Valli and The Four Seasons' rise to fame. He passed the gift counter where they were selling programs and an array of Four Seasons memorabilia in abundance and took his place at the end of the line intending to fill a gift bag full of Jersey Boys tchotchkes for his father.

The line moved slowly, and Sean was growing impatient. He began to look around the lobby to look at his fellow patrons — what a motley assortment of humanity they were. Most were senior citizens and nearly everyone was overweight and shabbily dressed; certainly, inappropriate for a night at the theater. Sean was undeniably the best dressed in the hall and he took great pride in that. He thought to himself, *There isn't a single theatre on Broadway that would let any of these people through the door dressed like this.* His New York elitism was beginning to emerge.

Sean's eyes suddenly set on a young woman who had just emerged from the theater. She was beautiful and alone. Foregoing his mission of filial duty, Sean left the line to push his way through the crowds to her. "Hi!" he eagerly greeted. "How are you enjoying the show?"

The curly-haired girl with luminous skin looked up from her trance-like state. "I am so loving this show. I can't get enough of it! I just love it! How about yourself?"

Sean was just about to answer her when he saw a man carrying two glasses of wine moving swiftly toward them. It was Ty Amaya. Dressed in an expensive Armani sports coat and similarly chic tailored slacks, Ty was annoyingly well-dressed. Understanding all too well the situation, Sean grinned.

Seeing Sean with Lucy consumed Ty with rage. He hoped the look on his face said, "Not you again. You try to get near my girl, and you'll be learning the meaning of a dirt nap, pal."

Without acknowledging Sean, Ty handed Lucy her glass and then grabbed her arm forcefully. "Let's go, Lucy. You don't want to be anywhere near this cretin." The girl looked bewildered by both his demeanor and words. Ty dragged her away.

Sean called after them, "Hey Ty, it was good seeing you twice in one day! Enjoy the rest of the show. I know I will!" He then added, "You may want to chill with the way you're knocking around your lovely girlfriend."

Once inside the theatre and back in their plush seats, Lucy asked Ty what that was all about, seemingly taken aback by his sudden change in mood.

"You don't want to know. He's just somebody I knew in New York. He showed up where I work today. I didn't like him there and I especially don't like him here."

Lucy surveyed Ty over the top of her glass. His once handsome face had suddenly taken on an ominous new dimension and contorted to form strange, disturbing angles. His brows contracted to force his eyes to bulge, making the skin under them look like empty, scooped-out shells. It was a hideous transformation and Lucy was horrified by his rapid change.

Throughout the rest of the show, Lucy sat uneasily next to Ty. He was distracted and squirmed continuously in his seat. At the end of the show, Ty behaved mechanically, and what little clapping he did, was robotic.

Bewildered and disturbed, Lucy knew she had to get the truth out of him or this night would prove to be futile. Lucy's thoughts were muddled, and thinking back to earlier, she was glad they hadn't moved too fast. How this night would end, Lucy could only wonder.

WESTERN NUGGET

It seemed to James that Macon had put up one roadblock after another and, no matter how hard he tried, he couldn't find his way around them. So, it was time for something drastic. Without giving it much thought, he booked a red-eye flight out of Hartsfield-Jackson bound for Las Vegas. Leaving Macon, Georgia was an unknown path for James. But he figured that even if it proved to lead nowhere, at least it was a nowhere he had never been before.

After a few days exploring the casinos, James was already bored. The glitter and lights of Vegas were enticing, but they were just that, glitter and lights. All the casinos were beginning to look alike too, leaving him to wonder what there was to do around Vegas once every casino had been visited. The old cliché "It's a nice place to visit, but I wouldn't want to live there" came to mind. James didn't know anyone. He needed to find a job and a place to live. He didn't even have a car. Maybe leaving Macon wasn't such a good idea after all.

One morning a week into his stay, he found himself wandering around the Western Nugget casino. Passing by a lounge, he was surprised to see it crowded with people. There was an attractive girl on the stage singing into a microphone. She was alone but singing against a musical track blasting over the lounge sound system. She wasn't all that good, and James didn't recognize the song she was trying to sing, but he decided to step in anyway and take a seat at one of the few empty tables.

After a few minutes, a waitress in a short skirt wearing a pair of shiny nylons in an apparent attempt to hide her thick thighs came by presumably to take his drink order. But the first thing she asked him was his name. Surprised, he told her. Then she asked him, "What's your song?"

Confused, James asked, "My song?"

"Yeah, your song. What song do you want to audition with?"

"Ma'am, I just came in to see what was going on." Looking around, he asked, "So, what *is* going on?"

"Auditions for the midafternoon show here. So, what can I get you? Screwdriver, Bloody Mary?"

James ordered an Irish coffee. As the waitress left his table, he called out to her, "By the way, my name's James and my song is 'Stormy Monday.'" The waitress smiled and jotted something on her order pad.

James sat for an hour sipping his drink. After enduring pathetic performances by all sorts of talentless people, he was about ready to leave. But not much later, his name was called and James hopped up on the stage. After a brief consultation with the sound engineer about which rendition of "Stormy Monday" he should load, James was left standing alone facing a real audience for the first time in his life. He nodded to the control booth to start the track and the Allman Brothers began to play the intro. He held his mic as natural as if he was holding an ice cream cone. After a few bars, he sang, "They call me stormy Monday, but Tuesday's just as bad." He sang with passion and had the kind of smoky, raspy voice that made for a good blues singer. It was as if he was on stage with the Allman Brothers and he was Greg Allman.

Sitting alone at a table in the far corner of the room was Bill Walters. He was the casino's entertainment director and sole judge of the auditioning talent. Until then, Bill Walters appeared more absorbed in playing his daily Sudoku on his iPhone than he was in listening to the line of mediocre singers parading across the stage. But as James began to sing, something about James' voice must have caught Bill Walters' attention, because he looked up and began to listen. After a few minutes, Bill Walters lifted his head and arms upward and uttered, "Halleluiah! Finally, something I can work with!"

Looking around the room, Walters saw a harmonica player for a band that occasionally played at the lounge. Motioning for a waitress, Walters directed her to ask the young man to come over to his table.

The young man made his way over and Walters asked him, "Do you have your harp with you?"

The kid slapped his hip pocket and replied, "Always."

Walters invited the man to join James on stage. "Look, I want you to get up with this guy and do a few songs. Are you up for it?"

"Wild!" The kid jumped up and caught James as he was leaving the stage. "Listen, the boss wants to hear a few more songs from you. Just me and you together, can you handle it?"

James was confused. "What? Where's your instrument?"

The newcomer pulled out a harmonica from his pocket and said, "You name it. I can play anything."

After a quick discussion, they worked through a rendition of "Room to Move" by John Mayall. Even though it needed some tweaks and refinements, they had something with substance. That was enough for Bill Walters to finalize an agreement with James, but only on the condition that he teamed up with the harmonica player. He booked them to work the weekday afternoon crowd at The Deerskin Lounge between one and five.

The auditions James had somehow stumbled into were over and Bill Walters had found his act. He led the duo out of the lounge to an elevator and pressed the down button. While they waited for the car, Bill Walters began telling them what he expected from them. "Look, you guys are young and probably like hip hop and metal and would rather be playing that. But hip hop is not what Deerskin patrons want to listen to over their drinks. In fact, it's the very last thing they want to hear. It's an older crowd. They're country-music oriented and probably wouldn't recognize any song recorded after 1975 anyway."

The elevator arrived and Bill gestured for them to get in while he followed behind them. "So, you get what I'm saying? Keep your playlists tight and stick to classic rock and roll. For the first few weeks, I want to approve your setlists before each show."

James replied dutifully, "Yes sir, Mr. Walters. No problem with that." The harmonica player smiled and gave Bill Walters a thumbs up.

The elevator stopped in the basement of the casino where the director led them down a dimly lit hallway to a small rehearsal room. Flipping on the lights, Walters asked, "So, besides singing, what else can you do, young man?"

James replied tentatively, "Well, I can play the guitar. I'm pretty good, but I've never actually played in front of an audience before."

Walters nodded his head and appeared deep in thought. "I see. I see. Well, you two have a week to get used to the idea. Now, I'll leave you guys alone to get to know each other. I'll send my assistant down in a little while to get your personal information. In the meantime, get busy."

Walters left, shutting the rehearsal room door behind him with a kind of finality. James stood silent, numb from the whirlwind chain of events that he had unexpectedly been sucked into.

James' new partner, on the other hand, smiled broadly, hopping from one foot to the other, apparently excited at the prospect of bagging another paying gig. James wouldn't have been surprised if the guy started doing backflips off the stage. "I can't believe it. I got two gigs now. Wow! I am riding a radical wave, man! We could be on our way. Dude, I am so happy that you walked in here wanting to do some tunes with a harmonica. That is so dope. Those are some long odds because I usually don't come here during the day. By the way, now that we are going to be a team, what is your name?"

James extended his hand and introduced himself. "You sure made that harmonica sing. You were good. I appreciate it."

"Thanks, dude. My name is Randy Kiefer. Now we got to come up with a name for ourselves."

To James, Randy came across as the quintessential surfer bum from California with his affected speech. Curious, James asked him where he was from and how long he had been playing the harmonica.

"Dude, I am from L.A. and I've been playing the harmonica and guitar forever. But L.A. was way too big and I couldn't make it. So, here I am, and *now* I've got two gigs on the Vegas Strip. It's a gnarly-good wreck, man! I caught the peak with my sled and I'm going off." He seemed to be rambling in his delight, and for crying out loud, James needed a translator to make sense of Randy's surf talk.

Still deciphering his partner's dialect, James mused, "We could be the Dudes from The Nugget."

Randy put out his fist and drove it into James. Their knuckles collided in a hard fist pump. It was then that James knew the name would stick like this guy's surfboard to his feet. Randy grinned. "Now let's get working and lay down some material." He pulled out his harmonica and started blowing.

James recognized the Allman Brothers tune "Ramblin' Man." The song put him in a good mood; he felt proud of his Georgia roots for the first time in a long time. "Hey man, I'm from Macon, Georgia. The Allman Brothers are Macon's own and one of the best rock bands ever! You do me proud." Randy nodded approvingly as James began singing.

Transitioning to another Allman Brothers song, "Sweet Melissa," Randy opened the song softly, and James started singing. After the first stanza, James walked over to retrieve an acoustic guitar hanging on the wall. He started picking a solo, and when they finished the medley, they knuckle knocked again. They had it and they knew they could ignite some interest at this Deerskin Lounge. They could play electric or unplugged. It really didn't matter because it was working.

After a few songs, they took a short break during which time, James said, "I'm impressed you know the Allman Brothers so well."

"Yeah, I know, man. They're older than dirt. Wasn't one of those old grandpas married to some lady with all that plastic surgery named Char or something?"

James stared at Randy, a bit defensive about the insult to his hometown heroes. "You mean Cher. Well, yeah, you're right. But you've got to admit they're one of the greatest rock-and-roll bands ever and they're Macon's own. Growing up there, I worshipped at the altar of the Allman Brothers."

"Sure dude, whatever. I like all kinds of music, including theirs. I'm just saying that pretty soon they'll all be in a nursing home playing 'Whipping Post' for a bunch of old ladies, dozing, and drooling in their wheelchairs."

"I can't deny that," James laughed. "It must be strange being that old and still rockin'."

They worked for another two hours before Randy looked at his watch. It was 1 p.m., the exact time that a week from now, the "Dudes from The Nugget" would be taking the stage at The Deerskin Lounge. Randy declared, "Let's go up and watch the lame-ass comedian we're replacing." James didn't understand, but Randy told him he had heard people complaining for weeks about how truly awful and unfunny this so-called *comedian* was.

Upstairs, they took ownership of some empty stools and ordered up snacks at the corner of the bar. Hidden by other patrons, James overheard Bill Walter's conversation with the bartender, "I can finally pull the plug on this no-talent, wannabe POS comedian. He shouldn't have quit his day job at Walmart. Shit, I bet he wasn't even good at being a Walmart greeter." The bartender chuckled as Walters continued, "I tried to give this guy a chance as an afternoon filler, but he couldn't cut even the proverbial happy hour slot. And let's face it, The Deerskin is for B-team players. It doesn't take a lot to play here, especially during happy hour. All people care about is getting shit-faced. They don't care what they hear and he *still* can't keep a crowd. Hell, I'll bet even his own family would walk out on him."

Leaning on the counter, the bartender agreed, "I am so sick and tired of hearing customers complaining that they are going to take their happy hour elsewhere if they had to listen to him one minute longer. A few even went as far as saying that their drinks should be on-the-house for having to suffer through his act. One irate guy came up demanding a refund on his scotch, saying he wanted his drink comped because the comedian sucked. The guy went on and on. He tells me, 'I don't know what kind of scotch you gave me, but it tastes like watered down piss.' I felt like saying, 'Pal, if I had a dime for every time I heard that, I'd be rich enough to buy the whole damn strip.'"

The bartender laughed again and Bill Walters took a sip of his drink, looked at his glass, and said, "I wonder if it really is this hack comedian or just this cheap scotch that's responsible for the slow sales."

The comedian didn't know it, but he was about to be replaced by the Dudes from The Nugget.

TREASURE ISLAND

The night after Lee and the guys had unwittingly bolloxed up Becky Dean's plans to shake up the band by appearing on stage as Delinda Delgado, she decided to do something drastic and resolved to move to Las Vegas. Earlier in the day, she spent several hours on a computer at the local library researching airfares and apartment rents in Las Vegas. As she signed off her computer session, Becky Dean had been resolute in her decision to leave Madison and the band behind and begin again in Las Vegas; only this time, she would fly solo. She calculated that between her credit cards and what little she had in savings, she could get by in Vegas for a few months. It meant living a spartan existence, but that wouldn't be any different from the life she had been living here in Madison.

Not only did Becky Dean not feel guilty about abandoning the band, she felt liberated and imbued with an odd sense of destiny. The one thing worrying her was that big-mouth Basil might have overheard her making reservations during their last rehearsal break and blab it to Lee and Javier. Even though she had tried to keep the conversation to a whisper, it was possible Basil had heard her while he had waited for her to come out of the bathroom. Becky Dean wanted to make a complete and untraceable disappearance. But if the band found out, so what? She didn't care. She was done playing low-paying gigs at dead end bars. The blue-collar drunks and barflies she sang for were the same everywhere; they showed no appreciation for her talent, much less respect.

Yes, it was time to leave. Staying any longer would be a slow suicide. Tired of her paltry income and constant hunger, Becky Dean couldn't think of a thing she'd miss about Madison, Wisconsin – except the Green Bay Packers. She loved football and had been a loyal cheesehead for as long as she could remember. But what the heck? She could cheer them on anywhere.

So, it was goodbye Wisconsin, so long to the Three Stooges Lee, Basil, and Javier, and hello Las Vegas and a solo career! Heck, she wasn't even going to bother saying adios. Her loyalty extended only as far as her football team.

In truth, it all happened pretty fast. Before Becky Dean even knew it, she was waiting at a bus stop outside McCarran Airport in Las Vegas on her way to book her next gig. The rest did not matter to her. She knew finding a place to live and all the other variables that came with moving would eventually materialize. She was never one to fixate on petty details. She was used to living meagerly and having few possessions. If she only could afford to buy more food for herself, all her other sacrifices wouldn't matter.

She had been told all about the world of Las Vegas buffets and she was anxious to experience that culinary delight for herself. "You can eat all you want at these buffets for only $5.00! And we're not just talking fried chicken with mac and cheese. I'm talking prime rib, roast turkey, and ham – the works! But that was then, it probably costs a damn sight more now." That had come on authority from Ted, an old man she'd met at a spaghetti dinner sponsored by one of the churches in Madison. Ted told her how he had lived in Vegas twenty years before and claimed that they bilked him out of all of his money during a two-week gambling binge. He blamed his downfall on the waitresses who kept plying him with too much liquor. "I lost my head and lost it all. Now I'm just another sad victim of Lost Wages, Nevada," Ted had had told her. "When I walked away from the table, I literally didn't have a penny left to my name."

Ted described how he had been forced to find a job bussing tables; he had been reduced to living out of his car for weeks until he had scrimped enough coin together to get back home to Madison. Becky Dean had listened to the man's story politely but unsympathetically. She knew she was too smart to let something like that happen to her.

Without much of a plan, Becky Dean got off the bus about midway along the strip. She walked into the nearest casino and spent thirty minutes searching for the personnel office, only to be handed an eight-page employment application with a don't-call-us-we'll-call-you attitude. She tried four more casinos, only to be summarily dismissed by every person she was able to speak with. They hadn't even bothered to offer her an application. Discouraged, she thought she probably couldn't even buy her way into a job and gave herself a quick lecture not to lose hope.

By the time Becky Dean walked into Treasure Island Casino, she was tired and needed a break. She sat on an empty stool in front of a slot machine called Nickel Haven. Even though this was the first time Becky Dean had been in Treasure Island, she still loved it. Since seeing a commercial that promoted the pirate show on the sinking ship with the fake explosives, Becky Dean had been fascinated by the place. She would make a point to see the pirate schtick later that night, but for now, she had other priorities. Buying a roll of nickels, she fed the voracious machine until the only thing left in her hand was the empty wrapper; coin wasn't going to rain down on her today.

She glanced at her watch and knew she had only a few hours to accomplish her objective in this strange land of Las Vegas. She left the slots and walked into a lounge for a glass of ice tea. There she found a couple sitting at one of the tables, but no one at the bar. Becky Dean took a seat at the bar; when the bartender came around with her tea, she asked if he knew of any place looking for a singer that could also play guitar and put on a fantastic show. "I'm damn good and whoever hires me won't be sorry." If there was a hint of desperation in her plea, she covered it well with her arrogant bragging.

Scratching his head, the bartender thought about it for a moment and told her, "Try the Western Nugget just down the street. They's always a'looking for someone cuz no one ever wants to play on Mondays and Tuesdays. They got a lounge there where they play. I think it's called something like The Deerskin. I ain't really sure for certain, miss. Them're bad days and ain't no way you make tips. Why don't you try bartending? I like to think of myself as just a hick from the sticks, but I do know they's money in it cuz everyone likes a drink now and then – even on Monday."

Becky Dean thought he sounded like he had just arrived from Appalachia. As it turned out, he *was* from a small West Virginia town. His name was Hal and, after talking with him for a while, she decided she liked this affable hayseed and promised to come around again. As the bartender watched her leave, Becky Dean sexed up her walk and sauntered out of the lounge; it was the only tip she could afford to leave.

She strolled confidently into the personnel office at the Western Nugget and demanded to talk to the manager in charge of entertainment. The lady at the front desk appeared unimpressed, and apparently mistaking confidence for arrogance, eyed Becky Dean with disdain. Undaunted, Becky Dean continued, "I heard that you are looking for lounge acts on Monday and Tuesday for some lounge by a dance hall. I could fit the bill. Tell them they need me!"

The receptionist rebutted sarcastically, "Well, of course. He's been waiting for your arrival. They need you because you are who? And you are from where? I'll call him and let him know you want to talk with him. I am sure he will be pleased that you are finally here." She picked up the phone and spoke in hushed tones so Becky Dean could only imagine what they were saying. Finally, she heard the woman say, "Yes, sir. Right away." She hung up the phone, gruffly pointed to the elevator door behind her, and told Becky Dean to take it to the seventh floor and ask for Bill Walters.

Becky Dean smiled triumphantly as she walked past the seething but nebbish woman. This was perhaps her only chance to showcase her talent. Bill Walters welcomed her into his office and asked for a demo disc. She apologized, explaining that she'd just arrived in town and it was packed away in her bags.

"Well, no worries." said Bill Walters. Within ten short minutes, she was standing in front of Mr. Walters with a karaoke mic in her hands singing "Sweet Home Alabama" by Lynyrd Skynyrd. When she finished, Becky Dean couldn't tell what Bill Walters was thinking. At least he hadn't thrown her out halfway through. But when he asked her to sing another song, Becky Dean knew she had impressed him. Next, she chose a blues tune by B.B. King called "Three O'clock Blues." Bill Walters seemed to enjoy her performance and asked her if she could sing some more blues for him.

Excited, Becky Dean sang "Every Day I Have the Blues" with verve and an energy level that surprised even her. It was like she was a theme park thrill ride and Bill Walters was along for the rush. She mused to herself proudly that she was "laying it down with everything I have, and it's working." Bill Walters was mesmerized.

When she had finished, Bill Walters sat quietly at his desk staring past her out of his office window.

Becky Dean didn't know what to think. Had Walters liked her singing or was she imagining it? Her forte was really country-western and southern rock. "Three O'clock Blues" was an impulsive choice on her part. She had always admired B.B. King and his love affair with Lucille, his black Gibson guitar. Had she blown it? She kept telling herself that the fact she was still there was a good sign. Still, Becky Dean was nervous.

Suddenly Bill Walters perked up and said, "I have an idea!" Becky Dean looked at him expectantly. "Are you available Monday through Thursday for the one-to-five afternoon show?" He went on to explain that he had just hired two new guys. "They wanted solo gigs like you, but I put them together and I have to admit, they make a good team and live up to the real meaning of the Western Nugget. I mean, for pity's sake, what do you think a nugget is anyway? Well, I'll tell you what it is. It's a solid gold rock star of a gem and that's what they can become. One even played the harmonica like you never heard."

Becky Dean asked him the obvious question, "Then why do you want me at the same time?"

"Because I think you should join their group. Together, you three could be one hot trio. You could go places. So, what do you think?"

Not believing her good fortune, she wanted to tell everyone she knew or ever knew how happy she was. "I'm all for it. I want to meet these guys right away and get down to business."

"I will get them over here as soon as possible. They're going to like you. You're going to rock the apple cart, as they say. I can't wait to hear the three of you together!" Bill Walters grabbed the phone and pressed it to his ear. "Veronica, get those guys I just hired for the afternoon gig in The Nugget on the phone. Tell them to be in my office tomorrow at eleven sharp."

Bill Walters slammed down the receiver and brought his hands together with a thunderous clap. He seemed drunk with enthusiasm, as if he had just discovered a new version of the Spice Girls or the Backstreet Boys. "So, it's all set, be here tomorrow at 11."

"But what if they don't want me?"

"We shall see. Let's get together tomorrow. I'm going to issue an ultimatum. Both seemed hungry for work, so they'd better drop whatever plans they have and be here. They need to meet the newest member of their group – pretty Miss Becky Dean."

As far as Becky Dean was concerned, it was all set for tomorrow at eleven. Becky Dean floated out of Bill Walters' office as if in a dream. She only hoped it wasn't.

DUKE OF SURREY

At precisely 11 a.m. the next morning, Bill Walters introduced James Donavan and Randy Kiefer to the newest member of their band, Becky Dean. James wasn't sure what to think about her. Sure, Becky Dean was pretty enough with her big brown eyes and little nose. She was thin but had a nice figure and looked like she kept herself in shape. Her legs were well-toned. Perhaps it was because she danced while performing on stage? All he knew was that he liked her legs.

But could she sing? Could she play the guitar or merely strum a few chords? Bottom line: was she a musician?

James knew that it was pointless to worry about it because none of it mattered. Bill Walters had already decided that this girl was going to be part of their act and Bill Walters was boss. He made all the rules. From the moment he and Randy were hired, James understood that they were just two more employees added to the casino's payroll. So, when he got the call from Bill Walters' secretary pleasantly asking him to be at the casino a couple of hours early, James now understood the request for what it was. It was an ultimatum they could not ignore: "Be at my office tomorrow morning come hell or high water! We have things to discuss and you are going to like what I am about to make happen. Be here, or else. No excuses. I can replace you in a New York minute."

Becky Dean smiled and took in her new crew. James was the good looking one. He had thick, wavy black hair, stood about six foot two, and had the kind of features that Becky Dean found attractive. Randy was younger than James and fidgeted like a sprinter waiting for the starting gun.

After exchanging some awkward greetings, Becky Dean took command. "Well guys, let's get to work!"

Randy and James looked at each other, surprised and clearly uncertain about how this was going to play out. Bill Walters smiled and told them that he'd reserved a rehearsal room down in the basement for them. He scribbled the room number and key code on a piece of paper and handed it to Becky Dean. "Take the elevator down to B2 and turn right." Becky Dean took it and motioned for James and Randy to follow.

Becky Dean punched in the key code to the rehearsal room and the door unlocked with a loud snap. Walters had ordered that the guys' instruments were plugged in and waiting for them. Becky Dean grabbed an old acoustic guitar from the corner and began tuning it. Again, she took the lead and suggested that they start with a blues number. Almost simultaneously, James and Randy called for the T-Bone Walker classic "Stormy Monday." They picked up their instruments, and Randy counted down the beat. He played one of the most soulful harmonica intros Becky Dean had ever heard.

As Randy moved into a sustaining rhythm, James took the lead on guitar and dropped a solo blues riff that perfectly progressed the mood of the song. Becky Dean was impressed. These guys were good. With The Madison Four, she was always looking for her cue, but not with these guys. Their progressions were not only amazing but so intuitive that she needed no signal for her entrance. At the end of James's solo, Becky Dean came in so naturally it was as if they'd played together many times before. After Becky Dean sang the first few bars, she saw James smile and Randy nod in approval. Even before they finished that first song, the chemistry between the three was evident. And after playing a few more songs together, James and Randy found out that Becky Dean was more than just a good voice. She could also play guitar, keyboard, and the harmonica.

An hour later, Bill Walters walked in while Becky Dean was singing "God Bless the Child" with Randy blowing a soulful harmonica accompaniment. He sat in the corner to listen. When they finished the song, Bill Walters jumped up excitedly exclaiming, "Can I pick 'em or what!" He strutted out of the room, evidently euphoric in his ability to discover fledgling talent.

James and Randy looked at Becky Dean as if to ask what that was all about. She shrugged her shoulders when Bill Walters barged back in to announce, "I liked what I heard. Keep practicing. Becky Dean, you go on stage next week." And he was gone again. They looked at each other and smiled. The trio was launched.

At practice the next day, their trio began to crystallize as their strengths melded. They went over the songs each of them knew. Surprisingly, there was a great deal of overlap in their catalogs and they were able to cobble together three solid sets of songs. They had but one problem – what to name themselves. Obviously, they could no longer be called "The Dudes from The Nugget."

Randy came up with the name "The Rajabede Trio," explaining that he took the first two letters in their names to concoct it. He seemed delighted by his cleverness but James and Becky Dean looked at each other dubiously. When they approached Bill Walters about it, he shrugged his shoulders and said, "Just mull it around for a bit."

Randy Kiefer affected people. At first glance, he looked every inch the California surfer dude with his bleached, blond hair, multiple piercings, tattoos, and stoner talk. But underneath it all was a gentle soul that people found downright likable.

He certainly did not fit just a single label and posed a conundrum in the minds of most of the people he encountered. Randy could turn from being a nonsense-spewing pothead to an innocent and honest young man searching fiercely to find his niche on this Earth. Even he seemed to grapple with who he was and what he was to become. But whatever Randy Kiefer was, he was a hard worker, willing to toil relentlessly to help take The Rajabede Trio to the pinnacle of success.

Not wanting to disturb the fragile cohesion of their merry trio, Becky Dean and James surrendered, agreeing to Randy's cockamamie name for their group. To them, it sounded like the name of some Indian guru, or a Silicon Valley startup, or somebody's computer password. Later they would confide to each other about how silly and ridiculous they thought the name was and share a good laugh. But for now, there were more important matters to concentrate on, so when Randy pressed them to decide on a name, James said, "Rajabede it is!"

Becky Dean echoed, "I agree! It's a keeper."

"Sweet!" Randy Kiefer said victoriously. "Let's go buy some beers. It's on me. How about the Duke of Surrey over on Harmon?" James and Becky Dean gave Randy the thumbs up and they proceeded to the Duke of Surrey.

The Duke of Surrey Pub was a replica of an English pub with thick wooden beams exposed in plastered walls and low ceilings with oak rafters. Their walk-in special was a "Pie and a Pint." But the menu included all the expected "pub grub" like shepherd's pie, fish and chips, bangers and mash, and pastries. The Duke of Surrey was authentic even down to the darts, skittles, and dominoes it offered. It also sponsored a local football (soccer) team for the ex-pat crowd. Prominently displayed throughout the pub were the team's trophies and photographs commemorating their victories.

As they stepped into the Surrey, Randy put his arms around his newfound partners, and in his best faux English accent said, "Blimey, you bloody wankers! Let's do something wonky! Let's get bladdered!

So onward The Rajabede Trio went. It was unanimous. They all wanted to catch a buzz or, as Randy Kiefer pointed out to them, "As they say in Britain, let's get legless." He seemed rather proud of himself that he knew a little bit of British slang; he was, after all, a cradle California boy.

But what he didn't tell them was that he had spent many summers across the pond in London and mumbled to himself, "Whoa! Got to stay in the pocket, can't blow my surf's up image and wipeout."

RADIO STATION KPLV

Immediately after they first took to the stage at The Deerskin Lounge, The Rajabede Trio could confidently boast that they were a success. "Man, we're causing a righteous commotion out there!" Randy Kiefer exclaimed one day during a break between sets. The Rajabede were drawing ever-increasing daytime crowds. So much so, that additional wait staff was hired to handle the surprising increase in business.

None of this went unnoticed by The Nugget management and behind the scene, Bill Walters was already busy planning out a promotional campaign to capitalize on his new sensation. Bill arranged for the trio to perform a live spot on Las Vegas's biggest country music station "Radio 95.8 – All Things Country." Between live radio performances, the colorful DJ host Tommy Bill Dillion would interview them. None of them needed to be told how important this opportunity was. It could just be the break each of them had always dreamed of; they were determined to turn every listener tuned to All Things Country into a rabid Rajabede fan.

Used to having her way, Becky Dean insisted they open up with Johnny Cash's "Ring of Fire." That was her song. Even though Johnny Cash had made the song a hit, it was his future wife June Carter who had written the song as she was falling in love with him. Written by a woman, Becky Dean knew she could style it the way only a woman could – with a passion that threatened to reel out of control. She could relate to June Carter Cash. Becky Dean owned that song and had proven it many times in the past. "Ring of Fire" was usually the song The Madison Four opened their shows with and it always won the audience over.

Thinking about the second song, she wanted to go with the blues and play "Stormy Monday." There was no disagreement with that. In the short time they'd been working together, that song had become their signature hit. With her and James' harmonizing vocals, their rendition was better than most, and Randy always revved up the audience with his fantastic harmonica. They quibbled a bit over the rest of the playlist until they settled on something that wasn't entirely country but demonstrated their range. Bill Walters approved.

Bill Walters and The Rajabede Trio arrived at the radio station in the hills outside of Las Vegas. They were met by Tommy Bill's disengaged producer who perfunctorily led them into an empty studio.

She explained that Tommy Bill was already on the air and would join them as soon as they were ready. They plugged their instruments into the station's system and, after a few sound checks, the producer announced from the control booth that they were ready. "I'll go tell Tommy Bill."

A few minutes later, Tommy Bill burst into the studio energetically and quickly made it clear that he was in charge. With a nod from the producer in the control room, Tommy Bill began.

"Well, we're back, Las Vegas and I'm joined here in-studio with the trio that is shaking up the afternoons over at the Western Nuggets' Deerskin Lounge. So, let's get to know them and find out what this brushfire is all about."

He walked over to each of them and asked the typical questions: their names, where they were from, how they got together, and the like. Each gave the expected answers that culminated in them getting together at The Deerskin Lounge. He cut to a commercial and instructed the trio to set up for their first tune. When Becky Dean told him they were going to play "Ring of Fire," she could see DJ Tommy Bill Dillion was getting a thrill just being near her and that alone boosted her confidence.

Back from the break, Tommy Bill announced, "Here they are, The Rajabede Trio playing 'Ring of Fire' by the indomitable June Carter Cash. Folks, buckle up your seatbelts or, should I say, sit tight in your saddles. Hit it, Rajabede!"

They began to play and they were fantastic.

When they finished, Tommy Bill, who appeared moved but never lacking for words, exclaimed, "Rajabede, that was so good it makes you want to slap your granny." He continued to get to know them by asking what their favorite music genres were. When they answered in unison – the blues – Tommy Bill squealed with delight.

"The blues are my thing too! Well, folks, let's take another break and when we come back, what will we hear? I'm going to throw it over to pretty Miss Becky Dean to tell us, 'cause lordy knows, I sure ain't got a clue."

Becky Dean responded, "Well, Mr. Tommy Bill we thought we'd play 'Stormy Monday,' darlin'."

During the break, Tommy Bill lamented to whomever would listen that he used to harbor dreams of singing the blues. "Kids, I ain't ashamed about it but there's something I just gotta fess up to. All my livelong life I wanted to sing the blues so bad 'cause I've had my very own bucket full of problems and they been a burr in my saddle for years. Believe me when I tell you that I haven't been able to give them the heave-ho even 'til now. They've been holding onto me for years, but my voice wasn't worth a pile of dried-up cow dung."

Tommy Bill cut for another break after they finished "Stormy Monday," but not before he asked if they would entertain his audience with just one more song. Becky Dean answered him with a forced southern drawl, "Well, you sure do know how to flatter us, Mr. Tommy Bill. You got us flying high in the clouds right about now." They knew their finale, "Sweet Home Alabama" by Lynyrd Skynyrd would cement their reputation. High-fiving each other during the commercial break, they didn't notice the frantic producer behind the glass motioning Tommy Bill to come into the control room to take an urgent phone call.

After what seemed like an abnormally lengthy break, Tommy Bill returned wearing a peculiar expression. He was looking at them, and particularly Becky Dean, rather hostilely. Suddenly the atmosphere in the room turned dark and the trio was taken aback, wondering what had changed. Becky Dean looked at Randy and James and whispered to them, "Give it all you got. Remember, this is live radio!"

Tommy Bill sat down and pulled his boom mic close to his mouth. "We're back and boy-howdy, do I have some news I've just got to run up your flagpole. I just got off the phone with some guy named Lee from Madison, Wisconsin. If you recall, that's where our pretty Miss Becky Dean told us she hails from. Well, this guy is making claims to be a musician, saying that he knows Miss Becky Dean very well. In fact, he told me that she was the lead singer in their group until one day a few weeks ago when she left them cold. Without so much as a word to the folks that she had played with for years, she disappeared, leaving them hanging and having to cancel all their gigs."

Tommy Bill took a breath and continued, "But here's the real deal. He says they are a slamming band and that Becky Dean stole all their arrangements. And listen here – they are out for blood. Well, folks, I say that's dirty dealing and this is where I come into the picture. I say let's resolve this with some piss and vinegar followed by a pinch of sugar. Here's my idea. Let's have us a good, old fashion Battle of the Bands. Y'all can listen and cast your vote. Each group will sing three songs and you, my good friends, will be the judges and jury. Folks, it seems to me that it's the only fair thing to do. It'll come down to a nail biter and someone's gonna have some chewed up fingers before it's all over. These guys have a score to settle and they want to do battle right here on my playground at KPLV."

Ignoring the expressions on the trio's face, Tommy Bill was animated, throwing his arms up in the air as he talked. "Folks, I'm all lit up. We've still got to work it all out, but we will, and we're gonna have us a good time. Them kinks got to get hammered out first. Then you can decide, Las Vegas, if Becky Dean is a 'baddie' and the dudes from

'Maddie' have a point. The 'Maddies want redemption and maybe Becky Dean can get vindication. The responsibility lies in the power of your ears. You guys are the sugar because you can help resolve this squabble. With y'all's help, you can make these two groups kiss and makeup."

Becky Dean dared a glance at James and Randy. They appeared stunned by Tommy Bill's pronouncement. And why not? She had been deliberately evasive when they asked about her past and sketched in only the faintest outlines of her life before Rajabede. She had revealed little about herself and had always turned the conversation whenever they pressed her too hard about things personal. "Look," She'd say, "Let's just be happy we have a job doing what we love to do." With that, Becky Dean was able to put them off, but now they looked at her, perplexed and bewildered.

Bill Walters motioned for the team to huddle around him and said, "Look, I brought you all together in a moment of inspired impulse and until now, I've been proven right. But even this can work in your favor and its great publicity. We couldn't have asked for anything better. Trust me. I'm like magic and I've made it all happen for you three. You all are a hit at The Deerskin. What can I tell you? You guys are stars! I knew it from the moment I heard you. We'll play this up for all it's worth and when it's all over, you'll be working nights."

Despite the Bill Walters pep talk, James and Randy still looked confused and shaken. But it was the look on their lead singer's face that demanded attention. Becky Dean was in a genuine panic. She felt like she was having a stroke. She leaned against the wall for fear of fainting. Looking down, she could not make eye contact with any of them in that small studio. She felt stranded and alone on her own deserted island of her own making.

The worst thing that could happen in a radio broadcast was silence. And already there had been too much of it and Tommy Bill crashed the quiet with his booming voice. "Enough with the dead air, Rajabede. Let's get on with it. You all got to get busy and throw it down. What are we going to hear?"

James quickly went over to Becky Dean, put his arm around her, and whispered in her ear, "Give it all you got! Remember, we're on live radio!" He winked and Becky Dean smiled. Her shock began to fade. It was as if James had thrown her a life preserver.

She stepped up to the mic and said, "Ladies and Gentlemen, we're going to sing 'Sweet Home Alabama.' But since this isn't Alabama, we're going put a Vegas spin on it just for y'all." There she was affecting that contrived fake southern accent again. Her stance had now changed and she hardened herself to perform. Becky Dean was ready to sing. Sure it took effort, but Lee Murphy had thrown down a formidable challenge she could not ignore.

Still, she couldn't keep the questions from swirling through her mind. Where was Lee? He certainly couldn't be in Vegas. But then how could he have known to call in? How did he know where she was? Why couldn't Lee leave her alone? For now, she brushed off these questions; she had a performance to give. Hopefully, the listeners would hear a fabulous group possessed with remarkable talent.

Tommy Bill clapped his hands and let out a whoop. "Oh man, good stuff. Y'all the best. I want to thank The Rajabede Trio for coming out to play for us all. But I guess I need to put it to the Rajabedes and ask them how they feel about battling the 'Maddies.'"

Becky Dean retorted, "Tommy Bill, we are *so* on. This competition can't happen soon enough. They are going to wish they had never called in because we are going to kick their...."

Suddenly James interrupted, finishing the taunt for her, "... their sorry Madison, Wisconsin butts!" Brushing up beside Becky Dean, he showed his unyielding support for her and their trio. "No one puts my girl down on live radio without payback."

"Okay. Randy, are you going to let these two do all the yappin' for you? What've you got to say for yourself, boy?" Tommy Bill had a few minutes left live on his show and he drew it out to the last second.

Randy Kiefer's eyes widened as he said assuredly, "Yeah, I'm in the mood for kicking some 'Maddie' ass cause I'm badass." Even though it was live radio, they were on a six-second delay but it was what it was. Tommy Bill signed off from his show, yelling into the mic.

"Stayed tuned to KPLV for the latest news on the competition. We're going to have us a barn burner between these two bands so hold on to your matches and lighter fluid and we'll see which of these two barns gets burned up. I'm only kidding, but I'm leaving it up to you country bumpkins to decide this. So, for now, this is Tommy Bill Dillion on KPLV radio – All Things Country. Saddle up Las Vegas; we got some hot new acts a'coming your way to the Valley. Here's The Rajabede's to take us out with 'Sweet Home Alabama.'"

Tommy Bill switched off his microphone and pointed to the trio who were ready and waiting. "One, and two, and .... Big wheels keep on turning..."

WHEATON, ILLINOIS

Nadine's hand shook uncontrollably as the policeman with the glasses handed her a crumpled envelope. It was from Frank. He had written a suicide note and addressed it to her. In it, he explained that for the last three years he suffered from aggressive throat cancer and, over the past year, it had progressed to stage four.

In the letter, Frank apologized that his cancer made him difficult to live with and rendered him all but unable to speak. He was terminal and his doctors had given him only a few more weeks to live. He was depressed and felt hopeless. A life-long addiction to cigarettes caused his cancer and his only regret was that he hadn't kick them sooner. He warned Nadine never to let her children smoke. Frank expressed his great love for her and her children, Dorothy and Robert. He told her he loved her from the very first minute he met her in Walgreens buying cigarettes. His letter was confessional but sentimental and explained how he realized the burden his grim prognosis would place on her during his final weeks and that was something he didn't want to put her and the children through. So, on that brutally cold November morning, Frank walked out of the house, sat down under a tree in a nearby park, and shot himself in the head. By the time the police found him, Frank was frozen solid.

Nadine wiped tears from her eyes and turned the page. Her eyes widened as the letter went on to explain the big secret that Frank wanted to tell her but had been unable to do so because it was too painful to talk.

Five years earlier, Frank had won the Illinois Mega Millions Lottery. It was an enormous jackpot but he kept his winnings a secret, disclosing them to no one. Frank waited for months after winning the prize before hiring a slick lawyer to claim it for him. He never had a phone and his only mailing address was a post office box he rarely opened. In this way, he was able to avoid the haranguing sycophants and vultures eager to con him out of his fortune.

Not keen on shopping or one to indulge in big boy toys, Frank banked his jackpot and lived his life as frugally as he could, as if he had never won anything. Afraid that some teller or banker might reveal his secret if he kept it all in one large account, Frank opened accounts at banks in Wheaton and all around the Chicago area, making small deposits in each.

He fooled them all. He went about his life living as a pauper in a one-bedroom apartment and driving a beat-up old Toyota with a weather-beaten paint job. Never once was he been mistaken for an eccentric man of wealth. Frank outwitted the whole town and Nadine thought it was something he was proud of. With his bedraggled appearance and dirty clothes, no one in the city had the slightest notion that the man they regarded as borderline indigent was, in fact, worth more than eighty million dollars.

As Nadine read the long letter, she began learning more about her husband than she had ever known about him while he was alive. Frank knew that someday he would put his money toward something good and charitable. But he wasn't about to waste it on just anybody or anything. Frank had trusted he would know what to do with it when the time came. And from the first time Nadine slid him his pack of cigarettes across the counter at Walgreens, Frank had known it would be Nadine who would share his treasure. He just needed to convince her that he was the one she needed without him having to reveal why.

Frank was not blind to the many obstacles of his plan, not the least of which was their difference in age. And God knows he had never been considered handsome, not even in his prime. But he was determined not to epitomize the phrase, "There's no fool like an old fool" and become that dirty old man chasing after some young girl barely old enough to be his granddaughter. Besides, his vigor had left him long before and he didn't have the energy. No, he had to make Nadine like him for himself.

It had taken some work, but somehow Frank convinced Nadine to marry him without ever having told her about his wealth. Whatever her reasons, Nadine accepted his proposal and in the few months they were together, Nadine worked hard to make Frank feel at home, in her home. His letter acknowledged that fact and he was grateful to her and hoped Nadine shared the same feelings. Similarly, he had never told her about his cancer and admitted that as his condition worsened, he had become irritable and withdrawn and thanked Nadine for remaining patient and supportive through it all.

As she read the letter, he thanked her for her kindness to him. His only regret was that he hadn't had enough time to spend with her. Hopefully the money she was about to receive would redeem him. Frank told her to make the most of the money and to spend it wisely. He wanted Nadine to improve her situation in life as well as her dear children.

As she folded the letter back into its envelope, Nadine sobbed. She couldn't quite believe what she had read. A tsunami of guilt consumed her as she wondered if she had been there emotionally for Frank. But it never occurred to her that Frank was that sick. She could have done more for him. In a sense, she felt that she slighted him. Her first priority was to bury Frank in the fashion he deserved.

Throwing her shoulders back and taking a deep breath, Nadine had to be strong. She had been blessed and given a new future thanks to Frank. It was necessary to approach this responsibly. After all, she had to worry about her children.

It was what Frank Spencer wanted for her. Nadine would honor his wishes.

BOISE, IDAHO?

Nadine was busy. After tending to Frank's funeral, her priority became to educate herself on how to manage her newly acquired fortune. At first, she didn't believe it. But everything Frank had said was true, only more so. What he hadn't deposited into a savings account, he'd invested and those investments brought Nadine's net worth to over one hundred million dollars. That many zeros and commas made it a sum that was intimidating and incomprehensible to her.

Fortunately, Frank had left her a blueprint of how he had invested his money and to whom she could turn to for solid advice. He warned her not to trust any single banker or broker. But instead to spread her portfolio across many different brokerages. For now, she wouldn't change any of the investments Frank had made until she had a chance to learn more about stocks and bonds. Just as her late husband had done, Nadine decided not to tell anyone about her newfound wealth, vowing to keep it a secret, especially when it came to men. Nadine didn't want to get involved with anyone just because she was rich. She understood how Frank had felt.

After selling her small house, Nadine went into Walgreens and said goodbye to Ronald and all of her co-workers. It proved to be an emotional moment and she made them promise to keep in touch by email. She told them how she had had some of the best times ever working with them and would never forget them. But when they prodded her about where she was moving to, Nadine remained silent.

Ronald told her he knew the manager at a Walgreens in Boise, Idaho, adding, "I could put in a good word for you. You'd like it there." He continued with praises of Boise, Idaho.

"Thanks, Ronald, but Idaho gets even colder than Wheaton. I want to be free of that forever. I'm trading in this icebox for someplace warm and exciting."

"Sure, it's cold and it snows just like here in Wheaton, but at least you can ski there. They got some of the best skiing, whether you like cross-country or downhill. You'd like Boise, Nadine. And your kids could turn on to skiing. They could become future Olympians." Nadine didn't understand why Ronald kept belaboring the point. What was he anyway, a rotary club booster for the Boise Chamber of Commerce?

Nadine just wasn't that interested in skiing and ignored Ronald's blathering. If anything, she liked figure skating, not skiing. Growing up close to Lake Michigan, she had spent many a day skating on the nameless frozen pond surrounded by oak trees near her home. Executing figure eights on the icy pond as the sun warmed her were memories that Nadine would keep forever. Learning to jump and spin on the cold hard ice had left her with a fondness for Wheaton that would remain with her no matter where she lived. Ice skating was something she wanted her children to experience, but she didn't have to move to Idaho for that to happen; nearly every mall in America had an ice rink.

After one last round of hugs with her coworkers, Nadine turned to leave Walgreens one last time. She was met with a bevy of questions.

"Come on, Nadine. Tell us where you are going. Why the big secret? What's the deal? We can't take it anymore."

"So, where are you off to? It's not fair that you are telling us to stay in touch, but you won't tell us where you're moving."

One girl put it succinctly, "We aren't going to text or email you unless you tell us where you are moving to."

Nadine looked around at all of their faces and finally relented, "Don't despair, I'll give you a hint: What happens there, stays there! Need I say more?" She flashed them a mischievous grin.

The girls squealed. "Oh my God, you are going to Las Vegas!" They jumped up and down with excitement. "Can we come out to visit you, Nadine? Please? Pretty please?"

Even Ronald appeared to have completely abandoned the idea of Boise. "You can have Boise, Idaho. I'll say it again. You can have Boise, Idaho. You're onto something good Nadine with Las Vegas. I hope Walgreens decides to have their annual managers' conference there. Who knows, maybe I'll run into you!"

Nadine felt like giving Ronald the biggest hug of all. "You never know, Ronald. Maybe we will." But even as she said it, Nadine knew she would never see these people again. She told herself, *It's just the way things are.* And as she walked out of the Walgreens for the last time, Nadine was okay with that.

Free from the anxieties and concerns of being a single mother to two young children trying to survive on a clerk's salary, Nadine could now enjoy looking forward to the future. Tomorrow at this time, Nadine Wall-Spencer and her children Dorothy and Robert would become residents of Las Vegas, Nevada. Nadine marveled at the changes in her life but couldn't imagine what being a multi-millionaire was going to be like.

THE CARRINGTON PALACE,

LAS VEGAS

Nadine and her children had been in Las Vegas for two weeks, enjoying and adapting to their stay at The Carrington Palace on the Vegas strip. A five-star hotel and casino, The Carrington catered to the world's rich and famous. There, guests could avail themselves of every luxury and indulgence imaginable. But in the rare instance a guest wanted something the hotel couldn't immediately supply, the concierge service never failed to find a way to deliver.

Nadine planned to stay there for a few months until she found a home for her and the kids. But for now, life at The Carrington was enchanting, full of luxurious trappings and furnishings. To say Nadine did not thoroughly savor her new wealth would be an extreme understatement.

In addition to ordering frequent room service, Nadine went on serious shopping excursions and had her hair done and redone on a daily basis. She quickly became a favorite client of The Carrington's beauty spa staff because of the generous tips she left behind. Enjoying watching how they'd scramble and push one another out of the way so they could be the first to wait on her, Nadine quickly learned what the phrase "money talks" meant.

She needed transportation, that much was evident. So, one morning she walked into the exotic car dealership in The Carrington complex to do something about it. When the salesmen saw her come through the doors dressed in a t-shirt and yoga pants, they snickered and could hardly conceal their disdain for what they saw as another flyover country gawker about to waste their time. The sales staff ignored her as Nadine walked around the showroom looking at motor cars whose lowest price was well north of $200,000. It was only when Nadine tried to open the swing-up door of a Lamborghini Aventador and climb into it that a salesman intervened.

"I'm sorry, miss, this isn't a department store where you can try on the car to see if it fits."

"Well, how can I know if I want it without sitting in it?"

"Ma'am, this is a $400,00 car. I'm sure that's beyond your price range."

"How would you know?" Nadine said as she approached a Ferrari and slid her fingers over the sleek machine. "Now, I like this one."

The man arrogantly replied, "This is a Ferrari 488 Spider drop-top. And it's priced at three twenty-five."

Nadine said, "But it seats just two. I have a couple of kids to cart around. Where do I fit them?"

"Well, maybe you'd like the Gran Turismo, it seats four and costs even less than the Ferrari."

"But I like the Ferrari," Nadine said, thinking out loud to herself. "I don't know; I could always get a limo when the children are with me."

"You could always buy them both!" The salesman snorted condescendingly.

Nadine looked at him seriously and said, "No, I don't think Frank would approve. But I'm embarrassed to admit that it did cross my mind." She laughed and told the salesman that she would have to think about it. As Nadine left the showroom, she gazed at the sky and thanked Frank for making this the most challenging problem she had to deal with.

However, Nadine was beginning to feel restless and she wasn't sure what the remedy was. Part of her wanted to try her hand at poker, so she decided to take advantage of the free lessons offered at the Mystic Hotel and Casino. Nadine took it seriously and soon was able to understand the mechanics of the game, even winning an occasional hand. But mostly she lost and then she would succumb to guilt and her stomach would seize as she pictured Frank looking down on her dismissively. Gambling was frivolous; she needed to find something noble to do with her life. While pondering what that philanthropy would be, she realized the first thing she needed was to have a night out. Tonight, Nadine would escape to her past. Since she was now able to affect the "rich-bitch" persona, she longed for something unpretentious, average, and normal. Her soul needed soothing. What Nadine needed was a night of country-western dancing.

She smiled as she remembered club nights with her friends in Wheaton, especially the country dancing. Though she was clumsy on her feet, she looked pretty good as a line-dancing cowgirl with her hat and boots. Unable to dance a simple two-step, Nadine had inevitably stomped all over her partner's feet. Laughing to herself, she thought Wheaton, Illinois seemed a planet far away, both literally and figuratively. It was a thousand miles from Las Vegas, even a million when you considered everything.

Still unaccustomed to her new riches, she was somewhat embarrassed when she plunked down over $2,000 for a pair of boots. But these were Lucchese Classics and she was able to rationalize her guilt away by scolding herself very sternly in the best West Texas drawl she could conjure. *Now girl! You have over a hundred-million dollars and that darn cowgirl hat didn't even cost you a hundred. And it's even genuine leather. Now you get real, you hear? Besides, you just got to look good because you know you can't dance for nothing. Not even if your life depended on it.*

Nadine was bound for the Western Nugget casino. It was in there that the Wild Bill Hickok Dance Hall, the famous country-western bar, that some described as a party on steroids for Vegas cowboys and cowgirls, resided. Squeezing into her tightest jeans and pulling on her new Lucchese classics that would have eaten up at least two months' worth of her Walgreen's paycheck, Nadine couldn't wait to make the acquaintance of the Western Nugget. Crowning her outfit with her off-the-rack leather, cowgirl hat, Nadine was able to assuage her guilt to a degree.

Pleased with what she saw in the mirror, she smiled so wide she swore it pushed her ears behind her head. She also approved of her new boots; cut from the supplest leather, they wrapped around her feet like soft butter. They were chic for the cowgirl set, smooth to walk in, and she loved the new leather smell. Nadine felt like a regal cowgirl.

The reflection in the mirror grinned back at her and then winked. She was ready for the Western Nugget.

WILD BILL HICKOK DANCE HALL

Nadine strolled into the Western Nugget Casino and made a bee-line to the bar by a row of slot machines. She wanted to get a little tipsy because she was nervous. Knowing a few drinks could ease her jitters, she ordered a strawberry daiquiri. A short time later, the bartender returned with her cocktail. She liked the little red umbrella that came with it and quickly took it out of the tall, slender glass and slipped it into her purse. Like her boots, her new purse was another temptation Nadine had succumbed to; it had set her back some $500. A Rebecca Minkoff, the purse was a masterpiece of hand-tooled brown, glazed leather adorned with meticulous stitching. The handbag sported a retro-western look that resembled a fancy saddlebag.

Nadine took a long draw from the straw. The drink was sweet and smooth, and before she had finished it, she knew she needed another. "Bartender, could I please have another one only this time I would like a blue umbrella to match my jeans." The bartender eyed Nadine's expensive boots and fancy handbag and threw Nadine a look as if she was some demanding diva. As soon as he brought her drink, she swapped her empty glass for the full one and drained it so fast that the bartender barely had time to tend to other customers before she demanded another one. He kept a watchful eye on Nadine, shooting her furtive glances as he hustled from customer to customer behind the bar. She was rapidly on her way to an alcoholic stupor. After her last demand, it was Nadine who now kept a watchful eye on the bartender. Slurring her words, she warned the bartender not to water down her drink and to once again not forget to give her an umbrella. This time she demanded a green umbrella and told him to hurry it up. She had somewhere to go.

Waiting for the bartender to serve her third daiquiri, Nadine noticed two guys sit down at the other end of the bar. She overheard one telling the other that it had been a long trip getting there and they needed to celebrate with a few drinks. They both ordered beers; only one kept staring at her as if he was interested.

Slobbering her words, Nadine asked him nastily, "What are you looking at, pal? Why do you keep giving me the once over? You never seen a cowgirl?" With that, she slurped the last of the daiquiri with her straw and let out a loud hiccup.

The one she had directed the question to chuckled, "Sure have. But you're the best-looking cowgirl I've seen here and that's about all I have to say about it, sugar."

His friend, who seemed to be the quiet guy, chastised him. "Come on, Leroy, give it a rest. Leave her alone. Do you have to make a scene everywhere we go?"

Leroy contorted his face with a chagrined look and then sheepishly looked down as he spun himself around on his stool. Nadine thought he reminded her of a little boy being scolded by his father. He seemed to acquiesce to his friend's orders.

Nadine got up, stumbled, and opened her purse clumsily. Fumbling around in it, she pulled out her red umbrella. Teetering on her Lucchese boots, she wobbled over to her defender. "I sure do appreciate you telling your big-mouth friend to shut up. So, for that I would like to give you my most recent prized possession, my little red umbrella. Just a small token from my daiquiri." Not entirely satisfied with this, Nadine finished with an invective aimed at the guy named Leroy. "Hey you, don't ever call me 'sugar' again. You got that?"

Leroy rolled his eyes and told his friend, "She's all yours, man. She's trouble and she ain't my type anyway. I'm going to shoot some craps. At least I know I can score there." With that, he rose from his barstool and headed toward the craps tables.

"Can I buy you a drink?" Nadine had lost all restraint. "I'm loaded in more ways than one." She laughed uncontrollably as she held out the umbrella offering. "By the way, I am Nadine. What's your name?"

Roy felt drawn to this Nadine by some mysterious, attractive force that emanated from her. She was pulling him into her orbit and he didn't care to escape it. Typically, Roy avoided sloppy drunks, yet Nadine intrigued him. There was something sad about her and Roy was puzzled. He took the umbrella and said, "Thank you, ma'am. I can always use another beer. The name's Roy, Roy Garner. I just arrived in Vegas in a cab – all the way from Houston, Texas." He pointed to the empty barstool where Leroy had been. "He was my cabbie."

As Nadine sat down, Roy motioned to the bartender for another round, telling the bartender to put it on his tab. He wasn't about to let a woman buy his beer. That would be something Leroy might allow, but that would be uncharacteristic of Roy.

Roy handed Nadine her daiquiri and lifted his beer, "Cheers."

After eyeing the tacky, black polka-dotted umbrella that adorned her drink, Nadine clinked her glass to his and exclaimed in disbelief, "Wait! Are you telling me you took a cab from Houston to Las Vegas? Are you friggin' crazy? Why didn't you fly? I bet that cost you a king's ransom."

"Oh well, someday I'll tell you all about it. Are you here to hit Wild Bill's and do some kicker dancing? With those fancy boots, you look like you're fixing to step out. You know what they say – 'Life's always better in cowboy boots!'"

Nadine lit up. "Yes, sir. I'm ready for the Wild Bill Hickok experience even if I ain't much of a dancer, but at least I look the part." While the contraction "ain't" wasn't part of her vocabulary, for some unexplained reason, Nadine felt compelled to use it. She thought it must be the western garb bringing out the hidden cowgirl in her.

Roy gave Nadine another close look. "Yes, ma'am. Yes, you do. And don't worry, I can teach you how to dance. I'm not half-bad." He put on his best 'aw shucks' act and hoped for the best. It was a strategy that seemed to be working.

Nadine grabbed his hand and pulled herself onto the stool Leroy had just vacated. She kissed him softly on the lips. "I'm going to need all the help I can get tonight because I've been knocking a few back as you probably noticed."

Nadine's sudden amorousness surprised Roy but left him feeling confident. He tossed down the rest of his beer and slammed the mug down on the counter so hard that it almost cracked in half. With that, he declared to Nadine, "Let's go to Wild Bill's and see if we can shake it up."

Roy watched as she took another long sip and emptied her glass. "Just want one more so I can stand up straight in the dance line," she joked. "Bartender, hit me with another daiquiri. This time, make it banana with a yellow umbrella."

The bartender leaned in to clear Nadine's empty glass and said, "I'm sorry ma'am, the bar is closed to you." He spoke slowly and enunciated his words precisely.

Nadine yelled back, wagging her finger at him. "No way. I'll have your job pulled, so you better get hopping and pour me a stiff banana." She laughed, apparently pleased with her none-too-subtle inuendo, and glanced at Roy. Roy managed a smile at Nadine's clever comeback, but he knew it was probably because she was drunk. She was intoxicated and based on the looks on the faces of the customers patronizing the bar, was becoming rude and annoying. All seemed to be in agreement with the bartender.

The bartender turned to Roy and told him to get her out of here or else he'd call security. He also warned Roy not to take her to Wild Bill's or they'd be thrown out for sure. Nadine got up from the barstool, her shoulders slumped, and she fell into Roy's arms. Roy was so alarmed that he wondered if she even had a pulse. That frightening thought left his mind quickly when she lifted her head to tell him, "Thanks for the gift you gave me. I'll never forget it." That was it. Her body went limp, and Nadine passed out in Roy's arms.

There he was holding an unconscious woman in his arms while people at the bar stared like he didn't know how to keep this belligerent person under control. And yet Roy had no idea who she even was. Once again, Leroy had left him to his own devices or, in this case, with a passed-out drunk.

Roy wondered what the hell she was talking about. "What gift?" This was not at all the way he had imagined his first night at Wild Bill's would turn out.

He was in a predicament and he found himself debating over what to do next. He had to get Nadine home. But he hardly knew her, so why had she suddenly become his responsibility? They had no past together; he had only known her for a short half-hour, and even that was an exaggeration. Besides, he didn't want to miss the scene at the Wild Bill. He wanted to dance. But what the hell! He had a pretty girl passed out in his arms and Texan chivalry demanded he rescue her.

Roy slung her limp arm around his shoulder and he more or less carried Nadine out of the casino. At least she was petite; she couldn't have weighed more than a hundred ten pounds. Together, they made quite a scene and Roy was uncomfortably aware of the stares as they headed out the door.

Leroy spotted him from the craps table, and immediately pulled his chips and left the game. Running after Roy, Leroy added to Roy's embarrassment. "Why are you carrying that crazy girl out of here?"

Once outside the Western Nugget, Roy set Nadine on a bench and propped her head up against the wall. He rifled through her expensive-looking purse, searching for some identification. Who was she? Where did she live? One thing for sure, the girl had money. Though Roy didn't know much about expensive handbags, he did know a thing or two about cowboy boots and he knew a pair of Lucchese boots when he saw them; hers were top of the line. He found her leather wallet.

Leroy chided him, "Brother, what are you getting' yourself into? Leave her here and let's hit the Wild Bill."

"Carrington Palace, room 777. That's where I live." Nadine, beginning to revive, started pleading with Roy to take her home. She said she was feeling sick. Roy instructed Leroy to bring his cab around.

Leroy protested. "She better not puke in my cab, man." Roy just looked at him, and Leroy stared back at him. "Just sayin'." Still, he sprinted to the parking garage, pulled his cab up beside Nadine and Roy, and opened the back door. Roy scooped up Nadine once again and carefully helped her into Leroy's taxi. She seemed lifeless and doll-like. With Leroy's heavy foot on the pedal, they left The Nugget at NASCAR pace and made it to The Carrington before Roy could say "Shiner Bock." He did not have time for any further thoughts about missing out on the Wild Bill. Dancing would have to wait.

They had to think fast about how to get Nadine through the lobby and up to her room without being noticed. The Carrington Palace was one of the classiest, most upscale hotels in Las Vegas and the staff probably would not appreciate them leaving an intoxicated woman in their lobby, even if she was a paying guest.

Together, Roy and Leroy managed to manipulate Nadine through the hotel's entrance past the check-in desk. They passed by the crowded lounge that boomed with laughter and loud chatter. So far, things were working to their advantage. Roy and Leroy formed a Nadine sandwich, holding her up by her belt loops, so she seemed to float above the floor. But her head bobbed up and down and Roy was forced to let go of his grip on her belt to steady her head. This left the smaller Leroy holding up more than his share of Nadine. Roy pressed the button to call an elevator. They were almost there.

"What's going on here? Is that girl drunk? Is she on drugs? Is she OD'ing?" A very demanding and outraged Carrington manager came rushing toward them. "Who are you? I am going to call security if I don't get some answers. I said I need answers, now!"

It was then that Roy discovered that there was at least a little bit of Leroy in him as he lied to the manager. "Sir, this woman is sick. She has diabetes and needs to get some orange juice as quick as possible because of her elevated blood sugar level. We need to get her to her room immediately. Thank you." Roy couldn't believe his acting skills. He deserved an Oscar for his role in this deception.

He wasn't sure why he didn't tell the guy the truth: that their hotel guest was stinking drunk and they were the poor schlubs stuck with taking her home. But it didn't matter at this point; Roy had to get her to her room. And then maybe he could still have a chance to try out the dance floor. The Wild Bill was still calling him.

"Do we need an ambulance for her condition? What room is she going to? I'll check later and see how she is doing. I need to make sure, sir."

Roy noticed the sudden change in the manager's attitude. Roy replied ever so politely "I think we'll be okay for now. If not, I will give you a call or you can call her room. She is in room 777."

This seemed to satisfy the manager as he held the elevator door open for them when it arrived and said, "I'll check in with you later after I attend to something in one of our restaurants." The manager watched as the elevator doors closed on Roy and Leroy and their Nadine sandwich. To Roy the manager seemed ultra-conscientious and wasn't about to let any balls drop during his shift.

Roy and Leroy reached the seventh floor still carrying a very drunk Nadine. They helped her to her hotel room door where Nadine started banging spastically on the door. Roy and Leroy were amazed at her sudden recovery, but it was obvious Nadine was too liquored up to find her room key. Roy was ready to retrieve it from her purse when the door opened wide and a very plain-looking woman with droopy eyes stared alarmingly at them.

"What happened to Ms. Nadine? Who are you two?" Two small children peeked out from behind each side of the woman. Their eyes were big and inquisitive.

Roy peered into Nadine's room, overwhelmed by its opulence. It was a huge and luxurious suite that had to go over two thousand square feet. There was even a grand piano in the middle of the living room. Roy's eye's bulged when he saw a diamond-shaped hot tub standing inside a Tiki-decorated porch.

"My little ones, how are you?" Stirring, Nadine cooed to her children. They looked to be about seven and five years old. Struggling to stand on her own, Nadine awakened from her drunken stupor and demanded that the droopy-eyed lady make her some coffee. "Now, I want coffee. ASAP!" She snapped her fingers and the poor lady made haste to serve her "spoiled mistress."

Roy figured that's how the woman thought of Nadine in her mind. He wondered what he had stepped in. This woman obviously had money, but he wasn't sure he liked what she was made of. He stepped back from the situation and said he needed to be going. Both he and Leroy asked the suddenly very mysterious Nadine if she would be okay; she told them she would be fine.

Roy struggled to make sense of everything: the drunk girl, this place, the nanny, and these children – but none of it made sense to him. Had he been duped? He wasn't sure. But he knew one thing. The Wild

Bill was calling out to him and he was in the mood for some good, old-fashioned stomping country-line dancing. Especially after this episode.

Holding the coffee pot in her one hand, the droopy-eyed subservient lady let them out the door.

Leroy later cracked a joke that she must have been the maidservant for Queen Nadine of The Carrington Palace. Roy had taken note of one thing. Nadine hadn't bothered to say, "Thank you!" or even, "Goodbye." And what was that about her thanking him for some gift?

BLUE GOOSE

Lee looked at the calendar being held by three dingy magnets on his rusted refrigerator. To him, it appeared like the band was out of business. Except for the following Friday at the Blue Goose, the rest of the calendar was empty of gigs. It had been that way the week before as well. And where was Becky Dean? She'd missed several practice sessions without notifying any of them, which was not like her. Worse, Lee hadn't talked with her for the last few weeks. He missed her and he wasn't happy. Sitting down on his frayed couch, he thought the whole situation smelled peculiar.

Pick up the phone and just call her. The thought kept running through his mind. Jumping off the couch, Lee grabbed his phone and punched in Becky Dean's number. It was no longer in service. He screamed at the phone, "What kind of shit show is this? Just exactly what the hell is going on?" The band was one thing. But Lee always had a thing for her. She could be abrasive and quarrelsome, but she could also sing and play an instrument better than anyone he'd ever heard. Becky Dean possessed all the elements to front a band. Having a stage presence that captivated an audience, she always kept them coming back for more. The Madison Four always drew a large crowd wherever they played and Lee knew quite well that it was mostly due to Becky Dean. On top of all that talent, Becky Dean had a figure that aroused men and women envied. Lee was attracted to her the moment they met.

Pouring himself three fingers of his reliable friend Johnny Walker, Lee looked forward to becoming comfortably numb. The numbness had barely begun when he heard a knock on the door.

"Hey Lee, its Basil. Let me in, bud."

Lee opened the door to find the band's drummer leaning in his doorway, wearing a troubled expression on his face.

Basil pushed past him into the apartment. "So why aren't we playing any gigs this week? I got to put food on the table. What happened to all our gigs and where the hell is Becky Dean? I got a wife and two kids. I don't know for sure, but I think 'ole Becky Dean dumped us and split to Las Vegas. What do you think of that?" Basil was raging. Lee could see it in his eyes and knew he had to tread carefully. "Big Basil" was the high school football phenom who had stirred fear in every offensive line he faced. When he felt ornery, it was best to avoid him.

Lee felt sucker-punched. "What do you mean she went to Vegas? What are you talking about? Are you telling me she took off for good? Where're you getting this man? Talk to me."

Basil got in Lee's face. "Dude, I heard her on her cell booking a trip to Vegas and then I heard her asking about prices on some long-term hotels. Face it dude, she's pulled a Casper on us. The bitch ghosted us!

Lee thought for a moment; Basil made sense. "You know man, you're right. I can't believe she ran out on us. I gave her way more credit than that."

Basil started ranting, but Lee wasn't listening. "I got kids and rent to pay, and this is what she does to us. That bitch! Who needs this?"

Lee had a blank look on his face and headed toward the corner of the living room to pick up his guitar. Strumming his guitar always helped him focus on a problem. As Lee bent over to pick up his guitar, he felt Basil's large hand grab at his neck. That got Lee's attention and he turned to face Basil.

"I need to know what you plan to do about this." Basil had tightened his grip on Lee's neck.

"If you'd get your damn hand off of me, then maybe I could think. This is no picnic for me either. I got bills to pay too, and grabbing my freaking neck won't help matters." Lee pushed Basil's arm away, and Basil eased off.

"Do we need the bitch? Most of the time she's more trouble than she's worth. Couldn't we trade her out for some other chick? You know, like they do in football? There's always someone else coming up." It all made sense in Basil's mind but to a musician like Lee, Basil's constant football analogies were tiresome.

But to Lee, this was a different set of rules than football. Lee turned to a furious Basil and quipped, "Who's better than Becky Dean? Man, Basil, you got to get real."

Basil stared back at Lee like he was conjuring up some ingenious idea. "You may be right, but I got a plan B. Right up there with the quarterback sneak."

Lee had to stop himself from rolling his eyes. *There he goes again, Basil and his world according to football.* With a sigh, Lee said, "Yeah, let's hear it."

Basil said, "Let's catch a plane to Vegas and find her."

Lee questioned, "Well, what about Javier?"

"What are you, batshit crazy? Javier has no life whatsoever. He lives for us and the group. He's got nothing tying him down. I'm the one with the baggage."

Lee turned away for a second, aiming his eyes on his lonely guitar in the corner of the room, then looked back to Basil with a sly smile, "Hell yeah, Basil! Let's do it! Vegas isn't such a bad idea after all. It will blow her mind when we show up on her doorstep." The more he thought about it, the more excited Lee felt. A confrontation with Becky Dean was in order.

"Now you're thinking, dude. I'll pound a beat on her front door and when she opens it, I'll beat a drum roll on her head. Let's get the hell out of Dodge as soon as possible. I just got to tie up a few loose ends first. Luckily, my lease is up so I can hit the road without any problem. Vegas, here we come."

Basil was out the door before Lee could retrieve his guitar. He wanted to play it for more reasons than one. Becky Dean had wounded him and Lee was determined to make her pay. The guitar would help him think and Johnny Walker would help him forget.

GENERAL MITCHELL
INTERNATIONAL AIRPORT

Basil drove Lee and Javier to General Mitchell Airport in Milwaukee. He stopped in the passenger unloading area and opened the trunk of his car. Lee pulled his bags out, set them on the sidewalk, and then turned to shake Basil's hand. "So, we'll see you in a week or two?"

Basil nodded. "Yeah. Track her down."

On that point, they were all in agreement. This was their quest and they would let nothing get in the way. Lee wouldn't stop searching until he found Becky Dean, no matter how long it took. Even Basil's wife Marie had signed up for the search.

But none of them bothered to think about what they'd do if they did find Becky Dean. Would they kidnap her, tie her up, put a sack over her head, and haul her back to Madison? Or would they just take turns swearing at her and telling her what a no-good Judas she was and then fly back home?

Javier laughed and grabbed his bag out of the trunk. "Come on, Lee. We better check-in."

Lee and Javier purchased a couple of cheap Vegas Players Packages at some casino. Neither of them had any intention of gambling, but the deal included airfare, five nights in a hotel, and a couple of passes to a 24-hour all-you-can-eat buffet, featuring 87 different food items to choose from. And five nights was enough time for them to find a more permanent command center from which to mount their search for the vicious, cold-hearted Miss Becky Dean.

On the flight out to Las Vegas, Lee and Javier worked out a sleuthing strategy. The first thing they'd do was scour the strip and inquire if a singer named Becky Dean was playing anywhere. If asked why they wanted to know, they'd claim to be her husband in desperate need to get in touch with her. The first places they'd check were the country-western venues along the strip. Lee always thought of himself as being lucky, or maybe he was just smart. He figured it was just a matter of methodical, systematic elimination before they found her.

As the hotel shuttle took them down the Las Vegas strip to their hotel, Lee looked out the window. They passed one giant casino after another on both sides of the boulevard. These huge gambling complexes had even sprouted along the cross streets. In every direction Lee looked, throngs of people flowed in and out of them.

He began to realize the impossible task ahead. In Madison, there were a finite number of places for a singer to work, maybe a hundred at most. It might take some time, but you could cover them eventually. Here in Vegas however, there must be thousands of lounges and taverns at which she could be working. He now knew their chances of finding Becky Dean amidst all of this humanity were about the same as him winning the $10,000-a-week-for-life grand prize from the Publisher's Clearing House Sweepstakes.

The shuttle had long passed the glitzy casinos of the strip and eventually turned down a narrow side street north of downtown. They were now in an area of town that resembled many other forgotten cities in America, where empty sidewalks and yellowed, curling "For Lease" signs papered over the windows of vacant storefronts like a ghostly echo of what used to be. The only real commerce was a nasty-looking bar and a few tattoo parlors. Oh, and of course, Lee and Javier's hotel.

They looked at each other warily as the shuttle left them standing in front of the ramshackle building. On the marquee, the plastic letters welcomed the International Association of Independent Pest Control Professionals.

Javier joked, "Hell Lee, at least we'll know who to call when we see the roaches."

Lee replied, "Well, it's only for a few days. You look for an apartment and I'll work on finding Becky Dean." They picked up their bags and walked into the hotel lobby.

Once they had settled into their room, Lee went to work. He planned to start with the major casinos on the strip and call his way through the smaller venues in town. Beginning with the A's, Lee called the HR department at the Aria. Then Bally's. Then the Bellagio's, Caesar's, and on and on.

Each call consumed at least an hour and, regardless of whom he ended up talking to, the script was always the same. After navigating through an automated answering service, he was finally transferred to a live voice in the personnel department. Acting the part of a concerned husband, he explained ad nauseam, "Hello, I'm looking for someone I was told in good faith works there. I am her husband from Wisconsin and I desperately need to speak with her. It's of a personal nature. Can you give me her phone number?"

The voice in the personnel department was always professional. "I'm sorry, sir, but I am allowed only to confirm employment and not permitted to divulge personal information. What is her name?"

"Becky Dean Silas."

The voice would then put Lee on hold for a painfully long time. Each time, Lee was forced to endure interminable Muzak tape loops, the worst of which was a cheesy rendition of "Muskrat Love" by Captain and Tennille. It accosted his ears.

After several days of calling, Lee finally reached the end of the alphabet. While waiting for someone in the HR department of the Western Nugget to tell him what he had become accustomed to hearing, that no one by the name Becky Dean Silas was employed at their casino, he contemplated his next steps.

When the girl from the Western Nugget returned, she told Lee that his wife was, in fact, employed at The Nugget in a group known as The Rajabede Trio. They played at The Deerskin Lounge Mondays through Thursdays beginning at 3 p.m. Lee thanked her profusely and after he ended the call, screamed, "Game on!" It was almost too easy. Lee couldn't believe his luck.

He thought about what Becky Dean's reaction would be when she saw him, Basil, and Javier sit down at a table in front of the stage while Marie captured it all on her cell phone. He couldn't wait to tell Basil and Javier the news.

Then he shook his head at the stupidity of their name – The Rajabede Trio. What kind of name was that? It sounded like Pig Latin or some Indian mystic. Maybe "Madison Four" was a boring name, but no one could say that it didn't make sense. Actually, it had been Becky Dean who had given them their name.

Come to think of it, Becky Dean's fingerprints were on pretty much everything that belonged to The Madison Four. Lee broke into a mischievous grin. *She's probably bossing her new trio around right at that very minute — pity for them.*

Lee wanted to confront her right away, but Javier convinced him to wait for Basil. The *three* of them would confront Becky Dean.

DAN THE PLUMBER ON

VALLEY DRIVE

Basil and his wife Marie flew into Las Vegas three weeks later. It had taken them a bit longer to arrange their departure from Madison than Basil expected. But when they arrived, Lee was there to meet them at the airport and caught them up on what he'd found out about Becky Dean. Lee dropped them off at their hotel and they agreed to meet later that day at Lee's apartment to work out the plan to exact their revenge. Even during the weeks that had passed since Becky Dean had abandoned their band, their boil had not diminished. Basil rubbed his hands together, imagining the inevitable scene when they finally went face-to-face with her.

A few hours after their arrival, Lee welcomed Basil and Marie into his musty-smelling apartment near McCarran Airport. Javier was already there. Lee found himself embarrassed about his unpleasant surroundings. The yellow paint was peeling off the walls, the heavy, dark orange drapes were frayed and worn, and the commode ran constantly in the background. Lee crossed his fingers, hoping no one would ask to use it because it was always clogging up. He saw Marie frown as he welcomed her into the apartment. The compressor on the refrigerator emitted a loud hum and half the time it dripped water on the kitchen floor. There was no furniture except for a director's chair Lee had bought at a thrift store. Lee offered it to Marie while he, Basil, and Javier plopped down on the floor in front of an old TV that probably wouldn't last another six months. Lee bragged he bought it cheap at the Salvation Army Thrift Store along with a radio and a pair of camouflage pants. He explained, "I'm in my minimalist phase!"

To kill the silence, Basil popped up and turned the radio on, joking that they would be lucky if he could find a station. Moving the dial-up and down, he only picked up static. "You really got a doozy with this one," he quipped. Everyone laughed, but he was finally able to zero in on a station.

Marie looked at Javier and said, "I think we have connected to Earth!" Javier scrunched his eyebrows as he listened.

"Welcome back to KPLV 95.8, All things Country! I'm Tommy Bill Dillon, the handsomest devil with a face for TV but trapped in your radio. But that ain't no how anyway, I'm here to turn y'all on to what's new in country music playing at the casinos and lounges right here in Vegas, and I'm going to pistol-whip y'all if you don't listen up. So, don't touch y'all's dial because I got a band with a real cutie of a singer and they're going to play their hearts out for you. Yes, sirs and ma'ams, this trio's got it. They may have a weird name, but you're going to love their style! Their name is The Rajabede Trio and you're gonna love their lead singer Ms. Becky Dean. Stay tuned 'cause they are going to bring it after this important message about a man and his toilet!"

All four of them stared at the radio incredulously, unable to speak. Hearing Becky Dean's name announced on a Las Vegas radio was just about the last thing any of them had expected. Then Dan the Plumber and his peppy jingle rang over the radio.

> *Have a problem with your can?*
> *Please call up Happy Dan.*
> *I'll get rid of your slime*
> *And I'll be there on time.*

> *I got the skills and the knack.*
> *And a great, big plumber's crack!*
> *Call Dan the Plumber on Valley Drive*
> *Call 1-800-233-FIVE!*

Lee wished he had a plunger right then. He would use it for something more than just unclogging his toilet. Where the hell had they dug up this clown? But that thought didn't last long because they were barraged by five more minutes of insanely annoying commercials.

Finally, Tommy Bill came back on the air. "Howdy cowboys and cowgirls. Welcome back. Have we got a show for you today and I'm just gettin' started! We've got The Deerskin Lounge's Rajabede Trio in studio and they're going to start us off with a song and then we'll meet them on the flipside. Here they are, playing 'Ring of Fire'' by the indomitable June Carter Cash. Folks, buckle up your seat belts or, should I say, cowboy belts. Hit it, Rajabede!"

Even through the tinny radio speaker, they all recognized Becky Dean's voice. Lee had to admit that The Rajabede Trio was pretty darn good. The lead guitarist had the talent and the harmonica player was one of the best he'd ever heard. In the few short weeks since flying solo, Becky Dean had gone higher and further than The Madison Four had in all the years they'd been together.

After a few moments, Javier gaped and then shouted that Becky Dean had stolen his arrangement, the one they always opened up with at The Blue Goose.

Lee felt like he'd been stabbed by a twelve-inch steak knife. "She's such a rip-off. She just traded us for those two losers. I'm going to call the damn radio station and tell them what she's really all about!" Lee's anger morphed into a frenzied rage.

Basil said, "I want to kill the bitch."

Marie shushed him, "Why do you always use that word?"

After "Ring of Fire," DJ Tommy Bill Dillon asked them how they liked playing together at the famed Western Nugget. Becky Dean answered with mawkish sentimentality that she felt pennies from heaven were falling on her. At that, Marie stuck her index finger to her mouth in mock jest like she was going to throw up.

Once again, this fomented Basil's anger. "I'd like to drop something on her fucking head."

"Basil, watch your mouth. Don't be like that," Marie scolded him again.

One of the guitarists who introduced himself as James said he was loving having Becky Dean as their vocalist. "She sure knows how to keep the customers coming. Randy and I feel blessed."

Randy, the harmonica player, agreed. "It's Becky Dean's talent bringing the people in and that's why she's calling all the shots."

"No, really?" Lee chortled sarcastically, "Becky Dean, a takeover artist?" For the first time, the remaining members of The Madison Four laughed contemptuously in a chorus of agreement.

"They can have the bossy bitch. Good riddance." Basil looked over at Marie, expecting her to rebuke him again. But this time, Marie just smiled at him.

DJ Tommy Bill asked them what their next number would be and Becky Dean replied that they would like to perform a little bit of the blues. This seemed to strike an emotional response with Tommy Bill because he said, "I heard all about you guys playing some of the best blues The Deerskin Lounge has ever heard. I myself am a big blues guy and, along with Ms. Becky Dean, you all are making my day. They ain't just making noise; they're planting the blues flag over at The Deerskin. So, what are you fixin' to play?"

"Well, Mr. Tommy Bill, we gonna play what I bet is one of your all-time favorites." Becky Dean was turning on the shine for Tommy Bill. "We gonna play 'Stormy Monday,' and we gonna put some grit into it. Randy here is gonna to tear it up on his harp."

"Stormy Monday" was usually The Madison Four's follow up number and hearing Becky Dean recite their playlist only inflamed Lee's determination to get even with her. He screamed at the radio, "So what are you going to do after that, Becky Dean? 'Sweet Home Alabama?'"

Lee noticed the affected accent Becky Dean had taken, mimicking the radio announcer's, "We gonna this... We gonna that!" What a fraud she was, shapeshifting into any form she needed to get what she wanted. But no matter the situation, Becky Dean always lauded her imperiousness over everyone.

Even DJ Tommy Bill seemed to be caught under Becky Dean's spell. He was using every superlative he could think of to describe her. He even went so far as to say that Becky Dean seemed like "the salt of the earth," claiming her to be "just a good ole country girl."

That did it! Lee grabbed his cell phone and pounded at it frantically. Finally, he put the phone to his ear. Agitation was heavy in his voice. "Let me speak to DJ Tommy Bill Dillon. I have something very important that he needs to know. Believe me; he wants to hear this. My name is Lee Murphy and this is very urgent. I just got to talk to him now."

The lady on the other end responded with a thick New York accent and haughty impatience. "You do know he is on the air right now with a live band? Gimme you's numba and I will have him call ya when he can."

"Yes ma'am, I understand. That's exactly the reason I am talking to you now. I am calling regarding this group. He can't go wrong talking to me before they do their next number." Lee wished he could dive into the phone, emerge out the other end, and toss this obnoxious gatekeeper out of his way.

But she was shrill and refused to let him speak with Tommy Bill. "No, sir. No way can I put you's through to him. The best I can do is take you's name and numba and have him call you's after the show is over. Now I have my pen, what's the numba?"

Lee exploded. "What is your problem, lady? How much are you getting paid to keep people away from Tommy Bill? Don't you think you're overdoing it a bit?"

Clearly the receptionist had heard it all before and was primed to unload her verbal pistol on Lee. "I told you's how it works. I don't need no attitude. Now eitha give me your numba or fagedda about it."

It then occurred to Lee that he was talking to a caustic New Yawker, making the whole situation quite ironic. Here was a country hee-haw in the person of DJ Tommy Bill paired up with a pain-in-the-ass Yankee receptionist from Da Bronx. Nevertheless, he was determined to get through to Tommy Bill. "Ma'am, I got something here to boost your ratings. I promise you, Tommy Bill won't be sorry."

Suddenly, he could hear Tommy Bill talking in the background. "What is it you want, girl? We got us a show to do and this is not the time to be taking personal calls. Who the hell are you talking to anyway?" There was a moment of silence before he said, "Well, now you got me curious. Tell me cuz I got a little bit of time before I go back on the air."

She held out the phone to him, covering the receiver with her hand. "I got a live wire here who demands to talk to you's. He says he has information regarding the group you's got on. Here. Take this guy off my hands and see what he wants."

"Tommy Bill here, what can I do for you?"

Lee couldn't believe it. Here was a chance to torpedo Becky Dean in a way none of them had ever dreamt of. "Yeah, hi. Listen, you don't know me, but my name is Lee Murphy and I know a little something about the group you have on the air right now. I especially know about that singer, Becky Dean."

Tommy Bill's voice was picking up volume. "Yeah, boy? What you got for me? What sort of information ya got that you gotta be harassing my producer over?"

"Mr. Dillion, Becky Dean is not the 'salt of the earth' person she pretends to be. She is not a good person by anyone's standard." There was a pause, dead air, and for a moment Lee thought Tommy Bill had hung up on him.

"Why's that? What'd she do and what do you have to do with it? Let it rip. So far, you ain't said nothing interesting. I'm running out of time, boy."

Lee took a deep breath and began spewing the truth about Becky Dean. "For the last five years, she was the lead singer for our group in Madison, Wisconsin. That was until four weeks ago when she up and left us cold. We had gigs scheduled that we had to cancel. Some of us have kids to feed and we all got bills to pay. So, what does she do but split to Las Vegas without saying so much as a word to any of us. This 'good ole girl' as you referred to her, is poison. She's a thief. Nothing but a nasty snake in the grass and now she's hooked up with another group.

"Those are *our* arrangements she's singing. She sandbagged us and now she's performing the material she stole from us. So, what's left of The Madison Four came out here to Vegas for payback. There's three of us. She cost us everything as well as destroyed our reputation in Madison."

Trying to sound somewhat sympathetic, Tommy Bill suggested, "Why don't you three get yourself another singer. Lady or guy, whatever you choose. Don't let her get you down. If she's as bad as you say, then you're a damn sight better off without her. Man up! Put some fire in your wire! In fact, I'll tell you what, boy. Go get yourself another vocalist and I'll host a competition, live, right here on this li'l, ole radio station. But! And there is a but! You all got to come down here and play a few songs for me, so I know you just ain't pissin' in the wind. I gotta go. So, what's it gonna be? If you are what you say you are, I'll announce it on my next show."

Lee thanked him profusely but was adamant. "But Mr. Dillion, you've just got to announce it in the next minute and set up the competition. It'll be red-hot publicity and you won't regret it. I promise we will come in and play for you soon, but I am telling you, sure as shit we can play. If you think we are punking you, then sue us sky-high from one end to the next. But I'm telling you we are good musicians. We were The Madison Four and I can give you the numbers of bars and gigs we played so you can know we are legit. Now, I admit they may have soured on us now since we had to pull out and cancel on them. But that was all Becky Dean's doing. I can give you a reference sheet that would wrap around your radio station a mile long. Mr. Dillion, please go back on the air and tell them we are up for a Battle of the Bands. I only wish I could see ole Becky Dean's face drop and turn four shades of red when you call her out on live radio."

Lee could hear Tommy Bill whistle between his teeth with a quick comeback. "Boy, you're on. I believe y'all. This will be da bomb. Stay tuned and listen up to what comes up next."

The line went dead and Lee shoved his phone into his pants' pocket. He smiled and gave everyone a thumbs up. Hearing Lee's part of the conversation they all gathered around him offering up effusive congratulations. Boxing the air, Basil screamed, "To sweet revenge. We came. We found her. And now we're going to kick her ass!"

There was only one thing that could make this day better. They all moved in close around the radio, waiting to hear the explosion after Tommy Bill dropped the bomb on Becky Dean.

Basil shouted out, "Man, I bet she won't be able to get through her next song. I know that's what we're all waiting for, dudes. Now *this* is what I call an ambush."

Lee, though, was lost in introspection. He knew Becky Dean was a consummate professional. He'd known her to work through a few tough times during their years together; she had never let her personal life affect her performance. In fact, hardship only seemed to motivate her.

He knew the three of them had to find a new singer fast. In a few weeks or so they'd be going up against Becky Dean's trio live on the radio.

While none of them realized it at the time, Tommy Bill had just given all of them the biggest break in their careers, a chance to appear on live radio in Las Vegas. As for Tommy Bill, this would be a ratings bonanza for him and KPLV – All Things Country.

DEERSKIN LOUNGE AT THE WESTERN NUGGET

Roy didn't know what to think. His experience with Nadine had been bizarre. She probably had a drinking problem which he wanted none of. He and Leroy had managed to get back to The Nugget that night and Roy had danced until the Wild Bill closed at 2 a.m. Roy was exhausted, but it was satisfied exhaustion. It had been therapeutic because, by the end of the evening, Nadine had pretty much faded into a forgotten episode. And in the days that followed, Roy made it a habit to frequent the Wild Bill.

One evening as he entered the dance hall through The Deerskin Lounge, he noticed a sign with big, bold red letters announcing:

COUNTRY LINE DANCE CONTEST
PREMIERING COUPLES LINE DANCING
ALSO KNOWN AS THE "JACK & JILL" CONTEST
FEBRUARY 22ND AT 7 PM
WILD BILL HICKOCK DANCE HALL
IN THE WESTERN NUGGET

1ST PLACE: $100,000
2ND PLACE: $50,000
3RD PLACE: $10,000

THE WINNER'S PICTURE
WILL HANG ON OUR WALL OF FAME!
SIGN UP NOW!!
http://www.wbhdh.com

The notice revived a long-forgotten dream of Roy's. The grand prize would give him the seed money he needed for his vision of opening a country-western bar of his own. The prospect made him think about Mindy back in Houston. She'd be the perfect partner if he were to have a chance at winning this line dancing contest. But the pang faded quickly.

The truth was that Mindy was one great big hassle; and that was something he needed to consider. And after putting in the energy to keep her happy, what if they didn't win?

Still, Roy needed a partner who could dance and the only person who came to mind was Mindy. He thought about calling her up in Houston to see if she would be interested in partnering for the competition. Mindy was good. She was a fierce competitor, unyielding until after even the last step of the dance. Mindy never surrendered. Roy had to admit that.

But then what? What about after the competition? He might be saddled with her and that was an alternate reality Roy was not prepared to enter. He would also have to do a lot of 'splaining' as to why he had suddenly left Houston without saying anything to her. That was a conversation he'd prefer never to have.

Even though the idea was an anathema to him, his quest to enter and win the contest overrode everything else. He wrestled out his cell phone and tapped it a few times. Before he was fully aware of what he was doing, Mindy's phone was ringing in Houston, Texas.

"Hello?" came Mindy's voice.

"Hey Mindy, this is Roy. How are you doing? Guess where I am." Roy detected her anger in the ensuing silence, but he could tell that she was still listening. At least she hadn't hung up. What the situation called for was a little deception. "I miss you, Mindy. I really do. It's not the same without you." He purposely cracked his voice a little to sound more sincere. There still was no reply. "Mindy honey, I'm in Las Vegas!"

"What?" the scream shook his eardrum.

Mindy found her voice and launched barrages of profanities at him, one after another. Roy held the phone far from his ear and waited for her to wear herself out. It took some time, but she finally used up all her ammunition and the line went silent again.

Roy felt twinges of guilt, not so much about leaving Houston without telling Mindy, but for what he was about to say to her. He reassured himself that this was the only way to get her out to Las Vegas, *I've got to say whatever it takes.* He reminded himself that she can dance and that together they could have a chance at winning it all. *Besides, a hundred grand will go a long way to healing a lot of hurt feelings.* Mindy always brought out his best dancing. With the wisdom of a philosopher, Roy arrived at a decision. Agreeing with the ancient Aristotle axiom, that 'the whole is bigger than the sum of its parts' Roy saw that it was true, at least when it came to the Texas Two-Step. Thanking Aristotle for sharing his insight, Roy thought he could convince Mindy.

"Mindy honey, I want you to come out to Vegas to be with me." He began to tell her about the contest and the prize money they could win and how only she could bring out his best. "Mindy, we're perfect together, and as dance partners, we're a slam-dunk to grab that payday."

Mindy's iciness began to melt. Roy heard it in her voice. Tentatively, she asked when the contest was, which he ended up repeating three times. "Well, I'll tell you what, Coy Roy, I sure as shit could use the money. A hundred-thousand dollars! That's more money than I've made in my entire life." Smiling to himself, Roy knew he'd turned her. Mindy only called him "Coy Roy" when she wasn't angry with him.

Within the week, Mindy arrived in Las Vegas and they were a team again, if only a dance team. It didn't take long before Roy's long-festering feelings about Mindy begin to stir though. These were unwelcome thoughts from the past that Roy tried to repress. But whenever Mindy did something to annoy him, which was often, Roy recited the mantra he'd made up to help him overcome just those times. *Mindy can dance and together we are unstoppable. Mindy can dance and together we are unstoppable.* Most of the time, it worked.

They began spending most evenings at the Wild Bill where they practiced with earnest determination and resolve. Some nights, as they sauntered across the floor, Roy noticed Mindy rubbing against him suggestively or lingering in his arms long after the music ended. She would not let go of him. Instead of "tripping the light fantastic," she was "snuffing it out!" Roy literally had to peel her off of him. Pushing her away, he scolded her, saying, "Look, Mindy, we're at work. This is a business. Our business. We've got to keep it that way." Mindy would sulk away until Roy reminded her about the prize money.

To compound matters, Leroy had begun to take an interest in Mindy, describing her as if she was some goddess. "The lady's got game, brother. I mean, the lady's *got* game!" It was tiresome to hear over and over and Roy wished he had some duct tape to slap over Leroy's mouth.

Wednesdays at the Wild Bill were Ladies' Night which meant women got in free. Roy could never get over how many cowgirls lined up at the door waiting to "boogie scoot." For guys, ladies' night was always a success. For every guy coming through the door, at least four or five unaccompanied women would come in. Roy liked those odds and he enjoyed the scenery.

Mindy, however, was unhappy. She mocked and ridiculed almost every woman who entered. "Look at that herd of heifers coming in now. I hope these floors are built to withstand that stampede!" She seemed threatened. Roy's eyes roamed back and forth, surveying the cowgirls in waiting. Standing against the wall across from Roy and Mindy, one cowgirl, in particular, received most of his attention.

Roy could not believe he was seeing her again. She looked the same except this time, she was standing steady. In her hand was a bottle of San Pellegrino Sparkling Natural Mineral Water. He was pleased to see she was not drinking. It was Nadine.

Nadine must also have caught a glimpse of him because she crossed the room with such ardency that she nearly knocked him to the floor. Acting as if nothing had happened, she gave Roy a warm hug. Her spice-scented perfume was intoxicating. Roy felt his legs crumble as he once again succumbed to Nadine's allure.

Nadine asked flirtatiously, "May I have this next dance, cowboy? By the way, didn't I give you a green umbrella?"

"It was red."

"Do you still have it?"

"Of course. I jazz up every Shiner Bock I drink with it." Roy was lying, but Nadine seemed pleased. Grabbing her hand, he led her onto the dance floor. "We never got to have our dance that first night. Now's our chance."

As soon as the music started, it was clear to Roy that Nadine had told him the truth; she couldn't dance. She was stiff and devoid of rhythm. Roy's attempts to teach her even the most basic steps, though gallant, were futile.

Nadine didn't seem to care she couldn't dance; she was relaxed and having fun. She seemed comfortable with herself and in her fancy boots too. Roy liked this new Nadine. This Nadine was fun and unpretentious.

Meanwhile, Mindy planted herself against the back wall and watched Roy and Nadine together while she attacked her drink, her fury building with every gulp.

Roy was alarmed. He'd seen that look before on Mindy and feared she was about to explode. A sudden, foreboding feeling overwhelmed him. Mindy's tantrums were violent and uncontrollable. She could morph into a psychotic banshee without a moment's notice. If she had a gun in her pocket, she would no doubt fire it and blow Roy and Nadine's heads clean off. But he quickly dismissed her, tired of her childish temper tantrums. Roy wanted to concentrate on the very enticing Nadine. But that thought did not last long; Mindy was unraveling fast.

Sensing impending disaster, Roy tried to hustle Nadine off the dance floor toward an exit, away from Mindy. But it was too late. Mindy plowed through the crowd like a runaway dump truck and began pummeling Nadine with her fists. Nadine fell and Mindy jumped on top of her, pinning her to the floor. Mindy swung her arms manically, pulling Nadine's hair and thrashing her face.

Screaming in shock and surprise, Nadine was stunned by the assault. But then her basic survival instincts emerged and she began to fight back. Somehow, she was able to free a leg and kick with the heel of her Lucchese boot; she connected with Mindy's nose. Blood splattered everywhere and now it was Mindy's turn to holler. Nadine had just begun and was exacting revenge.

By this time, the dancing had stopped and everyone on the dance floor was circling Mindy and Nadine to watch the catfight. Nadine was no longer pinned on her back and continued with her relentless leg kicks to Mindy. Instead, she was upright able to have a good look at her assailant. Patches of blond hair and spattered blood littered the Wild Bill Dance Hall floor. Some of the blood from Mindy's bleeding nose dripped on Nadine's Lucchese boots. When Nadine saw her blood-marred boots, she launched onto the woman, wildly mauling Mindy with flailing punches.

True to his uncanny timing, cabbie Leroy arrived and came to Mindy's rescue. Standing between Mindy and Nadine, Leroy reached for Mindy's hand and said, "Come on, baby. Let me take you home and get you fixed up." Mindy was trembling but seemed ready to give up the fight. Taking her hand, Leroy led Mindy away.

Nadine, however, was inconsolable. Roy, who had failed in his repeated attempts to break them up, reached out to Nadine and took her into his arms. Smoothing out her hair and wiping away her tears with his fingers, he tried to comfort her. But Nadine was sobbing uncontrollably and her tears dissolved her mascara into long black streaks down her face. Roy did his best to wipe it away. He kissed her gently on the forehead and told her he was there for her. Sobbing, she kept asking him who that lady was and why she attacked her?

"Who is she?" Nadine begged Roy for an answer. "What did I ever do to her? I am going to press charges. She's not going to get away with this. She'll be sorry she ever messed with me. Who is she? Do you know her? Just what the hell did I ever do to her to make her come up and attack me? My back is killing me. Oh my God, it hurts so bad. I need to get her name. Do you know her name?" Roy looked up to see Leroy whisk Mindy out the hall solacing her with his arms wrapped around tightly.

"Nadine, her name is Mindy, and she is, or was, a friend of mine. She's my dance partner. We've entered a dance competition. I knew her from Houston. I am so sorry she involved you."

Nadine was outraged "You mean to tell me you know that psycho? And you actually dance with her? Is that what you are telling me? That you're involved with her?" Nadine wanted answers. "Is *she* your girlfriend?"

Roy looked distressed. "No, I admit I did call her up to come to Las Vegas but only because she can dance. We've never had anything going and the only reason I called her was because of the competition. I swear to God, that is the honest truth. We're dance partners and nothing else. I am so sorry she acted like that."

Nadine was in pain, both physical and emotional. Roy could see it in her face and in the scratches on her arm that were visible through the torn sleeve of her blouse. He then realized the consequences of his ploy and was filled with guilt. Instead of Roy being punished, Nadine became the unintended target of his deception. She was the innocent victim in all of this. He was the one who had led Mindy into thinking there was more between them than there ever could be. Right then, Roy felt he would never be deserving of Nadine again.

Walking the wounded Nadine out of the dance hall with all eyes paying close attention to them, Roy held her tight and promised to make it up to her. "God, I wish these people would quit staring at us. How about I take you back home and later, if you feel better, maybe we can go out for dinner somewhere? Are you up for that?"

Looking up at him with her beat up face, she snarled, "What? Are you kidding? You drag me into the middle of your bullshit life and I'm supposed to act like nothing ever happened?" Then, with a weak, shaky arm, Nadine hailed the first taxi coming her way. She got in fast and took one last churlish verbal jab at him. "Here's to you and your certifiable nut-job dance partner. I hope you fall on your asses. You deserve each other. Choke on this!" And with that, she flipped him the middle finger as the taxi sped off.

Roy had to think fast to try to get her back.

DOWN TO THE WIRE BAR

The night after Ty's date with Lucy at The Jersey Boys, Ty decided to go to a bar. Grumbling aloud to himself, he said, "I need to put on a good buzz and then beat the shit out of Sean. I swear I'll rearrange his face." Seeing Sean at The Jersey Boys had ruined his date with Lucy. After that, it had been hard for him to pretend that things could continue where they had left off before the show.

Instead of accepting her invitation to come in for a drink, he had told her he would give her a call later the next week. He had seen the look of confusion on Lucy's face. Of course, she couldn't have understood the reason for the marked change in his mood. How could she? The only thing consuming Ty were thoughts of Sean and vengeance. "I'm going to hunt him down and teach that fuck a lesson." But that didn't happen. What did happen was Ty found himself walking through the door of a downtown lounge called Down to the Wire Bar.

Down to the Wire Bar was a living, breathing cliché straight out of a 1940s noir movie. Often described as a "seedy gin joint," it was dark, dirty, and smoky with vinyl upholstered bar booths and sticky tables. Keeping true to the noir genre, Down to the Wire was frequented by unsavory locals with the bartender being an-in-the-know ex-con able to get you whatever illegal substance you needed. Locals knew they could find anything inebriating there. Liquids? Powders? Pharma? It didn't matter; Down to the Wire had you covered. If you were unlucky, you might remember being there, but if you were fortunate, you'd wake up the next morning without any memory of being there at all.

Ty took a seat on an empty stool at the counter and looked at the bottles of liquor on the shelves behind the bar. He saw his favorite gin Tanqueray, but passed. He was in the mood for a more lethal intoxicant. In less than half an hour, Ty had tossed back four shots of cheap Black Eagle Kentucky bourbon, chasing each with a bottle of Coors. He leaned back into his barstool, waiting for the alcohol to begin its work. Ty knew it would take time, but tonight he was impatient. He wanted to be juiced, and he wanted it now.

Sitting next to him was a large man with sickeningly transparent porcelain skin and dyed orange hair. He looked to be in his late forties and wore an oversized hoodie zipped halfway up over his stomach in an apparent attempt to conceal his enormous gut. Beside him was a skanky girl with bug eyes. Her face was drilled with holes from multiple piercings. Four mini, curved barbell studs stabbed each eyebrow while a thick gold ring pierced her septum and a medusa piercing decorated the center of her philtrum. But what nauseated Ty were the two snake fang piercings on either side of her lower lip accompanied by two tattoos of black widow spiders. They looked like they were crawling out of the corners of her mouth. Being from New York, he thought he had seen every kind of screwy look imaginable, but this chick broke the glass on the freaky meter.

Ty just ordered another drink when the fat guy turned and remarked, "It looks to me like you're trying to get somewhere fast. You want to play some pool and talk about it?"

Ty had something different in mind. "What I really want is to score some blow."

The skanky girlfriend spoke up and said with a whistling lisp, "Tho what are you interethted in? Maybe we have it. What ith your pleasure?" She sucked a drag off her cigarette and released snorting sounds through her nose. Blowing smoke rings in the air toward Ty, she then asked if he wanted a blow job. Finding her utterly repulsive, Ty thought a game of pool might be a good idea after all.

The guy with the gut sat waiting for Ty to reply. With one scarred hand holding onto the handle of his beer mug, he stuck out his other to Ty in greeting. Proudly and loudly, the man proclaimed himself to be "Jake the Snake." Ty reached out his hand and the man shook it with a painfully firm grip. "I know I look like a fat ass and not like a snake, but there it is, man. That's my name and I make no apologies for it."

Ty eyed him with some reservations and then took a look at his disgusting girlfriend. "Hey, I'll take you up on that pool game, though I'm no money player. Even if my life was on the line, I couldn't deliver. I'm a piker when it comes to pool. How 'bout we play for drinks?"

Jake the Snake stood and hovered over Ty still sitting on his bar stool. He was feigning what he called his badass warrior pose. "Fair enough, my new friend. You better not be shitting me, because if you're bluffing, I've been known to turn a pool stick into an instrument of torture." Jake the Snake smiled jokingly, but Ty didn't doubt his boast.

After playing two straight games of pool and Jake schooling Ty in both of them, Ty's only consolation was that he wouldn't get a pool stick jammed up his ass. Oh well, at least he didn't scratch or worse, pocket the eight ball. But the games had slowed down his drinking, and he needed to get back to that.

Ty stepped up to a higher-shelf bourbon and ordered a double of ten-year-old Bulleit, an indulgence he usually sipped with great enjoyment. But not tonight. Intending to pay off his bet, Ty turned to ask Jake what he wanted to drink. But the fat ass had disappeared.

Ty looked around and saw Jake standing near the back door of the bar motioning for him to come over. Ty shot back his bourbon in a single gulp and slammed the glass on the bar. He could tell the bartender wasn't happy with that. "Hey man, don't break the freaking glass, okay?"

"Yeah, sorry about that," Ty yelled back and then he remembered he hadn't bothered to leave a tip. Running back to the bar, he pulled a five from his wallet and slapped it on the counter next his empty glass.

For that, he received a monotone, "Thanks, appreciate it."

Walking over to Jake the Snake, he said, "What's up, Snake? What are you doing? Where's your girlfriend?" Ty slurred his words and was having a tough time walking straight.

"Hey, I got a little something you might like."

Ty nodded at him and said, "You never know, I might just like it. What is it?"

"Well, I've got some foo-foo dust for you, my friend. And about my girlfriend, well, she's out turning a trick on some trucker who blew into town. Didn't you see her leave? She's out there doing what she does best, making money for old Jake the Snake. Truckers get lonely you know. And she said he's got a sweet rig and that means he's got a huge wad. But the hell with her. I've got some blow that will put you on a cloud to paradise. You'll be tripping my friend. You'll never want to leave. This cloud could be your new home."

"I'm game. I'm in, man." It didn't matter that he had never been there before, Ty was going there now and Jake the Snake was going to be his guide.

He led Ty back through the bar and out the front door, explaining, "They get hacked off if you try and go out the back door. There was this one f-upped guy who wouldn't listen to them and tried to push it anyway. By the time they were done working him over, the guy ended up with kidney damage from too many kicks to his gut. They threatened him and he was too scared to press charges. Now he's so full of holes that he can't even piss on his own. Last I heard, he's on dialysis. I'm telling you, you don't want to mess with anyone here. If they tell you to jump, you ask them how high. Hell, they use some of these guys to keep the cheaters in line at the casinos. "

"So, what's the big deal with the back door, Snake?"

With a piercing stare, Snake explained. "Supposedly, there is another door that leads to a secret room or office. A lot of shit goes down in there. Don't ask me what 'cause I'm not going there. And FYI. My name ain't Snake. It's got three words to it, and they are 'Jake' and 'The' and 'Snake.' So, don't screw it up, if you know what's good for you. Respect is the word, Pisano."

They went outside and walked down a back alley a block away. Jake the Snake pulled a small plastic bag and a glass pipe from his pocket. He dropped a few white chunks from the bag into the bowl and handed it to Ty. Putting it to his mouth, Ty used his index finger to block the hole at the end of the tube. Jake the Snake brought out a lighter, flicked it, and held the flame to the bowl. Ty sucked on the pipe and the small chunks of crack glowed brightly like the sun. Taking his finger off the end of the tube, a rush of air sent the crack smoke deep into his lungs. Almost immediately Ty felt himself simultaneously floating and falling into an almost trance-like state. He was on a high like he'd never been before.

Jake the Snake struck his lighter again and told Ty to take another hit. "Suck it in and you won't remember a better time." Floating himself into a new world, Ty ended up surrendering over a whole week's salary. Mumbling something inane to Jake, Ty complied with, "Shit, I don't mind forking it over for real estate like that cloud."

As they started walking back to the street, Jake the Snake told him he had got to thinking. With that, he stuck a toothpick in his mouth, rolling it around playfully with his index finger. "My man, Ty, I don't think you paid 'ole Jake the Snake enough for that goodie. I need more thanks than that. You've got to show me some love. You know I'm making a good point, so don't disappoint me."

Ty had no cash left and told him so.

"You telling me you don't have a bank card? Maybe this will help you remember that you do." Jake the Snake pulled out a Beretta stuffed in the small of his back and pointed it at Ty's head, saying threateningly, "Let's go find some cash."

The next thing Ty remembered was feeling numb, pulling a few hundred-dollar bills from an ATM, and handing them over to Jake the Snake.

Snake counted the cash and said, "No hard feelings, kid, but I got to learn you the rules. Now, you know who to come to when you need something. Just remember this one thing: if you act like a rat, I'll swallow you alive like a snake."

Ty now understood how Jake the Snake had earned his name. But Jake's threats didn't concern Ty because he liked how he felt. Nothing bothered him anymore.

HUMPHREY'S GOLD

Roy found himself in a dilemma. In just 15 minutes, he had managed to lose both his dancing partner and Nadine, the woman he suddenly couldn't stop thinking about. For years, Mindy was his dance partner. He had lured her out to Las Vegas, pretending to feel more for her than he really did, just to enter a dance contest. And now she was gone. Without Mindy, he knew he'd destroyed any chance of his winning the competition. As for Nadine, Roy couldn't believe that she had become the unwitting victim of his deceit. He knew he'd probably never see her again.

Roy was alone and had just finished dinner at the Humphrey's Gold Casino which housed Lafontaine's, indisputably the best buffet on the strip. Roy had hit the taco bar and found it to be some of the best Tex-Mex he'd had in a very long time. And then there was been the dessert bar, a decadent smorgasbord of high-calorie temptations. In an attempt to console himself, he decided to order a strawberry crepe. But as much as the buffet impressed his stomach, what he really appreciated was the Victorian elegance and the history behind the casino.

Humphrey's was named for a miner who had struck it rich during the California gold rush of 1849. His ancestors were prominent members of San Francisco society and virtually monopolized the mundane but nevertheless lucrative concrete industry in the city. Five generations earlier, Burton Humphrey had been one of the fortunate few who had struck it rich panning for gold off the American River flowing out of the Sierra Nevada mountain range. He arrived two weeks after the news circulated about James W. Marshall's gold discovery at Sutter's Mill. Humphrey's Gold casino was his family's memorial to him and the opulence of San Francisco society during the Gay Nineties.

Maybe it was the strawberry crepe that helped Roy to think differently. Surely there were other girls in Vegas who could dance. There had to be. All he had to do was find one. But how? Roy decided to place a classified ad in the Las Vegas Gazette.

Calling the newspaper, he was connected with a girl named Camille. She informed Roy that his ad would list in the paper's Help Wanted section. Not wanting the ad to read like a loser looking for an escort or hook-up, Roy tried his best to impress upon Camille that they get the wording exactly right. When it came to details, Roy could be anal-retentive.

He suggested that they add the line "No Hookers or Prostitutes Need Apply." But Camille suggested they change it to "Serious Inquiries Only."

With a syrupy voice, she told Roy, "Don't you worry. I've been working the want ads for years. I'll take good care of you. I'll make sure your ad gets a good response. We have a large circulation at the Vegas Gazette, so I can guarantee you will get results. I can do this job standing on my head with my eyes closed."

During the course of their conversation, it turned out that Camille could do more than just stand on her head. She could country line dance too. Camille boasted, "Mister, I can bust a move, and if you had a brain in your head, you'd pick me for your partner. Besides, you'll save the dollars it'll cost you to run this ad." Camille had a pushiness about her that Roy found annoying, but she seemed the type that would not take "No" for an answer. "I can do it all. Darlin', I was born with cowboy boots on!"

Roy was quick with a comeback. "Don't you mean cowgirl boots?"

Camille, so intent on becoming Roy's new partner, didn't even notice Roy's quip. "So, when do we start? As far as I am concerned, it can't be soon enough." Camille was not going to let Roy go without a fight. She pressed him for an answer; she was wearing him down with her tenacity.

Roy thought, *What the hell?* "Okay then, do you know about the Wild Bill Hickok Dance Hall? Have you ever been there?"

Before Roy finished his sentence, Camille screamed, "Of course, I do! I've worn out many a pair of kickers in that place."

Roy pounced with what he thought would be his Sherlock Holmes moment. "Funny, I've never seen you there. Do you dance someplace else or are you just invisible?"

Camille was silent for the first time and Roy thought he had her trapped. But after a brief moment, Roy heard her mocking laugh. "Of course, you haven't seen me there, dummy. You have no idea what I look like!"

Suddenly Roy felt very, very stupid. "Yeah, I suppose you're right. But seriously, do you go to other places to dance? Where do you go?"

"Look! I've been there many times. You can be sure of that. But it's mostly during the week. Ask any cowboy there about Camille. After one dance with me, they are weak-kneed and begging for more. On the weekends, I go out of town, so that leaves those two days out. But believe me. I know how to get my swerve on."

Roy interrupted her. "I don't mean to get personal, but I need a partner for at least Friday nights." Growing somewhat irritated, he added, "By leaving them weak-kneed, do you mean you're stepping all over their toes?"

Ignoring him, Camille told him she had a boyfriend who lived in California and that she spent her weekends with him. Roy had heard enough. "This definitely is not going to work out. You would need to be around to practice. The competition is on June twenty-second, and that leaves us only three months to prepare. That's not a whole lot of time."

Camille now had a question for Roy and practically blew out the speaker on Roy's phone yelling, "Then why the hell are you trying to get a new partner with just three months to go? Seems to me that's a no-win situation. You're going to be up against some of the best and your time is just about out."

Roy was through sparring with this order taker. "Well, if you're interested, then meet me next Monday night by the entrance to the Wild Bill at 7 p.m. I'll be wearing a cowboy hat with a snakeskin headband."

Again, Camille started laughing and taunting Roy. "Every guy there is wearing a cowboy hat with a snakeskin band. How original is that? I need more to go on than that. What do you look like?"

Roy chuckled and told her, "Okay then. I'm about six-foot-one and I have brown hair and green eyes. But you'll know who I am because I'll put a camouflage bandana on my hat. Good enough, Miss Camille?"

Camille laughed, and said teasingly "Did you just call me, Miss Camille? I guess you are getting familiar with me now. The only way I'll know who you are and the only way I'll agree to meet with you is if you make it a red bandana."

"No ma'am, I've got my principles. I'll agree to wear a camouflage bandana on top of the snakeskin. That's bad enough, but there's no way I'm going to wear a red one. No red on my head." Roy was serious. "And by the way, Miss Camille, what do you look like?"

Camille had a fast answer. "Just look for the cutest cowgirl there. I've got curly jet-black hair that goes all the way to my butt. I'll be wearing a country-style midriff top and tight jeans. Also, my cowgirl hat has a red bandana on it. So there."

They were all set to meet, Red Camille and Camouflage Roy.

CLARK COUNTY JAIL

John stared out from behind the bars of his Clark County Jail cell at nothing; he was in despair. He'd been booked on assault and battery charges and informed to expect an extended stay – through the night and into Monday. The bail judge was out for the weekend and there was no one to give him a hearing and set bail.

John reassured himself that he had enough money to post bail. But what if he was forced to hire a lawyer? That would force him into adopting an austere budget which would make it all the more urgent that he begin earning a living playing Texas Hold'em.

During the ride to the jail, the cop had said nothing to John and John wasn't about to engage him in conversation. He knew enough to keep quiet and not give the officer more fodder to escalate the charges. He pictured himself with a red "No Talking" sign slapped over his mouth. There was one thing that pained him, and that was the handcuffs clamped tight around his wrists. The cop was glibly sarcastic as he had pulled John's arms behind his back. "Here come the bracelets, son. You're not going anywhere now. And who knows, maybe you deserve them. I guess you think you're some kind of Rocky Balboa or stone-cold Steve Austin." John had said nothing, but thought the cop seemed old.

Once there, the booking procedures began. First, they searched John for drugs and weapons. They spread-eagled him, patted him down, and found nothing but a large hole in his right pants pocket. John did not resist at all, and in fact, tried to be cooperative with the cop. John responded to the officer's every command with, "Yes, sir." Jail was a nightmare he could not wake from. He was fingerprinted and had his mug shot taken. They Mirandized him and told him he could have one call. Humiliated, he wanted to get this torment over. Until then, all he could do was trust in the truth; that he was innocent.

The county jail on Stella Green Avenue had quite a reputation. It processed a lot of crazies, some of whom actually enjoyed being guests at the center. The 'three hot's and a cot' the county provided them came easier than panhandling enough change to buy their next sporadic meal, especially in the summer heat. It was well known among the down and outers that the jail provided good grub. It even had its own Twitter hashtag #GoodEatsAtClarkCtyJail where guests could tweet out reviews of their stays. One of the most recent tweets said, "Eggs, bacon, home fries. Hope I don't get released 'til the afternoon. Looking forward to lunch."

John knew of only one lawyer in Vegas. He was the famous one who had his face everywhere in the city. He was, in one word, ubiquitous. It was plastered on billboards along every highway, on local TV commercials as well as frequent TV appearances. Known to Las Vegans as "Thayer the Slayer," people often remarked how he didn't fit the picture of a rough and tough "Slayer" when they saw him in person. He stood only five-foot-four inches and weighed in at a mere one hundred twenty-five pounds; his stature was the furthest thing from imposing. But Samuel Thayer had a reputation of being a tenacious defender and of winning most of his cases, especially those deemed unwinnable by less able attorneys.

"Thayer the Las Vegas Slayer" was known for taking on some cases pro bono and John hoped that his situation might fit into that category. Apprehensive, John dialed 1-800-WIN-CASE. The phone rang and Slayer's answering service told John that Mr. Thayer was out until Monday morning and could not be reached. He left his name with the service and pleaded with the voice on the other end, "Please ask him to contact me as soon as possible. I'm in the county jail."

The voice assured him that the information would be given to Mr. Thayer as soon as he arrived at the office on Monday. "Thank you for calling Thayer Legal Services where we are here to serve you day and night. Have a nice day!"

The voice hung up leaving John to stare in disbelief. How could this be happening to him?

RHYOLITE, NEVADA

Thayer the Slayer's notoriety was founded on his defense of a wealthy Las Vegas socialite, Loralita Frost. Loralita was charged with the heinous murder of her equally wealthy boyfriend. Four witnesses came forward for the prosecution. Each of them testified under oath that she had bragged about drugging his iced tea with antifreeze and then taking his dead body into the desert and incinerating it with gasoline. By the time a rider on an ATV literally ran over and discovered the charred and badly decomposed remains, there was no way to positively identify whose remains they were.

Thayer fashioned Loralita's defense as a four-pronged counterattack against the prosecution. He never denied the anti-freeze poisoning allegations but instead deftly turned the murder on the victim's sister. He raised the issue of the sister's very public lawsuit between the siblings over their parents' will. His sister had claimed that the murdered man had coerced his parents into changing their will and leaving their entire one hundred-million-dollar estate to the son and nearly nothing to the daughter. "Ladies and gentlemen of the jury," Thayer argued forcefully, "the fact is that my client had no motive to commit the crime she is accused of. She is rich in her own right and it is the victim's sister, not my client's, the demure and unassuming Loralita Frost, who had the most to gain from this diabolical act of murder."

After successfully creating a reasonable doubt of guilt with the mind of the jurors (and, if the truth was told, also in the prosecuting attorney), Thayer launched the second prong of his defense – to attack the testimony of the prosecution's star witness. Through misdirection and several well-compensated expert psychological statements, Thayer the Slayer was able to convince the jury that Loralita had become so distraught at her boyfriend's disappearance that she began to imagine stories about what had happened to him. He convinced the jury that the trauma of the victim's disappearance had induced a form of schizophrenia where Loralita convinced herself that she was the perpetrator of such deeds. Therefore, she could not be held responsible for anything she said.

Third, Thayer pointed out that the prosecution was unable to produce a positively identifiable corpse. He argued that it was not uncommon to discover the charred remains of unidentifiable bodies in the desert near the ghost town of Rhyolite and went on to enumerate many such grisly discoveries over the recent past. So how could anyone be sure these were Loralita's boyfriend's remains anyway?

Finally, he worked the fourth prong of his defense on a more human level and relied on the basic instincts of the very carefully selected jury he had fought hard for during voir dire.

After Thayer's merciless cross-examinations of the witnesses, his closing argument persuaded the jury, and they returned an eight-four verdict of not guilty. Of course, the jury's composition of eight men and four women may have had something to do with their decision. For it was no secret as the local newspapers always pointed out, "Loralita was very, very easy on the eyes."

Loralita's acquittal not only cemented Thayer's reputation among Las Vegans but for a very short time, the town of Rhyolite became the weekend destination of curiosity seekers.

COUNTY JAIL OF DALLAS,

TEXAS

Father Lawrence had been the parish priest in Mariottaville for the past five years; the first Catholic church in Mariottaville was thriving. It had grown steadily since its beginning. He and Hank Mariotta were extremely pleased with the number of new parishioners and credited it all to Father Lawrence's tireless efforts to build a vibrant religious community.

But as of late, Father Lawrence had been filled with thoughts of beginning a new and different ministry. After weeks of prayerful introspection, there was no denying or ignoring it; the Holy Spirit was calling on Father Lawrence to serve the Lord in a new and different way.

Father Lawrence sensed God was calling on him to help those who had found themselves in trouble with the law. His new calling was to visit those incarcerated in county jails around the country, to act as a sort of spiritual first responder to minister to a person's troubled soul.

"Hank, I have never discerned a stronger calling from God since I entered the priesthood. I'll be a shepherd of sorts, trying to bring God's lost sheep back into the fold."

Hank encouraged him and suggested he start at the Dallas County Jail. A longtime friend of his, Ricardo Fernandez, worked at the Dallas County Correctional System. Hank offered to arrange for Father Lawrence to meet with him and went on to relate the story of how his friend Ricardo Fernandez came to work in the Dallas County penal system.

Ricardo Fernandez worked with Hank as a master welder during the early Mariotta Maverick years. Hank had great respect for him because of his welding skills. Ricardo could fabricate motorcycle frames better than anyone around, and Hank realized his value to the upstart Mariotta Motors. Ricardo's talent was widely recognized and he was routinely courted to join other shops with the offer of better pay. But

Ricardo remained loyal to Hank Mariotta and stayed with him until one day he came into Hank's office and declared that his days as a welder were over.

Ricardo had never been one to talk personally, so Hank stopped what he was doing and turned his full attention to Ricardo. A blue vein bulged out from Ricardo's forehead, but his eyes were expressionless. Ricardo matter-of-factly explained that he had sustained irreversible eye and skin damage from the welding light. His eyes were vacant, and he seemed unable to meet Hank's gaze while he spoke. Then his composure began to disintegrate. Ricardo fought to suppress his tears. He said there were days when he could barely see what he was working on. And his skin burned and itched. The pain was unbearable and left him unable to sleep at night. As much as he hated to leave Mariotta Motors, Ricardo had no choice but to tender his resignation. Hank asked him what he would do, and Ricardo admitted that he was concerned. Welding was all he knew, and he had his family to support.

Hank motioned for Ricardo to sit down while he picked up the phone. After a brief conversation with someone on the other end, Hank hung up the phone. He told Ricardo that if he wanted it, there was a desk job waiting for him in the Dallas Office of the Texas Department of Corrections. It wasn't charity, even though Ricardo was given the position under the Americans with Disabilities Act and was provided special viewing aids to assist him. For Ricardo, this was the panacea that could save his eyesight from further damage and still allow him to provide for his family.

That had taken place more than twenty years before, but through all that time, Hank and Ricardo remained in contact with one another. Ricardo had advanced through the years and was now a senior manager with the department.

When Hank placed a call to his old friend on Farther Lawrence's behalf, Ricardo Fernandez was only too happy to meet with him. He took the Father on a tour of the Dallas County Jail and offered to provide every assistance possible with Lawrence's new ministry.

Over the next few months, Father Lawrence made regular visits to every jail in the Dallas-Ft. Worth metroplex. He was doing God's will and he plunged into it without hesitation. The prisoners he counseled were men who had lost all hope and needed help in so many ways. The Father's role was to provide spiritual counseling and to show them that someone cared about them. Father Lawrence took the time to listen, give counsel, and pray with them. Some of them, unable to post bond, had been incarcerated for months pending their trial. Often, Father Lawrence was the only visitor they had seen since their incarceration so they would unburden their troubled consciences and let Father Lawrence see inside their anguished and depressed minds.

One troubled young man named Rue often called on Father Lawrence to seek direction. Facing up to life in prison for allegedly murdering his ex-wife and her boyfriend, he confided his innermost thoughts to Father Lawrence and even asked for absolution and forgiveness. Father Lawrence was humbly thankful to God for Rue's act of contrition and could already see God working through him to change this young man's life.

But as Rue continued with his confession, Father Lawrence realized he still had work to do with this young man. Rue whispered in Father Lawrence's ear, "Father, please bring me a gun next time you come." Then he began to sob quietly. "I've done wrong and I don't want to bring more shame on my family. Help me, Father Lawrence. Bring me a gun and let me do myself in. I want to kill myself. I want to die."

Father Lawrence studied Rue's eyes. In the sternest tone he could project, he told the young man, "What you have just said has rocked me to my very core. Son, you need to have faith and give this over to God. It is never up to us to take our own lives. That is God's decision. You must be strong, and God will see you through it. I will never bring you a gun or enable you to harm yourself. And if you ever ask me again, I'll report you so fast your head will spin. Don't ever insult God like that again. Nothing is ever too big for our God. He will be there for you always. Now let's pray together and ask for His help." They got down on bended knees and sent their prayers to the One who is Almighty.

LOBBY BAR AND CAFE AT THE ENCORE

Roy had to see Nadine but was uncertain how to make that happen. He knew he'd probably never see her at the Wild Bill again and the only thing Roy knew about her was where she lived. But he couldn't even be sure she was still staying at The Carrington. Whether she was or wasn't, Roy decided it wouldn't be a good idea to just show up at her hotel room door and announce, "Hi, remember me?" Instead, he loitered around the lavish Carrington Palace lobby hoping for an accidental encounter with her. But after several days without a Nadine sighting and tiring of the constant stare from the statue of the Greek goddess Venus presiding over the grand lobby, he ventured into the Encore Lobby Bar and Cafe at The Carrington.

Sitting down at the stylish bar, Roy decided to order a drink called an Earl Grey Mar-Tea-Ni invented by The Carrington's mixologist. Asking the bartender what was in it, the native Nevadan, who called himself the "Spirits Whisperer," promised Roy that he was about to taste something extraordinary. "You are in for a real treat. The Spirits Whisperer is going to make your day. Something special is about to happen." Describing the ingredients as he mixed the drink, Roy felt as though he was watching a Food Network cooking show. "Now, the Earl Grey Mar-Tea-Ni consists of a sugar-rimmed martini glass first moistened with a wedge of lemon. I set the glass in a freezer to chill, and now the real fun starts." The Spirits Whisperer pulled out a martini shaker. "Start with the lemon juice. Some simple syrup. Two generous jiggers of Beefeaters gin that Earl Grey tea leaves have been steeping in for several hours. Finally, an egg white." Spirits Whisperer saw the look of disbelief on Roy's face and said, "Yes, that right; I said an egg white. That's what gives it its punch. Now we cap and shake for 15 seconds and then put ice into it and shake some more. Strain it into the chilled glass and top it with a twist of lemon. Voilà, what a creation! You are going to enjoy this, buddy." He placed the completed concoction in front of Roy, clearly pleased with his performance. "A lot of folks think I invented this drink, but I just added a few twists to the basic recipe, and I guess that's what made me famous for this drink. But I believe in my past life it was me who invented this masterpiece."

The bartender hovered over Roy waiting for him to taste it. Roy took a sip. It was delicious; he didn't even notice the egg white! He appreciated the bartender's enthusiasm for the drink although, to Roy, his zeal for this liquid medley was a tad overdone. But Roy had to admit that it did trigger something in his mood. He smiled and gave the bartender an approving thumbs up. Satisfied, the Spirits Whisperer left to serve other customers.

As Roy continued to enjoy the drink, he realized it was making him happy, really happy. This Earl Grey Mar-Tea-Ni seemed to be the perfect anecdote for elevating one's state of mind and mood. The tea part helped him concentrate on coming up with a plan to find Nadine. The gin relieved the anxiety of not yet having a plan. Part of him wanted to ask the strangers at the bar if they had seen a beautiful petite brunette named Nadine, but common sense stopped him. It would make him appear desperate or worse – they'd think him some stalker or predator. No, he would sit there, lollygag, and enjoy his drink. He could people-watch and savor the scenery of the luxurious Carrington. And who knows, maybe Nadine would come walking by.

All the while, Roy strained his mind to come up with an ingenious plan to see Nadine again. Unfortunately, his brain wasn't cooperating and he failed to produce even one good idea. The only thing happening in Roy's head at the moment was the beginning of a nagging headache. It was only in a mild stage right now, but Roy knew from experience that he would need to get something fast to prevent it from getting severe. Once he developed even the slightest sign of a headache, they often escalated into mind-numbing migraines that could only be squelched by rest and large amounts of ibuprofen. That was the only thing that had a chance of working. But once they started, they never went away on their own.

Leaving behind his half-finished drink and a generous tip for the bartender, Roy went in search of a dose of Advil. Rubbing his temples vigorously, he rushed out the lobby doors without noticing the beautiful statue of Venus as he passed.

Was this the punch the Spirits Whisperer was talking about?

VEGAS RITE PHARMACY

Roy moved as fast as his legs would take him. The pain was worsening; he knew that if he didn't put some speed in his stride, he might crumble and collapse right there on the sidewalk.

He hurried to the nearest drug store a half-mile from the strip. Typical of the drugstore wars, a Vegas Rite Pharmacy occupied the right side of the street facing north while a CVS Pharmacy balked at it from across the street. Being the closest to him, Roy chose the Vegas Rite Pharmacy. Rushing through the automatic doors, he realized that he could have just gone to the hotel's gift store to pick up the relief he so desperately needed.

Roy's head now felt like a thousand sledgehammers were pounding inside his brain. The Earl-Grey Mar-Tea-Ni was having its payback. As his headache swelled in intensity, he began to feel dizzy. Barely able to make it inside of the Vegas Rite Pharmacy, Roy searched for something to help him stand. He spotted an empty shopping cart and leaned on it for support. The pain was excruciating. A blinding whirl of sparkling stars marred his vision and he began to slump over. Never before had he felt this bad.

The thought that he had been poisoned by that damn fool Spirits Whisperer, as well as a multitude of other disturbing possibilities, rambled through his throbbing head. But mostly, Roy blamed his current state on the Spirits Whisperer and wondered if he wasn't some malevolent mad scientist. Had he narcotized his drink or, as Roy grumbled to himself, "Did he slip me a mickey?"

What the hell was all that damn talk about that drink anyway? The more his pain intensified, Roy convinced himself that something evil was mixed into that peculiar beverage. But why? Something nefarious was going on and he'd been the victim. The thought nagged him as the migraine pounded with the pulse of his heart that was ticking down until his head blew apart.

The buzz of the store's fluorescent lights seemed to amplify to the point that Roy could hear nothing else. He covered his ears, trying to silence the noise. And now his olfactory system started to betray him. Glancing to his left, he saw a display of perfumed candles rich with the scents of pumpkin, strawberry, pine, and vanilla, all combining into a sickening mélange of assaulting sweet scents. The sensory overload was overwhelming and sudden nausea seized him. He couldn't think anymore.

The violence of the lights, perfumed air, and pain battered him like a perfect storm. Something ominous was happening. Roy felt himself slowly lose his grip on the cart handle, and he collapsed on the floor.

He didn't know how long he was on the floor, but gradually he became aware of someone talking to him. Leaning over him with her hand reaching out was a celestial being from heaven. This angel came in the form of a very pretty brunette with astonishingly green eyes tucked under prim eyebrows twisted up in concern.

"Roy, are you all right? What's the matter? What's wrong? Are you hurt?" Nadine blasted him with questions with the stuttering repetition of a machine gun. It was difficult for Roy to respond, and all he did was nod. Nadine helped him sit up.

By now, at least eight pairs of eyes had gathered around to stare at the strange man sitting on the floor. They were not there because of any real concern or interest in his wellbeing but they were just obnoxious onlookers. Roy felt like a lab rat and guessed that every Vegas Rite employee in the store was looking on him with the dispassionate scrutiny of a technician conducting a drug study.

One thin, anorexic young man with pink and green dyed hair had the basic decency to ask Roy if they should call for an ambulance. His Vegas Rite Pharmacy badge read "Lucas."

Roy grabbed on to Nadine's hand and, though quite wobbly, was able to make it back to his feet. "I think I'll be okay. I just have a terrible headache and I feel weak."

"Are you sure?" Lucas inquired again. Roy was beginning to feel embarrassed.

Nadine asserted herself and told Lucas rather sharply. "Young man, I've got this handled. I'll take care of him. But thanks just the same." Then she began to usher Roy out of the pharmacy. "I am going to take him to the doctor right now." She wrapped her arms around his chest as she guided him out the door and sat him down on a bench outside the store.

Roy stammered, "I've got to get an Advil," and started to get up. It was difficult for him even to say that. Now he was thinking that maybe he was having a stroke.

Nadine pulled him back down. "You just stay here." She ran back into the store and came out a minute later carrying the Advil and a bottle of water. She opened the bottle and put two tablets into Roy's hand. "Here, take these."

Roy complied and swallowed the pills, gulping down most of the bottled water hoping that it would dissolve the medicine faster. "Thanks, Nadine."

After a few minutes, Nadine whispered, "Come on, Roy. Let's get you out of here and find you someplace to rest." Nadine helped him slowly across the parking lot to her car. She stopped him in front of a brand-new, fire-red Ferrari with gold pinstriping. Even though the bright daylight sun made it painful to look at, Roy could not help but admire the gorgeous sports car.

It was a car that stood out and shouted, "Look at me! I am special!" It was indeed a work of crafted beauty and he thought Nadine had paused to admire it as well. But when Nadine unlocked the passenger door and helped Roy into it, he wished he felt well enough to ask if she was sure she had put him in the right car. But as he settled into the passenger seat of this engineered marvel, Roy thought for the first time in his life that he would enjoy being the one being stared at by envious eyes watching as this hot ride rolled past.

Nadine lurched the Ferrari out of the parking lot, throwing Roy's head forward and then slamming it back hard against the seat. Roy put his hands around his head, hoping to contain the jolt of pain. "I'm sorry, Roy. I'm still learning how to drive a stick shift." Then she took his hand and told him she was glad she had found him.

Roy managed a smile. "Have you ever heard of the drink called an Earl Grey-Mar-Tea-Ni? It is good and bad. It trashed me and literally brought me to my knees. But the twist was… that it also brought me to you. There's nothing else I wanted more than to see you again. They say it comes… with a twist and a punch. Though I could have done without the punch."

BEER BELLY'S LIQUOR

STORE

After Jill had finished talking with the cop and the two witnesses at Saldini's Sandwich Shop, she had gone to the police station to file charges against Derek Martin. Jill accused him of assault and rape and didn't care that without witnesses, the rape charge would probably be dropped. She knew what he did, and Jill wanted revenge. She wanted to see Derek crash like a skydiver whose parachute didn't open. Even if he didn't go to jail, Jill could destroy Derek's reputation by exposing him for the scumbag he truly was.

Despite the drama of the evening, Jill remembered she had to be strong for tomorrow. It was the second day of tryouts and she knew that even one missed step would be her last. Ironically, her confrontation with Derek only strengthened her resolve. She was not about to let anything, especially Derek Martin, prevent her from making the cut. She'd plow over the sturdiest oak tree if it was in her way and Derek Martin was just a shrub.

But Jill was preoccupied with something else, and it consumed her. She had to clear John. It had been several hours since the cops cuffed and hauled him away and Jill needed to speak to John in the county jail. But that wasn't going to happen until she could calm herself. She was emotionally drained, and right now, Jill needed something to steady herself. She was not unfamiliar to a drink every once in a while, but today was a day that called for several.

On her first day in Vegas, Jill had discovered a small liquor store near her hotel called Beer Belly's Liquors which was operated by a short, slight man from India named Samar. Samar was a talkative cashier and on her visit to Beer Belly's, he had explained to Jill that he had chosen to settle in Las Vegas because of the climate. The desert heat of Las Vegas mimicked the temperatures of his native village, Taj Ganj, just south of the Taj Mahal.

A minor tenant in a nondescript, cinderblock strip mall, Beer Belly's offered a surprising selection of beer and wines. To Jill's delight, they carried several vintages of Dona Paula Malbec, her favorite. She had made a big show of finding the last bottle on the rack and Samar had promised that he would continue to stock it just for her. Jill celebrated her first night in Vegas alone in her hotel room with a bottle of red wine, watching Wheel of Fortune on television.

The night was balmy and the walk to Beer Belly's gave Jill a chance to think about other things, like the fact that her feet felt like the victim of a Chinese foot binding. That was when she realized she was still wearing the same constricting heels she'd been walking on all day. Sitting on a bus stop bench, Jill replaced her high heels with a pair of flip-flops she had stowed in her bag. The rest of the walk home was now effortless and Beer Belly's was just around the corner. It was early, so of course, it would still be open. But that didn't matter because, as Samar had proudly told her when she had asked about his hours during her first visit there, "24-7-365! 24-7-365!" Beer Belly's never closed.

Walking through the door at Beer Belly's, Jill waved at Samar and headed straight for the beer cooler. She pulled out a six pack of Fat Tire and then went over to the wine rack for a bottle of Dona Paula. But the shelf was empty. She swore to herself and picked up a cheap but drinkable bottle of Australian Yellow Tail Merlot and took them to the counter. Jill asked Samar where the Dona Paula was, prompting him to apologize and explain that he was out. This seemed to bring all the day's frustrations together and Jill couldn't help but punish the store clerk verbally. "Jeez Samar, get it together. You're always out of something. Shit, you know that Dona Paula is my fave' and I need it after the crap day I've had. You've got to start doing something about your inventory control if you want my business."

Samar bobbed his head from side to side and looked at her quizzically. Smiling, he bagged Jill's purchase and handed her the change. "Thank you. Come again."

"Yeah sure, whatever." Jill blasted out the door and headed home. She couldn't wait to pop the cork off her wine, even if it was just Yellow Tail, and chase it down with a Fat Tire.

Once home, she poured herself a glass of wine and took a sip. It tasted good enough and already she felt that she was on her way to putting the events of the day behind her. But not entirely. The trauma pestered her like a splinter in her foot she couldn't find. She had some unfinished business to attend to and, with a full wine glass in one hand and her phone in the other, she thumbed the number for the county detention center and pressed the Call button.

The switchboard operator answered perfunctorily, "Clark County Jail. How may I direct your call?"

"I'd like to speak with John Sanger, please."

"John who? There's no one here by that name."

"He was just arrested. I desperately need to talk with him."

"This ain't no country club, lady, and I ain't no answering service for your daddy John whatever-you-call-him."

"Please ma'am, it's his mother. She's had a horrible accident and…"

"Save your breath, girlfriend. I've been working this switchboard for fifteen years and I've heard every story under the sun. And your 'mother's in a terrible accident' is the one I hear at least once a day. You could have at least done me a favor and come up with something new."

"Okay, but here's the real truth, I swear it." And Jill proceeded to tell the operator what happened in the alley behind Saldini's Sandwich shop ending with, "So you see, they arrested the wrong man and I need to let him know that I am going to get him out of this."

"What're you going to do, bad girl, break him out of jail?"

"No. I just need him to call me. Please, can you at least give him that message?" Jill pleaded with the operator but knew she was wasting her time.

The operator expelled an exasperated gasp, "Okay! So, what's the perp's name?" Jill told her. "And what's your name and number?"

"Just tell him to call Jill on my cell. He knows the number. And thank you so much."

"Whatever girlfriend. But just a word of advice: don't hold your breath!" The switchboard operator ended the call and left Jill sitting on the side of her bed.

Ignoring the operator's advice, Jill poured herself another glass of wine and stretched out in her bed waiting for John's call. Jill was asleep when the phone rang and woke her.

"Hello, this is John."

Jill was shaking. With a tremor in her voice, she mustered, "This is Jill."

"Yeah, I know, Jill. Are you all right? Who was that guy attacking you? Do you know him?" Jill took a deep breath; she had to ask.

"John, do you still care about me? I need to know." There was a pause. And the pause got longer. "John, we only have a few minutes. I want to thank you for coming to my rescue. But I need to know; do you still have feelings for me?" There, she did it. She finally got to ask him the question she needed answered, ever since John left her.

"Of course, I care about you. I always will. But I've got to be honest with you." He went silent for a moment. "But Jill…" Jill held her breath; she knew what was coming. John continued. "But I've moved on. We aren't good for each other. All we ever did was fight."

Jill had just one more question. "Is it that girl I saw you with at Bebe's? Are you with her? Tell me; I won't get upset. I just need to *know*." Jill stressed the word "know" even though she already knew the answer.

"Yes, I am. Her name is Mary and I want to marry her someday. I don't know why I'm telling you all this. But I've never met anyone like her. I know I just met her, but yeah, I think I want to marry her. There's something vulnerable about her and she needs me. We're comfortable together. We even finish each other's thoughts sometimes. You and I never did that Jill. I'm sorry how it all worked out."

Jill thought it was good they were speaking over the phone so John could not see the look of disappointment on her face. But after mulling it around for a few seconds, she knew he was right, painful though it was. Long before, she knew her future was not with John; he had just become a habit. But this was final. No regrets, no remorse. They'd built some good memories together, but they were never really together. Still, Jill would always be grateful for how he had protected her, but the fact was that Jill had already started her life without John. And he had done the same.

"Do you have a lawyer yet? The police and I spoke to witnesses that saw it all, and you will be exonerated. I filed charges against Derek Martin. You asked me who the guy was that did this to me and I'll tell you. He's some creep that has been bothering me since I got into town. The lowlife even had the nerve to call me and try to bribe me not to press charges. I told the little troll that he couldn't hide anymore under a bridge because they were coming for him. John, you're assault and battery charges won't go any further, I can assure you that. They're looking for this monster. They got a warrant out on him and believe me; they'll find him and bring him in." It made Jill feel good to be the bearer of good news.

John told her that he had called Thayer the Slayer and that the answering service had promised he'd contact him on Monday. "Jill, it looks like I'll have to be here over the weekend. Hopefully, Thayer will come through for me. The bad thing is that I'm stuck in here until then. Let me tell you, this is a new experience for me and one I don't intend to let happen ever again."

"But John, you helped me. If it hadn't been for you…" Jill imagined the worst.

"I didn't mean it like that, Jill. I only meant that I don't ever want to be in here again. This sucks more than you could ever imagine."

Jill tried to encourage him. "You mean you hired that Thayer the Slayer guy from TV? If he's half as good as he says he is, he'll do a beatdown on anyone!" She was happy for John. Then, as Jill had been warned, they were interrupted with a loud click on the line. Their fifteen minutes were almost up.

"You have one minute left," a monotone voice instructed them.

"Well, bye for now, John. And thank you. If you need me for any further help, let me know."

John responded sincerely. "Thank you, Jill. And the same to you. I'll be there for you also." They were cut off, just like that. But there was a poetic finality to it.

Jill remembered she had a few more Fat Tires and some Yellow Tail to finish.

D POD

It was a rainy day, unusual for Las Vegas, when Father Lawrence's flight touched down at McCarron Airport. Unlike most of the passengers disembarking from the plane heading for various casinos and hotels up and down the strip, Father Lawrence's destination was the Las Vegas County Jail. From the very beginning when he had first started his prison ministry, he had looked forward to this trip with great anticipation. He felt there was a great need for him in Las Vegas. After all, there was a reason it was called "Sin City."

The first thing he did when he entered the jail was to request a visit with a few of the most recent inmates. A burly cop with a crooked nose gave him a look of disbelief but handed him a clipboard with the list of the jail's newest occupants. Father Lawrence hesitated, taking it from him after the cop sprayed a wet sneeze all over the roster. Finding it difficult to decipher the names through the splatter of snot seeping through the paper, Father Lawrence wished he had a pair of latex gloves.

"There's a guy named John Sanger and he's really virgin. Uh, sorry, Father. I mean, he's only twenty-one years old, and I think it's his first time in jail. He looks scared. I'll have the guard take you over to D Pod where he's being held. The guard will bring him over to the visiting room there. If he agrees to see you, you will be allowed twenty minutes of visiting time. You won't be alone. There are also eleven other prisoners receiving visitors packed into the same room. The prisoners sit on one side of a glass window and visitors on the other. You speak to each other through a handset."

Father Lawrence was all too familiar with the setup. There would be visitors that may have been waiting hours to see their loved ones. Some of these people would be agitated and stressed. Other would be crying. Many of the women would have their young babies with them and others their entire family. Often, he had found himself spending as much time counseling visitors of the prisoners as he did with the prisoners themselves.

The cop continued, "I just want you to be aware of this and the rules. But back to this young man, John Sanger, I don't think he's said one word since he's been here. I mean, he is scared." The hulking cop had a gleam in his eyes when he stressed the word scared. "He was processed for assault and battery, and that's about all I know. Maybe you can help him out."

Another guard guided Father Lawrence down a long passageway that eventually opened into a large circular room. In the center was a guard seated at a desk and around him were four different heavy steel doors that led to the jail's different detention blocks. After signing in, they went to the door marked "D Pod." D Pod was the jail's minimum-security unit and housed up to twenty detainees. The door made a loud clunk and the guard opened the door. Father Lawrence stepped into D Pod. The guard followed him; the door shut solidly behind them. Once again, there was a loud thud of locks engaging. They took a quick right and entered a medium-sized room. Along one side of the room was a long, thick glass wall with a row of low cubicles and chairs where people sat and talked softly through a cabled receiver to inmates sitting across from them on the other side of the glass. Several guards were stationed at various spots around the room on both sides of the glass partition.

Father Lawrence's escort pointed to an empty chair and motioned for him to sit down. Through the glass, he saw a very dejected young man who appeared to be in a stupor staring past him, trancelike. The young man seemed focused on the dirty orange peeled wall on the other side of the glass. Father Lawrence was afraid the young man might be catatonic. He was about to meet the virgin inmate of the county jail.

The guard rapped the glass with his knuckles and John looked up slowly, still gazing off distantly. He picked up the receiver and motioned for John to do the same. "Sanger, this is Father Lawrence and he has traveled all the way from San Angelo, Texas to speak with you. Are you interested? Get with it if you want your twenty minutes."

Father Lawrence saw two big brown eyes look up at him, instantly erasing their far away fixation. John Sanger made eye contact with Father Lawrence through the glass partition. It was like the imaginary fog that had shrouded the forlorn young man had magically disappeared. Now, they were face to face with each other, even if their phone receivers impeded their intimacy.

The guard handed the receiver to Father Lawrence. "Hello, John. I'm Father Lawrence. It's nice to meet you."

John Sanger asked, "Did you really come all the way from Texas to see me? Is it because that is where I am from?"

Father Lawrence responded to him immediately with compassion. "Yes, I was told you are from Houston. I am the parish priest in Mariottaville, Texas," he said, waving his arms as if this might help communicate with the boy on the other side of the glass.

The good Father realized there was no reason to be so animated and commanded his arms to settle at his sides. After being a priest for so long, he tended to gesticulate while he spoke, as if he was delivering a homily. Sometimes, he felt that he might have picked up the habit from Hank Mariotta. Being of Italian descent, Hank Mariotta often gestured with his arms and hands.

To Father Lawrence, it was imperative that he reach this young man. It was obvious John Sanger did not belong in this place or this situation. And the longer he remained there, the more damage it would do to his psyche. He wasn't sure if it was divine providence that had brought him there, but he knew that he had to help John.

The guard stood behind Father Lawrence and looked at his watch as if he were counting down the minutes until he could send John back to his cell. John began talking, and in less than ninety seconds, he had told the good Father his entire story as well as explaining why he was in Las Vegas in the first place. John said shakily, "I was walking down the strip and heard a scuffle on a side street. I saw a man attacking a woman, and I went to defend her. I was merely trying to save a girl by beating off her attacker. I'm just here to play poker and now my dreams are over." John repeated it, "I came here to play poker, and I am totally innocent, Father. I was just being a Good Samaritan."

When John mentioned the subject of poker, Father Lawrence knew he had found the common denominator with which to engage the young man. Father Lawrence told him he was good friends with someone who was also very interested in poker.

"He's so far gone that he wants to create a poker channel, I kid you not," Father Lawrence said. "I pray for him, as I will for you, because I am not certain poker is from God. I am not sure that this is God's will for him, or you, for that matter. After all, son, you'd have to admit that if you hadn't come to Las Vegas to play poker, you wouldn't be here right now. You could almost say that it's because of poker that you are in jail."

Obviously curious, John asked, "Is this guy a good player? Is he famous? Do you think this guy could help me improve my game?"

Father Lawrence was amazed by how quickly the mention of poker transformed John from a nearly catatonic state of depression to a state of ebullience.

The priest was quiet for a few seconds and scratched the side of his head questioning how much he should reveal. "His name is Hank Mariotta. Being from Texas, you probably have heard him. He owns the San Antonio Antelopes and created the Mariotta Maverick, the most unbelievable motorcycle ever made. As far as I'm concerned, there is nothing that even comes a close second to that amazing machine. But John, don't miss my point, son. Poker is a game. The Lord never intended it for anyone to make a career out of it. Hank Mariotta is a man of God, and he understands that fact."

John completely missed the Priest's logic. The first part of Father Lawrence's comments had captured his attention and John was colossally curious; so much so, he could not get his questions out fast enough. He was rambling out of sheer excitement. Poker always did this to him. For a moment John forgot where he was.

Of course, John knew about Hank Mariotta. Who didn't? He was a household name, especially in the Lone Star State. Now to find out he likes poker and wants to start his own poker channel; John could only hope to meet a man as famous as Hank Mariotta. Maybe the Father could help with more than just concern and prayer. To John, this priest was more than a kindly visitor. He could be the catalyst to bring his poker dream into fruition. While John appreciated the priest's effort, for the present John was more interested in Father Lawrence's friend than this well-intentioned clergyman.

What happened next surely should have gotten the attention of one of the guards. John thought there were enough guards to go around to protect half the city of Las Vegas and they were all armed. It certainly would have rattled the good Father if he had witnessed it. But only John had observed it, and it made a formidable imprint on his mind.

An older woman who must have been an inmate's mother or even grandmother appeared to be the matriarch of this family. There were two young boys and a young girl who were likely the inmate's brothers and sister. They were in the partition on the other side of the room from Father Lawrence. The sister was probably all of thirteen years old and was standing behind the woman. A few chairs away, sitting between John and that inmate, was another prisoner talking through the phone receiver to a bald guy with a humongous brown birthmark on the top of his head. After the bald man said something, they both had a rowdy laugh. The inmate, who seemingly noticed the young girl on the other side of the glass, luridly laid his eyes on the thirteen-year-old. He fixed a leering glare on her, obviously wanting to attract the young girl's attention. He hung up the phone and stood, wagging his finger at the girl. She saw him and her eyes read terrified. He mimicked a kiss, licked his lips sleazily, and then mouthed the words, "Juicy booty." Grabbing his crotch, he stuck his dirty finger in his mouth and pulled it slowly out.

The young girl recoiled in horror. It was obvious she was too petrified to do or say anything. And while John saw it all, Father Lawrence was oblivious to what was happening. The guards did not seem to have noticed either, or maybe they simply chose to ignore what they knew would inevitably turn into a bad situation. Even the girl's inmate brother either didn't see it or did and wasn't about to start something with this depraved loser. Perhaps he was getting bullied around by him or this place. John thought to himself, *If I say anything, I'll only stir up trouble for myself. One way or another it'll blowback and bury me, and the last thing I need is an extended stay in this hell hole.* Besides, playing the role of White Knight was what landed him there in the first place. John ignored the disturbance; he was learning how to play the game inside the jail.

Father Lawrence brought John back into the conversation by asking, "John? Is there anything I can do for you? Do you have a lawyer?"

John replied, "I think so, Father. I mean, I called Thayer the Slayer Friday night, and his answering service said he'd call me as soon as he got into the office on Monday. But here it is almost ten-thirty and I haven't heard from him yet." Then John turned the conversation back to Hank Mariotta and asked the well-meaning but unobservant priest from Texas, "Can you help me to meet him? That would blow me away. I am in such awe of him. Please tell him about me." With that, he asked Father Lawrence to write down his phone number and give it to Hank Mariotta.

Father Lawrence said he would see what he could do and asked John if he would like to pray. "John, we must pray for temperance with your poker. If you must gamble, then you should donate some of your winnings over to charity. It would help other people." Father Lawrence was talking rather loudly through the phone.

Suddenly feeling very selfish and ashamed, John avoided direct eye contact with the priest but rattled off his phone number to Father Lawrence anyway.

"Please have him call me," John said. "Also, thank you, Father, for your concern. It was nice to meet you. Hopefully, I will be out of here real soon and you won't have to visit me here again. I wouldn't mind praying with you, though."

Father Lawrence began his prayer and kept praying and praying. John thought that he was surely sending a lot up to the Almighty. Father Lawrence continued to pray until a muscular guard barked, "Your twenty minutes are up. Let's go." The receiver clicked dead. John stood up and the guard slapped cuffs on him and led John back to his cell.

Father Lawrence waved goodbye through the glass, trusting God had heard his incomplete prayer. What he didn't know was that God had heard and he indeed had a plan for John. If Father Lawrence was a betting man, he would have gone all-in when it came to God answering his prayer.

GUARDIAN ANGEL

CATHEDRAL

It was late afternoon and John was still waiting on the cot in his holding cell. A guard appeared and announced without expression that he was to be released. Enlisting the help of Samuel Thayer had been the wise thing to do. And, although Thayer had not contacted him as quickly as his answering service had promised, John finally received Thayer's call while he was eating lunch.

Leaving the table and his half-eaten meal, John picked up the phone expectantly, "Yes, this is John Sanger?"

"Samuel Thayer here. I understand you're in need of a lawyer?"

"Yes sir, but I am afraid I do not have a lot of money."

"Well, the first consultation is free. Tell me what you did to get yourself in there in the first place."

John explained the incident in detail and ended his story with "… And that's why I called you, Mr. Thayer. I love your commercials about how you always fight for the little guy and, sir, I am that little guy." John was not too proud to stroke the lawyer's ego.

Thayer assured John, "Kid, this is a slam-dunk. You were doing right by defending this girl. There's a Good Samaritan Law and your actions are protected under this provision. The burden of liability is removed from you if you are helping a person under distress. I promise, I will drum up so much publicity on this, they will have no choice but to let you out. They know me and they sure as hell don't want to have me in their faces. If I have to, I'll hammer their little faces into mashed pulp. No one can work the press like me. And don't worry about the cost, kid, this one is pro bono. Meaning, it's on the house! That's how confident I am feeling about this, kid!"

"Thank you so much, sir. Can I ask you one favor? Would you contact my girlfriend Mary and tell her what happened?" He also told Thayer he did not want Mary coming to visit him. "I don't want her to come to this low-life place and have one of those dregs in the visiting room hassle her or say something. I saw that with some little girl when I had my one and only visitor, a priest. Some inmate in the middle of a visitation put his phone down, stood up, and tugged on his crotch in front of a young girl and her mother. He then talked trash to her and made some gross gesture toward her like he wanted to have sex." John went on to Thayer, "I'm telling you that this girl was too scared to even mention it to a guard and not even to her mother. Hell, not one lame-ass guard was paying attention. No one saw a thing or at least, pretended they didn't. That's exactly why the piece of scum did it. No way do I want Mary to have to go through that hassle or have someone do something like that to her. You want to talk about assault and battery? I would put a smash-mouth on him so fast I'd find myself rotting in here forever." He found himself thinking about Mary the same way he did when he talked to Jill about her. He wanted to protect her. "Just tell her that I'll see her when I can and not to worry about me."

Thayer interrupted him. "Whoa boy. Settle down. I'll let her know, but you needn't worry about her coming there for a visit; I'll have you out before you know it." Thayer the Vegas Slayer agreed to convey the message to Mary and assured John he would take care of business. He then went about his work. Thayer never flinched, maintaining he was one-hundred percent confident that he could get John off in a matter of hours. "Rest easy; you'll be out in no time."

Within hours, Thayer had brought the reports of the two witnesses and Jill in front of a judge. Based on that testimony, the judge found no probable cause to arrest the man in the first place and ordered John Sanger's immediate release. Concurrently, the judge also issued a warrant for the arrest of one Derek Martin.

The bailiff facetiously quipped, "You're free, boy scout, so get a move on it. Follow me as I take you over to the facility to begin the release process." John felt like a minion following the pied piper Guard of the Clark County Jail. But he knew it would ultimately lead out the jail's front door to freedom. All his praying to God with Father Lawrence had worked. God had heard his prayer. He would be forever grateful to Father Lawrence for invoking God in his time of tribulation.

After being released, John stopped at the Guardian Angel Cathedral to thank God for his release and to promise Him that he would try to spend more time at church in the future. Never particularly religious before, jail changed John and made him realize that he was powerless in a fight with the law. John needed the help of an even more powerful force. And for him, God was the most powerful force he could imagine. He was elated and his worries were behind. John was now free to attend to the two most pressing matters facing him – poker and marrying his Mary.

What John never found out was that neither "Thayer the Slayer" nor anyone on his staff ever saw John's message. It was buried under a stack of other urgent notes, all of them pleading for representation. After leaving the detention center, Father Lawrence had called Thayer's office and inveigled Thayer into action on John's behalf. Had it not been for Father Lawrence, John would have still been an innocent victim of the Las Vegas penal system and a reluctant resident at the Clark County Jail.

DANBURY MOTOR COURT

After one of the policemen drove off with John in a patrol car, Jill and the other left for the sandwich shop to look for witnesses. The crowd of onlookers disappeared and Derek was left alone in the middle of the alley. Since no one told him to stay and the ambulance had yet to arrive, Derek chose to leave the scene and meandered back to his car via a path that consciously avoided Saldini's Sandwich Shoppe.

Derek Martin looked at himself in the rearview mirror of his car. His eye was bruised and already starting to blacken. He pressed down hard on his swollen mouth as if the pressure would take the swelling away. Pulling a moist wipe from its tube, Derek dabbed away the blood drying under his nose and around his lips. He was hurting and had to admit that the guy could throw a punch. If the cops hadn't come as soon as they had, the guy would have pureed his face into the pavement.

But through the pain, Derek managed a smug grin as he pictured the cops hauling Jill's protector and savior away, "the asshole!" One look at Derek sprawled out on the pavement with his face all bloodied, the police jumped to the obvious conclusion that Derek was the innocent victim in all of this. Since it was Jill's boy-wonder they had slapped the handcuffs on, Derek felt he'd avoided the worst of it. He started humming to himself, confident that he'd outwitted them all. But damn, his eye hurt badly and now he was seeing double.

That whore-bitch Jill was his real concern. What would she tell the police? Even though nothing happened, she could damage or, more precisely, destroy his career. The morals clause in his contract had always been loosely enforced, just as long as his extracurricular staff exploits remained private. But Derek was under no illusion that the moment someone lodged a harassment complaint against him, they'd flush him like a floating turd. He'd seen it happen all too frequently and now it was his career in danger of getting caught in the drain swirl.

Derek began thinking about Jill. What was her problem anyway? Why didn't she just play the game like everyone else? Give a little, get a little. The rules are simple. Here I am handing her the chance that most girls would kill for, to some nobody from nowhere. And in return, all I wanted was just a little something, and suddenly she goes all nun on me like she was some blessed virgin. Yeah, she's cute, but she's nothing exceptional and doesn't come close to the others. I doubt she even finished high school. So why the hell did I let her get to me? Derek Martin couldn't figure it out.

Granted, he probably was overthinking it, but if Jill filed charges, he faced the prospect of being arrested. The last thing he needed was for a law officer frog-marching him out of his office through the Malai Casino in front of his bosses. Derek needed to settle things with Jill. But he also needed to hideaway for a few days. Not only to avoid the law, but also to nurse his battered face. Derek Martin started his car, put it in drive, and headed north on I-15 out of town.

About sixty miles out of Las Vegas, Derek saw a billboard for the Danbury Motor Court. Badly weathered by the desert sun, the sign had been there forever. Normally, if he even noticed it all, it was the kind of advertisement the far too cultured Derek would laugh at as he drove past. But the road sign promised "Pull-In Garages!" and that was just the kind of no-tell motel Derek needed to conceal his attention-getting sapphire Ford GT.

He took the next exit and drove down the service road until he saw the motel. It was starting to get dark, but there was still enough light for him to see that the Danbury was in just about the same shape as its billboard. He drove under a pitted, plastered archway up to the office door. Before getting out of his car, he looked around. The motel rooms were built around an empty swimming pool in the center of a courtyard. There was a chain-link fence around the pool with a sign on the gate that read "Closed." Chunks of white plaster peeling away from the exterior walls lay in piles against the flat-roofed buildings.

The place reminded Derek of a French Foreign Legion fort in the middle of the Saharan desert he had seen once in an old movie. But the Danbury did have pull-in garages just as the highway sign promised. He opened his car door and walked into the office to get a room for the night.

The office was dark and reeked of garlic. There was an old, ratty and stained wingback chair in the corner and Derek Martin shuddered at the thought of the state of the rooms. He walked up to the thick bulletproof window where a tiny Asian woman waited, eager to check him in. Speaking through an intercom, she asked in a squeaky, heavily accented voice, "Mista, you want room? Hundred-twenty plus tax. Free parking. Porn movie." A bank teller drawer opened from the wall in front of him. "Put license and credit card in here. I give you key."

Derek tried to smile, but it hurt too much. "Okay. One night, please." He put his Platinum Amex and Nevada driver's license in the tray.

The drawer slid back into the wall, and in a few minutes, she returned his license, card, and a key attached to a green plastic keychain.

Derek signed the charge slip and dropped it in the drawer. On his way out of the motel office, the woman asked him, "You want massage? I send you nice girl. She take care of you." Derek managed a smile and just waved goodbye.

After parking in the garage next to his room, he slowly stepped into the darkened room. He felt for the wall switch and flipped the lights on. It was like taking a step back in time. The compact room was sparsely furnished. There was a chair, a double bed with nightstands, and a dresser. The only things not anachronistic about the Danbury was the flat-screen TV bolted to the wall and the Asian madam hotelier who replaced the balding, middle-aged man sitting behind the office counter in his sleeveless undershirt. Derek was grateful for one thing; at least the room didn't smell of garlic. He pulled open the bed covers, took off his shoes, and laid down.

He fell asleep.

Sometime later, he was awakened by a soft but persistent knock on his door. "Who is it?" he asked through the door.

A soft voice answered, "It is Ping and Sen. You want party?" came the answer. Then he heard a brasher voice say, "Hey, don't forget about me, Cynthia. How 'bout all four of us have some hot fun?"

Derek opened the door slowly and poked his head out to see two cute, petite young Asian girls standing on his doorstep. One held an ice bucket and the other a bottle of scotch. Behind them stood a slight, very blonde whose hair was so bleached that it resembled a bottle of milk. Derek presumed this was Cynthia and didn't bother to find out who was Ping or Sen. He swung open the door and invited them in.

Derek had a wild Saturday night, then all day Sunday, and on through Sunday evening. On Monday morning, he woke up alone. The girls were gone and his brain was a foggy mess.

When he checked out of the Danbury, he signed for a bill far larger than just two nights for a room.

During the drive back to Vegas, he recalled with amusement the experience his friend Pauly once had on his way back from Reno. And coming from someone as cultured as Pauly, it was one crazy story.

On a Monday morning in August, Derek had been sitting alone in a conference room waiting on his coworkers to arrive to begin their weekly staff meeting. One of them was Pauly and he limped through the door. He plopped into a chair, badly sunburned and lobster boiled. He looked like he'd had a tough weekend and Derek couldn't help but comment. "Pauly, man, you look like hell! What happened?"

Pauly answered, "What a weekend. I'm driving back from Reno down 95, and I'm just about fifteen miles out of Tonopah when the

S.A. Craig

engine dies on my new Benz. Can you believe that? There I am, stuck out in the middle of nowhere on the hottest day of the year. I get no cell connection and I'm the only one on the road. So, I start walking. And walking. And walking. Finally, I come up to this wretched motel and just want to use a phone to call for a tow. But the manager is a real bugger and won't let me use the phone unless I check into a room. So, I get a room at the Coachella Motor Court, and Derek, I kid you not, this was the most dilapidated and squalid dive you could ever imagine. When I opened the door to my room, there was a scorpion waiting on the floor to greet me." Pauly shuddered, "God, I hate those things."

"Hell Pauly, you should have just kept on walking," Derek offered.

"Maybe, but that's not the worst of it. The only other guests there were two of the ugliest skankers I ever saw, and they kept walking back and forth past my window. I tried to ignore them, but when I went out to give the wrecker driver my keys, they cornered me before I could get back to my room. We start talking, and before you know it, we're in my room doing the nasty. And Derek, I mean *the nasty*! Now, I think they gave me the crabs. I've been itching ever since."

Derek laughed and said, "Well, I'll tell you one thing for sure; I'd never let myself get into a situation like that." At that point, other meeting attendees began to arrive and Derek and Pauly never talked about it again. Still, Derek had thought less of Pauly ever since.

Now as Derek neared the city, he thought about the hypocrisy of his situation. He rubbed his hand across his beat-up face and once again Jill's defender floated into his head. He had to have been some professional boxer because he knew what he was doing. A few punches from him had Derek crawling on his belly. Derek replayed the situation again. The guy had physically punished him, but he wasn't about to let it occupy any more of his time. He was the poor slob sitting in the county jail wearing an orange jumpsuit. It was good he'd been punched out because it made him look like the injured party and now Derek was the one free and walking around. The recurring stab of fear once again subsided. He needed normalcy and to get back to work. Heading to his condo for a shower and a much-needed change of clothes before showing up at work, Derek avoided thinking about the past few days.

Derek's condo was just on the edge of downtown. This particular area was under massive reconstruction and reclamation. Old buildings were demolished and new, upscale ones sprouted in their place. It was now commonplace to hear the sounds of heavy construction equipment roaring during all hours of the day. The area was undergoing rapid gentrification, and of course, Derek Martin saw to it that he had gotten in on the ground floor of what was anticipated to become the address to have in Las Vegas.

On the slim chance the police were looking for him, Derek decided to stash his car a few blocks away from his condo near where construction was beginning on a new mega-restaurant. He was interested in following the restaurant's progress as it promised to become the swankiest eatery downtown Las Vegas had to offer. He envisioned it taking on some of the finer restaurants found in the casinos on the strip. This mega-eatery would be able to be independent and stand on its own. Derek looked forward to becoming one of its best customers.

Then his memory unleashed like a dam, bursting over him. Derek was suddenly paralyzed; his entire body stiffened. Thinking that he did suffer some kind of concussion, he wondered why he just now remembered that Sunday morning phone call. Maybe it was all the weed and blow he had consumed, or else Ping, Sen, and Cynthia had worn him out. But only now did he recall the conversation. Panic and anxiety overwhelming him, he staggered as he remembered phoning Jill. What else could he have done? Derek had to find out whether Jill filed charges against him. And if she had, he would offer her anything she wanted for her to drop them. For all he cared, she could be the high priestess of the Malai Extravaganza showgirls or whatever.

But it was too late. Derek had hoped to reason with her, but there was no reasoning with the irrational. Jill had cursed him out and told him he would find it hard to sleep at night. She taunted him. "Too late, sleazebag! You can run, but you can't hide, asshole. You're going to see trouble like you never did before. The cops are already out looking for you. They're hot on your ass. And if you think I am not going to report this to the casino management, you're an even bigger fool than I thought."

Derek had ignored Jill as she screamed a tirade of shrill accusations through the phone, instead focusing on caressing Ping and Sen who had still been in bed by his side.

But Jill continued, "I not only filed assault charges, but you also have a rape hanging over you. There's a warrant out for your arrest right now."

Derek still had his pride and he was through with her lies. "I am not going to take any more of this. I never did anything to you, and you know that. Just try to prove it, bitch! I don't know why you won't let it go. I can make it *all* happen for you if you just relax. I will make sure you make it and not only that, I'll make sure you're the lead dancer in the whole damn show. I'll have you crowned the Queen, and you know what comes with that. You would get the choicest dance roles. You wouldn't just be wearing more bling and feathers on your head; honey, you'll be making more money than you ever dreamed of. How does that sound? What's so hard for you to understand? You could have it all. Just stop running your mouth off to the cops and drop that bullshit rape and assault rap and it's all yours. Do you get that? You know it never happened, but deep down, maybe you wish it had. Don't you? Because isn't that what sluts like you really want?"

There had been a long silence. Derek wished he could rewind the conversation and start over.

"I can make it on my own. I don't need your sorry ass. Besides, you won't even have your job, Mr. Entertainment Director. You're so done at the Malai. The cops are going to be picking you up in no time and you know wearing an orange jumpsuit just isn't your scene. And now, thanks to your little call, I might also go to the cops and tell them you tried to bribe me on top of everything else. I'm letting them know you're back in town."

Derek responded sarcastically, "You don't even know where I am, bitch!" Now he felt threatened. There was nothing left to say. This little slag had control over him and there was nothing he could do or say that would change her mind. Any further talk was useless. Slamming the phone down hard, it aggravated his already sore hand.

Derek thought back to when he called in sick to work on Sunday. He revisited the scene in his mind. They'd treated his bogus flu excuse with abject skepticism. Did they know something? Had Jill already reported him to HR? He had come close to asking for Jill's number until he remembered that it was somewhere in his messy wallet. He'd slipped it in there after Jill first interviewed with him. He didn't know why she impressed him the way she had. It must have been the tawdry little turn she had done for him in his office.

Walking at a brisk pace, it was almost as if Derek was hoping his swift steps could erase what happened. He knew he had to disappear entirely or else. His walk turned into a trot that took him past the construction site of the new restaurant. There were bulldozers, caterpillars, backhoes, and all kinds of workers wearing orange safety vests. A cloud of dust obscured the scene and signalmen with stop signs controlled the passing traffic. For a moment, Derek forgot about his present problems and envisioned a time when the restaurant was complete and he was enjoying elegant dinners there.

Then he saw the lights of a patrol car coming toward him. He stood frozen for a moment and turned to run the other way. But the lights from another patrol car were coming at him from that direction too. He heard the sound of sirens squealing over the noise of the construction. It was piercing. The LVPD had him cornered. Instinctively, Derek ran. He sprinted into the dust cloud of the construction area against the frantic objection of the workers. One of the patrol cars followed him onto the site. Out of the corner of his eye, he caught a glimpse of yellow swinging toward him. Something hard slammed his body. It knocked him to the ground on his back like a ragdoll. In a daze, he looked up into the dusty sky, unable to move. Through the haze, he saw the steel teeth of the earthmover descend on him in slow motion. He tried to move but was paralyzed with fear; his screams echoed back to him as the steel bucket sliced into his body like a juicy steak. The monster basket scooped up his body along with a half-ton of desert dirt and dumped it into the bed of a waiting dump truck.

The dozer operator never realized he had gutted Derek Martin until the horrified policeman who had followed Derek onto the site, rammed his cruiser into the backhoe, its red lights and siren still maniacally piercing the dusty air.

It had all been a gruesome accident, but Derek Martin's life was over.

ST LUKE'S 24-HOUR

EMERGENCY CLINIC

Nadine took Roy to the St. Luke's 24-hour Emergency Clinic on Paradise Road where Roy explained his symptoms to the attending physician. The doctor ordered a complete battery of blood tests and recommended Roy undergo a CT scan to check for bleeding in his brain. Roy was adamantly opposed to that, so after asking a few questions and having Roy perform a series of coordination tests, the doctor concluded he had not suffered a stroke, but just a debilitating migraine. However, the doctor warned him that he could suffer lingering effects and recommended several days of dark quiet and bed rest. Roy thought the doctor was overly cautious.

Roy was relieved to learn it was just a migraine and not some strange evil concoction mixed for him by a bartender intent on killing him. In his pain, he was sure he had been poisoned. He imagined himself the victim of any number of assassination plots even though he couldn't think of a single reason why someone would want to rub him out unless it was a case of mistaken identity.

As the pain began to subside, Roy's imagination finally stopped inventing bizarre conspiracies against himself. Maybe he'd been watching one too many spy movies like *The Bourne Identity*. Or perhaps paranoia was just one of the symptoms of extreme migraines.

As they left the clinic, Roy discovered his eyes were still sensitive to the blazing desert daylight and the ordeal left him weak and listless. Nadine opened the passenger door of the red Ferrari, and helping Roy get into it, told him, "You're coming home with me until you get better."

Roy tried to refuse, saying, "Thanks, but I'll be okay. I just need to lay down for a while. Besides, I don't want to impose on you."

But Nadine was adamant. "I won't take no for an answer. You heard the doctor say several days of peace and quiet. Besides, I'm driving and this car is heading back to The Carrington Palace." Roy didn't have the strength to object.

Roy stayed with Nadine at The Carrington where she played nurse and mother to him, doing everything she could to make him comfortable. That first afternoon, Nadine put him into her bed, pulled the drapes to darken the room, and left him to sleep. Immediately, Roy fell into a deep slumber, unaware that Nadine had looked in on him several times during the night. The next morning, Roy came out into the living room and announced that he was feeling much better and wouldn't burden her any longer. But Nadine ignored him, insisting that Roy stay until her doctor said he was well enough to go. Roy agreed, but only if he could sleep on the couch. He wasn't about to let Nadine give up her room. She had the maid make up the couch into a bed and arranged for the hotel doctor to come up and examine him. When the doctor recommended another day of rest for Roy, Nadine continued to dote on him throughout the day.

When he wasn't sleeping, they spent hours together talking and learning about one another. Roy told Nadine everything about himself. He explained his relationship, or lack thereof, with Mindy and regaled her with tales of his and Leroy's adventure coming out to Las Vegas and of his dream to open his own country-western dance hall. All he had to do was win the contest at the Wild Bill. Nadine listened intently and occasionally told him something of herself, always being careful to avoid the obvious question about how she could afford the luxury she was living in.

Another unexpected yet pleasant surprise for him was Nadine's two young children, Robert and Dorothy. Robert was seven years old and had already affectionately attached himself to Roy. He followed Roy around the suite constantly and was never without his toy toolbox. He asked Roy if he would help him build a tree house with it. Dorothy was five and strongly resembled her mother in both looks and personality. Green eyes and a sassy demeanor, she too was taken with Roy and called him "Mr. Roy."

When the time came and Roy was well enough to leave, Dorothy ran into her room and hid under her bed in a tearful tantrum. Robert held up his toy hammer and asked Roy when they could build their tree house. Nadine tried to explain to him that he wasn't living in Wheaton, Illinois anymore. Bending over to hug her son, she told him, "Someday we'll have a house with a big tree in the backyard, and Mr. Roy can come and help you build it."

Roy agreed. "You know what, Robert? We can build a great big treehouse two stories high! And we'll put a lookout tower on it. We can even make furniture for it. So, you just hang on. The next time I see you, I'll bring you a brand-new tool kit. Would you like that?" Robert seemed satisfied and his brown eyes grew two sizes larger. He high-fived Roy and said, "See ya. It was nice knowing ya!"

Amused at Robert's farewell, Nadine hid her smile with her hand and tried to sound serious. "Why Robert, you are demonstrating good manners to Mr. Roy." Then in a somewhat stern voice, Nadine called to her daughter, "Dorothy, child, you need to stop crying and come and say goodbye to Mr. Roy."

Dorothy stalked out of her room still sobbing and holding her cherished stuffed teddy bear she had renamed "Mr. Roy." Since he'd been there the little girl had begun holding her hand to her head, pretending that she and her teddy bear were experiencing what she called, "head-hurts." Dorothy had quite the imagination. She dropped her teddy bear onto the plush white carpet saying he needed to rest because he had another headache and she asked both of them if they had a thermometer so she could take the sick bear's temperature and see if he had a fever. But what came out of her mouth next was notable. With her small outstretched hand, she shook Roy's hand and said, "Good day, sir. Good luck with your deliberating headaches. I hope your recovery goes well."

Nadine and Roy laughed aloud. "Honey, you mean debilitating," Nadine corrected her. She looked at Roy and said, "I wonder where my little Dorothy learned such a big word." Roy told the children that he looked forward to seeing them soon. Then, taking Nadine into his arms, Roy told her how grateful he was for caring for him. He kissed her for the first time.

After that, Roy and Nadine were inseparable. They had been in their own private paradise at The Carrington. For Roy, there was no debating that he wanted to marry Nadine, but he wouldn't ask her until after the dance competition. And that was something Roy planned to proceed with immediately.

While recovering, Roy had missed his appointment to audition Camille as his new dance partner. He called her and explained what had happened and they agreed to try meeting again at Wild Bill's on Friday. If they were going to prevail and take the money, they had to begin their practice sessions right away. There was still time, albeit not much. This was especially true for a dancing couple who had never taken two steps together. Roy was apprehensive and only hoped that Camille could dance as well as she could talk.

Roy thought about the events of the last few days. He'd been really happy and at ease with Nadine and her children. The time he spent with Nadine brought him much joy. And now that she was in his life, winning the grand prize became even more important to him.

CVS PHARMACY

Roy stood outside the big doors of the Wild Bill waiting for Camille. Couples and groups of people passed by talking and laughing, but no one had a red bandana wrapped around their hat. Roy glanced at his watch. Camille was late, which didn't surprise him. Perhaps she went to California to stay with her boyfriend. That would be just his luck. Roy looked at his watch again before feeling a tap on his shoulder. He turned to meet a girl wearing a red bandana on her hat and a wide smile on her face. "Why are you standing out here, cowboy?" she asked, flipping a pointed thumb behind her back. "The party is in there."

Camille was cute in her cowgirl duds. Her red bandana was more like a wide red ribbon that fell off the back brim of her bull-hide Copper Creek leather hat. It looked good on her and gave her an added flair. So far, she was meeting Roy's expectations and he thought to himself, *If she dances like she looks, we might have a chance.* He took his off hat to introduce himself and saw the ridiculous camouflage bandana wrapped around the brim of his hat. After confirming that he was indeed talking to Camille, he tore off the bandana and stuffed it into his hip pocket.

Roy led Camille to an empty table. The waitress came around and he ordered a Shiner Bock for himself and asked Camille what she wanted. She answered, "I'll have the same as you. I've never had Shiner Bock. I hope I like it."

"I was beginning to think you weren't going to show, Camille. But you were in here all along."

"Don't you remember, dummy, we were supposed to meet at the bar?"

"Hell, those damn migraines must be messing with my brain. Oh well, we're here now."

The waitress returned with their beer and Roy lifted his mug for a toast. "Here's to smooth steppin'!" Camille clinked her mug to Roy's and they began to chit-chat. And just like their first conversation, Camille did all the talking. Her mouth flapped endlessly of all sorts of things about herself. Roy had no interest in any of it. With all her chatter, he barely had the opportunity to get in any chit of his own. Finally, Roy stopped her in mid-blab and said, "Let's have a dance and see what you're made of!"

He took Camille by the hand to the center of the dance floor and they lined up for a simple boot-scoot. Counting out a beat, they began stepping to the music. They were not exactly in sync with each other. Camille seemed to be a step behind the entire song. Roy thought that maybe Camille just had a case of the nerves. But their second dance together proved to be worse than the first. Camille had no rhythm and her footwork was a web of entanglements. "Downright awful" best described Camille's dancing. It was a wonder she hadn't tripped them to the floor. Before the song was over, Roy stopped and looked frustratingly at Camille. She had lost some of her self-assuredness. Her confidence disappeared and timidity took its place.

In the middle of the third dance, Camille tripped over her own feet and would have fallen on the floor had Roy not caught her. Screaming at her over the music, he told her, "I can't take this anymore. Camille, you're a lovely woman, but you're one lousy dancer. This just isn't going to work out. You are not going to be my partner. That's for sure." Roy surprised himself with his bluntness. Generally, he tried not to cause offense, taking care to load his meaning with innocuous niceties instead of blurting out what he truly wanted to say. At least that was his modus operandi when it came to talking to women.

Camille was outraged. Abandoning any manners, she stuck her middle finger in Roy's face and told him that he had a lot of nerve. "Don't trash me, man! You're the one who can't dance. Shit, you're the most uncoordinated geek I've ever met." She pushed Roy into another couple and ran off the dance floor. Then, grabbing her bag from the table, Camille fled out of the Wild Bill.

Roy chased Camille through the big doors of the dance hall after Camille when some guy stuck out his leg and tripped him. Plunging unceremoniously onto the floor, Roy rolled on his back and lay there, staring at the ceiling. Shit, the guy just about broke Roy's already aching back which was still sore from passing out at the Vegas Rite Pharmacy. First, he had that crazy Camille stepping all over his toes and now this jackass appears out of nowhere and drops him hard on the floor. Roy tried to move but the fall twisted his back and he couldn't move to confront whoever it was that put him on the floor.

Then Camille, the woefully incompetent dancer, knelt beside Roy and helped him sit up. Camille was sobbing. Contrite, she told Roy, "I know I can't dance, but I'm sick of my job and my boyfriend. This was my chance to get rid of both. I can't stand either one. That's why I lied about being able to dance. I just had to do it to get out of my pitiful life. I saw this as my way out when you called. I bought the ticket to the dream. Can't you just teach me to dance? I promise I'll practice and do whatever it takes."

Roy looked up at her from the floor. He sure knew how to pick them. Why him? Advertising for a dance partner with a classified ad was an idiotic idea anyway. Now he was stuck. With less than three months to go until the dance contest, he's got stumble-foot Camille trying to weasel herself in as his dance partner. Rubbing his sore back, he held out his hand for her to help him up.

"Camille, I don't like it when people lie to me. I really need a competent dancer and..." Roy paused, searching for the right words. "Aw hell. Let's face it, Camille; you can't dance at all. You're a pretender." Even as he fired Camille, Roy was formulating his plan B. Psycho Mindy was the only option he had left. But before he could think any further about it, a guy with greasy hair in a muscle shirt showed up and kicked Roy hard on his knee caps.

Once again, Roy found himself pasted on the floor, writhing in pain. He thought he might pass out and this time Roy couldn't defy the odds and pick himself off the floor. It wasn't happening. All he could do was lay sprawled in a heap. With his body seizing up he began to panic. Looking up at his attacker, he realized that this was the same guy who had tripped him just moments before.

Roy screamed up from the hard floor that had become his new home, "What's your problem, asshole? If I could make it up in one piece, you'd be on life support by the time I finished dismantling your face. Who the hell are you? What's your problem?" Roy glanced at Camille and back at his assailant. Then he understood. "Camille, do you know this guy? Is this the boyfriend you're trying to dump? Is this grease-ball looney your weekend loser?"

Camille's boyfriend gave Roy the fisheye and shook his fist, warning, "I'm going to beat your ass so bad if I ever catch you with Camille again. You understand? I'll cripple you if you so much as try to text her. Are we on the same page?"

Camille interrupted his tirade. "Oh Tony, I can't believe you! Why are you following me around and how did you know I was even going to be here?" Tony answered gruffly and grabbed her arm hard. She cried out. "Stop, you're hurting me. Leave Roy alone. He was going to make me his dance partner for a dance contest coming up. The prize for the winners would have given us a lot of money and then I could buy you a boat. Baby, I swear I was only thinking about you and what would make you happy."

Tony yelled back at her sarcastically, "Yeah sure, baby. Where are we going to float a boat in Death Valley? You stupid moron."

Camille seemed wounded and replied softly, "Well, you could just move in with me here in Vegas." Greasy Tony said he might consider it if she could find him a job.

By now, Roy had managed to get off the floor with no help from either one of them. It was a chore. Straightening up was a problem, however. He had withstood a hammering attack to his already ailing back as well as a painful whack to his kneecaps and was beginning to think that Las Vegas might be a jinx for him. Roy flashed back to all the bad luck he's had since leaving Texas. Things had better start changing for him, or he might still consider booking a one-way flight back to Houston. The one immediate thing he wanted was for Camille and her boyfriend to go away. Speaking up, he told them, "Look I've got to get going. Camille, thanks for nothing. This has all been one big waste of my time. Just another miserable mistake." Hobbling away, Roy brooded, "Damn, I'm sick of this shit."

Unwilling to slink away like a whipped dog, he looked over his shoulder. Feeling cocky and pissed, he threatened Greasy Tony, "Hey pal, it's been a real pleasure. Don't even think about coming at me again. I got friends that can find you and take care of business." There was no truth to that, but Greasy Tony didn't need to know it. But then Roy thought about Leroy. That guy was always ready for a fight and wouldn't mind waving his Glock around just to scare dirtbags like Tony away. Roy imagined contracting crazy Leroy for his services if he ever ran into Tony again.

But blowing hard to Tony worked. Tony shoved Camille out of the Wild Bill without saying anything more and together they disappeared. At least they were out of his life. A crowd of onlookers had gathered around him and as Roy dusted off his pants, he told one goofy gawker wearing dark sunglasses, "Talk about two good-for-nothings. They deserve each other." Tony and Camille, now those were two deranged people Roy would like to forget.

Once again, he needed Advil. But this time it wasn't for a headache. Roy's back and knees hurt something awful. He had read somewhere that getting capped in the knees was the most painful injury you could endure. They were right. He struggled out of the Casino in search of a pharmacy. He chose the CVS Pharmacy just across from the Vegas Rite Pharmacy where he had experienced all that drama the week before. The last thing he wanted was to see all those Vegas Rite employees again. Sure, they had all been helpful and professional, but it still was embarrassing.

Roy was sick and tired of floors. His trajectory was in need of change.

ETERNAL REST FUNERAL PARLOR

Fearing an encounter with a cockroach big enough to rope and ride, Roy and Leroy fled the La Hacienda Motel within thirty-six hours of arriving in Las Vegas. After driving around for a few hours, they found a complex that rented month-to-month furnished apartments. So, they became tenants at the Geneva at the Lakes on Starboard Drive. It wasn't much of a step up from the La Hacienda, but it did boast a better class of cockroach. It had a few unpruned palm trees bordering a lake with fountains that, when they worked, spit out a limp stream of water two feet into the air. Nor was it much of a lake. It was more like a holding pond whose stagnant water was dyed a bright blue. It looked ridiculous, and to Roy, it appeared as if someone had dumped a drum of fluorescent food coloring into it.

But Leroy was impressed by the lake and told Roy, "This place has got class. No need for us to look any further. This is the place old Leroy is going to plant his flag."

Roy thought to himself, *What does he mean* us*?*

After seeing the apartment, Roy signed the rental agreement and the manager handed him the keys. Roy looked at Leroy like he was almost sad to say goodbye. "Well man, I guess that's it. Good luck. Have a safe trip back to Houston."

"Hell, boy. Back at you. But I'm staying right here. I need my own place with a sweet little señorita to share my crib with." Leroy turned to the manager and said, "Give me one of those apartments too."

Leroy wasn't hard to find. His apartment was on the other side of the complex on the second floor. He complained incessantly about how his porch faced the afternoon sun, and he couldn't even use it because of the scorching heat during the day. "How did you get the good location while I got stuck with Hell's back porch? On top of that, take a look out my bedroom window." Roy looked out. "See that?" asked Leroy.

Roy wasn't sure what he was supposed to see. "See what? All I see is the back of a building with a loading dock attached to it."

"What the hell is wrong with you? Did you burn out your eyes staring at the sun? Look at that big neon sign in the front of the building. It's a damn funeral parlor! Eternal Rest, my ass. Ain't no way those corpses going to get any rest with that damn sign blinking all night long like a slot machine jackpot. I might buy some binoculars to look at some lady stiffs if I get lonely. No shit, man. Who knows, she might be just the one I'm looking for. Hey, I wouldn't have to put up with any backtalk." Leroy had another complaint. "Management keeps telling me I'm first on the list for an apartment on the other side like you, but since I tried to score with the super's wife, Zoe, they put me on hold. And now I got nowhere to go to drink my drink. Brother, my porch is like sitting in a pizza oven all day. And at night, there's nothing but funeral services and depressed people dressed in black lined up to check out the stiffs."

Roy's reply was always the same. "Just think, in the winter, you won't have any heating bills."

Leroy would look at him incredulously. "This is Vegas, brother. We're in the middle of the desert. Winter lasts a friggin' weekend!"

Roy had a plan, and it involved Leroy. That alone probably indicated that he was half-crazy. But if Roy was serious about entering the dance competition, then he would have to try to negotiate peace with Mindy, again. Ever since her fight with Nadine, whenever Roy visited Leroy's apartment for a few beers, Mindy would flee the room in a fit of rage. Leroy would look at Roy, shrug, drink his beer, and say, "You hurt her, brother, and now she's with me." And frankly, Roy didn't blame her.

After the melee at the Wild Bill, Leroy had taken Mindy back to his apartment where they spent the night together. The next morning, Mindy moved in with him. After that, the only time Roy saw either of them was when he went to Leroy's apartment which, given Mindy's frostiness, was very infrequent.

The morning after the fight, Roy had knocked on Leroy's door to find out what happened after he and Mindy left. Leroy had greeted him in his boxer shorts and let him in. Roy heard some pots banging in the kitchen and then Mindy calling out, "Leroy baby, how do you like your coffee?"

"Black, honey. I like it black. But I don't need sugar, baby. I'm sweet enough without it," Leroy had answered her, motioning for Roy to sit on the couch. Leroy sat in the chair across from him.

Moments later, Mindy walked out of the kitchen carrying two mugs of steaming coffee. She lurched a bit when she saw Roy sitting there, causing some coffee to slosh out of the cups and spill onto the aging carpet. But Mindy recovered quickly and sat in Leroy's lap without spilling another drop. She handed Leroy his cup and kissing him, turned to Roy and said, "After Leroy rescued me from that nasty chick Nadine, Leroy is *my* man now." She kissed Leroy again, gave Roy the finger, and stomped into the bedroom, slamming the door behind her. That was the last time Mindy acknowledged his presence.

Still, he had to do something to convince her to partner with him again. Roy needed a different strategy, a more subtle attack on Mindy's flank, so she wouldn't be aware of what was happening. And that's where he needed to enlist Leroy in the effort. Leroy could trick Mindy into being Roy's partner; Roy was certain of that. Roy just had to figure out how to con Leroy into doing it for him. But that would be easy as long as there was a little something in it for Leroy. Roy knew Mindy required coddling and knew that it would be better to leave that part to Leroy.

Roy planned to invest his half of the grand prize winnings into opening a dance hall and bar similar to Trudy's Roadhouse back in Houston. Vegas already had a Wild Bills; what Sin City needed now was some authentic Texan culture. With the prize money providing the necessary investment capital combined with the street credibility of winning the biggest title in the country-line dance world, Roy would have what he needed to realize his dream. "I'll be able to call the shots from now on," he said aloud as he smiled and fantasized about seeing his name on the Wall of Fame in the Wild Bill Hickok Dance Hall.

Leroy was well aware of his idea and not a day passed without Leroy begging Roy to include him in his plan. "We could be partners, man. We'll blow a hole in Wild Bill's. Shit, I can see it now, brother," as he waved his hand through the air in a wide arc, "Leroy's Line Dancing Company." All that did was irritate Roy, but he knew Leroy did it on purpose. Hell, he repeated the same damn thing every time Roy brought up the subject. "Man, I just love rattling your cage," Leroy crooned tauntingly.

Roy responded, "I was thinking more along the lines of 'Roy's Fine Line Dancing Club.' Leroy Hart, Janitor! Who asked you anyway? You can't line dance to save your life even though you spun a good story. Stick to cabbing, but even that needs some work."

But there was something true about their Abbot and Costello shtick, and they both knew it. Roy was serious about his plans for the club and equally so was Leroy about becoming a partner. Thinking Leroy was nothing but a liability, Roy always discouraged the idea. Trouble skulked about Leroy, just waiting for the right moment to pay you a visit. But now, Roy needed Mindy, and for that to happen, Roy needed Leroy. So, if it was necessary to ask Leroy to be his partner in his yet-to-form company, well, he would have to accept that as the cost of doing business.

Roy grabbed the six-pack of Shiner Bock sitting on his kitchen counter and left his apartment, intent on implementing phase-one of his plan. Even though the beer was barely below room temperature, it would help to prime Leroy. Since leaving Houston, both of them missed being able to toss down a Shiner Bock, or two, or three. Roy had stopped at every package store he passed looking for his Shiner Bock, but was rolling snake-eyes until one day when he walked into a small store hidden away in some side street called Beer Belly's. He had finally rolled his seven and was now a regular customer buying his daily ration of Shiner Bock like some stumble-down alcoholic. Roy was a lot of things, but being an alcoholic was not on that list. He was unusually disciplined. However, he did consider himself an enthusiastic devotee of the social lubricant; it reminded him fondly of Texas.

He tried to hurry across the complex and up the stairs to Leroy's apartment, but his knees hurt and would not cooperate thanks to Greasy Tony's footwork. With some difficulty, Roy limped up the stairs and knocked on the door of apartment #222. The door opened and he found himself face to face with Mindy. This was not the way he had imagined his diplomatic overture to begin. Her expression told him that her anger had not subsided in the least. In fact, maybe it had grown. Forcing him to stand outside like some door-to-door salesman, Roy began to think that maybe things between them were beyond repair.

"Oh, it's you! I wonder what you could want. If I didn't know better, I'd bet you came to beg me to dance with you. But you're all washed up, and you know it. First off, you can't dance if your life was on the line and you're nothing but a two-bit shit in so many ways. Hell, let me count the ways...." Mindy was enjoying every bit of it and continued to excoriate him with every thought that came into her head. Roy stood quietly in front of Mindy like a guilty prisoner hearing a judge recount his crimes before pronouncing sentence.

Fortunately for Roy, her tirade was interrupted by Leroy. "Hey, hey, hey! What's going on out here, Mindy-honey? They probably could hear your big mouth over at the funeral parlor. Hell's bells, baby, you're loud enough to wake the stiffs up from their big sleep." He looked out at Roy. "Hey man, what's going on? You better not be ripping on my little honey pot Mindy, or I'll have to do some ripping of my own."

Then Leroy saw Roy holding the six-pack of Shiner Bock beer and let out a loud whoop. "You found some Shiner! Man, are we back in Texas or what?" He pulled Mindy out of Roy's way and said, "Anybody bringing me glad tidings of Shiner Bock is more than welcome. Come in, my good man. Come on in and check out what the Little Lady's done to my digs. Where the hell did you find Shiner in Vegas?"

Roy smiled as he stepped into the apartment past a seething Mindy. "Ever since we got here, top on my to-do-list was to find out where they stashed the Shiner Bock."

Signaling for Roy to have a seat on his oversized leather couch, Leroy sat across from him in a sky-blue armchair. Between them was a very modern-looking glass coffee table. A huge poster from the 1980s of a very young Madonna with a hole burned through her left nipple hung on the wall behind Leroy. Roy said sarcastically, "Hey man, I just can't help myself, but I just got to say: I love what you've done with the place."

Leroy pointed up at the poster when he noticed Roy's staring at it. "It wasn't my idea to have that no-talent, hoe-bag stinking up my wall. I got high and tried to burn her titty with a joint. She ain't my type and she can't sing. Mindy likes her, but Mindy ain't got no taste except when it comes to me."

Mindy was still standing by the door, and Roy could see her temper mushrooming. Leroy tried to diffuse her before she detonated. "Now, you just calm down, Mindy, and have yourself a brewski. Either that or go light up a joint and smoke yourself silly, my sweet little honeysuckle." Mindy rolled her eyes and told Leroy to go fuck himself.

"Oh, come on, baby. You know you are my one and only. Now, darling, don't use that kind of mouth around our good company. Remember, you eat with that, dearest."

Roy was about to laugh when Mindy launched into more vitriol. "I wouldn't take a beer from that snake if you paid me. He's probably poisoned them."

Ever so tactfully Leroy once again told Mindy to take a hike. "Honey, you just got to stop working yourself into a snit and let me and Roy have a beer party. You go take yourself a little happy pill and have yourself a chill. You got your panties in a knot, and you've just got to untie them." Mindy fumed into the bedroom and violently slammed the door behind her.

Turning his attention to Roy, Leroy said, "You just got to know how to handle women. So, what's up, brother? Tell me what's on your mind."

Roy opened a bottle of Shiner and handed it to Leroy. He opened another for himself and said, "Bottoms up!" Leroy gestured a toast with his bottle and took a long drink. Roy began executing his plan. "Remember how you wanted to be my partner when the time came for me to open up my own dance hall? Well, I got to thinking and I want to cut you in."

Leroy was curious. "Why now? I thought my stuff stank and you didn't want anything to do with it unless, of course, it involved riding around in my tricked-out taxi. I'm not getting it."

Roy inhaled deeply and held his breath like he was smoking a joint. Only he wasn't, because Roy never smoked pot. He looked at Leroy for a moment and wondered if he was about to make the biggest mistake of his life. Finally exhaling, he said, "Well Leroy, it goes like this; I do have some conditions." Pausing again, Roy took a long drink of his beer.

Impatient, Leroy snapped back somewhat defensively, "Have at it, my brother. What conditions?"

Roy leaned forward and lowered his voice, so as not to let Mindy hear any of what he had to say. "I need Mindy. Together, we could take that prize. I need to have her get over it all fast and come back. She hates me and you need to wage an intervention. I need that money for the club and that's where you come in. If you want to be in business with me, then you need to help get Mindy to be my partner again. Make it happen, Leroy, and I'll bring you in. But do it fast, because time is flying by. We have less than three months now to be ready."

Rising from his armchair, Leroy murmured something obscene under his breath. "Roy, I get where you are coming from, but you just got to remember that Mindy can be a hard woman. She's all mine, but that's a load of baggage you heaped on her. I'd have to do a lot to get her to walk that line again. The dance line, that is."

Roy turned serious. "Would it be that difficult to bring her back? You can do it. You've got to do something. It's my turn to beg and now I'm doing it. Tell her to meet me at Wild Bill's tomorrow at eight sharp. Do whatever it takes."

Roy stood, emptying a full beer. His eyes focused on the *Las Vegas Gazette* lying on the coffee table. It was open to the sports section where the news was all about the San Antonio Antelopes and their quarterback Rebel Rebenack. He had taken them to the AFC conference playoffs for the first time in the history of the franchise. This Rebel Rebenack was beginning to be noticed nationwide, and Texans took great pride in him.

He said to Leroy, "Can you believe how good the Antelopes are this year? I've gotta say I miss being in Texas 'cause I would be going nuts with the rest of the crazy fans."

Leroy had a quick answer. "Let's fly out to Phoenix if they make it all the way. Man, I sure could handle partying at a Super Bowl. Good times. You in? Even better, we'll take my cab and get there in about six or seven hours. Hell, I won't even turn the meter on for this trip. Dude, you'll get a free ride all the way to the game, except for the gas. The buck stop's there. Maxi the Taxi needs a good workout anyway. How 'bout it? You game? Pun intended." Leroy appeared pleased with himself to have concocted the plan and Roy could tell he was already mapping out the route down to Phoenix in his mind. Now, he pushed Roy for an answer.

Roy hesitated. The idea of riding around with Leroy in his cab with another one of his half-baked ideas brought back a plethora of memories. Their road trip from Houston had been a series of perilously threatening, harebrained escapades combined with a near miss with the law. Opening up another bottle of beer, Roy took another big swallow, hiccupped, and replied, "I don't know. It's something to think about. I'll let you know."

Leroy mimicked Roy's drinking style and shot-gunned his beer. But instead of hiccupping, he followed it up with a loud belch. "Be there or be square. Is that what you want me to tell her; some corny shit like that?"

Roy smiled and said, "Yes, that's part of it." Then the smile left his face and he became serious, "There's just one more thing I need you to get her to do."

"And what's that?" Leroy asked skeptically.

"You've got to get Mindy to call Nadine and apologize to her for starting that cat fight."

Leroy's jaw dropped. "*Whoa brother*. Getting her to dance with you is one thing, but getting her to apologize? I'm good, but even I ain't no rainmaker. Just how do expect me to do that?"

"I don't know, buy her some flowers, or some jewelry, or something. You'll have her eating out of your hand. Do what you have to do, partner," he said with an over-the-top Texas drawl for effect. "If anyone can do it, you can."

Leroy thought for a moment and then accepted the challenge. "Consider it done. Mindy will be there tomorrow at eight sharp with all her bells and whistles on and she'll have patched it up with Nadine by then too.

"Thanks Leroy. I'll leave it in your hands then."

Roy moved to leave when Leroy announced, "But we're not done just yet, brother...."

Exasperated, Roy turned to Leroy and asked, "Now what?"

"Well, Roy, my new partner, how about I grab one of your suds for the road or should I say one for my couch." Snatching the bottle from Roy's hand, Leroy brought it up to the air for a toast. "Cheers. Here's to Leroy and Roy's line dancing club." He winked. "I'm messing with you man. That ain't gonna work 'cause that makes us sound like a couple of fruits." Then he joked, "That might make Mindy mad and the last thing we need is for Mindy to go on the warpath again. Just don't go throwing any more shade on Mon Cheri. Both of us need to stay on her sunny side."

Roy laughed and agreed, telling Leroy he'd see him at the Wild Bill.

As Roy walked towards the door, Leroy slapped him on the back and quipped, "And about the Super Bowl. If you got to think about me giving you a freebie to Phoenix and want to bail, well then that's okay because I can barely stand riding your ugly mug around now. You just ain't pretty enough."

Roy shuffled from the apartment leaving it to Leroy to work on Mindy. He accomplished what he had set out to do and felt better for the wear of it. Joking to himself, he said he wasn't feeling much of anything and that was good for his kneecaps. All it took was his secret weapon, Shiner Bock. It had been his ammo all along; it always led to good times and happy endings.

ABADDON'S DINER

Roy was waiting at the bar when he saw Mindy enter the hall at Wild Bill Hickok's. Mindy was alone and didn't look too happy to be there. Still, she was there, just as Leroy had promised. Roy waved her over and Mindy reluctantly joined him. Looking at him suspiciously, she said, "Okay Roy, you win. I'll be your partner, but don't go breaking my heart again. First, you up and leave me in Houston and then you lead me on to get me here. This old heart of mine can only take so much abuse. Anyway, it doesn't matter now because I'm in love with Leroy. So, let's get to dancing and take the money."

Roy was relieved Mindy wasn't going to let her feelings for him prevent them from attending to the practical matter of winning one hundred thousand dollars. Roy was dying to ask Mindy about Nadine but decided against it. He was afraid to upset the fragile truce they now had. Then, almost as an afterthought, Mindy announced, "Oh, and by the way, I patched things up with your girl Nadine. I like her. We had a good long talk, mostly about you."

Roy pulled Mindy into his arms and bear hugged her. "Mindy, you're the best."

Speaking like a coach, he warned her, "Everything from now on is going to be hard work and then more hard work. Let's get busy. Mindy, my incomparable colleague, we'll dance until our feet fall off." Roy explained their practice schedule and Mindy agreed to it. "Well then, let's get started." He led her by the hand to the center of the dance floor and they waited for the music to begin.

From the moment the first note played, they attacked the dance floor. They suffered a few missed steps at first, but soon they were back to moving as fluidly as they used to back at Trudy's in Houston. Roy led and established their pace while controlling the length of their stride with Mindy responding nimbly to Roy's direction. They both wore cowboy boots and together performed difficult dance steps and odd turn combinations like the wizard, the sailor, and cross-chasse, all in perfect synergy. They created a sensation as they moved across the floor melding various dance steps like Stroll Along Cha-Cha, Country Slide, and the Texas Slide into one fluid motion.

Mindy's favorite dance was the Pretty Baby Line Dance that they performed flawlessly to the song "High-Class Lady" by the Lennerockers. In deference to Roy and Mindy, the other dancers formed a circle around them as a show of respect for their exceptional dancing finesse and clapped enthusiastically after each dance, especially after finishing what Roy and Mindy considered their signature song, "Wagon Wheel" by Darius Rucker.

Another reason why Roy liked Darius Rucker was that he was a huge fan of Hootie and the Blowfish, of which Rucker was the lead singer. All things Darius Rucker helped put him and Mindy in a good mood which helped cement their dancing reunion. It was as if they had never stopped dancing together. They committed themselves to practicing every day from then on. They were, at the very least, a dancing coupledom once again.

After dancing for hours, they left the Wild Bill and headed for a restaurant a few miles off the strip called Abaddon's Diner. Leroy had texted Mindy for them to meet him there when they were done. Abaddon's was Leroy's favorite place to eat in all of Las Vegas. It was known for its red velvet pancakes. But like any self-respecting diner, Abaddon's menu was as long as a Russian novel and boasted exotic delights like frog legs.

Abaddon's design was an excessive amalgam of diner decor from all different eras. The restaurant facade resembled the long and shiny metallic Streamliner railroad cars from the forties. The red Naugahyde bench seats and tableside jukeboxes were reminiscent of the soda shop days of the fifties. The long service counter and stainless swivel stools were the first things Roy noticed upon entry. But the centerpiece of Abaddon's was the enormous art deco-style crystal chandelier that hung in the middle of the dining room. It was an elegantly excessive decoration that dumbfounded Roy whenever he walked into the diner.

There, swiveling on one of the counter stools, was Leroy gorging on a plate of jumbo fried shrimp. It was two in the morning which made no difference because like the rest of Las Vegas, Abaddon's never closed. Abaddon's made it possible for everyone to enjoy a sumptuous dish at any time of the day or night. Mindy and Roy joined Leroy at the counter.

Leroy always finished his meal off with a five-layer chocolate cake. For Leroy, the diner made him happy; he was simple like that.

The party of three ate so much that Roy had to loosen his belt. He patted his stomach and smiled at Mindy, saying, "From now on, Mindy, we need to put ourselves on a strict training diet." Mindy agreed and they set their cowboy hats on the prize.

Leroy laughed at them and declared, "Not me, man. I'm ordering another piece of cake to go!"

CHEVRON STATION

Nadine was awakened in the middle of the night by a grumbling stomach. She tossed about in her bed trying to get back to sleep, but it was no use. Nadine was restless, hungry, and longed for Roy. She missed having him around. They had grown close in the days since nursing him back to health. She knew she was falling in love with Roy and was even okay with him dancing with Mindy; but only after Mindy offered her profuse apologies to Nadine. Afterwards, she became their biggest cheerleader. Yet despite her growing feelings for Roy, Nadine was still reticent about revealing her financial situation, and Roy never asked her about it. And for now, that was the way Nadine wanted it.

Nadine got up and wandered through the quiet suite toward the nanny Ethel's bedroom. She had come highly recommended by The Carrington concierge when Nadine first checked in; Ethel had not disappointed her. She was fantastic with Robert and Dorothy, and the kids liked her so much that they began calling her "Nanny Eth." Ethel also assisted Nadine with other things like cooking and helping out with various errands. The suite included a well-equipped kitchenette that Ethel used to create tasty meals and snacks that were good enough to serve in a restaurant. It was like getting room service only better.

Knocking gently on Ethel's bedroom door, Nadine waited impatiently for the nanny to respond. Nadine knocked again and a sleepy Ethel slowly opened her door. Still in a drowsy stupor, she looked frightened. "Miss Nadine! Is something wrong? Is everything all right?"

"Everything's fine, Ethel. I'm just hungry and I'm going to get something to eat at Abaddon's Diner. I'll be back in a few hours. I just didn't want you to worry if you or the kids were looking for me. I can't help it; I'm starving, Nanny Eth."

"Why, Miss Nadine, I'd be happy to fix you something here. I could scramble you up a nice plate of eggs or anything you like. How about a western omelet? That's my specialty. I used to fix 'em for the rodeo boys when they came to town."

"That's all right, Eth. I need to get out for a little bit."

Ethel looked over at the clock on her nightstand and then back at Nadine, this time with a quizzical look. "Well, okay, ma'am, if you say so.

Five minutes later, Nadine was out the door and on her way to her favorite diner. The Ferrari needed gas so Nadine detoured to the nearby Chevron station a few blocks from the hotel. The staff at the Chevron always made a big deal over Nadine's car and treated her like royalty. No matter who was working the register, the cashier always fussed over her and occasionally offered her a fresh donut that was reserved for the staff. After filling up, Nadine headed for Abaddon's, already savoring the taste of the chicken and waffles that she was going to order.

As soon as Nadine entered the diner, she was surprised to see Roy, Leroy, and Mindy sitting at the counter. Behind them were chrome-rimmed shelves filled with bottles of fine liquor, beer, and wine. The red lights that framed the liquor cabinet reflected off the metal into the bottles, so they appeared to glow from within. It was an alluring sight and put Nadine in the mood to order a fancy drink with her chicken and waffles. Even though it was late, tonight was going to be a good night.

When Mindy saw Nadine, she spun off her stool and ran up to Nadine to give her a warm hug. Nadine returned the gesture and it looked to Roy as if they were best friends forever.

Nadine sat down next to Roy. He was in a happy mood. Putting his arm around her, he told her they were there to celebrate. "It's like we are better than ever. Mindy and I were literally cutting the rug!"

"Yeah, and it's a damn good rug too! No junky rugs here!" Mindy shouted with too loud a laugh. To Nadine, it seemed like Mindy had had a few too many.

"You should see us dance. We make one hell of a team. If we keep this up, I don't see how we don't come home with the big bucks." Roy was excited and Nadine was happy for him.

Nadine ordered a plate of chicken and waffles but felt funny when it came, because she ended up eating alone as the others had already finished their meals. Self-conscious, she politely ate, aware that the others were watching her. Still, their gawking gazes didn't prevent her from cleaning the last crumb on her plate and smacking her lips in contentment. It was now well past three in the morning. Leroy jumped up and grabbed Mindy, saying, "We need to get, girl. It's time to run. Roy and Nadine, we'll catch you later." The two lovebirds flew out of the diner and headed back to their "love cage." At least that's what Mindy called their apartment at Geneva at the Lakes.

Roy put his arm around Nadine and hugged her. "I'm glad we're finally alone," he said. He became serious and replaced his smile with a sober expression. He stared at Nadine until she turned away from his penetrating eyes. "Nadine, I've got some important questions on my mind. I would say they are some serious ones that I need to speak with you about. It's been bugging me. I know so little about you."

Nadine squirmed uncomfortably on her stool. She had an idea about what Roy meant by "serious questions." Frankly, she was surprised Roy hadn't asked about her lavish living before this. There she was riding around in a two hundred thousand-dollar Ferrari and staying in the swankiest hotel in Vegas in a suite costing more than fifteen hundred dollars a night, and there hadn't been even one question about where her money had come from. Not even a hint of it. The closest Roy had come to mentioning it was when they were in her Ferrari, and even then, all he said was, "Nadine, you bought yourself one hell of a machine. What a ride! I like your ride!"

Roy stumbled around for the words. "Nadine, I think I love you and think we should get married. But there are a few things I've just got to know."

At first, Nadine was thrilled that Roy wanted to marry her. But the condition he put on his proposal, "just a few things I need to know first," filled her with uneasiness and an odd sense of déjà vu. She had played this scene before with Frank. As she recalled, when Frank asked her to marry him, he too had some things on his mind.

The chicken and waffles were beginning to churn inside her and Nadine rubbed her stomach hoping to calm it down. "Well, what is it you need to know, Roy?" She pretended to be ready to answer anything he asked, but behind that facade, Nadine was pensive and nervous. If Roy was going to ask about her money, was she prepared to tell him the truth?

Nadine wasn't sure she wanted to reveal anything about herself, at least not now. Not here. What would he think once he found out she was worth millions from her first husband? It would change everything between them. Roy might not like the idea of being a "kept man."

During the time he had stayed with her to recover from his episode, Nadine had learned a few things about Roy. After three days, he had started getting fidgety and was always looking for some way to help around the suite. Somehow, he felt guilty about having to rely on Nadine to care for him through his migraine ordeal. She had sensed that. He wanted to be the provider in their relationship. She knew this about Roy for sure. On their dates, he never let her pay for anything. It was one of the traits she liked about him. Still, there were questions that needed to be asked and answered eventually, only not tonight.

Nadine sat waiting for him to ask his questions when Roy lunged violently at her, knocking her off the stool. He pushed her under the counter and shoved her head flat on the floor with his foot. Gunshots reverberated through the diner followed by the sound of shattering glass. There was more commotion in the front part of the diner. Nadine heard

someone scream and then more gunshots popping like firecrackers. Roy
threw his body over Nadine and wrapped his arm tightly around her,
wedging her between the counter stools. She struggled to free herself, but
Roy pushed her head down into the floor and whispered for her to lay
quiet and still. More shots. More screams and moaning. What was
happening? Paralyzed by fear, Nadine was going into shock.

Unlike Nadine, Roy was alert like a hunted buck. His eyes were
wide and all his senses elevated. Looking toward the front of the
restaurant, he saw three thugs in battle fatigues wearing outlandish latex
masks over their heads. One had an evil clown mask while another a
horse-head mask. The third sported a sickening white zombie mask with
one of its eyes dangling out of its socket. Several of its teeth were
missing. Two of them brandished handguns and the third carried a sack
and waved a high-powered hunting rifle with a scope in the air. Roy
forced Nadine behind him, trying to position his body as best he could
between her and them.

The clown gunman suddenly blurted out, "We're gonna blow
this dump sky-high. But first, we're gonna use your fat motherfucking
heads for target practice."

The horse mask cracked that the food was so bad it made him
want to kill someone. Pointing his pistol near the cashier's head, he
taunted, "I don't like no acid influx." Pulling the trigger, he squeezed out
a few rounds past the cashier's head that blasted more bottles and
glassware from the shelves behind him. Then he moved to the bar for
some more action. Shooting out a few bottles sitting on the top shelf of
the bar, they laughed as they watched the glass shatter, spilling out their
insides onto the floor.

Shouting and intimidating the innocent diners into stunned
silence, they turned back toward David the cashier. The first two thugs
trained their pistols inches from the poor guy's head, demanding the cash
from the register.

"Give me all you got, or you're gonna have your brains plastered
all over the wall." They tossed him a bag to empty the register into. As
David the cashier opened the drawer and dumped its contents into the
bag, they laughed and spewed vile expletives. As he handed it to the
gunmen, Roy noticed David's hand reach under the counter ever so slyly.
Roy hoped it was the panic button to alert the police. While the gunmen
focused on David's hand holding the bag full of money, David pressed
the button without the gunmen noticing.

As Roy climbed over Nadine to shield her better, he realized they were as good as dead lying there on the floor. A woman who had been sitting at the counter closer to the cash register began to wail with fear. She got onto her knees and began shrieking. This brought out the third gunman's wrath.

"Shut the fuck up, bitch! I can't stand your squealing." He walked over to her, raised his Sig Sauer, and pumped two rounds into her body. She went silent; her body slumped forward on the floor. Her life faded and she was soon gone, leaving a pool of red to form around her lifeless body.

Roy said a prayer for her. Fearing the worst, he wondered what it would take to get himself and Nadine out the front door. How he wished he had Leroy's Glock right now. His heart was pounding, but he had to stay alert and couldn't do anything stupid. He could only hope that the police were on their way. The thugs had their money and now they had their blood; maybe they would just leave.

But they weren't done yet. These murderers had more on their agenda. Cackling, they took turns shooting out Abaddon's magnificent chandelier so that glass and plaster flew everywhere. All three found this amusing and kept shooting until finally, the famous art deco fixture came crashing onto the tables below.

The zombie mask said he needed more action than "this motherfucking chandelier" and aimed his rifle at one elderly man shaking and quivering in the far corner of the diner. Roy closed his eyes as he listened to the elderly man desperately pleading for his life. "Please, don't do this. I want to live." It was too late. The sick killer marked him and shot him in the forehead. Roy thought about charging them when Nadine began to move. He had to keep her from doing anything to get their attention. He whispered for her to stay quiet and perfectly still.

Suddenly there was an enormous explosion accompanied by the crashing of glass from the restaurant's front window. A team of swat commandos as well as an impressive force of men in blue rained into the diner. Armed with laser-sighted assault rifles, the gunmen were no match for the task force and the police. There was a brief flurry of gunfire and the three masked men lay dead.

Good had prevailed, and evil had been taken down.

Roy stood up and helped an ashen-faced Nadine to her feet. She buried her face in his chest and sobbed quietly. When Nadine found the courage to look around the diner, she shuddered. Regaining some composure, she told Roy they needed to do what they could to help the others get through this horrific ordeal.

Roy agreed. For some reason, his concern was for the owner of the diner. Roy assumed that Mr. Abaddon named it after himself, but he couldn't be sure. He was convinced, however, that the owner had worked hard for years to build up a great business with a reputation for great food and service only to have it all destroyed in the span of ten minutes. Abaddon's would forever be known as a house of tragedy that had seen the slaughter of two innocent victims. And for the survivors of this traumatic event, their horrifying memories would haunt them forever. Roy doubted that Abaddon's could ever be the same.

People gathered at the entrance and watched in numbed silence as EMS wheeled away the two murdered diners. They had done nothing but come in for a late-night meal before they went on with the rest of their lives. Roy and Nadine stood among the survivors, overwhelmed by the surrealness of it all. They were still alive, but those people were dead. *Dead! Dead! Dead!* Roy kept repeating the word to himself as if it might reveal some hidden secret or wake him from a dream. Maybe all of this was just a terrible nightmare. It was all surreal, and Roy was confused and puzzled.

It was chaotic inside and outside of the diner. There were ambulances, police, and now news reporters from the local television stations. Crowds of people gathered on the street – all curiosity seekers gathering around to see what had happened.

Roy saw the cashier David walk over to a reporter for KTNV. The correspondent on the scene spoke with an annoying upspeak at the end of every sentence making even her statements sound like questions. Lately, it seemed that everyone talked like that and it grated on Roy. "I am here speaking with the owner of Abaddon's Diner, David Alexios Matthopolous, the real hero of this terrible ordeal. Mr. Matthopolous, were you nervous that the gunmen would see you when you hit the panic button? And how do you plan to go forward after this tragedy?"

David Alexios Matthopolous answered somewhat distractedly. "I did what I had to do. I'm no hero. I have great faith and I was saying a prayer to God the entire time this was going on. My heart goes out to the two who were killed by those cold-blooded murderers. My prayers are for the victims and their families. The Lord will see me through this. The real heroes are my customers and what they had to endure and…"

David seemed to be regressing into a mild state of understandable shock as he continued to speak. "I would be remiss if I didn't thank the elite swat team and police. They put their lives on the line. They are the real heroes." With that, his voice began to quake and choke. He walked away from the reporter, murmuring faintly, "Thank you. That's all I can say."

Roy couldn't help but admire David's courage and strength. Then a weird and peculiar thought coursed through his mind – perhaps the diner could be renamed. People wouldn't go there even after it was rebuilt because the name Abaddon's would forever be associated with this event. It needed to be called "David's" after its valiant and brave owner. That was his real name after all. "David" was a good strong name and a perfect example of a David was the great King of Israel in the Old Testament in the Bible. He was a courageous warrior who took on Goliath and won. David had defeated him by killing him with a rock from his sling. Abaddon, on the other hand, was a name that conjured up destruction as it was the name of a fallen angel who was known as an angel of the bottomless pit. Roy would bring this up to the intrepid proprietor as soon as things calmed down.

Then he wondered if he too was suffering some form of PTSD trauma because there was something wrong with his thinking. He couldn't help but wonder why he was worried about something as trivial as a new name for the diner. Maybe it was a simple defense mechanism. For tonight, it was the only way Roy knew how to handle this catastrophic tragedy.

SAN ANTONIO, TEXAS

Between anticipation of his date with Christianna and being the first quarterback in Antelopes' history to bring them a winning season, Rebel was in the mood to celebrate. Leading the Antelopes to victory over the Carolina Panthers, Rebel clinched a wild-card spot and brought the team one game away from outright winning their division. And now he had a date with the most beautiful girl he'd ever seen. Who wouldn't want to pop a cork and have a party?

Rebel left his apartment in the early morning to make the two hundred-mile trek to San Angelo. It was a spectacular day for December and Rebel lowered the top of his Corvette as he sped down the highway out of San Antonio with the music from satellite radio's Outlaw Country trailing in the air behind him. This was one appointment he would not be late for.

Rebel wasn't the least bit embarrassed or concerned about his Jumbotron kiss with Christianna. Sure, he'd endured some good-natured joking in the locker room. And the fact that it had provided another angle for sports journalists to report on, well, that was just one of those things you learn to accept when you are the hottest talent in Antelopes' franchise history. But if he had known about the trouble their little tête-à-tête had caused Christianna, he would have happily postponed it until a more private setting could be found.

Sensing a good story in the making, the star reporter for ESSN and his camera crew waited patiently in the Davy Crockett stadium parking lot. His name was Norton Hadley, but those around the league called him "Nosy Hadley." Nosy could pry a story out of even the most hardened and reluctant subject. This guy could make a mute talk, and when their interview aired, most of his victims wished they'd remained quiet. The one target that had eluded him was Hank Mariotta.

Mariotta had a reputation for being extremely guarded with the media. But he was particularly so with Nosy. After a question from Nosy, Hank would pause as if he was thinking carefully before giving an answer. Once he did respond, his words were so precisely metered that there was no ambiguity in his meaning. Follow-up questions were pointless since Hank always repeated his original answer. Because of this, Nosy usually left Hank alone when he was looking for a story. He had learned through experience that Hank Mariotta was an impenetrable wall, not to mention a lousy interview.

But this time was different. Nosy had seen the same Jumbotron kiss half of America had witnessed and knew he had a story. As Hank Mariotta was about to open his car door, Nosy and his crew ambushed him in the parking lot. Standing between Hank and his car door, Nosy stuck the microphone in Hank's face. "Mr. Mariotta? Just a few questions, if you please." Hank stared impatiently at Nosy. "How is your relationship going with Bruce Rebenack now that it is common knowledge he is dating your daughter Christianna? How do you feel about that?"

Hank gave Nosy a contentious stare. He had remained silent for far too long, and Nosy could see the anger building inside Hank. What a story! Finally, he was going to get something worth reporting from the elusive Hank Mariotta. Maybe Hank would take a swing at him. Nosy hoped he would. This was Nosy's "gotcha" moment. Nosy motioned for his cameraman to zoom in on Hank's face.

Face aflame, Hank took a deep breath and smiled menacingly. "Nosy, all I can say is that Bruce Rebenack has been playing his heart out. His passing stats far surpass anybody else in the league. He's got something going with Drew Perry, one of the best receivers around. It took them a while to get it together; now they've got that 'wow' factor." Choosing his words judiciously, Hank was careful to give Nosy nothing. "As for Christianna and him, what do you think? You've got to admit, they make a good-looking couple! Now, excuse me, Nosy." Hank elbowed past the reporter, opened the car door, and climbed into his car.

Dejected and disappointed, Nosy Hadley dropped his microphone to his side. Hank Mariotta had defeated him – again.

If Nosy had only known how angry Hank was, he might not have been so quick to cut off the interview. The fact was that Hank was on the verge of boiling over and with just a bit more probing, Nosy would have gotten the explosion he wanted. But as it happened, Nosy turned to his cameraman and said, "Let's pack it in, Russ. We got nothing, as usual."

Hank had learned of the incident between Rebel and his daughter through an off-hand comment made by the team's general manager.

Immediately, Hank had locked himself in his office and replayed the kiss on his television to see it for himself. Usually a model of self-control, Hank Mariotta could be positively terrifying when provoked and this public scene with Christianna enraged him like nothing ever had before. He slammed the remote on his desk causing the back to break and spill out the batteries.

During the long drive home to San Angelo, Hank's world remained tinted a crimson hue. After smoking the tires of his Porsche Cayman out of the stadium parking lot, he broke his personal best for making the trip home. Showing the Cayman no mercy, Hank red-lined the tachometer with every shift and nearly wore out the gearbox before turning onto the long drive leading to Big Sky Ranch.

As he entered the house, Hank saw Christianna sitting in the kitchen. His immediate thought was to lock her in her bedroom forever. She had disgraced herself and had embarrassed the entire family. That was not how he had raised her to behave. Hank was incensed with his daughter. But he was also infuriated with Nosy for his guerilla-style tactics, his GM for even mentioning it, and his sons for letting Chrissy out of their sight. But mostly he focused his wrath on Bruce Rebenack for having the temerity to kiss his daughter.

Christianna ran up to him excitedly and, wrapping her arms around him, said, "Daddy, that was the most exciting thing I have ever done. Thank you for letting me go to the game. I loved it and now I want to go to all of them from now on."

Hank pushed her away. "You've got your damn nerve! Don't try to cozy up to me after what you've done."

Christianna's eyes showed hurt. "Daddy, what is the matter with you? What have I done?" Her voice was meek and innocent, but she knew. She knew her father had heard about what happened. She was afraid, but she was beginning to feel something new. It was her own anger, anger at her father. She was of age and was starting to chafe at her father's oppressive and dictatorial control of her life. "Yes, Daddy, it's true about your star quarterback and me and I am going to go on a date with him. How about that?" It was the first time she had ever challenged her father; she could tell he felt betrayed.

Hank Mariotta's Italian ancestry surfaced and he began shaking his fists in the air. "You see that guy anymore, and I'll throw you out on the streets. I wonder how long you'd last as a street troll. How would you like that, young lady? He's not right for you, and I forbid you to see him again."

Christianna yelled back at him. For the first time in her life, she was confronting her father's authority, and it emboldened her. "Throw me out then. Maybe then I can learn a little something about life instead of going around scared all the time because you keep me caged like some pathetic songbird." Running out of the house, she slammed the solid oak door behind her so hard that her father flinched; jerking his shoulder in spasmodic response to the crashing door.

Outside and alone in the cool night air, Christianna knew that from then on she was going to seize control of her life, even if it meant being tossed out on the streets. As far as she was concerned, Tuesday and her date with Rebel couldn't come soon enough.

Even Christianna's brothers, normally her allies when it came to dealing with her father, now took their father's side and against her. Hank Mariotta had handed his boys their orders and he expected them to be carried out; they were to ignore Christianna.

Much to Christianna's dismay, Luke and Phillip became the most distant and cold. It was painful receiving this kind of treatment from Luke. Despite their difference in age, they were very close. Even when his responsibilities as the Antelopes' orthopedic doctor forced him to live in San Antonio for the season, Luke was never too busy to take her calls. Now, Luke hardly answered his phone. And when he did, he abruptly ended their conversations with, "Listen, Chrissy, I'm in the middle of something now. Let me call you back." Which, of course, he never did.

Her brother Philip boasted, "I'll lead the Mariotta brothers in a brigade to puree pretty-boy Bruce's face. But only after the season's over. We've got to acknowledge our priorities. And right now, we can't afford to put Rebenack on the disabled list. But as soon as it's over, I'll take one for the team!"

They were all against her. But as much as they ignored her, Christianna was just as determined to avoid them. And it was this mutual shunning that created an uneasy quiet for everyone at the Big Sky Ranch.

Christianna became secretive about her activities and kept to herself by either hiding in her room or taking long walks alone around the ranch. Tuesday was slow in coming. Rebel had called her the night before to confirm their date. She had told him yes, but that she preferred meeting him out by the front gate. Rebel's voice betrayed his confusion and he asked, "Do you mean that you don't want me to come in and say hello to your father?"

She didn't want him to know about the situation with her father and brothers, and she answered him almost too fast, when she thought, about it later. "No, that's not it. I just want you to pick me up where we first met." She realized it was a stupid thing to say, but it was the only thing she could think of and so now she had to invent a reason that Rebel would believe. "Yeah, I'll be out walking anyway. I love walking in December. There are so many pecan trees on our property and I like picking them off the ground. They are such a treat to eat and I make an amazing pecan pie." Where was this stuff coming from anyway? She piled one lie on top of the other and wondered if Rebel was buying any of it. Not only had she never cooked a day in her life, but she couldn't even microwave popcorn. It always burned.

"Well okay. If you say so, I'll wait out by the gate for you. Try not to eat too many pecans along the way. You wouldn't want to spoil your appetite." Rebel laughed, and Chrissy couldn't tell if he believed her or not. She would have to wait until Tuesday night to see if Rebel would say anything more about it.

Christianna had not spoken with her father since their confrontation. So far, he didn't seem to notice or care. In fact, Hank Mariotta seemed oblivious to his daughter. Neither of them was willing to try and mend the breach. For her part, Christianna was content to avoid her father until after her date with Rebel.

She did, however, have a nagging concern. What if for some reason her father happened to notice she was missing and wanted to know where she was? She needed a plausible diversion. She thought about saying she had gone to a movie, but then her car would still be in the garage. Then she thought about saying she was going to visit a friend for the evening; but the few friends she did have were away at college. Finally, she decided just to say she was out for a long walk which was something she often did.

Christianna spent hours walking the trails around the ranch. That had been the only true part of her concocted story to Rebel. She enjoyed the open sky, endless prairie, and wildflowers of every different shade. There were thousands of acres to explore and over the years Christianna had wandered through most of them. Unexpectedly, the same paths that once seemed so endless, now felt finite and confining.

TOE NAIL ROAD

Christianna jotted down a terse message on the notepad by the kitchen telephone before leaving the house to meet Rebel. It read:

Went walking. Need to sort things out. Back later.

She thought this would satisfy her father and brothers in case they wondered where she was – not that they would care. Nor did it matter anymore to Christianna if they did. Her deception and subterfuge were new and exciting to her. She slipped quietly out the back of the house by way of the kitchen door.

Spotting Rebel waiting for her by his car outside the wrought iron gate, Christianna sprinted down the drive and leaped into his car. The feeling of pride she had for defying her father gave her new confidence and seeing Rebel brought a broad smile to her face.

Magnoli's was located in the small town of Christoval, about twenty miles south of San Angelo. And if San Angelo was just on the edge of the middle of nowhere, Christoval was smack in the middle of it. Even Christianna commented about it on the way, saying, "I've lived here all of my life and I don't think I've ever been to Christoval. And I've never, ever heard of Magnoli's."

Bruce explained, "Just after your father signed to the Antelopes, I was cruising around exploring Texas when I got hungry. It was late and I had no idea where I was when I saw an old house with a bright sign in the front, promising Fine Italian Dining. I figured, 'What the hell?' I mean heck. 'Why not?' And Christianna, I had some of the best lasagna I ever ate. And get this; it's on a road named Toe Nail Road."

Chrissy laughed. "That's not exactly a street name that would make you think of fine dining!" She was having fun.

Magnoli's Restaurant was everything Rebel had promised. The lasagna was delicious and Rebel stuffed himself with a second portion. They settled into an easy conversation about all sorts of things that, thankfully for Christianna, did not include her father. Christiana thought Rebel was very solicitous of her. He made her feel like she was the center of his universe and it seemed that all he wanted was to concentrate on getting to know more about her.

Christianna liked Rebel's charm; they were easy together. For a girl whose only date had been with a pimply boy at the junior high school dance, she felt comfortable in his presence. He was funny and never once brought up football. For the first time in her life, Christianna's shyness receded.

Throughout the evening, Rebel regaled her with stories of his college days and the antics which he participated in or had the pleasure to witness. He told Christianna a story about something that had happened to his dorm mate. "This guy was abnormally large. Huge, you might say. Gargantuan! Enormous!" Rebel gestured enthusiastically, spreading his arms wide. "Well anyway, he came back from class one afternoon and said he was through with school. He had just bombed a test and threw his books across the room and climbed up on the ladder to his bed on the top bunk. In a rage, he threw himself onto his mattress, cussing and punching his pillow. The next thing you know, the whole thing came crashing down." Rebel used his hands to describe the scene and flapped them in the air like a bird, attempting to emphasize the crashing beds as his roommate plunged to the floor with a loud thud. Slamming his fists down hard onto the table, Rebel caught the tines of his fork with his left hand and sent it soaring into the air.

Christianna burst out laughing. As Rebel searched for the wayward fork, he leaned out of the booth, but fell, landing in a sprawl on the floor. Christianna was now in a twitter of unrestrained mirth as Rebel performed a quick roll to retrieve the fork. Picking it up as he popped to his feet, he held the fork victoriously in the air, saying, "Fumble, recovered, I've retrieved the fork!" Christianna clapped her hands appreciatively. Rebel seemed pleased to receive a loud laugh from her. "Can you believe I'm an NFL quarterback? "

Christianna chuckled, "Absolutely. I've never seen anyone fall so expertly in my life. They trained you well."

Unsurprisingly, Rebel's antics caught the waitress's attention and she hurried over to ask if anything was wrong.

Rebel explained that his silverware had taken flight and asked for a clean set, one whose wings were clipped. Still laughing, Christianna tried to hide behind a linen napkin she held to her mouth. As the waitress stood between them, Rebel asked, "Also, ma'am, do you have any Italian cream cake?"

The waitress's eyes crinkled and she smiled broadly. "This cake is delizioso!" She kissed her fingertips in mock-Italian. Christianna thought she was emulating shades of her father. "Do you both want a piece?"

"Yes ma'am, we sure need to celebrate this night. This is one for the books. I need to top it off with my favorite kind of cake. I think I deserve it."

"Okay, you got it. I'll be right back. You won't be disappointed. But first, what is your name?"

"Bruce. Why do you need to know?" He exchanged a bewildered look with Christianna.

"Well, it's about time I call you by your name." The waitress shrugged. "It's just a quirk I have. I like to get to know my customers and give them the personal touch."

"Oh, no problem, ma'am."

With a smile, she breezed off to the kitchen.

Rebel looked at Christianna and winked. "After recovering that fork with my very skillful and athletic tumble, I put enough points on the board to earn some cake."

Christiana agreed, "My stomach hurts from laughing so hard, and now, I don't need to do my daily sit-ups." She clutched at her stomach with both hands and dramatically told him, "Thank you for that."

A few minutes later, the waitress returned carrying two large pieces of cake. One had a flickering birthday candle atop it. Placing the candlelit piece in front of Rebel first and then setting the other one before Christianna, she had a peculiar look stuck to her face like a barnacle. "Happy Birthday to you, Mr. Bruce! I hope you enjoy your cake!" Once again, Chrissy and Rebel traded bemused looks.

Instead of leaving them to their cake, the waitress moved behind Rebel and began stroking his hairline before moving up to play with Rebel's thick and lustrous hair, tousling it into a mess. Then it began. Opening her mouth wide and pawing at his shoulders, the waitress sang in a startlingly loud, high-pitched soprano voice her rendition of Happy Birthday – In Italian opera. But to Bruce, it sounded more like an air raid siren.

Tanti auguri a Te,
Tanti auguri a Te,
Tanti auguri a Bruce
Tanti auguri a Te!

Rebel turned around to face her shrill intonations in an attempt to explain that it wasn't his birthday. But this proved futile as she was too preoccupied rubbing him down with her hands and singing. Rebel looked at Christianna and shrugged. Now they knew why she wanted to know his first name!

The waitress' voice was exaggerated, dramatic, and loud. It overpowered the soft music playing through the restaurant's sound system and caused the other diners to stop eating, their forks frozen in midair. As more people turned in their chairs to watch the spectacle, Rebel realized that he had become the costar in a floorshow he hadn't auditioned for and didn't want to be in. He experienced a feeling unfamiliar to him – profound embarrassment. As the waitress kept running her hands through his hair, her voice shrieked higher, growing ever more theatrical. It was apparent she had once performed on stage, and she was giving Bruce a birthday he would never forget. It was the reverse of the don't-quit-your-day-job wisecrack.

Exasperated, Rebel buried his head in his arms on the table. There was no stopping her. It was clear to everyone there that the waitress was off in her own world and would keep singing until she felt like ending it. Rebel hid even deeper into the table and surrendered to the embarrassment.

Like the rest of the diners, Christianna also appeared staggered by the sheer volume of the lady's voice, as well her histrionics. For a fleeting moment, Rebel wondered if Christianna had been in on it, but he knew she wasn't. It was, after all, their first date. Besides, she'd already said she had never heard of Magnoli's.

Finally, after one last fluff of his hair and a crescendo that could shatter crystal, the waitress finished. The entire restaurant broke into astonished applause as she took several obligatory bows and blew kisses. Her performance had upended Magnoli's and she savored their adulation.

Still flustered, Rebel managed a weak smile and a mild correction. "Well, ma'am, I sure did appreciate your singing to me, but it isn't my birthday. But thanks anyway just the same. You've got some set of pipes; that's for sure."

"What do you mean? It's not your birthday?" she panted. "You mean to tell me I sang my lungs out for a faker? I don't just sing for anyone, especially a pseudo-birthday-boy like you. Do you know who I am?"

The air turned frigid. Christianna looked at Rebel and began to tighten her grip on her purse as if she was preparing to do battle with the waitress.

The waitress pointed vehemently at Rebel and announced to the restaurant, "Folks, I just sang my guts out to this guy and it turns out he told me a bold-faced lie. What do you all think of that? I've heard of fake news before, but fake birthdays? Come on! We gave him the best cake in the house, Italian cream, and the best singing by me, the a la mode, and it was nothing more than a low-down birthday hoax. All this in an attempt to get out of paying for a piece of cake. All I can say is that I've served some cheapskates before, but this guy literally takes the cake! Give me a break! And to think I gave it my all for some guy who was playing me." Unaware of her own pun, the waitress glowered at the few patrons who dared to laugh.

Embarrassment fading, Rebel scrutinized the waitress. It was impossible for her to be so confused. This seemed like a scene she had played before; it felt deliberate, contrived, and phony. Perhaps she was trying to make a name for herself around the area and become an opera star. Maybe she pulled this stunt once a week or as much as once or twice during her shift. Rebel didn't know. There was no denying she had talent, but this was the wrong way to go about using it; at least Rebel thought so.

Nose tipped so high she would have drowned in a rainstorm, the waitress asked him once more, "Do you know who I am?"

Aware of the other diners' watchful, if not judgmental, gazes, Rebel scowled. He felt like he was on trial and, gauging by the looks of the patrons around him, he had been found guilty.

Before Rebel had time to scowl, Christianna stood up and said emphatically, "Oh please, ma'am, do you know who *he* is?"

She was met with a hard, icy stare from the singing waitress. "Yeah honey, I know. He's Brucey Goosey who tried to play fast and loosey with me and swindle a free piece of birthday cake."

Christianna retorted, "Hey, you're getting annoying. Have you ever heard of Bruce Rebenack, the quarterback of the San Antonio Antelopes?"

The waitress seemed rattled but quickly blurted out, "Yeah, I just bet he's Bruce Rebenack. Like I'm the famous Italian opera star Cecilia Bartoli! You only wish, honey. Get real."

"No, ma'am, you need to get real," Christianna ordered, motioning for Bruce to tender his driver's license.

"Well, let's see it, Mr. Star Quarterback," the shrill singer demanded.

Rebel was finished being polite. "Ma'am, you need to shush!" As he leaned against the table to dig out his wallet, his elbow caught the scoop of his spoon, launching it into the air.

This sent Christianna into a fit of uncontrollable hysterics. Once again, turning beet-red with embarrassment, he put his head into his hands. But that didn't last long as Christianna's laughter was infectious. It helped him to see the bizarre absurdity of the situation, and he began laughing with her to the point that they could barely breathe.

The party at the table where the flying spoon had landed were less amused, and the singing waitress let out a gasp. Rebel turned to the table behind him. "I am so sorry." Secretly, he wished the waitress would have been the one to take the hit. Maybe it would have dulled her cocky attitude.

His apology was met with a chilly stare by the couple. The young woman at the table had anger etched on her young face. "You could have poked my eye out. Are you from the circus? Are you some kind of knife thrower except your expertise isn't knives? First, you threw your fork and now your spoon. What the..."

With a grumble, her boyfriend turned around to defend his dinner date. When he saw Rebel however, his demeanor drastically changed. "You're Rebel Rebenack!" His girlfriend was speechless, her mouth open. "I guess you just can't help but throw a pass no matter what it is. The fork pass was incomplete, but the spoon pass should have scored a touchdown."

"That's why he needed to throw his spoon," Christianna playfully added.

The girl giggled as she got in on the fun. "I guess I'm not much of a receiver or else I would have caught it. Can I at least keep your spoon as a souvenir and can you sign my napkin? I promise I haven't even used it yet, so don't worry about it being nasty or anything like that."

Rebel told her it was the least he could do, but he did give the napkin a cursory inspection. "As far as you keeping the spoon, you'd have to ask the restaurant about that. Just tell them you have a spoon collection and you wanted to add one more!" The girl replied that she *did* have a spoon collection and that this spoon was the best one of them all!

Now, the entire restaurant was involved and many of the customers had crowded around their table asking Rebel for his autograph. He politely obliged. With a sly smile, Christianna warned the autograph seekers, "Be very careful around his pen when he signs his autograph. You might need a helmet." More laughter erupted.

Ignored and forgotten, the deflated waitress stood off to the side eager to be the star of the show again. Pushing through the autograph hounds, she told Rebel, "Please forgive me. Let me sing you another song. O Sole Mio." She fluttered her eyes, pleading with him to accept. "It's a song about what a beautiful thing a sunny day is and it will be my sun upon your face. I hardly ever sing this song for anyone, but I have decided to sing it to you because you are a very special person." Her insipid groveling was complete and it was, in a word, pathetic to witness.

The thought of sitting through another one of her performances made Rebel grimace. He was just about to decline her offer when the rest of the customers began to moan. Then someone told the stunned waitress what they all wanted to say. "We don't want to hear you, lady. Take a hike. You were rude to our quarterback, thinking you were all that."

Another diner cut in, "Yeah, lady, whoever you are, go bark at the moon with your damn songs. Why would anyone lie about it being their birthday to get a stupid piece of cake free?" Insulted and chagrined, Rebel and the crowd watched as the waitress fled to the kitchen.

"I wonder who the hell she really is," one customer mused.

Rebel opined, "I don't know, but I am sure of one thing; the only opera I like is the Grand Ole Opry."

Another patron offered, "I didn't like it either, no how. My ears are still ringing." He had a very, very long gray, dappled beard where he'd stored a few bread crumbs from his dinner; evidently intended for a late-night snack. And as he stroked his beard with his fingers, he rapped sharply about the waitress and her sham birthday cantatas. Taking his apparent ire out on his slovenly and knotty beard, he kept tugging on it as he continued to untangle it. It was all very unappetizing. "She's been pulling that birthday routine since she started here. For the past month, she'd bring out birthday cakes to people and begin to sing that stupid opera. And when the poor SOB explained that she was mistaken and it wasn't their birthday, she goes through that birthday-liar-stuff, trying to put them on a guilt trip. And you know what?"

Rebel and Christianna, as well as the crowd surrounding their table all inquired at the same time, "What?"

The bearded man seemed to be enjoying his newfound attention as they all leaned in closer to hear what he was going to say next. "I'll tell you what the customers do; they tip her like a queen. She walks away with more money than she ever could make delivering the poor sap his plate of spaghetti. But that's not the end of it. Even if they stiff the waitress, if they bothered to look at their check, they'd have seen a charge for something not even on the menu."

Fiddling with his bedraggled beard, he pulled out a chunk of garlic bread and flicked it on the floor. The bearded wonder continued. "You practically got to knock off a bank to pay the bill. Old Man Magnoli is in on it too; she's his secret weapon." He paused a moment for effect. "They add an entertainment fee to the bill. The owner gives her a cut of the entertainment fee and she pockets the tip. You have to admit; it's a pretty good scam. For them, that's the icing on their cake and they always end up with the last piece of it. Get it?" Tossing his head back, he bellowed, enjoying his own brand of humor. "Rumor has it she could never make it big in the opera world. She tried her voice in Italy and again in New York City, but she was just a big flop. Somebody told me that she was related to Aldo Magnoli, the owner, but nobody knows. Maybe she's old Aldo's girlfriend and that's why she can get away with pulling this tiresome ruse."

Rebel took the check the waitress had left on the table when she had delivered their cake. Christianna peered over his shoulder at it. When he looked at it, he saw that the bearded codger was right. The two pieces of Italian cream cake were there, and so was a one hundred-dollar *Entertainment Fee*. Rebel thought to himself that he'd been taken to the cleaners or maybe to the bakery with its gold-plated cakes. He didn't like Magnoli's style, even if they did have the best lasagna in the world. In all of the craziness, he hadn't even gotten to enjoy his stupid cake. But that no longer mattered, he was through with Italian cream cake.

As patrons gathered around their table chattered on about the charade, there rose a piercing wail from behind the kitchen doors. Everyone fell silent as "Ole Sole Mio" filtered into the dining area. After a moment, the waitress burst through the swinging doors, her ear-splitting soprano rattling the glassware. She headed for Rebel with her arms opened wide, clamoring like a cymbal. But this time it wasn't going to work. Now he was sure he wasn't about to give his usual generous tip to this operator. Stingy is how he felt toward her.

The one thing the woman had going for her was her voice. There was no denying the girl could sing. But why did it have to be opera? Rebel was through with the waitress and Magnoli's. The only thing "Ole Sole Mio" did was convince everyone to swear off opera for the rest of their lives. All he wanted to do was grab Christianna and get out. He couldn't bear another minute of her fingernails-scraping-a-chalkboard singing. "Damn the Italians for inventing opera," he grumbled.

Rebel looked at the dinner check again and mumbled something unintelligible. He wasn't about to pay the bill with his credit card; he could only guess what the final charges would be if he used it. And the only cash he had was in one hundred-dollar bills, so he'd still have to wait to get his change. That would only prolong the torture. So, he dropped three, one hundred-dollar bills on top of the ticket, snatched Christianna by the hand, and rushed her out of the restaurant with the singing waitress chasing them out the door. It was too much money, and though it left her with a tip more than the cost of their meal, it was all Rebel could do to get them out of that restaurant.

Outside it was quiet and the evening was pleasant, complete with a waxing crescent moon dangling in the sky like a sparkling jewel. At that moment, Rebel wondered how his life could get any better. He was, after all, on a date with the lovely, ingénue Christianna Mariotta.

Walking back to the car, they laughed together about the shenanigans going on at Magnoli's, not to mention their part in it. Rebel concluded that the waitress was pretty shrewd. "Talk about singing for your supper. What a con artist! That grifter saw me coming, marked me, and picked my pocket clean. And she did it all out in the open. She knew what she was doing, all right. Got me coming and going. But the funny thing is, I'd do it all again." Rebel looked over at Christianna. "Who knows, maybe she'll sing for you on your birthday."

MAGNOLI'S RESTAURANT

Christianna couldn't remember having a better time. She had enjoyed herself at Magnolia's and was sad their date ended so soon. Rebel had an early-morning practice, but she also knew that she better get herself home or else her father might think something had happened to her and call the police. After such a perfect evening, the last thing she wanted was another confrontation with her domineering father.

As he drove up to the entrance to Big Sky, Christiana told Rebel to let her off at the gate. Rebel stopped and looked across to Christiana, "You're confusing me. I thought we had a good time tonight. Christiana, I want to see you again and I thought you felt the same way. Is something wrong? How come you don't want me to see you home? Is it something about me? What's the deal?"

Christianna struggled for an answer. She blurted out, "Please don't tell anyone we went out on a date. My father can't find out." There. She had told him the truth. "He wouldn't like it if I dated anyone from the Antelopes. So please, let's fly under the radar and keep it quiet for now." Speaking calmly, she tried to make it seem like it was just an overly protective father watching out for his only daughter.

Rebel appeared satisfied with her answer but the pleading and desperation in her voice were unmistakable. "Well, in the future, we're going to have to change that because I want to see you again and again, for that matter. And that's an order. I wish you didn't even have to get out of my car."

He leaned across the console and pulled her into his arms. They kissed and he sighed, "Why do I have to be so gone on you? The playoffs are just around the corner and all I should be thinking about is football. But now you're all I can think about."

Christianna tossed her long blond hair back and whispered seductively, "I wish tonight didn't have to end." Rebel ran his fingers through her soft hair, nodding.

Christianna reluctantly pulled away from Rebel's embrace and stepped out of the car. She leaned in through the open car window to tell him, "I don't think I can handle a week without seeing you." She turned and ran up the road toward her house. Rebel watched as she disappeared into the night.

As Rebel drove down the empty road toward San Antonio, Christianna looked up at the twinkling stars and moon making its's way across the black sky. Tomorrow she would take her case to Father Lawrence. Maybe he could talk some sense into her father.

SAINT LAWRENCE CHURCH

Either Hank Mariotta was too preoccupied with his football team to notice Christianna's absence last night or else he still wasn't speaking to his daughter. Whatever the reason, Christianna heaved a sigh of relief when she awoke the next morning to find her note exactly where she had left it the night before. She did not know if he had ever seen or read it. One thing was apparent however – her relationship with her father and brothers was deteriorating. She hadn't spoken to the men in her family in days. She felt alone, like a castaway on a deserted island with only her thoughts of Rebel to keep her company.

Later that morning, Christianna went to visit Father Lawrence. Fortunately, he was in town and was able to see her. Since beginning his prison ministry, the priest was away more than he was present in Mariottaville. He'd been traveling from city to city, visiting jails around the country to counsel and pray with inmates who were awaiting trial or serving sentences. Christianna marveled at the selflessness of a man like Father Lawrence. He seemed to derive immense satisfaction merely showing many of these troubled inmates that they were not forgotten. His message was simple, "God was the only steadfast rock they could anchor their lives on."

Christianna could always tell when the Spirit of God moved Father Lawrence. His face radiated with pure joy and his enthusiasm was infectious. Today, his smile was for her when she walked into the austere parish office. Unlike most other offices she had seen, Father Lawrence's wasn't filled with plaques, achievement awards, and meaningless certificates. Instead, the walls were bare except a single Crucifix and a picture of "The Sacred Heart of Jesus." They hung low on the walls across from each other. The office was sparsely furnished with an old couch and a small neglected loveseat covered by a faded gold slipcover with red triangles woven into it around the frayed edge. The table between the couch and loveseat was nothing more than a TV tray masquerading as a coffee table. Father Lawrence was not one for pretentious furnishings; second-hand furniture had always been just fine for him.

Christianna walked briskly into his office. Something was troubling her, and it did not escape Father Lawrence's attention as he greeted her warmly. Father Lawrence's smile assured her that he was the person she could confide in. "I need to talk with you right away, Father. That is, if you have the time."

"Sit down. You know you can always come to me, Christianna. What's on your mind?" He gestured for her to have a seat and Christianna sat cautiously on the rickety couch fearing it was literally, on its last leg. Father Lawrence sat on the loveseat across from her. Ever since Christianna could remember, Father Lawrence had been the one person she could always take her problems to.

"Father Lawrence, it's my father. He won't and has never given me any freedom to do anything on my own in my *entire* life. For the first time in my life, I have a boyfriend and I have to sneak around behind my father's back like I am a little school girl to see him. Even my brothers won't talk to me. Daddy and I haven't spoken in days. I love him and my brothers, but it's not like I am doing anything wrong. I need your help, Father."

Father Lawrence leaned over and took her hands into his. "I know, I know. Your father came to me this morning and told me about it. Christianna, he is very concerned for you, but I must tell you he is also very angry. I am not sure how to mediate this problem. I had trouble reaching him. He did not seem to want to listen to me or take my advice." Then he looked at her intently. "I need to tell you something. I don't feel like I am going behind your father's back; but you need to know what is on his mind. I was planning to have a meeting with both of you later this evening. It is critical that you two mend this rift before it rips both of you apart."

Christianna's hands began to shake, and she asked pleadingly, "What is it, Father? Please tell me."

Father Lawrence raised his eyebrows and spoke softly, almost to the point of being inaudible. "Your father wants you to take up residence in a convent. He thinks you should live your life as a nun. I myself don't feel this is a bad idea, but only if this is something you would want. I know that in the past..."

Christianna interrupted him. "I know that. He has always talked about me joining that convent, Our Lady of the Mission. He's taken me there several times. I even met with Mother Ruth, the head Abbess. No thanks! As I recall, she didn't think I was good enough for her convent anyway. There might have been a time when I would have been interested but no longer. I really like this guy and I want to see more of him. But here's the problem –"

"Rebel Rebenack. Yes, I know. Why else do you think your father is so angry and conflicted? Put yourself in his shoes and look at the impossible situation this puts him in. I mean, think about it. An employee of his, the Antelopes' star quarterback, is now the supposed boyfriend of his only daughter. Your father is furious."

Christianna took offense at the priest's characterization of Rebel being her *supposed* boyfriend. "He *is* my boyfriend and I want to be with him. I am not going to go live in a convent, and Daddy can't force me into one. I am eighteen years old and an adult!"

Father Lawrence gripped her hand tightly as if to tell her to calm down. "Chrissy, let me try to get a hold of your father and maybe we can all talk together sometime later this evening when your father returns. Are you going to be around later, maybe around eight?"

He called her by her nickname and to Christianna, the way he said it sounded patronizing and condescending. She resented being called 'Chrissy' and now deemed it to be far too juvenile at this point in her life. Christianna was indignant. "Well, where else do you think I would go? I'm not supposed to leave the ranch unless I'm with him or one of my brothers." Fuming, she pleaded, "Father, please explain to me why it would be so bad for me to get involved with one of his players. Especially Bruce. I mean, he knows Bruce is a Christian. What problem does Daddy have with Rebel? Isn't he, after all, the star quarterback he is always bragging about?" Her question was laced with sarcasm.

Although Father Lawrence answered her almost as fast as she had challenged him, he stirred uneasily on the rickety loveseat. "Your father feels that Bruce Rebenack is a real ladies' man and is too sophisticated for you. He thinks he will break your heart and something bad will happen to you. He also does not want his star quarterback to lose his focus and be unable to concentrate on the game. Your father does not want any distractions for him. The fallout could affect the entire team. Do you understand that this could cause so many problems for your father?" Christianna nodded that yes, she could. "Good. Then why don't we close now and say a prayer together."

Father Lawrence bowed his head and the priest prayed for understanding between father and daughter. After his Amen, he rose to his feet and said, "Now, my dear Chrissy, you should go into the chapel and pray a Rosary for peace to settle between you and your father."

"Thank you, Father." Christianna walked to the office door, opened it, and looked back at the priest. "Father, my name is Christianna." Without waiting for a response, she closed the door behind her.

As she made her way toward the chapel, Christianna took a Rosary out of her bag and ran her fingers along the beautiful pearls that surrounded the solid gold crucifix which was inlaid with semi-precious stones made of garnet, opal, and amethyst. It had belonged to her mother

Matilda and had been designed for her by her father; she knew very well the story behind its creation.

Her father had been meticulous and exacting in its design and was just as particular in commissioning the jeweler who made it a reality. Creating it became an obsession for Hank and a symbol of his affection for his wife. He surprised Matilda with it on the occasion of their first anniversary.

Being the accountant behind his enterprises, Matilda always kidded him that at least this rosary wasn't a drain on their resources since he had designed it himself. She said this with a wink, knowing that the gift had cost Hank much more than they could afford to spend. Then Matilda would lead them in reciting the rosary and ending with a prayer that God bless their business with the success needed to find the money to pay for the precious rosary. His wife's playful banter amused and delighted Hank but he knew she cherished the gift. After Matilda died, Hank presented it to Christianna on the occasion of her first communion.

Christianna remembered how her father would reverently take the rosary out of its ornate, diamond-set case set and have her hold it while he led her and her brothers in praying every night after dinner. Hank Mariotta insisted that they pray together as a family. Christianna closed her eyes and remembered how they would send up their prayers to Mary for intercession in hopes that Jesus would hear them. Her father taught her to be good and emulate Jesus's mother Mary in all things in life.

A tear formed in her eye as she thought of the chasm that now existed between them. Wiping it away didn't help because more tears followed. As her fingertips moved across the smooth pearls of her rosary, she entered the chapel and kneeled in prayer.

SHELL STATION

All of his business interests kept Hank Mariotta traveling constantly. He needed something that would allow him to go anywhere he needed to go and to do it all very fast. He settled on a Gulfstream G650. Straight from the showroom floor, the private jet would have cost him nearly seventy million dollars, but being the shrewd businessman he was, he was able to procure the jet, capable of approaching Mach one, for little more than half that. And after spending a few million more in refurbishments, the aircraft was a flying mansion any business mogul would be proud to own. It not only boasted a spacious cabin with a conference area, but sleeping quarters for intercontinental travel.

The jet was perfect for business, but Hank often joked that it was the ideal family vehicle too since it carried fourteen passengers and anybody else who wanted to come along for the ride. Driving, he needed a small fleet to move his family. But flying was a different proposition. He just loaded everyone into electric golf carts for the short trip from their house to the ranch's private airstrip, ushered them into the waiting jet, and off they flew around the world on too many vacations to count.

And it was because of his hectic schedule that Hank was unable to meet with Father Lawrence that evening or anytime during the week. Christianna called Father Lawrence's office to tell him that her father was in San Antonio all week and they would have to plan to meet the next week. After all, it was nearing the end of the season and the Antelopes were on their way to the postseason for the first time in franchise history. Therefore, Hank spent most of his time in San Antonio monitoring his team's preparation for the upcoming big game before retiring to his high-rise penthouse in downtown San Antonio which showcased views of the Alamo and the River Walk.

Her father's persistent absence did not deter Christianna, however. She had a date with Rebel next week and nothing could stop her. Her father and brothers no longer controlled her. She was becoming increasingly self-confident and independent with each passing day.

Christianna put on her hiking boots, deciding that a walk was the best way to gather her thoughts. Her stroll took her by the big lake where she watched a flock of ducks paddle by, flapping their wings and slapping water to take flight. The wind blew from the north and it was getting cold. Huddling against the chill, she walked a little faster. Gray clouds dotted the blue sky. Maybe it was going to rain. After walking a mile and a half, she came to her father's private airstrip. His plane wasn't there since he had flown to San Antonio in it and the flight crew that was usually busy fussing over the jet was gone. Except for the wind that whistled through the empty hanger, Christianna was alone.

Her hike took her to the narrow trail of pebbles and stone Hank had designed. The path meandered for about a mile before leading to one of the highest points on the ranch where Hank had built a gazebo. Christianna loved to visit this spot. Here she could sit and watch the kaleidoscopic skies and ever-changing prairie vistas – as well as seek shelter from the wind. This was the most beautiful spot on the ranch and Christianna came here often.

The gazebo was a hexagonal structure with thick cedar beams supporting a copper roof weathered cobalt-blue. No detail was overlooked, even down to the handcrafted cedar furniture Hank had built specifically for its interior. Each window looked over a different scene which seemed to change every time she visited. There she sat and thought. It had been a while since she had been able to relax and reflect. Hopefully, she could resolve the ongoing struggle with her father. It was therapeutic being in this spot; it always helped her put things into perspective.

Christianna mused over the events of the past few days. Last Sunday seemed so long ago. Since then, everything in her life had been uprooted and proven fake like so many movie props. It was as if she was living through the days after a tornado had torn through the plains, annihilating everything in its path and forcing the survivors to begin their lives again. The tornado that stormed through Christianna's world came with the name Bruce 'Rebel' Rebenack. He unsettled nearly every foundation her life had been built upon.

For the first time, Christianna questioned everything around her. Especially her relationship with her father. Until recently, he had been like a god to her who was never wrong, but now she had her doubts. It was like a closed door she had walked past her entire life but been afraid to open. Today though, she turned the doorknob and stepped through that threshold into adulthood. In that instant, everything made sense to her. Her father Hank Mariotta was just a man. This sudden realization that her father was only human startled her. It was almost heretical. She tried to walk back through the door and shut it out of her mind but she couldn't.

Memories of her father making stupid mistakes just like everyone else came rushing back. Like the time he backed the car out of the garage without first opening the door. Or the time he stumbled over a chaise lounge and fell into the pool during a formal party he was holding for his board members. At the time, these were just funny things her daddy did, but now she looked on them differently; her father made mistakes and could be wrong about things just like any other mere mortal. This revelation frightened her because it fundamentally changed their relationship. Hank Mariotta was no longer her *daddy*; he had become just her father. She loved him but from then on, she would make her own decisions. Even if they turned out to be mistakes, they would at least be hers. She resolved that when he returned, she would talk to her father without Father Lawrence's mediation. Regardless of her father's reaction, Christianna was going to assume control of her life.

After a while, she ventured on and walked to the road leading into Mariottaville. She was in the mood for some hot tea and there was a little tea house in town. She and Luke often went there just to hang out.

Mariottaville's only Chinese family operated The Lucky Teahouse. They had emigrated from China on a hardship visa and ended up, in all places, Mariottaville. The husband, a coal miner by trade, had contracted black lung disease and was sent with his family to Dallas for treatment. There, they discovered the remarkable opportunities available to them and subsequently requested, and were granted, political asylum. He quickly adapted to the lack of mining opportunities in West Texas and opened up The Lucky Teahouse. It was a bustling little place where residents congregated to chat and gossip over a cup of hot tea or coffee.

Luke wasn't a big tea drinker, but he found other reasons to join Christianna. He was attracted to one of the owners' daughters who waitressed there, telling his sister, "I'd drink all the tea in China just to have one date with Mei."

Unfortunately for Luke, Mei's parents were traditional and very strict. They forbade interracial relationships and wouldn't let their daughter date at all until they found her a suitable Chinese husband. And now, her father was finalizing Mei's marriage to a young man from the same small coal-mining town in northern China they had come from. The last thing they would allow was for their daughter to marry a lǎowài (a Chinese pejorative for Westerners, particularly white Europeans). It didn't matter to them that their daughter's suitor was an accomplished orthopedic doctor and the son of Hank Mariotta, one of the wealthiest men in Texas. He was still a lǎowài. But none of this deterred Luke. As long as Mei Chan remained single, Luke saw an opportunity, even if it meant drinking a lot of tea.

Mei Chan was as American as Luke and Christianna. She had been quite young when her parents had brought her to the United States, and except for her home life where her parents had demanded strict adherence to their traditional ways, Mei had adopted the sensibilities of her native-born schoolmates. Mei and Christianna had become close friends. They both shared a common factor; their fathers were strict, controlling, and demanding and they often confided to each other. And though Mei's parents would never understand, Christianna knew that Mei was not about to enter into a marriage arranged by them; especially with a prospective husband from Jincheng, her birthplace. She was an American now, and her parent's ways were not hers. Mei's assimilation was not uncommon and happened with nearly every second generation of immigrant families.

As Christianna walked along the lonely road toward town, she had a feeling she was not alone. Turning around, she saw the headlights of a small, green car following slowly behind her some yards away. Suddenly the Mazda raced forward and screeched to a stop in front of her, blocking her way. Fear and confusion raced through her mind as well as her heart. The car door opened and a dark figure jumped out and charged toward her. Panicked, she ran into the scrubby prairie but heard the footsteps of someone running after her. Trying to outrun him proved futile, and he quickly grabbed her, wrapping both his arms around her in a tight viselike grip. Screaming and kicking, Christianna struggled to free herself. But her attacker was relentless and overpowered her.

Christiana could not break free as the man dragged her toward the idling car. He kept saying, "Come on, Chrissy baby, you're coming with me. Just cooperate and nothing will happen. You're going to end up in a better place than here." All she could think about was that he was going to stuff her in that small trunk. She told herself to stay calm and alert, all the while trying to kick and claw her way out of the man's hold on her.

Then a second man jumped out of the back seat of the Mazda. He screamed at his partner, "Don't be rough with her. Don't scare her either. And don't ever call her 'Baby!'" It was Hank Mariotta. Christianna understood. Her father was abducting her. Why? What was he doing to her? She was more frightened now than just moments before. Her father was *kidnapping* her. Then she suddenly remembered what Father Lawrence had told her and she knew. He was going to take her to the convent.

Ripping her away from her captor, Hank pushed her into the back seat of the small car and climbed in behind her, where they were crunched together. Christianna stared at her father and he stared back with a vacant look. He had become someone she didn't know, and at that moment, Christianna never hated anybody as much as she hated her father. Seemingly unsettled by his daughter's piercing glare, Hank turned away and stared out the car window.

"Christianna, I didn't want it to be like this, but you drove me to it. I certainly do not want to hurt you. I am doing what I know is best for you. We are on the way to the convent in San Antonio to see Mother Ruth."

Recovering from her initial panic, Christianna was defiant. "Where is your jet, Daddy?" She asked him sarcastically. "I thought you were in San Antonio to be with your beloved Antelopes. And who's your henchman who nearly choked me to death? Does he have a name? How much did you pay him to kidnap me!"

Hank groaned. "Oh Chrissy, this is Bobby Fieldbrook. You met him once and he did not put you in a chokehold. You need to calm down. You know I would never let someone hurt you." There was pain and remorse in his voice.

Christianna said a quick prayer and felt the Holy Spirit imbue her with a remarkable clarity. "Fine, Daddy. Whatever you say, but before we start this lovely trek where you will imprison me in a convent, I need to stop and use the bathroom. I've been walking for several hours. So, please stop. At least do that for me."

"I'm not about to fall for that. I will only allow it if I escort you to the restroom and wait until you're finished. I swear, I'll stand right outside the door the whole time. You're not going to get away with any shenanigans. *I will have my way!*"

"You're going to make a big scene, Daddy, because everyone knows you in Mariottaville and they're going to wonder what is up with 'Daddy Mariotta' camped outside the women's restroom while his daughter is inside doing her business."

Hank puffed his chest defiantly. "I don't give a damn who sees what or what they think. They wouldn't even be in this town if it wasn't for me." Christianna had never known her father to be arrogant and yet his response was laden with pride and condescension. This was a side of her father she never knew existed.

Hank ordered Bobby Fieldbrook to drive the small car up the road for a half mile and pull into the gas station; the same Shell Station that Hank had taken Father Lawrence to when they first met years before, after the priest's car ran out of gas. Bobby Fieldbrook brought the Mazda to a quick stop and all three anxiously got out. It was a bit of a struggle for Hank and Christianna to get out of the small rear seat. They had been packed in tightly and Hank seemed relieved to stretch his long, cramped legs.

Christianna looked disgustingly at the two men. The elaborate scheme her father had devised to abduct her was appalling. Flying to San Antonio, then secretly returning to town in a small car like this – she never would have believed her father was capable of such deception. But there they stood, the kidnapper and his hostage.

Hank directed Bobby Fieldbrook to get back in the car and leave it running in case they had to drive away fast. Walking into the store toward the ladies' room, Hank flanked Christianna. At the restroom door, she looked at her father as if to ask, "Are you going to follow me in?"

Hank leaned against the opposite wall and told her, "Don't be long."

Christianna shut the door behind her and bolted the lock. Commanding her hands not to shake, she quickly retrieved her cell phone out of her pocket. The number she wanted was programmed in. She hit the speed dial digit and prayed to the Almighty while she waited for the connection to complete. He answered on the first ring. Whispering and with a quivering voice, she told him her father had gone insane. She described what had happened and where her father was taking her. "You have to stop him. Please come to the Shell Station right away. I know you can make it here fast. I'm locked in the ladies' room and I'll to stay in here until you come. Please help me." She couldn't help the sheer panic in her voice.

Father Lawrence heard the desperation in her voice as he hurried to his car. It was always hard for him to walk fast because of his back condition. But Christianna was right; it would only take a few minutes at most to get to the station. He arrived there quickly and as he entered the Shell station saw a Hank Mariotta he had never before witnessed. Pacing back and forth in front of the ladies' room, Mariotta had transformed into a crazy man.

While Christianna was in the bathroom, a line of women formed outside waiting to get in. Clearly embarrassed, Hank made up some excuse that he was worried about his daughter because she was sick and that was why she had been inside the restroom for so long.

The door chime announced Father Lawrence's arrival and Hank Mariotta's pallor turned ashen when he saw who it was. Ignoring the wary onlookers, the priest went directly to Hank and stood in front of him, stone-faced and disgusted.

"What are you doing here, Father?" Hank asked feebly.

Father Lawrence looked him over. "I think you know. What you're doing is illegal. You're kidnapping your own daughter. Hank, you have to let her go. It's illegal and an offense to God."

Hank turned away and then looked back at his priest, telling him defiantly, "Stay out of my business. This doesn't concern you."

"Hank, either you call this off, or I'll bring in the police. You can't do what you are planning. Christianna does not want to go to this convent. And you can't do this without her permission. She is, after all, eighteen years old and entitled to live as she wants. Please, Hank, don't take this any further. You're destroying everything that's important to you. It's time to end this now."

The priest's words had their effect. Appearing defeated, Hank lowered his head and nodded his agreement.

Side-stepping the line of waiting women, Lawrence walked over to the restroom door and knocked on it. "Chrissy, it's Father Lawrence. I've talked with your father. Everything is all right. Please come out."

The door whipped open and Christianna dove into Father Lawrence's arms, crying and begging. "Help me, Father, Daddy's gone crazy! This is such a nightmare."

Father Lawrence wrapped a protective arm around Christiana. Meanwhile the small crowd that had gathered around the unusual scene stared accusingly at Hank. Hank scowled back. The tension building inside the station had not gone unnoticed by Father Lawrence, and he told Hank, "Let's take this outside."

Father Lawrence led Hank and Christianna out of the store and told Christianna to wait for him in his car. Christianna ran to the priest's car and climbed into the back seat, locking herself inside.

Turning to Hank, Father Lawrence spoke sternly. "You need help, Hank. Immediate help from a trained psychiatrist." Hank scoffed at the priest but the priest continued. "I'm not suggesting it. I'm demanding it. It is non-negotiable. What you're doing is criminal. Perhaps it was out of love for your daughter. But that doesn't matter. The fact is that you forcibly tried to abduct Christianna and there is no telling how it could have ended. For now, we'll leave the police out of it. But I am warning you, if you do not see a psychiatrist, I won't hesitate to bring the law in on this." Father Lawrence motioned to Mariotta's car. "Tell your accomplice he isn't needed anymore." Father Lawrence was now in command; replacing his humble servant persona with that of the strict master.

Hank nodded and gestured for Bobby Fieldbrook to roll down his window. "Go on home, Bobby. It's all over. Thank you." Fieldbrook shook his head incredulously but did as Hank commanded. Without a word, he peeled out of the gas station and tore down the road pushing his little Mazda hard toward San Antonio where he and Mariotta had hatched their ill-conceived plan.

Without making eye contact with his daughter, Hank Mariotta slowly got into the passenger seat of the priest's car. Father Lawrence drove them to his parish office in silence.

Once there, they talked and then prayed together. Christianna cried. After a long silence, Hank turned and confessed to them both, "I used to have all the answers, but now I'm confused with nothing but questions."

Both Hank and Christianna accepted Father Lawrence's demand for them to seek professional counseling. Hank also agreed to not interfere in Christianna's relationship with Bruce Rebenack. He was beginning to understand that his daughter was an adult, ready and capable of making her own decisions. This was the first step in healing the chasm that he had created between him and his beloved daughter.

The tension was palpable between father and daughter during the drive back to Big Sky Ranch. No one spoke. Father Lawrence drove slowly up the long drive of Mariotta's estate and pulled to a stop in front of the house. Christianna quickly left the car and ran up the steps as a cold gust tossed her hair like a flag waving in the wind. Hank lingered behind in the car and thanked Father Lawrence for intervening; he asked him to pray for him and his family.

Once inside, Hank paused to look up at the portrait of his beloved Matilda hanging above the massive fireplace. It radiated a wave of memories for him. He wondered. Would he have done this if Matilda was still alive? Was he trying to hang on to Christianna for fear of losing her as he had Matilda?

Sitting in his leather recliner, Hank Mariotta asked God to forgive him and to heal the rift he had created between his daughter and him.

THE CAFETERIA AT DESERT VALLEY HOSPITAL

Ty was walking a tight rope, and he was beginning to lose his balance. He was still working at Marks & Franklin but the job no longer interested him. If he never picked up his camera or created another grand photo layout again, it wouldn't bother him. Struggling up the corporate ladder had become banal and a waste of his time. Now there was something much more important to him. He had found the door to a new reality and walked through it as often as he could. Cocaine was the vehicle Ty used to transport himself on drug-fueled excursions. It launched him into a new and different world. Ty had discovered crack and it consumed him.

Down to the Wire had become Ty's new home. He was there almost every night on a bar stool, pounding down shots of cheap Scotch. Jake the Snake often surprised him by coming up behind Ty and slapping him hard on his back. "Kid, you sure know how to drink your face off on cheap booze. I've got the stuff that'll get you there quicker. Just follow me." And Ty would go outside behind the bar and get high with his new best friend and dealer Jake the Snake.

Ty's bank balance was shrinking as fast as Jake the Snake's pocket burgeoned. Ty had become a steady customer and Jake filled his pockets on the back of Ty's addiction. But this didn't faze Ty so long as the Snake kept him supplied. What good was money if you didn't spend it on a good time? And now Ty was doing both. Laughing as he'd hand a Benjamin over to Snake for the exchange, he said, "I'm running through a shit-load of money, but I am having a good time doing it." The only other thing that mattered to Ty was Lucy. They managed to see each other a few evenings during the week and on those occasions, Ty tried to be sober.

One evening when Ty arrived to pick her up on one of their rare early evening dates, Lucy chirped that she needed a few more minutes to dress and told Ty to help himself to a cold beer and disappeared into the bedroom.

He stood outside her closed bedroom door. "Lucy, I'll be out on the porch." Pulling out a beer from the refrigerator, Ty slid open the back door and sat down at the little marble ice cream table Lucy had on her patio. He looked out onto a small gravelly patch of desert earth bordered by a high wall. It was private and Ty was alone.

Knowing that Lucy would need more than a few minutes before being ready, Ty passed on the unopened beer waiting on the table and reached into his pocket to bring out a glass pipe and a small plastic baggie filled with chunks of creamy white goodness. Putting one of the smaller pieces into the bowl, Ty lit it, inhaled, and immediately floated into the new reality that was increasingly becoming home to him

Euphoria interrupted.

Lucy finished dressing and rushed out onto the porch. Ty was startled as Lucy materialized in front of his eyes. Doing a little twirl for him, she said playfully, "I'm ready." On the come around from her spin, Lucy saw Ty quickly slip something glossy into his coat pocket. She noticed an odd smell in the air sort of like burning plastic and commented, "Ty, something's burning."

"Hmm. I didn't notice. Maybe one of your neighbors is having a barbecue."

Lucy looked at him skeptically but did not press the matter further. But for the remainder of the evening, Ty sensed a growing distance between them, almost as if he was becoming a stranger to her.

Lucy knew that she did matter to Ty but had begun to notice a change in him. However, she wasn't exactly sure what was wrong. As a nurse, she kept an erratic schedule and sometimes the only time they could find to be together was late at night. It was then that Ty behaved differently, as if he was barely functioning. She tried to convince herself that he was just tired, but being a nurse, Lucy had her suspicions. Lucy cared about Ty, but someone else had begun to show an interest in her too – Ty's nemesis, Sean Stevenson.

Ty had never explained his strong reaction to seeing Sean that night at "Jersey Boys" no matter how many times she asked him about it. After receiving the same evasive response, she eventually forgot about the whole incident.

On one of her few afternoons off, Lucy decided to visit Marks & Franklin hoping to surprise Ty. But as she stepped out of the elevator to Ty's office, instead of meeting up with Ty, Lucy had literally run into Sean.

"Oh, I am so sorry," she said. "I should have been looking where I was going."

Sean apologized, "No, it's totally my fault. Don't give it another thought."

Lucy tried stepping around the man, still not recognizing who he was. Grabbing her arm, Sean stopped her.

"Excuse me. This may seem like a trite line, but we've met before. You were Ty's date that night at 'Jersey Boys,' weren't you? After seeing you, I didn't even care about watching the rest of the show. I couldn't concentrate on anything else except you."

Flattered by the compliment, Lucy blushed. "Yes, I remember you. I'm sorry, but I don't remember your name." Lucy lied. Of course, she knew his name. The few times Ty had talked about his work, it was always in a rant against this man.

Before Sean had time to answer, Ty appeared, rushing like a wave toward them. His agitation was obvious. Fists balled, his eyes were ablaze with rage.

Seemingly buoyed by Ty's reaction, Sean coolly said, "You're just in time, Ty, to watch me take your girl away from you."

Sean's arrogance incited Ty and he lashed out. "You? Lucy wouldn't give you the time of day. You're a scheming player and Lucy's too smart to fall for a grifter like you. Lucy doesn't troll for trash." Sean stared at Ty with a smug smile. He appeared to be thoroughly enjoying himself.

Pushing past him, Ty led Lucy back to the elevator. "Come on, let me see you out." With their backs turned to Sean, Ty pressed the button for the elevator while Lucy remained silent. She knew Sean was setting Ty up for something, though she didn't know what that could be.

Through his office window, Sean watched Ty and Lucy walk through the parking lot to her car. They were arguing. Ty smashed his fist on the roof of Lucy's car and walked back angrily toward the office. Sean smiled. Returning to his desk, he began typing an email to the HR department to begin building the case that would eventually lead to Ty's firing.

Just a few days later while Lucy was passing through the cafeteria line at Desert Valley Hospital, someone tapped her on the shoulder. Turning to see who it was, she blanched at the sight of Sean Stevenson standing behind her grinning like the Cheshire Cat. Used to handling unexpected situations, she quickly gathered her composure and put on her everything-is-all-right face. Nevertheless, Sean gave her a creepy feeling. "Why Sean Stevenson, what in the world brings you here to Desert Valley? And to the cafeteria no less?"

"Well, I've heard such good things about the cooking here that I decided to come by and check it out for myself. Besides, I was hoping to ask you to have lunch with me." Sean winked playfully at her.

"Why sure, everyone knows the Desert Valley Hospital cafeteria is rated three stars in Michelin's best Vegas restaurants."

Sean laughed and explained, "Actually, I came to check on a Marks & Franklin account."

Lucy frowned, puzzled. "I thought that was Ty's account."

"Perhaps you're not aware of this, Lucy, but Ty reports to me. And as Media Director, it's my responsibility to meet with our clients and see how my people are doing. And from what I heard this morning, I am glad I came."

This didn't sound good for Ty, but Lucy wasn't about to ask Sean what he meant. Thinking back, she fidgeted. Ty had never followed up on his so-called art picture that would supposedly hang on the walls of Desert Valley Hospital. Now, she wondered what had happened to all of those pictures he took of her. That had been almost two months ago, and she had never seen them. Lucy decided to ask Ty about it when he came to pick her up for their date that night. Sean caused her to have doubts about Ty, and she despised Sean Stevenson for putting them there.

As the cashier gave Lucy her change, she grabbed her tray and turned back to Sean. She wanted to get away from him as fast as she could and so made up a bogus excuse. "Sean, I'm sorry, but I have to run to an oncology meeting. But it was nice to see you."

As she walked away, he called out to her, "I'll see you again, Lucy. And I will let Ty know I saw you."

Pretending not to hear him, Lucy was beginning to understand why Ty lost his temper whenever Sean's name came up and thought to herself, *Wow! Ty's right. This guy is a problem.*

MARKS & FRANKLIN

Sean returned to the office and stopped at Ty's cubicle. "Ty, I've just been to Desert Valley Hospital for a meeting. I want to see you in my office immediately." Ty ignored the directive. With a shrug, Sean casually announced, "By the way, while I was there, I ran into Lucy. We had lunch together and, I hope you don't mind, but I asked her out for a date. She's cute." Seeing the look Ty gave him, Sean turned and took the short walk into his office wearing a checkmate grin across his face, but not before signaling his secretary.

Visibly annoyed, Ty shoved his chair under the desk and followed Sean into his office. He'd been there before. But now as he slammed the door behind him and saw the sleek, expensive furnishings, uncontrollable envy began to spread like cancer inside Ty. Stainless-steel legs shaped like girders supported a thick glass desktop; the thousand-dollar ergonomic mesh office chair overlooking the Vegas skyline completed the effect. This should have all been Ty's. Yet, somehow this weasel had stolen his job and all the trappings that went along with it. All Ty had was a laminated desk surrounded by half-height cubicle walls. It was barely a step away from working on a card table with a cardboard box for a wall. But what made the situation so intolerable was that Sean Stevenson was his boss. And now, this fuckhead was working on his girlfriend. It took every bit of self-restraint Ty could muster not to launch at Sean right then and there. What the hell did he want with him anyway?

Sean sat in his chair and looked at Ty. A sickening smile swept across his face as he combed his hair back with his fingers like some *GQ* model. "Have a seat." Ty obeyed. "This isn't easy for me since we've been friends for so long. But I have a responsibility to Marks & Franklin to see that our people deliver what our customers pay us for." Sean paused for a moment. Outside the glass walls of his office, a security officer stationed himself by the door. "And Ty, after my meeting with the management at Desert Valley this morning, it is clear that you are not delivering the quality product that we promised them. It took everything I could do to keep the account. They agreed, but only on the condition that I manage the account myself. What do you have to say about that?"

Ty wanted to throw a punch at Sean but only said, "Okay. So, they don't like me; put me on another account."

"Well, that response only confirms my concerns about you. It's that kind of attitude that does not belong at Marks & Franklin. I've discussed your situation with management and HR. They have left the final decision to me. I am sorry, Ty, but I am going to have to let you go. I have been documenting your poor job performance daily so if you think you have a wrongful dismissal case, well, think again. The truth is, pal, you don't have a prayer. I need you to get your things together and a security guard will escort you out of the building." Sean motioned for the guard who had stationed himself outside Sean's office to enter.

It took Ty a few seconds for him to realize what had just happened. But when the security guard grabbed his shoulder, he understood. He was being fired. It was then that his hatred for Sean metastasized into every area of his being. Sean had just launched a Pearl Harbor on him but Ty was ready for the battle. But with the security guard standing behind him, now was not the time. Maybe he could get some of his buddies at Down to the Wire to do a job on old Sean. Perhaps not. Ty could wait.

Ty stood and stuck out his hand to shake Sean's. "Well, if that's the way it is, that's the way it is! No hard feelings. I understand. This job just wasn't for me." Hesitating, Sean reluctantly shook hands with Ty.

Work in the office came to a halt as everyone stopped what they were doing to watch the security guard escort Ty through the office out of the building. Sean watched from the window as Ty walked across the parking lot to his car.

A wicked sneer engulfed Ty's face as he strode through the parking lot. He began laughing out loud at the thought that Sean Stevenson wouldn't have much longer to enjoy his fancy office.

FIT LIKE ADONIS CLUB

Ty became obsessed with thoughts of revenge. Sean had crossed him many times before. But this time, Sean had stepped over an imaginary red line that had pushed Ty into an almost psychotic state of mind. This was all-out war, and this time, Ty intended to win unconditionally.

Fit Like Adonis was arguably the most prestigious gym in Las Vegas but inarguably it was the most expensive. It had a reputation for producing bodybuilding kings and for four of the past five years, club members had won prestigious bodybuilding titles in national competitions. Ty knew about the gym and had made joining it one of the first things he did after moving to Las Vegas. Of course, he was not surprised when Sean too became a member shortly after arriving.

He had done the same thing in New York. Sean dogged Ty's every move. But unlike man's best friend, Sean was determined to beat him at everything they did. When Ty benched ten reps at two hundred fifty pounds, Sean would do the same; but at two-seventy-five. On their runs through Central Park, Sean would sprint the last leg goading Ty all the way. Now, Sean had followed him to Las Vegas to destroy his career and, Ty presumed, steal his girlfriend, Lucy. Ty knew what he had to do and phoned Sean from his car.

"Hey Sean, this is Ty. I wanted to let you know I'm okay with you letting me go. Yeah, I'm okay, man, but I still want to kick your ass in a game of racquetball. You deserve to have your butt kicked around the block for old time's sake. What do you say? How about you meet me at the Adonis tomorrow night at nine? I tried, but couldn't reserve a court 'til then. They were all booked up." Ty surprised himself at his composure. He was cool and knew Sean well enough to bait him with a lure he couldn't resist. He just had to let his catch run a while before he set the hook. "Oh, by the way, dude – bring your checkbook. The betting is on." Sean agreed to the match, and Ty said, "Okay then, game on!"

The next evening Sean arrived at the gym a little before nine. Ty was already there waiting for him in the lobby. As they looked at one another, both seemed to understand that this would be their final competition.

Ty knew all about Sean's philosophy of life: everyone was an adversary and needed to be vanquished. Sean's father had instilled it in him since he was a small child and the one thing that motivated Sean was pleasing his father. Ty knew that Sean Stevenson intended to shred him and wouldn't be satisfied until he brought about Ty's complete mental and physical humiliation.

Keeping up his pretense, Ty greeted Sean jokingly. "Well, hey there, Sean! Are you ready to get your butt kicked back to the Stone Age? How about we make this match interesting, say a hundred bucks? I win, you pay me and vice-versa; you win, you also pay me."

Sean shook his head. "I'm good with the first part of the deal, but you lost me on the second part."

Ty picked up his racquet and waved it through the air. "Relax, bro. I'm just busting you."

Ty thought it was funny, but Sean laughed at him mockingly. "C'mon, man. If you want to bet, let's bet. How about five Benjies. Best of three? After that, I have to go."

Ty thought to himself that this was going better than he could have imagined. He was leading Sean down Shakedown Street. "Let's shake on a thousand. Best of three."

Sean looked at him savagely and shook Ty's hand. "Done! Now let's get this thing going."

To determine who served first, Ty knelt and spun the head of his racquet on the floor, asking Sean as it spun to call up or down. Sean called, "Up." Ty looked at the letter on the butt of the racquet and showed it to Sean. It had landed upside-down. Ty smiled and won first serve. The game was on. As always, the competition was fierce. Both of them sustained long volleys back and forth, but Sean struggled to handle Ty's three wall returns and eventually lost the first game in a humiliating defeat.

His decisive fifteen-two victory made Ty ecstatic. But despite the score, it had been a long and hard-fought game. It had taken so long, in fact, that they didn't have time to play two more full games before they lost the court reservation. So, for the next two games, they agreed on shortened, eleven-point bouts.

As Sean readied himself to serve, he balled his fists and yelled, "It ain't over yet. There's still one more game; so, put your victory dance on hold, dude. There's still some mojo left in the tank. I've just been keeping it in the cooler for now."

"What the fuck do you mean in the cooler? Your cooler's empty."

Sean goaded Ty. "I ain't about to let you in my cooler. Just wait. I am going to ice you this game." Spinning the racquet in his and, Sean crouched to serve and with a twinkle in his eyes said, "You're going down in defeat like you always do. Get ready to write that check."

Ty squared off for the serve and Sean slammed the hard rubber ball into the wall at the other end of the court. The room was an echo chamber as the hard-hit ball ricocheted off the walls and their sneakers squeaked as they moved back and forth across the floor.

Ty was fatigued and admitted to himself that Sean was giving him more of a challenge than he had anticipated. But after two hours of arduous play, Ty won the second game and the match. He could hardly believe he had actually defeated Sean.

But losing was a first for Sean, and he was not willing to let it end there. Red-faced and dripping with sweat, he grabbed a towel aggressively and said, "Let's go for one more game! There's absolutely nobody near these squash courts. How about it? I'm not in the mood to say die. I'm not going down in flames. I don't know what losing even means."

"No, man. Game over. I won. You lost. How about we go out to my car and knock back some brewskies while you write my check?" Accepting defeat, Sean shrugged, and they began changing into their street clothes.

Sean reached in his gym bag, telling Ty, "I don't usually carry my checkbook around, but I know you don't take credit cards, so I brought it along just in case. But I never thought I'd be having to pay you off, but it is what it is." Sean wrote out a check for the grand and handed it to Ty. "Let it be known that Sean Stevenson never welches on a bet."

Ty grinned as he took the check from Sean's hand. "I hope this check won't bounce like the racquetball." As he stuffed it into his shirt pocket, he said, "It felt good opening a can of whoop-ass on you! We'll have to do this again real soon." He stuck out his hand for a handshake.

Shaking Ty's hand firmly, Sean said, "Okay, now let's go pound down some brews."

It was just a bit past eleven and the gym was still busy. Fit Like Adonis was not a club for the casual, once-in-a-while-when-I-feel-like-it health nut. Their members were fanatics who never missed a day of working out. And they all looked like it. Most were able to deadlift twice their body weight. Passing by the bodybuilders made both Ty and Sean feel like scrawny runts when, in fact, neither of them were small or out of shape.

The two men walked down the stairs and crossed the parking lot to Ty's Dodge Charger. "Hey man, let's drive over to that alley over there. The last thing I need is for a cop to catch me with an open can and haul me in on a DUI." Ty drove across the lot and pulled into the alley, out of sight. "I've got the Bud on ice in the trunk. I also got some sweet weed. You in the mood for some ganja?"

301

Sean gave Ty a puzzled look. "It sounds like you got a stash. Thanks, but I'll stick with the Bud."

"Suit yourself, man." Ty got out of the car to get the beer, carefully checking their surroundings to make sure they were alone. The last thing he needed was somebody sniffing around and he sure as hell did not want the "po-po" up in his business. Grabbing two beers out of the trunk, he also pulled a silk tie from his gym bag and shoved it into his hip pocket.

Walking over to the passenger side, he rapped on the window with a beer can and signaled for Sean to open it. "Here's a cold one, dawg. Cheers!" Sean thanked him, popped the top, and started guzzling. "Hey, why are you drinking like that's the last beer you'll ever have? Put it on slow-mo, bro. There's more where that came from." Ty feigned hospitality. "Two hours of racquetball fatigued me too. I'm with you on the beers. I feel dehydrated. You want another one since you sucked that one down in two seconds flat?"

Sean begrudgingly agreed and Ty went back to the trunk to fetch more beers. He looked up at the sky. It was black; not a star could be seen. This time, he returned carrying the ice chest and wrestled it into the back seat. He slid into the back seat next to the cooler and behind Sean. He shook the cooler, pretending to grab another beer while he pulled the tie from his pocket. Wrapping an end around each hand, Ty pulled it tight to be sure it would hold.

Sean was getting impatient. "Where's the brew, man?"

Ty leaned forward and, almost whispering, said, "Hey Sean, baby? Remember when I said you were drinking that beer like it was your last? Well, I hope you enjoyed it because guess what?" With a single swift move, Ty wrapped the silken noose around Sean's throat and kept pulling it tighter and tighter, digging his feet into the floor for better leverage.

Gasping and struggling to free himself, Sean tried to fight back. Somehow Sean was able to pull out a switchblade from his boot. It opened with a snap and Sean began slashing and stabbing at the air behind him. Ty laughed and grunted out, "A switchblade? What the shit is that going to do?"

But Sean's knife connected and several times it dug deeply into Ty's hand. Blood squirted everywhere. Ignoring the pain, Ty pulled the silk death rope ever tighter around Sean's throat. Sean continued to struggle, thrashing the knife feverishly behind his back, but Ty was relentless. He could feel the life in Sean Stevenson slowly ebbing. Ty's evil knew no end. "You're going to die, motherfucker!"

Ty wrenched down on the noose until Sean's struggling began to subside. Suddenly, Sean went limp. Ty released his hold and Sean's lifeless body flopped sideways, hitting the car window with a thud. Sean Stevenson was dead. It was over. Now, Ty needed to get rid of the body.

Still panting, Ty got out of the car and looked around, blood dripping from his hands. His footsteps on the loose gravel that paved the alley pounded loudly like the beat of a bass drum. The last thing he needed right now was to draw attention. Convinced that there was nobody around, Ty stepped carefully to the back of the car and opened the trunk.

Grabbing a gym towel from his bag, Ty wiped off the blood from his hands and pressed hard on the worst of the wounds to stop the bleeding. Opening the passenger door, he pulled Sean's lifeless body out of the car. Too big to sling over his shoulder, Ty wrapped his arms around Sean's chest and dragged his body to the trunk of his Charger. The noise was dreadfully loud and Ty's eyes darted maniacally back and forth, making sure no one was watching. The thought that never again will Sean Stevenson ruin his life rushed through his mind. He should have done this long ago. "Good riddance, bro."

Sean's lifeless body was like a six-foot bag of cement and Ty struggled to stuff it into the trunk. Hurriedly, he located Sean's bloody knife in the front seat, closed it, and tossed it on top of the body. With a grunt, he pressed the trunk lid shut and wiped the sweat from his brow. One last look around satisfied Ty that nobody had seen what he had just accomplished.

As he drove out of the alley, Ty felt exhausted and anxious. He needed a hit. Maybe that would steady him. His only thought was to get to the Wire and meet up with Snake. If only he could smoke some of the good stuff, he could calm down.

LAKE MEAD

The parking lot at Down to the Wire was full and that meant the bar was packed with people; Ty did *not* want to have to go in there to find his man. But luck was with him as he saw Jake the Snake slither out of the bar just as Ty arrived. Jake saw Ty and they both nodded at each other at the same time.

Snake looked at Ty with contempt. Ty was hooked and that's just what every dealer wants. Addicts made good customers. "Yeah, I got what you want, as long as you got the cash. Otherwise I don't want to see your fucking face!"

The transaction was routine and quick. Ty handed Snake the cash and Snake slipped a small plastic baggie into Ty's hand. The only time the Snake's face cracked even the semblance of a smile was when he stuffed cash in his pocket. Both of them had what they wanted.

Making his way back to the car, Ty pulled a glass pipe out of the glove box. Again, he was careful not to be seen firing up his crack. The last thing he needed now was to be seeing sirens and smelling bacon dressed in blue. He dropped a small rock into the bowl and struck his lighter. One deep toke and Ty was flying.

He pulled out of the Wire and steered the car toward Lucy's apartment. Being a nurse, she could bandage his cuts. All he had to do was tell her a little fib about how he had cut his hand in the kitchen and that would be that. Lucy would fall for anything as long he used his boyish charm. She was hardly ever disagreeable.

Knocking on Lucy's apartment door, Ty couldn't remember if she had the evening off. It was past midnight. Oh well, he'd soon find out. It only took a few knocks before Lucy appeared at the door wearing a slinky negligée. Ty wondered if she was expecting him and he temporarily forgot about the baggage in the trunk of his car. Lucy immediately focused on his hands.

"Ty, what is the matter with your hand? Oh my God, it's both of your hands. What happened? Come into the bathroom with me right now. Geez, I get one evening off and here you come around knocking only to be my next patient in waiting! What did you do?"

Ty could sense that, although she was genuinely worried, she was also suspicious. He wondered if she interrogated her ER patients when their stories couldn't quite explain the injuries that brought them to the hospital in the first place. Through his haze, he remembered that

Lucy was an oncology nurse and not an emergency nurse. But didn't emergency nurses and doctors have to inquire what happened? It was a good thing he had Lucy to help him treat his lacerations. But what the hell could he tell her?

Lucy led him into the bathroom and turned on the faucet. She told Ty to hold his hands under the water. She opened her cabinets and pulled out hydrogen peroxide, cotton balls, and gauze. Lucy looked intently into his eyes. "I'm waiting for an answer. Seriously. This looks like you got into a knife fight. I want to know, Ty, who were you fighting with? God, it looks like you almost sliced your fingers off."

"No, I went fishing with some dudes the other day at Lake Mead. I caught some striped bass. I was gutting them and the knife slipped. I kind of had a buzz going on and I ended up filleting myself. I also caught a channel catfish and it finned me. Damn, it hurt. That'll teach me to mix drinking and cleaning fish at the same time. My bad, but I'll live."

"Ty, I'm not a fool. You're not telling me the truth, and I don't appreciate it. These wounds are fresh. They *just* happened. I'm going to ask you one more time, and if I don't get an answer, I am going to pick up the phone and call the police. What do you take me for? A stupid fool? Don't insult me!"

Ty insisted, adding detail to his story. Lucy slammed down the cotton balls she had in her hands and rushed out of the bathroom. Grabbing a towel, Ty followed her into the living room. He watched her pick up the phone. Ty hoped Lucy had no intention of calling the police. Maybe she was trying to scare him, but it looked like the bitch really was going to make the call.

He panicked. Lunging at her, he ripped the phone from her hands and threw it across the room. Grabbing her arms, he began to shake her. He was angry. He was upset and surprised at the violent way he grabbed her. He loved her and he thought she loved him too. Her betrayal angered him. He had not expected things to play out like this.

Screaming loud enough to strain her vocal cords, Lucy confronted him. "You're on something and you're on it tonight. You're lying to me."

Pushing her to the ground, Ty began kicking Lucy in a blind rage. He knew he was acting like a crazed monster. Why was she making him do this to her? Feeling like he was in some deranged nightmare, he wasn't even sure this was real.

Lucy tried to get up, but Ty shoved her hard again onto the floor. In her hysteria, she yelled, "I know who you got in the fight with. It was Sean Stevenson, wasn't it?" Triggering an earthquake in Ty's mind, he lunged toward her with even greater force and raised his leg above her head. Lucy rolled away just as Ty smashed his heavy boot into the floor. Lucy screamed out in terror as Ty lifted his boot again. This time he wouldn't miss.

Frantic knocks erupted at the door followed by pounding and yelling. "Lucy, are you all right in there? We've called 9-1-1. Let us in. Are you okay?" They wouldn't stop banging on the door.

Ty fled out the back of Lucy's apartment into the small yard. He tried opening the gate, but it was locked. He launched himself up and over the high wall of the courtyard and fell down hard on the other side. He thought it lucky that Lucy's apartment was on the ground floor.

Running to his car, he fumbled with the key to start it, and for some inexplicable reason, it wouldn't turn over. "Shit!" he yelled. Ty heard police sirens some blocks away and knew they sang for him. He tried the engine again. This time, it started. He jammed the gas pedal and raced out of the parking lot into the night.

But the men in blue would be looking for him. Once they talked with Lucy and her neighbors, they would soon be putting out a warrant for him. It was only a matter of time, and Ty couldn't waste his. He began babbling to himself, "Shit, I hate pig-cops. I smell bacon and this time, it's the whole damn slab."

HOOVER DAM FLYOVER

Ty intended to lose himself in the nighttime traffic of the strip while he figured out a plan. His first and only plan – to lie low with Lucy – had just exploded in his face. He needed get out of Las Vegas fast.

His mind raced like shit through a goose. There was a lot to think about. Why did Lucy turn on him? He still couldn't believe it. Plan B. Sean's dead body was in the trunk. What was he going to do with it? Had he really killed Sean? Maybe he had just hallucinated it all. Damn, that crack was playing tricks with his brain. Maybe Sean wasn't even there. It all seemed like some weird dream. Maybe none of it happened. But it had, and Ty had the stab wounds on his hands to prove it.

But what if Sean wasn't dead? Maybe he had just blacked out. Ty had not felt for a pulse. What if Sean regained consciousness and was still alive? No. If he was, there would be pounding and screaming coming from the trunk. But what if he *was* still alive? What if Sean found the trunk release and let himself out while he was at Lucy's? Holy shit! Ty had to be sure.

Pulling into the parking garage of the New York-New York Casino, he drove up several levels until he found a dark empty area to park in. Turning the car off and pulling out the keys, Ty rushed to the trunk. He put the keys into the lock and turned it. The lid popped open and Ty jumped back ready for Sean to spring out at him like a jack-in-the-box. But nothing happened. Taking a breath of relief, he approached the trunk, and in the night glow, peered down at Sean's motionless body. Pigeons rustled nervously in the ceiling. Refusing to go through that kind of uncertainty again, Ty reached for Sean's wrist and searched for a pulse. The hand was cold and lifeless. Sean was indeed dead. He wasn't going anywhere except where Ty wanted him to.

Ty closed the trunk lid on the dead man and got back into his car. For a moment he just sat there. It had been a busy night and he was suddenly tired. But there was still so much left to do. The main thing, he kept telling himself, was not to get caught. "Fuck that bitch Lucy anyway. She ruined everything."

Ty began to plan. He'd head south for Hoover Dam, stop halfway across the flyover, and toss Sean off the bridge into the Colorado River nine hundred feet below. With any luck, the river would float the body well downstream before daylight; it could be months before anyone found it. And the chance of him being noticed was slim. It was late and traffic was bound to be light. But if someone did stop, he could always fake car trouble or a flat tire. From there, he would cross into Arizona and hide in Somewhere, USA though he hadn't yet figured out where that somewhere was.

It was the perfect plan, sheer elegance in its simplicity. Hoover Dam was only about thirty-five miles southeast of Las Vegas and on the other side was Arizona. He had time because it was still dark and he had outrun the police. Laughing out loud, he thought, *I'll be so outta here before they even post a warrant out for me. I'm the man.* Smiling, Ty closed his eyes and fell asleep.

Ty was awakened by a heavy rap on the car window. Looking up, he saw flashing blue lights dancing against the walls. A cop stood looking into his car. *Shit*, he thought. How long had he been asleep? Rolling down the window, Ty squinted against the glare of the flashlight and said nervously, "Hello, officer?"

"Casino Security," came the gruff reply. "You can't be camping here, buddy. It's time for you to move on."

Ty relaxed just a bit. "Oh, sure. Sorry, sir. I must have dozed off."

"Just move on, pal."

"No problem, sir. Thank you." Damn, that guy sure took his flunky security job seriously. In reality, he barely had the power to make a citizen's arrest.

Ty started the car, backed out of the space, and drove slowly down the ramp and out of the garage with casino security trailing him all the way. The streets were empty and Ty realized it was early morning. Looking at the clock, showed he had pretty much slept the night away. It would be light soon and if his plan had any chance at all, he needed to get on with it.

His head was beginning to hurt. Another hit was what he needed. Ty leaned over and grabbed the glass pipe from the glove box. Fumbling with the baggie he scored from Snake, he squeezed out a pebble-sized piece of the cocaine and lit the pipe. The rock glowed a soft orange as he released his finger from the end of the tube and took the hit. Immediately, he felt better.

The Charger breezed down Las Vegas Boulevard past McCarran Airport east onto 215. A few minutes later, Ty caught Interstate 515 at Henderson and turned south. To his left, he could see the hint of dawn beginning to show on the horizon and already the dark of night was lifting to reveal the murky hills around him. Shortly past Henderson, the interstate turned into US-93 and a traffic light brought a halt to the Charger's progress. Already the Vegas-bound lanes across from him were becoming busy but traffic in his direction was still light, and Ty sat alone waiting for the signal to change. The light turned green. He saw that as a good sign and lit up a joint for what he deemed a cause for celebration. Hoover Dam was now only a few minutes away. Feeling renewed with weed, Ty thought his escape was guaranteed.

At Boulder City, US-93 took a hard left at another traffic light. The Charger nearly missed the turn and Ty had to cut across three lanes to make it. Ty looked around nervously and behind him in the rearview mirror. There was nothing, only a sedan lazily turning out of a shopping center lot. It pulled up into the left turn lane next to him. He looked over and saw that it was a Ford Mustang GT being driven by what appeared in the growing light to be a middle-aged man with a mustache, no doubt trying to relive his glory days with a muscle car. The signal light flashed a green arrow and the Mustang sped on ahead of him and was soon out of sight. Off in the distance, Ty could see the first sign of the waters of Lake Mead.

There were just a few miles more to go but dawn had already broken and the southbound traffic was beginning to build. No longer alone on the road, he started to have doubts about his plan. Maybe it would be better to rent a boat at the marina, motor out to a secluded spot, tie a few rocks to Sean, and toss him overboard to sink into the depths of Lake Meade.

But how does one take a dead body out of a car trunk and carry it onto a boat without drawing attention? And how to explain hauling a couple of boulders along for the ride? He could drive up along Lakeshore and maybe find a place where he could stash the body and then swing by and pick it up in the boat. Hell, why bother to sink the body anyway? Maybe he was overthinking the whole thing.

Now Ty wasn't sure what he should do, but whatever it was, he knew he better hurry. Scrunching his brows to concentrate, a rush of anxiety attacked him. Trying to think so hard was bringing on a headache. He massaged his temples and loaded the pipe with a big chunk of crack and lit up. Within a few seconds after exhaling the hit, Ty reasoned that simple was best and he would stay with his original plan – fake car malfunction, wait for the traffic to clear, and dump Sean's body off the bridge.

A few miles from the Hoover Dam flyover, Ty noticed a car coming up fast behind him. It raced up to his rear and began tailgating him. Ty slowed, hoping to let the car pass, but it only slowed down with him. Ty sped up and the car kept pace. Ty braked hard; the car behind him fell back, but quickly rode up to his tail again. This guy was gaming him. Something about it looked familiar. As it came up to drag on his tail lights again, Ty finally recognized it as the same Ford Mustang he'd seen at the traffic light in Boulder City. He began to worry. He wanted to see who was driving the muscle car and stared into the rearview mirror. Yep. It was the same guy with the mustache. Ty thought, *Woah! This guy is gunnin' for me!*

Then his worst nightmare was realized. Two police cars drove down an entrance ramp onto the highway as he passed it to fall in behind him and the Mustang. For a moment, he thought this might all be a bizarre coincidence, but then red-and-blue flashing lights flashed through the grill of the Mustang with its siren blaring. The cops behind him followed suit and turned on their noise as well.

Ty was ready to run. He jammed the gas pedal to the floor and the Charger rocketed forward, leaving the police behind him in a puff of black exhaust. Almost as quickly, the Mustang was up alongside him in the other lane; the two patrol cars were fast catching up too. The car pack raced past yellow warning signs as they negotiated a broad curve around a rocky brown knob before blasting onto the bridge. The blue ribbon of the Colorado River threaded through the chasm one thousand feet below.

It was now a straight run across the bridge to Arizona and Ty smashed the gas pedal to the floor. But the Mustang had the jump on him and they drag raced to the other side. Suddenly, the Mustang raced in front of him and braked hard. Ty swerved to pass, but the Mustang blocked him. One of the patrol cars behind made a move to come up alongside in an attempt to box him in. Ty lurched right to cut him off and was able to break out in front of the Mustang. Suddenly the cars behind him slowed and Ty sped on alone. Arizona was just ahead. But a hundred yards at the other end of the bridge, he saw a blockade of flashing lights. He was caged.

Realizing he was cornered, he jammed on the brakes and skidded to a stop. He jumped out of his car and dashed along the bridge guard toward the center of the flyover.

The blockade of police cars at the other end of the bridge dissembled to form a line of flashing lights moving slowly toward him. Meanwhile, the cops and the unmarked Mustang behind him skidded to a stop and began chasing after him on foot. Weapons drawn, they ran after Ty, shouting, "Stop and get down on the ground!"

Crazed with panic, Ty ran as fast as he could. His lungs were about to burst.

"Stop, or we'll shoot!"

Ty heard the gunshot echo off the canyon walls. The two cops behind him were gaining on him. His agitation was apparent. Ty waved his arms frantically and began running back and forth across the road, unsure of what to do. Two more shots were fired. The police were closing in on him from both sides. There was no escape. Two more shots – and Ty stopped. He turned his focus on the canyon below. In an instant he ran to the side of the bridge.

"No, no! Don't jump!" screamed an officer, gun drawn. More pleas rose from the chorus of police gathering around him. But Ty didn't hear them. He was only aware of the pounding of his heart and the panic threatening to swallow him whole.

Ty vaulted over the barrier into the sky and for a moment he was flying.

The police were everywhere along the bridge. No one could believe it. The man had jumped nine hundred feet to his death. The plainclothes officer, the one driving the unmarked Mustang GT, went to Ty's Charger, turned off the car, and pulled the key from the ignition. He moved swiftly to the trunk of Ty's car and opened it. What the officer saw sickened him and he stepped back as the patrolmen came up behind him to stare at Sean's lifeless body in silence.

It was over, except there was still one person the police needed to contact – the young lady named Lucy, who had reported the violent assault.

Lucy recounted the details of her confrontation with Ty. But that wasn't necessary; the investigators could see the bruises covering Lucy's body for themselves. Lucy went on to tell them about Ty Amaya, the misguided person whose life had taken a tragic turn, and his uncontrollable hatred for his nemesis Sean Stevenson. They now understood, and placed the final piece of the puzzle that led to a horrific murder and senseless suicide.

SERIOUSLY COSMOPOLITAN

Waking up that Sunday morning, Jill sat on the edge of her bed and rubbed her temples in an attempt to massage away her hangover headache. Last night's drinks had helped her forget the strain of the day, but this morning the memories came rushing back. The tryouts, Derek Martin attacking her, and now John sitting in a jail cell on her account left her feeling hopeless. Awash in self-pity, Jill felt vulnerable, and that was a new feeling for her. For several long minutes she worked to hold back tears. Then her phone rang.

Jill looked at the cell display. She didn't recognize the number but answered anyway. "Hello?"

It was Derek, and he sounded like he was high on something. Jill listened silently as Derek promised to give her the top spot in the Malai's Extravaganza if she'd be willing to forget about what had happened.

But Jill remembered everything all too well and told him, "Too late, you piece of shit! I'm pressing charges and won't rest until your ass rots in jail." Derek lost all control and began screaming through the phone, calling her a slut and promising to ruin her. That was all the motivation she needed to crush the audition.

By the time she arrived at the Malai for the second day of tryouts, she had vanquished any thought of defeat. At the end of the day, Jill was one of a hundred women asked to return for the final cut on Monday.

On Monday, when she arrived for the final day of tryouts, something was different. Instead of all the girls stretching and warming up around the big hall, everyone was huddled together peering up at a television monitor. They watched with rapt attention as the breaking news reported on the untimely death of Derek Martin.

The television reporter was interviewing one of the police officers at the scene. He stated that the deceased had been wanted by the Las Vegas police on an alleged assault charge and went on to explain that the dead man had tried to evade police by fleeing into an active construction area where he had met his demise.

The reporter thanked the officer and turned toward the camera, "Well, there you have it. Derek Martin, Entertainment Manager at the Malai Casino, met an untimely and tragic death today when he ran into a dusty construction area and was killed by the swinging bucket of a backhoe. I am told the backhoe operator will not be charged and that

Derek Martin's death is being ruled as accidental. This is Kevin Joliet reporting."

Everyone was silent while the judges gathered in the corner of the room in conference. Jill watched as they debated whether to cancel tryouts or at least postpone them until tomorrow. After some discussion, the judges agreed in true show-biz spirit that "the show must go on."

The fishnet lady found the remote control for the monitor and turned off the television. "Ladies, ladies." She spoke loudly to get their attention. A well-dressed and distinguished man stood next to her. "This is Mr. Otto Dietrich, General Manager of the Malai and Derek Martin's manager. He would like to say a few words to you."

"Ladiees, deese ees a tragic ting to 'appen, but vee must be all beezzness now. Vee begin in ten minutes." Jill had never seen him before but immediately recognized his voice as the man who had first made her appointment with Derek. It seemed odd to Jill that Derek's boss scheduled interviews for his managers, but that was definitely the man she had spoken with.

Jill felt numb but also strangely relieved. She would never have to deal with Derek Martin again. Her only concern was whether anyone at the casino could somehow connect her with Derek's death. Even though she was the victim, she knew companies didn't like scandals. And this one had the makings of exploding into a notorious fiasco. She knew the truth would eventually come out about what Derek had done to her, but she hoped that day would wait until well after tryouts. A hopeful thought came to her. She reasoned that it was too soon for anyone in the room to know anything more about it than what they had just seen on television. Furthermore, the judges and the dancers were sequestered in the vast hall and would remain there until the end of the tryouts. By then, the cuts would be made. Jill wasn't about to let the news about Derek Martin literally biting the dust stop her from becoming one of the chosen.

The judges worked the girls harder during this final tryout session than in the previous two days. The dance moves became more complicated and demanding and the judges showed little patience for those who could not keep up. Of the several hundred girls who had started, Jill reckoned there to be less than a hundred remaining. And that number was being steadily whittled down as those who missed a step were summarily disqualified and told to leave. This process continued until only fifty remained. And of that group, fifteen of them would serve as alternates or understudies.

Jill, however, performed flawlessly. There wasn't a routine or dance step she couldn't complete; she could tell that the judges seemed impressed. Jill's body pumped adrenaline. She was able to jump higher with greater form than anyone in the room. With toes pointed and her back arched almost like a folded jackknife, Jill's talent and skill were evident. But she also danced with grace and fluidity that all but assured her selection for a place somewhere in the chorus line.

The audition came to an abrupt halt after the fifty-first dancer was sent home. The girls were told to form into a chorus line and come forward when their names were called. When she heard her name, Jill stepped up to be fitted for her costume. Two Extravaganza alumni came up to Jill and placed the Malai Extravaganza crown on her head. It was a glittery white-beaded skull cap replete with brightly-dyed, dangling red drabs and two ostrich plumes shooting two feet into the air. They hugged Jill and the rest of the people in the room broke into applause for her. Expected to take a bow, Jill did so with a triumphant face. Her coronation was complete.

The girls were told that they were free to leave for the day but to come back tomorrow for introductions and the first of many rehearsal sessions. It was indeed a momentous achievement for Jill and should have been a time to bask in her accomplishment. But after many hugs and congratulations, Jill rushed out the door. Up until then, there had been no further mention of Derek Martin, and she did not want to be drawn into any gossip about the man that might make others suspicious of her. No, Derek Martin was gone and she was now a dancer in the most extravagant show on all of the Las Vegas Strip.

Jill used her three-day pass to catch a red, double-decker bus outside the Malai. Intent to celebrate on her own, she headed downtown to a trendy upscale bar called Seriously Cosmopolitan. It was a favorite hangout of lawyers, doctors, and wealthy businessmen. Now, with her new pedigree, Jill would fit right in with all the other assorted professionals who frequented this fashionable establishment. She could already taste the large pink cosmopolitan, double vodka she was going to order.

Taking a window seat on top level of the bus, Jill watched the passing crowds and the casinos with their fancy signs announcing their entertainment line ups. She felt like the queen of all of Las Vegas and looked forward to the day when the famous double-decker bus, known as the "Deuce", would boast a picture of her posing with the other Malai Casino Extravaganza showgirls, pasted along its red sides. The thought made her eyes crinkle with delight. It seemed fitting that she was sitting high up on the bus now that she was part of an elite class of performers in one of Vegas' premier stage shows. She would toast herself at Seriously Cosmopolitan and make that martini glass full of her pink cosmopolitan shimmer and shake just like she planned to do as a Malai Extravaganza showgirl.

THE RED ROOM

In a single weekend, Jill's life had gone from dull and monotonous to new and exciting. There were daily rehearsals and grueling sessions of choreography. But with the show opening in just three weeks, there was a lot to do. She met new people all the time and mostly got along with the other girls picked for the chorus line. Of course, there was some friendly, and sometimes unfriendly, competition between the ladies. But the one thing they all agreed on was that they couldn't trust the understudies.

Fortunately for Jill, most of the dressing room talk revolved around the show or boyfriends or food; there was scant mention of Derek Martin. Whenever his name did come up in conversation though, Jill kept quiet or lied, saying something like, "Yeah, I guess it's too bad what happened to him. But I only met the guy the one time in his office to sign up for the auditions." That seemed to be the only memory any of them had of Derek Martin, and even that memory quickly faded like a rain puddle evaporating under the desert sun.

Jill was grateful the media and newspapers had chosen to protect her privacy and refused to mention her name. Even the Malai management seemed inclined to move on. The very day after he was killed, they cleared out his office and within a week, filled his position with a new Entertainment Manager. Jill took this as a sign that she had nothing to worry about and could concentrate solely on making the Extravaganza the best show on the strip. By opening night, no one remembered Derek Martin. It was like he had never existed.

The chorus line girls queued up behind the curtain and Jill fidgeted nervously as the orchestra began to play. After weeks of hard practice, she could not wait to kick up her legs and sashay around the stage wearing elaborate and colorful costumes. This was it – opening night.

Every number required a costume change with each costume more dazzling or risqué than the one preceding it. Throughout the show, the special effects lighting spotlighted the dancers from all sides to not only give them the illusion that they were glowing, but to emphasize the sculpted qualities of the dancers' bodies.

The Malai brought in legendary Broadway choreographer Jason Gleeson to direct and produce the show. The man was a frenetic cyclone of energy with a reputation for consistently delivering innovative entertainment to audiences and returning very handsome profits to investors.

Big, bold, and flamboyant was an apt description for Jason Gleeson's productions, and the Malai Extravaganza was no exception. With no big-name entertainer to headline the show, Jason relied on the collective talent of his cast and confidence in his ability to create and deliver a successful show. His stage choreography was often described as "Bob Fosse meets George Balanchine." Fosse was known for his inventive jazz dance creations while Balanchine was the primary choreographer for the New York City Ballet. Jason Gleeson's productions were a hybrid of the two. Both men had long since passed on, but their legendary contributions to dance gave them an immortality few men have achieved.

Another factor that made Gleeson's show so successful was the talented stage crew whose special effects expertise never failed to astound audiences across the country. They employed glitter and confetti bombs, streamers, fake snow, smoke, and an array of pyrotechnics that would be the envy of every small-town July Fourth fireworks committee in the country. Special effect machines shot fireballs into the air while tall columns of flame were set around the stage. Through this spectacle, the showgirls in their feathered costumes maneuvered in four-inch heels and danced seamlessly. When it was all brought together, the result was the "Wow" effect expected of a Jason Gleeson production.

But the rehearsals were not without problems. The singers and stage crew missed their cues often and the chorus girls couldn't keep their line straight. With each mistake, Jason Gleeson would erupt into uncontrollable tantrums that terrorized the cast members. During the final dress rehearsal, one dancer stumbled into one of the flame columns. In a flash of fire, her feathered headgear burned down to her scalp, leaving her to scream in panic as stagehands rushed out with an extinguisher to hose her down.

Unconcerned, Gleeson bellowed, "Suck it up. Your costumes are fireproof. You should be grateful your clumsy feet didn't dance you off the stage for good. But your butt is where you are going to have a problem because it is going to become mighty sore sitting in the front row watching your fellow dancers perform. In a word, you're grounded." He pulled her from the line, replacing her with an understudy on opening night.

The theme of the Extravaganza was "Happy Days Are Here Again." They put on two shows a night, Wednesday through Sunday, and the production was booked to run six months. But already there was talk of extending it for another six months because of the immeasurable amount of pre-publicity and strong advanced ticket sales. It looked like Jason Gleeson had another hit on his hands and Jill was a part of it. It thrilled her every time she came to work and passed the life-size picture of herself in the chorus line with the other girls.

The theater was full of influential people throughout the entertainment world. Local casino executives intent on evaluating their competition and celebrities from Hollywood and Broadway, all came to see the latest Gleeson production. Jason, of course, did not disappoint. Despite so many critical eyes in the audience, when the curtain closed on the final number, the cast of the Extravaganza received two standing ovations. Then chants of "Jason, Jason, Jason!" ensued. Running out from behind the ornately beaded curtain, Jason was all smiles, taking bow after bow. He finally turned and swept his hands to acknowledge the cast standing behind him. The girls in the chorus line were center stage dressed in their two-foot flocked headpieces and stiletto slides. The entire line bowed in perfect unison and then kicked their legs up to perform a quick can-can, much to the delight of the audience. Enthralled by the audience's reaction, Jill couldn't wait to read the reviews of the show.

After nearly two hours of high-intensity dancing, Jill's feet hurt and the smile she was required to maintain throughout the show now felt as if it was permanently glued on her face. She was reluctant to join the by-invitation-only celebration at the Malai Casino's opulent restaurant known as the Red Room. But in the dressing room, she was told the entire cast and crew were expected to make an appearance. So, she followed the rest of the Malai Extravaganza organization behind an effusive and buoyant Jason Gleeson down a long corridor to the elegant Red Room restaurant.

As Jill milled about moving from group to group, talking and laughing and receiving congratulations from the guests, she couldn't help but notice one man appearing to be in his early sixties staring at her. She tried to ignore him, but every time she moved to another group, he seemed to follow. She thought the man looked distinguished and important. He was impeccably dressed in formal attire and handsome – for a man old enough to be her grandfather. Jill wished he would stalk someone else.

Rip Rumple was a well-known billionaire. A businessman who made his fortune in real estate and venture capital, Rumple also had a reputation as an eccentric playboy. He loved gambling, and the casinos competed with each other to cater to his every whim. It was probably because Rumple was such a reliable loser.

There was an abundance of stories surrounding Rip Rumple's epic losses at the gaming tables, the most famous of which had him lose three million dollars in a single hand of baccarat. According to those who were there, Rumple pushed himself calmly away from the table and stood. Smiling at his fellow players, he had pulled his empty pants pockets out and told them jokingly, "Well, my dear friends, it would appear that I am out of chump change, it's no big deal. But now, I must extend to you all my fond farewell and retire to my room where I hope my head will find my pillow and not the floor." Everyone at the table laughed because they understood the joke.

His nickname was Rip 'Van' Rumple because Rip Rumple suffered from a malady known as narcolepsy. Sufferers of this rare sleep disorder were suddenly consumed with severe drowsiness and prone to falling asleep at unpredictable moments. Though unlike his namesake Rip Van Winkle, who slept for twenty years after imbibing on a glass of Dutch gin called Jenever, Rip 'Van' Rumple was known to fall into deep slumber at the most inopportune times and without the assistance of any medicine or alcohol.

Just as the stories of his gambling escapades were legend, so too were the stories of those who had witnessed Rumple fall asleep. At important business meetings where billion-dollar deals were negotiated, Rip's head would unexpectedly drop to his chest in a narcoleptic spell while influential corporate executives waited patiently for him to reawaken. Of course, many of them were skeptical. They thought Rip used his well-known condition as leverage to get what he wanted. But even they needed to wait until the eccentric billionaire decided to come back to life.

Rip had even fallen asleep standing up at a craps table right after doubling his bet with thousands left on the table. The players next to him had had to wake him up to let him know that the shooter had just made him a fortune. Letting out a high-pitched whistle, he woke up for a fleeting moment to say, "Take all my bets off the table!" only to crash into sleep again after receiving his winnings. A young waitress doing her best to be sexy wiggled on over and tried to wake him by offering him some strong coffee. It was futile. Taking one sip of the coffee, he nodded back out and slept through it all until the next shooter came up and tapped him on his shoulder. This shook Rip into wakefulness once more but not for long. Standing up for a brief second, he soon toppled over and bounced off the craps table careening into the young waitress carrying drinks. She let out a yelp as the glasses fell off her tray and smashed to the floor. This time, Rumple was awake and apologized profusely. He then asked if someone wouldn't mind escorting him back up to his hotel room.

Malai Casino management made sure to indulge Rumple whenever he came to Las Vegas. Free lobster and steak dinners were common and though he had his own private Vegas penthouse, Rip was always offered the casino's most exclusive penthouse suite along with every other spoiled demand he made. One time, he requested an expensive Steinway baby grand piano be brought to his room. The hotel staff obliged even though the joke was that Rip 'Van' Rumple couldn't play a single note. Rip Rumple was just that kind of man.

As Jill took her place at the large Red Room dining table, an older man moved in fast to take the seat next to her. Winking at Jill, he told her it was about time they finally met. Not finding him very exciting, Jill did her best to ignore him. But he was persistent, evidently unaccustomed to a brush off. Taking a small Post-It pad from his coat pocket, he began to scribble something on it. He folded the paper and tucked it back into his jacket.

Jill looked around the room and noticed that the show's cast was sitting together and Malai management had taken most of the seats around the Extravaganza dancers as if to fence them off from the other guests at the table. There was a reason behind that.

A key clause in the employment contract that everyone in the show was required to sign was the morality clause. It was unambiguous in its prohibitions, stating: "No member of cast or crew may fraternize in any way with Malai guests where such actions could be construed by a corporate panel to bring disrepute or scandal to the Malai Corporation. I understand that such action will result in my immediate termination and I agree to accept the panel's final judgment and I accept that decision. I, therefore, waive any demand to arbitrate said decision."

The clause was explicit. Jill had readily initialed that statement on her contract. Becoming involved with a Malai patron was unimaginable to her, especially after hearing the dressing room chatter of previous dancers summarily dismissed after being seen consorting with some of the casino's high-rollers. Gauging by the man's swagger and apparent unfamiliarity with her objections, Jill concluded with some exasperation that her suitor was the infamous Rip Rumple.

Rip Rumple would not stop staring at Jill. He leaned into Jill and pretending to reach for a bread basket, slipped the piece of paper he had written onto her lap. It read: "Meet me at the Gold Café on Fremont. Tuesday at seven-thirty p.m. Nod if you agree." It was signed, "Rip Rumple." In passing her the note, he whispered in her ear, "I know about your contract. No worries my lovely, I will protect you."

Jill laughed to herself at the thought of a billionaire reverting to schoolboy note passing. She was flattered at being the recipient of his childlike approach and was touched by the charm of it all. Without looking at Rip, she nodded her head agreeing to a Tuesday night rendezvous. What could it hurt? Under the table, Rip touched Jill's leg in confirmation and then turned his attention to Jason Gleeson sitting to his left. Jill appreciated Rip's discretion.

Jill was tired and wanted to go home. She covered her barely eaten steak with her napkin to signal the wait staff to take it away and got up to leave. As she did, she thought she saw some of the Malai executives staring at her. Maybe it was her imagination, but the stares seemed to be critical. Did they know it was she who Derek Martin had assaulted? Had they seen Rip Rumple's flirtation? She couldn't be sure.

Making her obligatory goodbyes to all the important people she worked under, Jill thanked them for her wonderful dinner. She lied convincingly. Her barely cooked steak was just like everything else in the room – too bloody red. They had even put red beets with a radish garnish on her plate.

She took a last look at the Red Room. What else could they have named it? Everything in it was some shade of red. The lamps as well as the curtains, carpet, walls, tablecloth, napkins, and the plates and glasses were all red. The centerpieces were red vases full of red roses, and the butter dish was a transparent candy-apple red. Jill wondered if there wasn't anything in the room that wasn't red. Even the wooden chairs and table were stained dark cherry. It was ridiculous, and she was convinced that the interior decorator had to have been color blind. The wait staff dressed in their red uniformed pants and red button-down cotton shirts wished her good luck as she passed them. Rip Rumple gave her a knowing smile as she hastily left the dining room. Of all things, there seemed to be a red flush to his face.

GOLD CAFE

Jill waited impatiently at a bus stop for one of Vegas' double-decked buses to take her downtown for her date with Rip Rumple. She wondered what small talk would be like with a billionaire. "How many millions did you make today?" Or, "How big is *your* yacht?" She laughed at her double entendre.

As the bus rolled to a stop in front of her, she gasped with excitement at the advertisement emblazoned along the length of it. A near life-size picture of herself linked arm-in-arm with the Extravaganza chorus line colorfully festooned it. She looked around, expecting someone at the stop to recognize that she was one of the girls in the picture. But no one did, and all got into the bus without noticing her at all. Disappointed, Jill climbed in silently behind them.

The Gold Cafe was located next to a florist shop, and as soon as Jill entered, Rip Rumple was there to greet her with a bouquet of yellow roses. She was glad they were any other color but red. "My dear, you look wonderful. These are for you. My guess is that you have seen enough of red for a while."

Jill laughed as she took the bundle from Rip. "Funny you should say that; I was thinking the same thing. These are beautiful. Thank you."

Rip escorted Jill to a table near a window where sun-splashed rivers of glowing yellow and orange lit the tablecloth. A large and delicate butterfly-shaped sun catcher hung above them. Beams of light streamed through its glass wings, splitting them into spectral colors that danced around the room. And as gentleman Rip sat Jill in her chair and seated himself next to her, the suncatcher bathed the couple in pools of lustrous colors. Pastel hues of blue, pale green, and soft reds illuminated the couple to make it look as if they were glowing.

It was beautiful. The fantastic sight caught the attention of everyone in the restaurant, so much so, that a young, somewhat effete man walked up to their table and asked if they wouldn't mind if he took a picture exclaiming, "I've never seen anything so spectacular!"

Jill agreed and thought about asking him to take a picture from her phone. But then she smiled slyly and whispered to Rip, "I don't think it's a good idea. I've got to be careful about being seen with you."

But Rip told her, "No problem, sweetness. I'll protect you." That did little to alleviate her concern, but she surrendered to Rip Rumple's bold confidence. Rip allowed the young man to take the photo. He did, and showed them the picture and then left them alone. As he did, Rip told Jill, "You know, my dear, I do think that that young man steps a little too light in his loafers for me." Rip winked but Jill was flabbergasted at his blunt, flagrant slur. Feigning a lukewarm laugh, she thought to herself that maybe all this sunlight was an omen of good things to come.

Throughout dinner, Rip asked Jill all about herself. He seemed to be genuinely interested in what she had to say and sprinkled his questions with affectionate names for her. "My love, how did you come to live in Las Vegas?" or "What is it like, my pet, to be in a show as popular as the Extravaganza is certain to become?" Or "What do you want in the future, my love?" And as they finished their dinner, Rip asked her, "Would you like a piece of carrot cake for dessert, my darling?"

Normally, Jill would have laughed mockingly at such sappy sobriquets but somehow coming from Rip Rumple, they seemed charming and sincere. However, when he affectionately called her "Jiggly Jill," well that was a name she was sure she didn't like. One thing was obvious – they were captivated with one another and Jill readily accepted Rip's amorous invitation to breakfast the following morning. "Will you join me for breakfast tomorrow morning, my Love?"

After their breakfast date, Rip asked Jill for another date, and then another after that. Before too long, Jill had become Rip Rumple's paramour, albeit a very secret one.

The next few months spun into a blurry whirlwind for Jill. She performed nightly in the Extravaganza and afterward would return to her apartment, change, and step into the long dark limousine waiting outside her apartment. It would whisk her to Rip's penthouse for late-night dinners on the balcony followed by clandestine trysts. They were careful, extremely careful not to be seen together in public. Loving her job and all that went with it, Jill refused to take the chance of jeopardizing it. For the first time in her life, she felt a sense of accomplishment and pride. She was now in complete control of her future. Her decisions were her own. But the trappings Rip Rumple placed before Jill were irresistible.

One evening, the limo took an unexpected turn and pulled to a stop in front of a posh high-rise condominium. The chauffer escorted Jill to the thirtieth floor where Rip waited for her in front of an open apartment door. He ushered her into a spectacular fully-furnished condo unit and declared, "This, my love, is for you."

Kissing him passionately, "Oh Rip! Thank you!" Jill moved in immediately.

Rip continued to indulge Jill with expensive surprises. One night, while they were sipping wine on the porch of her new condo that had a fantastic view of the strip, Rip reached into his pocket and said, "My dear, I have been thinking. It is not fitting for a star such as you to rely on public transportation to get you back and forth to work. And since you won't let me send my chauffeur to deliver you, well, I thought that you might be more comfortable getting to work this way." Rip pulled a key fob from his pocket and said, "Let's go down to the garage and see what that might be."

"Rip, I'm fine with the bus," Jill answered coyly. But secretly, she couldn't wait to see what Rip had waiting for her.

Her excitement grew as the elevator door opened into the garage and there parked in front of her was a sleek, silver Z06 Corvette with a big red bow on it. Jill screamed with sheer excitement and began jumping up and down like some wacky game-show contestant. Pleased with himself, Rip steadied Jill's hand long enough to place the key in it. "Now, tell me, my dear, which would you prefer to go to work in? This or a smelly bus?" Instead of answering, Jill threw her arms around Rip and smothered him with kisses.

And the gifts kept coming.

"Mi amor, how about a trip to Tiffany's in New York City? I have some business in the morning but after that, we can stroll the shops on 5th Avenue and I'll buy you whatever you want. Darling, I know New York like the back of my hand. Let's give it a whirl. You'll return with so much 'bling-bling,' we'll need a cargo jet to bring it all back."

"Oh Rip, I wish I could, but you know I have to work tomorrow."

"We'll take my jet and I promise to have my pet home in plenty of time for her to don her beautiful costumes."

Jill wriggled into Rip's lap and began kissing him and running her fingers through his hair. "I can't, Rip, but you go and come back and surprise me."

"Ah, my love? We could have such a good time. But I understand that work is primary. No worries, dearest. I will return with something scrumptious." Squeezing Jill with a hug, he eased her off his lap and led her into the bedroom.

Rip returned the next evening bearing gifts in the form of a fifty thousand-dollar yellow diamond necklace from Tiffany's. Jill held her breath as Rip fastened it around her neck and then ran to a mirror and modeled the expensive bobble.

Six months ago, she was just some girl from Houston, Texas who had to budget to buy a cheap pair of jeans from Ross. Jill smiled as she realized that those days were now forever behind her.

BROADWAY, NYC

Because of its popularity, the Malai decided to extend the "Happy Days Are Here Again" Extravaganza for another three months even as planning for the next production was underway.

Jason pitched the new production as a modern adaptation of the fifties' Broadway hit musical "Guys and Dolls." In the original play, the protagonist, vice-racketeer Nathan Detroit and his gang were turned from their life of crime by a group of nubile Salvation Army sisters. Jason's idea was to portray the Malai chorus girls as a group of well-intentioned prostitutes intent on turning Nathan and his gang toward good. It was a controversial concept for any producer to tackle. But for a Las Vegas show where audiences from fly-over country expected a wholesome and non-controversial message, it was an exceptionally delicate balance to attempt. The Malai executives were not worried; they just expected Jason Gleeson to deliver another hit production.

But Jason was being courted by theater backers in New York City to produce the next season's run of "The Lion King" on Broadway. Backstage gossip at the Malai talked of trouble brewing between Jason and casino management. Some of the tension was due to creative disagreements. Jason was notorious for staging hissy-fits over the smallest problems and his volcanic tantrums resulted in more than one complaint to human resources about his treatment of the cast and crew. In Jason Gleeson's world, there was no such thing as compromise. He was a talent and arguably a genius, but his talent came in a too tightly wound package. To some, Jason was becoming more trouble than he was worth.

But as it usually did, in the end, it all came down to money. Contract negotiations to produce "Guys and Dolls" broke down when Jason demanded a sizeable cut of the box office on top of an enormous salary increase. He felt disrespected when the CEO and Board of Trustees at the Malai refused to counter-offer his demands. They wanted nothing more to do with Jason Gleeson and showed him the door.

So, off Gleeson went to do battle in the jungles of Manhattan with "The Lion King" and join his waiting boyfriend. The boyfriend was cast in an off-Broadway production and didn't like the idea of a long distant relationship.

Now, the Malai production managers were left with a big decision: without Jason Gleeson, should they continue with plans to stage a risqué production of "Guys and Dolls" or decide to do something else? After some heated arguments, the Malai proudly announced to the world that the "Happy Days Extravaganza" would be extended for another six months. This was good news for Jill and the rest of the girls in the chorus line. It meant their jobs were safe and they wouldn't have to audition again at least for another six months. And in Las Vegas, six months seemed like a lifetime.

Then one late Thursday afternoon, as Jill was leaving for the Malai, her phone rang. It was from the Malai. Why would they be calling her at home? They'd never done that before. Nervous, she touched the button to answer. "Hello?"

"Jill. This is Jack from the HR team at the Malai."

"Sure. Hi Jack, what's up?"

"Jill. We've received evidence that you have violated the customer fraternization clause of your contract. It is my duty to inform you that the Malai is taking steps to void your contract. And your employment with the show is suspended without pay until a complete investigation is concluded. "

Jill screamed into the phone. "*What*? What are you talking about? You can't do this to me! I don't know what you are even talking about." Not wasting a breath, he got right to the point and told her she was being fired because they had positive proof that Jill was intimately involved with one of the casino's important customers. Jill fiercely denied everything the man accused her of, but her protests were futile. Finally, in desperation, Jill threatened, "I've read my contract and demand that we go to arbitration!"

The man responded calmly. "Yes, you certainly have the right to arbitrate this decision, but let me remind you of an amendment to the contract that we had you recently sign. It states that, and I quote, 'If it is determined during arbitration that the Malai Corporation is within its legal rights to terminate the contesting party, that party will assume the full responsibility for all costs incurred by the Corporation during the arbitration process.' End quote."

Jack paused a moment. He seemed to be waiting for Jill to digest what he had just read to her and then continued. "We've got incontrovertible evidence against you and are confident that if you bring this to arbitration, you will lose. Believe me, arbitration costs rack up fast, and before it's over, the Malai's costs alone will be more than anyone but Rip Rumple could afford to pay. Face it; it's over, Jill. We've already replaced you with your understudy, Lorie."

Jill's entire body convulsed in spasms and she screamed into the phone, "You're bluffing. I don't believe you. I want to see your so-called incontrovertible evidence."

She was met with a smug and curt reply, "Little missy, I'll be here with your proof ready to shove it up your nose. And believe me, it's a slam-dunk. Come in tomorrow for your check and to collect your things. After that, you are banned from setting foot in the Malai again. Till tomorrow." Jack ended the call.

Trying unsuccessfully to muffle her wails of anger. Jill screamed at the phone, "Who saw us together? We were so careful And I deliberately never drove the 'Vette anywhere near the Malai! Who the hell ratted me out?"

Jill picked up the phone and dialed Rip. Sobbing uncontrollably, she said, "You told me you would protect me. You've got to do something, Rip."

"Yeah, baby, I hear you... Oh yeah, well, that's too bad..." Then Rip's voice faded and was followed by a combination of snorts, loud snoring, and whistling noises coming through the phone.

"Rip, are you there?" Jill's anger festered. "Rip, dammit, I said are you there?" All she heard was a tepid answer of "Yes, baby," and then more snoring and finally a loud crash. She could tell he had hit his head or something. The next thing she heard out of him was vague stammering of "shit" and "damn."

Jill kept screaming at him through the phone until it finally dawned on her that Rip had gone narcoleptic and was useless. Enraged, Jill shouted through the receiver, "Have a good sleep, you stupid old man!" and then she threw her phone against the wall with such force that it shattered. "Piece of shit," she yelled even louder. Jill retired to her lavish bedroom and hurled herself on the bed filled with self-pity.

She began beating her pillow with her fists. Pity parties might give solace to some, but not her. Getting up, she went to the kitchen and opened a bottle of her most expensive Cabernet Sauvignon. It cost $150 a bottle and tonight, she would drink to forget. But tomorrow? Well, Jill was armed with a 650-horse power Corvette that she could easily turn into a guided missile once she found out who the mole was that sank her career.

MALAI PARKING GARAGE

Jill went to the Malai Casino to collect her last paycheck with a hangover and spent most of the morning nursing it. After losing her job, she was in despair and had nearly drank herself into a coma. But that was last night. Now, Jill made a silent pledge to discover who the snake was that had betrayed her. She had her suspicions and somehow would exact her revenge.

It was late in the afternoon before she felt well enough to venture into the Malai. Coincidentally, it was about the same time the girls began arriving to warm up for their first show. She went to the changing room to empty her booth. Many of her friends were already there and greeted her warmly. Apparently, they had not heard the news that she was no longer with the show.

This gave Jill the chance to do some sleuthing. She needed to confirm what she already suspected. Careful not to arouse the suspicions of her former co-workers, she flitted from girl to girl, making casual conversation with each. After she worked the entire dressing room, Jill was sure that Honey was the one who had ratted her out.

Honey was one of Jill's closest friends at the Extravaganza. Jill trusted Honey with her life; at least, that was how Jill had felt. Now, she wasn't sure she could trust her to hold her purse. Honey was the only one Jill had ever told about her liaison with Rip.

Her first name was Olivia, but she swore that Honey was her real middle name and not just some stage name she'd invented for herself. "That's the God's honest-truth!" she had insisted when Jill smirked on first hearing the name. "Honeywell was my mother's surname and she wanted to give me some part of it. I'll swear to it on a stack of Bibles, if you don't believe me."

Jill didn't care then and couldn't care less now what Honey chose to call herself; she was still a Judas.

Having been able to speak to everyone *but* Honey, Jill waited for her former friend to settle at the makeup table adjacent to her own. As always, Honey greeted Jill with a warm embrace before turning to the vanity to primp. It was then Jill told Honey that she'd been fired, insinuating not-so-subtly that it was Honey who had betrayed her.

"Jill, I swear it wasn't me. I've kept your secret, but I do know what happened." Pulling her close and in a soft, faint voice, Honey, insisted, "I'll call you in the morning and tell you everything I know." Honey looked devastated.

"You can't; I got so mad I broke my phone," Jill admitted. "Meet me down in the parking garage tomorrow before work."

The next day, Jill drove her silver Corvette into the Malai garage with the top up, wearing a scarf and large dark sunglasses. She had to be cautious. While picking up her check, Jill had been warned never to set foot on Malai property again or run the risk of being prosecuted for trespassing. It was a devastating humiliation for Jill but her need to get at the truth outweighed any threat made by her former employer.

Jill felt like she was starring in a scene from an old movie she had recently watched called *All the President's Men*. The film came out long before her time, but she felt like she could relate to it in a way. Her situation was similar to the movie as Jill was about to meet Honey, AKA "Deep Throat" on the lowest level of the Malai's underground parking garage.

All the President's Men was about the Watergate scandal and subsequent cover-up which eventually led to the resignation of President Richard Nixon in 1972. It involved a government informant, known only as Deep Throat, who funneled details about the scandal to two young *Washington Post* journalists, Bob Woodward and Carl Bernstein. Using Deep Throat's information, their reporting brought down the President of the United States by exposing his complicity in the scandal. It was well-known that Deep Throat would often pass the journalists damning information during clandestine meetups deep in the bowels of a subterranean garage.

As Jill walked through the dimly lit parkade looking for Honey, she heard someone whisper her name. She stepped around a column to find Honey waiting for her. As they huddled there, Honey squeezed Jill's hand to let her know she was in complete solidarity with her. Pulling her hands away from Jill's, Honey began to tell the story, that to Jill, seemed to be carefully crafted for dramatic effect.

"Do you remember when you first met Rip on your so-called secret lunch? Well, you do remember when he bought you the yellow roses at that florist shop next door, right?" Honey was looking for confirmation from Jill.

"Yeah, I remember. That was our first date," Jill confirmed. "But I wasn't with him in the flower shop. That means someone from the Malai had to have seen Rip there and then followed him over to the restaurant? That's creepy. Who would do that?" Jill was still skeptical of Honey's story.

Honey leaned in to Jill and dramatically enunciated, "It was Jason Gleeson's boy-toy." Honey paused to let Jill take it all in. "His boyfriend just happened to be at the flower shop when he spotted Rumple. He didn't know for sure, but he had a sneaking hunch that the guy talking with the florist was Rip 'Van' Rumple. Let's face it, everyone on the planet knows what Rip Rumple looks like. It wasn't like he was a rocket scientist or some kind of ace detective cracking open a great mystery.

"But I guess Jason's boyfriend knew he was right when he heard the florist talking to Rip. She said his name so many times because she couldn't believe he was really in her store. I guess she was so excited to have him in her store that she just about flipped out. She asked Rumple to sign a picture she had of her posing in front of her store during her grand opening.

"Rip couldn't have been happier to oblige and began flirting with her, saying stuff like, 'Where is your pen, darling? I would love to autograph your lovely picture of you and your wonderful store. You are like a bouquet and just as beautiful as the flowers you sell.' Then he let her take a selfie of them embracing. I guess he wanted to keep his options open just in case you didn't show up.

"Oh, and the way she was panting over Rip! All it would have taken was the most subtle suggestion on his part and she would have hauled him into the back room for a little you-know-what. But of course, he had his date with you, so Rip let it out that he was going next door to Gold Cafe to surprise someone with his large bundle of 'love flowers.' That's what he called them, 'love flowers.'

"After Rip left, Jason's fiancé asked the florist if that was really the billionaire Rip Rumple. Oh – and by the way – his name is Troy. Anyway, when the florist confirmed that is *was* Rip, Troy tailed him into the café. And Jill, that's where he saw you with Rip."

Jill cut in immediately. "But I don't remember ever meeting him." Jill thought back quickly. Nope, she had never met this Troy before in her life.

Honey didn't bother to respond and carried on with her story. "Well, he has flown out three times and watched the Extravaganza and he even mentioned you to Jason the last time he was here.

Jill's eyes grew large, as did her curiosity. "When in the hell was that?"

Without blinking an eye, Honey exclaimed, "He's got you and Rip together twice on video."

Jill was aghast. "What the? How? Where?"

Honey cut her off. "Let me finish. Jason told me he was so excited to see Troy and that they were going to get married soon. He had a lot of anxiety over what Troy, being a great actor and all, would think about the show. Well anyway, when he showed up, he sat in the front row, and I guess you didn't know who he was or maybe Jason never thought to introduce you to him but anyhow." Honey kept talking, hardly pausing to take a breath.

"Troy liked your dancing. Don't worry, he didn't like you. I mean, your plumbing is all wrong." Honey laughed but kept unloading information. "Anyway, that's when Troy made the connection between you and the show. He told Jason he had seen you twice with Rip and he had video of you and Rumple together to prove it. But neither one of you even knew it. I guess he had followed Rumple into the cafe and took a quick video under the pretense of capturing the beautiful light coming off the sun catchers where you guys were sitting. He got you and Rip and the roses on his phone. And when he saw you on stage, the little prick knew he had caught you fraternizing with the Malai patronage. You broke their golden rule, girl!"

Jill gasped. "I *do* remember some guy walking up to us out of nowhere and asking to take a quick picture of the light coming through the window. What a shit! Done in by a damn freaking window!"

"The second time he spied on you two was from the inside of his car. Troy saw you two kissing and getting amorous at a 7-11 while tanking up his car. He snapped another picture for his collection and told Jason you guys were acting like a couple of teenagers in heat. When Troy showed the pictures to Jason, Jason was furious and reported you to HR. That's how this all came down, Jill."

Jill was incredulous. "And how the hell do you know all of this? And especially all of these details? I mean, shit! How did you know every single thing that happened and why didn't you tell me? Or maybe *you* told them about Rip and me? You are the only one I ever told my business to."

Honey swallowed hard and looked wounded. "Jill, I swear I never told a soul! I got in early the other day before anyone else and I overheard Jason and Troy talking to some HR people in Jason's office. The door was open and Troy was dishing all the dirt on you and showing them his videos. I hid in the corner and heard everything they said. I was so nervous and my heart was pounding so loud that I thought they would hear me too."

"Why didn't you tell me, Honey?" Jill pleaded. "I could have gotten Rip to stop it all. Now it's too late!"

"I was going to tell you yesterday, but it was already too late. But Jill, that's not the worst of it. After the top execs left Jason's office, Troy cooked up a scheme for them to really cash in. He wanted to blackmail Rip into buying those pictures of you two or else he'd sell them to that tabloid *The American Scuttlebutt*. And that weasel Jason loved the idea because he said they could use some extra money for their honeymoon. So, it might not be too long Jill before you see you and Rip on the cover of that gossip rag having a good smooch. What a pair of creeps! You do believe me, Jill, don't you? I couldn't make all this up." A tear slid down Honey's cheek.

"I'm so sorry I didn't trust you, Honey. I really am." At that, Jill took Honey's hand in hers. "You have been such a good friend. And you were brave to stay there and listen, if not a little crazy in the head. I just wish I knew what I'm going to do now."

Honey told her, "Don't worry. There are lots of dancing jobs in Vegas even though they're probably topless or worse. But what do you have to worry about anyway? You've got a billionaire Sugar Daddy. Good luck and call me if you need me." The two women hugged, promising to remain the best of friends and left the garage in different directions. Both knew they would never see the other again.

HILLER'S GROCERS

Jill didn't waste any time looking for another job. Early the next morning, she cruised south on Las Vegas Boulevard in her Corvette to Brandon Casino. If Honey was right, Jill might have to work topless. Though she had never actually stripped in front of an audience, she felt no qualms about doing it. She was proud of her body, and after months wearing suggestive costumes in the Extravaganza, Jill found that she was now prepared to take the stage in any state of undress the situation required. Jill was becoming something of an exhibitionist.

Brandon Casino was a smaller road-house casino with a big sign in front that screamed "Dancing Girls!" in swaying LED lights. Jill drove into the parking lot and pulled into an empty parking space. She knew the kind of dancing Brandon wanted was more of the pole dance/striptease kind rather than the choreographed stage numbers she had performed at the Malai. But she preferred the freedom of expression that modern dance encouraged compared to the strict and rigid demands of the chorus line. So, when she was offered a job on the spot and asked to start immediately, Jill thought her timing most remarkable. She was sure her bona fides from the Malai Casino Extravaganza had played no small factor in her getting the job.

So once again, Jill was gainfully employed, and as the weeks passed, she began settling comfortably into her new but significantly less prestigious job.

However, a rupture developed in Jill's life. Rip. She called it "Her Ripture." Lately, Rip's visits to her had become noticeably less frequent and his stays briefer. But for Jill, the worst of the matter was that he was neglecting to make regular deposits into her spending account which he had opened for her shortly after their first date. His gifts became less extravagant and more mundane and pedestrian.

Jill knew he was losing interest in her, but when he surprised her with a Kitchen Aid stand mixer, Jill knew that Rip was looking to exit their relationship. "My dear, normally I'm not a fan of re-gifting, but this thing somehow found its way to me; I think it is meant for you." Jill shoved the stand mixer into a corner on the counter without ever plugging it in.

Rip was conflicted over how to deal with the whole fiasco with the Malai. For years, he'd been a steady customer of the casino and had been rewarded for his patronage with unparalleled perks and concierge services. Rip thrived on that kind of attention; it proved to be difficult for him to abandon his years-long relationship with the Malai over a six-month fling with a chorus line girl. It was an unfortunate situation that he wanted to avoid confronting and dealt with it by blaming it all on Jill, especially now that she was pole-dancing in a sleazy night club.

It also annoyed Rip that Jill never showed the least bit of interest or compassion over his struggle with narcolepsy. In fact, she seemed to mock it. She never made any attempts to educate herself about his disability, nor did she even consider the problems it caused. For instance, narcolepsy and driving could be just as lethal as driving drunk, and for that reason, Rip relied on his chauffeur Lloyd. But there were rare times when Rip was forced to drive himself, and even then, Jill hadn't shown the slightest concern for his safety. In truth, Jill couldn't be bothered with what she considered Rip's personal problem, except when Rip visited bearing gifts. However, the irony wasn't lost on Rip that Jill made darn sure she was never in the car when he was driving. "No way, Rip baby! I'm not getting anywhere near that car as long as you're driving. Paging Lloyd to the rescue!"

By now, Jill had grown accustomed to the kind of good life Rip's money could buy her and to a certain extent, even the fame. *The American Scuttlebutt* indeed ran a series of articles using Troy's pictures of her and Rip sucking face. It also covered her downfall firing at the Malai because of it. At first, she had been upset and embarrassed about the exposure, but soon learned to revel in it. Even if the reason for it was somewhat dubious, the articles had helped Jill achieve a degree of notoriety as "the eye candy" latched onto the billionaire Rip Rumple's arm. Jill quickly learned there was no such thing as bad publicity.

While walking downtown, Jill ran into John again and even *he* had mentioned it. "Hey, I saw you on the cover of *The American Scuttlebutt* at Hiller's Grocers. You're a star. You've reached the top now, Jill! I guess I should be asking for your autograph. But since I don't have a piece of paper, will you sign my T-shirt?"

Laughing, Jill ran her fingers sexily through her hair and asked him if he had a sharpie. "That way you'll never forget my name even if you wash it a million times over."

They laughed. Jill felt good that John had jokingly asked for her autograph. But as she looked at him, he was like someone she barely remembered. It had not been all that long ago that they were living together in Houston. Standing before him on the streets of Las Vegas though, she had to strain her memory to even see herself with him. It sounded like he hadn't changed.

He still had big dreams of making a living as a poker professional. "I'm busy practicing all the time. As a matter of fact, I'm on my way to a game now." Jill wasn't surprised to hear that, but was caught off-guard to hear that he was married. "Yep! She's the girl I told you about when you called me in jail." John's eyes sparkled and a broad smile filled his face. "She's my poker babe, and we're very happy together." His news brought an unexpected sting with it and Jill found it difficult to manage even a polite smile.

While Jill may have seen benefits to *The Scuttlebutt* coverage of their relationship, she learned that Rip Rumple did not. He thought the tawdry exposure was an invasion of his privacy and told Jill he thought she should feel the same way. When she disagreed, Rip began breaking their dates and finding reasons to avoid her. And as Jill and Rip's relationship began to chill, Jill found it harder to keep up with her pampered lifestyle. Rip still paid the bills, but that was about all. He used to play the perfect sugar daddy and would transfer money into her account whenever she asked. But he had stopped doing that weeks ago and she could tell that her constant demand for money was wearing thin with Rip. It was then that Jill noticed his affection for her began to wane and when they did see one another, he made her feel like trailer trash.

Jill was no fool and realized that Rip would soon stop calling her altogether and when that day came, she needed an insurance policy she could cash in. So she conceived of a plan to capitalize on the interest that *The Scuttlebutt* had in her and Rip. She decided to become her own paparazzi and began selling pictures of her and Rip to the highest bidders. Besides *The American Scuttlebutt*, there was another smarmy tabloid called *The Tell Me All Wire* that she could sell the pictures too. If she had learned anything while living in Vegas, it was that she needed to strike while the opportunity presented itself before it vaporized altogether. Jill knew it was time to seize the offensive and that realization brought a broad, toothy grin to her face, the kind she flashed when she was onto something big or important. Jill had a plan that promised her a big payoff.

Sure, she could supply snapshots and selfies of her and Rip stepping out on the town like any paparazzi. But she could provide so much more. What would pictures of her in compromising positions with old Rip 'Van' Rumple be worth? And even better, why not sell or leak a sex tape out on the Internet? If Jason and Toy or Troy, or whatever his name was, could do it, she didn't see why she couldn't play the game too. Why the hell not? Jill consoled herself that there were plenty of celebrities who had made their fortunes in this manner. Right now, she and Rip were the hottest, sought-after tabloid fodder at grocery checkouts across the country. They were guaranteed front-page news. And at least for now, there seemed to be an insatiable appetite for stories about the eccentric billionaire and his alluring but dethroned showgirl.

Of course, she had to be careful not to let Rip find out. He hated that type of publicity. He didn't object to business articles hailing his latest acquisition or financial success. But never before in his entire life had his picture appeared on the cover of a cheap supermarket rag like *The American Scuttlebutt*. When Rip saw the photos Jason Gleeson's boyfriend took of them in the tabloids he had been appalled and furious and let Jill know he held her responsible for this intolerable public humiliation.

This irritated Jill. Rip was the one who let the little twit take their picture in the first place. He was the one who had started all this. If it hadn't been for him, she would still have her job at the Malai. But Rip never acknowledged his responsibility for what had happened.

Further, Rip made it clear to Jill that he was no fan of her working as a lowly pole dancer in a sleazy casino. It was obvious he didn't want to be seen with her. Jill was an embarrassment to him and he told her so outright. One night they had gotten into an argument and Rip had asked her, "Really, darling, how are the poles treating you at Brandon's? It must be hell having to rub up against them for paltry tips."

The nastiness in his words was like a declaration of war. It was time to go viral on all the gossip rags and social media sites she could find. By the time Jill was finished with Rip 'Van' Rumple, he'd be the joke of every penthouse party between New York City and L.A. If Rip wanted to burn the bridge, Jill was ready to blow it up.

The next morning, Jill purchased a half dozen video cameras hidden in clocks and various knick-knacks and set them up in strategic locations around her apartment, especially in front of her bed.

Ready, set, let the videoing begin.

BEER BELLY'S LIQUOR
STORE, AGAIN

    Jill tried everything she could to rekindle Rip's interest in her. She even went so far as to study up on narcolepsy. But Rip wasn't fooled by Jill's sudden adoption of the three A's – affection, amorousness, and attention. He met her attempts to revive their relationship with utter indifference. Jill wouldn't have been bothered by Rip's inattention as long as he had continued making regular deposits into her bank account. But even his infrequent contributions were surprisingly meager and for the first time in a long time, Jill began to have to watch her spending.

    The show at the Brandon Casino was, in reality, an erotic dance show. Jill harbored no illusions about that. She no longer had to perform the intricate dance steps that she mastered and performed routinely at the Malai. At the Malai, Jill had honed her dance skills. There was always a challenge, and the various dance coaches made sure she was kept on her toes, literally. They pushed Jill, and she was always at risk of being replaced by her understudy. It had been intense – and Jill didn't miss the pressure. But now, she was bored. The Brandon crew did not concern themselves with perfect dance performances. As long as Jill showed the audience the skin they wanted to see, her bosses were happy.

    But between boredom with her job and a faltering relationship with Rip Rumple, drinking had become Jill's new best friend. The funny thing was that it did not impact her performance. But then her new audience was not the most culturally discerning. Their love of the fine arts did not extend to the appreciation for the nuances of creative dance techniques. Jill thought that their collective ambitions did not venture much beyond the hope of winning first place in an Oktoberfest beer-belching contest.

    Though the liquor didn't impact Jill's performances, it did affect her weight. Her excessive drinking combined with far fewer grueling workouts and rehearsals caused Jill to expand. Her stomach became puffy, and her waist grew noticeably. She even began to see cellulite develop on her thighs. Unfortunately for Jill, her weight struggles did not go unnoticed by her bosses at the Brandon. There was only one rule that the Brandon enforced and Jill was in danger of violating it.

Like prizefighters, the girls were required to submit to a weekly weigh in. The first time the scale's needle climbed past the "Too Heavy" mark, she received a casual admonition from the staff, "Jill, you are a bit over. You'll need to work on losing it and keep it in check."

But at the next weigh-in, instead of losing weight, the scale tipped even further past Brandon's red line. After five more weigh-ins, Jill had put on an extra fifteen pounds. She was placed on probation and given two weeks to take off the first five.

It was a challenge that required the kind of extreme discipline Jill no longer possessed. She knew the wine was responsible for her weight gain, but it was too comforting to give up. It was not unusual for Jill to fall asleep and wake the next morning with an empty bottle of Dona Paula Los Cordos and a half-filled wineglass on the nightstand next to her. If only she had a man as reliable and comforting as her Dona Paula Los Cordos, she'd marry him and live happily ever after.

Because of her drinking, Beer Belly's Liquor Store had now become something of a constant in her life. The only problem was that they were sometimes out of stock of her favorite wine which caused Jill's temper to erupt. Samar, the store owner, was always on the receiving end of Jill's wrath and tried hard to keep it on his shelf. It didn't seem possible that she could consume a case of wine in a week. But his order sheet didn't lie; he made sure to keep at least several cases in his inventory.

Instead of cutting back on her drinking, Jill drank herself into a haze every night after she finished her last performance. It was obvious she was unconcerned about conquering her weight demons. Living on raw carrots and celery sticks sustained her well enough before her shows. But after work, when Jill began drinking, her appetite was insatiable.

Rip even took to insulting her about her widening girth. "My love, why are you such a glutton? They are going to boot you out of the Brandon if you keep up with your hearty appetite. You, darling, will bend the pole when you straddle it. Personally, I feel sorry for the skinny pole."

It was no surprise to Jill when she failed to lose the weight demanded by the terms of her probation. She couldn't knock off the vino. Jill's last round on the scales at the Brandon was humiliating. All eyes watched the scale as the needle shot through the maximum line and raced deep into the red zone. There were a few gasps as Jill stepped quickly off the scale. Not only had she not lost the required five pounds, but she had managed to put on another three. As a result, her termination at the Brandon was curt, decisive, and immediate. Since her departure at the

Malai, she had packed on close to twenty pounds. And based on her recent weigh-in, that upward trend was likely to continue.

Now that Jill was through at the Brandon and knowing that Rip 'Van' Rumple was pretty much through with her as well, it was time to execute her plan to capture all of Rip's peccadillos in full hi-definition video. But first, she had to make a stop at Beer Belly's. This time, she grabbed more than her usual bottle of wine and six-pack of Fat Tire. She also added a bottle of Absolut Vodka to her purchase and asked Samar to snatch a bottle of Kahlua from the shelf behind the counter. Samar scanned the bottles standing in front of him and looked at Jill quizzically as if to ask, "How are you going to mix all this up into something drinkable?"

Jill didn't need to explain it to Samar, but she did anyway. "Now that I'm out of work, I figure I might as well add a little kick to my morning coffee and start my day off with a White Russian."

Samar smiled but didn't seem to understand anything she said. "Thank you. See you next time." Jill grabbed her bag and wished him a good night.

As she stepped out the door, Jill looked down and saw something she hadn't noticed before. She laughed out loud and thought to herself that Beer Belly's was aptly named. Looking down again, she saw her stomach protruding out of the gap between her top and her tight jeans. Jill had to admit that she sure as hell was developing one heck of a large beer belly.

THE MERMAID CLUB

Waking up to a throbbing headache, Jill realized she'd drank herself to sleep again. She trudged into the bathroom and took two Advil. Her thoughts were foggy and disconnected but memories of the night before punched through the pain. Something about being offered a job kept coming to mind.

After the humiliation she had suffered at the Brandon Casino, Jill needed to do something to make herself feel good. She needed a night out on the town. But as usual, Rip was nowhere to be found. So, it was up to Jill to make her own party. Her crazy night stretched all over Las Vegas, and she had the receipts to prove it. The cab fares alone set her finances back considerably as she had taxi-hopped around town. But Jill didn't care; she had just been fired again. She thought to herself, *Oh, what the hell is a girl down on her luck supposed to do but party!* And party she did.

After leaving Beer Belly's, she had gone back to her apartment and drank a beer. Too early to turn in, she decided to treat herself to a night out and drifted into a cruddy out-of-the-way club a few miles from downtown.

Jill had to think for a minute what happened after that. She could remember dancing and drinking with some guy, but couldn't recall his name. What was it? Nick or Mick? Or was it Rick? No. That wasn't it, but his name did start with an R. Maybe it was Randy. Yeah, that was it. It was Randy-something. Randy Kiefer. Jill recalled that he talked like he was straight out of the 1980's Los Angeles Valley scene, using phrases like "totally bitchin'" and "gnarly." Jill had tossed him off as just another flaky-flake to forget.

But as the Advil began to work its magic, last night's events came into focus, and it seemed that Randy Kiefer figured into most of them. She remembered being in his dingy apartment listening to him talk about playing for the Western Nugget in a bar called The Deerskin Lounge. He was a member of a trio group with some foreign-sounding name that she would never be able to remember. He'd told her they had even been on the radio. She remembered having sex, but it must not have been that good because she could barely recall any details other than that he kept telling her that she had "a totally awesome body!" and that he was "ripping radical waves" by scoring with her. What a freak! She swore an oath to herself never to frequent the Western Nugget. For Jill, that wouldn't be a difficult vow to keep; she hated country-western music anyway.

But before she had met Randy Kiefer, Jill had bounced into one bar after another looking to start a party. After a drink or two in each, it was clear to Jill that the clientele was more interested in playing pool or watching sports on the big screen than talking to her, so she decided to move on.

Jill had hailed a taxi to take her to the Duke of Surrey. It was an English pub some of the girls at the Malai raved about for their authentic British pub grub. Since Jill was hungry, the Duke of Surrey was her destination.

Pushing open the heavy, brass-strapped oak doors of the Surrey, Jill stepped into the bar and was transported into a convincing replica of a dimly lit English pub. Thick oak beams supported a low, rough plastered ceiling and as Jill searched for an empty table, the wood-planked floors creaked to complete the illusion. She pulled out a menu wedged between the napkin holder and a carafe of malt vinegar. As she thumbed through it, a waitress came around to take her drink order and Jill ordered a pint of pale ale called "Old Speckled Hen." While she waited for her drink, she mulled over an important decision; should she order Fish & Chips or the Shepherd's Lamb Pie that she'd heard good things about? The waitress returned with her pint and took Jill's order for the Shepherds Lamb Pie.

Waiting for her food, Jill sipped her beer and looked around the pub. There was a group of men playing darts, others were at the long shuffleboard table, but most were screaming at the soccer game playing on the widescreen. None of them even noticed Jill sitting alone at the table except for one guy with bleach-blond hair who was staring at her from across the room. Jill stared back at him, but their silent banter was interrupted when the waitress placed Jill's meal in front of her.

As Jill prepared to take the first bite of her meal, she looked over to where the blonde was sitting. But he was gone. She thought to herself, *Oh well, easy come, easy go!* Jill drove her fork into the pie and took a savory mouthful of mashed potatoes, lamb, and vegetables. It was delicious, and her only thought was of taking another bite. But as she was just about to take it, she became aware of someone standing over her. Jill looked up to see the blond guy holding two pints of beer.

"Hi! Do you mind? I saw you were running low on your Speckled Hen and thought you might need a refill." He handed her the ale and pulling out a chair to sit down, he continued, "Ale's not my bag. I like my beer stout and warm. A lot of people think warm beer is like, kind of gnarly. But you learn to like it. Just like me."

Jill wasn't sure if he was talking about learning to like warm beer or if he was trying to say he was like a warm beer that she would learn to like. Either way, she was pretty sure neither was an option for her. "I don't think warm beer is my thing. But thanks for the Speckled Hen."

Randy Kiefer smiled and lifted his mug. "Cheers!" Jill responded in kind, and they both took a drink. "My name's Randy. I've got a gig over at the Western Nugget in The Deerskin Lounge."

"I'm Jill. I just got shit-canned from my pathetic job. Now I'm out to celebrate." She took a big forkful of her pie and washed it down with a gulp of beer. "But that's not the worst of it. I was a dancer in the Malai Extravaganza before that."

"Wow! Bummer, man! You look max dope to me." Jill smiled at the compliment. Randy thought for a moment and blurted out excitedly, "So you're shit-canned ex-dancer? Did I get that right?" Jill nodded absently and continued devouring her meal. "Dudette, I know exactly where you could make the scene. I'm tight with the manager at the club." Snapping his fingers, he said, "I can get you a job there presto."

Just then the waitress came around, and Randy ordered them another round. "This town will shred you into confetti if you let it. The trick is not to let it. Let's have a go at it!" Randy Kiefer seemed eager to get her to this mysterious club. After a few more drinks, it was off to the gentlemen's club with her surfer dude.

It was the first thing she noticed when they entered this grimy-looking club. There was no way you could miss them. Statues of topless mermaids and mostly naked mannequins of all shapes, sizes, and colors were ensconced throughout the room. Jill thought she was on an acid trip and she had Randy Kiefer to blame. Maybe he spiked her drink while she had finished off her pints at the pub. Hell, if he wanted to sabotage her, why hadn't he thrown a dart into her eye during their game of darts? But when they sat down at a table next to one of the mermaids, she knew her eyes were not deceiving her. It was then that she realized that she had stepped into Randy Kiefer's reality and not a drug-induced hallucination after all.

Before long, a man joined her and Randy at their table. Randy introduced him as Manny Sessums, the club's owner and manager. Jill remembered feeling a little repulsed by the bizarre atmosphere of the bar, not to mention the repugnant owner.

Mermaid mannequins dominated the entire club. They were dressed in scantily clad costumes, and some sported macabre and creepy S&M themes. The mermaids had motorized eyeballs that would move back and forth to follow the customers. Some of the mermaids were programmed to talk and said scary and suggestive things in shrill voices. Jill also noticed the many mermaids positioned in compromising positions with other mannequins. She could not believe the tackiness of the place. It was a mash-up of a horror show and robotic eroticism. Jill asked Manny Sessums where in the world he acquired all these mannequins, especially the mermaids.

Manny, with his low baritone voice, took her question as an insult. He immediately hit back with a surly, "Why, you got a problem with my mermaids? You jealous? They help my girls dance. My girls sway with these here mermaids. They talk to my girls. These mannequins make my girls what they are."

Starting to feel drunk, Jill fired back at him. No way would she let some wretched porn hustler like Manny Sessums disrespect her. "You need to relax about your mermaids. I am just getting to know them, okay?" Jill figured her best bet was to humor this lunatic psychopath. "I mean, if that's okay with you?"

Manny leaned back in his chair and gave direct eye contact to Randy Kiefer. To Jill, it looked like he was giving Randy the stink eye. His look to Randy amounted to, "Who is this and why did you bring her here? Who is she to prance into my club and disrespect my mannequins?"

Apparently keen on getting to the point, Randy said, "This beautiful woman is looking for a job. She used to be a dancer in the Malai Casino Extravaganza show. Manny, you got something here! She could bring in the money for the club. You said you're always looking for a so-called Head Mermaid that will put the cha-ching in your cash register."

Manny eyed Jill again, taking in every detail of her as if he was taking copious notes. "She's got a ton of junk in her trunk. And she's busty to make the men lusty. I'd pay a deuce to see her caboose turn loose." Throwing back his head, Manny gave off a dirty laugh to match his oily, black hair. Her gut told her that he must have used that seamy, moronic rhyme many times before. Jill felt queasy.

So now, the morning after and as the Advil continued to work on Jill, she began recalling more of last night's events. Had she really accepted a job stripping at the Mermaid club and was she supposed to start tonight? Jill hung her head as the events of the last few months played through her mind. She imagined herself free-falling into a bottomless dumpster. She'd started as a respectable Malai dancer and was now forced to strip down with a bunch of creepy robotic mermaid mannequins. It was like going from tenderloin to ground chuck. But still, it was a job. All it would take to handle the Mermaid Club was to be as loose in the head as she was in the booty. Jill knew the prescription for that was to remain extremely intoxicated.

As if dancing with mermaid mannequins wasn't sinking low enough, Jill had somehow ended up in Randy Kiefer's bed. After sex, she recalled seeing a fat rat scampering around Randy's squalid apartment. Rolling up a newspaper, he had tried to swat it, "Can you believe we got us a little critter that wants to get in on the action!" It was at that point that Jill ran out of Randy's apartment and caught a cab back to her condo.

Her memory was surging and thinking about it was making her want to vomit. Jill wanted to forget all of last night. She ran immediately over to the refrigerator and popped open a Tallboy. Now she was into the twenty-four-ounce cans. They were the best memory erasers.

Jill checked the refrigerator and confirmed she had an ample supply of Pabst Blue Ribbon Tallboys on the shelf. She'd need them as fortification for her debut tonight at the disgusting mermaid club.

THE AMERICAN

SCUTTLEBUTT HOME OFFICE

Rip worked hard to avoid her, but after being dumped by the Brandon, it seemed that Jill became something of a nightly rendezvous for him. Her constant invitations to her bedroom not only exhausted Rip, but began to bore him. And after a few weeks, Rip started to decline her persistent calls and ignore her frequent texts. Then one afternoon, in a momentary lapse of caution, he answered his phone without first scanning the caller ID. "Rumple here."

"Rip? It's Jill. Where have you been? I've been calling and texting you 'til I think my fingers are going to fall off."

"Well, my dear, I have been busy with work, and in fact, I'm waiting for an important call right now." It was a lie, but Rip wished to cut short his conversation with her. "What is it you want, Jill?"

"I just wanted to let you know that I miss you and want to invite you over. Believe it or not, I am going to make you dinner. I might even use the stand mixer you gave me to make a cake."

Rip laughed to himself. He knew Jill's game but felt like playing along. "Well, now that is quite surprising. Tell me, my love-dove, what's on tonight's menu? Frozen TV dinners?"

"That's a low blow, Rip." But it was true. Jill couldn't cook. And if it weren't for the invention of the microwave, she would probably have starved to death by now.

"Seriously Jill, let me take you to dinner tomorrow night. That way we can both avoid the risk of ptomaine. I'll pick you up around eight. But my call is coming in now. I have to go." Rip abruptly ended the call.

The next evening Rip arrived to take Jill to dinner. She opened the door with a glass of wine in her hand. Wrapping her arms around him and giving him a suggestive kiss, Jill sloshed some wine and it spilled on the floor behind Rip. He pretended not to notice, but it was evident that Jill was in her usual inebriated state.

When she stepped back to let Rip see her, he was shocked at how bad she looked. She was considerably overweight and had lost her sex appeal. Her flab pressed out against the strained fabric of her evening dress begging to be set free. It was as if Jill had traded her once svelte figure for that of a frumpy hausfrau.

At dinner, Rip was appalled as Jill literally shoveled her meal into her mouth and then proceeded to order two pieces of cake for dessert. Rip asked her sarcastically, "My love, would you like me to ask the waiter to bring you a second fork? That way you can eat both of your desserts at the same time!"

Jill snarled at him as she devoured her second piece of cake. Rip watched in amazement while she scraped her fork across the empty plate for the last bit of icing. He wouldn't have been surprised if Jill picked up her plate to lick it clean. She then asked for an after-dinner liqueur like a mocha kalua or was it a hazelnut kalua? Whatever it was, Jill was not disciplined enough to control either her eating or her drinking. Rip was disgusted and now determined to rid himself of Jill once and forever.

As his chauffeur pulled up to Jill's condo, Rip made his apologies. "My dearest penguin, I am sorry, but I will not be able to see you to your door tonight. I have to leave early tomorrow for an extended business trip. But I hope to see you sometime in the future."

Even as Rip plotted to untangle himself from her, Jill was equally busy assembling her portfolio of Rip Rumple pictures. Surreptitiously snapping as many photos of Rip as she could before he gave her the final dust-off, Jill was counting on a big payday from *The American Scuttlebutt*. Armed with hours of video from her hidden bedroom camera as well hundreds of pictures of Rip, Jill had spent her spare time assembling a salacious dossier to use against him. Now was the time to cash in her insurance policy.

The following morning, Jill gathered her portfolio and stashed it in her bag. Standing in front of her bathroom mirror, she pulled a fiery red wig over her head and slipped on an oversized pair of thick, black glasses. She then rubbed her lips with an equally red lipstick and walked out into the gloriously warm Las Vegas morning.

The home office of *The American Scuttlebutt* was nothing like Jill imagined it would be. Instead of the gray-windowed skyscraper monument to American journalism, *The Scuttlebutt* was stuffed away in an aging, low-profile office building on the edge of town. Jill began to wonder if the outlet would be able to deliver on the windfall she had in mind. As she walked into the shabby lobby, a frowsy receptionist eyed her suspiciously. "May I help you?"

Confident in the value of what she had in her purse, Jill responded, "It's more like, how I can help you?" She pulled a stack of photos out of her purse and slammed them down in front of the receptionist, saying, "And there's a lot more than this. Maybe even a sex tape! That is, if the price is right."

The receptionist began to thumb through some of the pictures and then looked up at Jill and asked, "That's Rip Rumple, isn't it? How did you get these?"

"Does it really matter to you? Let's just say that I have enough material for months of stories and it's available to the highest bidder."

Startled by Jill's bizarre appearance and arrogance, the receptionist looked up at Jill with alarm and asked timidly, "Will you excuse me for a moment?" The receptionist stood up and left the room with the pictures in her hand. Once Jill was sure she was alone, she slid her fingers under her red wig and scratched her itchy scalp. Her long fingernails provided welcome relief from the tight-fitting cove but they also shifted the wig so that her real hair spilled out from under it. She hurried to stuff it back when the receptionist, accompanied by a man dressed in blue jeans and a sports coat, stepped into the room.

When he saw Jill frantically trying to readjust her fire engine-red wig, the man couldn't help but stare. Jill hoped he didn't recognize her. "Good morning, miss. I'm Allen Farmer, a reporter for the paper. You have some very interesting material here."

Jill responded confidently, "Hello, Mr. Farmer; my name is Tawny Ladeaux." She became alarmed when Allen Farmer tried but failed to choke back a laugh. Jill attempted to hide the concern from her face as even the receptionist covered her mouth to conceal her mirth.

"I'm sorry, I'm not sure I heard you correctly. Did you say Toni Labeaux?"

"No, Mr. Farmer! Tawny! Tawny Ladeaux. That's 'Deaux.' With a 'D'!"

"Oh yes, of course. My mistake. Well, Miss Ladeaux, you have something that *The Scuttlebutt* might be interested in. But first, I will need to see some identification and have you sign some papers. It's something our lawyers require."

"Oh, well certainly, Mr. Farmer, I understand. Just a second." Jill pretended to rummage through her purse for an ID. But instead of producing identification, she pulled out another stack of photographs. "You know, Mr. Farmer, in my haste to get here, I must have left my license in my other bag."

"Ha!" scoffed the receptionist. "Who walks around without identification these days?"

This angered Jill. She was not about to take crap off of this lowly receptionist and snapped back. "What's it to you? Don't you need to get back to answering the phones or something?"

The receptionist was indignant. Allen Farmer turned to her and answered, "Evidently Evelynn, Tawny Ladeaux doesn't see the need to carry identification." Then turning back to Jill, said, "If that's even her real name."

Jill raised her right hand as if to swear an oath and said it was the God's-honest truth that it was her given name. "But of course, if you're not interested, there's always *The Tell On Me Wire*. I've got a gold mine in my hot little hand, and if you peons play this right, you might just get a piece of the pie." Jill shoved the pictures back in her bag and reached out for Farmer to give her the batch he still held.

Farmer clutched the folder tight and refused to let it go.

Jill was getting impatient. "Look! I don't have to take this shit from you. Where the hell is the editor? I've got the goods. Either he wants to make a deal with me or not. Get the damn publisher, or I'll take what I have to your competition."

Just then the door to the back office opened and a distinguished looking man in his fifties stepped into the lobby. He took the folder from Farmer's hand and shuffled through the pictures. He looked at Jill and said, "Miss Ladeaux, I'm George Trumball, the managing editor." Returning the folder to her, he instructed, "Please come to my office."

The American Scuttlebutt editors didn't appreciate being played as fools, but that didn't stop them from negotiating a deal with Jill. It was going to prove lucrative for both parties. Over the next few weeks, a series of embarrassing and humiliating headlines and photos about billionaire Rip 'Van' Rumple began appearing on supermarket checkout racks across the nation.

THE SCARED GHOST

It had been some weeks since Rip had last seen or spoken to Jill. Thankfully after their last date, she had stopped harassing him with her texts and calls. Now, as Rip pursued new love interests, Jill became just a fading memory of his past. Rip Rumple's life was back to normal again.

Lately though, it seemed that wherever Rip went, whether to a show, a private dinner, or even walking down the street, he noticed people staring strangely. Someone would point at him, whisper to their friends, and then they'd all snicker. He thought they might be laughing at him, but could not understand why. Rip Rumple wasn't a man necessarily prone to self-consciousness, but all of this new-found attention had him concerned. What in hell was going on? Rip was baffled.

As Lloyd drove his employer to a business appointment, Rip directed his chauffeur to pull into the mini-mart ahead. Lloyd pulled alongside the store curb and opened the passenger door for his boss. He watched as Rip hurried into the store. Rumple had done this before, and Lloyd waited patiently for his employer to return. A few minutes later, Rip rushed out of the market clutching a stack of colorful newspapers and jumped into the back seat. He couldn't hide the look of panic on his face.

Shutting the door behind him, Lloyd pulled the limousine back onto the road and headed for their destination. Rifling frantically through the magazines, Rumple muttered, "My God! Oh my God!"

Lloyd tilted his head back and asked, "Something wrong, sir?"

Rip couldn't answer. He was mute and could only stare at the cover page picture of him asleep in a bed, completely nude. A naked woman was pictured sitting next to him, but her head was cropped and he couldn't be sure who it was. A black block censored his privates while the bold, blaring headline read mockingly, "RIP 'VAN' RUMPLE. THE TRICK EVERY HOOKER PRAYS FOR!"

Rip had now become the target de jour of the gossip rags and the laughing stock of Las Vegas. He was the constant subject of ridiculous stories that more often than not included more unflattering photographs than actual text. All this attention was new and unwelcome and all his overpriced lawyers told him the same thing. "We can sue. But you would lose and only drag this embarrassment out even longer."

He scoured the photographs for any clue about who he was with or where he was when they were taken. But any hint of that had been expertly photoshopped away. He was certain Jill was behind it, but since he never actually saw her with a camera or using her phone to take his picture, Rip didn't have the proof.

Fortunately, one of Rip Rumple's valuable assets was the extensive network of friends and acquaintances regardless of social status he had developed over a lifetime. He had sources in high and, in this particular case, low places. Finally, an insider at *The American Scuttlebutt* and one of Rip's contacts informed him that the one feeding the tabloids their fodder was, "your flabby girlfriend looking to cash in before you finally put her out to pasture!"

Rip had to be sure and pressed his contact for details. "Rip, you've got to believe me. The guy who told me all of this was there when Jill waltzed into *The Scuttlebutt* office. She slammed her pictures down on the receptionist's desk and implied that there was a lot more where those came from. He said she tried to disguise herself by wearing a crazy, red wig and huge, black nerdy glasses and called herself Tawny Ladeaux."

Over the next few weeks, more embarrassing stories and pictures appeared in the pages of *The American Scuttlebutt*. Now, Rip didn't need secret sources to prove it was Jill who was behind this disgrace, because *The Scuttlebutt* no longer attempted to conceal Jill's identity. There were pictures of her and Rip together; they even began quoting her in some of their captions and using Jill's real name. Despite all of his billions and angry outbursts, he was powerless to put a stop to the seemingly endless stream of sewage spewed out for the whole world to see.

But Jill had only just begun. Her hidden cameras had captured hours and hours of video of Rip in every embarrassing situation imaginable. All Jill had to do was find a salacious frame, print it out on her computer, and then auction it off to the highest bidder. And lately, *The Scuttlebutt* was being outbid by *Tell on Me Wire*. They too wanted to get in on the Rip Rumple craze while it still had 'legs' and was selling papers at checkout stands nationwide. Jill was more than eager to oblige. Her plan was panning out better than she ever dreamed.

Jill's pictures became so popular, that she even began suggesting captions for her pictures and was getting pretty good at it. In one image, Jill was sitting up in her bed with her arms crossed and looking frustrated while Rip was conked out beside her. She suggested the caption, "Rip 'Van' Rumple, Not UP for The Job! The Only Thing He's Good for Is Sawing Logs."

Another of Jill's captions to an embarrassing photo was one the editors felt they couldn't improve upon was, "Warning! Sleeping on The Job, Will Not A Baby Rumple Make!"

It was this headline that irritated Rip the most. It implied that he wanted Jill to have his baby and this was the very last thing he wanted from her. A child meant that he could never rid himself of Jill and it would give her a permanent hold on him and his bank account.

This last article was Jill's piece de resistance and Rip resolved to put an end to this public humiliation. Deaf to the objections of his lawyers, Rip ordered, "Hire a private investigator and dig up whatever dirt they can on that ungrateful witch! This has got to stop *now*!"

A few days later, the investigator's report was given to him; there wasn't much in it that Rip didn't already know about Jill. "She'd come from Texas, got a job in the chorus line at the Malai, and was later seen around town as Rip Rumples latest arm candy. Fired from the Malai Extravaganza, she next worked as a pole dancer at the Brandon where she was terminated due to uncontrolled weight gain. Now she strips at the Mermaid Club." There was nothing new there except the last bit about the Mermaid Club.

Advertised as a sophisticated men's club with the latest in AI sex robot technology, to Rip Rumple the Mermaid Club was just another Las Vegas titty bar – the kind of degenerate hole Jill deserved to land up in. Comforted by the schadenfreude of it all, Rip Rumple hatched his scheme.

Rip laughed aloud at the thought of visiting such a place. *But then, there was always a first time for everything. It could be another box on my bucket list that I can check off!* he told himself sarcastically. *Was the Mermaid as he hoped it was?* Rip had to see this for himself.

Deciding he would pay this dirty, perverted strip club a little visit to see for himself just how low Jill had plunged, Rip borrowed a few tips from Jill's modus operandi; he too would go incognito. He relished seeing her have to writhe, squirm, and twist her body around in the slime, and God knows what else, just to get a few dollars thrown her way. She was now reduced to working for chicken feed… or was it fish food since mermaids lived to consume fish?

Rip amused himself by contemplating the taxonomy of mermaids. Kingdom, Animalia. Phylum, Vertebrate. Class, Osteichthyes. Order, Mythical. Family, Mermaidia. With genus and species yet to be named. It would be a mythical paraphyletic animal, something Jill couldn't begin to pronounce even when she was sober.

He would wear a hat and a fake beard with a mustache and glasses so nobody would recognize him. Even Jill. He was going to witness her downfall and humiliation, being careful not to contribute to his own. He figured what goes around comes around and payback was fair play. Rip needed to run some errands to accomplish this trickery and so, called Lloyd from his office desk. "Lloyd, fetch the car. We're going shopping!" Their first stop was The Scared Ghost Party and Costume Store.

Rip walked into the store and up a flight of stairs leading to a balcony that overlooked a massive warehouse. The long steel trusses supporting the roof stretched before him into infinity, like a mirror reflecting another mirror. He reckoned that the roof covered at least a half-acre and took up most of a city block. Rip gazed around in amazement. Large signs hanging from the rafters identified what the shopper would find down every aisle. The store was a walk-through of every holiday, party event, and significant occasion that could be celebrated during the calendar year.

Rip was struck by how cleverly the store was organized. Despite its intimidating size, shoppers could easily find the exact department they wanted without having to wear out a pair of shoes wandering around hoping to stumble upon the right aisle.

One half of the store followed the months of the year, boasting décor for each corresponding holiday. So, if you wanted something for Valentine's Day, you would go down the February aisle. Need a roll of patriotic bunting for Independence Day? Well, you would find that in the July aisle. Personal occasions organized the other half of the store that more or less followed the path of life, beginning with birth announcements and birthday decorations, followed by Graduation, Wedding, Anniversary, Divorce, Retirement, and finally a Funeral aisle. Then, set off to the side of the building was a large room, really an auditorium, filled with racks and racks of greeting cards and office supplies.

There was nothing you couldn't get at The Scared Ghost for any party theme or holiday. And if you walked out of there without finding what you were looking for, well then it probably didn't exist.

The Scared Ghost impressed Rip Rumple; part of him wanted to return to his office and draft an offer for immediate purchase. This kind of operation was waiting for someone to franchise it. There was money to be made here and identifying new business opportunities was what made Rip Rumple his billions. He lived for acquiring new businesses and The Scared Ghost would be a fun enterprise to build up. It was certainly something to think about. Rip made a mental note to meet with his acquisitions team about it and run some numbers on the Scared Ghost financials.

But now to get back to the reason for his visit. Rip was looking for a realistic disguise like a beard and mustache so he would not be recognized. Walking down the "October" aisle, Rip passed sections marking World Smile Day, Columbus Day, the Indian festival of Diwali, and finally Halloween. There, he saw every conceivable costume and disguise. Realistic mannequins modeled the elaborate costumes. Rip had to admit he found them kind of creepy. For a brief moment, he began to wonder if this was what it was like for Jill. She would be on the lookout for deranged and rogue mermaids prowling the place as she salaciously stripped in front of the licentious men.

Rip found a fake beard and mustache ensemble that required some wig adhesive to secure it. He found a mirror and held it to his face. *Yes, this will work!* he thought to himself. Someone would have to carefully scrutinize Rip to detect it as a fake. Now he needed to find some glasses and the right style hat. It was all there at The Scared Ghost, displayed by the assorted mannequins.

One mannequin, in particular, caught Rips attention. Talk about staring at you; it looked so real that Rip's heart started to race. This place was giving him goosebumps. The mannequin, wearing a fedora hat and black-rimmed glasses, began talking to him. The freaky mannequin kept repeating the same lines over and over. "How do you like my fedora? Maybe it would look good on you. Why don't you give it a try?" It let out a sinister laugh and asked, "Do you like me? Do you want to be me? You know you do because you can't take your eyes off of me!" Then the mannequin rolled its eyes and said, "I'm watching you watching me!"

Funny thoughts crossed the billionaire's mind as another peculiar idea wandered around his brain. Maybe he should buy The Mermaid Club and The Scared Ghost and mix the mermaids with some of these crazy mannequins here at The Scared Ghost. He could have them programmed to whisper absurd things to Jill as she performed. It would undoubtedly unsettle her and who knows, she might even take a swing at them, thus giving him grounds for firing her for destroying company property. Rip enjoyed himself immensely as his vivid imagination devised all sorts of revenge scenarios to unleash on Jill.

Rip's shopping basket was near capacity when he remembered to make one more stop in this playland of a store. Always the businessman, Rip needed some office supplies. He went back to a separate room that sold cards and stationery and loaded his basket with several reams of paper and ledgers along with some post-it notes. Still not quite finished, he made one more purchase and selected a friendship card with daffodils on the outside and blank on the inside.

The card was perfect for jotting down some nice sentiment to Nikki, the eighteen-year-old girl he had met just a few weeks earlier at The Palm Tree Oasis Casino. Nikki was the lounge singer there and she had quite the voice. Besotted by her youthful beauty and mesmerized by her hypnotic delivery, Rip planned to help launch her career and was now dating her.

But as he was exiting the store with all his goodies for tonight's grand plan, he wished there had been something to buy for his new love, Nikki. She had captured his affection, and she deserved more than just a card. If he owned The Scared Ghost, he might add a line of unique jewelry that would cater to the fanciful whims of the occasional billionaire. But that would have to wait. For now, a card with a sappy, hand-written sentiment inside would have to do.

NEVALLA LUXURY
APARTMENTS

According to the investigator's report, Jill's work day at The Sexy Mermaid Club usually began around nine p.m. and Rip intended to be there. Some might consider it petty, but Rip didn't care. After the public humiliation she had caused him, he wanted to witness Jill's spectacular degeneration for himself. And tonight, he was going to grab a front row seat to see the train wreck named "Jill."

Lloyd pulled the limo up to the front entrance of Rip's penthouse building and waited for his boss to emerge from the well-lit lobby of the luxury high-rise. By Vegas standards, it was still early, only eleven p.m. and for most people, the night would be just beginning. But for Rip Rumple, it was unusually late to be stepping out on the town. Normally his chauffer would be shuttling the billionaire back home for the evening. But Rip had instructed Lloyd to have his limousine waiting, and so there he was. The doorman opened the doors and a somewhat elderly bearded gentleman sporting a fedora and black framed glasses walked onto the sidewalk. The man walked up to the limo and knocked on the driver side window. Lloyd rolled down the window and told the man, "I'm sorry, sir, but I'm in service waiting for…" Lloyd's voice trailed off and then he began to laugh as he recognized his boss. "I'm sorry, Mr. Rumple, I didn't recognize you." Lloyd jumped out of the limo and opened the back door for his boss.

As Lloyd pulled the long car into traffic, he called to the back, "Costume party, Mr. Rumple? For a moment, I thought I was opening the door for Sigmund Freud."

Rip chuckled. "No Lloyd, not tonight. Tonight, we're going to the Sexy Mermaid."

"Oh?" Lloyd said quizzically as he scratched his head under his cap.

Lloyd pulled the limo in front of the Sexy Mermaid and Rip told him to wait in the parking lot for his text to pick him up. "Yes sir, Mr. Rumple. But don't you think I should be going in there with you? This place doesn't exactly look like it attracts a high-class clientele."

"Don't worry, Lloyd; you won't be missing anything special. Anyway, I shouldn't be long." Rip stepped out of the limo and disappeared through the doors of The Sexy Mermaid.

Rip was surprised by The Sexy Mermaid for exceeding even his lowest expectations. It was more debased and more disgusting than he had imagined. The mermaids disturbed Rip and the air alone made him feel as though he should be wearing a hazmat suit to protect himself from contracting any number of infectious diseases lurking in the place. Music blared as naked girls performed their gyrations to the hoots and hollers of the clientele who pressed up against the stage to get a close-up view of the show. Rip looked around the room. The Sexy Mermaid reminded him of a catch basin, the collection point for all the garbage and refuse that washed into the city's sewers. He was amazed by the agglomeration of perverts, winos, homeless vagabonds, and general losers assembled there.

As the music continued to roar, it seemed to Rip that the volume was gradually being increased to a point that it would be futile to try and have a conversation, even if there was someone worth talking to. Rip watched the show from a table as far from the stage as he could get. On stage the dancers posed with sordid-looking mermaid mannequins in various sexual positions. The mermaids themselves stared at the lecherous customers with their creepy eyeballs, occasionally winking and flapping their tails. It sure was an interesting visual to watch as some of the girls up on stage took their clothes off and danced around. One mermaid, in particular, seemed to be relegated for use as a clothes rack as the dancers would toss their tops and G-strings on it as they stripped down to bare skin. The music hit a crescendo as several dancers came out on stage for the set's finale. Rip watched it all, impatiently waiting for Jill to begin her performance. Finally, the music ended. It was over. The house lights brightened while the staff set up for the next show which amounted to the bartender retrieving the panties and bras hanging on the mermaids.

Rip waved his hand to catch the attention of a passing waitress. When she came over to the table, he ordered a scotch on the rocks. Before she returned with his drink, the house lights dimmed once more and another bout of blaring music rocked the building. The song was an old seventies hit, "Do You Think I'm Sexy" by Rod Stewart. The stage curtain opened and there was Jill. She was dressed in a too tight, white teddy. Her weight problem was obvious and Rip noticed plump bulges of skin poking out from under the silky fabric.

He watched as Jill concocted a series of provocatively stimulating moves, bumping and grinding her hips and even twerking with one of the mermaid mannequins. Rip had to concede that Jill had learned the fine art of exotic dancing from her work in the adult show at the Brandon Casino. She danced without inhibition. There wasn't anything she wouldn't do on stage. And apparently Jill had won over her raucous audience as they cheered and whistled at her every move.

With the things she did on stage, Rip thought she surely had to be on something. No one could be that uninhibited without at least some artificial fortification. But then again, this was Jill, and she had long ago proved to Rip that there was nothing she wouldn't do for money. And tonight, she was raking it in. Her fans waved fifty and one hundred-dollar bills in the air. She would shimmy over to them, turn around, and stick out her ample ass so they could slip their money under the strap of her G-string. She was taking home a bundle, at least five hundred dollars by Rip's estimation. Not a bad haul for a few minutes of dancing, if dancing was what you could call it.

Jill was now The Mermaid's "It Girl" and she made sure every pound of her extra curves rocked the Richter scale. She killed it and her audience drooled and begged for more. She must have realized she had the crowd on her side, because Jill went up for another go-round of even raunchier moves. She spread her legs more than Rip thought humanly possible and left every guy in the place completely enthralled by her titillations.

When his drink arrived, Rip took a sip and immediately spit it back into his glass and pushed the swill off to the side. It tasted like castor oil. He had seen enough, enough of The Sexy Mermaid and enough of Jill. He had seen what he came to see and had enjoyed witnessing Jill squirm for tips. As far as Jill was concerned, there was just one more thing he needed to do. But for now, he had to get himself out of The Sexy Mermaid. Rip pulled out his phone and texted Lloyd to pick him up in front of the club. As he made his way toward the exit, he took one last look at Jill who lay on her back while the audience pawed her with their hands and threw money on the stage. That was strictly illegal, but no one seemed to care, least of all Jill. It was repulsive. Rip turned, shaking his head in disgust.

Outside, Lloyd was waiting. Rip, the mustached and bearded wonder, entered the limo and they drove away. After peeling off his mustache, Rip struggled to dispose of his fake beard. It itched fiercely and was proving impossible to shuck it off. Deciding that could wait until later, he instructed Lloyd to take him home.

Rip walked into the kitchen and poured a glass of water. As he came back into the living room, he suffered another attack of narcolepsy. Tripping on the leg of an antique cherry-wood hutch, he crashed to the floor. Fortunately, the thick carpet made for a soft landing and Rip avoided serious injury. The only casualty was the spilled water; the carpet had saved the glass from shattering into a million pieces.

It was after two in the morning when he woke and realized he had been sleeping on his carpet. Somewhat disoriented, his chin felt irritated. When he touched his face, Rip felt the beard and scrambled up from the floor in alarm. Hurriedly, he raced over to a mirror and peeled the hairy disguise from his face, scraping off pieces of glue with his nails. He rubbed his hand across his face. Removing the costume beard left his cheeks ruddy and red.

Rip made the call he had told Lloyd to expect. Fifteen minutes later, Lloyd was again waiting in front of Rip's high-rise with the engine idling. Rip warned him that he might be in for a long night waiting for him in Jill's parking garage. But Lloyd didn't mind because Mr. Rumple always made it worth his while. Rip donned a sports jacket and made his way to the waiting limo. Lloyd knew where to go without being told.

On the way to Jill's penthouse apartment that Rip was still grudgingly paying for, Rip reached into his inner pocket and took notice that he had stuffed his card for Nikki there as well as the post-it notes. Lloyd maneuvered into the parking garage of the Nevalla Luxury Apartments and slowed to a stop in front of the building's lower lobby. Without waiting for Lloyd to open the limo door for him, Rip jumped out of the car and disappeared into an elevator.

Jill's condo was on the thirty-fifth floor. It had a glass-walled porch that provided a panoramic view of the Las Vegas strip. It was quite a stunning visual – and it was all on Rip's tab.

MEDITERRANEAN AVENUE

In his mind, Jill had reached obsolescence. Well, almost.

Using his key, Rip let himself into Jill's condo. Closing the door behind him, he staggered and leaned against a wall for support. His olfactory nerve was assaulted by overwhelming odors. The apartment reeked of cigarettes and pot. From the foyer, Rip looked around but didn't see anyone. He stepped into the living room and there laying on the eighteen thousand-dollar Victoria Palace sofa designed by Michael Amini, was a very drunk and passed out Jill. Bottles upon bottles were strewn all over the Brazilian cherry hardwood floors. It looked like the morning after a fraternity party.

Jill's breathing was shallow and the only way Rip knew she was alive was from the saliva bubbles that popped from her mouth when she exhaled. Her expensive silk nightgown was torn, exposing one of her breasts and it was stained with streaks of what Rip guessed was vomit. Thinking she may be overdosing, Rip tried to wake her. Jill was a mess. Pieces of puke stuck to her hair and mascara racooned her eyes and smeared down her face.

For a moment she rallied, but her face made a scowl when she saw Rip. Slurring her words, she was only able to mangle, "Rip gives bad sex. He's so old. You make me sick!" She hung her head over the edge of the couch as if she was indeed going to puke. Rip watched the back of her head bobble and he stepped back to avoid the inevitable vomit stream. But instead of becoming ill, Jill suddenly realized that Rip was standing in front of her. "Rip, baby, what brings you here? An hour earlier and you could have joined me and my two mermaid friends, Pete and Jamal. Or should I say *merman* friends? We sure had us a party, baby." Her words were barely decipherable.

Across the floor, Rip noticed a crusty pair of men's briefs and a balled-up pair of socks. An ashtray on one of the end tables overflowed with cigarette butts. The room smelled so rancid that Rip had to escape into the kitchen for relief. Once again, he held onto one of the tall cabinets and took deep breaths to keep from becoming sick himself. He noticed the door to the right of the kitchen was ajar. It was Jill's bedroom, and a soft light was streaming through the opening. He could make out a naked man passed out on her bed with slaver oozing out of the corners of his mouth. Another man wearing only a shredded UNLV Rebels T-shirt snored thunderously on the floor while cradling a glass bong that looked ready to fall out of his hands. Rip could see the inside of the man's mouth and his large crooked, yellow teeth. His torn shirt exposed a full-torso tattoo of a lion's head bearing a feral grin. Ironically, the tattooed lion had its mouth open as well and baring its own fearsome canines. Both men were out cold; even an exploding howitzer shell over their heads wouldn't wake them up.

What a fool Rip had been, paying her rent and furnishing her condo with extravagant furniture. He surveyed the living room and then the bedroom. He was appalled at the debauchery that besieged him. With the insight that made him a multi-billionaire, Rip distilled the situation down to bare facts. Comparing it to the game of Monopoly, Rip saw Jill as a Mediterranean Avenue whore who had momentarily landed on his Park Place. It was just an unfortunate chance that he had happened to be there when she strolled through his corner of the world.

Rip fidgeted. He needed an upgrade. Why was he still here? Without thinking, he put his hands inside his sports coat pocket and the post sticky notes tumbled out. Picking them up off the floor, he retrieved a pen from a kitchen drawer. Empty beer bottles and wine glasses filled the sink. Cluttered everywhere on the granite countertops was an untidy mess of empty beer and wine bottles. Some were high-end wines like the Dona Paula Jill so enjoyed. But alongside this, on the other end of the wine spectrum, was a bottle of Mad Dog 20/20 and tallboys of Pabst Blue Ribbon apparently used as chasers. He remembered MD 20/20 was the choice of wino-bums when he was a kid. It was cheap and fortified with that extra kick of alcohol that got you there faster. Cripes, he even saw a half-full bottle of Thunderbird. Talking aloud to himself, he said disgustedly, "What a joke! How the heck could darling little Jill swill that rotgut?"

Returning to the living room, he stood over his former lover who had again lapsed into an alcohol-induced stupor. Rip used two sticky notes to accomplish his task. On the first one, he scribbled, "Thanks for services rendered!" Jill moaned a little when he pasted it on her bare breast, but she didn't wake up. On the second post-it, he wrote, "As of this date," and he put the exact date and time, "Your services are terminated." Bonding the second sticky to her exposed pale leg hanging over the couch, he noticed Jill flinch, but it was her other leg that moved.

Rip decided to leave her one last remembrance and quickly penned another sentiment on a third sticky: "Enjoy Mediterranean Avenue." Then he stuck it to Jill both literally and figuratively as he sealed the note across her chubby abdomen. Even this did not arouse Jill, and as Rip left, he heard only the sound of her gurgling and baby snores.

Closing the apartment door behind him, Rip speed-dialed Lloyd and told him to have the car waiting for him out front. Stroking his chin, he noticed it once again felt velvety and smooth.

Lloyd was standing by the open car door when Rip strode from the building. As Lloyd drove them home, Rip asked Lloyd how he liked his new iPhone. As soon as Lloyd began to answer, Rip fell into a deep sleep. Lloyd drove on in silence and pulled into the underground garage of Rip's penthouse and tried to wake his employer. "Sir, are you okay? Wake up. We are home. Let me help you to your room."

Rip fumbled, "Are we at Boardwalk or Park Place? I want it. It is expensive. I'm going to put a hotel on it to keep out the lowlifes." He closed his eyes, and his head fell back on the limousine's headrest.

Lloyd's take on his eccentric boss was that he must be having a dream about Atlantic City. He smiled thinking about it, but he was confused by Rip's sleep talking. He thought Rip must be really out of it and thoroughly confused because why else would he think he was in New Jersey instead of Las Vegas?

Lloyd had spent some time at the Jersey shore in his younger years, in Atlantic City to be precise, and it was there where he met Rip Rumple. Memories of his out-of-control party days in Atlantic City floated back through his mind. Working as a blackjack dealer in one of the boardwalk casinos, Lloyd had spent his money frivolously. It had been good until the casino he was working at went bankrupt and closed its doors. Lloyd's cash dried up, and he was forced to find work as a driver for a limo service. Fortunately for Lloyd, one of his first passengers was Rip Rumple. Mr. Rumple took an immediate liking to Lloyd and offered him a permanent position as Rip's private chauffeur. That had been the best thing that had ever happened to him.

Rip mumbled something again, forcing Lloyd to stop reliving his past escapades, snapping him back into the present. Lloyd helped Rip Rumple out of the car and up to his penthouse.

Being loyal to his employer, Lloyd was left confused by Mr. Rumple's recent uncharacteristic behavior.

HAIGHT-ASHBURY, SAN

FRANCISCO 1968

Immediately after Tommy Bill threw down his challenge to a Battle of the Bands against The Rajabede Trio, Lee and the guys realized they had a lot of work to do if they didn't want to make fools of themselves on live radio.

The next day, they rented a small studio where they could practice and audition lead singers. After spending hours rehearsing and rebuilding the dynamics of the band their sound was tight and Lee thought they never sounded better. But after auditioning numerous singers, he became discouraged.

Finding a replacement for Becky Dean was proving to be a more daunting task than any of them had thought. Almost a dozen singers had responded to their Craigslist post, but not one of them had come close to being the vocalist that Becky Dean was. Finally, after watching the last prospect on their list walk out the door, the guys sat around their makeshift studio, downcast. They were ready to concede defeat and call off Tommy Bill's challenge.

Then Isabella, or Izzy as she called herself, strutted into the studio. Izzy exuded a confidence that seemed to announce, "See me! Hear me!" She told them their search was over; she was their new vocalist. Lee looked at Basil and Javier and shrugged. "What have we got to lose, guys?" Lee handed her their play list while they plugged in. When they were ready, Lee asked her, "What will it be?" Izzy chose an old standard popularized by Billie Holiday, "God Bless the Child."

While Basil tapped out the beat with his drum sticks, Lee and Javier started playing. Izzy stepped confidently up to the microphone and began to sing. Her voice was raspy and intriguing, utterly unique. She had a presence and style that Lee later called 'Joplinesque' after the late, great Janis Joplin. But now, as Izzy launched into the second stanza, Lee looked over at Basil and smiled. Basil nodded approvingly. When they reached the final refrain, Lee knew they had found their lead singer.

Unlike Becky Dean, Izzy didn't play any instruments. But the girl had a voice unlike anyone they'd ever heard. Her long, wavy hair and sultry voice gave her the illusion of being almost ethereal. Izzy was fascinating and her retro-hippie style suited her, telling the guys how she wished it was still the sixties because that was where she belonged. As it was, Izzy went around flashing the peace sign, wore Indian bead headbands, and used stale idioms such as "groovy" and "far out, man." She was a real walking, talking anachronism straight out of 1968's Haight Ashbury. It was as if Izzy had been transported into the here and now by a time travel machine.

The connection between them all was immediate, almost symbiotic. Isabella already knew most of the songs in The Maddies' repertoire, and as they continued practicing, Lee began to see a much-improved Madison Four develop.

At Isabella's prompting, they even decided to cover some Janis Joplin's tunes from her days with Big Brother and the Holding Company. And after a few false starts, "Cry Baby" became the new standard in their setlist. Possessing charisma and talent, Isabella infused the band with a new vivacity that Becky Dean had never brought.

At the end of one of their rehearsals, Lee turned on the radio to KPLV. DJ Tommy Bill Dillion was on air and promoting the upcoming duel like it was as important as a presidential election. He had taken to calling them the "Baddies from Maddie," and for now, Lee was content to be billed as such. All of them wanted redemption; revenge was foremost on their minds.

The showdown was set for Saturday night, just two short weeks away and The Baddies from Maddie still had a lot of work to do.

CLUB FLOWER POWER

After weeks of fevered promotion by Tommy Bill Dillon, all of the country-music listeners in Las Vegas tuned in to listen to the big event. The Rajabede Trio and, as DJ Tommy Bill called them, The Baddies from Maddie were set to face off in the KPLV studios for a Battle of the Bands extraordinaire. It all fell to the judgment of the listening audience to decide which group brought the sauce to take home the honors.

Each band arrived hours before the show to set up its equipment and perform mic and sound checks with the station's broadcast engineer. Tommy Bill had scheduled his meetings with both bands separately to go over the contest rules. He wanted to avoid any pre-broadcast clashes between the groups. Always the consummate showman, he wanted to be sure that if there were any fireworks, they would explode while they were on the air. But despite his careful planning, just as The Rajabede Trio was leaving the station, the Baddies arrived for their appointed meeting with Tommy Bill.

Basil was the first to spot Becky Dean walking out of the station between Randy Kiefer and James Donovan. He elbowed Lee, who was removing their equipment from a rented van. "Look who it is, Lee. It's the traitor." Lee turned around just as Becky Dean noticed them. Their eyes locked and Lee stared at her with pained determination. He said nothing but Lee's caustic stare told it all. Lee turned back to the task of unloading their equipment while Becky Dean hustled the Rajabedes to their car without ever acknowledging Lee or any of her former bandmates.

That evening when Tommy Bill opened his show, both groups were in the studio and ready to jolt the airwaves. The first thing Tommy Bill did was introduce the bands and then the members of each. He tried his best to be diplomatic. "Now, folks. What we got here is two groups a'wanting to claw each other's eyes out. But let's at least start this fight out on a good *note*." Tommy Bill paused a moment for effect. "Get it?" he asked and then started whooping and hollering at his cleverness. Tommy Bill didn't notice that no one else in the room was laughing. Instead, mocking stares and rolling eyes shot from one to another in unanimous disapproval of his pathetic pun.

But among his many other talents, Tommy Bill was a showman. "Folks, let's meet the home team, so to speak. This-here is The Rajabede

Tribe." Becky Dean threw him a stern stare. "Oops! I mean, Rajabede *Trio*. They're here for a second time. Put your hands together for pretty Miss Becky Dean, James Donovan, and Randy Kiefer." Tommy Bill pointed to his producer sitting in the control booth behind a wall of glass. Without hesitation, the producer punched up an applause loop.

Except for their brief encounter in the station parking lot, Lee had not seen Becky Dean since she left Madison months before. Now he found himself looking over at her more often then he dared to admit. It seemed to Lee that this James guy was paying a little too much attention to her. He could tell something was going on between them. Lee also couldn't get past beach bum Randy Kiefer who seemed like the quintessential California pothead and one wave short of a surfboard.

At one point during Tommy Bill's introduction of the trio, Randy Kiefer told Tommy Bill, "It was totally rad working with James and Becky Dean at The Deerskin Lounge." Lee thought he was listening to Jeff Spicoli from *Fast Times at Ridgemont High*, a 1980s movie he had just recently watched. He turned to watch how Becky Dean would react and was a bit annoyed when he saw James wink at her and then squeeze her hand.

Tommy Bill turned his attention to Becky Dean. "What we have been a'hearing is that you're no damn good, Little Miss Becky Dean, and that you plundered The Madison Four's setlist and ideas and then done ran away with them. You stole their boodle and I don't mean the kind you little gutter rats are thinking about. Get out of that-there stenchy sewer and think in terms of bounty. Little Missy B.D. ran off with song merchandise, so The Baddies from Maddie are here for vengeance."

Becky Dean stepped forward to the microphone to respond, but Tommy Bill ignored her.

"Now you're here in Vegas with a new group and setting The Deerskin Lounge on fire. But there is a problem. One very *big* problem. And that is 'The Baddies from Maddie' say you done them wrong and never looked back. Yes ma'am, you never told them where you were going, where you were, or that you were the least bit sorry. No sir, uh, I mean, ma'am. You couldn't pull it out of yourself to be sorry in the least. Hey Maddies, if you think she's sorry, y'all barking up the wrong dang tree. Miss Becky Dean, you left their big fat fanny's in a world of hurt, but they tracked you down and now they come to pay you back. You flamed them good and now, they're here fixin' to burn *your* house down to ashes." It pleased Tommy Bill to see two of the three Rajabedes squirm uncomfortably under his withering attack but he could tell that Becky Dean was smoldering. He could feel the heat from across the room. It was hot enough to melt the ice clinking in Lee's water glass. Tommy Bill was having fun.

Keeping the drama going, he continued. "Now! Baddies from Maddie, what do you want to do about this little ole situation? Do you all have some tunes you want to pull out of your pockets? I hope y'all been boning up. Are you gonna rock the house and put Miss Becky Dean to shame or are you all just gonna break a bunch of guitar strings and slink back home? Well? What's it gonna be, Baddies?"

Javier Ramos stepped up and fist pumped the air. Basil immediately responded, "Pump it harder" as he put his fist up to Javier's. "We're going to win because she's a fraud through and through." Then the newest Baddie, Isabella, went to her mic and, looking straight at Becky Dean, simply said "Meow!"

Tommy Bill jumped in excitably with, "Well folks, it sounds like we got us a real cat and dog fight on our hands." At that, both Becky Dean and James Donavan barked out "Woof! Woof! Dogs beat mangy cats any day, any time."

"Well," Tommy Bill continued, "I got the power and here's how it's gonna go down." He explained that each group would play three songs after which the audience could call and pick a winner. "Call up 702-COU-NTRY if you're for The Rajabede Trio or 702-BUC-OLIC" for The Baddies from Maddie. Your vote will register automatically. It's important. This, folks, is earth-shattering. Do you want The Rajabede Trio or The Baddies from Maddie? Lines will be open immediately after the show is over. I will keep repeating these cute little numbers, but I'll put them in plain telephone language now. Punch and crunch 702-268-6879 for The Rajabede Trio or 702-282-6542 for The Baddies from Maddie. So, remember to smile and dial and pick yourself the winner. Fasten your seat belts 'cuz here we go. I decided to let the defendants up first just like we're all here sitting in court with Perry Mason. The Rajabede's got to defend themselves. There's still meat on that bone, and you, the jury, got to make the choice. Up first, pistols packin' and loaded is The Rajabede Trio singing 'Stormy Monday.' Hit it, Rajabede!"

With the strike of the first chord, Lee could tell The Rajabede Trio was tight. Randy had his harmonica blazing and Becky Dean was singing and swaying, pulling it out from deep within herself.

Accompanying his so-called girlfriend in the refrain, James harmonized well with Becky Dean. *Damn*, they were hot. Lee thought he was going to faint from the pressure. But Isabella whispered in his ear, "Don't freak out, man. We're going to nail the whole shebang. They'll be loading our equipment by the time I finish singing. Dig it; they'll be our road-toadies." Stepping back and giving Lee the peace sign, she then decided, for some crazy-ass reason, to flash Lee her boobs. Pulling up her tie-dyed Jerry Garcia T-shirt, she jiggled her puppies in front of Lee who just about keeled over from the thrill.

Becky Dean saw it and for a moment was noticeably distracted. Tommy Bill saw it too and after The Rajabede Trio was done, told the audience, "You wouldn't believe what I just saw. After the commercial break, I'll keep you *abreast* of the situation." Once again, he laughed wildly at his joke while the others in the studio just kind of looked at each other. But as before, his pun was a bust, undoubtedly because no one listening had seen Isabella in action.

Lee knew they were up next to perform their rendition of "Stormy Monday." The contest rules were simple and dictated by Tommy Bill. There'd be three songs. Each band would start by playing "Stormy Monday." The second song would be of each band's choosing and the finale would be a surprise decided upon by, who else but Tommy Bill Dillon. But to be fair, Tommy Bill had given each band a list of the songs he would select from, so at least they knew it would be something they had practiced.

As The Baddies began their interpretation of "Stormy Monday," Isabella entrancingly edged up to the mic. Draped in a fringed skirt that dusted the floor every time she swayed to the rhythm and a floral headband, she grabbed it as if it was a natural appendage. Her voice was raw and powerful, yet she hit every note with subtle and startling nuance.

Lee responded with solo riffs that were equally inspiring and his backup harmony with Basil fused into a single sound. Javier's harmonica solo was mesmerizing. Undulating, Isabella twirled intermittently as her fringed skirt swirled in the air with every pirouette. As they closed the song, Lee knew they had won the first round.

Becky Dean also seemed to have taken notice. At one point, Lee was sure he saw her mouth clench in disbelief. Tommy Bill, however, seemed transfixed by both groups. After The Baddies from Maddie finished, Javier whispered loudly to Isabella, "I think we are tied so far."

In return, Isabella gave him a puzzled stare. "No way are we tied. They sure as hell didn't play 'Stormy Monday;' all they played was 'Boring Monday.'"

It was break time and Tommy Bill took to the air. "Well, hallelujah! We got us a competition to beat the band." And then he did it again. "Get it, folks? Beat the band? I am just full of the clever puns today. Y'all gotta agree. I'm like the Picasso of double-entendre, only my paintbrush is my yapper. I'll tell you what, folks, that first round was chock full of some mighty fine playing by both of these groups. Gracious me. We'll be right back after we pay a few of those annoying bills. Hang with us and then we're gonna come right back and kick up a ruckus!"

During the break, Lee watched James put his arm around Becky Dean and kiss her. She seemed to be cozying up to him for effect. Lee saw her glance at him and then flash her big eyes at least three times. He wasn't sure what message Becky Dean was trying to send him.

They were back on, and so was Tommy Bill. "Howdy, folks. Welcome back to All Things Country! We're gonna get on with these two bands 'cuz they got a hankering to sing y'all their favorite songs. They done picked out their own songs to play for y'all, so listen up. Both groups are gonna be hotter than a goat's butt in a pepper patch. So, once again, here is The Rajabede Trio with Lynyrd Skynyrd's "Sweet Home Alabama."

Rajabede started well enough, but when Becky Dean tried to punch up her vocals on the refrain, she fell flat. The energy just wasn't there; it seemed Isabella had siphoned off Becky Dean's confidence. One thing was sure – she didn't have the voice to match Isabella. Becky Dean seemed to be having an old-fashioned cat fight with Isabella being the instigator. Halfway through their song, Isabella stuck her tongue out at Becky Dean and then blew James a kiss. Her flirt threw James off and he missed a chord. Isabella's antics were distracting and The Rajabede Trio was on the verge of imploding. Finally, they turned their backs to ignore Isabella and were able to finish the song. But there was no question that Isabella's stunts had impacted their playing and whittled away at Becky Dean's self-confidence.

But even before Rajabede played their last note, Becky Dean jammed the microphone into its stand and after singing her last note, sauntered across the studio to stand in front of Lee. Wrapping her arms around him, she began kissing him passionately. When she was done, Lee's knees buckled and he almost fell to the floor. Becky Dean looked at Isabella as if to say, "Top that, sister!"

Tommy Bill took to the mic, and exclaimed excitedly, "Lord All Mighty! Folks, if you could see what I'm a witnessing, well, you just plain out wouldn't believe it. These-here young'uns are giving me a show and a half. I'm about to have a conniption fit. Dadburn it! One of them is a'flashing her stuff and the other is planting long kisses on the competition. Well, shut my fool mouth, but they are both a pair of hoochie-coochies. But I ain't saying no more except saddle up 'cuz we got The Baddies from Maddie singing their song. Just like baseball, it's the bottom of the second inning. And if any of you are half-wits, that just means we're on round two and The Maddies up next. Give 'em a hand 'cuz they're about to strut their stuff. What're you gonna sing, you Maddies?"

Isabella pressed up to the mic and, in her most condescending voice, answered, "Buckle up, Tommy Bill, 'cause the Maddies are going to sing 'Sweet Home Alabama.' But we're going do it right. What you just heard was the first-round casualty from an *America's Got Talent* audition. Now you're going to hear how it *should* be done."

Isabella wasn't joking. The Maddies played with an energy and precision that left everyone in the studio speechless. Becky Dean looked visibly distressed. Tommy Bill almost fell off his chair. Finally, after a few seconds of dead air, Tommy Bill shook himself enough to exclaim, "What can I say except you sure done Lynyrd Skynyrd proud. I'm getting' all riled up, and here we are near about done. We got us one more song and I'm going to surprise both bands with it just as soon as we pay a few bills. So, stay tuned, I'm telling y'all, these two bands are a pair of pistols."

During the commercial break, James told Becky Dean about the air kiss Isabella had blown him. "That chick ought to be locked up in a nut house," he concluded. Eyeing Becky Dean, he then asked, "What was up with you drowning that Lee-guy in kisses? Especially when he was the one who dropped the dime on us live on air? What do you have for him anyway? I thought maybe we were getting something started; but now I'm not so sure. Oh, and by the way, you acted like a surrender-monkey during 'Sweet Home Alabama.' You sang like you were on ludes."

Randy Kiefer jumped into the conversation. "Yeah, like, did you just rise from the dead? Man, like, what happened to your punch? You better bring it on the next number like it's your last meal, dudette, and up your game."

Becky Dean gave them an icy stare. "Well, you two didn't exactly set the stage on fire. Neither one of you saved the day, so don't climb on me." She tossed her head back defiantly. Becky Dean was clearly angry.

Tommy Bill was back on the air. "Hey, folks! I'm back with All Things Country and once again, let me tell you what – we got us a good, old-fashioned fight going on between two groups. We got The Rajabede Trio versus The Baddies from Maddie, and we got us a melee of a bunch of deranged cuckoos throwin' hissy fits all over the place with each other. They may be ignernt, but they can sure bust loose when it comes to the music."

Both bands looked like they didn't appreciate being called ignorant, or ignernt, as Tommy Bill pronounced it. But it was Randy Kiefer who confronted Tommy Bill. "Hey Mr. Dillon, like, we aren't ignorant. Like, we're just musicians."

Tommy Bill shouted him down. "Same difference, boy. I'll tell you what! Just you go back and play possum and shut your dadgum mouth until I tell you to get up and play. Do ya hear me? You've been taking too many hits to your noggin' with that surfboard 'cuz, boy, you ain't right in the head. You're about as sharp as a mashed potato." Randy Kiefer sunk silently back into the woodwork.

Having brushed away the pesky musician, Tommy Bill continued, "We're purt near the end, but I still got to tell you the next song I want to hear from y'all. Well, I've been a thinking and the last time I heard someone sing this song, he couldn't carry a tune in a bucket. Well, let me cut to the chase. The song I want y'all to sing and play for our country audience is a little something by Waylon and Willie. You all know it – 'Mama Don't Let Your Babies Grow Up to Be Cowboys.'"

Becky Dean gasped and there was a groan from the other side with Basil shaking his head. Isabella cut them both off and spoke up, "I love those country outlaws, and I applaud you, Mr. Tommy Bill, for your choice." Then she started whistling Willie Nelson's "On the Road Again."

Now Tommy Bill slammed the hammer on Isabella. "This is my show and I don't need no hippie girl tellin' me how to run it. I got a mind to come over and take you out to the woodshed for a good whooping. First, you try to butter me all up, and then you go off half-cocked a'whistling up a storm without being asked. Girl, I declare, you do let your tail wag your mouth. Now, let's get back to business. Rajabede's, you're up to bat." DJ Tommy Bill Dillon was getting cranky.

Before Becky Dean stepped up to the mic, she took a deep breath. She needed to sing them out of the hole she had dug. Deciding to sing it with a blues style, Becky Dean threw herself into her music. This was her last chance, and she wasn't about to let the Rajabede-ship go down.

Cradling the microphone in her hand, she sang the song the same way she did at The Deerskin Lounge. It was one of their signature songs and the crowd at The Deerskin Lounge always enjoyed their unique arrangement. She could tell Tommy Bill enjoyed it too. His mouth was half-open as he watched them in a hypnotized state. The Rajabede's were rallying. Becky Dean knew it was about the best the group had ever played that song. Bowing to an imaginary audience when the song was over, Becky Dean snuck a peek at Isabella. She hoped the woman got the message: "Try and beat that, you sixties freak."

But Isabella didn't appear intimidated one bit by the Rajabede's performance. She looked to Basil to count out a beat and away they went. Lee knew it wasn't one of Basil's favorite songs, but he laid down an intricate drum track that at first seemed too complicated for such a simple song. But when Javier entered on bass, it all made sense and together added a deeper dimension to the song. As usual, Lee made his guitar sing and Isabella was outstanding. Once again, her phrasing and style were perfect.

It was over and Tommy Bill returned to the microphone. "Man alive, both these two groups brought it, and I don't know what to say. Well, shut my mouth and let's go to a break. We'll be back in two shakes of a sheep's tail." During the break, both bands began tearing down their equipment. Now and then they would glance over at each other, but no one said a word. They seemed consumed with anticipation and now that it was over, a feeling of relief.

Returning from a commercial break, Tommy Bill began instructing the audience to get on their phones and text their votes. Once again, he recited the two numbers and told his listeners to pick the group they thought had played the best. "The phones will be open for two hours. After that, the people will have spoken and decided who won this epic battle between The Rajabede Trio and The Baddies from Maddie. We'll announce the winner on tomorrow's show during the six o'clock hour, and after that, maybe they can mend fences with each other. But I got news for y'all! The winner is invited back for their congratulations party. They will be playing for us some more. We gonna have a shindig with them 'cuz they deserve it!"

Speaking loudly and enthusiastically into the mic but addressing the bands, he said, "I reckon I ought to send these musicians home so they can hunker down and wait for y'all's verdict. I know one thing, they sure are a talented bunch, and they went in whole-hog with their playing. So, off you go to your respective corners." Speaking now to the listeners, he said, "And now it's up to you, the audience. So, get your fingers moving." Then he repeated the numbers. "Well, now once again, you are listening to 95.8, All Things Country and for your listening pleasure, this-here is Tommy Bill Dillon. I'm gonna play us out with some sweet Patsy Cline. Here's 'I Fall to Pieces.'"

Even though the winner had yet to be decided, the sour faces on The Rajabede side of the studio said it all. Lee deliberately slowed packing up his equipment to look over at Becky Dean. There was an expression of defeat in her face that he had never seen before which made Lee oscillate between relishing in her disappointment and feeling sorry for her.

But he was also curious. He wanted to ask Becky Dean why she had kissed him. They had been The Madison Four for years and never once had Becky Dean so much as even given him a peck on the cheek. And now this? Lee couldn't get it out of his head. There was something more to it than just a harmless flirtation. Had it been for show? Had she been trying to make that James guy jealous? Part of him missed Becky Dean. He wanted her back, at least as a friend.

Lee was lost in his thoughts when a flurry of angry words flew between James and Becky Dean. He watched as James stalked out of the studio, angrily waving her off leaving Becky Dean struggling to break down a mic stand.

The mood on The Maddies' side was far different. A confident Isabella wanted everyone to go and party. She was heading for the Club Flower Power, a club that had recently opened downtown. It was the new *hot* place and had quickly become the place to go for Vegas locals. Club Flower Power played all sixties music from Jimi Hendrix to Moby Grape. Sometimes a DJ would spin the tunes while other nights a live band would relive the golden era of rock-and-roll. Isabella explained, "Thursdays are test nights, like the Acid Test they used to have back in the day. Everyone dresses hippie, and they play nothing but Grateful Dead. Everyone loves it, and we all smoke a lot of dope, and no one cares. It's a ton of fun." Javier chuckled and told her he was game. Basil waved her off, saying he had to get back to his wife and kids. She turned to Lee and asked, "Well, I'm waiting. Are you in?"

A puzzled Lee looked at her. "Don't you want to see how the votes are coming in"

"Lee, that'll take hours and we all know we won. Besides, I'm no old fogey. And I sure as hell don't want to sit around here listening to any more of that Tommy Lee Dipstick or whatever his name is."

Lee replied, "I don't know; let me think about it."

"Well, you better decide pretty quick, sweet pea, because I'm splittin' this scene in about thirty seconds." Isabella had taken to calling him 'sweet pea.' Lee wasn't sure what to think about that one.

He glanced over at Becky Dean who was still wrestling with the mic stand and seemed to be taking her time about it. He went to help her; he didn't miss the slight smile that crossed Becky Dean's face. Lee wrapped his hands around hers and said, "Here, let me help you with that."

"Thanks, Lee." Becky Dean let go of the mic stand and stepped back a bit. "You guys were great. And I have to admit, that Isabella is something else. She's got talent and style to boot. You guys did all right coming up with her."

"Yeah, you got that right. She's good stuff." He broke down the mic stand easily and looked at Becky Dean expectantly.

Becky Dean had a serene expression and spoke in a soft, almost contrite voice. "Go on, ask away. I owe it to you. I was wrong to walk out on you guys without a word. I know it's not much, but if you can accept it, I am truly sorry."

Lee had replayed this scene over and over in his mind and thought he knew what he wanted to say to her. Now that she was standing in front of him all he could ask was, "Why?" It was more like he was pleading with her to help him make sense of the incomprehensible. "We were together for *years*. We were family! We trusted you and you deserted us. For crying out loud, Basil has a wife and kids! Why? I just don't understand how you could do that to us. To me!"

Becky Dean stood very still for a few seconds then said, "Okay! I'm going to tell you like it is. I left Wisconsin and the group because I felt like we were stuck in neutral. We were going nowhere, and I couldn't take it anymore. Las Vegas sounded like a good place to find work, and I liked the whole idea of it. I know I messed up by not telling you. I guess I was afraid of what you guys would say and maybe change my mind. And to get to the very truth of the matter, I didn't want to look at you after I told you. I mean, I didn't want to hurt you."

"But you did. I never felt a hurt like that before."

"But there's something you need to know. I mean, I'm enjoying Las Vegas and playing a gig on the Strip, but something is missing, something I didn't count on. So here goes." Becky Dean turned away from Lee, and seemed to struggle for the words she wanted to say. Then she suddenly blurted it out. "Lee, I miss you, and now I know you mean something to me. I know it's too late, but that is how I feel." She looked up at him and their eyes connected.

Lee opened his arms and put them around her. "Is that why you kissed me?" Becky Dean nodded. He pulled her close and kissed her. His heart was pounding and he could feel hers doing the same. They kissed again and became lost in each other's embrace.

It took Isabella's ire to drag the couple back into the present when she landed a playful punch on Lee's arm. "Um, I know I am interrupting, sweet pea, but are you coming with me and Javier to check out this new club or not?" She squeezed her eyebrows together expressing disapproval about what was going on, but she dared not say anything.

At that point, Randy Kiefer interjected, "Dudette, I know we're on different teams, but there's no reason we couldn't party together. Do you mind if I tag along?"

Isabella pointed at Lee and didn't wait for him to answer. "Sure, come on. It's plain to see he's not coming." She grabbed Randy by the arm and, as she made her way through the studio, she snagged Javier with her other arm. As they left the studio Lee called out to the trio that he might catch up with them later.

When they were gone, Lee turned to Becky Dean and asked her if she was hungry. "Remember how you used to get the spaghetti special at that church in Madison? Well, how about we go to my apartment and I cook you up some of the best spaghetti and meatballs you ever had in your life?"

Becky Dean moved close to him and kissed him with a quick tap to his lips. "Yeah, I can always eat, and you're right. I love spaghetti and meatballs. It's my all-time favorite. But I know the real reason you want me to go to your apartment is so you can ravage my voluptuous body." Flirting and laughing, Becky Dean seemed at peace.

But Lee surprised her with his answer. "No, Miss Becky Dean, I want to go back to my apartment so I can listen to the radio. I can't wait to hear that The Baddies from Maddie are the winners of the Battle of the Bands. I know we won and that's a fact!"

Becky Dean shook her head. "I'll bet you one meatball that the Rajabedes won!"

Lee laughed. "You must not have the confidence of your group winning if you are only willing to bet *one* meatball. I mean, after all, this is Las Vegas. Put your meatballs where your mouth is."

He was waiting for Becky Dean to up the ante. Her eyes filled with mischief and she replied, "Okay, I'll bet you two meatballs."

    The betting ended with Lee raising the stakes. "Okay! I'll see your two meatballs and raise you a sausage." He flashed her a coy smile.

    Becky Dean pulled Lee close and whispered in his ear, "I fold." He knew and he knew that *she knew* that the Baddies from Maddie would be crowned the victors of Tommy Bill's little Battle of the Bands.

    Lee also knew that The Baddies from Maddie were sorely in need of a new name.

WAFFLE HOUSE

Early the next morning after The Baddies from Maddie battled against Becky Dean and Rajabede on KPLV, Lee was awakened by the buzzing of his cell phone. Rolling over in the bed, he groggily searched his nightstand for his phone. "Hello."

"Lee Murphy?" the voice asked energetically.

"Uh-huh?"

"Lee. Tommy Bill Dillon here! Just calling you to let you be the first to know that The Baddies from Maddie smoked the phone banks last night. It wasn't even close, boy. I'm telling you, that little girl of yours was a sensation and you all did right by yourselves to boot. The Rajabedes will be spitting out that dirty dust you left them for a long time to come. We'll be talkin' soon, but now I've gotta give Miss Becky Dean a call and break the news to her. Congratulations, boy." Tommy Bill abruptly ended the call.

Lee sat up against his headboard, staring at his phone. Next to him, he felt a warm arm wrap around his chest and a soft sexy voice whisper, "What is it, Lee?" Before Lee could answer, the phone on the other bed stand began playing its "Stormy Monday" ringtone. Becky Dean rolled away and stretched her arm to answer her phone.

"Becky Dean? This is Tommy Bill Dillon. I'm just calling to let you know that you and The Rajabede put on a humdinger of a show yesterday and to let you know that we've had an overwhelming response to both bands."

"Well thank you, sir. Hopefully, everyone enjoyed us."

"Well, they did. But the plain and simple fact is that they enjoyed The Baddies from Maddie even more. You win some, you lose some. You had your time to shine, but you couldn't walk the line."

Becky Dean glanced at Lee. "Well, I guess the people have spoken. Who am I to argue with the people? Thank you, Mr. Dillon." Becky Dean put the phone back on the nightstand and pulled herself close to him. "Congratulations, Lee. I guess the best band won after all. What's for breakfast?"

He kissed her and asked, "How does Waffle House sound?"

DOC HOLLIDAY POKER PARLOR

Shortly after his release from county jail, John entered the heavily promoted Doc Holliday Celebrity Poker Tournament, determined to take the next step in his career and mix it up with the big boys. Despite her constant worrying, Mary went with him to the Laredo Casino to sign up. On the way, she gave him a look that asked, "Are you really sure you want to do this, John? It's a lot of money."

Knowing what she was thinking, John smiled and told her, "You can't win if you don't play." At the registration table, he counted out five $1,000 bills and laid them on the table. In exchange, he was given a fifty-page rulebook and assigned a seat at the table.

Two weeks later, John joined a thousand other entrants in the Doc Holliday Poker Parlor searching for their assigned table. He ended up sitting across from a big Hollywood celebrity. Looking around at the other tables, he recognized a few more famous people. Some were good players, and some just wanted to be there for the fun of it or to be stared and gawked at by ordinary players.

Well-known businessmen and financiers also sat uncomfortably on hard, steel folding chairs that were packed tightly around the one hundred or so tables in the crowded room. The setup was a far cry from the plush top-floor offices they were undoubtedly accustomed to. But regardless of their reasons for being there, John was sure of one thing – to each of them, the five grand entrance fee had been pocket change for them.

Without a doubt, John had become a better poker player. Practicing daily at the Julian Villa Apartments with other aspiring poker players, his game had seen a marked improvement in a very short time. With Mary by his side, he began to believe that he would someday reach his goal of ranking as a top player. Unlike Jill, Mary had confidence in him which allowed John to concentrate on developing his game. She made it easy. She made *everything* easy, and he fell more in love with her every day.

The funny thing about Mary was that she had come to Las Vegas to become a poker shark, but a poker player she was not. At first, John tried to teach her but quickly become frustrated when even some of the most basic game strategies seemed beyond her grasp. Mary also lacked the one quality that he could never teach her and it was probably the most important thing she needed to learn. That was patience. Mary played every hand and played it to the river, hoping to flop a flush or straight. Most of the time she lost and never learned to play the odds. Accepting reality, Mary had abandoned her poker aspirations and instead settled on the notion of supporting John and his goals. She became his biggest cheerleader and president of his fan club, of which she was the only member. And this, she was good at.

Sitting across the table from John was the famous infomercial pitchman known to many as Mr. As-Seen-on-TV who was undoubtedly the star at the table and clearly reveled in his recognition. When John asked if he actually believed in the products he promoted, the man scoffed, "Oh, hell no. There ain't a one of 'em worth a shit! Especially when they glued that guy wearing a hard hat to a steel girder and hoisted him a hundred feet in the air with a crane. Give me a break. But don't get me started. I like the paycheck. Let's just say that the Hollywood special-effects people could learn a thing or two from the infomercial directors and leave it at that." John thought the guy was arrogant and unprofessional, talking down the products he peddled to make a living.

Eager for the first hand to be dealt, John fidgeted nervously in his seat. He hoped he would end in the money, but realistically the odds were against him, and he knew it. Fifteen minutes until the tournament began, John saw a priest approach his table. Something about him was familiar, but John couldn't place him. Dressed in clerical black, the priest stared at John like he had found the one person he was looking for. Then John remembered! It was Father Lawrence, the priest who had visited him while he was in the Las Vegas detention jail.

Father Lawrence stopped in front of him. "John Sanger, how are you doing? I am so happy to see you again."

Surprised, John stood and greeted the priest, shaking his hand. "Well hello, Father. It's nice to see you again. But I have to admit that you are the last person I expected to see today." John hadn't given their jail meeting another thought. He hadn't even mentioned it to Mary. While he appreciated the Father's concern and for taking time to meet and pray with him, John hadn't thought it was anything more than the man just doing his job.

Father Lawrence laughed, "Yes, I suppose so. But I have been looking for you and took a chance on finding you here."

"You're looking for me? I can't believe it. But I need to thank you. Shortly after you left, they let me out and dropped all the charges against me. On my way home I stopped at a chapel to thank God for it."

S.A. Craig

Father Lawrence told him, "You see, young man, that prayer we sent up to Our Father in Heaven was answered. Truth won and you were vindicated. Praise God!" Father Lawrence motioned to the man behind him. "I have brought the friend along you had asked me to introduce you to. Do you remember?"

A man stood beside Father Lawrence. He was tall, thin, and wore a cowboy hat. It was Hank Mariotta, the creator of the Mariotta Maverick. But John knew him as the owner of the San Antonio Antelopes who, for the first time in the history of the franchise, were heading to the playoffs. Hank Mariotta was imposing and impressive, and John was more than a little intimidated standing in front of him.

"John Sanger, this is Hank Mariotta, the man you wanted to meet."

Hank Mariotta extended his hand and gave John a firm handshake. "It's a pleasure to meet you, John. Father Lawrence told me about your situation. I am glad things worked out the way they did."

"Well thank you, sir. I am too. It's an honor to meet you." John felt the eyes of everyone on him. Suddenly Hank Mariotta had made John the most important person in the room. His focus on John was intense, which didn't go unnoticed by the other players at the table. Even Mr. As-Seen-on-TV appeared annoyed at being upstaged.

They were even getting more attention than the barely clothed Ava Allende who used to be a B-list Hollywood actress and had become semi-famous for starring in a comic book action movie that became a big box office hit. It went on to become one of the most profitable movie franchises in Hollywood history. Unfortunately for Ava, her character had been killed off at the end of the first movie which had destroyed her acting career. Now she was just a casino troll, living off her royalties, poker winnings, and whatever tips she could make posing for selfies with the few fans who recognized her.

She walked around in a see-through dress that left her all but naked, except for the two pasties covering her nipples and a small gauze patch for her crotch. She exclaimed in a breathless voice that this was her designer dress made exclusively for distracting her fellow poker players. When she turned around, the back of the dress was sheer except for a razor-thin black thong. It seemed Ava couldn't get enough of herself as she sashayed back and forth on the bright red carpet of the parlor. Surprisingly, no one paid her any notice and players and spectators alike swarmed around Hank Mariotta to meet him. He was the real star in the house. Apparently humbled by the attention, Hank Mariotta told them he would be happy to visit with them as soon as he was done talking with the young man.

Mariotta pulled up an empty chair and sat next to John. He studied John for what seemed like forever before finally saying, "Father Lawrence tells me you are very interested in poker and that you intend to turn pro someday. Is that correct?" He never broke eye contact and seemed able to block out all other distractions.

John couldn't help but be confused. Why in the world would Hank Mariotta, owner of an NFL team and pretty much an American business icon, bother to take the time to talk to a nobody like him? John forced himself to answer. "Yes, sir. I love poker. That's why I came out to Las Vegas from Houston."

Hank Mariotta scratched the back of his right ear with his large hand. "Well, I like poker too, and I'll tell you a little something. The reason I am here with the good Padre is to scout around Las Vegas and check out the poker that's going on in all of these casinos. I am considering a broadcasting venture dedicated exclusively to poker. It would cover competitions like this one, provide guidance and tips for the beginning player, and the like. Father Lawrence told me that you had impressed him as the kind of young man that might just fit in with my plans and I have learned to respect his judgment. What do you think? I wouldn't mind talking to you more about it. How about we discuss it over lunch? How does tomorrow at the Tiger Tearoom sound? Do you know where that is?" Hank looked at his watch. "I hate to rush, but I've got to get going, and you have a game to play." He rose but waited for John to reply.

Incredulous, John stood. Here he was being invited to lunch by the great Hank Mariotta. "Yes, sir. I know it's by the Sand and Shell Casino. I think it is behind it, kind of in a remote location. Right?"

Mariotta nodded. "Then I'll see you tomorrow. Eleven-thirty at the Tiger Tea Room." They shook hands again. Hank wished him luck before turning for the exit. Because of his height, John watched as Hank Mariotta passed through the crowd and out of the hall, all the while unsure that any of this was really happening to him. Was he really going to have lunch with a living legend like Hank Mariotta?

The hall lights dimmed and the spotlights flickered on to illuminate each table. The MC welcomed everyone to the tournament and wished them all good luck. With that, the dealer shuffled the cards and dealt the first hand. John held a three of spades and a six of clubs. The ante was only $10, but when it was his turn to bet, John folded. The player next to him raised $25. Several others subsequently folded. When it was the big blind's turn, he saw the bet and raised another $50. Before the flop, the pot stood at over $1,250 and John was confident he'd made the correct decision to fold. Then the dealer flopped the three community cards; an unsuited Two, Four, and Five and John began second-guessing himself. Betting continued on the turn.

On the river, one of the players wearing mirrored sunglasses pushed all in. At that, everyone folded except Mr. As-Seen-on-TV who called. When the mirrored-sunglasses player turned over a low two-pair followed by the pitchman's three-of-a-kind, John felt sick to his stomach. He had thrown away the possibility of a straight and lost out on a chance to more than triple his stack and knock out two players on his first hand. Determined not to miss another opportunity like this again, he resolved to play every hand from then on. Like he'd told Mary when signing up for the tournament, "You can't win if you don't play!"

It was only a matter of time after that. At first, he decided to play to the flop and fold if he didn't have a hand. But it didn't take the more experienced players at the table too many rounds to size John up for the beginner he was; they began to steadily siphon off his stack by check-raising him at almost every hand. Mr. As-Seen-on-TV in particular seemed to have John's number and showed no mercy. After all, this poker was serious business – there was no room for amateurs.

As his chip count fell, John lost all control. He found himself chasing straights and flushes down to the river. His final hand was a humiliating loss going all in on a King high-bluff only to be beaten by a pair of deuces by, who else, but Mr. As-Seen-on-TV. Embarrassed, John left the table without a word. As he walked away, he heard the pitchman say, "Yeah, best go home to Mommy. Your diaper needs changing, little boy." He cringed as everyone at the table erupted in laughter.

Crestfallen, John waited outside the casino for the bus to arrive. It had been a painful lesson, and three thoughts consumed him. First, he resolved to double his effort to become a student of poker. Second, he needed to make the most out of his lunch meeting with Hank Mariotta. Finally, he needed to get home to his Mary.

As the bus rattled down the Strip toward his apartment, he thought about what he'd done wrong. He played terribly. Impatient and reckless, he'd cut himself bloody and those card sharks, sensing a wounded prey, had gone in for the kill. Who could blame them? He knew where he went wrong. His strategy of trying to force something instead of being patient and waiting for the cards to happen for him had left John defeated, profoundly humbled, and five grand poorer.

And there was the bluff. John knew that bluffing was a sure loss unless you had the respect of the players at that table. John's play had not commanded their respect and only proved him to be the blundering amateur he was. It was humiliating when one of the other players called him out. The guy read him perfectly and called John's bluff. As the man had pulled the large pot, consisting mostly of John's chips, toward him, he had given John a bit of sage advice. "Boy, I'm going to quote you a little bit of Benjamin Franklin. 'A man wrapped up in himself makes a very small bundle.'" The others at the table had snickered. It was a swift kick to John's psyche as he realized the point the guy was trying to make. John was trying to show off his bluffing skills but the rest of the players at the table could see that he didn't know when it was the right time to bluff or how to do it.

John took his quick loss as a teachable moment. More studying was needed; he needed to pick more games suited to his level. Maybe he wasn't ready for such a high-stakes game. Thinking he needed to change course, John shifted to a new strategy – play in lower-stakes games and keep learning. He had been going at it all wrong. He needed to forget about playing the big-stakes tournaments, at least for now. Those guys were pros, and they would eat him alive and spit out his bones. And that's precisely what they did.

As John stared out the bus window, he wondered about the timing of his lunch date with Hank Mariotta. How had Mr. Mariotta known he would be knocked out on the first day and therefore be available for lunch the following afternoon? After all, the Doc Holliday Celebrity Poker Tournament was a multi-day event and the final table was still days away.

TIGER TEAROOM

John couldn't believe he was about to have a lunch meeting with the mighty Hank Mariotta. He was nervous but knew he had to keep a sharp mind and show confidence. He only hoped he didn't say something stupid. Arriving at the restaurant about ten minutes before the appointment, John selected a table so he would be able to spot the big man when he came in. The aroma of garlic and other spices permeated the air.

The Tiger Tearoom was a Chinese restaurant known for serving authentic and savory Dim Sum. Heavy velvet, royal-red drapes lined the walls of the dining room from floor to ceiling. They were pulled closed except for one small section left open to allow a bit of daylight into the restaurant. The decor created a strange, almost mysterious atmosphere that resulted in giving customers the illusion that they could be the dinner guests of some ancient Chinese emperor in the Forbidden City.

Waiting for the most important meeting of his life to begin, John watched as a little boy played hide and seek with his mother in the folds of the heavy drapes. The boy would slide behind the curtains through one section and then spring out of another to his mother's enjoyment. The boy's mother laughed so loudly at his antics that many in the restaurant couldn't help but turn to look at them.

"Ricky, our contestant has selected curtain number three. Will it be a new car? Or maybe a trip to Cancun? Ricky, show us what is behind curtain number three!" his mother announced. The little boy ran to the drapes and, finding the edge of one of them, pulled it aside to expose an unfinished cinder block wall. The mother cupped her hands to her mouth like she was holding a megaphone and belted, "Whah, whah, whah. Oh, I'm so sorry. You've won a brick wall." John thought the woman was more than a little bit self-absorbed. Couldn't she see she was bothering the other guests? What kind of game was she playing?

Ricky ran excitedly to his mother. "Let's open curtain number three, Mommy."

She laughed, "But you already opened that curtain. What comes after three?"

"Four!" he squealed proudly. "Mommy, let's go open curtain number four!"

John noticed the restaurant staff gathered together near the kitchen staring nervously at the woman and her child. Surely, they were discussing how to calm the unruly boy. Oblivious to the disruption they were causing, the woman said loud enough for everyone to hear, "Okay, Ricky, let's go see what's behind curtain number four." She stood up and was just about to cross the room when their waitress hurried over with a tray full of food. "Ricky, curtain four will have to wait until we finish our lunch."

As the waitress began setting their lunch on the table, the mother continued to indulge her son's imagination.

"Ricky, what do you think is behind curtain number four? Could it be a big tractor or a bulldozer? Could it be a train?"

Ricky shook his head. "It's a tiger, Mommy."

The waitress interrupted them to explain in hushed tones that the curtains were there to hide the bare walls. "There is nothing more to it than that."

Imitating a TV game show host, the mother said, "Oh come on. What is really behind that curtain? Is it a new car or twenty cases of Spam? "

Little Ricky responded to his mother's musings and insisted, "No, Mommy! It's a tiger! A real live tiger! Come on, and I show you."

Again, in the best game show host voice she could muster, his mother relented. "Okay, let's go over to curtain number four and see what is really behind it."

It was clear that this woman was engrossed in the game she was playing with her little boy. But as mother and son started to head to curtain number four, the waitress quickly said in a polite but emphatic manner, "Ma'am, I need to ask that you please stay at your table and please keep your little boy from playing in the curtains. We are expecting a big dinner party any minute now and we respectfully request that you do not disturb the other customers or the *drapes*." The waitress particularly stressed the drapes. She then remarked that their meals were getting cold and asked if there was anything else she could get them.

The waitress' admonishment seemed to subdue the woman and she set little Ricky back into his seat, telling him that it was time to eat and curtain four would have to wait. Realizing that maybe she had been too disruptive, she replied in a muted tone, "I'm sorry, I was just playing. The curtains remind us of *Let's Make a Deal*. It's Ricky's favorite show; every time he sees a closed curtain, he pretends that he's in the show. We have a good time."

A sympathetic smile grew on the waitress's face and she told her that *Let's Make a Deal* used to be one of her and her mother's favorite shows when she was young. A comradery crept in as the waitress relived her past watching the host Monty Hall command the "beautiful Carroll

Merrill" to reveal what was behind the curtain. The waitress added another trivia tidbit. "Did you know that the show was Monty Hall's brainchild and he had a tough time getting it started? And now it's one of the longest-running game shows in history."

"I didn't know that. I thought we were watching something brand new. But isn't that the way it always is? When you think something is new, you find out that it's just a recycled rerun." The mother's response seemed to appease the waitress who left to wait on her other tables. The mother and her young son concentrated on eating their lunch without further theatrics.

With the commotion over, John returned his attention to the menu and began scanning The Tiger Tearoom's novel-sized menu, an eclectic hodgepodge of offerings, almost like that of a Greek diner. The first pages of the restaurant's menu highlighted dumplings, egg rolls, and, of course, Dim Sum. There were the other expected Chinese dishes as well. But the subsequent pages took the reader on a culinary world tour, offering a variety of quiches, an array of hamburgers, organic pizza, and vegetarian Indian and Thai cuisine. Despite the multicultural menu, all their dishes were prepared with a Chinese spin and promised the customer a unique dining experience.

The Tiger Tearoom dining room was small and quaint by Las Vegas standards but could easily seat several hundred guests. It was somewhat hard to find if you were looking for it for the first time. But it helped that the restaurant was just behind the Sand & Sea Casino which was known for its sandy beach and three-foot wave machine that budding surfers could ride even though the nearest ocean was three hundred miles away. The casino provided The Tiger Tearoom with a reliable stream of customers.

After deciding what he would order, John glanced around the restaurant only to find Hank Mariotta strolling up to the hostess station. John stood and waved to get Mr. Mariotta's attention who acknowledged him with a smile and made his way toward John. They shook hands and Hank surprised John by thanking him effusively for taking the time to meet with him. John replied, "Really, sir, *I* should thank you for taking the time to meet with me."

After taking their seats, John learned that Hank Mariotta was a straight-to-the-point kind of guy. Dispensing with the pretense of pleasantries, Hank immediately got down to the purpose of their meeting and peppered John with questions. He continued to probe until he received an answer that satisfied him. Before he was through, John felt that Hank Mariotta had picked his mind clean.

"John, I want to buy a poker channel that is going to put poker on the block once and for all. How would you feel about working for my station in some capacity? I just haven't figured it all out yet. Of course, we'd cover all the major tournaments. We'd do in-depth profiles of all the poker greats. We'd analyze the game from all points of view – from the dealer to the player, and maybe even down to the manufacturing of a deck of cards. We'd produce documentaries on historical figures like Earp and Holliday and Hickok, discuss theory, odds, and strategies of play." Hank's mind seemed to whirl as he barely finished explaining one idea before replacing it with another one.

"It's all just conceptual at this point, but I am excited about it and think it could catch on. Of course, I need to be careful about NFL regulations and I'm working to get the go-ahead from the commissioner. My lawyer, and he's never steered me wrong yet, thinks it's all workable. In the end, it all comes down to a single question – is this a viable venture? So, John, that is one of the reasons I wanted to meet with you, to learn what a greenhorn poker player such as yourself thinks of the idea. Is this a channel you might watch with some kind of regularity?"

John was momentarily speechless. Who was he to be giving business advice to a man like Hank Mariotta? And yet the man seemed to be genuinely interested in hearing what he thought.

"Sir, I am flattered that you are interested in hearing my opinions. I think it sounds like a great idea! And since I want to get into poker, I would watch all the time. I think most other serious players would as well. But frankly, sir, I wonder how many people there are like that." Hank Mariotta watched him intently, and John noticed him nodding slightly in agreement.

Encouraged, John continued, "But then again, sir, the way you are describing the programming, I think it could have a broader appeal. After all, if you look at the number of popular reality shows out there now, your idea could tap into that space in a new and different way."

Hank Mariotta seemed pleased and an approving smile swept across his face. "Exactly!" he exclaimed, smacking his hand on the table. "That's *exactly* my tack. And John, that is where you come in. I have this idea of creating a show to follow a beginning poker player, trying to make his way to the final table. It would be like a reality show, though it would not get personal and the cameras wouldn't follow you into the bathroom or anything like that. We'd have cameras following you around from game to game, have professionals analyze your plays, interviews with you and the other players at the table. Things like that. It's only conceptual at this point and of course, needs to be developed, but meeting you yesterday gave me the idea. What do you think?"

John couldn't believe what he was hearing. The events of the last few weeks traced through his mind like a lightning bolt. It had to be more than serendipity that he had met Mary. Was it more than chance that he had been walking by the alley when Jill was being mugged? Even being jailed had led to his meeting Father Lawrence who was responsible for John sitting there now. John never imagined something like this could happen to him and began to suspect that there was some mysterious and powerful force at work in his life.

Hank continued. "Of course, this all takes time and my sons and I have been planning it for what seems like years. My sons are building the casino and my television station will use that as our broadcast base. Now, while the casino construction is underway, we need to create content and have some shows already in the can, so on the day they open, we launch the station at the same time. Lots of work. Lots of work to do, my boy." As Hank's voice trailed off, he kept his gaze on John – *through* John. He was deep in thought. John squirmed under his gaze until eventually Hank asked, "John, do have you a journalism or communications degree?"

"No, sir. I have two years of community college and an okay GPA. Unfortunately, I couldn't afford to finish. But if needed, I'd be more than happy to get my degree."

Mariotta seemed pleased with John's response. "I'd reimburse you for your tuition and expenses. In exchange, you need to commit to maintaining a GPA at or above a 3.0. And secondly, that you agree to stay on with my organization in some capacity for two years after you graduate. Some might consider that indentured servitude. But I can assure you that not a single one of my employees feels like they are treated like, nor remunerated, like a servant. We can work out the details later, but what about your plans to become a professional poker player? You should always follow your dreams. I firmly believe in that as a principle in life."

John understood what Mr. Mariotta was saying to him. But after his abysmal play in yesterday's tournament, he had some doubts not only about his abilities but about whether he could afford it. He loved poker, but as a career, maybe it wasn't a very realistic goal for his life. "Mr. Mariotta, as I was sitting here waiting for you to arrive, I thought about our meeting. And all I could think of was 'How did he know that I would be able to meet him today?' After all, the final table probably won't be played until Friday or Saturday. How did you know that I would be knocked out after only a few rounds?"

Hank Mariotta smiled knowingly. "Young man, you can't expect to wake up in the morning and say, 'I'm going to be a poker player' and that evening win a tournament. It's like my coaches when they develop the perfect play. Their whiteboards are full of X's and O's, but it takes weeks of practice to perfect it. The same is true of any goal; unless you put it into action, all you have is a bunch of X's and O's on a whiteboard. Maybe we can write into your contract that you have X amount of practice while you study O number of hours."

A smile began to grow on John's face. "I never thought about it like that. What you are saying is that I need a game plan if I ever expect to reach my goals? And not only that, but just like football, a player needs a coach to help improve his game. Do you think poker is a lot like football?" John stated boldly, "You know, Mr. Mariotta, I don't always want to be a piker in poker."

Mariotta paused for a second and then replied, "You've got something there. I can see a lot of parallels between poker and football. I can see where you might think that. Good job, son, with your analogy."

They ordered a large pepperoni and mushroom organic pizza – Chinese style. It meant that instead of a crust made with the usual double-zero wheat flour, the dough was an unleavened flatbread mixed with olive oil and minced scallions. It was Mariotta's idea to order a pizza and he asked John if he would mind splitting a large pie, explaining that he'd been coming to The Tiger Tearoom for years and as odd as it sounded, it's Chinese-style pepperoni pizza was a fantastic dish. "I always order it. I don't know what they do, but it never disappoints." The last thing John wanted to do was to contradict Mr. Mariotta, even though he had wanted to order a plate of General Tso's. John didn't want to appear disagreeable.

Continuing the conversation, John shared with Mr. Mariotta that he had read that The Tearoom had a reputation for being the place where famous people came to dine. "I also heard that Rip Rumple who was at the tournament yesterday likes to come here too. I hear that he's always falling asleep in the middle of a hand. I guess he can't help it." John purposely failed to mention that the only reason he even knew about Rip Rumple came from thumbing through the tabloid material that Mary had left behind in their bathroom.

Hank remarked, "Funny that you should mention Rip. I bumped into him in the lobby as I was coming in." From his seat, John was able to see everyone in the restaurant and discreetly scanned the tables to look for the tabloid sensation. But Rip Rumple was nowhere to be seen.

Hank continued his story. "In this very restaurant in fact. We were discussing politics when all of a sudden Rip slumped and fell face-down onto his plate. The man was sound asleep." Mariotta laughed sympathetically. Then he quickly made a disclaimer that he didn't mean to make light of Rumple's infirmity. "But by the grace of God, there go I. I could have been born with that malady just as easily, and we should keep him in our prayers."

John felt he was being admonished. Then John recalled his and Father Lawrence's conversation about Hank Mariotta being a religious man. Mariotta was devoutly Catholic but as Father Lawrence confided, "he had a devil nipping at his heels." And, being a Godly man, Father Lawrence had expressed his internal conflict about condoning the path Hank Mariotta was taking to start up a casino and poker channel promoting gambling. John remembered the priest saying through the glass wall at the county lockup, "Son, there's a fine line between Bingo and gambling."

Their waitress brought their pizza to the table and set it on a stand before them. John looked at their lunch trying to conceal his surprise. The pizza looked like something that could have been delivered by Dominoes. But as John was about to comment, Hank Mariotta rubbed his hands together with anticipation and said, "Let's dig in!" John and Hank pulled slices from the pan before them, deftly catching strings of melted mozzarella before they fell onto the table.

Just as John was about to bite into his slice of pizza, a woman's shrill scream stopped him, and a brouhaha erupted throughout the restaurant. It caught the attention of all of the diners. Even Hank Mariotta turned around in his chair to see what had caused the commotion.

Little Ricky and his mother were back to playing *Let's Make A Deal*. His mother had permitted him to open up curtain number four. He had pulled the large drapes open only to reveal two closed, double-wide doors behind them. Ricky looked over at his mother who announced, "Ricky, show us what is behind those doors!" Obediently, Ricky turned the handles and pushed them open just like the models on the show would do.

What they saw next was never meant for a child's eyes. The little tike hollered across the room to his mother, "Mommy, Mommy! Look, Mommy! A secret room with people! And they don't have any clothes on! Where's the tiger?"

Hank Mariotta stabbed his unused fork into his pizza and exclaimed, "What in the world? This is unbelievable! I've been coming here for years and now it appears that they've been serving something more than just food in this debauched place." What Hank and every other diner in the restaurant saw were naked women in the act of rubbing and kneading naked men laid out on massage tables.

In full view of everyone in the restaurant, nude women and men scrambled about looking for cover. Old and flabby men pulled sheets over their heads to hide their faces while naked women posed like statues using their hands and arms to cover their most interesting parts. The restaurant staff desperately groped for the doors, but little Ricky was keeping them open with all his force, screaming. "Mommy, look! There is people here and they have no clothes on!"

Everyone in the restaurant had stopped eating to watch the spectacle little Ricky had revealed behind curtain number four. Many, clearly enjoying the sight, hooted and laughed. Startled mothers frantically covered their children's eyes and fled outside onto the street. One father dragged out his reluctant teenaged son who couldn't strip his gaze away from the surprise floor show playing out before him. Most guests just watched the scene jaw-dropped in stunned disbelief.

The shock of being revealed quickly wore off on those being serviced behind the curtain and full-fledged pandemonium erupted. Naked women ran, screaming and ripping the sheets off their male clients to wrap themselves in. Deprived of their fig leaves, some of the men tried to cover their faces; several others rushed the door in full frontal nudity trying in vain to close the doors and thus end the show. But to no avail.

Fearing for the safety of her boy, Ricky's mother ran over to protect him. She began thrashing away at the naked men swearing that she was going to call the police. One of the men wrapped his arms to subdue her and she let out a frightened scream, "Help! Rape!" Two stout diners rushed over to rescue the hysterical mother. Using their muscle, these men kept the doors from being closed, keeping the spotlight on the bizarre spectacle.

Realizing that there was no place to hide, the uncovered fled for the only other exit in the back of the secret room. The pileup of naked and sheet-wrapped bodies fighting to funnel through the narrow escape route looked like the panicked participants of a toga-themed 1930's speakeasy being raided by the police.

That evening, the local newscast reported that startled pedestrians had witnessed a number of men running through the restaurant parking lot and into their cars, "naked as jaybirds." Two women in their birthday suits streaked through the dining room out the front door, heading for who knew where. Inside The Tiger Tearoom, it was chaos.

In amused silence, John watched the scene play out before him. He had always wondered what a nudist colony was like, but this show had more the feel of witnessing a group orgy. He now also understood why the background music was so loud. Too loud. It was a clever foil to smother noise from the antics happening behind closed doors.

Ricky's waitress looked as if she was having a nervous breakdown. She shook all over and ordered customers to get back to their "damn tables." She repeated it a few more times before realizing it was hopeless. She abruptly untied her apron and threw it on the floor. With a sense of urgency, she declared that she was getting the hell out of there before the cops came.

Little Ricky sobbed uncontrollably. When he opened the curtains, he'd expected to see a real tiger and was bitterly disappointed when all he saw were naked people. "I want to see the tiger. Where is he?" He was inconsolable. Running away from the reach of his outraged mother who was engaged in a conversation with the recently arrived police, Ricky ran around the restaurant asking diners still at their tables, "Where is the tiger? I want to see the tiger!"

Mariotta left his seat to also talk with the police. John overheard him saying, "My God, I have been coming here for years and I would never have figured anything like this. You've got to throw the flag on this place." John thought it funny that Mariotta was using another football analogy. That thought disappeared when he found himself being stared at by a five-year-old boy with the saddest, biggest blue eyes he had ever seen. Little Ricky was all tears.

Crying out to John, he wailed, "I want to see the tiger. I want a tiger right now. Why are my mommy and everyone running around? Are they policemen? Will they arrest my mommy?" For someone so young, Ricky had already developed an inquiring mind. John tried to comfort the sobbing boy and looked around the restaurant for something to distract the boy's attention. He hadn't noticed them before, but behind the cashier's counter at the front of the restaurant, was a wall full of stuffed tigers of all shapes and sizes. He pointed to the wall and told the little boy, "Look! There's your tiger. Let's go up there and pick one out for you."

John's ploy worked and Little Ricky pulled him by the hand out of his seat excitedly, "There's the tiger! Come on!"

Dragging John by the hand, Ricky adroitly dodged fleeing customers and the hastily toppled chairs that blocked their path to the cashier's desk. John took stock of the tiger menagerie on the wall behind the counter. Large and small stuffed tigers lounged comfortably on their glass shelves, their paws dangling over the edges. There was even a ferocious, but extinct Sabertooth tiger. There was a classic poster of a car speeding down a desert highway with a tiger's tail sticking out of the gas cap; the caption read, "Put a tiger in your tank!" Another picture boasted a photograph of a magnificent Bengal tiger roaming free through a luxurious penthouse and looking out onto a stunning nighttime cityscape.

The caption on it read, "Take a tiger home and see it roam." The smallest of the toy tigers was strategically placed to promote one last sale.

Little Ricky's eyes immediately focused on the Sabertooth and even before John had looked the wall over, the little boy was tugging John's arm and pointing to it, screaming, "That's him! That's *my* tiger!" When John saw the price tag on the big cat, he gulped and pulled one of the smaller ones off the counter and asked Ricky if he wouldn't be happier with this one? But little Ricky knew what he wanted, and he wanted it now. He began to cry again.

Outwitted by a five-year-old, John admitted defeat and tried to get the attention of someone, *anyone* capable of letting him buy the tiger for the boy. Finally, after a few attempts, John got the attention of a manager being questioned by a policeman. When the policeman saw John and the little boy standing beside him, he allowed the manager a break from his interrogation to go and ring up John's purchase. But not without the policeman following close behind in case the manager tried to escape.

Grabbing the stuffed animal in his arms, Ricky hugged it tightly. Ricky's mother joined them. She had finished talking with the cops and returned to take ownership of her child and chided him to remember his manners. "Ricky, you need to thank this nice man for buying you that wonderful tiger. What do you want to say to the nice man?" Ricky looked up at her and shrugged his shoulders squeezing the tiger with all of his might. She reiterated her order, "Ricky, before you can take the tiger home, you have to say the magic words to this man." Ricky hugged the animal ever tighter and stared at John bewildered. "Abracadabra! Abracadabra!" The adults laughed at the boy's answer, and it injected the first bit of levity into a very extraordinary situation.

The Tiger Tearoom was like a bamboo house on fire that would soon be nothing but ash. It turned out that Hank Mariotta was one of the first people to call for the police and they had taken what little information he had. After the cops stormed and raided the place, several arrests were made. The scandal was the talk of the town for a while and even managed to make it to the national news. Hank Mariotta's name was mentioned as being a patron at the restaurant and the one responsible for calling the police. This only served to enhance his reputation with the public, though he tried to downplay his involvement. *The Vegas Sun* quoted him saying, "I simply was doing my civic duty. They had thirteen men on the field, and someone needed to throw a flag." To Hank Mariotta, his meaning was clear. But to someone unfamiliar with football, it was all gobbledygook.

On the surface, there was nothing about The Tiger Tearoom that seemed out of the ordinary. Diners watched as the wait staff went into the kitchen to place their orders and come out with their meals. To be sure, some patrons had their suspicions about the place and would remark about the smallness of the dining room given how large the building was on the outside. And from time to time, there were complaints from diners about the volume of the music and could they please turn it down – which of course they never did. Still, from the vantage point of the average Tearoom customer, everything looked right. Not even the most skeptical cynic would have imagined that hiding behind Curtain Number Four was a whole other world of adult activity.

In the days to follow, local newscasts reported on the scandal from every angle imaginable. It was a media frenzy that even made a mention on *The Drudge Report*. Reporters needed the help of interpreters to interview the mostly foreign women who were involved. How did they get into the country? Where did they come from? Were they victims of human trafficking? Most of the girls remained silent and those who did answer, gave confused and contradictory responses. Consumer reporters talked about public health violations and even suggested other local businesses that might be engaged in similar nefarious activities. And though the police insisted that they were doing everything in their power to identify who The Tearoom's clientele might be, they were unable to name a single person.

News cameras filmed every aspect of the illicit sex room. A series of cubicle dividers provided some semblance of privacy for presumably special guests who had more than lunch on their minds. There was a small dining room served by naked wait staff. The kitchen even had a hidden door that led to the secret dining room. It was a given that sexual activities were being traded for money transactions as evidenced by the smaller rooms. The rooms were filled with massage tables and small rosewood Korean nightstands jammed in next to them. The tiny tables were topped with small, colorful scented candles inside a glass jar.

The complex operation, once curtained in secrecy was now fully exposed to the light of day. Standing in front of the shuttered restaurant draped in yellow crime scene tape, one television reporter summed it up for his viewers: "How sad and sordid! The Tiger Tearoom, once known to Las Vegans as a place to enjoy a quirky, yet consistently good meal, has turned out to be nothing more than a false front for what adds up to be little more than a brothel for an elite but degenerate clientele. The Tiger Tearoom catered to a subculture of men who demanded more than just good food at lunchtime.

"Here, men were served by young, au naturel women, who, by the way, also happened to be the dessert tray, literally. Clients were served their desserts on a woman's bare breasts, stomach, and other parts of her anatomy. And from what we have been able to determine through the help of interpreters, the typical post lunch experience started with a sensual massage on an open table leading to the restaurant's ultimate money maker – sex inside one of the private cubicles. Yes, ladies and gentlemen, this story does appear to have legs and our investigative reporting has confirmed that the FBI and ICE, in particular, are investigating the three owners: Mr. Miles Percy, Fu King, and Larry Friedman for suspected sex trafficking. This is a case of pure greed. Nothing more than that. Not content with enjoying a thriving legitimate business and, I might add, having the respect of everyone in our community, the three owners turned to other more unsavory activities. You can be sure that there is much more to this story, and as officials continue to investigate, I, your humble news correspondent, will be here to bring it all to you."

As far as John was concerned, the entire situation worked in his favor. Hank Mariotta had jotted down John's phone number and he, in turn, had given John his business card. As for John, that card was as good as gold. Hank Mariotta had been very impressed, and, after learning of how John had calmed the little boy down with his act of kindness, said, "Kid, you got something special. That was a good thing you did for that little one. You're going be a good addition to my team. I'll let you know the direction we go next. You better get researching journalism classes at UNLV. Get on it, son."

John watched as Hank Mariotta left The Tiger Tearoom. He was colossal in John Sanger's mind.

JULIAN VILLA APTS.

All Mary wanted to know about was what John and Mr. Mariotta had discussed during their lunch at The Tiger Tearoom. But John kept talking about a spectacle that had happened. He became so animated that Mary had to tell him to calm down so she could at least try to comprehend the surreal scene he was trying to describe. But there was one thing Mary was sure of, and that was John had witnessed something so outrageous that he couldn't find the words to explain it. "I mean, there's this little kid just playing in some drapes, and he pulls open the curtain on a bunch of people in the middle of having an orgy. And here we are just eating our lunch and suddenly we see a bunch of stark-naked people diving behind anything they could find to hide. I mean, Mary, it was unbelievable!"

Mary smiled but was exasperated with him. "Okay John, I'm sure it was everything you said it was. But!" She paused until she was sure she had his attention and then blurted out, "What happened with Mr. Mariotta?"

"Oh yeah, I almost forgot. Mr. Mariotta offered me a job with his new poker channel."

Mary screamed with excitement and threw herself into his arms.

John's eyes flashed big as he told her some of the responsibilities for the new channel would be interviewing famous poker personalities. "He's even going to pay for me to go back to school and get a degree."

Mary hugged him tightly. "John, I can't believe it. Stuff like that never happens. I'm so proud of you."

"But that's not all; this is the best part. Mr. Mariotta said he'd hire a poker pro to take me under his wing and get me up to speed in poker!"

Mary hugged him again. She knew John was most excited about getting a poker tutor, but she was more excited about Mr. Mariotta offering to put John through college at the University of Las Vegas.

Not long after his release from jail, John and Mary had married. Having nothing to do but lay on his bunk and stare at the ceiling of his cell, all John had been able to think about was Mary. It was after his phone call with Jill that he had realized that Mary was the woman he wanted to spend his life with.

So, after his release, John and Mary made it legal in a tacky whirlwind marriage ceremony at the Elvis chapel. They were rabid Elvis fans even though Elvis died decades before either of them were born. After the wedding, Mary told John they needed to thank God for so many blessings. He knew where to go and the following week they reaffirmed their vows in a small ceremony at the Guardian Angel Cathedral.

One evening while they were watching TV, Mary had fallen asleep on their couch. John watched her sleeping and scratched his head. She was a mystery. He thought back to the first time they met. Then, he had thought that Mary might be a grifter. But after less than a week as husband and wife, that thought seemed comical to him. Mary was the furthest thing from a grifter. She was pure innocence and sweetness. Ironically, that was his first impression of her when he had first seen her in the McCarron Airport restaurant. Still he wondered why she lied to the cashier about not having the money to pay for her meal. Why did she let him pick up her check? And then, when they shared the cab ride, why had Mary tried to make him pay the cab fare, especially after he she knew he saw her fifty-dollar bill fall out of her purse? John smiled while Mary slept. He loved her without reservation, but these were a few of the questions he had for his new bride.

A few nights later, John and five others guys were jammed around a friend's rickety kitchen table playing Hold'em. They called themselves 'The Poker Posse,' and this was their regular weekly game. John felt guilty about being there without Mary, especially after only being married for a few days. But Mary had insisted that he go and not miss his Thursday night game.

John looked at his cards and tossed a few chips into the pot to call the big blind. He hoped something would come to him on the flop. But the flop brought him nothing except another losing hand. He pushed away from the table and tossed his cards into the pot. "I've had it! I'm going home to my wife."

"Come on, John. You can't quit now. Don't you want a chance to get your money back?" implored one of his friends. So, John sat back down and after a couple of beers and a few more losing rounds, none of them could talk him into staying any longer.

The apartment was dark when John got home. Thinking Mary was asleep, he was careful not to make any noise as he slipped under the covers beside her. He tried to settle into sleep but the game's hands still played in his head, and after a few moments, John sat up and turned on his nightstand light. "Mary?" he asked. "Why did you pull that act in the restaurant?" He waited for her to answer, but she didn't. John couldn't tell if she was really asleep or just pretending.

That was the only question mark in their relationship. Ever since that first day, Mary had always been there for him, and she had given him no reason to doubt her loyalty. She had been there when he was in jail on that trumped-up assault and battery charge. It was Mary who encouraged him in his poker. She had even given up on her dreams of becoming a poker star and had gone all in to help him realize his goal. He liked that Mary was always there to provide moral support. They worked. But Mary remained silent so John dropped the subject. He drifted off to sleep, leaving his unanswered question for another time.

During the weeks following their nuptials, John's poker losses continued to mount. One evening after a particularly bad beat, he came home dejected. The look on his face told Mary everything she needed to know and Mary welcomed him with a kiss and a hug. "I'm sorry, Mary, but I lost our rent money for next month."

Mary tried to console him, but John was depressed. "Don't worry, John," she assured him. "We're good for now. Mom, left me enough money in her estate to last us at least for the time being. I'm the furthest thing from rich but at least it will help us get by for a little while."

She sat him down into a chair and climbed into his lap, wrapping her arms around him. Mary's azure eyes stared compassionately into John's and she broke the truth to him gently but firmly. "You need to stop bluffing. You're no damn good at it, and another thing is…" She paused for a moment.

John looked attentively at her, "Yeah? I'm listening."

"John, you don't know how to *read* a bluff!" Now she really had his attention. "I need to tell you something, and this is as good a time as ever. Do you remember a few weeks ago when you asked me why I made a big scene in that restaurant? You accused me of lying to that waitress and letting you pick up the tab for my breakfast. Well, I wanted to see if I could bluff you. Remember what I told you about my Uncle Tad and all his talk about bluffing?" John nodded. "Well, I came to Las Vegas to try to make my mark, and this restaurant-thing was my first attempt. I did that pretty good. You've got to admit that, right?" Her eyes searched his. "But guess what? You failed. You failed miserably. I bluffed you bad. Even in the cab together, you thought you were with a scam artist. I saw you give me the evil eye when I let the fifty drop on the seat. I dropped it on purpose. Don't you get my drift? I bluffed you, and you never figured it out. Not until today that is."

John gazed at her in wonder. "Well, I was at a disadvantage. You had me from the very start. It was your angel face and blue eyes." Then he thought about it for a few seconds. "But you do make a good point." Mary indeed had him flummoxed and bamboozled.

THE CARRINGTON PALACE,

ROOM #777

Despite the blazing desert sunshine, Las Vegans struggled to understand the horror from the massacre at Abaddon's diner. A dark pall shrouded the entire city, especially in the downtown area where businesses expressed their mourning by hanging black sashes across their storefronts. The newspapers reported that the deceased gunmen were recently released from state prison around the same time and that they had all been members of the same prison gang. Evidently the men had made plans to meet in Las Vegas to celebrate their freedom.

Police briefings revealed that the trio was also responsible for a series of home burglaries which was how they had acquired their weapons. Autopsy reports showed that all of them had high levels of methamphetamine in their blood samples. A spokesman ended a press briefing by stating, "This appears to be nothing more than a senseless drug-fueled incident that unfortunately ended with tragic consequences that this city will, in time, ultimately recover from but never forget."

As for Roy and Nadine, they remained locked inside Nadine's suite and refused to leave. For days, Nadine walked around the room shocked and in a daze. She couldn't shake the vision of blood pooling beside the dying woman or the sound of gunfire. They clung to each other as if they were the last remaining survivors of an unspeakable holocaust. Roy was never far from Nadine and always there to hold her tightly as she crumbled in his arms, reliving the horrible ordeal. They barely spoke even as the bond between them grew. Both were silently grateful to be alive.

Finally, one morning, as they sat on the veranda of her hotel suite, Nadine emerged from her shock and abruptly put her coffee mug down on the table. She looked at Roy and said, "I think it's time for you to leave."

Roy was confounded. They were having morning coffee together, and for the first time since the shootings, it seemed like it might finally turn into an average day for them. But Nadine had just handed him an eviction notice. Her tone was hard to discern. It was somewhere in between "Who the hell are you anyway?" and "I'm doing this for your own good!" Roy dropped his cup hard, splashing a bit of coffee onto the lace table cloth covering the expensive Verano glass table.

Blotting the spill with a napkin, he snapped back, "What is this? I don't understand. What are you trying to tell me? Are you sick of me? I swear I can decipher Egyptian hieroglyphics better than I can figure you out. Shoot, if I want crazy, I could go visit Leroy." Roy stood up and told Nadine he'd be out the door as soon as he found his dang boots. As he left the balcony, Roy mumbled to himself in utter frustration, "I need this shit like a hole in my head."

Nadine ran after him and turned him around by the shoulder. "Roy, you've got to get back to your dancing. No more of us wallowing in this. We're alive and there is nothing we can do to bring those people back. We were saved for a reason. I've been thinking. As a matter of fact, I've been thinking a whole lot." Nadine paused, searching his eyes. "Your purpose is to win that contest and then go on and build your dream. You know you want to start your own club, so light the fire and make it happen. I want you to call Mindy and get back to your practicing. You're my superman hero. Baby, promise me you will go back today to the Wild Bill and dance your boots off. It's time we start living again."

Roy melted. Whenever Nadine used that soft, sweet voice on him, he turned into a fumbling child. She was irresistible. Roy smiled and pulled her close. "Nadine, you have no idea how happy I am to hear you say this. I've just been waiting for you to realize it too. It makes no sense for us to stop living just because we came close to dying. Just the opposite! We should be living every minute of our lives to the fullest!" Roy pulled her into his arms and kissed her passionately. He held her tightly and whispered, "I love you."

His first order of business was to find his favorite pair of dancing boots. Remembering he had left them in the kitchen when he went to get his coffee, he couldn't help but think he had turned into a bit of a space cadet since that night at the diner. Before leaving Nadine and their cocoon of safety, Roy called Mindy, asking her to meet him at the Wild Bill that afternoon. "We still have a lot of work to do."

On his way out the door, Roy shouted to Nadine that he would come back later and take her to dinner. Roy left The Carrington, and for the first time in days, stepped back into the world and the bright lights of Las Vegas. His first stop was the bank to get some cash for the evening ahead.

FREDDY'S HOT DOGS

Roy watched as the bank teller counted out six crisp, fifty-dollar bills behind the thick glass and pushed them through the drawer. After confirming the count, he stuffed his wallet with the cash, slid it into his back pocket, and left the bank to meet up with Mindy at the Wild Bill.

As Roy walked through the parking lot toward the bus stop, he heard a commanding voice call, "Sir! Sir!" He turned to see a heavyset security guard with a kind face waddle up to him, holding what looked like Roy's wallet in his hand.

With the swelling desert heat reflecting off the black asphalt, the cop appeared out of breath from the short jaunt from the bank. The man was so out of shape that Roy wondered how he was able to keep his job. Then again, being a security guard wasn't exactly the most demanding job in the world. It mostly required sitting or standing in a corner and watching people come and go.

"Sir, I may have something you need. Did you lose your wallet? You were just in the bank and may have dropped it on the floor."

Roy felt his back pocket and realized that he had indeed lost his wallet. With a displeased smile and feeling annoyed with himself, Roy nodded. "Thank you, sir. Yep, I must not have secured it very well." He reached out for his wallet.

"Whoa! Wait a minute! I can't just hand it over willy-nilly. You have to keep something in mind; I never actually saw you drop it. What is your full name?"

He gave the cop his full name, birthday, and address. "Now can I have my wallet back?"

"Not so fast. How much money do you have in your wallet?"

Roy couldn't believe this. Why the hell did this cop want to know how much money he had in his wallet? "What does that matter? It's my wallet, and I would like it back. Just look at the picture on my license."

"Well, it does matter. I am the authority here and that kind of information is just another way to verify that this wallet does indeed belong to you."

Part of Roy wanted to take what was his – grab the wallet from the cop's fat hand and get on with his day. But he thought twice about it and decided to play the guard's game, which was always the prudent decision whenever dealing with law enforcement. Roy took a deep breath and politely answered, "I have exactly three hundred dollars in there. And to be precise, it is in the form of six fifty-dollar bills."

"How much did you say you had?"

Roy was unable to conceal his impatience. "I said I have three hundred in there. Why don't you count it for yourself if you don't believe me?"

"Where are you heading with a roll like that? You look like you're on foot. That's not a good idea to walk around here in Vegas carrying that much green. You might get rolled."

"I've got my plans. Just now I'm on my way to grab lunch at Freddy's Hot Dogs."

The fat cop started salivating. "You know Freddy's is more than just hot dogs. They've got everything under the sun in there. They even got, what do you call it? Oh yeah, Korby beef burgers. The only problem I got with it is that it's just too much walking around. It's a big place, and you have to go around to all of these different stations to get what you want. One station to get your meal, then another for your dessert, and yet another one for your drinks. And then on top of that, you have to wait in line at another station just to get some ketchup and mustard. It makes me tired just thinking about it. If I just had a walking cane that I could lean on when I got tired, I would be a happy man. I got my eye on one of them fancy walking sticks in one of those sporting goods stores. The only problem is that I'd have to jack this bank up for the money to pay for it. Man, that walkie stick – that's what I call 'em – would set me back some, and I'm none too flush just now. But I ask you, how would it look if I knocked off the very bank I'm supposed to be guarding? I'd be fired for sure. But it would sure help me out if I had one."

It was becoming clear to Roy that the guard was angling for some kind of reward for returning his wallet. "Don't you mean Kobe beef?"

The doddering cop clenched Roy's wallet and shrugged. "Kobe? Korby? Hell, what difference does it make? It's damn tasty beef from Japan. How about you and me get some lunch at Freddy's? Like I said, I got my stomach set on a Korby burger. I'll drive us over there and, on the way, we can pick up that walkie stick. I'll need it to navigate Freddy's lines." The guard wagged Roy's wallet in his face and said, "I'll just keep this safe here inside my pocket."

Roy watched helplessly as the cop slid his wallet into his shirt pocket. He had done it. The chiseler cop was getting his way. "Okay, I get it. What the hell. But you'll need to give me my wallet back if you want me to pay for your lunch."

"Well now." The cop paused for a moment, scratching his chin. "Well sir, that's a tempting offer, but not before you take pity on me and buy me that walking cane. You'll see how hard it is for me to walk around. I mean, consider yourself lucky that I picked up your wallet and all your money was intact."

"Isn't this what's called a bribe or kickback? This is nothing but a shakedown!"

Insulted, the cop remarked, "How is this a bribe? You're crazy. I haven't asked you for anything. You just strike me as the type of person who would be grateful to have his property returned by rewarding the honest cop who found it."

Roy sighed as he realized that the only way he would get his wallet back was to surrender, and invite this con man to lunch. The bank guard smiled and told Roy, "Thank you, sir. The least I can do is drive us there."

On the way to Freddy's, Roy was not surprised when the cop first turned into the sporting goods store. Unfortunately for Roy, the walking stick the bank guard wanted cost much more than the twenty-dollar stick with a leather strap that Roy thought it would be. Instead, the cop picked out a fancy walking cane with a shaft made of exotic ebony wood tipped with a chrome cup and topped with a fox head handle made of solid pewter sitting atop a designer, braided pewter collar. As the cop pulled out four fifty-dollar bills from Roy's wallet to pay for the cane, Roy saw the elaborate fox head handle grin up at him slyly. He grimaced at the irony of it all; he had indeed been outfoxed. At least Roy managed to get his wallet back from the charlatan cop.

After lunch, they stood outside Freddy's where the cop offered to drive Roy back to the bank. Roy declined the offer and watched as the portly bank guard walked away, assisted by the aid of the expensive walking stick Roy had just paid for. Roy shook his head and counted his money. His wallet was $225 lighter than when he had left the bank. The worst of it was that the Kobe burger had been awful and tasted like ground bologna.

Roy was disgusted with himself. He had been a sock puppet in the hands of that cop. Nadine would have called him a "sucker." He swore that his days of playing the chump were over. He needed to make up for lost time, and now he was on a mission. Flashes of David Alexios Matthopolous charged through his head. That man was not about to let anything defeat him and neither would he.

More than ever, Roy was determined to overcome any obstacle to win that dance competition. But what he needed now was a strategy.

ABADDON'S DINER

Roy met Mindy at the Wild Bill Dance Hall and they wasted no time getting back onto the dance floor. With the competition fast approaching, they had lost precious practice time and so agreed to meet every afternoon for the next month to prepare.

Roy was silent as they stepped around the dance floor, his thoughts elsewhere. To be back dancing felt surreal. As they waited for the next song to begin, Mindy turned to Roy and, with a sincerity he didn't know she possessed, said, "It's good to have you back with us. We were worried about you; Leroy was even talking about taking us all back to Texas in Maxi the Taxi. But you gritted through it and that's what counts. We'll be a stronger team because of it and that makes me proud to be your partner. Remember we're joined at the hip for now."

Roy hugged Mindy warmly. "Thanks, Mindy. It does change the way you look at things."

The next song started and Roy led Mindy across the dance floor. As they swayed, Roy couldn't help but think about the goodness of life and the pleasure he felt from just being alive. As the afternoon progressed, their confidence swelled. By session's end, he was feeling his cowboy boot legs again.

Roy decided to take the long way back to Nadine's hotel, and it was not by accident that his detour led him past Abaddon's Diner. Reconstruction of the diner was already underway and Roy saw David Matthopolous, the diner's owner, talking to one of the workers just outside the restaurant's entrance. He waited for David to finish his conversation before walking up to introduce himself, explaining that he had been there when the gunmen burst into the diner. Roy told Matthopolous that he was glad to see David planning to reopen the restaurant. The restaurateur replied that he had never considered not rebuilding and was hopeful that the doors would open again in a few months.

"But I want to know – how are you doing? I'm really worried about the people who had to endure that nightmare," Matthopolous admitted. "I'll certainly never forget that night. We all have different ways to cope and I just hope everyone is okay. Do you know what I mean?" Without waiting for Roy to respond, David smiled. "How about we go in and I'll make you something to eat? It's not a full menu yet, but I can cook you up something that I promise you'll enjoy."

Roy pulled off his sunglasses so he could see the man eye-to-eye. "I'd love to, sir, but I got a woman at home who was also there that night and I need to get back to her."

David understood and said, "Of course. I understand, but I want you to know that you have an outstanding invitation that would be my honor to fulfill."

Roy was impressed by the man's concern and responded, "Thank you and one day we will sit down and tell you everything."

Matthopolous seemed genuinely pleased to see Roy and began confiding to him about the changes he planned to make. "The big one is to add a memorial fountain in the foyer in memory of those who were killed. I also am planning on adding a porch across the front of the building for outdoor dining." He chuckled a bit. "I know that some might think adding outside dining to a traditional diner is heresy, but I want to put a few new spins on the same old diner-thing. I think the customers will like it."

Roy nodded in agreement. "Yeah, I like the porch idea, especially at night after the sun goes down. But…" He hesitated.

Matthopolous lifted his hand to shield his eyes from the glare of the sun. "But? But what?"

Roy fidgeted. "Have you given any thought to changing the name of your restaurant? Just, I've been thinking that, you know, the incident is tied to Abaddon's Diner and… Well, 'Abaddon' actually means –"

David finished Roy's sentence for him, "I know. Abaddon means 'the destroyer.' I named it that to signify that we were here to stay and were ready to crush any competition. I just wanted it to be the best diner around. I suppose it did take on the bad guys in a way and I feel like it won to a certain extent. I mean, it's damaged, but we're still standing and coming back better than ever. The bad guys aren't. But I know what you mean, that name will always remind people of the evil that happened that night."

Roy asked him, "So what do you think you'll rename it? How about using your name? David?"

David stared at the ground for a moment and answered. "You know, I hate the name David. I don't get how I ended up with it anyway. I mean it's not like its Greek. And my parents were one hundred percent Greek and very proud of that fact. Go figure. They must have been hitting the sauce when they came up with that one. Heck, if they didn't care about preserving our heritage, why didn't they name me Dino? It's the name of my all-time favorite performer, Dean Martin. But everyone called him Dino. This guy ruled the Strip in the sixties. He was one of the original Rat Pack and just straight-up cool. After Frank Sinatra, Dean Martin was at the top of the famous Rat Pack. He was hip and funny and had a singing voice like no one else. People used to think he was drunk on stage, but that was just an act, and instead of drinking scotch, he was sipping apple cider. I read that he used to be a semi-pro boxer as a teenager going by the name Kid Crochet. He was a card shark too. I've read all about him."

It was obvious David was a Dean Martin buff and there seemed to be no end to the detail he knew about the guy. Roy didn't care but politely listened as David prattled on about his Hollywood hero. "He filmed a scene in the original *Ocean's Eleven*, right here on this spot over fifty years ago. Man, that was a great movie! Nothing like the remakes with George Clooney and Brad Pitt. The original movie dripped cool!"

Roy smiled, only vaguely recognizing the name of Dean Martin. But after hearing David Matthopolous' laud the man, Roy felt like he had just finished reading Dean Martin's autobiography. He nodded his head in agreement and then shook David's hand. "Well, Good luck to you, man. And good luck with the renovation and your new place. Next time I come here, I hope to see a big flashing neon sign hanging up there, screaming 'Dino's Diner' and underneath that, 'Never Closed!'"

David shook Roy's hand vigorously. "Remember, I owe you a meal and you owe me a story." He looked Roy in the eye and added, "But only if you feel like talking about it."

Roy headed back to Nadine's. He thought about what they could do to get their lives back to normal. Maybe they could stream an old Dean Martin film. The only movie he knew with Dean Martin in it was *Ocean's Eleven*, and that was thanks to David Matthopolous' Dean Martin tribute.

Later that night, even though Nadine had drifted off to sleep in the middle of the movie, Roy watched the film to its end. Matthopolous was right. If ever there was a movie that personified an earlier time in Las Vegas history and the cats that got it going, it was this one. Roy turned off the TV and kissed Nadine goodnight without waking her. He thought about a time when he and Nadine would be sitting in the new Dino's Diner enjoying a meal prepared exclusively for them by none other than David Matthopolous. Though they could order virtually anything on the menu, Nadine would no doubt order the chicken-and-waffles special.

RESTAURANT PIERRE FRANCOIS

Roy and Mindy maintained the arduous schedule they had agreed to nearly a month before. Despite their dedication however, even their renewed partnership hit some bumps in the road. Roy was a stern taskmaster and it didn't take long before Mindy began to bristle at his criticisms and snap back at him that Roy needed to improve his stage presence. "Roy, if you're going to call yourself a cowboy, you've got to start dressing the part." Despite the small squabbles, each of them remained solidly committed to their goal. And now that the big day was drawing near, Roy confidently admitted they were ready. They had never been more in sync. Their steps were crisp and precise and their transitions smooth and fluid. Roy was confident he and Mindy had more than a good chance of walking home with the top prize.

But for Roy, there was now more at stake than just the prestige associated with being crowned the national two-step champion. The reality of his financial situation was beginning to flash warning signals. Since arriving in Vegas, he had been living off the steady sale of his dwindling stock portfolio and the rent he received from leasing his house in Houston. The time for Roy to find a new income source was fast approaching. Not only was Roy counting on winning, but now he and Mindy *had* to win that prize money.

Roy had big plans for his future, and one of those was to ask Nadine to marry him. But it was clear Nadine had money. Lots of it. He could never hope to afford to give her the kind of luxuries she seemed to enjoy. But somehow that didn't seem to bother Nadine. Even with her money, Nadine was one of the most down-to-earth and unpretentious women Roy had ever known. Once, after selling off a few stock lots and coming out with a big gain on his investment, Roy had offered to take Nadine out to celebrate with a fancy dinner at Restaurant Pierre François in the French-themed Casino Château Versailles. With a few bottles of wine, the check would have quickly closed in on several hundred dollars. It would have been a nice meal, but Nadine admitted that she'd be just as happy going to In-N-Out Burger. Date night cost Roy all of fifty dollars, and that included Nadine's children.

Roy often talked to Nadine about how his club would be unique; with his contest winnings providing the seed money, he saw his dream soon becoming a reality. Nadine encouraged him to pursue his goals but never offered to finance them which Roy and his Texan pride were grateful for. The club was something he would accomplish on his own, and it would be something that would make Nadine proud of him.

The one thing about Nadine he could not understand was why she had never once visited Roy at his apartment. The only time she had been there was out of necessity, when he had collapsed at the Vegas Rite pharmacy. Insisting he stay with her at The Carrington to convalesce, Nadine had made the obligatory trip to his apartment to pick up some of his clothes. But that was it. She had never once mentioned anything about his living arrangement. It wasn't that Roy was embarrassed about his digs. He only hoped that the stark difference between Nadine's lavish suite at The Carrington and his hovel at the Geneva Lakes would not prove to be a 'bridge too far' for her to cross. But then again, when Roy was honest with himself, given a choice between spending a night or two at The Carrington or a night in a Motel 6, the question answered itself.

Roy was no mystery to Nadine. He hid nothing about himself and answered honestly everything she asked him about. Yet the only thing she had shared about herself was that she had moved to Vegas from Wheaton, Illinois and had been married to an older man. She was even reluctant to talk about her children. To his open book, Nadine was a safe-locked diary, the combination to which only she knew. Getting Nadine to reveal anything significant about her past was futile. So, after a while, Roy gave up trying to find out anything about her and contented himself with the fact that she was with him now.

The one secret Roy was not about to pry into was the source of Nadine's money. Sure, Roy wondered about it, but it didn't occupy his thoughts. He really didn't care. It might be old-fashioned, but the way Roy saw it, it was the man's responsibility to provide for his family. If they ever married, they would live in a house he paid for and he would support her children as if they were his own. Anything less would make him feel like a gigolo.

This fact drove Roy even harder to win the dance competition. The title would give him legitimacy in the world of country-line dancing and the prize money would give him the funds to build his dream. His win would be the catalyst on which to establish his club's reputation. Roy's desire to marry Nadine was what ignited the fuse in his cowboy boots.

BUCKAROO WESTERN WEAR

A few days before the competition, Roy decided that Mindy was right; he needed a wardrobe change. He knew that a new shirt was what he needed to stand out and grab the attention of the judges. For the last few days as he and Mindy had finished their practice sessions and walked out past the shops inside the Western Nugget arcade, Roy had caught sight of a shirt on display in the window of Buckaroo Western Wear. Buckaroo's was an upscale clothing store catering to the well-heeled Texan wannabe, offering custom-made Stetsons and an exclusive bootery where the entry-level price began at five Franklin's. You could also customize your own belt buckles with any number of precious gemstones designed and executed by the nation's best silversmiths. It all depended on the customer's taste and, of course, the size of their bankroll. But for Roy, he was on the hunt for a shirt that made a bold statement.

After telling Mindy that he had some errands to run and that he'd see her tomorrow, he walked into Buckaroo Western Wear. Telling the attractive greeting clerk that he was looking for a shirt, she pointed him to the men's department. Roy nodded his thanks and walked over to the neatly organized racks where he hesitated, assaulted by an overwhelming assortment of styles, colors, and embroidery. He scratched his head trying to decide where to start. It was then that a middle-aged salesman wearing a wide Stetson appeared beside him. He was very tall and lanky, and the man formed his fingers into a gun and pointed to a sign that advertised "The Ultimate Rock and Roll Cowboy Shirt." That was it. Roy saw what he wanted. He pulled a black, gray, and red plaid shirt off the rack and told the guy to ring him up.

This shirt was the perfect topping for the competition. Its long sleeves had extra wide cuffs with three rhinestone snaps on each. The front boasted an elaborate two-point western yoke while the back had a one-point yoke. Roy was conservative in every way, including what he chose to wear. And for any other occasion, this shirt would have been so outrageous that he would have dismissed it as nothing but a clown shirt. But this competition was not just *any other occasion*. He needed something that would set him apart from the crowd. He wanted – no, *needed* – the judges to notice him. He liked the way the wide collar flared out with two rows of large rhinestones. And if that didn't get their attention, the extremely large black and red plaid certainly would. It screamed, "Look at me!"

There was absolutely nothing understated about this shirt. Embroidered into each plaid block were elaborately stitched western scenes that ranged from a cattle drive to a high noon gun duel in a dusty prairie town, and every other wild west cliché ever imagined. At the corners of each block were embroidered brass nail heads giving the impression of pictures nailed to a wall. And this was just on the back of the shirt. On the front of it across the chest was another detailed, elongated oval embroidery. This one depicted a peaceful Indian village on the banks of a river. The teepees had smoke drifting out of their tops toward soaring mountains in the background. Bright gold piping framed the elongated oval scene.

When Roy got home, he tried on his new shirt and mentally went through his dance steps in front of the mirror. He looked good. From every side, Roy liked his new look and made a pact with himself. Mindy would be proud of him. He had found a "rock star" of a cowboy shirt and had to admit that she might be right after all. This shirt would make all the difference.

He decided that If he and Mindy did win the competition, he would buy some Buckaroo Western Wear stock.

WILD BILL HICKOK DANCE FLOOR

The big evening finally arrived. It was time for the Country Western & Line Dancing Association's national finals held at the Wild Bill Hickok Dance Hall. Along with three hundred other couples, Roy and Mindy waited impatiently outside the closed solid oak doors of the hall. They were supposed to open at six-thirty but already it was close to seven o'clock. Nervous chatter between competitors echoed through the hallway and ended in a sigh of relief when at last there was a loud click and the doors were flung open wide.

As the dancers filed in, they were instructed to line up to sign in and receive their identification flag and a large safety pin which was to be used to fasten the flag on the back of their costumes. The flag was simple, a square piece of paper with a large number printed on it. Roy signed them in and walked back to Mindy who pinned the flag on Roy's back. As Roy pinned Mindy's flag to her back, he told her, "They said we're in the third group. That means a long wait."

The couples were allowed a warm-up dance to an old favorite by Billy Ray Cyrus, "Achy Breaky Heart." It was a lively song from the past and intended to relax the couples before the real competition got underway. Grim and nervous faces transformed into fun-loving smiles as they frolicked around the dance floor to the light-hearted song. It helped ease tensions and limber up stiff muscles.

When the song finished, the master of ceremonies strolled onto the stage and called the competitors to gather around him. Standing in front of a long table stretching across the stage he began to introduce the judges. As he called their names, each judge walked onstage to a ambivalent of applause until fifteen had assembled. Taking their assigned seats at the table, the judges' faces were grim and unsmiling, supposedly meant to convey the seriousness with which they regarded the task before them. Pointing at the judges, Mindy jokingly told Roy, "Here come the Terminators."

The MC explained how the competition would proceed. "As you know, tonight is the final night of the Country Western & Line Dancing Association's signature dance event. And at the end of the evening, our esteemed panel of judges sitting behind me will crown a winner and award that lucky couple the $100,000 grand prize." There was an eruption of applause and the MC waited for it to subside before resuming his introduction. "Now, as you know, this dance contest has been going on for the last three days, and most of you have made it to this final night by winning a series of elimination heats. But tonight, you'll be joined by a small number of couples who by virtue of their past performances or reputations have been invited to bypass the preliminary eliminations and advance directly to tonight's finals. But never fear, tonight everyone starts over, the slate is clean, and everyone here has an equal shot at being crowned champion.

The MC told the dancers, "So, here's how tonight's going to work. There will be three rounds and the winners from each round will move on to the next. In the first round, you will be divided into three large groups where you'll perform five dances, each with their own required dance steps. The top thirty from each group will then move onto the second round. At the end of the second round, the field will be whittled down to just twenty teams, and these twenty couples will then advance to the third and final round. Simple, huh?" Then he asked, "Any questions?"

Roy didn't like that they were in the last group. He was anxious and ready to begin, but for now, all he could do was wait. Then surprising Mindy, he shouted at the MC, "Yeah! Just wondering how the groupings were decided." Startled by the question, the MC groped for an answer and then looked to the judges for assistance.

Annoyed, one rotund and surly judge stood and stared straight at Roy as he answered the question. "If you had bothered to read the rules when you registered, which clearly you did not, the answer was right there. The group assignment is based on the order in which you registered. Yep, we operate under the FIFO principle here – first in, first on. It's all about your timing and with our great technology, we know the exact date and time you signed up. It's recorded in stone or, should I say, megabytes; take it or leave it. If there are no more time-wasting questions, let's get this show going!"

Even though it was a snarky response to a reasonable question, Mindy gave Roy a look and asked, "Why the hell did you open your mouth?" Roy just shrugged wishing he hadn't.

The bad-tempered judge continued. "Okay! With that out of the way and in case more inane questions come up about something that you should already have read in the contest rules, here are the criteria you will be judged on. You will earn points on how well you technically execute the required dance steps. You will also get points for style, rhythm, and musical interpretation. The last category is your overall presentation, your appeal. How well do you move together as a couple?

Does your presence on the dance floor command attention? We take all of this into account including your costumes. If anyone has a problem with this, then you can leave right now and march over to The Deerskin Lounge and get yourself a liquid dinner. Get yourself shellacked for all I care."

The judge went on arrogantly, "All of us here on the judging panel are certified international judges and have worked our way up through the ranks. We are the best of the best. The top three couples coming out of here tonight will secure their places in the World Line Dancing Championship. This Las Vegas competition is a fully-sanctioned, qualifying event for the best in the world. This fall, the Hoe Down Dance Stampede World Championships will be in Nashville, Tennessee. We will work tonight's event like the Olympics with first-place winners taking gold, second place taking silver, and third place getting bronze. Sorry, but there is no participation medal for fourth place. And don't even get me started about the stack of money the winner will win. You second and third-place contenders will make some decent money also. So, how about we get this party started? Are there any questions?"

Roy noticed that nobody had any questions and after the way the pompous judge had shut him down, he really couldn't blame them. He also noticed that the other judges on the panel were not exactly enthralled with this egotistical guy either. Some buried their faces in their hands while others just shook their heads in disapproval. It was evident that to them, this was a tiresome act they had endured many times before.

Mindy whispered to Roy, "What an asshole! He thinks he's Mr. International Judge Extraordinaire. And it ain't like he's Garth Brooks or moves like Robert Royston. Just look how large he is!" Brooks was Mindy's favorite singer. She idolized him but worshipped Robert Royston, the five-time line-dancing world champion. Back in Houston, Mindy had turned her apartment into a virtual shrine to both. She had covered the walls with literally hundreds of pictures of her idols. The floor to ceiling homage had looked as if the walls were covered with a Brooks-Royston wallpaper pattern. She never tired of talking about them and could always find a way to work them into any conversation no matter how remote the association. Roy always teased her about her obsession, calling her a one-woman fan club who singlehandedly kept the Garth Brooks Tchotchke Emporium afloat. Her response was always the same, "A girl can only wish! Those are the only two I would even consider marrying. But that might pose a problem since they're already hitched. Oh well, I'll just have to wait until one of them unhitches himself."

414

Mindy began speaking louder so the others around could hear her. "Look at him. I bet the only line he ever stepped in was a lunch line!" Everyone who heard began to laugh and as they passed it on to those who hadn't, amused chuckles spread. Soon everyone around Roy and Mindy erupted in a contemptuous mirth that was loud enough to get the attention of the rotund judge.

Evidently, this was not the response the judge was hoping for and immediately turned his glare on Roy and Mindy. Pointing a crooked finger at them, he said, "Do you two have something you want to share with us? By all means, please let us know. Go ahead. I'm waiting…"

To Roy's dismay, Mindy answered. "Yeah, just one thing, where did you get your personality from?" Roy pinched Mindy arm to shut her up, but it was too late.

"What did you say, miss? I'm not sure I heard you correctly. Would you care to repeat it?"

"I think you did, but I'll say it again." Stepping toward the stage, Mindy raised her voice and shouted, "I said, where did you get your personality? I really like it!" Her sarcasm was palpable and everyone on the dance floor gasped with surprise. It was then that Roy saw his dream of winning disappear like a mirage in front of him. Months of hard work for nothing because of Mindy. Maybe he had taken out the grenade, but it was Mindy who had pulled the pin. Roy shut his eyes and waited for it to explode.

The judge left his high perch on the stage and walked over to Mindy and Roy. He stared menacingly, doing his best to intimidate Mindy out of the competition. He told her gravely, "And lady, I'm not sure I like *your* personality. I'm guessing this will have an effect on your score on presentment."

But Mindy was unimpressed and clearly unconcerned about incurring the judge's wrath. Not about to back down, she retorted, "Well, kind judge, as you can see, we haven't started dancing yet so how can you give out a score for personality? Unless of course you already know who's going to win. And if that's the case, then unless you want a giant scandal on your hands, I suggest that you recuse yourself." A murmur of agreement spread through the crowd and Mindy asked him, "I mean, didn't you ask if we had any questions? So, what did I say that was so bad?"

Unprepared for Mindy's accusation, the judge realized he was on the verge of losing control of the situation and said condescendingly, "Young lady, you and your partner have already wasted too much of my time, so I'll just let it be for now. We'll have to see who is left standing at the end of the night. Won't we?" He clapped his hands together to signal that the discussion was over and walked back to the stage. Roughly grabbing the microphone from the MC, he instructed those not in the first heat to clear the dance floor.

Roy and Mindy left but not before Mindy gave the judge one last defiant stare. She told Roy, "Shit, you couldn't fat-shame this guy if you tried!" Roy didn't comment. He was busy trying to figure out how they could recover from the shrapnel wound they had received from the explosion.

While those in the first group remained on the dance floor, the dancers in the later groups were ushered into an anteroom where they were to wait until their heat was called up. Since Roy and Mindy were in the last group, they had a long wait ahead of them; their anxiety began to escalate.

In the back room, their competition made no attempt to conceal their contempt for Roy and Mindy. Their icy stares said it all. Roy wondered why the animus but then realized that Mindy's antics had put them in the center of the spotlight and that could be to their advantage. Now the attention of every judge would be fixed on Roy and Mindy. But was Mindy that sly? He always thought she was as thick as a four-by-four block of wood. But even if it was some kind of strategy on her part, it provided Roy little comfort; he imagined that Mindy had put them on a tightrope the width of a razor blade. While the judges would indeed be watching them, it would be to catch them in even the most subtle misstep. Resentment surged within him, and now he didn't want to look at Mindy, let alone dance with her. He was seething. But Roy had a capacity for allowing bad things to blow past him like the wind, and he let his anger escape with a loud exhale. There were fourteen other judges on the panel. They couldn't all be petty and vindictive. Besides, what could they hold against him? He wasn't involved. His only crime was being Mindy's partner and he had always paid dearly for that unfortunate fact. Roy would try to remain civil with Mindy, at least for tonight.

After waiting nearly an hour and a half, the third group was summoned to the dance floor by a voice that came through the room's PA system. Keeping his composure, Roy squeezed Mindy's hand and said, "Let's go get 'em, girl." From what he could see of their competition, Roy felt pretty good about their chances. One of the couples in the group was a beefy pair and obvious connoisseurs of all-you-can-eat buffets. The guy's gut burst out between the straining buttons of his shirt. His partner wore the shortest skirt of anyone in the group exposing a set of enormous cellulite-ridden ham hock thighs. Even standing still, her fat dimples jiggled up, down, and around her legs as if they had a life of their own. Every step she took revealed peeks of her panties. Roy saw

London, France, and, as the children's rhyme continues, "I see the fat lady's underpants!" It was indeed an assault on the eyes. Her outfit only served to emphasize her flaws instead of hiding them. As revolting as this couple was, they walked out onto the dance floor with a commanding confidence, as if they already knew the outcome of the competition.

The couples order in the dance line was also based on the chronology which the entries were received. And as fate would have it, the corpulent couple set up right next to Mindy and Roy.

The MC announced, "Dancers take your marks!" The music began and the line moved in step. At times, the heavy couple drifted perilously close to Roy and Mindy, a deliberate attempt Roy perceived to intimidate and maybe even sabotage them. While setting up for the next dance, Mindy stepped in front of the girl and warned, "Look, you cow! Keep out of our way." Roy laughed aloud; Mindy had pegged them right. To her way of thinking, they were indeed a pair of heifers who thought they could muscle Roy and Mindy out of the competition. The woman smiled smugly and turned away.

The second dance they were to perform was the Wooden Nickel and the 10-Step Shadow to Alan Jackson's song "Good Time." It was one of Roy's favorites and the dance steps were more or less rote for Mindy and him. But as the music started, Roy saw the bovines swerve into their space to sabotage them. When the dance called for the gent to twirl his girl, the bull-cow swung his Elsie perilously close to Mindy. So close in fact that on one twirl, their heads almost smashed into each other.

Roy finally understood what was going on. These folks were professionals, as was probably everyone else in this final night of competition. Many of them had undoubtedly competed in dozens of other dance competitions before this one. In doing so, they had established standing in the world of country dancing that allowed them to advance directly to tonight's final rounds.

What puzzled Roy was how he and Mindy had been able to bypass the elimination rounds. They weren't professionals and had no standing. In fact, this was the first real competition they had ever entered. The only reason Roy and Mindy even had a slot in this final was that someone had chanced to see them rehearsing during one of their practice sessions.

Roy hadn't thought much about it at the time, but as they were stowing their gear to go home, a stranger had approached them and asked if they intended to enter the Wild Bill's dance competition. Of course, they'd answered yes. The stranger seemed pleased and handed them a piece of paper that read, "Final Round!" signed in an elaborate but indecipherable scrawl. The stranger told them to attach it to their entry application and then disappeared. Roy folded the note and stuffed it into his pocket, promptly forgetting about the encounter. But when Roy submitted their entry form, he remembered to staple the folded paper the stranger had given him.

Before tonight, the only other dance competition Roy and Mindy had entered had been a local event held in a Houston bar called the Eyes of Texas. Roy remembered working so hard only to come in second place. He never had liked that club. It smelled of stale cigarettes and had a mold problem so pronounced that it would have blown up the spore counter if the county health department ever decided to inspect the place. What a waste of time that had been. For coming in second place, Roy had hoped for at least a month's supply of Shiner Bock. Instead, they had won two free passes to the club and five BOGO coupons for Blizzards at the local Dairy Queen. The insult to the injury was that Mindy was diabetic! Roy ended up giving the DQ coupons to his neighbor's little boy.

Roy had blamed that disappointing finish on Mindy's hair. She had gotten a perm the day before and come out of the beauty parlor looking a bit too cute, like that child movie star from the 1930s, Shirley Temple. The curls in her hair had been so tight they could have been used as suspension springs on a heavy-duty pickup truck. After that, Roy and Mindy had avoided entering any more competitions, especially when all they stood to win was stupid stuff. But here they were now, finalists in one of country music's premiere dance competitions.

The third dance was a line dance, a standard Cha Cha slide but with a funky beat which introduced a twist that many couples had difficulty coping with. Roy and Mindy adjusted expertly. The fourth dance was a couple's dance, the Whiskey Wiggle, which Roy and Mindy stepped through flawlessly. The final song in this first round was the Travis Tritt tune "Put Some Drive in Your Country." It was another line dance called the Electric Slide, Mindy's signature dance. She had a way of owning the dance floor with it, and she alone made every other couple on the dance floor look like amateurs. The girl had rhythm in those hips, and when it came to stepping the electric slide, Roy just moved aside and let Mindy shine.

When the song ended, so did the first round. Of the one hundred couples who had come out in the last heat, only thirty would advance to the second round. The dancers fidgeted anxiously on the dance floor as the master of ceremonies announced the winners. Roy and Mindy were among the first teams to be called. They had made it. Maybe crazy, loony

Mindy hadn't damaged them after all. Roy hugged Mindy. He felt pretty good until Mr. and Mrs. Buffet Table were announced as the highest scoring couple of their group.

The large and enthusiastic audience piled on the bleachers along the walls congratulated the winners with robust applause. Despite the size of the crowd, it was easy for Roy to locate his and Mindy's cheering section even though their fan club consisted of exactly two people, Leroy and Nadine. It was Leroy who made their presence known. At the end of each dance, he'd jump to his feet and hoot and holler and spray long blasts from an air horn. He told Nadine that it would bring Roy and Mindy good luck because it was the same horn he had taken to the final regular season game the Astros had played in the Astrodome. The Astros had not only won that game, but had clinched their division title. Since then, Leroy kept the horn in the taxi glove compartment next to his trusty Glock, bringing it out for special occasions only.

But typical of Leroy, he took things too far, and the air horn proved so obnoxious that more than several people complained to management about it. Security had no choice but to send a detail over to Leroy and strong arm him out of the dance hall. Cussing and screaming all the way, he embarrassed Roy and Mindy even more by shouting that he was going to "open up a bigger dance hall that will put this Wild Bill Hiccup dump to shame." Then he let out a forced, drunken belch as he was unceremoniously ejected from the dance hall.

Roy just shook his head, but of course, the sight of two muscled bouncers hustling her man out of the dance hall rattled Mindy. She seemed mad at everybody and scowled first at the security that bounced her man, then at the judges, and then at the bloated folks standing next to them. Roy took her aside and told her to snap out of it and get with the program. "Girl, you got to let it go for now. We've got a real shot at this! Now we just have to get through these next two rounds, and we're home free. We're better than all of them."

As the finalists from the first two groups filed back onto the dance floor to the appreciative applause of the audience, Roy worried about his and Mindy's stamina. They had just completed five tiring dances and were now moving to the second round with sixty other couples who, unlike he and Mindy, had had ample time to rest between rounds. But he knew there was a fine line between well-rested muscles and muscles that atrophied from disuse. Roy looked over to where LeRoy had been blowing his horn. Nadine was there, and she blew him a kiss. Roy smiled and any concern he had about fatigue setting in disappeared.

The second round was more or less a repeat of the first except that the combined scores from both rounds would determine which couples would advance to the third and final round. Again, each team was to perform five dances. But in this round, the required steps were more technically challenging. The songs were not only longer but drew from genres as far removed from the country-western scene as New York City was from Nashville. It was apparent that this round was designed to confuse the less experienced couples and force them to commit mistakes and errors, thus making it easier for the judges to eliminate the majority of those still standing.

Surprisingly, the closest song selection to country western was what caused the elimination of a dozen or more couples. It was a fast-step line dance to a zydeco tune by Mamou. By the end of the song, parts of the line were so out of step that a few teams simply threw up their arms in frustration and dropped out of the line completely. That stumble forced their immediate disqualification from the competition.

The subsequent songs also caused difficulties. A slow Cuban medley from the Buena Vista Social Club, an Irish folk song by Ewan MacColl, a Brazilian samba by Astro Gilberto, and an exhausting ten-minute finale featuring James McMurtry's "Choctaw Bingo" all combined to create one of the most confounding dance segments any of the couples had ever endured.

By the end of the second round, the judges had a relatively simple task ahead of them. Nearly all of the couples had missed steps; those who stumbled on at least one of the songs were the easiest to rule out. When the MC announced the finalists, Roy and Mindy's combined score was high enough to send them into the final round.

After the applause for the finalists subsided, the MC explained how the rest of the competition would play out. Again, there would be five songs, and as with the previous round, the song selection held a few surprises. But only the scoring in this final round would determine the winners; all previous results were thrown out. It was a brand-new contest, and every step they took from here on in would decide their fate.

The final round consisted of a few surprise twists and dance steps. One was a Steve Earle line dance to the song "Wild Hurricane" in which they had to demonstrate scissor steps, boogie walks, the wobble, cupid shuffle, tush push, the sleazy slide, and the cowboy boogie. None of these steps were difficult for Roy and Mindy. They had practiced them many times, and at this point, it was elementary for them. Mindy whispered to Roy, "It's in the bag. We're kicking butt, and they all know it. Did you see how they all stared at us in the back room? We're what they hadn't counted on!"

The last two song selections made Roy smile with confidence. "Boot Scootin Boogie" by Brooks and Dunn set the standard for country-line dancing songs. Roy moved in such a way that onlookers couldn't help but watch him to the exclusion of everyone else in the line as they shuffled across the floor.

"Mama's Broken Heart" was the last song of the competition. The couples were required to demonstrate their mastery of advanced steps like laces, double and triple steps, four-count swings, and the lindy hop. These were all tricky moves by themselves, but the order in which the dancers were required to execute them was designed to see how proficiently the couples managed their transitions from one to the next. Mindy and Roy performed the intricate footwork without missing a single beat and glided through each step as if they were weightless and floating in space.

When the last note of the song hummed, Roy let out a whoop and swung Mindy around in his arms. His broad smile and excitement were contagious. "We did it, Mindy! Get used to it, girl. From now on we're going to have our pictures on the Wild Bill Hall of Fame. So much gold will be hanging around our necks that we'll need braces to hold our heads up."

As the judges filed off the stage to tally their decision, the audience showed their appreciation for the dancers with lengthy applause. Confident they had won, Roy and Mindy, along with everyone else in the dance hall, turned toward the leader board above the stage to impatiently wait for the announcement.

But when the final score was posted, there was no win, place, or show for Roy and Mindy. They finished in dreaded fourth place where there was no glory, no honor, and, most of all, no prize money, just a, "Thank you for coming and don't let the door hit you on the way out." Devastated, Roy and Mindy stared at the board in disbelief. How could this be happening? They had performed each dance step flawlessly and with far more style than any of the others.

Roy's plans to open his own dance hall dissolved into a confused blur. He always knew that opening his own club would be a difficult undertaking even with the money. But without it, Roy's Dancehall & Drinking Emporium would remain just another unfulfilled dream.

But after taking a closer look at the judges scoring, Roy became convinced he and Mindy had been cheated out of the win. His suspicions were confirmed when Mr. and Mrs. Heifer were awarded first place.

As the rotund couple accepted the congratulations from the other finalists, Roy glowered. The crowd didn't appear to like it either. When they saw who had won, they booed loudly and held their thumbs down at the decision. And more than a few people went further by throwing their half-full Solo cups of beer at the stage.

There was a particularly vocal section of the audience where Leroy had been sitting. Roy looked over and saw Nadine leading a cheer that he later learned was one that she remembered from her high school days. Sitting in the stands and watching a bad call against Wheaton High's Bulldogs basketball team, the team's cheerleaders would lead the crowd in the taunt, "Lollipops! Lollipops! Judges, you suck!" while they pretended to lick the palms of their hands as if they were candy suckers. In the entire history of Wild Bill's dance competitions, this was without a doubt the most divisive and controversial decision, and the crowd was not about to keep its disapproval silent.

The leader board clearly showed how each of the judges had scored the couples. All of them were remarkably consistent except for the absurdly low scores given to Roy and Mindy by one particular judge. That was the same judge Mindy had sparred with prior to the evening's competition.

Understanding the disparity in scoring, Mindy immediately convicted the pompous judge. There was some 'splaining' to do. She wanted revenge, and nothing could stop her. Arms swinging, Mindy broke away from Roy and marched up to the stage to confront the cheating judge. But he was nowhere to be found.

Where was the little worm? She had no idea where she was going and mindlessly ran out of the dance hall down the hallway, through the casino, into the lobby, and then out into the desert night. She ripped off her cowboy hat and whipped it into a hungry saw-tooth palm. The sharp teeth of the palm branch caught the flying accouterment and sliced into it, leaving it lodged there like some odd fruit. Her only thought was to find that judge and beyond that Mindy had no plan. She ran down the middle casino driveway blinded by rage, the tears pouring from her eyes. It took her a moment to realize that she'd run straight into Leroy's arms.

Leroy had been sitting in his taxi when Mindy had blasted through the casino doors and ran down the middle of the casino drive toward Leroy's cab. He quickly jumped out of the cab and made sure it was locked before he corralled her into his arms and forced her into Maxi's front seat. Not realizing it was Leroy, Mindy resisted and tried to break from his grasp, but Leroy had her good. Still, it proved to be difficult, and he had to use one hand to hold her while he used the other to click open the locked car. He was able to force her into the cab all the while repeating, "Mindy baby, it's me, Leroy."

Mindy sobbed and blubbered undecipherable epithets before telling Leroy, "That fat-ass judge sandbagged us. I gotta get my hands on him!" She was hysterical and Leroy had his hands full trying to calm Mindy all the while keeping a careful eye on his other passenger sitting in the back seat.

"Mindy, honey, calm down! I have a surprise for you. Guess who is sitting right behind you?"

She turned around and saw him. No longer pompous and arrogant, the judge looked like a terrified fawn afraid to move even a muscle. Mindy screamed with confused surprise. Leroy shouted at her again, and this time Mindy listened.

"I got the goods on this little puke. I snuck back in and watched the rest of the competition. I saw it all and how he cheated you and Roy. Baby, it was rigged from the start, and now we're going to blow this whole thing into a million pieces."

HANDICAP PARKING SPACE

With the help of the security staff he had befriended, Leroy had indeed been able to sneak back inside the dance hall. After being bounced from the Wild Bill, he made his way to the loading docks behind the casino where two of his friends, Rico and Sam, worked security. Leroy explained what happened and asked them for a little help. They told him that there wasn't much they could do. But when they continued their rounds, Sam winked at Leroy and nodded toward the back door. After they disappeared around the building, Leroy slipped quietly through the door his friends had left unlatched.

He followed the signs through the maze of basement hallways back to the dance hall where he found a safe hiding spot just off-stage behind the judges to watch the final round unobstructed. When the contest was over, even discounting the fact that he might be a bit biased, there was no doubt in Leroy's mind that Mindy and Roy had won. But after seeing the final scores, Leroy smelled a scam like rotten eggs. He watched as the judges mingled in a glass-walled reception room backstage smiling, sipping wine, and munching on hors d'oeuvres. Leroy pledged he would avenge this abomination wrongly perpetrated against Mindy and his future partner Roy.

Keeping a keen eye on the judges in the glass room, Leroy saw one of the few female judges leave the reception room and walk down the hallway to the ladies' room. Leroy followed and stepped in front of the restroom door before she was able to open it. Amaryllis Starr – as her nametag identified her – was surprised and frightened. "What's this? Who are you? You are in my way!"

Leroy smiled charmingly. "Don't be alarmed, ma'am! I just want to find out what dance contest you judges were watching up there. You certainly didn't see the same thing everyone else in the hall saw. You judges sandbagged my friends. They were the best couple out there and yet you gave first prize to those two porkers! Now, I want to know why."

Amaryllis Starr stepped back. "Look, I don't know who you are and I certainly don't know why I am telling you this, but I agree with you one hundred percent. It's Dennis Bales; he's nothing but a big cheat. And you're right! He marked them way down and ruined their chances. It wasn't the least bit fair. Here, I got a copy of the card that shows how he graded them. You can see how off it is. He didn't even try to hide it. It is so blatant. The proof is right here on the card. Take a look."

Leroy grabbed the card and studied it. One certain judge, Dennis Bales gave Mindy and Roy zeros on personality and overall presentation just like he had threatened. Conversely, that same judge significantly overweighted his scores for the obese winners. This was the smoking gun Leroy was looking for. "Miss Starr, may I have this card? It has all the proof I need to nail that cheatin' fraud."

She told Leroy he could have it but that it wouldn't matter much because the results were already officially recorded.

"That may be, ma'am, but there's something about holding Exhibit A in your hand when you are face-to-face with the accused. Well, thank you, Ms. Starr, and I apologize for interrupting you."

Leroy stuffed the scorecard into his shirt pocket and started back toward the judges' lounge, intending to confront Dennis Bales with his evidence. But before that, Leroy decided to avail himself of the service of the men's room facilities. He thought it an ironic twist as he envisioned the other judges would now act as the jury in his prosecution of this corrupt and unethical judge.

As Leroy dried his hands, the restroom door opened and in walked Dennis Bales; talk about serendipitous encounters. Leroy watched as Bales stood in front of the mirror, smug, arrogant, and sweating from the short walk from the lounge. Bales himself seemed oblivious to Leroy's presence. Leroy came up behind him and asked, "How ya doing?"

Bales didn't respond and splashed his face with water instead.

Leroy persisted. "Hey! Aren't you one of the judges in the dance contest? Man, I envy you. It must be a lot of fun getting to travel around like you do. But still, it's got to be a tough job judging all those dancers. That's a big responsibility to make sure you get it right."

The judge scrutinized Leroy in the mirror for a moment. "To tell you the truth, it gets old. Tomorrow, I go to some bumpkin town in Texas to judge another contest, and I'm getting tired of living out of a suitcase. But right now, I might be doing better if I had something to smoke." Dennis Bales looked at Leroy expectantly.

It was the lead Leroy was looking for. "Well friend, I got just the thing for you out in my cab. I just got back from Denver and scored some of the best medicinal herb I've ever smoked. I used to suffer from splitting headaches and so the doctor prescribed it for me. And you know what? It worked. One hit and you blast off, and you no longer care if your head hurts or not."

The judge looked suspicious. "Let me get this straight: you drove clear up to Denver to see a doctor to give you a prescription for some medicinal pot when all you needed to do was to walk into any one of hundreds of pot stores and buy it? You are aware that pot is legal in Colorado these days, aren't you?"

Playing the amiable fool, Leroy exclaimed, "Well shit! Just shit, man! Are you telling me I gave that quack doctor a hundred dollars to get a prescription for something I could have just gone in and bought like a bag of M&Ms? God, what a moron I am!"

Dennis Bales seemed amused and suddenly held out his hand. "Dennis Bales is my name. Glad to meet you. Now, let's go fire up that doobie I need something to work on this headache of mine. Maybe I should jet on over to Denver or Portland or Seattle. Now that it's legal, pot stores are becoming as common as Starbucks up there."

As they left the building and headed toward Maxi, Leroy said, "Better not take it into Texas, man. They got laws there that'll put you away forever." He had parked Maxi in a small paved area just outside the front of the casino in a spot marked "Handicapped Parking Only." He always backed into these spots in case he needed to make a quick getaway.

Leroy unlocked Maxi's doors with the key fob and opened the back door for Dennis Bales. The judge climbed in and Leroy ran around to the driver's side, discreetly locking the doors behind him, all the while keeping up his idle chatter. He didn't want Dennis Bales to suspect that he was locking him in for good. But Dennis Bales only laughed when he saw the tag hanging from the cab's rearview mirror that read "Handicapped Passenger."

"Well, let's light up some bud, smoke and toke, and we'll get this party going." Leroy reached over and opened the glove box. But instead of producing a joint, Leroy wrapped his hand around the cold steel of his Glock and, slowly turning around, pointed the gun in the panicked judges' face.

"What is this?" Bales yelled as he frantically tried to escape the locked cab. "Let me out of here!"

"No way out, man! I control those doors so losers like you can't bail on me! And I've been known to use this, so sit back and don't jack with me."

Frightened, Bales shriveled into the corner of the back seat.

Leroy pulled the judge's card out of his pocket and shoved it into Bales' nose, almost nicking it with his fingernails. "I bet you felt like a big man cheating the best couple and making sure they finish with nothing. And I mean *nothing*! Where do you get off hurting people? Oh yeah, that's right, you're some big-ass international judge! You're just some stinking cockroach. I ought to blow your brains out the back of your head like a Pez dispenser!"

Dennis Bales shook visibly. "You psychopath. You're going to spend the rest of your life in jail by the time I'm done with you. You can't get away with this. You're sick in the head." The judge wouldn't stop, and it only provoked Leroy all the more.

Leroy shoved the Glock into Bales' nose. "Hey, how 'bout shutting your pie hole! I always leave a round chambered, and you know that Glocks have no safety."

It was then that Leroy saw Mindy through the back window of the car, running toward them down the pavement in a wild panic. Leroy shoved the muzzle harder into Bales' nose and warned, "Don't move an inch!" He jumped out of the car and in within seconds had wrestled Mindy into the front seat next to him. He turned around again quickly and pointed the Glock on Bales while he tried explaining to Mindy what was going on. "Mindy, listen up! This scam artist robbed you and Roy, and I have the proof right here. I found one of the lady judges and..."

Mindy was rabid, "I don't want to hear about your lady judges. I don't give a …" Then she saw Leroy holding his pistol and turned and saw Bales sitting in the back. She screamed.

Leroy cupped his free hand over her mouth and with a tight grip, told her, "Shut up! Listen and let me finish. I stopped the judge, and she showed me the evidence we need to get this whole thing fixed up right."

Mindy pushed Leroy's hand away and demanded, "What's he doing here? What the hell are you doing? Quit acting like the mafia. What evidence?"

"Like I was telling you, the judge gave me this clown's scorecard. And the proof's right here. She was so upset that she gave me his card. I have it right here, and it proves how crooked he is. I got gold in my hand, and we'll use it to prove how he rigged the results. It'll ruin him. I'll let him out of my taxi, but only when he admits to what he's done. Here's the plan; he needs to make it right and fix it now. Otherwise, he's a dead man. That's his only hope."

Mindy shook her head. "Leroy, you idiot! Everyone knows! They posted the scores of all the judges up on the board. We all saw it. You've got nothing except a whole lot of trouble." In a moment, Leroy had gone from hero to criminal. Leroy stared venomously at the pompous judge in the back seat wondering what to do next.

Seizing the moment, the judge warned Leroy, "I'm going to tell the police you took me hostage at gunpoint. That's kidnapping, Rambo, and you're going to rot in jail for the rest of your life. You've gotten yourself and now your girlfriend into a no-win situation. Let's all just settle down and go our separate ways. No hard feelings. We'll let it all just drop."

Leroy stared at the judge in silence, and Dennis Bales, sensing his advantage, continued. "Come on, man, don't ruin your life over a stupid dance. The money's not worth the price you'll pay! And believe me, I know." He placed his hand on the door handle expecting Leroy to relent, "So, what do you say? Unlock this door, and I'll go back into the casino like none of this ever happened."

There was something in what the judge just said and a menacing expression grew on Leroy's face. "What about you, judge? What's in it for you? You certainly aren't so stupid that you'd risk your reputation over a pointless little dust-up between you and my girl Mindy here." He motioned with the Glock slightly toward Mindy who was now too scared to utter a word.

The judge squirmed uncomfortably. "What do you mean? Look, I get nothing out of this. My pay barely covers expenses."

That was it! Leroy heard what he wanted and asked accusingly, "So, how much, Judgey?"

The judge pretended to be insulted by the question, and Mindy stared at Leroy completely confused. "How much what?" the judge replied, knowingly.

Once again, Leroy plunged the Glock into Bales to reinforce that he meant business. "Don't play stupid with me. How much of the prize money are those two blimpsters paying you to hand them first place? I'm losing my patience, man, and remember, this gun has no safety."

Bales quickly crumbled like stale bread under Leroy's foot. "They were going to give me half of whatever they won. I am so sick and tired of all this cowboy dance bullshit! This was my payday out of the nightmare of judging inbred yokels like you. So there. Now let me out. Besides, you can't prove anything, and I'll only deny I said any of it."

Leroy ordered him to shut up and told Mindy to go and get the other judges right away and bring them out to the cab. "Hurry up, honey, before it's too late. And don't forget to herd those two underhanded cows down here too!"

Mindy dashed out of the car and ran into the ballroom just as the judges were about to crown the winners. She barged onto the stage frantically screaming for them to stop everything. Breathless, she told them the judge who had screwed her and Roy had admitted to conspiring with the winners to split the prize money. Mindy wasn't making a lot of sense, but Dennis Bales was indeed missing. The only thing they could determine from her ramblings was that Bales was sitting inside a taxi parked in the front of the casino.

The head judge looked perplexed. "What is he doing in your boyfriend's taxi?"

Mindy looked at the fourteen attentive judges and shrugged her shoulders. It was obvious she had no idea how Leroy had lured the duplicitous judge out to his cab. "He said he wanted to score some pot, so he went out to my boyfriend's taxi."

One of the judges snapped at her, "You mean to tell us your boyfriend's a dope dealer?"

Mindy shot back excitedly, "Look! I really don't know how he got out there! All I know is that he is there and he admitted to rigging his scores so those two beached whales could win and split the prize money with him!" Mindy pointed a vehement finger at the colluding couple. "They are cheaters, and because of them, Roy and I were duped. The guy admitted it all."

Then Amaryllis Starr interjected, "She's right! Dennis is corrupt, and he's in this for himself. Think back on all the other contests we've judged together. Our scores are all pretty much in line with one another. But his scoring is always way out in left field."

Amaryllis Starr continued, "Oh! And another thing that's always bugged me – look where he stays during these contests. Our per diems barely cover a room at Motel 6 while he somehow finds a way to afford some swanky digs and dinner at the best restaurants in town. The proof is staring us in the face; he's on the take." She gestured to Roy and Mindy to make her point, "This couple was very talented, and he marked them way down. Throw his scores out and this couple, Mindy and Roy, are standing up there in the winner's circle. Dennis is corrupt and I, for one, am sick of it. He makes us all look bad and impugns the integrity of our profession. So, guess what I did?"

Some of the judges had always had their doubts about Dennis Bales' integrity, but they had kept those doubts to themselves. Now though, as Amaryllis verbalized their private suspicions, they nodded their heads in agreement with her. Some of the newer judges considered Bales a legend and thought that Amaryllis Starr was committing blasphemy, bordering on apostasy. Regardless of which camp they fell into, Amaryllis had captured the undivided attention of all the judges, and they waited with for Amaryllis to tell them what she had done. The head judge, Marshall, suddenly developing an eye twitch said, "What, Amaryllis? What did you do?" There was impatience in his voice. He wanted an answer and wanted it quickly.

Amaryllis continued. "On my way to the restroom, I slipped Dennis' scorecard into my purse so I could compare his scores with mine. I wanted to be sure I was right before I came back and confronted him. But I ran into this woman's boyfriend on the way. He stopped me and I gave him Bales' scorecard. If that gets me in some trouble, then so be it.

I don't like how he treats these dancers like they're some dirt under his feet. If it weren't for them, we wouldn't have a job! Dennis Bales is dishonest and needs to go."

Marshall waved an impatient hand at her and then said, "It's time we hear from the accused." In unison, the judges turned a collective stare, or rather glare, toward the podium where the fleshy winners stood sweating and trembling nervously. The lead judge stepped forward. "Well? What do you two have to say about all of this?" But his tone had the ring of, "How do you plead? Guilty as charged?"

They stood like stone statues in front of the eyes of the jury of judges. Under their relentless stares, the woman suddenly crumbled and bolted from the stage into the curious crowd. Marshall declared his verdict, "Guilty! Let's get out to that taxi and settle this once and for all."

With Mindy leading the way, Roy kept pace. Behind the judges followed a growing contingent of curious bystanders that trailed after them like some nineteenth-century Texas cattle drive – destination Abilene.

Leroy saw Mindy and Roy blast through the front doors of the casino. Behind them followed the fourteen judges as well as what appeared to be everyone else in the casino. Grinning wolfishly, Leroy climbed out of the cab to greet them. Bales must have thought the crowd was coming to rescue him because from the back seat, he sang, "Just one word of advice, genius! When you're in the prison shower, don't bend over to pick up the soap."

Leroy considered letting the quip pass but then thought better of it. "Shut up you fat slob. Lard-asses like you become prison queens, and that's right up your alley." He stuffed his Glock into the small of his back, unlocked the doors and stepped out of the cab to greet the approaching mob. If there was going to be a lynching, it would be Dennis Bales whose neck was in the noose. He leaned casually against the passenger door while Dennis Bales frantically pounded on the back window to be let out.

Mindy and Roy rushed to stand on either side of Leroy. Stealthily, he slid the Glock out and pressed it into Roy's back. Roy discreetly stowed the gun in his belt as he pretended to tuck in his shirt. The judges assembled around them. Behind them, a large and enormously curious crowd gathered.

Leroy cried out in a loud and confident voice, "Greetings, judges! I have a member of your team who has admitted to conspiring with one of the dance couples to split their prize money. Together, they rigged the game, and by any standard, this is fraud." Then, as if he was speaking at some political rally, announced confidently, "Ladies and gentlemen, I give you Dennis Bales, the most corrupt and dishonest judge to walk the Earth!" There was a smattering of boos and hisses as Leroy stood aside and opened the back door with a flourish for Dennis Bales to make his appearance.

A beleaguered Dennis Bales rolled out of the car as fast as his plumpness permitted. When he turned and saw the angry mob surrounding him, he immediately began his lamentations. "Help! Call the cops! This crazed lunatic abducted me at gunpoint and was holding me hostage." Leroy smiled coyly, holding his empty hands in the air and spun around as proof, "What gun? I don't have any gun"

Amaryllis stepped forward going face to face with the unscrupulous judge. "That's bullshit, Bales, and you know it! I ought to smack you one. We know what happened! Your scores and your conspirators' behavior are all the proof we need! We have come to make restitution for the couple that you decided to mess up just because *you didn't like them*!"

Marshall, the head judge added, "Quit your damn lying, Dennis. We've heard it all before. Man, you got more stories under your belt but we're calling you out on this one. Remember when you told us that you wouldn't be able to judge the World Championships last year because your wife was going to have surgery?"

Another judge interrupted and said, "Yeah, what a crock. Your wife called in the next day looking for your ass. When I asked her how she was doing, she had no idea what I was talking about. That surgery-thing was completely made up. The truth was that she hadn't seen you in weeks."

Dennis Bales pleaded with them, giving it another attempt. "I tell you, this guy has a gun and he kidnapped me with it. Look, you can probably still see the marks where he shoved it up my nose." Bales pointed a fat finger at Leroy.

Mindy screeched at Bales. "No way does my boyfriend even own a gun. Search his car! Search him! This guy is a lying, corrupt bag of shit!" Even Mindy knew when to play smart.

Ignoring both Mindy and Dennis, another judge added, "How about that time in Des Moines when you scored down that couple after the girl wouldn't lay down on your casting couch? You act like you're some big Hollywood producer. She found you repulsive. Unfortunately, I found out too late to do anything about it."

It was as if they were at confession when one more judge stepped forward. "Yeah, and don't even go the held-at-gunpoint route. You've used that one before too. Remember when you pleaded with the Judges Federation for a pay advance because you said your landlord held a gun to your head and kicked you out on the street? Once again, your sweet wife debunked that lie. She said the landlord did no such thing and that it was you who had brought it all on by writing a rent check that bounced like a rubber ball."

Bales visibly cringed when one more judge said he too had heard the same story only with a different gun. "You told me some guy in a bar threatened to shoot you with his .45 because you were coming onto his wife, as if any woman would give you the time of day. You were probably harassing the poor woman, and just lucky she didn't knee you in the balls. So, forget that old, tired gun story; we've heard it too many times before."

Some of the female judges appeared thoroughly disgusted by those last comments. And so had Marshall, who now stepped forward to put an end to the discussion. "I think we have all heard enough. As the lead judge, I have the authority to throw out Mr. Bales' scores and order a recount. Which is what I will do." To his peers, he said, "We'll announce that the results will be recalculated based on some judging irregularities." Leroy and Mindy locked eyes. Leroy had a devilish grin.

Dennis Bales pounded the roof of the cab with his fist, shrieking in disbelief. "This is *not* fair. I am going to go to the Federation and tell them what happened. I'm telling you again; this man held me hostage in this freak'n damn cab at gunpoint. Go ahead, search him if you don't believe me." Leroy stepped in front of Marshall and held his arms out to offer himself for a pat down.

Marshall told Leroy, "That won't be necessary." Then he turned back to Dennis Bales and smiled. "Mr. Bales, you can rest assured that you will have an opportunity to appear before the Federation. But it will be a hearing for gross misconduct." Then he added, "I guess you're not aware of it, but five of us here were just appointed to the Federation board. There are only seven members, and five of us are here now. Do the math. You don't have a chance! We have a rap sheet on you that is loaded with so many of your infractions and improprieties you should be grateful that we haven't taken action well before this. There's a morality clause in your contract, and from what I see, you have violated it in so many ways that I have lost count. Pending a hearing, you are immediately suspended."

The crowd applauded and Marshall motioned for the judges to reassemble inside. "The clock is ticking and we've got work to do. We need to round up the accountants and recalculate the scores from the beginning of the night. They better still be around. They are required to stay until the medals are awarded." The crowd followed the judges back into the casino leaving a speechless Dennis Bales outside and alone.

Leroy threw a smug look at Bales before ushering Roy and Mindy inside.

When they arrived at the glass-walled judge's room, the four accountants responsible for computing and certifying the results had disappeared. Two came from Deloitte, the number one accounting company in the country while the others were from Ernst & Young, also ranked in the top ten. Without their official certification, the award ceremony could not be held. Marshall hastily summoned the MC into the room and explained the situation.

The MC bolted out the door, and within moments his voice was broadcast through the casino's PA system. "Attention! May I have your attention please? Will the accountants for the Jack-and-Jill dance competition report back to the judges' room immediately?" A few minutes later, the announcement was repeated. Fortunately, the CPAs were still in the casino and made their way back to the judge's room.

Meanwhile, the crowd inside the Wild Bill had grown impatient and began rhythmically clapping and stomping their feet on the bleacher floors. What was going on? A few were heard speculating that "The best dancers didn't win. How could that happen unless the whole thing was fixed?" Someone in the crowd started chanting, "Hey! Hey! Ho! Ho! All these judges got to go!" Others in the audience picked up the chant, and soon the entire dance hall reverberated with the unsavory refrain.

With a nervous grin, the MC took to the stage to appease the anxious crowd. "Ladies and gentlemen, in exactly one hour we will hold the medal ceremony and announce the new winners. Due to a computing glitch, all the scores need to be recalculated. We appreciate your patience and ask that all the contestants remain until the official results are announced." The excuse did not satisfy the skeptical crowd, and they expressed their disapproval by booing.

While the losers in the early rounds had little chance of moving into the winner's circle, no one was certain how the scores would recalculate after taking Bales scoring out of the calculations. Protocol dictated that all the couples were asked to remain, just in case. But now they had reason to come back more than it just being one of the rules. Maybe they had a second chance of getting a medal or moving up in the leader board, at the very least.

Mindy and Roy bounced back into the dance hall with new energy. With Bales out, Roy asserted that they had won. They were glad-handing each other. Mindy told Roy that she had never seen him smile so much. "Roy, you might just break your face if you keep that up." Mindy was elated every bit as much, declaring, "We got the gold, Roy. I can feel it!"

Finally, the MC jogged back onto the stage and announced that the results had been tallied and certified. There was scattered applause as he handed the mic to a man whom he had introduced as the Chairman of the Board of the Line Dance Federation. Roy nudged Mindy. "Don't we know him?"

Mindy peered at the man for a moment and then said, "Isn't he the guy who handed us the pass straight to the finals?"

With an earsplitting voice, the chairman thanked the audience for its patience. "Ladies and gentlemen, we have new results for the Jack-and-Jill Competition." His voice was so loud that Mindy covered her ears. "We do apologize for the inconvenience we have caused all of you and regret to inform you that one of our judges did not act with the integrity befitting his position. After disqualifying his scores, we approached the matter with the utmost scrutiny and had our accountants again recompute everything from the start of the contest. We would be remiss if we did not rectify this situation as soon as it came to light. I am proud to say we have resolved the problem and we now have the new results. There have been some changes in the initial results from the first and second rounds. Those results will be available online later tonight."

The judge continued, "Ladies and gentlemen, let me say that there is a big change in the placement of the final contestants. I will now announce the winners, starting with the fourth-place winner, then proceeding to the couple who will take the gold medal and the one-hundred-thousand-dollar grand prize. How about that!" The man's voice was so loud, Mindy figured he could be heard in Reno.

Mindy and Roy waited nervously. Barely able to contain themselves, they listened to the names of the couples being called out. So far, they weren't fourth place. Nor were they in third place. It was looking good for them. A couple of more seconds listening to this big mouth and they would take their rightful place on top. It was time for their coronation.

But when second place was announced, Roy and Mindy's faces turned ashen, and shock overwhelmed them both. They had placed second. Somehow gold had eluded them; they would have to settle for silver. Oddly, it hurt more placing second than it did when they had been out altogether. Jumping up two spots was a good thing, but how had they lost the crown? This was supposed to be their coronation. They were the anointed couple with all the great moves. Throwing hissy fits wasn't going to work this time, but admittedly, there was a sting to it. As Roy and Mindy stepped onto the second-place spot, Mindy wondered what did the first-place winners have over them.

Following the celebrations at the award ceremony, Mindy sure-footed herself over to the judges. Roy followed behind, desperate for an answer. "Okay, I don't mean to not sound appreciative for what you all did for Roy and me, but I just got to ask. I've got to know, and so does Roy. What was it we did wrong? Why did we come in second? I know we had better dance steps over the winners. We out-danced them, and you all know it!" Mindy's voice quaked as the judges exchanged emotion-loaded looks.

The head judge Marshall came forward once again. He seemed vexed. Something was up. The judges made eye contact with each other, as if there was something that they were trying to cover up. "Okay, Mindy and Roy, here it goes." Even Amaryllis seemed reticent. She studied the floor as if she was checking out her shoes. Suspecting another fix, it seemed to Mindy there was some secret between these judges.

"Come on. We can handle it," Mindy urged.

Roy fidgeted, dread swelling in his gut – he knew what was coming next.

Marshall sighed, "It was close, but you lost on style points." Looking at Roy, he said, "It was your shirt, young man. It didn't do you any favors. It was absurd and over the top. I wouldn't even suggest wearing it as a Halloween costume."

Amaryllis cut in. "It was ridiculous. It was too flashy. You look like you're wearing a history book. You overthought that shirt and that was the deciding factor. Those were the few points you needed to take first place."

In disbelief, Roy looked between the others. "Is that how... all of you feel?" To his dismay, they nodded in vigorous agreement.

One of the more flamboyant judges on the panel interjected, "Hell, I'm always up for doing your own thing. But cowboy, I just got one thing to say – you have to burn it. Put a blow torch to that shirt. It just didn't work. We had a hard time watching you dance with that clown shirt getting in the way. I know, I tried, but I couldn't get past all those cows. I swear, I could almost smell the cow dung. Hell, I thought I was walking through the Museum of Natural History!" Roy wobbled from embarrassment.

Melissa, a tiny and demure judge, shared in a mousy voice, "I was afraid that cattle drive was going to come alive and start stampeding. I swear, I could hear the cows mooing!" All the other judges laughed.

After seeing Roy's embarrassed expression, Amaryllis chided, "Oh, come on, Melissa. That's just rude, and you're just piling on."

Melissa bit back, "Okay, Miss High-and-Mighty, how come you didn't jump on anybody else's case with their criticism? Why just me? After all, the man asked."

Roy tried to swallow the hard lump in his throat. "Yeah, I messed up. To tell you the truth, the shirt was embarrassing. I thought it might be the trick that would put us over, except it put us…"

Then Mindy jumped into the fray. "Yeah, Roy, your shirt was the culprit. What in the world were you thinking?" Realizing it was time to take their leave, Roy thanked the judges for their honest, constructive criticism and for being so candid.

As they walked away, Roy gave Mindy a hard stare and said, "It was your big idea for me to buy a new shirt. That's the last damn time I listen to you."

Mindy jerked from his grasp and met his stare with a chilly gaze. For a long moment, nothing came out of her mouth – a first for Mindy. Then the silence broke. "Roy, you're right! It was me who kept nagging you. I should have gone with you to help pick it out. When I first saw you with the shirt on, it was too late." She started to laugh, "But I've got to admit, those judges were right about that shirt. Roy, were you off your rocker when you bought it? I mean, you had cattle roaming around the front of it and Comanches smoking peace pipes on the back of it."

The tension easing between them, Roy chuckled. At least he was certain about one thing; he sure as hell wasn't going to buy any stock in Buckaroo Western Wear. He might even consider shorting it.

That night, Roy went home a silver medalist. He took off his $300 hand-embroidered 'History of the West' shirt, grabbed a pair of scissors, and cut it into rags. They would come in handy when it came time to clean out the can.

ST LAWRENCE LOBBY

(MARIOTTA CASINO)

Hank Mariotta was busy putting together his new poker network. He had hired the production teams who were already developing content for cable television's first and only 24/7/365 poker channel. He had successfully negotiated exclusive broadcast rights to cover the World Poker Tour by offering to give it a permanent home. He was in constant meetings with all the major cable companies to include his network in their line ups. Both of the satellite providers had already signed with him, but the cable companies proved an unexpected challenge. Finally, after weeks of negotiations, he was on the verge of signing contracts that had the potential of bringing millions of eyeballs to his infant network.

Meanwhile, his sons Mark, Simon, and Andrew Mariotta were equally hard at work turning their dream of opening a poker casino into reality. The Mariotta brothers envisioned their casino becoming a destination for card players, *the* place where people came to play poker. The Mariotta Poker Palace was never intended to compete with the larger casinos on the strip. They wanted simplicity, something reminiscent of old west saloons where a saddle tramp could ride into town after a long day on the range, hitch up his horse, and come in for a drink and a friendly game of poker. There would be no slot machines, dice games, or any other form of gambling. The theme was poker, poker, and more poker. And after Hank's shrewd negotiations with the NFL commissioner, there was now a poker channel to help promote their venture. Once again, as with so many of his business undertakings, Hank Mariotta had demonstrated his ability to bring ideas into reality.

With a loan from their father, the brothers purchased a very large but rundown slot casino and began renovating what was to become the new Mariotta Poker Palace. After meeting with his lawyers and financial advisors, Hank had the loan contract drawn up and presented to his sons. The terms were generous, the interest low, and it came with a thirty-year repayment period.

Nepotism? Perhaps. But this was all part of Hank's master plan. Hank's sons needed the capital to open their poker room, and he needed a base for his operation. The synergy was perfect. The Mariotta Poker

Palace would become broadcast central for the network. It would provide the ideal backdrop for his production crews to discover a never-ending stream of human-interest stories by following the wins and losses of its players with their cameras.

Hank was well aware that as an owner of an NFL franchise, there were strict rules that prevented him from having anything to do with gambling and that he could not be involved in the ownership of a casino. So, before he had spent any money on equipment or hiring, Hank had directed his lawyer Teddy Washington to clear his plans with the NFL commissioner Boris Perry.

At first, Perry had stalled, drawing out his decision at an annoyingly slow pace and frustrating Hank. He was determined to launch his poker channel the same day his sons opened the doors to their casino, and Perry's decision had taken longer than Hank thought necessary. Fortunately, Teddy Washington was a dogged lawyer and had relentlessly pestered Commissioner Boris Perry for his approval.

Washington's main argument had been that the casino was a poker-only venture. There would be no other gambling of any kind, particularly sports betting. If you wanted to be precise about it, the Mariotta brothers weren't even opening a casino, particularly in the tradition of the behemoth structures that lined the Vegas Strip. Besides Hank was starting a cable television station; his only affiliation with the casino was to use it as the base for his operations.

Perry finally relented, but expressed concern about appearances despite Hank's reputation of uncompromising integrity. "I'm sorry, Hank, but these days, it seems that every decision I make is met with cynicism and scrutiny from the sports press. So, I have to be careful." It was for the media that Boris Perry had laid down restrictive parameters around Hank's new business venture; it was certainly more than he had ever demanded before from any other owner.

Hank would only be allowed in the network's production facilities. Everywhere else in the establishment was off limits. The NFL could not control where the network's production teams went but it could and would put a tight leash on Hank Mariotta. Perry did allow one exception, however – that these restrictions began the day after the grand opening of the casino.

Perry also required a stipulation be written into the loan contract with his sons stating that aside from the loan interest he received, Mariotta Enterprises would not benefit financially in any way from the casino's revenue. It was a non-negotiable condition before the NFL commissioner approved Hank Mariotta's plan. Hank was warned that the casino would need to keep scrupulous financial records and that the NFL retained the right to audit both his network's and his son's casino books on demand. The NFL intended to ensure that Hank could not blur the lines between NFL franchise ownership and the gambling world. Teddy Washington and Boris Perry had agreed upon the framework of what Hank Mariotta was allowed to do with his poker channel. And where he was not allowed to venture. Hank found the commissioner's terms acceptable and was particularly pleased to hear that his channel would not be prevented from using his son's casino as his own base of operations.

When the time came for Hank to meet with Perry and commit to the NFL commissioner's conditions, Boris Perry looked Hank Mariotta in the eyes and in a deep voice issued a stern and concise warning. "Hank. If you step over the line an inch on any of these stipulations, your next step will be to put the Antelopes up for sale. I will not tolerate even a whiff of scandal." Hank agreed, and as they shook hands, Hank understood that Perry's firm grip meant that he was deathly serious.

Hank conscientiously avoided having anything to do with the gambling part of the casino as his lawyer Teddy Washington constantly reminded him of the cost of violating his agreement with the commissioner. Despite the contractual shackles imposed on him, Hank was able to help get the renovation of his son's casino started while simultaneously coordinating the build out of his own production studios. It was no coincidence that the same general contractor supplied both construction teams. In fact, the foreman for both operations was the same man.

If his negotiations with Boris Perry had been tough, Hank Mariotta discovered that Father Lawrence was one tenacious pit bull that never let go when it came to granting his approval for the Mariotta's poker ventures. Father Lawrence spent a lot of time talking with Hank and his sons about the woes of gambling, repeating the phrase, "I don't care if it is only poker! It is still a tool of the devil." But even after Father Lawrence's admonishments, Hank remained determined to build his poker network while Andrew, Mark, and Simon simply brushed off the good Father's warning.

Although committed to his realizing his goals, Hank was concerned Father Lawrence might be right. Maybe he and his sons were indeed "dancing with the devil," as Father Lawrence had put it. But Hank rationalized the dilemma by committing ten percent of his earnings to Catholic charities. To curry the blessing of Father Lawrence, Hank also hired an accountant whose only job was to make sure that the ten percent reached the allotted charities. Hank then appointed Father Lawrence to oversee the charities and the accountants of that allocation. This seemed to appease Father Lawrence and he accepted Hank's compromise.

One other thing that Father Lawrence insisted on was that Hank Mariotta broadcast a public service announcement about the dangers of gambling and that he, Father Lawrence, was there to help or counsel any poker or grieved gambler in need. Hank agreed to this and even promised to broadcast similar PSA's throughout the day.

After their struggles, Hank playfully nicknamed Father Lawrence "The Patron Saint of Gamblers." Hank may not have been far from the truth. Father Lawrence's reputation was already growing and he found himself counseling distressed, broken gamblers before the casino or Hank's network even launched.

As for Mariotta's sons and their casino, the Father insisted that they create and provide staffing for a gambling crisis center right there in the casino. The brothers agreed and built a special room right off the main lobby for Father Lawrence and his counselors. They placed a large picture of Father Lawrence above the entrance and arched above the portrait in bold lettering was a sign that read: "Father Lawrence's Gamblers' Counseling Center."

The brothers' new casino was located just north of the strip in the downtown area which was undergoing a revitalization effort that only served to reinforce the Mariottas' conviction that they were embarking on a great new venture. It was a fact that mass development was giving way to a much-needed injection of new vitality to the district. The renewal of this area was another positive for the new casino and the brothers intended to put on a grand opening celebration like none other.

The three Mariotta sons were hard at work planning every detail of their grand opening. They hired bands, arranged for an endless string of celebrities to make appearances, and booked caterers with orders to create a feast like Vegas had never seen. Meanwhile, Hank was busy planning for the rollout of his new network. He wanted the cameras to cover it all. Mariotta's plans for the channel were endless. But what he needed to do right now was to focus on the network launch. If it was going to be successful, he needed to trust in the talents of his carefully assembled production staff and remain focused on his end goal.

BIG SKY RANCH

Hank had more on his mind than just a new poker channel however. Managing his far-flung business interests from Mariotta Motors to the San Antonio Antelopes kept him constantly occupied. Still, through it all, Hank made time to work on repairing the rift that had formed between himself and Christianna. Thanks to Father Lawrence's intensive counseling, he had come to realize the damage he had wrought on their relationship. So, Hank dedicated himself to mending the gaping fissure in his family. Because of this, he and Christiana were doing much better. He had finally accepted the obvious, that Christianna was no longer his "little girl." Gradually he began to unlock the doors that he'd always prevented her from opening and remained silent as Christianna made the most of her new-found freedom.

He had given his daughter free reign to pursue whatever she wanted – and what she wanted was Bruce Rebenack. With the season over for the Antelopes, Christianna and Rebel became inseparable. And it was only a short time later that Christianna flew into her father's office and ecstatically announced to her stunned father that, "Rebel asked me to marry him. Daddy, I am going to become the wife of Bruce Rebenack."

Unlike so many first-time teams that make their way into the playoffs only to implode in the first round, Rebel had remained cool under the postseason pressure. The Antelope's postseason wins had been decisive and they appeared unstoppable. The sports world talked of nothing but Rebel, and the line on the Antelopes put them on top by six points to be a Super Bowl contender.

Rebel had not disappointed. And now, the Antelopes were up by twelve going into the fourth quarter of the AFC conference playoff. With this win, the Antelopes would be going to the Superbowl. The Antelope locker room staff were already celebrating victory and started uncorking the champagne bottles while liberally imbibing themselves.

Midway through the fourth quarter, Rebel took the 'Lopes on a long drive inside their opponents' twenty and threatened to put the game away. On an end-run play that produced a first and goal, Rebel was hit hard; brought down by a flagrantly late tackle from a defensive lineman.

With whistles blowing and penalty flags flying the lineman was ejected from the game. Rebel lay motionless on the field.

The Antelope medical staff rushed out from the bench to attend to Rebenack. They helped him to his feet, but the attending physician determined that Rebel suffered concussive injuries and must leave the game. Rebel was greeted with resounding applause as he was helped off the field. When play resumed, the Antelopes had the ball on the one-yard line. The game seemed to be all but over.

As soon as he saw Rebel being assisted off the field, Hank had left his skybox and made his way down to the Antelopes' locker room. He found Rebel sitting on a bench surrounded by staff doctors who peppered him with a concussion diagnostic quiz.

Thinking their questions stupid, Rebel answered patiently and correctly but finally had enough. "Look, I am fine! Let me get back into the game."

That was when Hank stepped forward and the doctors moved aside like Moses parting the Red Sea. Looking up in surprise, Rebel only said, "Mr. Mariotta."

Hank peered down at Rebel and smiled warmly. "Son, you played a great game, and you've made us all proud – win or lose. But you took a brutal hit. We've got a lot of years ahead of us, and you need to stay healthy. Listen to the doctors." Rebel nodded reluctantly before Hank gathered the doctors aside to conference. They were all in agreement that Rebel should stay out of the game. Hank concurred and sat on the bench next to Rebel. He said kindly, "Son. Your season is over. Let's go and watch the rest of the game in Coach Kirby's office."

Hank turned the game on and he and Rebel settled in to watch the final minutes together. When play finally resumed, it became clear that the Antelopes' backup quarterback couldn't handle the pressure. On the very first play, he fumbled the snap and the other team recovered the ball. After that, the game momentum shifted dramatically and the Antelopes watched helplessly as their lead disappeared. Rebel begged Hank to let him back on the field. "I can turn this around, Mr. Mariotta. Please, I am okay!"

Hank shook his head. "I am truly sorry, Rebel. I want this game as bad as you. But I'm not going to let you go out there and risk further injury. Between you and me, a season's suspension for that tackle is what's called for."

Rebel looked at him pleadingly. "Sir, I mean this with no disrespect, but I really think that all these new rules are taking the soul out of the game." Hank hadn't seemed to take offense at his quarterback's comment. Together they had watched in silence as the

Antelopes' lead disappeared in the waning minutes of the game and then to lose it in the last seconds by a field goal.

With his season over and now that he was going to be part of the family, Rebel found himself welcomed into the Mariottas' very private inner circle. He was suddenly included in family dinners, parties, and even given a seat at the Mariotta family poker table.

Bruce was Christian but not Catholic. Knowing but not understanding why being Catholic mattered to Christianna, his conversion to Catholicism became his new priority. Under the tutelage of Father Lawrence, he would become Catholic during the vigil mass on the night before Easter Sunday.

Christianna and Bruce wanted a small wedding the following week after Easter. The Sunday after Easter, a sacred day for Catholics, was known as Divine Mercy Sunday, the Octave of Easter which was founded by Saint Faustina Kowalski, a humble nun from Poland who had had many visions of Jesus. The Divine Mercy Chaplet was one of Christianna's favorite devotions, and she could think of no more appropriate day to be married in the presence of the Lord.

It was Christianna's idea to keep the wedding a small family affair. The engaged couple wanted to keep the press out of their day of bliss. It would remain a secret, with the family members being the only ones notified of the special event. But with a family as large as the Mariottas, there still would be a large number in attendance. Hank had brothers and sisters and their children as well as his own extensive immediate family. Bruce Rebenack, on the other hand, only had his mother and virtually no other family members to invite. When asked about why so few, he told them, "They're all dead. My mother had two brothers, and they died before I was born. My father's gone, and I am an only child. My grandparents on both sides are deceased. So, this wedding is going to be a full-on Mariotta shindig!"

Christiana had her heart set on a traditional Catholic wedding with Father Lawrence presiding. She was equally adamant that the reception be held at The Big Sky Ranch. The date set for the wedding coincided closely with the grand opening of her father's poker channel and her three brothers' new poker casino which they had aptly named Three Brothers Casino. Hank didn't want anything to interfere with his business plans, but he also did not want to disappoint Christianna.

Somehow, he found the time to attend to the details that both important events demanded.

Of course, Christianna hired a wedding planner but time was running out, and there was still much left to do. For Hank's part, he brought on several more staff to spruce up the Big Sky's grounds for the wedding reception. Big Sky Ranch would be the perfect backdrop for the occasion. He gave the wedding planner full control of the preparations during his first and only meeting with her, stressing only that cost was of no concern. His one requirement was that the guests have a full bar stocked with top-shelf alcohol.

"Oh yeah, one more thing," Hank added. "We need the couple to arrive in a fully functioning antique stagecoach." Christianna looked at the wedding planner imploringly.

"An antique stagecoach?" the wedding planner mused. "Okay. I'll see what we can do with that."

Hank explained. He planned to use ranch horses for the ceremony to drive the coach — Hank's stable included quarter-horse racers, Appaloosa, and American Paint horses. The guests, particularly the children, would have a kick riding on the stagecoach and exploring the vast beauty of the Big Sky Ranch. Everything would work out if the weather cooperated, but there was always the chance it wouldn't. If they did run into unpleasant weather, the plan was to erect massive air-conditioned tents. Hank wasn't going to miss a thing. His only daughter meant everything to him, and he wanted her wedding day to reflect this.

Unfortunately, Christianna's crippling shyness began to return and she begged her father not to turn her wedding into a Wild West show. All she wanted was a simple ceremony, but in usual Mariotta fashion, the intimate event was becoming an out-of-control circus. As her father continued to add people to the invitation list who were not family, Christianna's anxiety swelled. The more people they invited, the greater the chances of someone leaking it to the media. In the end, her father must have sensed her increased nervousness and so compromised, saying, "Let's just have the stagecoach available to ride the children in."

The one decision Christianna had made was about her wedding dress and that brought her great happiness. The dress was first worn by Christianna's grandmother and then by her own mother, Matilda. She found a seamstress to restore and update it, making the dress suitable for a young, modern bride-to-be.

It was a Depression-era wedding dress made from rayon. Silk was an unaffordable luxury at the time and rayon had been fifty percent cheaper. Although it had faded yellow over its long life, the dress maker was able to bring it back to its original white color. It was a lined dress featuring a scoop neck adorned with a row of embroidered beads. Although it had a narrow waist and a clingy skirt, the rayon fabric gave it a flowing appearance.

Growing up, she had often tried it on in front of the mirror, dreaming of the day she would be wed in it. Now she would be the third generation of Mariotta women to wear it for her wedding. The dress was special, something tangible of the mother she never knew, something that she could actually hold onto. The simple fact was that knowing she was wearing the same dress her mother wore was as close as Christianna would ever be to her.

YIPPI'S HOT WHEELS

Lucy was having difficulty coping with Ty Amaya's death. When the detective came to her apartment and informed her of Ty's demise, Lucy had staggered and grabbed hold of the officer's arm. He had led her to a chair. Still in pain from the beating, she felt relief that she would never see Ty again. But since she had reported him to the police, she also felt responsible for his death. Then the officer told her about the murdered man they found in the trunk of Ty's car. Lucy gasped, knowing immediately that it was Sean. When the detective left, Lucy found herself drowning in a pool of muddled thoughts and confused feelings.

She didn't need her nursing degree to diagnose what was wrong with Ty. Like flashing neon in the darkness of a Death Valley night, the signs had been unmistakable. Ty's autopsy told the story. While the fall obviously killed him, Ty's blood test read like a Walgreens' pharmacy shelf. There had been high levels of cocaine, fentanyl, methamphetamine, and alcohol, among other drugs in his body. This came as no surprise to Lucy and only served to confirm what she already knew. It explained the change in his personality and his ultimate brutality. She remembered their first date at "The Jersey Boys" and how everything about him seemed perfect. That was, until Sean had showed up and ruined it all. Whatever might have been between Ty and her would now never be.

Wanting to leave those horrible memories behind, Lucy considered returning to Seattle. But there was nothing for her back there except gray skies, so she decided to give it a few weeks before making a final decision. For the moment, she would immerse herself in her work at Desert Valley Hospital and shut out everything else in the world.

Lucy was fortunate in one respect however. Thankfully the police had treated Ty's assault on Lucy separately from their murder investigation. Though media coverage was intense and consumed local reporting for days, it failed to link Lucy to any part of the murder-suicide. Lucy was spared the scrutiny and glare of the local television news reporters and their cameras.

In the weeks that followed, Lucy continued to complete her shifts dutifully. Gradually, her work became more than just a perfunctory series of services rendered in exchange for a paycheck. She came to realize that nursing was now more than just a job to her. She thought it peculiar that after all the years as a nurse, only now could she empathize with a dying patient's desire to wake up to the dawn of just one more day. It was strange that it had taken Ty's destruction for her to understand how precious life was. She had new-found compassion for those in her care, especially those who were terminal. And when she came to work to see an empty bed where someone had been the night before, she found herself truly saddened and said a prayer for their soul, and for the comfort of the surviving family.

This was not normal for Lucy. Before when a patient lost their battle and succumbed to their cancer, she simply began caring for the next patient in the ward. There was always another. She took a cold, fatalist approach to death as something everyone would have to face in the end. But now, Ty's demise seemed to have given her a new perspective on life, death, grief, and guilt. Lucy didn't quite understand it, but she felt a genuine empathy when her terminal patients' pain and suffering finally came to an end. Most of them left this world with a degree of acceptance and peace. To the surviving families, Lucy gave them words of comfort and hope that helped them through their grief.

On lunch break one afternoon, Lucy went down to the hospital cafeteria where a large crowd was gathered. It was quite a commotion. She chuckled and wondered if there been an upgrade in the food. Cameras clicked and flashed, focusing on one person in particular. It was Rip Rumple who had recently made a ten-million-dollar endowment for a new oncology wing of the hospital. It was also known that he had been visiting Desert Valley for help with his narcolepsy. He had seen a prominent neurologist who had diagnosed him with the worst form of narcolepsy known as cataplexy narcolepsy. Without warning, Rip would experience a sudden weakness of his muscles in conjunction with acute sleepiness. In layman's terms, his brain would decide to sleep. No warning, no sign. It could happen at any time, anywhere. It was a malady fraught with potential danger, and there was not much that modern medicine could do to prevent it.

Lucy observed Rip Rumple carrying a bowl of soup on his tray and heading for an empty table. He was intercepted by a journalist who began shouting questions about his generous donation to the hospital's new cancer ward. "Mr. Rumple, what's in it for you, except for the publicity?"

Rip rolled his eyes. The reporter's question was insulting but typical of the press. After a long silence, Rip answered slowly. "My first inclination was to ignore your question by faking a narcoleptic attack. But then I realized that intentionally dropping my face into a bowl of hot soup wouldn't be a pleasant experience. So, let me answer you this way." And with measured seriousness Rip continued, "My fervent hope is that one day, when you find yourself out of a job because some basement blogger replaced you at a lower wage, and you suddenly feel a wrenching pain in your stomach that your doctor diagnoses as pancreatic cancer, that you will have a place to come to receive the care you need without having to worry about how you will pay for that treatment. That's what this is all about."

Speechless, the reporter folded up his notepad and said, "Thank you for your time, Mr. Rumple." He left Rip to enjoy his soup in peace.

Dressed in purple scrubs, Lucy sat a few tables away from Rumple, consciously ignoring the hubbub surrounding Rip's presence. He was a billionaire; he could do and say whatever he wanted. It didn't bother her. But as she walked past Rip's table toward the coffee station to refill her mug, Rip Rumple stopped her by sticking out his empty coffee cup. He stood and introduced himself. Asking her politely, "Excuse me, my dear, but would you do me the honor of having your coffee with me?" He pulled out a chair, inviting Lucy to sit next to him. "Darling, after you get us some coffee, please come and sit with me." His charm enchanted Lucy and despite his decidedly sexist expectations, Lucy was not offended and took his cup.

Lucy returned carrying two steaming refills and sat down across the table from him. With mocking sarcasm, she announced, "Darling, I've brought you your coffee. Now just tell me where I can find your slippers and pipe." Rip laughed.

They played give-and-take with their banter. Lucy easily returned whatever quips Rip served up. And for his part, Rip didn't seem surprised by Lucy's lobs and returned as good as she served. After several minutes both of them realized that they were in a game that could go on forever. Rip was enjoying himself and didn't want the game to end when he suddenly served Lucy a lob she couldn't handle by asking her, "Sweetness, will you do me the honor of dining with me tomorrow evening?"

Rip's invitation was utterly unexpected and Lucy almost reflexively declined. It wasn't just about their age difference, even though Rip was old enough to be her father. But she was also struck by the eerie similarity of their meeting; it was just as it had been with Ty. Despite this, Lucy told him, "Well, you're in luck because tomorrow night my calendar is open." It was just dinner after all. Anticipating something fancy, Lucy worried about what she would wear and asked him where he planned to take her.

Rip was pleased and answered with a charming smile, "Dearest, I want to take you to Yippi's Hot Wheels!"

Again, Lucy was surprised. "Are you serious? You're kidding, right? You don't mean Yippi's, the roller-skating rink, do you?" Lucy knew Rip suffered from an extreme form of narcolepsy. Also, he was a man in his sixties, and although he appeared fit, she couldn't picture him in roller skates. What was worse, Lucy couldn't skate. Only once in her life had she been roller skating. That had been in seventh grade at a friend's birthday party. Lucy remembered spending the entire time gripping the railings as she had inched her way around the rink. Then another frightening thought came to her. What if Rip had an attack of narcolepsy and fell on the hard floor while he was skating?

"No, my charming nurse, I'm quite serious. Yippi's has great food and my doctor has prescribed roller skating as a way to treat my well-publicized malady." He asked Lucy for her address and told her that his limo driver would call for her at seven p.m. "Now, my dear, I have to run to a meeting." As he rose, Rip took Lucy's hand and kissed it, "Until tomorrow night."

Lucy thought to herself, *Taking a limo to a roller rink? If nothing else, this will be an interesting night out.*

The next evening a man named Lloyd knocked on Lucy's apartment and escorted her to the limousine where Rip waited. Taking her hand in his, Rip squeezed it and said, "So very nice to see you, my angel. I am glad to see you have dressed for the occasion. But I see that you forgot something." Lucy looked at Rip quizzically. "Yes, my love, I think you forgot this." Rip leaned over the car seat and brought out a rather large square box. It was wrapped with gold paper, and there was a bow on top. "Here, this is for you, my turtledove."

Lucy took the gift. "Thank you, Rip. But I don't know what I forgot." Tearing off the paper, Lucy opened the box and pulled out the contents. She held it up between them and began to laugh. "I guess you're right; I did forget to bring my crash helmet." Lucy strapped the helmet on and modeled it for Rip. "Well, how do I look Rip?"

"Stunning, my love!"

Lloyd turned the limousine into an empty parking lot and pulled to a stop at the steps of Yippi's Hot Wheels. Lloyd opened the door for them, and as they stepped out of the limo, Lucy saw the closed sign on the door. Relieved, she said, "Aw, that's too bad, Rip! It looks like they're closed."

Rip smiled and took her by the arm saying playfully, "Not to worry, Nurse Lucy. Rip Rumple has the power to open closed doors." He pushed open the unlocked door and led Lucy into the lobby of Yippi's Hot Wheels. Music boomed through the sound system while colored spotlights flashed off the spinning mirrored ball above the darkened rink.

It all looked perfectly right for a roller skate rink except for one thing – there was nobody there.

Located near downtown, Yippi's Hot Wheels was a nostalgic throwback to a time when recreation and entertainment were self-propelled and not the physically inert electronic fantasy world of today. The building itself was massive, covering nearly half an acre of prime desert real estate where the land was worth much more than the building sitting on top of it.

Rip seemed to know everything about the business and told Lucy more about the roller rink industry than she ever wanted to know. For a time, Yippi's owners had seriously considered closing the business and selling the parcel to an eager development group who had presented them with an offer almost too good to be true. Negotiations for the sale had been underway when Yippi's owners learned of a major supermarket chain's plans to build their first ever Mega Market in the empty lot directly across the street from Yippi's.

Rivaling Yippi's Hot Wheels in square footage, Mega Market was an enormous grocery store that offered foodstuffs from every culture around the world. From the moment the first customers walked through Mega Market's doors, Yippi's owners saw their own business begin to grow. The Mega Market became a destination for nearly everyone in Vegas if only to walk around and marvel at the astounding array of international and often bizarre foods stocked on their shelves. And when they came for groceries, they couldn't help but notice Yippi's across the street. The sight took parents on a nostalgic trip back to their childhood. The next time they headed downtown, instead of buying groceries, they turned into Yippi's and, dragging their kids away from their iPads and smartphones, laced their skates and pushed them out onto the rink of Yippi's Hot Wheels.

But tonight, only one person was working the entire complex. He emerged from behind one of the many concession counters. Lucy assumed it was the rink's proprietor. He knew Rip and yelled out a cordial greeting. "Hello, Mr. Rumple. How are you doing? Are you ready to skate all night long? It's all yours. I've set up the music and you don't have to worry about a thing. It's entirely automated."

Looking at Lucy, the man pointed to a counter and told her, "The Skate Shack is over there and you're welcome to help yourself to try any of the different types of skates back there. We've got speed and roller derby skates, recreational skates, and inline skates. Take your pick."

Then turning back to Rip, he added, "I have some bookkeeping to work on, but please let me know if you want anything, anything at all!

If you want any food, just come and knock on my office door. Otherwise, it's all yours! Have fun and be safe." The manager left them.

Lucy still couldn't believe any of this was real. This was unlike any date she had ever been on and it was the last thing she expected to be doing on a date with a billionaire. Surprised and somewhat confused, she asked Rip, "So, I guess this place is all ours, right? Is this where you take all your dates or are you just trying to impress me?"

Rip's eyes twinkled. He wrapped his arm around Lucy and led her over to the Skate Shack. "Come on, darling. Let's get you a pair of skates." As Lucy studied the racks of skates for something in her size, she saw Rip withdraw his gear from his gym bag. First, he pulled out his helmet and fastened it onto his head. Then he pulled out a pair of knee pads and, slipping them on, cinched the Velcro fasteners tight. The realization finally came to Lucy that this was for real! Rip was serious and she was about to skate around an empty roller rink like a junior high school girl. But if this was a billionaire's idea of a first date, she figured she might as well be dating a McDonald's fry cook.

Oh well, she was there and she only hoped it would be over soon. Lucy scanned the shelves for something she could stand in. She found a pair of recreational skates in her size, reasoning that the four wheels would be easier to balance on than the straight blade inline type. She pulled the skates off the rack and came out the Skate Shack reporting, "I found some!"

As Lucy caught sight of Rip, she began to laugh. Except for the face mask and a blue Rangers' jersey, Rip was padded up like a hockey goalie. He had donned elbow pads, wrist pads, and a butt pad that looked more like a thick chair cushion. He seemed hurt by Lucy's response, and she explained, "I'm sorry to laugh, Rip, but I have to say that you look like a giant blue marshmallow. If you fall, you'll bounce right back onto your skates. But what if you have a narcoleptic attack?"

Rip scrunched his eyebrows and stood straight, "Thus the padding, dearest. I have been seeing a neurologist at Desert Valley. You probably know him or have at least heard of him. He thinks I need to work on my balance due to my weak muscles. He recommended skating because it helps with balance – and it's good cardio. He stressed the importance of adequate padding for that very reason. As you can see, I have taken his learned advice to heart. I've been coming a few nights a week to practice and get a fun workout. These are slow nights for Ken and so he closes the place down and I make it worth his while. I can't say for sure, but I think it is helping."

Lucy's asked Rip who his neurologist was. Rex replied, "Dr. Harvey Lowenstein. He's the best in his field." Lucy agreed. Dr.

Lowenstein was a skilled neurologist and highly respected throughout the medical community. He was also known for his humanitarian efforts around the world. Flying to third-world countries, Dr. Lowenstein used his skills to save the lives of the impoverished sick who otherwise would have a very bleak prognosis.

Lucy sat on the bench next to Rip and laced up her skates. In the meantime, Rip pulled a pair of knee pads from his bag and suggested that Lucy put them on as well. Feeling dutifully obligated given her profession, Lucy obliged. "And the helmet," Rip chided. "Precious, I would hate to see you fall and crack open your pretty little head."

Once properly protected, Lucy stood and bravely announced, "Well, it's now or never, my dear Mr. Rumple."

Holding hands, they clutched the railings that led them into the rink. Rip looked at Lucy, smiled, and asked, "Are you ready?" Lucy nodded and together they pushed off to take their first lap. Lucy wobbled and squealed, groping for Rip for support. She was suddenly grateful for Rip's gift of the helmet because she was convinced that a crash was inevitable. Instinctively trying to walk, she slammed her skates down hard on the floor as if she was taking steps. Rip coached her, saying, "Glide, darling, just glide. Let your wheels do the rolling."

By their third lap around, Lucy felt more confident and began to ease her grip on Rip's arm. She was impressed by the old man's skating. He was actually very good. To her surprise, she was having a good time. Enjoying the music and conversation, they held hands and skated in circles to a soundtrack Rip said he had prepared just for her. Lucy was familiar with only a few of the songs he had chosen, but she liked them and Rip had an interesting story behind choosing each of them.

One of the songs Lucy did recognize was a 1975 disco hit, "Love to Love You Baby" by Donna Summers. Lucy told Rip that she knew the song and Rip brazenly told her that he specifically chose that song because that was exactly what he wanted to do with Lucy. "I want to *love* to *love* you, my lovely roller-skating goddess, just the way the song says." Rip purposely emphasized the two Love's in the title. Lucy was startled but not surprised at Rip's forwardness. She shrugged and remained noncommittal in her response.

Sometime later, Lucy commented that she was growing hungry and Rip suggested they stop and have a slice of Yippi's pizza. "We've been working out so hard, we deserve some good food to keep us going, darling." He led her to the edge of the rink and asked, "My sweet love, would you mind telling Ken that we are ready for some dinner while I find us a table?"

"Of course, my darling man!" Lucy chirped playfully, "Anything for you." She smiled and clomped toward Ken's office.

She knocked gently on the door before poking her head in and asking Ken if he would mind coming out to make them some pizza. Looking as if he was surprised, Ken asked suspiciously, "Where's your better half? Did you two play roller derby and knock the old man out? Is he laying on the floor with a concussion?" Lucy wasn't sure how to take Ken's question. She didn't appreciate the insinuation that she was some sort of gold-digging woman. She was insulted. If he was joking, it wasn't funny.

Rip appeared behind Lucy and told Ken he and his date were now ready for some of Yippi's excellent pizza.

Eager to please Rip, Ken got up from his chair, saying, "Let's get this pizza going. I'm on it." Behind the counter of the pizza station, Ken entertained them with his pizza-making skills. Stretching the dough with his fists, he formed a round disk and tossed it high into the air to the delight of Lucy and Rip. After several more throws, Ken lay the dough onto a wooden pizza peel and topped it with sauce, cheese, onions, olives, and pepperoni. He slid the pie into the oven and then brought them two large iced sodas. A few minutes later, he set a large, piping hot pizza on the table in Yippi's nook where Rip and Lucy waited. Both barely talked as they consumed the entire pizza.

Lucy gestured to the empty pizza pan between them. "You're right, Rip. It was quite good. It had a unique taste to it. But I am afraid that I may have eaten way too much." Patting his stomach, Rip agreed and suggested that they hang up their skates and take in a show at the Malai. To this, Lucy had no objection and in fact, couldn't wait.

As they began taking off their skates, Lucy's stomach growled ferociously and she felt a sharp pain rip through her abdomen. She looked up at Rip for help only to see him holding his stomach, doubled over in his own agonizing pain. It was strange they were both experiencing these terrible stomach pangs at the same time. Lucy felt faint and began to moan.

Rip looked at Lucy and grumbled, "I knew I didn't like that pizza. My goodness, what is happening to us? I think we've been poisoned."

Lucy said, "Something is wrong here. I think I am going to vomit. It's food poisoning. I know that much." Rip looked at her helpless to do anything for her. "Oh Rip, I'm going to be sick!" Lucy dashed toward the woman's room in her socks, hoping to make it in time. She didn't realize that Rip was close behind, heading for the men's room to deal with the demands of his own urgent gastronomical issues.

Lucy reached the restroom in time to throw up her pizza in violent heaves into a toilet bowl that was anything but sanitary. Once the worst of it was over, she had a fleeting moment of embarrassment – after all, this was their first date and she had ruined it. But when another wave of nausea swept over her, appearances no longer mattered. She was weak and feverish and staggered out of the restroom, hugging the walls as she tried to get Ken's help. Rip was nowhere to be seen.

Lucy opened the door to Ken's office and leaned against it for support. Ken was alarmed at Lucy's appearance. All color drained from her face and she could barely stand. Ken rushed over to her. "Miss, are you all right?"

Lucy struggled to answer his ridiculous question. But it was Rip, now standing behind her, who responded sarcastically. "Does she look all right, Ken? You need to call 9-1-1 immediately. That pizza gave us food poisoning. Get on with it." Ken picked up the phone and he punched 9-1-1 as Rip helped Lucy onto a chair. Rip seemed to be doing slightly better than Lucy as he played nurse to Nurse Lucy.

Apologizing profusely, Ken said he couldn't understand what had happened with the pizza and then he remembered. "I just changed suppliers and took my first delivery from them today. They gave me such a good deal over what I was paying with my old vendor; I couldn't say no. Some deal, huh?" Ken's only concern seemed to be how this would impact his business.

Still tending to Lucy and feeling ill himself, Rip looked up. "Let me guess, Ken; your new supplier is named Assorted Foods."

"Why yes, it is. They made me a deal too good to pass up. But how could you possibly know about Assorted Foods?" Ken appeared genuinely impressed at Rip's knowledge.

Rip sighed in disappointment. Assorted Foods was new in Vegas and still trying to carve a niche in the restaurant and food supply business. According to its representative, Assorted Foods' strategy was to focus on serving the smaller establishments in town. They promised to provide the same quality product and service that the large casinos received but at steeply discounted prices.

Looking over at Lucy, Rip saw her beautiful face as white as a cloud. He stroked her sweaty forehead. She was hot with fever. He told her softly that the ambulance was on the way. "You'll soon be in good hands, my dear."

Beginning to feel ill again, Rip hurriedly explained to Ken, "I make it my business to read the local news and to know what is going on. Lately, there have been a series of unexplained food-service delivery truck accidents. These accidents caused the potential spoilage of tons of perishable food. But instead of destroying the tainted food, it was sold below cost to an unknown buyer. My guess is that Assorted Foods was that buyer. Only that can explain the dramatically discounted pricing they offered you. Ken, my advice to you is that you re-sign tomorrow morning with your previous distributor."

Ken was livid. "I knew it all seemed too good to be true. But I figured it was just a promotional stunt to get my business. You know, loss-leader and all of that. It never occurred to me that they'd deliver ptomaine-laced food. Mr. Rumple, I am truly sorry for this."

The poison in Rip's system surged and he weakened. Unsure how much more he could take until the ambulance arrived, Rip kept his balance by gripping the edge of the office desk. "They've poisoned the wrong people and ruined my date with this lovely young lady. By the time I get done with them, they won't even be able to set up a lemonade stand in this town."

Lucy writhed in agony, cupping her mouth for fear of throwing up again. "Where is the ambulance? They need to hurry. Please!"

They finally heard the ambulance siren. Rip told the paramedics that he wanted to ride with Lucy. He said there was something rotten in the pizza they ate. Laying them both on stretchers, the paramedics locked them into the ambulance. Immediately, their vitals were checked. They tested their pulse rate, blood pressure, and respiratory rate. Lying side-by-side on their stretchers, Rip held Lucy's hand and tried to make light of the situation. "Darling, let's not a let a little food poisoning come between us?"

Lucy managed a smile. "And to think I was worried about your narcolepsy!"

Stroking the hair on the side of her head, Rip said, "My lovely roller-skating queen, what doesn't kill you makes you stronger." He smiled through his nausea and had one more request of her. "When we come out of this, will you accompany me to the grand opening of Hank Mariotta's new poker casino? He won't be serving up that wretched pizza we had tonight. I promise you that I'll have the last word on that."

Lucy tried to smile but couldn't. Thinking they must have given her something for her stomach pain, she drifted off to a restless sleep. In her sedation, she dreamed that she was roller skating down a road only to sink to the bottom of the Colorado River. She was sliding on the river bed when she saw Ty waving to her ahead. Just then, Rip Rumple appeared beside her and they skated together. Still underwater, Rip told her that Dr. Lowenstein had the antidote. In fact, Dr. Lowenstein had given Rip three slices of pizza that Rip had put in his pocket – one for Lucy, one for Ty, and one for himself. Rip handed each of them a slice and they started to eat the pizza. With the first bite, Lucy emerged on the river's surface, but Ty never did. She saw Rip floating comfortably next to her on a lounge chair. Lucy thanked him for the pizza and he told her that his slice of pizza triggered his narcolepsy.

As she was taken into the emergency room, Lucy cried out, "Dr. Lowenstein, the pizza killed Rip!"

It wasn't the doctor but an emergency nurse who knew Lucy. "No, Lucy. I'm not Doctor Lowenstein and Mr. Rumple's not dead. He's just sleeping.

Before she passed out, Lucy responded, "Okay. Then, can you please remove our roller skates. But please don't remove Mr. Rumple's knee pads just in case he falls down."

DEERSKIN LOUNGE

The Madison Four became an immediate success after Tommy Bill Dillon declared them the winners of the Battle of the Bands contest. They were booking play dates months in advance, and it seemed that there was more work than they could handle, at least for now. But Lee warned his crew, "We all know how fickle audiences are and just as quickly as we became this morning's hot new sound, tonight they could be saying, 'I can't believe I ever liked that music.'"

Of course, Tommy Bill Dillion had helped their case by promoting them constantly and promising his audience he would bring them back into the radio studio. "Just as soon as they can catch their breath, they need to come back here and shake their tail feathers for you and me. Those rascals owe us a debt of gratitude," he declared.

The Madison Four's popularity did not go unnoticed by Bill Walters, either. He'd been more than happy to use Tommy Bill's radio show to promote The Rajabede Trio and in turn, The Deerskin lounge. He had even encouraged the Battle of the Band's contest and was pleased by the increased business he saw in the days leading up to the competition.

However, after The Rajabede Trio's broadcasted loss, interest in the band quickly faded, and it wasn't long before Bill Walters began considering changes to his afternoon lineup. But it wasn't just business at The Deerskin that was declining. The receipts at the Wild Bill had remained flat for some time, and Bill Walters was under pressure to build them up and to start posting profits. As the casino's entertainment director, it was up to him to book entertainment that brought feet into the casino and once they were in, to keep them there. Realizing something needed to change, Walters waited for The Rajabede Trio to finish their gig one afternoon and called them into his office for a meeting.

He watched silently as Becky Dean sat in the chair in front of his desk while James and Randy took seats on the dark leather sofa set against the wall behind her. "You wanted to see us, Mr. Walters?" Becky Dean asked warily.

Walters answered her matter-of-factly. "I did, and I'll get right to the point. It's time to shake things up across the board. The acts are getting stale and I need to drive more traffic through the casino." Randy Kiefer squirmed nervously on the leather sofa making an embarrassing squeaking sound. Becky Dean turned and frowned at him. "So, I'm making some changes. I no longer need The Rajabede in the afternoon."

All three sat paralyzed, unable to speak. After a moment, James stood. "It's all your fault, Becky Dean. Ever since we lost the contest, you've been dragging us down." It had been a humiliating defeat for each of them. Bill Walters was well aware of the tension and resentment building between The Rajabede.

He had happened to overhear one of their arguments during a rehearsal. James broke off in the middle of "Sweet Home Alabama," their signature song, taunting, "Hey Becky Dean, too bad there isn't a *Singing for Dummies* book. I don't mean to jump in your chili, but you could learn a thing or two from Isabella. She brought it!" It seemed to Bill Walters that finding flaws with Becky Dean had become James' new pastime.

Becky Dean stared blankly at James then turned to Bill Walters. "So... today was our last show?"

Walters nodded. "As Rajabede, yes. Well, almost. Your last show will be in two weeks." The trio looked at him puzzled. "Like I said, I'm doing some spring cleaning across all of our venues. That includes the Wild Bill."

"What has that got to do with us?" James asked. "You just fired us."

Walters held up his hands. "Hear me out. I'm looking for a house band to play the Wild Bill. Now, of course, a trio like yours isn't big enough to fill that stage, but if you added a few more musicians to the group, you might have just what I need."

Bill Walters had their attention.

"I've been talking with Tommy Bill Dillon. It seems that little contest of his created quite a stir around town. And it also put your competition – The Madison Four or as Tommy Bill calls them, The Baddies From Maddie– on the map. But you all didn't do too badly for yourselves either. So, I thought that maybe it wouldn't be such a bad idea for you to team up with them and become Wild Bill's house band."

He understood the drama the contest had created between the two bands. But if he didn't do something soon, casino upper management would drop him for someone with a flashier resume. Pitching the idea to them proved a difficult sell. James sulked and announced that he wanted no part of the idea. But then Randy took an uncharacteristic stand, "Dude, take your meds and chill. What's your malfunction? You'll get to see Isabella again and I know you got a thing for her. I can just tell. And as for me, I just want a job and some moolah."

Everyone then focused on Becky Dean, who up to that point had kept silent. She squirmed in her seat before telling them that while her and Lee's relationship was secure, the same could not be said about the rest of The Maddies. "At best, there is a cold truce between us and I'm not sure if they'd cross that bridge again.

After several long minutes of discussion, it was decided – and Walters got his way. The opportunity to become the house band at Wild Bill's was too big for the trio to ignore. It meant larger crowds, notoriety, and most importantly, a bigger payday.

The only obstacle now was getting the rest of what used to be The Madison Four to agree to the merger. For this, Bill Walters relied on Becky Dean and asked her to remain behind as he dismissed James and Randy. After a suspicious James shut the door behind him, Bill Walters warned the lead singer, "You know, this is only half of the deal. You've got to get your old team back on board as well. From what I hear, they are finding work all over town. Do you have any idea how we can bring them in?"

Becky Dean smiled. "Look, Bill, what you are offering is every musician's dream – a steady gig, no travel, guaranteed salary. Trust me. It's a done deal."

A few days later before The Rajabede was set to take the stage at The Deerskin Lounge, Becky Dean poked her head into Walters' office once more and told him, "Rajabede and The Madison Four are now one!" They would have their first practice together next Wednesday afternoon.

With the hard part now behind him, Walters turned to the promotion phase of his plan to recharge the casino's entertainment lineup. The increased business Tommy Bill's Battle of the Bands contest generated for The Deerskin Lounge was noticeable. It was enough to convince Bill Walters to maintain a constant radio presence. And for this, he needed Tommy Bill Dillon and his radio show. But with a limited advertising budget, Walters had to find a way to get what he could afford – free publicity. He had a plan.

At heart, Walters knew Tommy Bill Dillon was a showman. He loved a stage and Walters wanted to give him a live one. The idea was to recreate something like the Grand Ole' Opry in the Wild Bill Hickok on Friday and Saturday nights with Tommy Bill Dillon starring as the Master of Ceremonies. It would give the radio personality a stage he so craved plus an audience he couldn't reach with radio. How could he resist? And the casino would get free weekly plugs when Tommy Bill reminded his radio audience to join him at The Wild Bill Hickok every Friday and Saturday night. Bill Walters was pleased with himself.

When he approached Tommy Bill with the idea, the only thing they couldn't agree on was Tommy Bill's compensation. He didn't like Walters' offer and let him know. "I know you're game. I want a piece of that advertising budget you won't be spending on my radio show. My God, you're tighter than a gnat's ass."

Walters stammered and carried on for a few minutes before landing on a figure that Tommy Bill felt appropriate for a man of his talents. But it was evident that Tommy Bill was still feeling fleeced from the negotiations. When he told his radio audience that he was going to be the new weekend MC at the Wild Bill, he expressed his frustration with Bill Walters. "He sure knew how to put a burr in my saddle, but we finally worked it out. He's lucky to have yours truly and he can't be getting so darn greedy. Because as the saying goes folks: 'Pigs get fed, and hogs get eaten!'"

It was another week before the two groups got together in the practice room by The Deerskin Lounge. They were all determined to make it work but who was going to emerge as the leader was still unanswered. James had led The Rajabedes and Lee had directed The Madison Four sans Becky Dean.

After a few tense moments, Becky Dean stood up and laid it all out for them. "Look, we all have our pasts, but we all know what we are capable of. We have an opportunity here to do together what we'd never be able to do on our own. We all have our strengths and weaknesses. To be sure, Isabella can belt out a rock anthem like I could never do. On those songs, I'll sing backup. On the blues, let's audition and you all can decide who will sing the lead."

Becky Dean's speech impacted all of them. In an instant, their animosities disappeared and they began to talk among themselves about the direction they could take their new band. At the end of their first meeting, they hadn't even played so much as a note, but at Isabella's suggestion, they all agreed to meet up at the Flower Power Club later that night.

Bill Walters's idea of what musical direction he wanted them to take was entirely different from theirs. In addition to a healthy dose of country music, he wanted them to add more of an edgy pop sound, and with two strong and distinctive female vocalists, Walters was thinking Fleetwood Mac. The Mac boasted two female lead singers, Stevie Nicks and Christine McVie. "Now, *there* was a group if there ever was one. They were one of the best to come out of the 1970s; Fleetwood Mac sold more than one hundred million records worldwide." Bill Walters dreamed of the commission he'd receive for managing a group like that. His folks were just as talented. Most of them could pick up any instrument and make it sing. Isabella was the only one-trick pony. But that pony could sing. She had beguiling down pat.

Walters followed their practice sessions closely. After a few weeks, they were beginning to produce a tight and cohesive sound. Pleased, he told them they needed a few more days and then he would let them take the stage at The Wild Bill. The combined group came up with the name The Thrillers. It was Isabella and James' idea because Isabella said it was the group's purpose – to thrill the audience. Nobody liked the name but acquiesced and The Thrillers were on.

The group's debut performance at the Wild Bill was a rousing success. The dance hall was packed, and Tommy Bill had certainly done his part to generate the kind of publicity that filled cash registers. And Bill Walters was now being viewed by Nugget executives as some entertainment guru.

The Thrillers proved they had the musical versatility to keep a large audience's attention for the evening. Their newfound fame brought them to the attention of business magnate Hank Mariotta who approached them to headline the gala kick-off of his new poker channel. The Thrillers were going to perform live in front of a worldwide television audience and they intended to thrill.

Becky Dean looked back at the last few months of her life. Since she had come to Vegas, there had certainly been some strange and unexpected turns. But one thing was certain – she no longer had to stand in line for a five-dollar spaghetti dinner with soggy noodles and runny tomato sauce.

MARRIAGE LICENSE BUREAU OF LAS VEGAS, NEVADA

In the days and weeks following their second-place finish, Roy became a simmering stew of anxiety. Taking second place was his fault, something he considered a personal failure. Roy had failed Mindy. He had failed Nadine. He even felt guilty about failing Leroy. But most of all he had failed to win the grand-prize money needed to fund his dreams of opening a country dance club of his own. To be sure, the prize money that went with second place was a welcome addition to his dwindling savings. But after splitting it with Mindy and the IRS, there was barely enough left to open a street-corner espresso cart let alone bankroll a viable night club in Las Vegas. Roy felt like he had driven his life down a long road only to reach the end of it and be no nearer to his destination. Because of this, he was none too enjoyable to be around.

Several weeks later, Roy visited Nadine at The Carrington. He was still depressed and moped around her suite like he had lost any hope for the future which, in fact, he had. That second-place finish destroyed Roy's confidence. All he could think about was how that lousy, gaudy shirt had cost him everything. He even thought about filing a lawsuit against Buckaroo Western Wear for his pain and suffering, and taking a swing at the lanky salesman who sold him that stupid shirt.

Sitting on the couch and staring at nothing, Roy barely noticed Nadine as she reclined nearby. After a moment of tense silence, he blurted, "Damn it, Nadine. This isn't working."

Perplexed, Nadine asked him, "What isn't working?" Roy wasn't in the mood to share his concerns with her since she was so mysteriously opaque herself. She then fired one last probe. "Come on, what is it?" Roy tried to ignore the pleading in her eyes. "You're worried about not having the money for your dance club, aren't you?"

Roy debated whether to answer. He took a deep breath and without looking at her said, "Well, it does concern me. I put everything on the line, and I crapped out. Now I've got nothing."

Nadine wrapped her arms around him and hugged him. "Roy baby, you don't need to worry. I've got your back."

Roy looked at her and asked stonily, "What the hell does that mean?"

Nadine's smile was wider than the sky. "Honey-baby, I've already bought you your dance hall!"

"You did what? What the..."

Nadine didn't let him finish. "Yes baby, you're sweet li'l ears heard me correctly. I purchased a building downtown and it's a perfect spot for you to open your dance club. It has plenty of parking and there's lots of restaurants and other entertainment to drive traffic. It's yours if you want it. Any questions? Is there anything you want to ask me?"

Roy went straight to what he saw as their real problem. "Nadine, where does all your money come from? I need to know. I want to marry you, but I also don't want you taking care of me. I am not a gigolo and I won't be kept. I am perfectly capable of taking care of you, your children, and ours. And that's what I intend to do."

Nadine's expression flashed surprise at his response and her face turned ashen. She stood and confessed, "Roy, I don't need you to take care of me. I have millions. My late husband died and left me a bundle. I can buy anything I want. And if you don't want the dance hall space, then I'll rent it out and make some money off of it that way. I don't care; it's my investment and a pretty darn good one, even if I do say so myself. As for me, I'm starting up my own cosmetic company. I've got big plans and I'm going ahead with them on my own. Now, if you don't want to marry me because I'm rich, then that's your problem. But if we were to marry, you wouldn't be 'kept' as you put it. I would expect you to work hard and make a success of the club. That would be your thing, and I would have mine. Think of it as me helping you to get it started. The rest is up to you. So, hop to it and quit moping. Call Leroy and get the ball rolling."

Dazed, Roy sat silent. But as he allowed her words to penetrate his self-pity, he knew she was right. Nadine tapped her foot impatiently, "Well? I'm waiting!"

Roy knew what to do. He got up from the couch and grabbed his blazer draped over the back of a high-back chair. Nadine looked at him with dread in her eyes. She asked him, "So is this it? Are you walking out on me?"

Roy didn't answer, but instead reached inside the blazer's breast pocket and pulled out a Churchill-sized Romeo y Julieta cigar. She watched curiously as he slid off the paper ring and tossed the cigar over his shoulder behind him. He approached Nadine and knelt on one knee in front of her and asked, "Nadine? Will you be my wife?"

Nadine screamed excitedly and began jumping up and down. "Yes, of course, I will!" Roy told her to stand still long enough for him to place the cigar ring on her finger. Once he did, Nadine smothered him with kisses, exclaiming that she wanted to get married right away.

Roy asked her, "I thought we were going to the Mariotta Casino grand opening? I never mentioned it before, but I'm a big fan of Hank Mariotta."

Nadine said playfully, "Of course, we'll go, but only after you make an honest woman out of me."

Roy smiled broadly, grabbed his jacket, and on his way to the door, told her "Come on! What are you waiting for? No time to waste. We need to grab a marriage license and then get to the chapel."

Nadine leaned back onto the couch. "I am just imagining what it's going to be like being Mrs. Roy Garner." She looked up at Roy and said quizzically, "Here we are going to be married, and I don't even know your middle name!"

Roy laughed and introduced himself, "Hi, I'm Roy Crockett Garner and you are soon to be the new, Mrs. Roy Crockett Garner. Now that we've got the introductions out of the way, let's go and get ourselves hitched. Let's speed it up and get going. We can get it done today." For the first time since the contest, Roy was happy. "We'll get the license, and then go to that little chapel with the doves on the window."

As Nadine grabbed her purse, she asked, "Any relation to *the* Davy Crockett?" Roy told her there wasn't. Then they hurried out of The Carrington together into what would be their new lives as a married couple. As they took their seats in Nadine's Ferrari, Roy joked that he had just one more important question for her. Nadine started the car and looked at him with a hint of concern. "Yes Roy, what is it?" Wanting to prolong his antic, Roy pretended to be serious. "What is it Roy, *please* tell me!"

Clearing his throat, he asked Nadine in the sternest voice he could affect, "Since we're going to be man and wife, do you think you could let me drive *you* sometime?" They laughed their way to 3rd Street in her revved-up convertible Ferrari. By the end of the day, Roy drove them back as Mr. and Mrs. Roy Garner. It was true; things happen fast in Las Vegas.

THREE BROTHERS POKER PALACE

The night of the premier opening of the Three Brothers Poker Palace finally arrived. This was the biggest night in the lives of the Mariotta brothers. The local media intended to cover it like Oscar night in Hollywood. Every Las Vegas television station sent crews out to do live remotes of the gala event. While the public was invited to join many of the grand opening festivities, an invitation to the private grand opening reception became one of the most coveted passes in recent memory. VIP invitations had been sent out to local dignitaries, politicians, and businessmen alike. The opening of the Poker Palace represented the first significant investment in the Las Vegas economy since the Great Recession and was hailed as the city's first step toward economic recovery. Every Las Vegan wanted to see it succeed.

With so much still to do and so little time left to get it done, the Mariotta brothers worked eighteen-hour days. Despite the pressure, not even the slightest detail was overlooked. Each brother had different responsibilities in overseeing the casino's completion, and each drove his crews hard. When Mark was blocked from completing his tasks because Simon was unable to finish his own on time, they were able to work it out amicably. And even though it meant pushing an already overworked staff even harder, Mark loaned out some of his crew to Simon so they could get back on schedule. But in the end, the Mariottas succeeded in transforming a rundown slot-machine casino in a long-neglected part of town into a destination for visitors and locals alike. The Poker Palace fit in well with the district's ongoing revival plans. The community pulsed with new businesses and the Three Brothers Poker Palace was, in large part, responsible for that.

The new gaming venue wouldn't offer hotel accommodations. The hospitality industry was one line of business the Mariotta brothers assiduously avoided. Dealing with cranky guests and piles of dirty towels and daily linens would distract from what they loved most. And, that was poker. They wanted their establishment to become the first-place people thought about when the topic of poker came up. If there could be such a thing as the Washington D.C. of poker, they wanted the Three Brothers Poker Palace to be that.

But the brothers realized that not all card players played poker. High rollers played Baccarat, others liked Gin Rummy, and nearly everyone played Black Jack. Wanting to appeal to all card players, they decided to make accommodations. They had even built a special room named the Tombstone Parlor which was dedicated to the memory of Wyatt Earp and Doc Holiday and decorated in the fashion of a nineteenth-century western saloon. From the swinging doors and brass spittoons, to the creaky wood-plank flooring obtained from salvaged building suppliers, the room was authentic in every detail. The card dealers were even costumed in western wear. Male dealers were encouraged to sport handlebar mustaches or wear fake ones if they couldn't grow one out themselves. Female dealers were dressed in cleavage-revealing colorful dresses typical of the saloon girls of the old west. As far as the Mariotta brothers could determine, their Tombstone Parlor was the only room in Vegas that dealt the game of Faro, a card game more popular than poker during the nineteenth century. Nonetheless, poker remained the prime focus of the Three Brothers Poker Palace.

From the beginning, they had resolved to become the center of the Texas Hold'em universe. Hank Mariotta's new poker channel would help establish the Poker Palace as that epicenter. Mark Mariotta was in charge of furnishing the casino and ordered custom card tables with special cameras that could see the players' cards as they were dealt. He designed the entire table to be one big camera that never missed a dealt card. The design was revolutionary and his father encouraged him to patent it, which he readily did. And as if a gift from the government, Mark opened the letter from the U.S. Patent Office granting him exclusive rights to his design on the very day the casino opened.

The tables were very expensive to manufacture, but Mark required each of them to be fitted with his patented camera and wired to the control room to record every hand dealt. There was also a video feed into the control room of his father's new poker channel. Mark viewed this as double protection against cheaters; if his people didn't detect it, his father's television audience certainly would. They could undoubtedly back their boast of "Hosting the most honest card games in town."

The cadre of directors, producers, cameramen, and technicians Hank hired had worked hard to be ready for the debut of the new network while Hank had availed himself of every opportunity to promote his new venture. This included sitting down to an interview with Tommy Bill Dillion on his radio show, All Things Country. Hank was more than happy to answer Tommy Bill's questions about his plans for the new network, but when the host began to focus on the Three Brothers Poker Palace, Hank looked to his son sitting beside him to answer.

Simon Mariotta told all the country-music lovers out there to be sure to come and check out their new poker digs. "The Three Brothers Poker Palace is going to have it all. If you're not a card player, we still have you covered. We've got a stage where we plan to bring in some fantastic bands for you to dance the night away. You can come in, have a drink, and then dance the two-step. And when you get hungry, you'll have two restaurants, a café, and a coffee shop to suit every taste. We'll deliver a spectrum of culinary experience from fine dining to the greasy spoon." Simon paused for a brief moment then, with a broad smile, declared enthusiastically, "And Tommy Bill, I have an announcement to make. And since you are responsible for making it all possible, we wanted to let you and your audience to be the first to know."

Naturally, this caught Tommy Bill's attention and he clapped his hands excitedly. "Well, bring it on, Simon Mariotta. What're ya going to dish out to me and mine?"

Satisfied that his tease had produced the intended effect, Simon continued, "Well, Tommy Bill, everyone knows that the hottest local band in Vegas right now is The Thrillers and that it's all because of you and your support of the local music scene." Tommy Bill moved to the edge of his seat with anticipation while Simon explained, "Tommy Bill, I'm proud to announce tonight on All Things Country, that we have booked The Thrillers to headline the grand opening of the Three Bothers Poker Palace. And more than that, The Thrillers will be playing to a global audience thanks to the coverage of Hank Mariotta's fledgling network. Yep folks, your favorite local group is going global and we hope to have the man who brought it all together to be our Master of Ceremonies." Simon paused for a moment and, speaking to the radio audience, added, "So ladies and gentlemen, we want to invite all of you to come out and celebrate the grand opening of the Three Brothers Poker Palace."

Hank interjected, "Tommy Bill, now that's what I call a two-point conversion. Congratulations!"

Never lacking for a quip, Tommy Bill was caught by surprise at Simon's announcement. With unaccustomed humility he accepted. "Well, Simon Mariotta, I don't know what to say. Except that it would be an honor and it makes me strut like a rooster in a hen house." Hank and Simon looked at one another and smiled at Tommy Bill.

The Mariotta brothers had planned their grand opening for the second Friday in April. But Father Lawrence had reminded them that that date fell on Good Friday. And since Holy week was an integral part of their lives, Mark, Simon and Andrew Mariotta moved the grand opening forward. Father Lawrence was thankful but it meant that they had to push their already overworked crews to work even harder to meet the accelerated schedule.

It was a beautiful spring day in late March, and the Mariotta brothers could not have been blessed with better weather for their grand opening. The temperature was a perfect seventy-seven degrees with plenty of sunshine. Everything that could bloom in Las Vegas had decided that this was the time to do it. In the deserts outside of town, wildflowers of every kind burst out of the brown desert dirt in brilliant colors and subtle fragrances. Wild sage and prickly pear cactus were in full bloom and vast expanses of delicate flowers blanketed the desert floor. Not to be outdone by Mother Nature, Las Vegas had prepared itself for spring in the carefully cultivated landscapes and gardens that erupted with colorful flowers, blossoming in every shape and size. Spring was a time for new life and hope for the future. It was an interesting juxtaposition. Just as the seemingly barren desert floor was now bursting with the promise of rebirth, so too was the opening of Three Brothers Poker Palace promising the hope of renewal to a long-neglected district of Las Vegas.

Meanwhile, the town pulsed with curiosity over the new downtown casino attraction. For the Las Vegan resident, the big casinos on the strip were places they religiously avoided unless they had out-of-town guests to entertain. But there was something different about what the Mariotta brothers were bringing to their city that they were determined to support. Casual citizens followed the casino's progress closely; some even marked their calendars so they were sure not to miss all the grand opening excitement.

Two Las Vegans in particular couldn't wait for the grand opening. Roy and his new bride Nadine invited Leroy and Mindy to join them. Roy had not spoken to Mindy and Leroy since the dance competition and he and Nadine had a few surprises for them. It would be fun to see their reaction.

As Roy and Nadine passed through the Poker Palace's front door and stepped into the lobby, they had the sense of entering something comfortably familiar yet compelled to explore every room to find its hidden surprises. The Mariotta brothers had used ornate nineteenth-century furnishings but had finished them with modern technology. For example, the massive chandelier with leaded crystal drop beads was lit by LEDs and contained a hidden high-resolution surveillance camera.

With awe in her eyes, Nadine took it all in. It was an upscale casino with a historical bent. There were replicas of old U.S. maps and rooms filled with antique furniture and artwork filled every room. In one sense it felt like a museum but with a twist to it. The design was an eclectic mix of the old west and the modern. It was all tastefully done, and somehow the Mariotta brothers succeeded in melding the past and present into one very consistent and compelling space.

In the corner of the lobby stood a huge, fully-restored grandfather clock that was certified to be the same clock that had stood in the entrance to the Dodge House during Wyatt Earp's time in Dodge City, Kansas. Manufactured in Philadelphia and shipped west by steam engine, it personified American history and certainly deserved museum status. The vintage pool tables, made from exotic woods, were meticulously restored to reveal intricate ebony, walnut, and maple inlays of unparalleled craftsmanship, wide rails, and woven leather pockets. These beautiful tables sat on heavy iron legs cast in the form of lion heads. Placed inside each of the three bars, the tables completed the scene. It was hard not to imagine that you had stepped through the swinging doors of an old west saloon.

In the largest of the card rooms, the brothers Mariotta replicated the flamboyant Victorian grandeur of the late nineteenth-century saloon halls found only in bigger cities like San Francisco, Denver, or New York. Intricately etched mirrors lined the wall behind the solid, hardwood bar, and gold-fringed royal blue drapery was drawn to expose the massive oak wall panels covering the rest of the room. Around the perimeter of the large hall, the floor was covered with a carpet of complex, woven oriental designs. The carpet gave way to a checkerboard floor of beautifully veined black-and-white marble in the center of the room. Distributed throughout were vintage leather wingback chairs with hand-carved, Brittany oak legs. When stepping through the doors into the Three Brothers Poker Palace, you were immediately taken back to a time long-past where strangely enough, you felt quite at home.

For the grand opening, long fancy tables had been set up in various spots around the casino and loaded with a smorgasbord of impressive hors d'oeuvres. But what wowed the guests was the astounding assortment of cakes set before them. Behind each table was a pretty hostess who was there to serve guests the slice of their choice. The cakes looked fabulous. But unlike most catered cakes that never taste as good as they look, these cakes were delicious. There were five-layer chocolate decadence cakes, red velvet cakes, and lemon and coconut cakes, not to mention the carrot cake supreme and Black Forest cakes. It was enough to tempt even the most conscientious diabetic. As expected, these were the most popular tables in the house. Throughout the night, lines of guests waited to dig into their first, second, and third helpings of the delicious confections.

It seemed the Mariottas had invited the entire world. Famous opera singers from Italy arrived ready to perform their signature arias for the more high-browed guests. The opera singers had been Hank's idea.

Hank Mariotta felt it important to acknowledge their family's Italian roots and had an idea for doing that at the grand opening. But since his agreement with the NFL commissioner prevented him from directly engaging in casino operations, Hank had been careful how he let his sons know what he wanted.

One evening over dinner with his sons, he began musing aloud, "You know who I would pay good money to see perform on your grand saloon stage?"

His sons looked at him, curiously and waited for their father to continue. Mark smiled to himself. This was the way their father got involved with their business without actually getting involved. Simon asked, "What's that, Dad?"

"Opera!" Hank announced.

Andrew, taken by surprise at the suggestion, began choking on a piece of his steak. Mark and Simon glanced at one another incredulously. Again, it was Simon who spoke. "Uhhh. Okay, Dad! Opera?"

Hank smiled. "I can think of no better way to pay homage to our Italian ancestors than to see the two biggest names in opera, Georgio Tucci and Alfredo Antoniotti, perform on that magnificent stage." Again, the brothers looked at one another dubiously.

There had been no more talk of opera that evening, but on opening night Georgio Tucci took the stage to sing "Habanera," one of the most famous arias from the 1875 opera *Carmen* only to be followed by Alfredo Antoniotti sporting a shiny, waxed black mustache that curled up to his cheeks. Alfredo sang Hank Mariotta's favorite song "Ava Maria."

VIP luminaries and invited guests began to arrive later. One in particular, was the mayor of Las Vegas Gwendolyn Sussman. After greeting the Mariottas, Gwendolyn spent the rest of the night standing in line for yet another slice of cake to shovel into her face. It appeared she was wearing the cakes as many of the crumbs were clinging to the collar of her dress. A few other local politicians in attendance kept busy, glad-handing every local constituent they found. Hank's friends, CEOs, and board members from numerous Fortune 500 companies came over to extend their best wishes for success in Hank's new venture.

A young billionaire CEO from a well-known internet company stepped out of a stretch limo wearing flip-flops and ripped cargo shorts. He approached Hank and began pitching what he saw as a mutually beneficial opportunity for their companies. But almost immediately, he started bragging about himself and the great success he'd made of himself and his company. While it was true that he ran one of the most popular social networking sites in the world, the man-boy also had a reputation for being the consummate bore. It seemed that his goal in every conversation was to leave the person he was talking with as impressed with the wunderkind as the wunderkind was with himself. But rather than being impressed, his victims were more likely to be relieved to escape the wunderkind's inane prattle.

As the boy CEO babbled on about himself, Hank was desperate to make his escape. Claiming he had to attend to some details in the control room, Hank politely excused himself and left the young CEO standing alone. Oblivious to Hank's abrupt departure, the wunderkind turned to shake hands with anyone who came within his reach like a politician campaigning for office. He corralled the first hapless couple that happened to pass by.

As the couple tried to move past, the boy CEO grabbed the man's shoulder, held it with a tight grip, and, with a car salesman's smile, declared, "Hi. I'm Chipper Stone. CEO of Get Connected. But you undoubtedly already recognized me. I bet you never thought in your wildest dreams you'd be shaking hands with a laidback CEO like me. Yep, that's exactly how I conduct business too. If you work for me, you can come into work in your swimsuit, for all I care. Just as long as you get your work done!"

Unimpressed, the man twisted himself out of the boy's grip and stared annoyingly at the CEO. "Well, my name is Leroy and I am the CEO of Maxi the Taxi Company! And I bet meeting a tycoon like me is just about the highlight of your punk-ass life. I just got only one rule too – if you get in the back of my cab, you damn better have the money to pay your fare when you get out, or you're gonna get a nose full of Glock." The stupid grin on the boy CEO's face never left as Leroy demanded, "Now, let my date and me pass. You're standing between me and the bar and anyone who knows me, knows that's not a safe place to be, especially when the first drink is on the house." But the pesky little CEO wouldn't budge and continued to brag about himself.

Mindy could see that Leroy had had enough and was just about to shut the guy up with his fist. She stepped in quickly and began to verbally pummel the CEO. "Why don't you find someone else to bother? And I've got a news flash for you, soy boy! Nobody trusts you or your stupid company! You're both phony! Just like those phony holes in your shorts." The irritating grin along with a little bit of color disappeared from the boy CEO's face and he sheepishly stepped aside. As Mindy and Leroy headed toward the bar to get their free drinks, Mindy sang, "Free is good and free is for me."

At the bar, she exchanged her drink voucher for a Tequila Sunrise while Leroy traded his for a Shiner Bock. As they began looking for a place to sit, Nadine and Roy waved them over to their table. They hadn't seen one another since the dance contest, so there was a lot for them to catch up on. Roy and Leroy immediately started talking football, almost to the point of arguing whether the Antelopes could make it to the Super Bowl next season.

Mindy noticed Nadine smiling coyly, conspicuously drumming the fingers of her left hand on the table top. It took only a moment for Mindy to spot the gold wedding band. She looked at Nadine and squealed excitedly, "Nadine! Really?" Nadine smiled and shook her head yes. Mindy screamed again, and they hugged. Then Mindy looked at her and asked gravely, "Nadine, you didn't have to, did you?"

Leroy quickly figured out what the girls were screaming about and congratulated Roy by slapping him on his back. "Congratulations, Roy. Does this mean there's a baby Roy-boy bakin' in the oven?"

Roy and Nadine laughed, and Nadine said, "Not yet. Someday maybe." Mindy pulled her chair close to Nadine to hear all the details ignoring everyone except Nadine.

While Nadine recounted the proposal and marriage, Roy leaned on an elbow and nodded to his friend and told him that he had some huge news for him. "Leroy, do you remember when I said if you got me and Mindy back dancing, I'd make you a partner in my new business?" Roy was hoping that Leroy hadn't taken their agreement seriously, but felt obligated to see what would dribble out of the man's mouth.

"Yeah, boy! I've been meaning to talk to you about that. Hell, kiss off the Wild Bill. That was nothing but a screw job, but you got to admit that shirt of yours didn't do you any favors. What a doozy, dude!"

Roy laughed. "Yeah, I know. I swab the can out with it now. But listen, I've got to tell you something. Nadine..."

Nadine cut away from Mindy to interrupt Roy. "Listen, I bought you all a great big space for your new club and it's just a quick walk from here." Her eyes sparkled as she explained, "This part of town is where all the action is right now. And it's big. Plenty of room for people to dance their tushies off. I'm not kidding." Nadine spread her arms wide to emphasize the point and Roy swore he saw Nadine's ears move back to make room for her broad smile.

Usually Leroy was quick on the uptake, but this time he was confused. "Are you telling us that you bought us a place? You bought Roy and me a place?" He repeated himself as if he was trying to make sure he understood. Nadine nodded. "Well, boy howdy, this must be my lucky day! I always knew you had some loot stashed away. I mean, you don't stay at The Carrington for months on end and trip around in a Ferrari chariot if you don't have yourself a big bank."

As much for Roy's benefit as it was for Leroy's, Nadine added, "Look, I do have some money and this is something I want to do for all of you. I'll be your banker and lease the space to you and loan you whatever you need to get the doors open, but it's up to you to make it work. I bet it will be a big success. Just call me 'Money Bags' Nadine."

Roy fidgeted uneasily at the "Money Bags" moniker.

Mindy blurted out, "And to think I tried to kill you in that catfight. Now I think I love you, Nadine!" She reached over and gave Nadine a hug that about knocked them both out of their chairs.

Leroy offered to buy a round of drinks to celebrate. Roy suggested they go over to the new Dino's Diner after the premiere and cap the evening with some good eats.

Just a few days before, Roy had run into David Methoapolis at the checkout counter at the CVS pharmacy. David recognized Roy and told him that he'd taken Roy's advice and officially renamed his restaurant "Dino's Diner" and it was now open for business. David reminded Roy that he still owed him a dinner and promised, "I'll make you and your friends a dinner you'll never forget. And you're going to like the diner's new digs." David paid the cashier and, as he left the store, told Roy, "It was good to see you again. Come by soon to check us out!" Roy laughed to himself; David sounded like he was doing a television commercial. But he was flattered the owner had taken his advice and renamed the restaurant to Dino's.

The new business partners Roy and Nadine and Leroy and Mindy began to jovially feel the effects of their celebrating. Leroy had long since made good on his offer to buy their second round. And now, with their glasses again empty, Nadine ordered three magnums of Dom Perignon Rose 2002 at $319.00 a cork.

Mindy began gulping it as soon as the sommelier filled her glass and held it out for a refill before he had finished pouring champagne for the others. She noticed that after taking a few skeptical sips, Leroy and Roy both pushed their glasses to the center of the table and resumed drinking their Shiner Bocks. Mindy reached for the nearly full glasses of champagne and proclaimed, "It looks like these poor orphans need to find a home. And I know just the place." She pulled the glasses in front of her and quickly drained them empty. Rubbing her stomach, she announced proudly, "There! Now these poor abandoned children have found a loving home – in my stomach."

Struggling to her feet, Mindy began to make a speech. "Attention everyone! I have something to say. I think my honey here, Leroy, needs to get his hack license so he can start driving legal here in Vegas. He's been riding people around under the radar and I don't want him to get busted. He needs to get real. I don't care. He can still run a dance hall and drive a taxi. And you never..." Mindy hiccupped. "There's always a chance the dance hall could flop. I mean, I'm not trying to be negative, but you never know." She hiccupped once more and then poured herself another glass of champagne.

Leroy admitted, "Yeah, that's an itch I've wanted to scratch," and promised he'd get legal and make an honest woman out of Maxi the Taxi. Roy stood and, holding his bottle of Shiner in the air, offered a toast, "To Leroy getting legal! It's about damn time!" Brown beer bottles and yellow-stemmed crystal champagne flutes clanged and together they chorused, "To Leroy getting legal."

Everything was falling into place.

BROTHERS 12 LOUNGE

The Mariotta brothers had booked The Thrillers to open the Brothers 12 Lounge. It was a win-win deal for both of them. The Thrillers were building a reputation for themselves around the city. And after being asked to headline the grand opening of the most celebrated event of the year, their standing as the hottest local act in town had been solidified.

As for the Mariotta brothers, they were confident they had booked the kind of local talent that could help establish the reputation they wanted for the Brothers 12 Lounge. They wanted to create a destination for permanent Las Vegans who sought an edgy club a cut above the average tourist fare.

Hank Mariotta had suggested they name the stage and dance floor after his twelve sons. He was not supposed to be involved, but he couldn't help himself on that matter. Mariotta could not have wished for more loyal and devoted sons and so had suggested the simple name of "12 Brothers." Despite some initial reluctance, the brothers ultimately relented and the Brothers 12 Lounge was born. Hank Mariotta approved and smiled proudly.

All of the Mariotta boys lived in Mariottaville. Seven of them were involved with the Antelopes franchise in some capacity. Except for Luke, all of them had built their homes around the lake in Mariottaville. Still single, Luke was a physician for the Antelopes and resided in the large ranch house with Christianna and Hank.

Christianna's brother, Matthew, was the one who had first seen The Thrillers at the Wild Bill Hickok. Afterward, when it had come to talking about the band, Matthew was never short with accolades. "The two female singers have great voices and, believe me, they are *good*. I think I want to marry the one with the hippie skirt and long wavy hair." Matthew didn't know her name and, of course, he was kidding about the marriage bit. But he did want to meet her and had decided the best way to do that was to book them to play the grand opening of Three Brothers Poker Palace. She had consumed his thoughts for some time and he hoped tonight would be the night he would finally get to meet her.

The Thrillers began working on creating original material. With their growing notoriety, they had become emboldened to sneak an original song or two into their sets at the Wild Bill. They were all quite good and each contributed original material, particularly Becky Dean. Recovering from her Delinda Delgado days, Becky Dean had learned the futility of copying another musician's style and had since begun to embrace her own creativity.

She loved songwriting and felt it was one of her most significant contributions to the band. Composing music transported Becky Dean into a different world. She loved laboring over the entire songwriting process. There was the challenge of writing a lyric and discovering the perfect melody for it and vice-versa. It was like popping in the last piece of a complicated jigsaw puzzle – there was only one way to make it work. Then, when the song was ready, she played it for the band on her acoustic guitar, hearing it grow into a song with Lee's bass lines, Basil's rhythms, and Lee's guitar solos as she harmonized with Isabella. It was hard work, but when the time came for the band to debut her song in front of a live audience, Becky Dean savored the moment. She couldn't wait for the audience's reaction.

THE RED CARPET

It was around nine p.m. when the long, black limousines began to pull up alongside the red carpet that had been rolled out to welcome the Mariotta brothers' special guests. VIPs dressed in black tie and evening gowns emerged from their chauffeured limos to the applause of the crowds gathered on both sides of the velvet rope line. Many strolling up the red carpet to the casino were unknown to most in watching from the spectator side of the rope line. Still, they politely applauded each one of them. Waiting at the end of the carpet was John. With microphone in hand, cameraman behind him, and connected to his producer in the broadcast room via wireless ear plug, he was there to interview the poker luminaries on their way into the Poker Palace.

As instructed by his producer, John let several well-dressed couples pass before an excited voice screamed into his headset, "John. Manuel Borgata is coming your way. Get him!" It was the first interview for Hank Mariotta's infant channel and it was about to be John's first live interview. Looking toward the street, John found the flamboyant Manuel Borgata. Dressed in black tails and sporting a large black Bolero, Borgata was slowly making his way up the red carpet with the help of a long, silver skull-topped cane to the cheers of the appreciative crowd. Manuel Borgata was one of the most famous poker players on the World Poker Tour. He was a stealthy card player who often annoyed his opponents with his incessant chatter, an obvious ploy to distract their attention from his play.

But John also knew Manuel Borgata personally. Several months earlier, Hank Mariotta had called John into an important meeting at his hotel suite. When John arrived, he met a man with a sophisticated air about him sitting comfortably in a wingback chair tossing a skull-topped cane between his hands. Hank had introduced him to John. "John, this is Manuel Borgata. He's going to teach you how to play poker."

Needing no introduction, John had flattered Borgata by telling him that he was his poker idol. "It's an honor, Mr. Borgata. I've followed your plays and studied your every hand." Once again Hank Mariotta surprised John. Hank had promised to get John a poker tutor, but John had never imagined that his teacher would be Manuel Borgata. Hank was keeping his promises to invest in John's future. Only weeks earlier, Hank had given John the tuition to enroll in some key communications classes at UNLV. John was humbled and appreciative especially now that Hank had kept his word to provide him a poker tutor. Now, more than ever, John was determined not to disappoint Mr. Mariotta.

As a teacher, Borgata had been impatient and demanding. But just the same, he treated John as his protégé. And John had not disappointed. He was a quick study and had soon learned more about playing good poker in one session with Manuel Borgata than he ever had in playing hundreds of hands with his poker posse.

As Manuel Borgata made his way toward the Palace's doors, John cornered the celebrity. "Mr. Borgata, can I have a word with you? Tell me, what do you think this opening of the Mariotta Brothers Poker Palace, as well as the launching of our new poker network, will do for the game of poker?"

"Of course, John. I'm glad to see you. I think the Mariotta Brothers Poker Palace will become the epicenter of the world of poker. Poker is a game of skill and strategy and the fun thing about poker is that every hand is a game to itself. And when it's over, you just might come out with a pile of money. No one is carrying you off the field on a stretcher. It's the kind of game you can play anywhere, and people have for over a hundred years. But it never really had a proper headquarters, and I think this venue will rectify that unfortunate oversight."

The producer screamed into John's ear, "Perfect. That was great. Now let's move inside and set up to cover the tables." John thanked Manuel Borgata for his insight and quickly moved inside to the main lobby. His assignment for the night was to roam the casino and conduct interviews with all the well-known players he encountered. The producer knew what celebrities were in attendance and where they were in the building. All John had to do was follow his direction and shove the microphone in his targets' faces.

But John also knew that this was his first chance to prove to Hank Mariotta that his faith in him had not been misplaced. He was already off to a good start with his brief interview with Manuel Borgata, but there was a long night still ahead before he could sign off. The grand opening was a live broadcast. He knew that even a slight mistake could blight the network's image. So, if something was to go wrong, John was determined not to be the cause of it.

Directed by the producer to cover the Ante Room, John made his way to another well-known player, Justin Tully, who was joking with a group of friends. As Tully raucously laughed, John rushed up to him, microphone in hand and cameraman in tow. "Mr. Tully, I'm with the Mariotta Poker Channel. Tell us, what is it about you that lets you win the big tournaments?"

Tully looked at John and then the camera. With his big brown eyes, he played coy for the cameras. "Cuz I can bluff your mama!" He laughed and then added, "No, it's more like I'm dragging a lot of years behind me. When I was coming up, I played every game under the sun. I had to chew on it and learn my ABCs." That was a wrap and John thanked Justin Tully.

Moving on with his cameraman in search of another celebrity to interview, John turned a corner and walked right into the ample breasts of fame babe Ava Allende. He recognized Ava from the first and only poker tournament he'd entered at the Doc Holiday Poker Parlor. It was impossible not to notice her in her tight dress that left nothing to the imagination. The transparent see-through material exposed all of her treasures except for the coverage of a well-filled black bikini bottom. This was what Ava did, and as John pulled his head out of her cleavage, he couldn't help but stare. Anticipating an interview, Ava put on a seductive pose and John asked his producer through his headset, "Do you want Miss Ava?"

The producer responded, "Hell yeah! But don't bother interviewing her." John laughed and stepped around a surprised Ava.

As he waited for instructions from his producer, he struggled to regain his composure. Ava had caused quite a sensation. Men were having difficulty concentrating on their cards and women couldn't help but glare at the scantily-clad woman who was famous only for being famous. Ava strutted her assets back and forth through the room, now and then twirling to give her audience the full view. John took a deep breath and willed himself past the alluring distraction and the carnage she left in her path.

With his cameraman trailing him, John wandered into another room and came across one of poker's most entertaining players. He was a spindly Texan known for his prowess and his familiar ten-gallon hat with a ten-mile brim and a twenty-mile wide smile. Sitting at a nearby table that was dealing Texas Hold'em, he shouted over to John, "How is y'all doing on this fine first day? This place is great. I'm getting a good feeling about being here and I'm honored that you'd pick me to jaw with." Bubba Devereaux was his name and from the start, Bubba was the one in control of the interview. Bubba loved cameras, particularly when they were pointed at him. He always had, and this made things easy for John.

John signaled his cameraman to roll and began, "Ladies and gentlemen, I'm talking with poker legend Bubba Devereaux and I'm going ask him his secret for always calling with the winning hand. Mr.

Devereaux, you've won at least three world championships. You're amazing! How do you do it?"

Devereaux grabbed John's mic and turned toward the camera. Letting a smile engulf his face, he told the audience, "It's all because of my dang-good looks. I got a face so pretty that it should be on every one of the dadgum cards. Players get all flustered playing with someone as purdy as me and I ain't kidding." He ended with a wink to the camera. Bubba was a card, just like the cards he played with. That was his secret. His disarming charm and skillful play proved lethal to his opponents. More often than not, they left the table completely broke. But you had to hand it to Bubba – he managed to keep them laughing, even while he slid all of their chips into his stack.

The producer told John to stand down for a while as they cut to a commercial and switched coverage to the lobby to cover the VIPs who were walking down the red carpet at an increased pace. But before he went silent, John heard the producer say through his earpiece, "Good stuff, John!"

Hank Mariotta's new poker channel was broadcasting and so far, so good. Some directors had argued against giving John such a prominent assignment on the network's debut broadcast. After all, he had never been in front of a television camera in his entire life. If he froze, it would be a disaster. But Hank Mariotta had insisted that John fit the demographic the network wanted to target. In the end though, he had agreed to make John available for countless rehearsals and private coaching sessions. The fact that John had landed such a plum assignment attested to Hank Mariotta's unfailing instincts, not to mention John's natural talent.

The cameras were now trained outside the casino on the entourage making its way up the red carpet. They were some of NFL's most exceptional players, Hank Mariotta's San Antonio Antelopes. The procession was led by wide receiver "Velcro Fingers" J.C. Stewart. Alongside him was GM Lou Danner. The two were heavily engaged in conversation and barely acknowledged the cheering crowd. Following them was Coach Curt Coby and Rookie of the Year, tight end Darius Michaels. Behind them trailed a group of beautiful women assumed to be the wives, girlfriends, and, for the cynics in the crowd, the paid escorts of the players.

Then Paul Mariotta, the assistant defensive line coach marched past with his eight brothers. The crowd was enthusiastic, but the big question remained, "Where was Rebel Rebenack?" He had become a national sensation of sorts after the illegal hit that took him out of the playoff game. Nearly every sports commentator agreed that had it not been for that hit, the Antelopes would have made it to the Super Bowl and very likely would have won. The rumor making its way through the crowd was that Rebel was dating Mariotta's reclusive and beautiful daughter. Would she be there? Christiana herself was an enigma. The only picture anyone had ever seen of her was a freeze-framed shot from the jumbotron many months before.

Behind the Mariotta brothers came the Antelopes' secret weapon, their game-saving placekicker Edmond Gerry. Gerry was an incredible talent. During the past two seasons, he had led the NFL in field goals beyond forty yards and his ninety-percent success rate was impressive. Gerry also held the NFL record for completing sixty-five consecutive field goal attempts. Hank Mariotta paid the man well. Gerry's salary averaged more than $100,000 each time he kicked a football. But Edmond Gerry was worth every penny of it to the Antelopes.

Off the field, Edmond Gerry gave freely of his time and money to help with a variety of worthy charities. He was highly respected by both his teammates and his community for his tireless philanthropy. His wife, however, did not share her husband's generosity.

Shay Gerry held onto her husband's arm as they walked down the red velvet carpet. Adorned with a stunning diamond heart necklace and white gold bracelets, Shay sparkled under the lights and had achieved a modicum of fame for herself in a short-lived reality television show playing the part of a conniving gold digger "Shay Elegant." She had a reputation of being a temperamental diva and those who knew her were not surprised when she refused to be involved in any of Edmond's many philanthropic causes.

Shay's indifference was a festering wound to Edmund and he had confided to a close friend that he feared he had made a horrible mistake marrying her. But his friend had committed the ultimate betrayal and leaked Gerry's confession to the media. The next morning, the lead story on all the sports stations had been that the marriage of newlyweds Edmond Gerry and his reality-show wife was on rocky ground. The public disclosure caused him untold anguish. It was an accepted fact that their divorce was only a matter of time.

The procession of prominent sports stars stepping down the red carpet finally came to a rousing culmination when Bruce Rebenack emerged from a long black limousine. He acknowledged the crowd's applause and then turned to help his guest out of the limo. An elegant arm reached out to grab Rebel's hand and suddenly there stood the enigmatic Christianna Mariotta. She was stunning and the crowd went quiet as all eyes gaped at the royal pair. Standing arm in arm, these two had to be the most aesthetically perfect couple on the planet. As they made their way down the red carpet, Christianna did not make eye contact with the audience but smiled shyly. Still, now and then she would wave to the adoring crowd.

Bruce Rebenack, on the other hand, was used to being in front of screaming crowds. He welcomed the cheers as he smiled and waved. Giving the thumbs up, he told the fans that he was interested in playing a few rounds of poker. "I think I've got a chance of winning." He squeezed Christianna and said, "I brought along my lucky charm."

They did make a beautiful couple.

THE FORBIDDEN CITY

As they entered the lobby of her brothers' Poker Palace, Christianna became unnerved by the commotion and told Rebel that she wanted to be alone for a bit. Rebel seemed to understand and led Christianna through the doors of the first room he could find. As it happened, they stepped into the small chapel her brothers had built for Father Lawrence. Rebel closed the heavy doors behind them and with the snap of the latch, the din and commotion of the lobby disappeared leaving the couple alone in complete silence. Christianna genuflected before the gold sacristy while Rebel stood beside her. When she got up, she smiled and kissed Rebel. "I just need to catch my breath for a moment. All this hoopla is overwhelming for a poor country girl like me." Rebel laughed and hugged her tightly.

After her father had come around to accepting that his only daughter was now an adult, he no longer objected to Bruce Rebenack dating Christianna. Without her father's tight grip to slow them down, the bond between Christianna and Rebel quickly developed into something more than just a trivial romance. Not long after, Rebel asked Christianna to marry him. She had thrown her arms around him screaming, "Yes! Yes! Yes!" That had been nearly two months ago and Christianna was still floating in a blissful haze where all she could see was Rebel. The date was set and their wedding day was now just three weeks away, and neither one of them could think about anything else.

When Christianna was young, her father would take his family to some exotic destination for Christmas, the most memorable of which was their trip to China. The family had walked on the Great Wall of China, toured the Forbidden City, and walked around Tiananmen Square in Beijing. They had floated down the Li River on bamboo rafts beneath the beguiling karst mountains of Guilin. They had celebrated Christmas in Shanghai by walking around the Shanghai World Financial Center and being dazzled by the Yu Garden in the Old City. There had been ponds and towers and magnificent gardens. The Mariotta kids looked forward to these vacations, and whether Hank intended their excursions to be educational or recreational, they were always fun and something that none of them ever forgot.

When Rebel had asked her where she wanted to honeymoon, Christianna had thought back on her childhood trip to China. But after recalling another Christmas vacation favorite, she had decided that she wanted to honeymoon at an exclusive resort on the island of Saint John in the U.S. Virgin Islands.

Two-thirds of Saint John remained untouched and preserved as a National Park. The resort was on the undeveloped side of the island and was very private and secluded, reachable only via the resort's private launch. Christianna had fallen in love with that island paradise and had never forgot the beautiful empty beaches and wildlife preserves.

Once composed and mentally prepared to face the bustle of the crowded casino, Christianna was ready. She looked up at Rebel and said, "Let's go see The Thrillers and check out Matthew's new infatuation."

As they left the chapel, an announcement came over the PA system explaining that Father Lawrence was going to bless the grand opening of the Mariotta Brothers' Poker Palace in fifteen minutes in the Father Lawrence Lobby. Bruce kissed Christiana on her cheek and told her they could get to The Thrillers after the blessing. "After all, they were going to play for four more hours."

The "Saint Lawrence Lobby." That's what the Mariotta brothers initially wanted to call the grand entrance to their casino. They had named it to honor the priest who had been so much a part of their lives for as long as they could remember. Of course, this honor had flattered Father Lawrence but embarrassed him all the same time. Guilt-ridden, he did not want to be exalted in any way. No matter what the Mariottas thought of him, he was not a saint, especially when compared to the real Saint Lawrence of Rome.

As a disciple of Jesus Christ, Father Lawrence lived by the rule that God must come first before anything else. And that he, Lawrence, must be last. More importantly, however, Father Lawrence felt that using his name only served to glorify himself and not God.

Yet, despite his vigorous protestations, the Mariotta family insisted on giving him this honor. They would not take "no" for an answer. The only concession Father Lawrence had been able to negotiate was naming it the "Father Lawrence Lobby" instead of the "Saint Lawrence Lobby." This was important to the priest. The Mariottas had reluctantly agreed to it, though in their minds he was already a saint.

THE AMBROSE

The liquor was flowing freely at the grand opening of the Three Brothers' Poker Palace. The Mariotta brothers were staggered at the number of people who were there. They all agreed that if their first day in business was any predictor of the future, then they were embarking on a venture that was assured of many successful years to come.

David Matthopolous was just one of the many locals who had come to be a part of the gala event. Roaming the various rooms and enjoying the atmosphere, he was impressed by the transformation the Mariottas had accomplished. They had turned a drab, concrete-block warehouse that used to house a slot machine parlor into a classy destination which Matthopolous looked forward to returning to when he had more time to enjoy himself. But before returning to his restaurant, David Matthopolous had a free drink voucher that required redemption.

He entered a room with a stately and formal atmosphere named the Ambrose where Roy, Nadine, Leroy, and Mindy were partying.

Most of the people in the lounge had already consumed enough alcohol to fail a field sobriety test and were not behaving in a manner fitting the decor of the Ambrose. For a moment, David took in the crowd before noticing the foursome. It seemed Mindy was working through her third bottle of champagne. Shortly, she staggered to the ladies' room. When she returned, her heel snagged the corner of a Persian rug and she went tumbling, nearly missing a waiter carrying a tray full of drinks.

The waiter wasn't pleased and was about to flag security when Mindy picked herself up from the floor and began to berate him, blaming him for the mishap. "Why don't you watch where you're going? You're lucky I wasn't hurt. And what's the idea of these rugs just lurking on the floor waiting to trip someone? Screw you and your fricking rugs. You're lucky I don't sue you." The waiter looked perturbed and rushed off to deliver his drinks.

Exchanging his ticket for a Scotch on the rocks, David heard someone call his name and turned to see Roy motioning him over. Happy to see someone he knew, David found an empty chair and pulled it up to Roy's table. Relaxing, he sucked his whiskey down so fast his cheeks puckered inward. Grabbing the arm of a waitress walking past him, David ordered another.

A few minutes later, David's drink was delivered by the same waiter Mindy had almost knocked down. He looked frightened when

Mindy recognized him and started in on how he had deliberately tried to trip her. By now, Leroy was feeling generous and threw a twenty-dollar bill on the intimidated waiter's tray. "Don't worry, brother. She's just drunk. Don't pay her any mind. Now take the damn money and I don't want to see your ugly mug back at our table anymore." Leroy gave the wimpy waiter a threatening look and added, "Or dude, I might just have to drop a can of whoop ass on ya."

Debating whether he made the right choice sitting down at Roy's table, David gave Roy a look like perhaps he should move on. One thing was for sure – David had some catching up to do in terms of drinking. He stood to leave, but Roy offering to buy him another drink, convinced him to stay and enjoy the party.

Even Nadine had gotten into the party spirit. David counted three paper toy umbrellas lying on the table alongside Nadine's half-empty strawberry daiquiris. Nadine swirled her drink; David figured she was working on her fourth. Eventually, Nadine drooped her head on Roy's shoulder and told him she needed to talk with Hank Mariotta about "a little something." When he asked her what about, Nadine said, "I know I may be a little bit bombed, but I want to buy into his station and become his partner!" Nadine stood suddenly and declared, "Where's Mariotta? He needs me. He needs a partner! He needs me! I've got to find him." She was tottering.

Roy tried to calm his new wife down. Holding her arm, he told a wobbly Nadine, "Didn't you hear the announcement? Mariotta is at the blessing in the front lobby. This is no time to talk with him. You're high as a kite. Wait 'til later to talk to him." For the time being, he was able to restrain Nadine, and he helped her sit back in her chair.

Seeing a way out, David Matthopolous shouted, "Did someone say a blessing? Where? I'm done here. See you all later!"

All of them answered him at the same time as if they were in a chorus. "It's going on in the Father Lawrence Lobby."

THE PEOPLE'S PARKING LOT

Though still feeling a bit queasy from his bout with ptomaine, Rip Rumple felt strong enough to attend his friend Hank Mariotta's launch of his new poker network. He asked Lucy to accompany him to the gala as long as she felt up to it.

He and Lucy had both spent two days at Desert Valley Hospital for treatment. Lucy had suffered the worst of it; Rip felt responsible for the torment she experienced. He demanded Lucy be given the best care possible and insisted on adjoining rooms. That way Rip was sure she received the attention she needed and this gave him the excuse he needed to look in on Lucy, which he did constantly. That first night, Rip stayed by her bedside all night long and by the time they were released from the hospital, their shared ordeal had transformed into a blossoming relationship.

Rip automatically assumed Lloyd would be on duty to chauffeur Lucy and him to the grand opening celebration. But when Lloyd unexpectedly asked for several days off to attend to some personal business, Rip was forced to change his transportation plans. "Mr. Rumple, it is my mother's seventy-fifth birthday and my brother, sister, and I are going to throw her a party."

Rip understood that being there for his mother was important to Lloyd and told him to take whatever time he needed and to enjoy himself thoroughly. Tonight, Rip would be his own chauffeur.

Because of his narcolepsy, he rarely drove himself but instead relied on Lloyd to transport him around town in the luxury of his stretch limousine. Rip loved his car. It was a home on wheels complete with television, Wi-Fi, plush leather chairs, and a well-stocked bar and humidor. He felt safe and comfortable and with Lloyd behind the steering wheel, Rip barely knew when they were moving. But Rip did drive on occasion and tonight would be one of those occasions.

Lloyd's absence gave Rip the excuse he needed to take his new Cadillac Ciel out for a ride on the town. The Ciel was a luxury concept-car Rip had seen on display at the Las Vegas Auto Show. It wasn't in production yet, but Rip had fallen in love with it the moment he saw it; he had to have one. Being a billionaire had its advantages so Rip had called in a few favors from his pals at GM. And now, long before the Ciel was scheduled to roll off the assembly line, Rip was admiring his new baby sparkling under the lights of his four-thousand-square-foot private garage. He was an avid collector and had built up an impressive collection of automobiles. Of the thirty or so cars in his stable, the Bugatti Chiron and the row of fully restored vintage Corvettes were the stars of his collection.

It was about eight-thirty when Rip got into the Ciel to pick up Lucy. Adjusting his seat, he looked over the controls and pressed the ignition button. Being a hybrid, the car's engine barely made a sound. Rip maneuvered out of the garage and onto the street heading toward Lucy's apartment. As he drove through the gates and into the parking lot of Lucy's apartment complex, he laughed at the bizarre sign on the gate. It read "Welcome to the People's Parking Lot." Below that, some enterprising graffiti artist had painted a hammer and sickle. Rip felt like he was crossing the Iron Curtain.

Despite their bumpy beginning, Lucy was fond of Rip and was excited about her first real date with him. She thought about those two days in the hospital. Rip had never left her bedside and together they had watched old movies late into the night. They had talked about seemingly everything. Lucy found Rip to be charming, intelligent, and unpretentious despite his billions. But Rip knew a lot of successful people and she fretted about meeting his rich and famous friends. Lucy worried about what she would say to them.

There was a knock on the door and with a smile, Lucy opened it to find Rip standing there. "Hello, my darling. Are you ready? We have a party to attend." Rip was dressed in a fine-tailored black-tie suit by Yves Saint. He personified class and sophistication. Helping her slide into a white silk coat, Rip Rumple opened the door for Lucy and they walked arm-in-arm to his Cadillac. Ever the gentleman, Rip knew just what to say. "My dear, you are a vision tonight."

Lucy found the Cadillac a dream ride and told Rip so. He seemed pleased that she appreciated it and said, "It drives even better than it looks." When they arrived in front of the Poker Palace, Rip pulled up to the red carpet. He looked over at Lucy and explained, "I'm sorry, my darling nurse, but I need to drop you off here while I park the car. The only person besides myself I would trust to drive it is Lloyd. I certainly cannot leave it in the hands of a valet. If you only knew the strings I had to pull to get this model, you would understand. I will join you soon, my lovebird. I promise."

Lucy gave Rip's hand a squeeze and said warmly, "Don't worry, dear Rip. I'll be waiting for you in the lobby."

FATHER LAWRENCE LOBBY

Father Lawrence stepped onto the riser that had become the makeshift altar where he would conduct the brief blessing ceremony. To his surprise, a large crowd had gathered and he quieted them down by announcing, "The Lord be with you!"

The Mariotta family stood in front of him and responded, "And with your spirit." Behind them, a contingent from the San Antonio Antelopes organization along with their wives and dates stood respectfully silent.

Father Lawrence continued, "Let us pray." The Mariottas bowed their heads and clasped hands. There were some in attendance who actually knelt on bended knees. "God, from whom every good thing takes its start and receives its steady and full growth, grant, we beseech you, that what we commence for the glory of your name, may be carried to completion by the ever-present aid of Your fatherly wisdom. In Christ's name, we pray. Amen."

Following the opening prayer, Father Lawrence picked up a small silver pail of water and a wooden wand with a silver ball on one end of it. The good Padre then walked around the lobby, dipping the silver ball into the bucket and sprinkling the entire hall as well as its patrons with water. Catholics in the crowd understood what Father Lawrence was doing and crossed themselves as the droplets of Holy Water landed on them. Non-Catholics naturally wondered why they were getting wet.

When Father Lawrence stepped back up on the altar, he began his blessing, "God's peace be in this place of business. And all who assemble here." Sprinkling more holy water in the room, he prayed, "Lord Jesus Christ, bestow your peace and blessing on this building and business with your graces. Help your angels to keep watch and drive away evil. Pour out your Holy Spirit in the hearts of the people who run and organize this business. Let your love and protection flow. Amen."

Father Lawrence then scooped a heaping spoonful of frankincense into a burning censer. Immediately the incense began to smoke. He waved the burner toward all corners of the lobby and the room filled with a pleasant scent. At his instruction, the people repeated, "Our help is in the name of The Lord."

Father Lawrence saw Hank Mariotta standing in the audience and understood why tears were welling up in his eyes. Nearly two years of planning and hard work had brought Hank Mariotta to this night, quite an accomplishment. Standing next to Hank was Christianna and her fiancé. She too appeared to be moved by the ceremony, and she gripped Rebel's hand tightly for support. The solemnity of the service was suddenly interrupted by a loud voice in the back of the lobby exclaiming, "Can I hear a shout out for God? And an Amen?" While not strictly Catholic, the sentiment was sincere. David Matthopolous wanted to praise God and again shouted out in full-throated passion, "God is great!"

With one voice, the burly Antelopes showed their support with a stout, "Amen to that!" The entire audience, including Father Lawrence, burst into applause.

Father Lawrence smiled broadly and dismissed the crowd with an invitation. "Ladies and gentlemen, join me at the dessert table to celebrate this special day. I'm told that there is a beautiful vanilla coconut cake with the words 'Bless this House of Business' waiting there for us to enjoy."

He was first in line to receive his piece of "blessing" cake. Though all the tables in the lobby offered a variety of tempting treats, the coconut cake was something special. And it did not take long for the server to hand out the last piece.

As Lucy waited for Rip near the lobby entrance, she heard someone call her name. It was some of her friends from the hospital. They were all eager to meet Lucy's new boyfriend and pestered her with questions. The group had been respectfully quiet during Father Lawrence's dedication, but as soon as the priest finished his blessing, the girls did their part to contribute to the lobby's increasing noise levels. The Desert Valley nurses were quickly joined by several of the hospital's resident doctors.

Dr. Lowenstein came over to the clutch of nurses and Lucy greeted him with a friendly hug. Another ER doctor Lucy knew only by reputation joined him. Marcos Perez was his name and the whisper about him was that he could be more than a bit brusque with people coming into his emergency room when there wasn't a real emergency.

Usually, when a patient came in with a headache or simple cold, he would keep them waiting as long as possible and often ended his shift without even seeing them. But there was one incident when a young man looking for a doctor to write him an excuse from work had come into the ER with a superficial cut on his hand. After taking a quick look at the wound, the doctor had become enraged, saying, "Man up and quit behaving like a little girl!" The doctor had literally chased the man out of the emergency room and badgered him into the parking lot, shouting, "And don't come back unless you're dead. You're wasting my time and putting the lives of those who really need my help in danger." When the doctor had returned through the ER lobby, it was to the cheers of nurses and waiting patients alike. The doctor had become a Desert Valley ER legend.

Lucy promised herself to find out more about the irascible and righteous Dr. Marcos Perez. But for now, she waited, anxiously looking out the casino doors for Rip Rumple.

LAREDO CASINO

Taking advantage of the brief downtime his producer had granted him, John joined Mary in the lobby. She was happy to see him, but John could tell she was troubled. They had both witnessed the blessing by Father Lawrence, a man John revered and whose counsel he often sought. More than once when John began to drift off course, Father Lawrence had been there to help steer him back in the right direction. Father Lawrence's latest intercession was no exception.

Lately, Mary seemed to be uncustomarily melancholy. But whenever John tried to find out why, she artfully changed the subject and began blathering about something else. Then, one day he came home early and was surprised to find Mary watching TV and crying over a silly reality show. The program followed a group of successful career women through their pregnancies into their first-year post-partum to discover how each coped with the demands of her career and motherhood.

It seemed Mary hadn't heard John come in because he overheard her cursing at one of the complaining ladies who was confessing that if she knew the trouble being a mother would be, she would have had an abortion. Mary screamed at the TV, "Oh, you need to get over yourself. I'll take your beautiful baby off your hands if you can't handle it. I wish I had that problem." Then she put her head in her hands, cradling herself, and began to weep. John knew then that Mary wanted a child and not having one was the cause of her sadness.

He wondered what the problem was, but didn't dwell over it. After all, they were just getting started; there was plenty of time to start a family. But after seeing Mary at that moment, John knew he had been wrong not to take it more seriously.

One night after losing another sizeable chunk of his money at the poker table, a dejected John left the Laredo. He wasn't eager to face Mary. He knew she would not be pleased, but would hug him anyway, telling him it was just another teachable moment in the game of poker. Still, he felt ashamed he was not supporting her and very soon would be depending on her for his livelihood.

Outside the casino, John needed to think a bit and decided to take the long way home, walking down the nature trail behind the Laredo. During the day, the half-mile trail was lush with flowers, shrubs, and palm trees and usually crowded with people. But the night was late and

John walked the path alone, the moonlight casting strange shadows around him.

The trail led him to a pond with a wooden bridge and that is where John spotted it. Even though there wasn't a full moon, it was light enough for him to discern a wad of rolled up cash held together with a thick rubber band. Next to the money was a brown paper bag with more cash spilling out of it.

What had he stumbled onto? John could only imagine. Someone must have tossed the bag over the bridge in panic. Looking around to make sure no one was watching, John scooped up the bag and stuffed it into his pack. He then turned and headed back out toward the strip to catch a bus home.

Even though he and Mary had a car, John often took the metro bus that stopped in front of the Julian Villa Apartments. But this time John wished he still had his cherished Jeep Wrangler Sahara. He missed riding high off the ground and off-roading along trails he could never explore now that he drove a practical and reliable Chevy Impala. At least he could be proud that once again he had purchased an American-made car.

He stuffed the bag of cash safely away in his backpack but still, John felt that every eye on the bus knew what he carried and worried that he was being followed. He had no idea where the money came from, but he could speculate. Questions coursed through his mind. Was it drug money? How much was there? Was he safe? Was Mary safe? He had stumbled onto something big and he wasn't sure how to handle it.

Knowing Mary wouldn't bother looking in his backpack, he decided to leave the cash where it was and, if she did happen to find it, he would have to tell her the truth. It would be safe for now and in the morning, he would tell Father Lawrence. The good Father would know what to do. And as far as John was concerned, he couldn't see him soon enough.

SAINT ANNE CATHOLIC CHURCH

When John got home, he went straight to the bathroom and locked the door behind him. From the other side, Mary knocked and asked him if there was anything wrong. John answered quickly, "No babe, I just need to take a shower." He turned on the water and, sitting on the closed toilet seat, opened his backpack and counted the money. Each rolled-up wad contained only one-thousand-dollar bills. In total, he counted $750,000 in cash. John was afraid and couldn't hide it from his face. When he came out of the bathroom, Mary asked him again if he was all right. John kissed her on the forehead, explaining that he was just tired.

That night he hadn't slept, nervously waiting for dawn. At the first hint of morning, John grabbed his phone and texted Father Lawrence:

URGENT I C U ASAP!

Almost immediately, a reply dinged his phone. "St. Anne's. 30 Min." John slipped out of their apartment without waking Mary.

Father Lawrence was waiting on the church steps when John arrived and led him to a private room in the basement of the church. Father Lawrence listened intently as an agitated John showed him the cash in his backpack. "I'm scared, Father. What should I do? What if someone saw me pick it up and now wants me dead? Worse yet, what about Mary? She has no idea about this."

Father Lawrence stared at the contents of the open pack. It seemed to John a very long time before the Father spoke. "John, I don't think there is any way possible to return the money. Obviously, it came from a dubious source. My take is that it was money begotten illegally. I think we need to resolve this quickly and in a manner befitting of God. The Lord will protect you if you give it to charity. But John, I share your concern. This could get dangerous. We need to go to the police immediately."

John agreed, but he wasn't finished. There was something else he needed to ask the priest. With his eyes firmly fixed on the Father,

John asked, "Please pray that Mary and I have a child. Mary is unhappy and desperate for a baby. I don't know why she is in such a rush since we've only been married a few months, but there it is. Please keep us in your prayers."

Father Lawrence closed his eyes and lifted his head upward for a few seconds. John wondered if he had heard him. Suddenly focusing on John, the Father told him, "John, I believe it is done. You were honest about the money and did not try to keep it for yourself. God will reward you. The victory is won. Soon you will have a new baby. Let's pray together and then I think it is urgent that we go to the police immediately and take this money off your hands. I'll drive us."

After he and John passed through the metal detector at police headquarters, Father Lawrence approached the officer on duty and asked if they could speak to the captain. After a few minutes of waiting on a hard-wooden bench, they were shown into the captain's office.

The captain appeared to be finishing up some paperwork and did not immediately acknowledge his visitors. John glanced at the brass nameplate on his desk: Captain Jack McGuire. John exchanged nervous glances with Father Lawrence.

When the captain finally sighed and looked up at them, he appeared bewildered by the priest and his cohort standing before him. "Well, to what do I owe this honor, Father?"

Father Lawrence cued John with an elbow jab to the stomach. "Uh. Well, sir," John began, "I was walking home and as I was crossing the footbridge, I found this." John opened his pack and pulled out a rolled-up stack of bills. I counted it last night and it came to about seven hundred and fifty grand!"

The captain blinked at him. "Say that again. How much? I'm not sure I heard you right."

John repeated the sum. "Three-quarters of a million dollars. All in thousands."

In a husky, gravelly voice, Captain McGuire thanked the Father and John profusely for doing the right thing and reporting the find, theorizing, "I could be wrong, but most likely this is mob or drug money. And assuming that it is, we need to proceed very carefully." He looked at John gravely. "Besides the Father here, does anyone else know about this?"

John shook his head, "No."

Captain McGuire continued. "Good, let's keep it that way. You are to tell no one about this. You see, we usually keep the money for sixty days and wait for someone to come and claim it. If no one does, we turn it back to the finder or donate it to some of our various charity programs. But with this amount of money, there are two things you can be sure of. First, someone, perhaps many people, are looking for it and will not stop until they find it. And secondly, these aren't the kind of people who would offer a reward through an ad in the Lost and Found and they sure as hell won't be reporting it to us."

John understood the captain perfectly. Father Lawrence remarked, "That's pretty much the way we figured it too. And if it does end up that the money is not claimed, then I believe John would like to make an anonymous contribution to charity."

"That's a wonderful idea. We support an important program that is helping children and adolescents stay off drugs. I can assure you that the money would be well spent." Captain Jack had nothing left to say and curtly ushered them out of his office. "Thank you again. We will keep you apprised of the situation."

During the drive back to St. Anne's, John and Father Lawrence barely spoke to one another. John's thoughts teetered between dreaming about keeping the money for himself and Mary and what could happen to them if he did.

Father Lawrence suggested they stop in the Adoration Chapel to pray for God's guidance and direction. He was uneasy about the abrupt way Captain Jack had ended their meeting. Could the police really keep the news of John's find from leaking to the press? And would they be honest brokers when the time came to return the money? Already he felt pressured by Captain Jack to let the police decide what to do with the money. But was that God's will?

God's answer came not five hours later when a Catholic church on the north end of the city burned to the ground after a parishioner knocked over a rack of burning votive candles in the chapel. The flying candles landed on a pew cushion and caught fire. The flames spread and quickly developed into an uncontrollable inferno. The firemen had had no choice but to let the fire burn itself out.

Convinced that God had answered his prayer, Father Lawrence called John and discussed his plan to donate the money. John readily agreed and the next day, Father Lawrence returned to the police department to see Captain Jack. He mentioned the church burning down at which the captain proclaimed he was well aware of the event. "But what you might not appreciate, Captain, is that more than five thousand families are now without a place to worship. They desperately need to rebuild but are sorely lacking the funds to do it. I know it hasn't been sixty days yet, but if you could release the money to the parish's restoration fund, it would go a long way toward helping them recover."

Captain Jack looked at the priest in a thoughtful manner. "You know, Father, I too am Catholic. Saint Bartholomew's was my parish. But you are asking for something I simply cannot do." Captain McGuire leaned forward across his desk. "Look, I have to be honest with you. I believe the money is drug money. I didn't want to alarm the young man yesterday, but he could be in more danger than what I let on. We need to handle this very carefully. I've got ears on the street listening for anything that might give us a clue about where the money came from and who's looking for it. For now, I can assure that it's best the money remains in our control."

Father Lawrence sat in stony silence while Captain Jack continued. "And if it does turn out to be drug money, then I am inclined to recommend we use the money for Drug Prevention Awareness programs for schools. The two are intertwined. That's about all I can say right now regarding the situation." Captain Jack stood, walked around his desk, and opened his office door. "Thank you for coming, Father. You'll be hearing from me."

Once again, Father Lawrence was hustled out of the captain's office. The priest was beginning to develop a complex and thought that maybe he smelled bad. He then dismissed the thought because he had used deodorant that morning. This Captain Jack was puzzling and left Father Lawrence with a concern for John's safety that could only be answered with prayer.

Father Lawrence called John to tell him about his meeting with Captain Jack and then asked him to pray with him. "Son, you must remember what Jesus said when two or more gather in his name. Do you know what he said?"

"No sir, I'm not sure."

"'Whenever two or more of you are gathered in my name, there I am amongst you.'"

John said that sounded pretty good to him.

LAS VEGAS POLICE DEPARTMENT

In the days and weeks that followed, the media focused on the unfortunate loss of St. Bartholomew's and the impact it had on the local community. The church had operated a shelter and soup kitchen for hundreds of the city's indigents. Local news stations continuously ran human interest stories about the plight of those suddenly left without this much-needed assistance. Rebuilding the church became the community cause célèbre and donations poured in from everywhere.

It took longer than sixty days, but Father Lawrence finally received the call he had been anxiously waiting for. "Father Lawrence? Captain Jack here. Can you and the young man come down to the station at one-thirty today? I have some news I would like to share with you." Captain Jack hung up on Father Lawrence without waiting for a response.

As John and Father Lawrence entered the captain's office, they were greeted by a smiling Captain Jack who gestured for them to take a seat. "As I suspected, no one has come forward to claim the money turned in by this young man and unfortunately we are no closer to learning whose it is. The Las Vegas Police Department would like to donate the money toward the rebuilding of Saint Bartholomew's." Thanking God for answered prayers, Father Lawrence crossed himself.

Captain Jack continued. "We've planned a media event in a few minutes where I will hand over a check for $750,000 toward the reconstruction of St. Bartholomew." Captain Jack picked up his phone and handed it to Father Lawrence. If you would call Father Moran to be on hand for the ceremony, this will all be over."

Father Lawrence was more than happy to tell his friend and priest of St Bartholomew's parish the good news. Within the hour, Father Moran was sitting with them in the Captain's office. Astounded by the unexpected donation, Father Moran could only exclaim, "Praise be to God!"

"Now gentlemen, let's go out and meet the press." Following Captain Jack out of his office onto the steps of the station, they were met by a waiting gaggle of television news cameras and reporters. Captain Jack took his place behind the hastily-installed podium and began to speak. "Ladies and gentlemen, I have an important announcement." The cameras recorded everything as Captain Jack relished his moment.

"Several months ago, the Las Vegas Police Department received a package in the mail. There was no return address, and despite our efforts, we could not trace its source. In the package was a letter stating that the contents were found and that it should be turned over to its rightful owner or failing that, to a worthy religious charity. Along with the note, there was $750,000 in untraceable cash. And now, since there has been no claim on the discovered cash, the Las Vegas Police Department is pleased to deliver this find as directed by the anonymous finder toward the rebuilding of Saint Bartholomew's."

At first Father Lawrence was shocked at the captain's blatant and outright lies, especially the part about receiving it in a package; then he realized that the deception was necessary. It was the only way to keep John's name out of the spotlight.

One reporter called out, "Captain McGuire? Captain Jack? How is this donation not a blatant violation of the constitutional mandate for the separation between church and state?"

Captain Jack seemed prepared for that kind of question and responded, "Not at all. These are not taxpayer funds. It is found money and was turned over to us anonymously. There were instructions about what to do with it if it was not claimed. The letter specifically stated that we donate it to a religious charity. And in light of all the tremendous good Saint Bart's has done for our city, well, it's time we give something back in their hour of need."

The reporter pressed the captain with a follow-up question. "Sir, who was responsible for making this decision?"

"This was my decision. It's something I wanted to do."

"But did you consider spreading these funds to other religious denominations?"

Captain Jack feigned the most pious answer. "I have wanted to give this plagued church a new start, particularly when you consider the enormous good that parish has done for our city's homeless population. It all came from above." Captain McGuire pointed his finger toward the sky.

The perceptive reporter then asked Father Lawrence what he thought about this generous donation. Father Lawrence wasn't about to dispute Captain Jack but he was offended by McGuire's self-aggrandizing speech. Father Lawrence wasn't sure what he should say. "Well, I..."

But Captain Jack interrupted him. "As I stated before, it was all my idea and I got in touch with this good Father. It seemed the Father loved my idea and so will the parishioners when they see their place of worship rebuilt. Of course, we've had city attorneys review the decision and they have put their blessing on the donation. Thank you. That is all I have to say at this time. But I would be more than happy to pose for pictures. Thank you."

With that, the news conference was over and reporters snapped shots of Captain Jack handing a jumbo ceremonial check to the parish priest while John and Father Lawrence stood awkwardly behind them.

Father Lawrence appreciated the captain's deception about how the money came into the possession of the police. But he struggled to hide his anger over what he saw as being recklessly exposed by Captain Jack. There was no need for John and him to be there. It could only serve to pique the curiosity of those who were no doubt searching for the hundreds of thousands of dollars they no longer had. And it wouldn't take a Sherlock Holmes to realize that their presence was pointless unless they had some connection with the money. Father Lawrence tried to block John from the seeing eyes of the press cameras.

The next morning, Father Lawrence began his day like he did all of his mornings – start brewing a pot of coffee, fetch the newspaper, wash the face, pour a cup, and sit down to read the morning news. Doing just that, Father Lawrence opened his paper and saw what he had prayed he would not.

Above the fold, the banner headline screamed:

LOST & FOUND MOB MONEY DONATED
TO CATHOLIC CHURCH REBUILD FUND

Below that was an exploded photo of the check ceremony with John standing recognizably in the background. Father spit his coffee all over the paper. He had lost all confidence in Captain Jack McGuire so Father Lawrence did the only thing he could do; he prayed.

THREE BROTHERS CASINO

Guests and curious gate-crashers alike milled about the lobby, feasting on the impressive array of delectable cakes and petit fours. Laughter and chatter filled the new casino, so no one noticed when the wine steward took to the podium where Father Lawrence had delivered his blessing and waiters began to wheel out table after table of magnums of champagne. Attempting to get the crowd's attention, the wine steward spoke through the mic, "Ladies and gentlemen! May I have your attention, please? I have a very important announcement." The crowd quieted and turn toward the podium.

The sommelier introduced himself and said, "Ladies and gentlemen, I have been given the honor and privilege to invite you all to join in a very special toast to the Mariotta brothers. Please come forward for a glass of vintage of Louis Roederer Cristal and join our special guest to raise a toast to the success of this establishment and the men who are responsible for it all." Immediately, lines began to form in front of the waiters who poured the expensive bubbly into plastic flutes.

John and Mary joined the line that had materialized near the front of the lobby. As they stood together, Mary whispered into his ear that she had something she wanted to tell him. Just as John was about to ask what it was, his producer broke in and ordered him to the Three Shuffles Poker Room to cover a big hand that was in play. John gave Mary a big kiss and said, "Work is calling, and I have to go!" Hurrying toward the Three Shuffles room, John turned and waved goodbye. A beaming Mary waved back.

As the champagne lines began to dwindle, the sommelier stepped up to tell the crowd, "Ladies and gentlemen, I have the honor to present to you Mr. Hank Mariotta. He has arranged this surprise for his sons and wishes to send them off onto their new venture in style. Please give a warm welcome for Hank Mariotta!"

The crowd erupted in applause as a dashing Hank Mariotta stepped onto the stage and took a champagne glass from the sommelier. Standing in front of the microphone, Hank looked out on his audience. "Thank you very much. I want to start by saying that this is a proud day for me and I want my family to join me up here on stage to toast to the success of my sons' new casino."

Again, there was enthusiastic applause as the entire Mariotta family stepped onto the platform and lined up on either side of their father. Hank Mariotta smiled and held up his champagne glass to propose a toast. "Friends, this is a proud moment in my life and I want you to join me in wishing my sons Mark, Simon, and Andrew, the greatest of success in their new venture. May God grace and shed His blessings on this establishment!"

As the audience raised their glasses to affirm Hank Mariotta's toast, a chilling scream of terror erupted near the lobby entrance followed by a thundering crash as the glass doors shattered to the floor like heavy rain on a metal roof. Champagne and flutes flew through the air as the crowd panicked, screaming and running in every direction.

On the podium, Hank Mariotta watched in horror as he saw a car explode into the lobby at full speed, its headlights glaring like two diabolical eyes in search of innocent victims. People dove left and right, hoping to avoid the deadly projectile. Pandemonium and hysteria reigned as it plowed deeper into the lobby. Loud moans rose from the people on the ground, and still, the car kept rolling mindlessly along. It sideswiped a wall and plowed through everything in its path. Shattered glass flew through the air; tables and chairs splintered into pieces with loud cracking sounds.

The car suddenly veered off the wall to take aim at the cake table. Terrified servers screamed and dove out of the way as the vehicle crashed through the heavy maple tables, overturning them and launching cakes and pies into the air. Nothing slowed the car as it took out everything in its path, including people.

Ava Allende was the first apparent victim as she had lost her dress in the melee and now wandered mindlessly in the car's wake wearing nothing but a tattered bikini bottom. Rubber butt pads peeked out from under it and now Ava Allende's celebrated and prodigious derriere was exposed for the phony it was. As she walked, the two butt pads worked loose and fell to the floor.

With everyone rushing to get out of the way, no one had thought to try to stop the car. Now, a few of the Antelopes attempted to flatten the tires by placing pieces of splintered wood in the vehicle's path. The car steamrolled over them like toothpicks and continued to exact its relentless devastation. Other players tried grabbing the door handles, hoping to open a door and jump in. But their hands just slid across the smooth metal because the car had no door handles.

J.C. "Velcro Fingers" Stewart jumped onto the hood and started pounding on the windshield with his fist. The machine was unstoppable and Velcro Fingers was forced to hang on for the ride of his life. His teammate grabbed a table leg from the floor and lined up in front of the oncoming car, intending to swing the heavy maple table leg into the windshield. But he misjudged the car's trajectory and the horrific crunch of his leg as the car passed over it was devastating. It was Edmond Gerry, and his kicking leg had been shattered. Even from a distance, it was apparent that he was in real danger as a steady stream of blood pooled around the femur that poked out of his torn pants and mangled leg. His wife Shay ran over to him and screamed in fear, "Someone stop that fucking car."

She cradled Edmund in her arms, trying to comfort him. Writhing in agony, he kept repeating, "It's over. It's over. It's over."

Shay looked at the wound and she knew her husband's injury was indeed career-ending and couldn't help but think to herself, *What's he going to do now? Sell used cars?* But then she got a notion that put a sly smile on her face. She squeezed her husband's hand, and whispered in his ear excitedly, "You know what, baby? It's a good thing your leg got mowed over. You got yourself some good insurance. We're rich! I mean really rich!" Despite his pain, Edmund smiled because it was true. He had taken out a hundred-million-dollar iron-clad insurance policy on his kicking leg with Lloyds of London.

Hank Mariotta, Lou Danner, and Coach Coby rushed over to Edmund, their faces taking on the same look of sheer, frantic terror upon seeing their star kicker's mangled leg.

Coach Coby swore, "Nothing better be wrong with my kicker. I'll kill that son of a bitch." Hank looked mortified. "Someone *stop* that damn car!"

It was too late. The car had made it through the lobby and was on course toward the Three Shuffles Poker room.

But first, the car had a date with the Ambrose Lounge where Georgio Tucci was on stage entertaining his audience with the arias that made his tenor voice famous. Unfortunately, his voice wasn't protection enough as the two-ton steel-and-muscle wrecking monster took aim and headed straight toward him. From the stage, Tucchi watched the car blast into the lounge, tossing chairs, tables, and people aside like dollhouse toys with its headlights trained straight for the stage.

The Thrillers were on a break and Lee and Becky Dean sat at a table near the lounge entrance. Grabbing her with a mighty force, Lee pulled Becky Dean out of the way of the thundering car. They ended up on the floor with Becky Dean complaining, "Ouch! You pulled half my hair out!" And indeed, Lee saw that he was holding a handful of Becky Dean's long brown hair. At another table, Roy and Leroy were helping their girls Mindy and Nadine up from the floor.

Leroy watched as Georgio Tucchi leapt off the stage just before the car crashed into it – then through it. It blasted through the back wall of the stage into the adjacent room, announcing its arrival in the Three Shuffles Poker Room. Leroy announced that he'd had enough of this car and chased after it.

Flying sideways through the air, Tucchi crashed hard on the floor. His arm twisted unnaturally behind his back, cracking loudly. Leroy followed after the car through the hole in the wall while Mindy rushed over to Tucchi who told her, "My arm! It's a'keeling me. That car, eet's a'crazee!"

THREE SHUFFLES POKER ROOM

While the rogue automobile continued its rampage through other rooms of the casino lobby, players in the Three Shuffles Poker Room were only aware of the cards they were holding in their hands. John and his cameraman were there covering the card play at a celebrity table. His tutor Manuel Borgata was playing a big-stakes hand with several other poker legends including Justin Tully. Relying on his gift of gab, Borgata used it to disarm and sometimes even charm his opponents. On this particular hand, Borgata focused his banter on Justin Tully.

"Tully, what's that you got in your hand? Is it whiskey on the rocks like the kind you got in your head?" Borgata smiled at Tully's obvious annoyance and added, "I bet you thought I was talking about your cards. I'm one funny dude, huh?"

Tully knew Borgata's tactics and had learned to let it blow by him like an ill wind. He also knew that he had pretty much won the hand after the river card gave him his third ace. Tully kept his face down. Borgata was hooked, and now he had to play him just right in order to land the big fish and net the pot. All he needed was to get Borgata to raise and then Tully would be all in, certain to reel in a sweet catch.

"Well Tully, it sure is getting hot in here, but the temperature on the sun's surface is eleven thousand degrees." As he slid a stack of thousand-dollar chips into the center of the table, Borgata looked at Tully and taunted, "Feeling the heat, Tully?"

Tully was ready to set the hook and go all in. But he forced himself to appear concerned. Borgata grinned like the cat that ate the goldfish. Tully slid his entire stack into the pot and said, "Let's see who gets burned."

Just then the demonic car exploded through the wall and burst into the room. Instant chaos erupted in the Three Shuffles room as it veered toward Tully and Borgata and crashed through their table. Poker chips, cards, and players went flying through the air, and over the din, Justin Tully swore, "Shit! Shit! *Shit*! I had an ace-king boat."

Suddenly gunshots echoed through the room. *Pow! Pow! Pow!*

Armed and standing defiantly in front of the oncoming car, Tommy Bill Dillion emptied the clip of his Ruger .45 into it. "Stop you, ignernt sum'a bitch! I'm gonna take you out!"

Bang! Bang! Bang! Bullets ripped into the black car, flattening the front tires and shattering its headlights. Tommy Bill concentrated the rest of his shots into the engine compartment. Steam began spitting and hissing from the grill. The car was about done.

A man rushed through the hole in the wall waving a gun. He ran up behind the car, swearing, "Just for good measure, I'm going to finish this mother off." It was Leroy. With two shots of his Glock, he hit both rear tires. Air rushed out of them as the back end of the car sank like a slain marauding rhino. The demon car was dead.

For a few moments, everything was quiet and those caught in the ransacked room began to peek out from where they hid to look at the car. Based on the emblem, the pitch-black car was undoubtedly a Cadillac, but it was a Cadillac like none had ever seen. The car windows were heavily tinted, obscuring the car's interior. On the lower side of the door was the word "Ciel."

Mindy ran up behind Leroy and began kicking the car with her high heels, screaming, "Get out of the car, you crazy fuck!"

Tommy Bill and Leroy crouched low and carefully approached each other along the driver side of the car. They met on either side of the door, and Tommy Bill whispered to Leroy, "You got it done, boy. Now let's get on with it and rip this shittin' door' off! I'll open the door and you get ready to shoot." Leroy nodded and Tommy Bill said, "Okay. On three. One. Two. Three!"

Springing to their feet in unison, Leroy trained his Glock on the door as Tommy Bill reached for the handle. Just then, the car door opened and out slumped Rip Rumple – sound asleep.

Leroy holstered his gun and he and Tommy Bill dragged Rip out of the car. "Wake up and face the music, boy," Leroy ordered. They were intentionally rough on him until stopped by Dr. Lowenstein.

"Let me handle this. I'm a doctor from Desert Valley Hospital. This man is a patient of mine. He has a disability called narcolepsy. Sit him over there in that chair and then see if you can help someone else. There are a lot of people who need help. Somebody call 9-1-1 and have them send ambulances. We've got injured people." Dr. Lowenstein took control.

Until that moment, everyone seemed paralyzed. But Lowenstein's call to action pulled them out of it and they began to carry out his commands.

By now, Lucy had made it to the car and ordered Mindy to quit kicking Rip's Cadillac. For some strange reason, Mindy obeyed. That was a first. Lucy hurried to Rip's side.

Hank Mariotta and his sons rushed into the poker room. They were followed by a security contingent who immediately surrounded Rip Rumple. Hank Mariotta could be heard over the commotion exclaiming, "My God, it's Rip Rumple."

Rip was becoming somewhat aware of the destruction he had wrought. He tried to look up at Hank, but he was still disoriented. His face was bruised and cut. Dr. Lowenstein declared somewhat sympathetically that Rip had received multiple contusions and most probably suffered from a concussion. "He probably bounced around in that car like a rag doll. No telling how many times he banged his head on the steering wheel and dashboard." But as they surveyed the damage he had caused, the Mariotta brothers found it hard to feel the least bit of concern for an old narcoleptic like Rip "Van" Rumple.

Leroy stood next to Tommy Bill Dillion and said, "This grandpa is as loopy as a mofo loony bird."

Tommy-Bill agreed. "You got that right, boy. He's more confused than a cow on Astroturf. The dude's probably on ludes. Narcolepsy, my ass."

The police and EMTs arrived and Lucy's nurse friends began triaging the casualties. They directed the EMTs to rush the most critical cases to the ER. Rip Rumple was among them.

As he was lifted onto a stretcher, a young woman pressed her way through the crowd carrying a wine glass in her hand. Unsteady on her heels and drunk, Jill staggered up to a dazed Rip Rumple and peered at him. Turning to the crowd, she slurred, "Who invited this old man to the party? As you can see, he has to be the life of the party at any cost." She looked at Rip strapped into the gurney and began laughing uncontrollably. "You ruin everything and everybody you ever touch." She threw her wine in Rip's face and screamed, "Was the party so boring you couldn't stay awake, my love?" Then leaning in close, she spit on him with boozy breath and said shrilly, "I hope this wakes you up, lover."

Dr. Lowenstein demanded, "Get security and get her out of here."

Hank Mariotta snapped his fingers and armed security quickly grabbed the drunken woman by both arms and dragged Jill out of the destroyed casino.

John and his cameraman had captured every bit of the action. They had set up behind Borgata's table which happened to be the perfect position to film the car crashing through the wall into the room. They had even captured the showdown between Tommy Bill and the oncoming menace. And through it all, John had kept up with his description of the scene like a seasoned pro. His producer was wildly ecstatic and nearly broke John's eardrum screaming, "This is fantastic! Keep on it, John. In a million years we couldn't have scripted a better launch for the network!"

As security hustled Jill out of the room, they passed John and his cameraman. She could barely walk and looked to be on the verge of passing out, but upon seeing the camera, contorted her face into a strange grin. Then she noticed John holding a microphone. Confusion flashed across Jill's face as she tried to focus her eyes on him. "John? Is that you?" She gave him an awkward wave that almost took her to the floor. But the security guards caught her and kept her upright. John felt sad for her. It was hard for him to remember the Jill with whom he'd shared an apartment in Houston, Texas.

In the meantime, Hank Mariotta and his entourage kept busy helping their guests who had sustained injuries. Fortunately, no one had been killed. For that, Hank Mariotta and his entire family thanked God. However, there were body and limb injuries that needed immediate medical attention. Mariotta was most concerned about Edmond Gerry. With a broken femur sticking out of his leg, Hank worried the Antelopes might lose their star kicker.

Dr. Lowenstein's friend tended to Gerry. Without the aid of x-rays, his diagnosis, though qualified, was dismal. He surmised Gerry's leg was fractured in three places – his femur, fibula, and tibia were in pieces. Privately, he told Hank he thought Gerry's injuries would include damage to the knee and the tissues wreathed around the bone. "I doubt he ever plays a game of football again. At best, he'll have a limp, but most probably will need the use of a cane for the rest of his life."

Hank was not surprised and took the unsettling prognosis in stride. He told the doctor, "Spare no expense. I want the best surgeons brought in to put this boy back together."

The famous and talented tenor Georgio Tucci still lay on the floor. His arm was broken and he was in incredible pain. In Italian, he cried out, "*Questo fa male! Aiutami! Aiutami!*" It hurts! Help me! Help me!

Inside the Three Shuffles, Manuel Borgata nursed a sprained ankle. Then there was Justin Tully. As far as he was concerned, he'd been the most injured of all. He couldn't get over being screwed out of that big pile of money. "I had the big boat. I would have won! Who paid this guy to take me out?" Tully had been on the verge of landing the biggest catch of his life only to watch helplessly as a bigger fish came in to rip it off his line just as he was ready to net his prey. Tully looked over at the beached, dust-covered Cadillac. He swore an oath then and there. "As God is my witness, I will never buy another Cadillac again!"

Other guests had been bruised by the big car as they had tried to get out of its way. But for most, they would end their day as healthy as they began it, but with a fantastic story to tell. Still, there was some drama to play out even as those in the casino began to recover from the initial horror of the scene.

Ava Allende followed through the path of the wreckage dazed, confused, and, with the exception of a deflated bikini bottom, naked. A younger woman rushed to her side and handed her one of her missing butt pads. The girl mocked Ava, telling her that she was lucky she was wearing the Spanx because it protected her backside from the wrath of Rip's ruthless bumper. "Honey, this butt pad protected your rear bumper. You should donate it to the Smithsonian for the sake of 'posteriorotomy.' Get it?"

Ava got it and covered her bared breasts with her arms. It was a humiliation beyond recovery. Another person in the crowd added, "What you should really do, Ava, is a PSA telling how your butt pads saved your life!"

To further compound her obvious embarrassment, someone else taunted, "This time you could really earn your star on Hollywood's Walk of Fame. It's about time because no one knows why you are famous anyway."

With that, Ava fled toward the refuge of the nearby women's room. All eyes were on her near-naked body.

The devastation in the Three Brothers Poker Palace was complete. The Mariotta brothers knew they could rebuild and were already discussing between themselves how long it would take before they would reopen. For his part, Hank harbored no ill will toward Rip Rumple. Rip was his friend and Hank knew full well of his disability. Whatever his failings, Rip Rumple honored his obligations and would be ready to make good for the damage he had caused.

Hank Mariotta was busy attending to the injured when Father Lawrence found him. Hank asked, "Father, how is everyone?"

Father Lawrence answered with a smile. "But by the grace of God, things could have been much worse.

Relieved, Hank breathed, "Well, thank God for that."

The Padre seemed to have something on his mind. "Hank, I would like to gather everyone in the lobby again to thank God for protecting us and pray for the speedy recovery of those who were hurt. It won't be long, but I think we owe a debt of gratitude to our Savior for his hand in guiding that car in a way that spared everyone's lives."

"That's a good idea, but it's not my call, Father. My sons have to okay that. Run it by Simon. You can tell him I think it's a good idea, but it's his decision to make." Father Lawrence left to look for Simon Mariotta.

It was then Hank noticed the young woman who had been standing next to Father Lawrence was still there. She was pretty with bright-blue, expectant eyes. Hank had no idea why she was staring at him. He was about to ask if she was hurt when she blurted out, "My name is Nadine and I would like to speak to you about investing in the Three Brothers Casino and your poker channel. Mr. Mariotta, I don't care about what just happened here. Your insurance will pay for the rebuilding. I believe in the idea you started here and would like to be a part of it. I could bring a lot to the table."

This was the last thing Hank had expected to hear. Still, she seemed sincere, if not a little drunk. Her timing, however, was terrible. "Ma'am, you're coming at me at the worst possible time. I'll tell you what – give me your card and I will call you once things settle down. Surely you can understand that this is not the time for a business meeting." Hank looked past her, surveying the ruination. The place was a mess, but it was salvageable. The comely brunette handed him her card and told him that she would be waiting for his call. Hank watched her as she walked into the arms of a man Hank assumed to be her husband.

Everyone was beginning to wander into the Three Shuffles to see where the wild beast of a car lay dead. People took selfies standing triumphantly next to the lifeless carcass like big-game hunters showing off their prey. Then they would post the pictures to their Facebook, Twitter, and Instagram accounts. Someone even tweeted their photo with the caption "I *am* The Beast Slayer."

As the crowd began to build in the Three Shuffles, Hank's family encircled their father as if to protect him from further catastrophe. Matthew was standing next to Christianna when he saw The Thrillers milling around the Ciel. He nudged her and said, "There she is. The girl in the hippie dress. Isn't she a knockout?"

Christianna looked Isabella up and down, concurring with her brother. There was something almost celestial about her. And she didn't have any tattoos, at least none that were visible. She thought to herself, *What would Daddy say?* But she knew Matthew had been stuck on her for some time so she told him, "Yeah. She's cute. Why don't you go over and talk to her?"

Matthew told her, "What's the use? She's got something going with one of the guitar players in the band. Even on stage, she can't keep her hands off him. I can tell they are gone on each other. Besides, we're going to be up day and night for weeks getting this place ready for our second grand opening gala."

Christianna agreed, "You sure have some serious work on your hands repairing this mess."

Everyone in the room suddenly ran for cover when they heard the roar of another car coming into the room. But they quickly recovered when they realized that it was only a tow truck backing through the hole in the wall to drag the Cadillac Ciel away.

Like a funeral procession, people lined up on either side of the tow truck as it slowly dragged the battered Ciel out of the room. What started as a stylish automobile had turned into a weapon on wheels, and was now an ugly block of steel. Covered with dust and stripped of its bumpers with folded fenders and a splintered windshield, the Cadillac had lost its luster.

Lucy stayed with Rip and held his hand as the ambulance took him to the hospital. He drifted in and out of consciousness like a faint radio signal. Lucy looked at Rip, perplexed. "Who was that vile woman Rip?" But in his condition, this was obviously not the time to probe. Squeezing his hand, Lucy told him not to worry, that he was in good hands with Dr. Lowenstein.

Lucy cared for Rip, and she had to laugh when she realized that all roads in their relationship either began or ended at Desert Valley Hospital. They had met in the hospital cafeteria and ever since, had been either coming or leaving the hospital's emergency room.

For a brief moment, Rip was lucid. His cheeks were flush and his eyes were glassed over. "Lucy. Lucy. Please tell Hank Mariotta I am going to pay for the damage and that I want to sponsor a reality show showcasing the progress with the new casino. Please, darling, do this favor for me and go back and tell that to my good friend. Tell him it's all on me. I owe him that much. I hope he'll understand." Rip closed his eyes and drifted back into peaceful oblivion.

Once Lucy saw to Rip's admittance in the ER, she returned to the damaged casino in pursuit of Hank Mariotta. She had a message from Rip Rumple.

ST LAWRENCE LOBBY AGAIN

When Lucy returned to the Three Brothers Poker Palace, she found police and security personnel blocking all entry and exits. No one was allowed in or out. And that included Lucy. After explaining that she was a nurse at Sunshine Hospital and had been called in to assist the doctors inside, she was allowed in. Once inside the lobby, Lucy noticed a crowd gathering around the priest who had blessed the place scarcely an hour before. Looking around at the devastation, she couldn't help but think, *God sure didn't bless this place today.*

Spotting Hank Mariotta loitering near the gathering, Lucy hurried over to him. With a strong hand, she took him by the arm and pulled him away, saying, "Mr. Mariotta, if I could have just a moment with you. I'm the girlfriend of Rip Rumple. He has a message he wants me to give to you."

Mariotta cocked his head in interest. "How is Rip doing? Please tell him I don't blame him for anything. I know about his condition. Please tell him not to worry. We'll all get through this just fine."

Lucy couldn't believe his response. Mr. Mariotta seemed not to harbor even the slightest trace of ill will toward Rip; on the contrary, the man only had concern for Rip's wellbeing. Hank Mariotta intimidated Lucy, but she forced herself to tell him Rip's idea about the reality show.

Hank smiled. He had a whimsical look on his face and enthusiastically told Lucy, "You tell Rip that I like the idea. Yes! Tell him I like the idea and we will work out the details in due time. Meanwhile, tell him to rest up and get well. I'll come in and visit him at Desert Valley sometime this week." Lucy felt relieved. Hank told her they were going to have a prayer session that was going to begin in a few minutes and earnestly said, "Things could have been much worse, but God looked out for us and thankfully no one was killed. We need to praise God and thank him." He invited Lucy to join him.

Lucy thought about how events had brought her to where she now stood. Something, or maybe someone, had guided her there. Not particularly religious, more than once Lucy had witnessed the inexplicable curing of a terminal patient. Their recovery could only be described as miraculous. She paused for a moment and sent a tepid thanks to God, including only one plea – that Rip be all right.

John squeezed Mary's hand tightly as Father Lawrence began the impromptu service. The lobby seemed more crowded now than it had been at the blessing service. John looked at the people around him. All were in solemn reflection. He glanced at Mary who seemed to be radiating joy for the first time in a long time.

She pulled him close to her and whispered in his ear, "You and I are going to have a baby girl! And I am going to name her after my mother, Elizabeth! That's what I have been trying to tell you." John grabbed Mary in his arm and twirled her around with excitement. He wanted to run over and tell Father Lawrence the good news. But instead, he went to his knees and coached Mary to do the same. "We've got a lot to be grateful for. We need to thank the Man upstairs." John pointed upwards and then folded his hands to pray. It was a short prayer, and when they were done, John helped Mary to her feet.

Roy and Nadine and Leroy and Mindy were there. With their hands interlocked, they became one. Leroy prayed aloud, "Thank you, God, for my Glock. If it wasn't for her, that car would still be on the rampage." Roy and Nadine burst out laughing but quickly composed themselves in a way fitting the occasion. They too had many things to be thankful for. Roy flashed through everything that had happened over the past year. The road trip with Leroy, the migraines, the nightmare at Abaddon's, and, of course, that competition-losing shirt. It was strange how all of that had led him to Nadine. Now she was his wife.

Like so many in the crowd, The Thrillers hung together. Becky Dean clutched Lee's arm for comfort. They had a history together; they belonged together. They had been making music together for years, but it took Las Vegas for them to realize that they were playing for each other. Next to them stood Isabella and James. Despite the drama of the evening, it was the happiest James had ever been. He was in a band that had potential, and to top it all, he had snatched Isabella, the babe of the group.

As Father Lawrence fell silent in preparation, Rebel held Christianna close and thought about their big day. Soon they would be starting a new life together. They felt grateful that no one had been seriously hurt.

The good Father then began to lead the gathering in prayer. First, he thanked God for guiding the car in such a way that spared the lives of those in attendance and then asked for the swift and complete recovery of the injured. He mentioned Edmond Gerry, Georgio Tucci, Rip Rumple, and other guests who had been hurt. "We ask You, God, that you heal them completely according to Your will. Please help us and give us the strength to rebuild. Please give Hank, Andrew, Mark, and Simon Mariotta the stamina and resolve they will need from this day forward." The lobby was quiet as everyone bowed in prayerful reflection.

Hank Mariotta shifted on his knees as he thought of his beloved Matilda.

As Father Lawrence prayed, he thanked God for Mabel, his very own Angel!

Amid this solemn celebration, a well-groomed man in a blue suit pressed his way through the crowd, and came up behind Mary. Nobody noticed when he pulled a gun from his pocket and shot her once in the head.

Mary's body crumpled to the floor. She and the baby she was carrying died instantly.

EPILOGUE

John cradled Mary. Gone, just like that. Bloody and limp.

Why?

Who had shot her?

John knew.

Closing his eyes for a few seconds, he held her tighter as if that might keep her from leaving him. But it was no use; Mary was gone.

In the ensuing pandemonium John glimpsed a well-dressed man in a navy-blue suit pushing through the crowd toward the exit. Disturbing memories flashed through his mind. All night long that man seemed to be wherever John reported from, watching him. It was obvious he was sending John a message, and the message was, "We want our money back."

Tears streamed down his face as he realized that Mary, his gentle wife, had become a sacrificial lamb.

ABOUT THE AUTHOR

S.A. Craig enjoys living in the South with her husband. She loves all the magnificent coffee houses, tearooms, and grand ole restaurants where she wrote *Some Saw an Angel in Las Vegas* and many volumes of poetry. She also loves popcorn.

To learn more, visit: www.sacraigauthor.com.

www.ingramcontent.com/pod-product-compliance
Lightning Source LLC
Chambersburg PA
CBHW071628260626
47170CB00001B/4